THE STALKER'S TALE

CHRISTINE WOOD

The Stalker's Tale

A NOVEL

First published 2020

by Zuleika Books & Publishing

Thomas House, 84 Eccleston Square
London, SW1V 1PX

British Library Cataloguing in Publication Data

A catalogue record for this book is
available from the British Library

ISBN: 978-1-9161977-4-9

Designed by Euan Monaghan
Printed in England

CHAPTER 1

A man waits in the rain for a bus he refuses to catch. It is six thirty in the evening; he has been there since 3 p.m. And still she has not noticed him.

People begin to get suspicious. Yet he scarcely sees them. He was also here on Tuesday.

His age is difficult to guess. Wide-frame glasses lend his features anonymity. He may once have been handsome, but the oval of his face is now carved viciously in arabesques; the bridge of his Roman nose thickened with fat. Only his mouth remains beautiful; a taut, curvaceous design that remembers its own sensuality. His amber, gold-flecked eyes search constantly, yet are strangely unseeing.

He glances at his watch. Twenty minutes since he last rang her bell. He crosses the road to the handsome Victorian villa, now converted into six apartments.

At the front door, he hesitates. Bianca's neighbours cast querying glances at him, before allowing the door to slam in his face. He shields his face from them with his cupped hand.

There is something distraught in his way of holding himself; a tall man jack-knifed from his waist to an angle of thirty degrees. A beige anorak puffs up around his bulk, like a child's duvet; his loafer shoes, beneath concertinas of white sock, appear to tap-dance the air impotently, like those of an uncoordinated marionette. From around his neck hangs a soft leather pouch.

Eventually, timidly, he presses Bianca's bell, promising himself not to speak; only to listen to her voice on the intercom.

Hearing the doorbell ring, Bianca sits very still, her breath suddenly heavy in her throat. She recognises Hesketh's light touch on the bell; knows each sound he makes like a signature. She is instantly alert, sensing danger. Although alone, it feels as though someone has just entered the room. She is infected by a sudden escalating anger. The bell rings again, this time a little more insistently. Bianca holds her breath, praying for him to go away... Once more... Still, she does not answer... The silence grows longer and a brief moment of blessedness descends, the space around her no longer feeling invaded.

Hesketh retreats to the bus stop. Yet he knows she is there. He unzips the leather pouch... In the powerful eye of his new binoculars, he can spy her sitting in the window of her first-floor sitting room, framed between clouds of white silk curtaining; a standard lamp casts a pool of light across a polished walnut table. Scavenging for more details, the binoculars focus briefly on the trembling, scintillating drops of a chandelier, before alighting greedily on Bianca herself, her hair a mass of golden curls... Held, poised in her hand, is a silver fountain pen...

Hesketh draws in his breath. So delicate is the geometry of her face that it might have been put in with the hesitant marks of a 2H pencil. Her eyes look innocent, the colour of cornflowers, yet her mouth, a melting smudge of raspberry sensuality, contradicts them. She raises her head, gazing directly at him, causing Hesketh to step back in shock. There is something both sorrowful and joyful about that face, even in solitude. She starts to write, with an intense, rapid energy.

Taking a Sony Walkman from his breast pocket, Hesketh presses Play.

'Why would I wish to have dinner with someone who has done me so much harm?' she asks in a low-pitched, musical voice.

Hesketh looks momentarily enthralled, before the machine crackles in his ear, incoherent with static.

That was the last time they spoke, two years earlier. The tape had picked up only some of her words; the recorder concealed in his overcoat pocket. Nevertheless, certain phrases emerge distinctly. Driving on his own late at night, Hesketh often replays the tape, each angry word remembered and lovingly anticipated. Listening to the strained, defiant heartbeat of her voice, he frequently discovers he has an erection.

Whenever the recording deteriorates through overuse, he has it transferred to a new tape.

Why does it thrill him so to hear her say he had done her harm? He does not himself understand why. Yet every time it excites him. Nor could he have imagined such exquisite pleasure. He still expects her to be kind. Closing his eyes, he can remember the taste of her, the scent of her skin, the normal soothing tempo of her voice. The Walkman erupts into life again:

'The reason I don't go to the police is that I no longer want the hassle,' she spits furiously. 'But if you persist…'

A sudden shudder passes through him. He remembers the last time they met in court.

Gripping the pen, Bianca forces herself to write against the rapid pace of her heartbeat. Flooded with hatred and fear, her mood accelerates towards panic. She is fairly sure Hesketh can't access the building, but, with him, nothing is certain. She still remembers the days when he would climb scaffolding to reach her.

If one of my neighbours lets him in downstairs and he comes to my door, should I call the police?

In the past, she had always called them. But then she stopped; their mood, when they arrived, always out of kilter with the distress of the occasion. Liking to plead a prosaic ABC of common sense, they existed solely for information, notebooks ever at the ready. Extremes of emotion embarrassed them. Even their own emotions, Bianca eventually realised, embarrassed them. And in their guarded stares she always detected the shadowy camaraderie of men, united against the hysterical effrontery of women, which is partly why she eventually became so reluctant to involve them; that and their huge fondness for witnessed information, plus their undiplomatic tendency to share it indiscriminately. They always wanted written answers:

'Are you married?'

'Do you own any properties other than this one?'

'What is your profession?'

If forced to call them, Hesketh would have more intimate information about her life within half an hour than he had hoped to discover in several years.

Yet Bianca must know I've changed?

Hesketh sinks back into the relentless debate he conducts with himself, the camera now hanging loosely about his neck. In the elastic scope of his mind, where anything is possible, he speaks to Bianca daily. He has taught himself to tune into her, much as if she were a radio station. Occasionally, sitting next to her in his thoughts, he can actually feel her physical presence. Sometimes, in the mornings, he wakes to find her in his arms. Then, for a few seconds, he experiences the sensation of having come home, before reality reinfects his mind, and his arms refold emptily about his chest.

I always understood Bianca better than she understood herself.

A distant memory of a row in a college forecourt causes him to frown.

Those wayward, intellectual parents of hers also had a lot to answer for…

Her father, William, had never liked him and Anya, her mother, who had begun by liking him…?

But she must be elderly now?

She, also, no longer answers his letters, although for numerous years had done so.

Hesketh refocuses his binoculars, wondering: *Do Bianca and her mother still speak?*

He is almost certain Bianca now lives alone. He prefers the idea of her being alone.

She may yet feel grateful to me for caring?

Only rarely does he remember the glitter of the diamond ring on her wedding finger, that evening two years earlier.

Bianca's voice explodes in his ear with spiteful disdain:

'How dare you impose your hideous, incontinent emotions on me for all these years?'

Hesketh throws back his head and laughs. A young woman waiting at the bus stop looks around in alarm. There is something

4

both ugly and violent in that laughter. He switches the Walkman to Play.

'You are like some filthy piece of flotsam that won't wash clean,' she hisses imperiously.

He smiles uncertainly to himself.

Of course, she didn't really mean it... She knows, deep down, that she loves me too.

Dwelling in the depths of her hatred and fear of Hesketh, Bianca feels both ashamed and empowered by it. There is no one else whom she so loathes. He has forced her to become part of his anar-chy of madness, forced her to understand – understanding having been her only means of survival – but that had not made it any more desirable. She thinks of her own hatred and Hesketh's ugli-ness as something conjoined, as if in hideous collusion. She knows intellectually that when they first met, Hesketh had been dashing, desirably handsome even. But it was like remembering someone who no longer exists. Her sense of his fatal repugnance had long ago overridden any perception of beauty. To Bianca, Hesketh feels like filth... Even the sound of his voice is a contamination.

His hair is plastered to his skull in the driving rain, yet Hesketh takes no notice. His pale, golden eyes now hold an otherworldly look of inspiration and triumph. Undying passion has elevated him into spiritual aristocracy... Bianca has become his life's work... That desire has not always nourished his body is irrelevant. The skin around his star-struck eyes might be that of a drunk's, red and crêpey, but his mind is perpetually enraptured by its own fervour, by the dialogue of delusion and pain he has chosen for them both. Everyone else's experience strikes him as pitiful in comparison. He feels no shame, no sense of trespass. On the contrary, he is proud of his own tenacity.

Bianca belongs to me... She always has and always will.

His thoughts tumble over one another, like greedy fish.

Thank God for wealth.

Over the years, private detectives had become much more expensive; some had begun to turn him down. Even sleuths, it seems, operate professional codes of conduct, and his story about her needing to find him and not knowing how was beginning to wear thin. One man had told him straightforwardly he did not like doing business with people who were mad.

Years earlier, he had persuaded a man he met in a pub to pose as an insurance claims adjuster and confront Bianca at home. But she had seen through him immediately. Demanding to see a business card, still unconvinced, she had refused to let him into her hallway. Later, she had checked up on him. His ploy was to accuse her of causing whiplash to another driver... Hesketh had assumed, after all these years, that Bianca must drive. It turned out that she did not even hold a driving licence.

The genuine claims adjuster, whose card it was, knew nothing about it. Yet the vociferousness of Bianca's complaints almost lost him his job, until he suddenly remembered her name, 'Bianca Johnson', and where he had last heard it. Tracing the episode back to his friend, Hesketh James, Hesketh eventually admitted stealing the card from his desk one lunchtime to pass to the amateur sleuth.

Hesketh bursts out laughing at the absurd memory of it all. He and the claims adjuster no longer speak. He shrugs... A far more subtle worry etches his thoughts; he used to more easily persuade women friends to spy on Bianca...

Am I losing my touch?

Fast forwarding the tape: 'Break down the door, why don't you? Isn't that your style?' she asks coolly.

He hears himself mumble something about being 'thick' and remembers Bianca's whole body recoiling in contempt. He cups his hand protectively over his face. He can still feel her scorn, even though he knew she hadn't meant it. He wishes he liked the sound of his own voice better. He can never control it. Words leap out and lie on the ground before him like blemishes, making him sound sinister and threatening, when all that he wants is to be loved.

He refocuses the binoculars. Bianca stands silhouetted against the light, head held characteristically to one side.

How slender she is...

She is dressed in jeans and a soft angora plume of a jumper. He can still imagine the circumference of her waist, the feel of the skinny knots of her lower backbone against the splayed fan of his fingertips, the warmth of her breasts as he held her close, her heart fluttering against his with the beat of a bird's wing.

Does she know that I'm watching her?

Her face is in shadow, indecipherable. In the lens, only the wide, happy shape of her mouth is traceable. His hand makes an involuntary gesture, as if to reach out and touch its gentle surfaces. She moves out of view.

Bianca moves about the room, angry with herself for not having the strength to ignore Hesketh's predatory rings, furious with him for interposing himself, yet again, between the pages of her life. Thoughts lash at her in a torment of frustration. Guiltily, she wishes he would die, longs to know her life free of his interference.

'How did I ever imagine him lovable?'

All she is left with is repugnance, grotesque feelings of distaste. Beyond which are only fear and loathing.

What aberration of mind makes him think such violent pursuit might lead to success?

She too, once upon a time, like the police, had expected common sense to turn a corner in Hesketh's mind and for him to let go. But now even the very thought is prosaic. Bianca knows that he can't. He has invested his whole life in a memory of lust. The fatal difference between them is that he calls it 'love' and she names it 'hatred'. He wants it back, and she never wants to look it in the face again.

Hesketh sighs, a deep exhalation of air, almost a sob. He used to write to Bianca daily; now, only every three weeks or so. He recalls his thousands of unanswered letters… although, since their conversation two years earlier, the mood of his writing is changed.

'Year after year of writing about what *you feel… you want…* and *you need?*' Bianca had mocked.

'I can be thick sometimes,' he'd faltered.

She had recoiled in disdain. 'Perhaps they don't use expressions like "thick" in Holland Park?'

A trickle of rain runs down his neck. He glances up at the mansion block behind him; next to it, a garage.

Maybe I should buy a flat here? Then I could watch her in greater comfort?

He smiles. Even the money had, in a roundabout way, been her blessing. Early on, trusting him still, she had related the family anecdote of how her aunt and uncle kept an emergency fund of £25,000 in banknotes, hidden in the seat of a kitchen stool, in their quaint, rose-shrouded house on Highbury Fields. Bianca primly refused to tell him the address, but he had traced it easily enough through the family name. It was that £25,000, stolen from her aunt, which had given him the basic sum to set up his travel business.

He had bought a run-down cottage on Ibiza and done it up, then a second on Majorca. It was travelling back and forth to the Balearics that had first given him the idea. Tourism was booming. It also gave him an excuse to place a business in the small town to the east of London, where her father, William, still lived. Bianca's family had always travelled. He had assumed one or other of them would come in to book a holiday; that he would then have all their details: credit cards, bank accounts and, best of all, telephone numbers. All her family were ex-directory. He had driven his staff mad, making them go through their receipts each night, checking for information on either Bianca or William Preston Johnson. But nothing had surfaced.

Perhaps they spotted my name over the door, 'heskethjames TRAVEL', in spite of my instructions to the sign writers to keep the lettering small?

The business itself had flourished. He subsequently opened branches elsewhere, until eventually Thomas Cook had approached with an offer to buy him out. Overnight, he became a multi-millionaire, with homes all over Britain and abroad. Emotion had robbed him of much, but never any of his instinct for business. He continued to operate his formula of buying cheap properties in unlikely places and watching them grow fashionable. Years earlier, he had written, hinting at his good fortune and enclosing a cheque for £10,000, but Bianca had never cashed it.

That uncashed cheque still worries him. *Had she torn it up at the time?* He rewinds the tape:

'The reason I don't go to the police is that I no longer want the hassle. But if you persist...'

He hears his halting ridicule of her assertion they might be interested, followed by Bianca's calm reply: 'Why don't we let them decide?'

A shiver passes through him. After their last court appearance, his brief explained that it was she, and not Patrick, 'that pathetic boyfriend of hers', who insisted things could no longer be 'settled out of court'.

Does she keep my letters?

He wishes he knew. These past two years, he had been more careful to write unthreateningly, fearing them being read by the police. They were intended for her alone. One Bank Holiday Monday, during the extravagant revelries of the Notting Hill Gate Carnival, convinced she was away, he had tried to break into her flat. Getting through the main front door had been easy... Unfortunately, none of his skeleton keys fitted the Chubb lock of her internal door. He even tried to lift it off its hinges. But one of her neighbours grew suspicious and he was forced to retreat.

Bianca glances at her watch. Getting late, she forces herself to abandon her anguished reveries.

Stephen will be here soon to collect me...

Needing to bathe, change and wash her hair, she does as she has numerous times before... She makes herself practise normality. It is getting dark.

Maybe Hesketh has left by now...? At least twenty minutes since he last rang my bell.

She switches off the standard lamp overlooking her desk and runs a bath. Sweeping her long blonde hair into a ponytail, she applies first one, then another face mask. Minute by minute, as the familiar routines assert themselves, she finds herself thinking of Stephen, not Hesketh. It is for him she plans to make herself beautiful.

Just as he is starting across the road to ring her doorbell again, the lights in her flat suddenly extinguish. Hesketh prowls agitatedly up and down the kerb.

Is she about to leave?

The binoculars tell him nothing.

Hesketh runs through his checklist: no back exit to the street, no fire-escape, except through the top-floor balconies... No way she can leave without his knowing.

Bianca is still in the bath when the phone rings.

'Everything okay?' Stephen asks, sounding happy.

'Yes, fine.'

Only later, perhaps, will she admit to her afternoon with Hesketh. Finished bathing, she dresses carefully, then applies her make-up with habitual speed. In five minutes, Stephen will be here to collect her. She extinguishes the rest of the lights.

Her front door opens and, suddenly, there she is, at the top of the steps. Hesketh's mind somersaults... Breathlessly, he witnesses the benign composure in Bianca's face; no trace of anger now. This is how he remembers her, sweet natured and kind.

She pauses, as if expecting someone. His breath catches in his throat. She is dressed in an elegant black suit, which moulds exactly to her slender figure. Miniature pearls dance flecks of light at her throat and ears, the only colourful notes her suede vermillion gloves. On tiptoe in high heels, she scans the street, at one point looking straight at him. Hesketh's heart breaks with the intensity of her gaze, but she has not recognised him. He knows himself to be more changed physically than she is. That night when they last spoke, it was dark. She had twice recently passed him in broad daylight without recognising him. No matter, nothing could alter the significance of today...

Today will always be ours.

A sleek, black car, its windows of smoked glass, draws up below her steps. Hesketh cannot make out whether the driver is male or female. Thoughts of it being a man ricochet through him, scattering his attention. He forces himself to take deep breaths, just as his doctor had taught him to. Briefly, his mind is a minefield of miniature explosions. He raises his hand protectively to his mouth, trying hard to remember.

Bianca would probably prefer us just to be friends, at least to start with…

He blushes; at times, his feelings are as coy and sentimental as those of a young girl.

As Bianca descends the steps smiling, he still can't see the driver. Hesketh watches her face light up in greeting. That sudden, aggressive thing his doctor has warned him of moves within him. Kicking out viciously at a stray Coke can, he sends it bouncing into the gutter, causing a small boy waiting at the bus stop to burst into tears.

As Bianca gets into the car, it moves off smoothly, only to be detained at traffic lights. Unthinkingly, Hesketh trudges after it. He can just make out the silhouettes of two heads turned towards one another, before the lights change and the car speeds away. He has lost them. Turning back, cursing, he had stupidly forgotten to note the number plate. He sits down heavily at the bus stop, his breathing now fast and uncontrolled, his diaphragm heaving visibly inside his duvet jacket. Behind his glasses, his eyes swim with tears; within the bow shape of his beautiful mouth, his teeth chatter unrestrainedly.

Until now, he had not noticed the cold and wet. He glances at his heavy bracelet Rolex, registering actual time for the first time that afternoon. Four hours have vanished in what felt like minutes… Gradually, his heavy breathing subsides, to be replaced by a sloppy, self-indulgent grin. He feels proud of his capacity to dispense with time.

One of these days, Bianca will come to her senses and realise the good friend I could be… After all, who else is going to care for her?

A violent sob racks his frame. He now feels the cold acutely.

Opposite, a policeman is questioning an elderly woman and glancing in his direction. Trying to cross, the traffic forces him to wait… Suddenly, Hesketh throws back his head and laughs loudly. Then, like someone coming to from a dream, he walks off rapidly, taking a familiar route through a half-concealed passageway running between the garage and the mansion block, his blue-silver Saab parked two streets away.

As he gains momentum, Hesketh's tap-dancing feet appear to

dawdle behind his powerful, jack-knifing frame. Punching his mobile phone with a familiar number, a voice answers softly.

'Sorry to be late, darling, I lost track of time... But I'm on my way home now.'

The voice at the other end is youthfully hesitant and querulous. 'Where are you?'

'I got detained.'

There is a small silence on the line...

'You've been to her house again, haven't you?' the voice asks unhappily.

He does not reply... That morning, in the moments of half waking, he had pulled her into his arms and called her 'Bianca' again. He had not known how to apologise.

'Bruno is refusing to speak,' the voice counters.

'I'll be right back.'

A disfiguring tiredness now controls Hesketh's features, leaving his face bereft of illumination. She has mentioned the only thing, other than Bianca, that really matters: Bruno, his nine-year-old son, who, like Bianca, also refuses to speak to him. How Hesketh's heart weeps for this handsome, clever boy, who plays the piano with exquisite precision but never speaks, except when his back is turned and, even then, only in riddles. When he was a baby, Hesketh had despairingly accused the Swedish au pair of having put a spell on him.

Driving south towards his home on Chelsea Embankment, he replays the tape.

'Do you imagine we've all spent our time becoming more unintelligent like you?' Bianca's voice asks scathingly.

Momentarily, the haunted look in Hesketh's eyes clouds resentfully.

Pathetic bitch... hadn't even remembered what day it is. Yet she dares mock me...

Driving through Sloane Square, the flower stall is shutting up for the night. It occurs to him that what he needs most is a stiff drink... Then, precipitously, his mood somersaults, and he grins boyishly. Shaking himself free of negative thoughts, he prepares instead to be graciously indulgent of Bianca's daft mistakes.

The silly billy, beautiful darling, hadn't even remembered her own anniversary.

He raises his voice above the fury of hers: 'Happy Anniversary, Bianca – 2 September 1971, twenty-seven years to the day since we first met. To us, now and always, my sweet love.'

CHAPTER 2

Early morning, and Bianca has not yet drawn the curtains. The delicate lines of her face are pale, and without make-up; her blonde hair tumbles about her shoulders, like a child's drawing of the sea. She picks up her silver pen to write: *'How to do this intricate thing of telling the old, familiar stories, without shrouding myself in the past and getting coated in its mud?'*

A bunch of roses, wrapped in Christmas paper, lies discarded at her feet.

Last night, for the first time in two years, she and Stephen had gone to a London hotel to make love. It was partly nostalgia... they used to do it often... partly circumspect. Leonardo is due back today, but he might have just as easily arrived yesterday. He often turns up unannounced – a film shoot finishes ahead of schedule, he gets to an airport early and takes the first available plane. On some journeys, it can make a difference of twenty-four hours. His first marriage to his Parisian wife, Lisette, had ended in divorce after he had twice caught her in bed with other men. That was years ago. Now, in the abstract, infidelities no longer signify with him hugely. Bianca knows it... He is, perhaps, unfaithful himself. Only its details are capable of hurting him, and it is precisely these miniature truths from which Bianca so assiduously protects him.

The phone rings. Startled, she glances at the large Ormolu clock left to her by her grandfather: 7.35 a.m. Few people ever ring before eight; she is again dressed simply, in jeans. The apologetic tones of Matthew, her oldest friend – and art dealer – greet her, sounding both gleeful and anxious, the guttural edge to his voice always most pronounced on the phone. He explains delightedly: 'I received a fax during the night, commissioning a new portrait by you.'

Bianca can hear the excitement in his voice. He mentions the words 'great honour', full of enthusiasm for the project. She feels a sudden rush of panic.

'Must I? I still have the Cavendish children's portrait to finish.'

His startled silence rebukes her.

'How can you not?' he eventually asks. 'Think of all the publicity.'

Reluctantly agreeing to talk later to arrange sittings, she thanks him almost too formally, before gently replacing the receiver.

In half reverie, she scrutinises the brushwork of a miniature Rouault watercolour, propped up on the mantelpiece, next to a calendar – 3 September 1998.

How had he done that? she wonders, before resuming her place at the polished walnut table and almost stepping on the roses.

Suddenly ashamed for having neglected them, she deposits them out of sight in the lavabo sink of her hallway toilet.

Bianca's apartment is a sequence of white rooms, with pale carpets and baroque drapes of oatmeal silk curtains defending its tall windows. From the street, it appears smaller, as though only one half of the raised ground floor, whereas, in reality, the sitting room, thirty-six feet long, extends either side of a central staircase to straddle the balconied front of the building; a room in which delicate antiques juxtapose with sumptuous sofas covered in white brocade and supported on carved claws of limed oak. Bianca draws back the extravagant curtains, ready at last to greet the day. It is no longer raining, the expression on her face strangely sad.

Portraits are like short stories, she thinks.

She has not yet told Matthew she has been writing and publishing stories under yet another pseudonym. All her professional work is pseudonymous. It is another of Hesketh's legacies in her life; a constant, watchful need for secrecy. As a portrait painter, she uses her mother's maiden name, Turvey. She is reluctant to tell him. As her dealer, Matthew would only consider it valuable time away from her painting. It would be difficult to explain, even to him, her oldest friend, how the two activities complement and galvanise one another. Even last night had been a short story of sorts...

As Stephen's car swept her from her door, she had turned to see a figure bent double against the wind and rain on the far side of the road. The man's head hung, lantern like, in front of a wid-ow-humped body, clouded in baby duvet; his right hand gesticu-lating forward; the other crouched like a small animal against his cheek, concealing a rictus of broken smiles. At first, she did not recognise him…

In fact, not until this morning, in quiet recollection, is she certain that it was Hesketh…

Bianca shudders. How changed Hesketh is. Years earlier, his sophisticated looks had been intriguingly, deliciously throwaway; a bruised, random kind of handsomeness. Nevertheless, that half-recognised figure, battling with the wind and rain last night, had registered deeply with her.

Was it emotion that had corrupted and stolen his looks?

She yields briefly to memory, acknowledging the very truth of Hesketh, before deliberately, almost painfully, switching thoughts. She has trained herself to never dwell too long on Hesketh… She thinks of him as an illness, whose symptoms are contagious by thought. Whenever forced to remember, she quickly rehearses the name of someone she admires, but has never yet met, repeating the name like a mantra, until all thoughts of Hesketh are obliterated…

'Max Holland… Max Holland… Max Holland…'

* * *

Picking up her pen to write, Bianca visualises herself and Stephen entering the chandelier-lit hotel foyer the night before. A tall man, with craggy features, places his hand possessively on Stephen's sleeve, asking amiably: 'How are you?'

Stephen's eyes grow steely and concentrated in reply, Bianca recognising the look he assumes when either annoyed or about to tell a lie. Nevertheless, he forces his features into gracious smiles of introduction: 'Do you know Bianca Vescarro-Johnson?'

'Bianca… John Harvey. We sit on the Castleton Board together… He also used to work for me at CERvello.'

'CERvello' is the publishing house Stephen started in his twenties and still owns. Bianca stretches out a vermilion-gloved hand to his. But the man's handshake is limp and elusive, and strangely at variance with the rugged lines of his face. Only his eyes sweep over her in an acceleration of interest.

'Vescarro? Any relation of Leonardo Vescarro?'

Bianca smiles decorously. 'Yes, I am his wife.'

The man's eyes open wide suddenly, his crooked face boisterous with questions he dares not voice.

'Do you know my husband?' she asks gently.

The look in his eye is now covertly hostile.

'Well no, not exactly,' he retreats apologetically. 'I've never actually met him, but I know his name, of course, and have heard him speak... Brilliant man,' he concedes.

She smiles quietly. 'Yes, I think so.'

Bianca returns the man's gaze steadily, her demeanour serene. But she is not deceived. She knows there is no creature more jealous, nor more cruelly moralising, than one who feels his own failures highlighted by another's success. She has also sensed Stephen's dismay. With the slightly apologetic stoop typical of tall men, he is smiling down on them, lopsidedly observing the tennis match of their exchange while trying not to look exasperated. She glances at John Harvey. Fleetingly, his face is bruised by jealousy. Peeking sidelong, he is embarrassed to catch the remnants of contempt in Stephen's eye. He begins to stumble his words, jabbing at thoughts, until the one uppermost surfaces unhindered: 'Leonardo Vescarro was recently on the cover of *Forbes* magazine.'

His voice is almost accusatory. Bianca's serenity performs a sudden volte-face, starting to apologise.

'Poor Leonardo. It's all part of the wretched publicity machine he has to submit to.' She pauses, wondering how useful sincerity is right now. 'He actually finds it endlessly intrusive,' she ends lamely.

'Really?' John Harvey raises an eyebrow sarcastically. 'Can I quote you on that?'

He dances backward a step or two, like a boxer considering his next move. 'I hear Vescarro is only too willing to brag about the money he makes...'

His comment is almost a shout, followed by silence. Bianca looks startled.

'Are you a journalist?' she asks.

Having chanced his arm so rudely, John Harvey lets out a soft, apologetic whinny of a laugh. Bianca smiles bittersweetly at him; she is used to people feeling they understand her husband better than she does.

Emboldened by her smile, he adds: 'I also hear Vescarro gets no time for a life of his own, the poor bastard.'

He glances down at the polished toecaps of his black brogues, as if in wonderment at his own acres of time. Bianca smiles guardedly, vaguely impressed now by the unconscious extravagance of his insolence.

'That's not true,' she states loyally.

She glances up at Stephen. He is wearing a look of urbane, smiling mockery, his long eyelashes fluttering furiously against high cheekbones; his face lightly flushed, his expression one of unmitigated contempt, as he battles against the temptation to denounce the man for his idiocy. Then, returning Bianca's anxious glance, his face suddenly stills into a sweet smile of deep concentration, the look in his eyes rushing, as always, to heal her distress.

'I say…' John Harvey begins, his voice trailing to a halt.

He has intercepted their look of complicity.

A familiar magic of reversal now starts to take effect. So strong is the impression of unity between Stephen and Bianca that people always capitulate to it, as though finding it irresistibly persuasive. Years later, still haunted by the image they had made together in public, people enquire hesitantly: 'Do you still see Stephen?'

To which Bianca always replies elliptically: 'Yes, we'll always be best friends.'

'Are you attending the conference here on Economics?'

More business-like suddenly, John Harvey addresses Stephen a little more formally. He gestures to the crowd of dark-suited men spilling from the elegant bar into the marbled hotel foyer.

'They're serving us cocktails, before Milton Friedman gives his talk.'

Bianca flinches slightly. She and Leonardo had had dinner with Milton Friedman and his wife only a few weeks earlier at their place in Siena. Noticing her startled look, he misinterprets it.

'I imagine even the great Leonardo Vescarro has something to learn from the Milton Friedmans of this world?'

Her face relaxes into an amused smile.

'Yes, I expect so,' she agrees effortlessly.

A doorman from the hotel passes by, bowing from his waist and smiling widely.

'Good evening, madam. How are you?'

John Harvey again looks at her quizzically. This time, she laughs openly at him. 'I come here most mornings to swim.'

But Stephen's patience has finally deserted him. Beyond the easy charm of his smile is a boisterous, barracking anger.

'You know the rules, Bianca… Never, never explain.' He pauses. 'Especially not to riff-raff like this.'

He punches John Harvey playfully on the shoulder to lessen the blow. Nevertheless, a deep barometer flush creeps up his crooked features. But Stephen has decided. 'We must be going.'

Looking around him, he takes possession of Bianca's arm. 'We need to find the lift.'

He turns back more politely towards John Harvey: 'How extraordinarily nice to have seen you.'

Bianca smiles simply. 'Goodbye.'

She again places her vermilion fingertips in those of John Harvey's.

'Will you not stay for Milton's talk?' he asks, anxiously reluctant now to let them go on so ambivalent a note.

'No, I have a client to see,' Stephen lies. 'He's expecting us in his suite on the sixth floor.'

John Harvey glances from one to the other of their smiling faces, suddenly brimming with understanding and jealousy. Yet also crestfallen and ashamed, as though feeling for them all the shame and sorrow he assumes them incapable of feeling for themselves. He raises his hand to stroke the air in a strange capitulatory gesture, half smile, half frown, then turns away peremptorily to be absorbed back into the crowd.

'I don't think he believed you… And as for "extraordinarily nice to see you", what was that? Politeness intended as ambush?'

Stephen smiles, linking her arm fondly in his. 'Years ago, I had to give him the sack. He's still resentful, but unlikely to say anything.'

'Shouldn't you have told him a more convincing lie?'

Stephen looks at her sharply. 'I'm sick of all the lies, aren't you?'

Bianca looks up in surprise, unsure of having heard him correctly. Although a fluent public speaker, Stephen aims to match much of his private conversation to the lightning speed of thought, with his sentences often turning into a bumpy ride of jumbled sound. She detaches this single thread, as if from a skein.

Sick of all the lies...? Can that be true?

She shrugs hesitantly. It occurs to her that her own mind is too ruthlessly on the side of those whom she loves to care hugely about any lies she might tell to protect them.

The lift doors open, and they step into a miniature TARDIS of oak panelling, inset with mirrors. Bianca concentrates instead on the familiarity of their twin reflections... Stephen's tall frame leans towards hers, darling gracious at her side. She traces the precise aquiline of his profile, set against the laughing, rippling, curvaceous mouth and smile; his sun-kissed cheeks of evening stubble. As she gazes into the transparent turquoise of his eyes, she smiles in secret anticipation of the somersault alchemy that will turn them dark blue in moments of fierce emotion and back to pale ice in moments of supreme intellect. Despite Leonardo's worldly reputation for cleverness, she is in far greater thrall to Stephen's intellect than she is to Leonardo's. An edge of white card emerges from his pocket. She looks at him questioningly.

'Later,' he says mysteriously.

Instinctively, she veers away from too much scrutiny of her own reflection to again concentrate on unravelling the question. It is not the lies they have told, but the sacrifices they have made for one another that worry her.

Can sacrifice brutalise?

As the lift doors close, Stephen takes her in his arms, the warm, familiar scent of his skin against her cheek.

'I know,' he whispers. 'Ducking and weaving; we've become too good at it.'

The irrational anxiety that can escalate in her immediately quietens. It is as though he has read her thoughts. She gazes undaunted into his eyes. Only in Stephen's eyes does Bianca ever know herself completely. She brushes one of her long golden hairs from the sleeve of his jacket.

They have emerged onto a deserted corridor. From his breast pocket, Stephen produces a sliver of plastic – Room 625. Green lights flash enter and they find themselves in a mock-up of a Belgravia drawing room, curiously doll's house in scale. To the right of the cavernous street below stretch the green banks of Hyde Park, where Bianca had once seen a helicopter land...

Feeling vertigo suddenly, Bianca steps back from her memories into Stephen's arms, also a trophy from the past. A current of warmth absorbs them. Gazing uninterruptedly at one another, they watch a fierce breath of intimacy embroider itself between them. Briefly, they hesitate... Too late... Stephen's arms tighten possessively about her. Bianca can taste the sweetness of coffee on his breath. She closes her eyes...

'Let him decide.'

Beyond, is the inviting smile of a high packed bed, but the distance feels too great... Stephen's hands start to explore her... He holds her wrapped against him, peeling her free of clothes; the funereal chic of her jacket, followed by the straight confines of her skirt. As she steps from its fallen circle at her feet, Stephen turns her round in his arms, watching joyously, his eyes creased in happiness. Beneath the demure severity of her tailoring, she is dressed like a creature from a carnival, in frou-frou confections of delicate black silk and lace. He propels her towards a full-length mirror, knowing she hesitates to think of herself as beautiful... In the mirror, her eyes and skin glisten with excitement.

'Dance for me,' he insists.

She obeys, gently swaying her hips to an imaginary rhythm. Circling her throat with necklaces of kisses, beneath the light worsted cloth of his trousers, she feels his erection dance with her. Suddenly, it is as if a switch is thrown. She glances up at Stephen, recognising the expression on his face; an abstract dream briefly inhabits its contours, before returning it to full focus. She feels the rasp of his stubble graze her skin, his mouth against hers, angry and pleading. Tonight, she knows, will be a rapturous debate... In the mirror, towering above her, Stephen's eyes are now a deep navy blue.

* * *

Later, just for a few minutes, Stephen sleeps. Bianca watches him, the graceful angle of his profile tucked into the raised cavity of his armpit. He will not slumber long; his energy and restlessness are formidable. Deserting his side to run a bath, she clambers back into bed, curling herself, shell-like, against the warmth of his back. As he stirs slightly, she raises herself on the mountainous pillows to glance around the room, half impressed, half amused by the forced gentility of it all. Bianca adores all the details that spell luxury, without feeling any fundamental belief in them.

For fifteen years, except whenever they had tried yet again to leave one another, evenings like these had been their adventures. She threads her arms lovingly about Stephen's waist.

Should I mention Hesketh's ringing my doorbell all afternoon?

She decides against it. Even after years of being hunted down like quarry, Bianca still feels ashamed to admit how much she hates Hesketh. He is like a dirty film over their lives that never wipes clean. Nor will she allow either Stephen or Leonardo to go to the police on her behalf. She had seen Hesketh on his days in court. For him, they mark triumph, not failure; silence, she knows, is his greatest punishment. It is also her only chance of ensuring his ignorance, her method of protecting not only herself but those whom she loves. If Hesketh knew who they were, he would persecute them too. Of that she is certain.

Stephen has woken and is watching her intently. 'Why are you frowning?'

'Hesketh,' she replies, but says no more. 'I have run us a bath.'

He grins happily.

They sit soaping and splashing one another like children, enjoying the hotel's ecstatic excess of mirrors and lighting; discussing bath taps, as though they were important pieces of sculpture. As they contemplate the restaurant where they plan to eat, before again returning to the hotel to make love, the phone rings. Not the landline, but the more urgent sound of Stephen's mobile.

Stephen lifts himself from the bath so quickly that sheets of water pour down his lean legs, splashing over its sides. The clamorous sound of the phone saws into their senses. Bianca hears Stephen say, 'Hello.' Then, in answer to a question: 'I'm in the street.'

She runs more hot water, hoping to drown the sounds of his conversation. But as she turns off the tap, she hears him ask: 'Just how late is he?'

His amused voice now sounds clipped and faintly irritable.

But when he reappears at the bathroom door, his face is stricken, all the high adrenaline he is capable of transforming it into an instrument of tortured concentration.

'Henry's missing,' he blurts out. 'He was at school all day, supposed to be home by six for a music lesson and never showed up. That was two hours ago. None of his friends seem to know where he is, and Sarah is distraught.'

Bianca looks up at him, sharing his sense of anxiety. It is as though he had suddenly lost several inches in height.

'You'd better go,' she states immediately.

There is no hidden moodiness in her suggestion.

'Would you mind?' he asks hopefully.

She smiles. 'No, of course not. We can do this another evening.'

Stephen's handsome face is full of dismay. 'Sixteen years old… a teenager for God's sake… He'll probably just turn up.'

His face is written with apology.

'But until he does…' She does not finish her sentence. 'Just go. I'll ring and cancel the restaurant.' She smiles up at him reassuringly.

'If you're sure?' His eyes, icily pale again, sweep over her in consternation but are already occupied elsewhere.

'Of course I'm sure.'

She thinks of how long they had loved one another, far longer than either of their marriages to Leonardo and Sarah. There is little jealousy. Instead, every moment is a bonus, reclaimed from what could and should have been their own past. When Bianca was seventeen and Stephen twenty, they had planned to marry. Bianca had got cold feet a few days before their wedding.

'I left the brochures for China on the table,' he suddenly remembers.

She smiles. 'No problem, I'll take them home to read.'

Wrapping himself in a huge white towel, he starts to rub his athletic limbs dry. He is six foot three. Dotingly, Bianca notices the light dusting of freckles on the fair skin of his shoulders as he starts to dress. She turns on the hot tap and remains in the bath.

'Have you paid for the room?'

'Yes, I did it earlier. I also ordered a taxi to pick us up here at nine to take us to The Ivy.'

'Okay, I'll deal with it.'

By now he is dressed and ready to go, his dark suit one she had chosen for him. He bends over the steam of the bath to kiss her gently, a moment of sweetness.

'Let me know if Henry's okay.'

'I will.'

He smiles lopsidedly and disappears.

* * *

Bianca dresses slowly. Alone in all this false luxury, the room begins to lose some of its charm, its doll's house loveliness reduced to embarrassed silence. She glances out of the window. Raining again, it would probably be difficult to get a cab.

Perhaps I should wait until nine, and ask the pre-booked taxi to drive me home, instead of to The Ivy?

She glances fleetingly at Stephen's haphazard spread of brochures. China is to be their most daring trip yet. They plan to leave in late October.

Will Henry's disappearance make a difference?

Bianca dismisses the thought. They had lived from day to day, with the expectation of 'something making a difference' to their plans for fifteen years. Yet they had always survived, teaching themselves to bend, like trees succumbing to the wind.

Once dressed, she makes herself up carefully. In the mirror, her head inclines naturally to one side, as though a *contrapposto* S runs through Bianca's body, lending it movement, even when still. A similar energy controls her face; quizzical movement seeming to constantly disrupt its symmetries, leaving anyone watching to play catch-up with the changeful weather of sorrow and smiling delight that chase across its surfaces, marking it bereft with despair one moment and beautiful with compassion the next. Contradictions which often match what she feels about herself; a shy uncertainty.

The room now feels oppressive, her presence there faintly ridiculous. She jumps as the doorbell rings. It is a maid checking the room. Unthinkingly, Bianca lets her in and together they silently survey the storm of sheets and pillows left by hers and Stephen's lovemaking. Suddenly feeling like an interloper, rather than a guest, Bianca decides to go downstairs to wait for her taxi.

Despite the crowded foyer, one of two yellow leather armchairs flanking the fireplace is vacant. Bianca decides to sit there and wait. It feels indecorous this late at night to buy herself a drink at the bar. The doorman again passes by and smiles.

As she searches in her bag for a handkerchief, a shadow eclipses her light; a dishevelled-looking man, towering above her. She recognises him instantly. The handsome, broken features of the playwright, Max Holland, glance down at her in amused silence.

Max Holland... Max Holland... her mantra against thoughts of Hesketh.

'I feel as though we've already met,' he begins suavely.

Studying him closely, as if sweeping a lamp across his features to memorise them, her scrutiny forces him to stand a fraction taller... He checks himself.

'Appalling of me... That must have sounded like a line,' he apologises, instantly willing to edit his own words.

Bianca smiles back sweetly, rescuing him. 'It's true we have almost met. I saw you last week in the distance at the Millers' party.'

He smiles happily, relieved.

'How were you dressed?'

She giggles. 'In pale blue.'

'More details,' he demands, suddenly boisterous. 'More details...'

'My hair was in pigtails and I was wearing a pinafore,' she says seriously. 'I was a waitress.'

'Were you?' he asks, flabbergasted.

'No.' She smiles, no longer teasing. 'I had on a blue suit, with fluted collar and cuffs...'

Her sentence trails to exhaustion. 'I don't know how to describe myself.'

She glances up at him. His face is beaten up and sensual, its impassive, impacted planes written across in a calligraphy of exquisite detail; the full-lipped, self-contained curve of his mouth, identical in pallor to his cheeks; the eloquent delineation of his dark eyes, juxtaposed with the curious laziness of one eyelid; the intelligent height of his brow, the rough and tumble of a hairdo that remembers its student days thirty years earlier and the swagger of a red scarf around the neck of his Armani suit, making it appear more casually throwaway than Armani may have intended.

'Whereas you are just as I have always imagined you,' she says gently.

He is flattered.

Suddenly remembering her booking at The Ivy, she half rises from the yellow chair. 'I meant to cancel the restaurant...' she explains. 'I was here with a friend. Our plans changed last minute.'

She glances disconcertedly at her watch. 'I've almost left it too late... Do you think they'll be furious with me?'

He watches this conflict weave through her frame, infecting every gesture, yet without robbing any of her sweetness and elegance.

'Ring them on this – it will be easier,' he says, handing her his mobile phone.

Then, as she begins to dial: 'Could we not retrieve the situation by going to the restaurant together, but at my invitation?' he asks.

Bianca hesitates, looking confused.

'We could discuss all the parties where we almost met, and the people who got in the way,' he argues persuasively.

He checks himself, suddenly composed. He has noticed the diamonds sparkling on her left hand.

'What I should have asked is if it is appropriate for me to invite you? Whether you still have time this evening for dinner?'

She holds the phone listlessly in her lap. 'Yes, I do have the time,' she eventually replies. 'Although, I was just intending to go home.'

'So was I... I came here to listen to Milton Friedman's speech.

You just looked so beautiful sitting there...' He does not finish his sentence. 'Can we not see if we can be friends?'

He pauses, observing her closely. 'Where is your reservation for?'

'The Ivy.'

Suddenly, he laughs, a great joyous sound, and she laughs with him. With a theatrical flourish, he bows deeply, sweeping the floor with an imaginary feathered hat.

'You shall go to the ball after all, Cinders. But as my guest,' he insists.

She smiles happily.

The doorman reappears.

'Madam, your cab is here.' He glances at the man as he speaks.

'What's it to be?' asks Max Holland.

'If you're sure?' she agrees stumblingly.

'Yes, much more than sure...'

As she and Max cross the foyer, she turns to find twin pairs of eyes upon her, one set abstractly interested, the other warm, welcoming and pretty. Sitting just beyond the entrance to the bar are the diminutive figures of Milton Friedman and Rose, his sweetly smiling wife. The latter nods and gives a half wave. She is wearing the same black outfit with diamante lapels she had worn in Siena a few weeks earlier. Max Holland follows her gaze and smiles.

'Twenty-five years ago, we had a period of galloping socialism; now we have a period of creeping socialism,' he quotes. 'What we now want is a period of declining socialism...'

'Do you agree with that?' she asks, returning the old lady's wave.

'No, not entirely,' he replies, 'but it's very eloquent and some subtle truth seems to lurk in its corners.'

She laughs with him.

Together, they dash out into the rain, scampering under the doorman's vast umbrella to avoid getting wet. Then, cocooned in the dry warmth of the taxi, Max and Bianca chatter easily, genially, like old friends.

At the restaurant, Max is greeted by a spontaneous round of applause from the other diners. A new play of his has just opened in the West End to superlative reviews. Once seated, people dash up to him, kissing him proprietarily, their eyes sliding over Bianca in mute, irritable envy. Bianca waits patiently for their drama to settle. These sycophantic dances are all-too-familiar territory. She experiences them, although more covertly, with Leonardo. She smiles ubiquitously. Finally, they are left alone to concentrate their attention exclusively on one another. As they do so, some magic of instinctive feeling, some strange sense of belonging, patterns itself between them. They talk easily, joyously, heedless of time. They discover a mutual delight in the work of Lawrence Durrell. They discuss the philosophy of Gaston Bachelard. Not until one in the morning do they think of leaving. When, finally, they look around them, the restaurant is almost deserted. Max pays the bill and asks the waiter to arrange a cab, insisting on accompanying her home safely before taking the taxi on to his own address in Islington. At her door, Max steps briefly from the taxi to say goodbye. Neither of them notices the rain. Taking her hand gently in both of his, he kisses her on both cheeks, then clambers back into the cab, and waves goodbye. They have not exchanged phone numbers.

* * *

By next morning, Bianca has hardly slept. At 7.35 the phone rings… It is Matthew, reporting having received a fax in the middle of the night from the playwright, Max Holland, commissioning her to paint his portrait.

'Such a great honour,' he whispers breathlessly.

Bianca does not explain… Promising to speak later in the day, she returns to her desk, feeling suddenly depressed. Noticing the roses at her feet, she takes pity on them. She had found them outside her door last night when she returned. Inside their Christmas wrappings, was scrawled: 'All my love, Hesketh.'

She sighs. *Why Christmas paper when it's only September?*

She dumps them out of sight in the lavabo sink.

At 8.30 the phone rings again… It is Leonardo. He is at the airport; Lily, his driver, is with him. He will be home within half an hour. Replacing the receiver, she runs herself a bath.

They circle one another smiling, taking stock, neither hugging nor kissing. Conversation between them is stilted, hesitant.

'Would you like your favourite breakfast of smoked salmon with scrambled eggs?' she asks.

Bianca has not seen Leonardo for seven weeks; spoken to him only intermittently on the phone. She glances at the heavy undertow of bruised shadow beneath his dark eyes, the white-grey ringlets that run like unravelled knitting across his skull, to curl in tight tendrils above his collar; the elongated mauve of his smile, in which are elements of both irony and conspiracy.

He is all chiaroscuro... she thinks, seeing him clearly, as if for the first time.

Beneath his tan, his skin is curiously bleached, with heavy thumbprints of mauve either side of his nose and temples, a daub of shadow beneath his lower lip and chin. He scarcely glances at her.

'No breakfast; I just want to sleep...'

She returns to bed with him... It occurs to neither of them to make love. Yet, beneath the subduing warmth of the duvet, they snuggle automatically, one to another, like two cats, their bodies making cosy peace. He is as warm and sweet smelling as freshly baked bread. They sleep until 11 a.m., when she makes coffee and scrambled eggs, which he eats ravenously, sitting up in bed.

He's like a Roman version of Pooh Bear, she thinks fondly.

Still, their chatter is only intermittent; the fact of their being back together in the same room far more important to them both than anything said. Two people feeling their way to heal a divide of absence, without actually mentioning it. Neither of them cares about the details of that absence. All that matters is the resurrection of their status quo; their entire marriage is based on nothing being allowed to get in its way. It is one of the principal things on which they agree, tacitly and passionately. Gently, they set about fitting back into their life together, before absorbing their next separation.

When, at lunchtime, Bianca eventually checks the various messages that have accumulated on the answer machine while they slept, one is from Stephen. His voice sounds lifted and glad. His son, Henry, had got drunk with a new group of friends on his way home from school and lost track of time.

'I'll phone you later... All is well.'

Bianca repeats the phrase, sighing to herself: 'All is well?'

She wonders... *Can that can be true? Not altogether, maybe?*

CHAPTER 3

Twenty-four hours later, the police arrive, looking for Hesketh. Overlooking the river, next to the Chelsea Physic Garden, his fifth-floor apartment on Chelsea Embankment is in a building vaguely French in style. Its street entrance buzzer barely works, forcing visitors into a fight with the door. Stranded midway within its gloomy pentagonal hallway stands an oak refectory table, spread with disorderly accumulations of mail, some of which spill onto dusty parquet, never to be picked up.

A short staircase leads to a timed light switch, exposing scraps of torn matting in front of an old-fashioned lift, with collapsible grille doors; the lift itself tiny, no more than a dumb waiter. An intimate encounter, even for two, as it judders slowly to the top, to open directly into Hesketh's apartment.

The policeman, and woman, revolve from its confines like tops onto a corridor. Silently framed in a doorway sits a nine-year-old boy, his face deliberately turned away, his features strangely swaddled, as if bandaged against the truth.

Readjusting her black-and-white cap, one half of the policewoman's face is smooth and pretty, the other stained by a strawberry mark that has made a map of her right cheek. The tall policeman, his natural bulk accentuated by the square cut of his uniform, grins at the boy.

'Is your father at home?'

His manner is that of someone who had hoped to be ordinary, yet failed. Some light of compassion in his violet eyes gives him away.

The child, whose face is a rumour of Hesketh's, continues to avert his gaze. In his features, silence. Only his fingers are animate, as if dancing to some inner tune. They are also strangely long and expressive in someone so young; as though a nine-year-old's vitality were channelled exclusively through his hands.

The policeman repeats his question. In reply, the boy turns his back on him. Disconcertedly stepping back, like someone recoiling from a blow, the radio on his lapel crackles suddenly, barking an indecipherable tannoy of information. Still, the child does not look up.

He glances questioningly at his colleague.

'Someone must have let us in,' she reminds him.

They have emerged into the narrow hallway of a flat, spread equally from left to right of the lift shaft. To the right, a handsome room with views of the Thames; to the left, obscured by a turn in the corridor, a kitchen and dining room leading to a miniature roof terrace overlooking the Physic Garden. Doors to other rooms are deceptively concealed behind panels in the corridor walls.

'Perhaps the child let us in?'

The policeman studies the boy carefully. 'Is he old enough to be left on his own?'

Baffled, they begin to feel nervous. As if to reassert authority, the policeman swaggers his bulk into the handsomely proportioned room overlooking the river. On one wall, jumbled chaotically, is a collection of British paintings, dating from the 1940s; some quite valuable. He bends to scrutinise a model of an ancient plough displayed sculpturally to his right, before turning towards the high stone mantelpiece, on which rests a modern triptych, composed of twelve small pictorial panels flanking an abstract central panel. Scattered at its base are various invitation cards. One particularly attracts his attention; requesting the presence of Mr and Mrs Hesketh James at a fundraising dinner for the local Conservative Party, at which the Chief Commissioner of Police promises to speak.

Although hearing no sound, some instinct causes him to suddenly spin round... He backs away in alarm. Stealthily bearing down on him is the tall, naked figure of Hesketh, an intent, aggressive look on his face. The vicious curves carving Hesketh's cheeks, plus the angry pout of his beautiful mouth, give his face a look of astonishment. But in the depths of his golden eyes is only cunning, masquerading as outrage.

With scant apology for his appearance and as though to dress, Hesketh puts on his wide-framed glasses. The policewoman, her raspberry stain turned towards the room, watches circumspectly from the doorway. Noticing her, Hesketh's laughter skids through the room like an insult.

'If you could just put some clothes on, sir, I'd like to ask you some questions.'

Raising a hand to half shield his teeth, Hesketh leans forward to his favourite angle of thirty degrees, stabbing the air with his forefinger, his voice now a sneer.

'I'll dress as I please in my own home.'

The lady PC blushes, uniting her face in a brief symmetry of colour.

'How did you two get in here?' Hesketh demands.

'Someone let us in.'

'Not me.' His voice is honeyed with sarcasm. 'I wouldn't dream of letting any of you in.'

His laughter is disparaging, violent.

'The boy, perhaps?' suggests the policeman. 'Did he let us in?'

Suddenly, a look of anguish breaks the aggressive fixity of Hesketh's stare, shuffling through his golden gaze like a deck of cards before reasserting itself.

Distantly, a washing machine fast spins its load, followed by a soft flurry of footsteps.

'Darling, what would you like for lunch?' asks a youthful voice.

From the doorway behind Hesketh, a young woman suddenly appears, her light auburn curls piled high over submissive grey-green eyes, as she struggles to thread her arms through a white towelling robe to cover her slender nakedness. Her face is round and unblemished, apart from sleepless traces of mauve beneath her eyes, her skin an even blush. She has a mouth almost too wide for her face, which spills with uncertainty and the promise of soft kisses. She is perhaps thirty-four years old, yet appears much younger. On noticing the two policemen, her face freezes in terror. Only her eyes darting between them register movement.

'Can't a man even make love to his wife without you lot interfering?' snarls Hesketh.

'Where were you two nights ago, sir?' counters the policeman.

The young woman's face blanches, her petal-like prettiness dissolved in panic. From the corridor suddenly emits a strange ululating sound, haunting and desperate.

'Bruno,' states Hesketh breathlessly. '*My son*... You are distressing MY SON.'

His voice, begun on quiet notes of menace, rises to a distraught, pitiful shout.

'Go to him,' he snaps at his wife, who looks back at him transfixed in sluggishness.

'For God's sake, Chloe, just go to him...'

Chloe suddenly pulls her robe tight about her tiny waist and scurries slavishly, tripping over a tear in the carpet in her hurry to reach the distressful sound.

'You're causing serious disruption here,' states Hesketh smoothly, standing momentarily tall, in uncharacteristic retreat from his thirty degrees. 'I shall want to know the name of your superior, in order to file a complaint.'

The policeman is unperturbed. 'Either answer my questions here, sir, or put on some clothes and come down to the station.'

His perceptive eye sweeps over Hesketh's lean body. He is shivering slightly, goose pimples on his thighs. He sees that anger had provoked Hesketh into a half erection.

'Where were you the night before last, sir?'

Hesketh plays for time. 'Do you know who I am?'

'Yes, sadly I do... This isn't the first time, is it, sir? Were you at the Anglesea Arms near Sloane Square, the night before last between 7 p.m. and 8 p.m.?'

A lightning change, almost of relief, infiltrates the hazel gold of Hesketh's eye. As the policeman turns squarely towards him, he is suddenly reminded of someone. Struggling to retrieve this lost page of memory, hovering at the edge of his mind, he detects a secret smile in Hesketh's face before it vanishes again into pantomime.

'Now, let me think... that night... where was I?'

Chloe re-enters the room, leading the reluctant child by his long, sensitive hands, the boy's face remaining averted from them all, as he taps his toes rhythmically against the spines of a 1911 edition of *Encyclopaedia Britannica*.

'Hesketh was here with me,' she answers abruptly for her husband.

'Between 7 p.m. and 8 p.m.?' the policeman queries.

She looks up momentarily, as if astonished by his question, before nodding and glancing away distractedly, saying nothing more.

'Our information is that the night before last between 7 p.m. and 8 p.m. you may have been involved in an incident at the Anglesea Arms?'

The policeman notices what may be a faint purple bruise in the shadow beneath Hesketh's eye.

'Do you ever use make-up, sir?'

Hesketh ignores this long shot. 'What am I alleged to have done?'

'Made remarks of a racist nature, calculated to incite a disturbance,' states the policeman, glancing at his notes.

Hesketh's penis, he notices, has now dwindled to a corkscrew of withered flesh. In his face, however, is renewed confidence. It occurs to the policeman that Hesketh was anticipating a different kind of accusation.

What's it like to be this man?

He had read Hesketh's recent file: 'A successful businessman and collector of paintings, capable of turbulent outbursts of racial hatred.'

His violet eyes appraise the strange mixture of aggression and mewling tenderness that are the rapidly exchanged currency of Hesketh's personality.

Can a man like that ever be happy?

'You must be confusing me with someone else,' states Hesketh.

His eyes bulging, the glutinous, hyperthyroid veins are suddenly caught unfairly amplified by the two-way action of his glasses.

'I was here with my wife.'

'Are you prepared to confirm that, Mrs James?'

As he turns towards her, Chloe's face drains of colour, yet she nods automatically. Her eyes stray anxiously towards her son, who has now picked up some knitting and is producing a long ribbon of tautly knit bright-blue wool at an astonishing speed.

35

'Would you be willing to take part in an identity parade, sir?'

Hesketh laughs at the absurdity of this question. There is, both he and Hesketh know, little that he can do. The racist remarks had been made in a half whisper, spoken insidiously, and only heard accurately by the young medical student for whom they were intended. Even if Hesketh could be identified as having been in that pub at the correct time, it would still be his word against that of the student. The 'incident' had resulted in little more than a scuffle. Hesketh is too smart.

'May I remind you, sir, that making racist remarks in public is a punishable offence?' he states hollowly.

'Perhaps you should leave,' retaliates Hesketh dryly, 'and come back when you have more reliable information. Harassment and entering a property without a warrant are also offences, I believe? Is it enough to remind you of that or should I take my complaint to your superiors?'

Leaning forward, Hesketh spits each word in the policeman's face like an insult. Only the policewoman notices the mottled grey of his flesh beneath its light friction of hair

'Someone let us in,' she reminds them.

'Well it wasn't me and it certainly wasn't my wife. We were in there, making love.'

Hesketh glances cruelly at the policewoman. 'Don't suppose you get many lovers with a face like that?'

The policeman flinches, rocking back on his heels, his fists clenched in anger; out of the corner of his eye, the hunched shape of the child.

'No need for personal insults, sir...'

'No need for either of you to be here is what you mean!' shouts Hesketh.

Chloe blushes deeply, her head hung in shame, tangles of curls parting to reveal her slender neck.

'Consider yourself cautioned,' states the policeman.

Yet he realises himself beaten. Not so much by Hesketh, whom he could easily have manhandled to the ground, but by the presence of the child. He prides himself on his capacity for calm. Retreating backward towards the lift, he shoos the policewoman ahead of him, like a small child.

'Take the stairs.'

Hesketh opens a panel in the hallway onto a darkened stairwell.

'This apartment is like a Chinese box,' comments the policeman in mild surprise.

'There doesn't seem to be much light,' objects the policewoman. Eleven o'clock in the morning and already she feels exhausted.

'No, unfortunately, the bulb has gone,' states Hesketh cruelly. 'Just keep your hand on the banisters and feel your way to the bottom.'

'Is this absolutely necessary, sir?' asks the policeman, quelling his anger.

'Yes, I have neighbours... My wife and son to think of. Your presence here is indiscreet, intrusive. No one uses the stairs. No one will see you leave.'

The policeman casts one last lingering look at the enclosed features of the boy, his hands still knitting mechanically fast, as though independent of the immense silences in his face; his whole being capitulating to compassion.

'Very well, sir.'

Hesketh holds the door open, briefly illuminating their descent.

The policeman's final glimpse is of Hesketh, bending in naked supplication before the diminutive figure of his son, followed by pitch darkness as he lets go of the door. Suddenly, he remembers... A court case he had attended many years earlier, as a young constable in Knightsbridge... That distraught, handsome, violent man in the dock, he now realises, had been Hesketh twenty years earlier, accused of causing grievous bodily harm to his former girlfriend's new boyfriend.

'Take my hand,' he orders his colleague. 'I promise to catch you if you fall.'

* * *

'Were you there, that night, in that pub?'

Hesketh pauses, looking Chloe in the eye, as if to assess the depths of her passivity. In certain lights, she still reminds him of Bianca.

'Of course, not. I was on my way back here from a business meeting.'

Turning away, as though to shed herself of him mentally, she says: 'I'll prepare lunch, shall I?'

Her voice is dull with exhaustion.

'Yes, shortly, but first there is a letter I must write.'

Still naked, Hesketh disappears into a small cupboard of a room, adjacent to the lift and furnished like an office, with desk, computer and files. Taking a sheet of A4 paper and red biro, he returns to the sumptuous room overlooking the river. The distant figure of Buddha in Battersea Park gleams in the morning sun. Positioning a white swivel armchair in front of the fireplace, he drags a small table alongside it to improvise as a desk, meanwhile gazing up at the triptych above the mantelpiece, as if for inspiration. It is an early painting by Bianca, one he had stolen from her many years earlier. She had never known. She had left it briefly in the basement of his former house for safekeeping. He told her it had been damaged in a fire, along with all her other early paintings and drawings. She has no idea they still exist.

Glancing at the miniature configurations of painted figures, predominantly a man and woman, in each frame, dispersed about its twelve smaller panels, he has always believed these figures to depict himself and Bianca, even though Bianca had denied it. Taking a sheet of paper, he starts to write.

'Darling Bianca...'

Behind him, in the doorway, silently watching, his face no longer averted now that his back is turned, is Bruno.

CHAPTER 4

The following morning at breakfast Leonardo tells Bianca he had visited a doctor in Singapore.

'It seems...'

Bianca glances up at him, urgently scanning for what he is about to say. It is 7 a.m. Between miniature cups of strong black coffee, he has already smoked his third cigarette.

He's Italian, she thinks indulgently. *What else would he do?*

She observes the lilt of his eyebrows, his dark, currant-bun eyes looking at her questioningly. He is both the ugliest and most beautiful thing she knows; the Roman head, with its high narrow forehead, smaller in width than his pocked marble cheeks. Plus the chiaroscuro dance of shadows, which only animation sends fleeing, like puffs of smoke disengaging from the contours of his face, to leave behind a curious radiance. He is sitting up in bed surrounded by magazines, in that moment caught betwixt modes, neither solemn nor joyous. He takes another draw of his cigarette.

'I've been suffering migraines.'

She holds her breath against the tide of his voice. 'You didn't say.'

'I passed out one night from the pain in Singapore.'

'What did the doctor say?'

'There is no shadow, no brain tumour visible on the X-rays.'

'Is that what he feared?'

He pauses. 'Yes, I think so.'

Bianca looks down at her hands. She is kneading them back and forth unconsciously, one upon the other, forcing blue veins to the surface with her spiteful pressure, bending back the fingers acrobatically. A kind of sick panic possesses her. She glances up at this elusive, beloved man with whom she has chosen to half share her life. She has no illusions. She knows their marriage to be deeply flawed, that perhaps it had been right from the start. She also knows he does not love her exactly. Or if he does that it is a love despite himself, something which takes him unawares. Nor is she proud of her infidelity to him; in fact, she is repelled by it. Yet she also accepts it as inevitable, her allegiance to Stephen final. If anything, she is grateful to Leonardo for making the story of her life easier by neither inspiring nor strictly deserving fidelity. He is a man too self-absorbed, too capricious at other people's expense; incapable, if ever he was, of losing himself in unconditional devotion to another human being. He is also emotionally opportunistic, capable of giving away any depth of emotion and relationship to a passing fancy and then imagining, like Pangloss, that his actions are invisible. Bianca had accepted long ago that Leonardo was essentially fickle, that no woman who had ever really known and understood love would choose to remain faithful to him.

And yet, she also knows that he deserves and commands the utmost loyalty. There is a sweetness and generosity of altruism in Leonardo Vescarro that no one surpasses. It often occurs to her he is a man who understands the rules of friendship superbly well and the rules of passion not at all. He longs for people to feel passionately towards him, but without the hassle of his ever needing to feel the same in return. A man cloaked in the ermine of self-adoration, who, despite moments of acute shyness, thinks it more fitting to receive love than to give it. Bianca finds him a never-ending set of contradictions.

When they first married, she had been shocked by the tales of his first wife Lisette's flagrant infidelities, but in time she had come to understand them. He would gladly turn any wife into a dormouse and not really notice her despair; a dormouse who knew how to strew his path with rose petals would strike him as ideal.

Yet, despite all these undecorated truths residing in her perception of him, as Bianca waits for him to divulge his illness, she feels deeply afraid for them both. How to explain, even to herself, the soaring gift of freedom his contradictory nature had brought her? People are so steeped in longing for some conventional version of security. But for Bianca, that security exists only in the dependability of Leonardo's contrariness. He does not deliberately set out to hurt; he is incapable of malice. He simply wants to be surrounded by people sufficiently robust and elastic enough to make some sort of philosophical pudding out of pain, as he has had to. And the challenge to submit to being simultaneously shackled and free is, she had discovered, a strangely rewarding one.

She thinks of the freedoms within her marriage as glorious leftovers; generous crumbs from a banquet. When all her duties towards Leonardo are fulfilled and he chooses to turn away to follow some miniature programme of fun from which she is excluded, then, and only then, does she dare turn joyfully quick-silver and vanish into a theatre of her own; as baroque, beautiful and daring as any her maestro captor can imagine. She lets out a half sob. The true heartbeat of her life is Stephen, but Leonardo is the fabric. She loves him too, and the thought of his suffering acts like an immediate blight on her emotions. Her mind races with pain at the prospect of what he is about to say.

'They think it may be my eyes causing the migraines, that I may be developing a cataract. I'm going this morning for an eye test.'

Such is the depth of her fear that it takes her a moment to absorb what he just said. She smiles hesitantly, anxiety slipping from her. Leonardo picks up a piece of toast, pinching it delicately between his thumb and forefinger before biting voraciously, as though fear-ing its being snatched away. She sighs, smiles and gets up to give him a kiss on the crease in his earlobe. He grins up at her wickedly, mischievously, like a naughty child. He has witnessed the depth of her anxiety and it has given him immense pleasure. He relaxes a little more regally against the pillows. Now, at last, he feels prop-erly at home again. Adoration... What heaven...

'Why don't we eat out tonight?' he beams beatifically.

'We have guests, remember?'

'Oh yes,' he replies distractedly. 'So we do.'

* * *

That evening, Bianca lays a table for dinner in their hallway; a long rectangle, from which all other rooms of the apartment lead. Between its panelled doorways, hang tall rococo framed mirrors;

presiding grandly from one end is Bianca's most recent portrait of Leonardo. The painting has great presence, yet Leonardo dislikes it. He distrusts its absence of flattery. Bianca has replaced his easy-going charm with something magisterial, almost desolate. Plus his friends tease him about it.

'Didn't know you were capable of such unhappiness, Leo,' they say, laughing.

Their first guest to arrive is Robin Holderness, a tall crag of an American, and English academic. Carrying a biker's helmet under one arm, his angular figure wrapped in yellow plastic, beneath this plastic shell, he is dressed in a sandy coloured corduroy suit; bone dry, except for his drenched face and hair. Bianca considers Robin a friend, yet she is never completely sure. He lives to do battle. She had known him in her own university days, remembers him tenaciously standing still, watching philosophy turn fashionable, while, for amusement, he had numerous affairs with his students. Looking at him now, she suspects the amusement has begun to wane. She detects in him despair, tinged with desperation. Also, that alarming dislocation between what a person perceives philosophically and feels privately. How different from a painter, she muses, whose intellectual ideas might easily be wrong-headed but would nevertheless act like a creed... Action, identical with belief.

'How are you?' she asks merrily, her eyes scanning every inch of his corduroy body.

Watching her sternly from his great height, his eyes melt suddenly, to reveal the soft underbelly of affection he feels for her.

'Give us a kiss, while no one's looking,' he suggests.

She raises her cheek to his, but instead his lips graze against hers. Briefly, her eyelashes flutter and close, as she recognises the secret gentleness in him.

'Now take me to that charlatan husband of yours.'

Her eyes fly open again, startled. 'Leonardo is next door,' she replies, instantly formal again.

He laughs naughtily, taking a sip from the glass of champagne she offers him.

'Lead me to him then... Let's find out if he knows anything about chaos theory?'

Despite herself, Bianca smiles. *Leonardo is himself a little bit of chaos, at times,* she thinks fondly.

As Robin follows her into the long drawing room, Leonardo rises from a great throne of a sofa to greet him.

'Hello, Robin, how's philosophy?' he asks teasingly. 'Still stuck on logical positivism?'

Bianca leaves them to joust, running to answer the doorbell.

As she does so, the phone rings… Picking it up, someone at the other end listens to the silence between them, then replaces the receiver carefully, as though attempting to tiptoe away from the call. The doorbell rings again, this time more insistently.

Damn, this only ever happens when Leonardo is at home.

Bounding up the stairs to greet her is the tall, blonde, athletic figure of Aubrey Byng, right-wing English political correspondent of *Le Figaro*, his handsome boyish features overwritten with suspicion and false eagerness. His friends all call him 'Byng', as though his Christian name. Although he thinks like an Englishman, his manner and style are elegantly French, his kiss on Bianca's cheek slightly rough. Glancing obliquely at her, she returns his gaze doubtfully. He suspects her of knowing the details of his most recent affair, leaving him feeling uncomfortably exposed. The false eagerness in his face, however, is less in response to herself than a product of the conflict governing his personality. More than simply a journalist, Byng prides himself on being an intellectual. He greets Robin Holderness with effusive shows of deference, from which Robin, the purist philosopher, backs away in repugnance. In fact, Byng is intellectual, but the absurdity and greed of journalism have ruined it for him. The hunger for information, his instinct to immediately turn it into news, have rendered the more speculative side of his nature stillborn.

Beatrice, his glamorous Swiss wife, dressed like a bejewelled odalisque, follows him into the room, cutting a swathe of smiling, perfumed self-confidence; it is an immaculate performance. Yet Bianca knows that her discovery of her husband's affair and subsequent forensic pursuit of his chequebook stubs and credit-card details have almost destroyed her.

Drawing her to one side, she asks: 'How are things, Bea?'

The exquisite beauty's eyes darken with sorrow. 'As soon as Byng is out of sight, I start to hate him,' she confesses. 'Then, the moment he is with me, I fall in love with him all over again.'

'Surely it will get better?' Bianca soothes.

'I hope so…' Her voice is a whisper as she chokes back tears.

Witnessing just how fragile that hope is, how defeated and sad Beatrice feels, Bianca watches in admiration as she recovers herself, deliberately fixing her smile and turning it joyously towards Jocelyn Carpenter and his wife, now making their entrance in the long drawing room. It had been listening to and sympathising with Beatrice's distress that had caused Bianca her greatest misgivings in her own relationship with Stephen.

Can love ever be as final and justified as ours feels?

Briefly, she ponders it again now, but her mind refuses the melancholy thought. She and Stephen… They are like complex pieces of machinery, difficult to switch off. She turns to fetch more champagne. As she does so, she suddenly notices Leonardo isolate himself to speak on his mobile phone.

Jocelyn Carpenter is a former QC and silk, knighted for his philanthropy. A charming, wonderfully urbane man, he makes no effort to disguise the flapping stump of his left arm, amputated above the elbow. Bianca is fond of him but never knows whether he remembers and recognises her. It hardly matters. Although, occasionally, she catches him watching her intently. It had always felt too indecorous to mention. Not even Leonardo knew they had first met in court twenty or so years earlier, with Jocelyn presiding as judge and herself as chief witness. Yet, even during those distraught, distant days in court, he had felt familiar somehow… More than anyone else she knows, he has kept faith with the altruistic ideals of his student years, some of them identical to those she had inherited from her Bohemian parents: William and Anya Johnson. Especially Anya… Always so denunciatory cruel when faced with pretension, yet forever devotedly championing of the underdog. For thirty years, while ruling over the lives of people driven to extravagance by their unruly desires, his compassion had remained genuine and unaffected. Repudiating any sense of his own superiority, Jocelyn still reminds himself: *There, but for the grace of God…*

Bianca kisses his diminutive wife, Laura, herself a JP, warmly. Although not exactly beautiful, Laura's voice is so delicious, it seems to fill her face and personality with exquisite charm. Serving them both champagne, before introducing them to Robin Holderness and the Byngs, by now a buzz of affable, animated conversation prevails in the long drawing room. Leonardo is quoting statistics in an Italian accent. 'Did you know…?'

Just as Bianca starts to quiz Jocelyn about a recent case, the doorbell interrupts again. Simultaneously, the telephone rings twice, then stops, before either she or Leonardo can reach it. They glance questioningly at one another.

Voices call from the top of the stairs… Robin turns, knocking over a vase of arum lilies, just as the Russells, two soigné plump pigeons of husband and wife, arrive. David, a merchant banker, advises the Palace; Adriana, Greek and a restless scholar, also paints. Walking straight up to Bianca's portrait of Leonardo to scrutinise its intricate surfaces, she turns away without comment. Bianca knows she is jealous.

'Don't waste time on that nonsense, Adriana,' she says, laughing. 'Come and have some champagne instead.'

Fetching two tall flutes of the golden liquid, she leads them towards her other guests.

'You're looking beautiful, Bianca,' says David appreciatively.

She smiles happily. He is an intelligent man, who likes to take time over his opinions, laying them out lavishly like a smorgasbord, each element separate from the next. He and Adriana are both ardent Zionists.

The doorbell rings again. Leonardo shakes David's hand, then turns to Adriana, asking: 'Have you met Beatrice Byng?'

From the kitchen now emanate delicious cooking smells of garlic with lemon thyme.

Slowly emerging from the stairwell, each step an effort, is Nicholas Rowe, a dark-haired giant of a man and architect, famous for his robust, John Bullish denunciations of modern architecture in favour of Georgian pastiche. Plus Solange, his delicate-looking, clever, half Russian girlfriend. He kisses Bianca enthusiastically.

'How pretty you are.'

Bianca knows he says the same thing to every hostess in London. Meanwhile, Solange shrinks from Bianca's kiss, her skin cool and unwelcoming.

Reptilian... thinks Bianca.

Solange's husband, whom they have left at home reading a book, smiles benignly on their affair, while Nicholas's wife complains as bitterly now as she did when it first started ten years earlier. Yet nothing seems to make any difference to Nicholas and Solange. They are like two people, who, having found their reflections in a mirror, narcissistically won't let go.

'I have known that trollop, Solange, for most of my professional life,' confides Robin Holderness to a startled, embarrassed Laura. 'She calls herself an academic, but has never yet succeeded in gaining tenure, you know?'

Overhearing him, Bianca makes the excuse of standing on tiptoe to adjust his loosened tie, to whisper: 'This is a dinner party, Robin. Not one of your moral debates.'

He looks momentarily shamefaced.

'Come and help me mop up these lilies.'

Their last two guests arrive together: Giulietta Raine, the film star, famous for the storms of intrigue in her beautiful face that dash between fragile perfection and unhappy defiance – both in her superlative acting and in real life. Plus Hanan Badr, an exotically beautiful Palestinian lawyer.

* * *

From opposite ends of their long table, Bianca observes Leonardo's face, all reserve abandoned now. Forgetting the severity of his portrait standing sentinel behind him, his hands, with their dark, silky stroking of hair, fondle the wrists of the two most beautiful women in the room, each seated deliberately either side of him: Giulietta Raine and Beatrice Byng. But it is Solange, two places away, Bianca notices, who continuously engages his eyes. The bleached thumbprint hollows are now banished in wide smiles of happiness. Even his tan seems suddenly restored to full colour. His conversation becomes discursive, fast paced and urgent, quite different from his and Bianca's desultory conversations, in which only the warmth of skin on skin seems to pass as fluent communication.

Reflected in the numerous hallway mirrors are two vast chandeliers of opaque Murano glass, their glow caressingly gentle, turning faces more youthful, while intensifying the shiny delight in bright talkative eyes and enhancing the sparkle of jewellery. The mirrors also allow extra glimpses of one another, simultaneously revealing front, back and side views, as though re-conjuring the principles of Cubism. Bianca watches Leonardo's profile turned towards Solange, their images fractured and multiplied.

Bianca has done all the cooking herself. The endless courses fulfil some ancient ideal of Francophile ritual in her mind. Bianca was born in Paris; the rituals of food feel natural to her. Nevertheless, occasionally cooking overambitiously, she can absent herself too long in the kitchen and reduce herself to slave at her own banquets.

Relaxing now in conversation with Robin Holderness, she glances teasingly at him. 'Do you still think of yourself as American, or are you honorary English by now? Minus the accent, of course?'

'Without the accent, I'm stuffed don't you think?'

She grins. *With or without it*, the cruel thought crosses her mind. But she says nothing.

'It was the welfare state, the post-war ambitions of the Labour Party, which first intrigued me into leaving America. I fell in love with the idea of a government, inheritors of a bankrupt nation, remaining determined to afford all these new benefits of health and education, while still maintaining their great endeavours abroad.'

'Surely the truth was they couldn't afford them?'

'Perhaps, but I can't tell you how deep my disappointment, now that is all betrayed.'

His corduroy arms wrap around his chest in resentment.

Bianca lets out a sigh. She agrees with him… And yet, there is something about this heavy handed, cloth-cap socialism of Robin's that now seems otherworldly.

47

Suddenly, the doorbell rings again. Bianca looks up startled. They are expecting no other guests. Much to her surprise, Leonardo rushes to answer it.

Bianca's first thought is that it might be Hesketh intruding again, but the ring had been long and insistent, quite different from his timid presses on the bell. She glances the length of the table. Everyone is talking animatedly: Byng and Nicholas, discussing politics; Robin berating David Russell for refusing to answer his question properly. His gravel voice overleaps the heads of three intervening guests accusingly. Bianca sighs…

He conducts dinner parties, like one of his seminars…

Nevertheless, the juxtaposition between the architectural serenity of the room and the wayward ebullience of her guests is precisely what Bianca loves. Beneath the delicate lights from the chandeliers, her table is like a musical score, designed to be disrupted. Its confections of white lace tablecloth and napkins, laid with old-fashioned silver cutlery, inherited from her Yorkshire grandfather, plus the polish and gleam of tall-stemmed glasses, set against delicate blue china, licked in gold, all seem to invite glorious ruin.

Ten minutes elapse before Leonardo eventually reappears. With him is Laetitia Norton, who occasionally acts as his assistant, depending which film he is working on. She is also one of his oldest friends, from long before either of his marriages to Bianca or Lisette. Bianca distrusts her.

'Haiiiii,' Laetitia greets everyone. 'See you've started without me… Noooo problem, darlings…'

She smiles charmingly, Bianca about to protest…

'Leo invited me, didn't you, darling?' she states breezily.

'I'm so sorry, I didn't know.'

'I think I tell you… but maybe no?' comments Leonardo.

Briefly abandoning English syntax for Italian shorthand, it is something he only does when embarrassed.

'Let me find you a chair,' says Bianca, immediately hospitable. 'Where should I put you?'

'Next to Byng,' Leonardo replies. 'Laetitia loves journalists.'

His mauve mouth elongates into a wide smile of secret amusement, shared exclusively with Solange. Beatrice's glamorous looks darken in anxiety. But she need not have worried. Laetitia immediately takes charge of the entire table, as though she, and not Bianca, were the hostess and Leonardo's wife, barely stopping short of stating how delighted she is that all has been done to her satisfaction, now she has finally arrived.

She breathlessly explains to the room: 'I was delayed by my busy schedule... Guess what, Leo, darling? I've just been at an early evening charity performance of Max Holland's new play, and Max himself was there... What a wonderful, wonderful man he is.'

Bianca witnesses a shadow of dismay register, in varying degrees, on the assembled masculine faces. Only Robin notices the tremor that passes through Bianca at the mention of Max's name. Saying nothing, she continues to observe the newcomer's every move. Laetitia's eyes are like pale, opaque stones, indecipherable, vaguely unseeing.

They match the Murano glass, thinks Bianca disaffectedly.

Laetitia turns her full attention on Byng. 'You simply must invite me to stay with you in Paris some time,' she cajoles, swinging her ecstatic gaze to encompass an alarmed Beatrice. 'We can arrange to meet up with Barry Unwin, the Australian ambassador; as much an old friend of mine as he is yours... What beaut fun we'll all have together,' she confirms with a smile, inadvertently revealing her Australian roots.

'Second secretary, actually,' corrects Byng.

Beatrice nods uncomprehendingly, while Laetitia starts picking off Bianca's guests with her instant charm and quoting incidents from the distant past, when she and Leonardo had been on location together without Bianca.

'Do you remember that time in Cuba, Leo, when we stayed up dancing in the old town square until four in the morning? Wasn't it wonderful? We were so happy that night... You must remember?'

Leonardo barely looks up from his plate.

'Was it wonderful?' asks Solange in a halting, tremulous voice.

Robin Holderness has remained silently watchful throughout all this. Bianca now senses a volt of energy react in him.

'Until you arrived, we were having an intelligent discussion,' he interrupts.

'Excuse me?' asks Laetitia's sing-song voice, with its pretensions to English vowels.

Yet, failing to notice the subtlety of his rebuke, she recovers almost instantly.

'Leo says you're a philosopher. How exciting. I once met that chap, thingamajig, what was his name, A.J. Ayer... He was soooo sweet. I remember him saying that I was the best, best...'

Robin groans, dropping his knife and fork with a deliberate clatter, and folds his arms tightly across his corduroy chest.

'Why don't you *shut up?*'

'Excuse me?' bleats Laetitia.

'When ignorant of what you're talking about, it's best to say nothing,' states Robin unapologetically. 'Besides, "sweet" is not a word I would use to describe Freddie Ayer...'

A sudden, concentrated silence fills the room, as the group absorbs the force of Robin's insult. Leonardo lets out a low chuckle that is almost a gurgle from a well-fed child. Bianca recognises the familiar sound. It is one of amusement, meaning that Leonardo, although astonished by Robin's rudeness, will do nothing to rescue Laetitia from it.

Bianca scrutinises Laetitia, anticipating her next move. Laetitia is one of those women, immaculately beautiful when sitting still, but curiously, discordantly vulgar the minute she either moves or begins to speak. Caught now in momentary fear, perfectly still, she reflects the image she had fashioned earlier in the mirror. That, Bianca knows, accounts for the ten minutes elapsed between her arrival at the door and her getting to the table.

Perhaps she doesn't know about this more vulgar creature, who exists when the mirrors are taken away? Bianca glances around the room... *Little chance of that here – mirrors everywhere.*

A sudden thought occurs to her.

'Was it you who phoned earlier?' she asks, breaking the silence in the room.

Laetitia replies petulantly: 'I just wanted to talk to Leo...'

Why, oh why, thinks Bianca, *does Leonardo devote so much time to these aggressive airheads...?*

And yet, really, she knows why. They are like a memory of his youth, these women, before society had dictated the hierarchy of his success. He finds their company uncomplicated and relaxing. They are also the principal reason why Bianca rarely travels with him while working. She doesn't suspect him of sleeping with them necessarily. But whereas their company bores her, he seems to rejoice in their prattle. At her most unkind, she thinks of them as his *nostalgie de la boue*, much preferring to be at home, with Stephen and her friends, rather than spending lonely evenings in hotel rooms, chaperoning Leonardo's exquisite delight in the rituals of flirtation.

* * *

With Laetitia temporarily subdued, Robin enlists the help of Giulietta Raine to launch an attack on Nicholas Rowe and his girlfriend, Solange. Unbeknown to Bianca, Robin had savaged the design of one of Nicholas's complex of claustrophobically small flats, masquerading behind a sumptuous pseudo-Georgian facia, in *The Guardian* two weeks earlier. Known for his right-wing journalism, linking architecture to politics, Nicholas is anathema to Robin, who, regardless of whether he feels American, thinks like an old-fashioned British socialist along the ethical lines of: 'Either ye are for, or agin' us.'

Egged on by their desire to impress the beautiful Giulietta, the exchanges between the two men become increasingly bitter. Laetitia attempts to intervene.

'I would have thought—'

They both hold up their hands to silence her.

The crux of Robin Holderness's rebuke is that journalists like Nicholas, who use their tub-thumping abuse of minority social groups to foster their own careers, regardless of any pain and fear they might peddle, 'are dishonourable, barbaric vulgarians, who only know how to climb tall when casting others down'.

'And you, Robin,' replies Nicholas. 'Is it not vulgar of you to accept a civilised invitation to dinner, then turn it into a circus of vicious debate?'

'Oh, Leonardo doesn't mind...' interjects Laetitia.

'Shut up,' threatens Robin darkly.

'You behave like some political naive who never knew society's rules, let alone how to obey them,' continues Nicholas imperiously.

'And as for your professorship of philosophy, what a joke that must be, Robin. A man who teaches truth tables like some ABC of minimalist meaning in the morning and fornicates with his students in the afternoon? What kind of truth are you teaching them? You are nothing but a Tartuffe, a hypocrite wrapped in your own faeces of self-adoration.'

All the smaller conversation at the table stops so the others might listen. Bianca and Leo's parties are known for their pungent debate, but this is extraordinary. One or two people glance at Bianca to see what she will do. She and Leo exchange a long look that excludes the rest of the room in a touchstone of mutual understanding. This is the strength of their marriage; their willingness to accept everything, to not disturb the will of others. Bianca picks up some dishes to take to the kitchen, Leo approving her decision with a smile.

Reflecting on Robin's need for fury, Bianca is reminded of her own volatile mother... the beautiful Anya. Occasionally, as he casts his blows, she catches a last-minute look of sorrow on his face, as though the blows he inflicts on others are identical with the pain he inflicts on himself. As she returns to the table, a familiar, breathless preoccupation haunts her thoughts. Mostly, she has it under control, but a chance comment can trigger it into unruly blossom.

Where is my mother hiding? she wonders bleakly.

Bianca had been brought up with these paradoxes of intelligent people... How no amount of intelligence can rescue them from self-destruction.

Will I ever see her again...?

Another of the paradoxes is that Robin is an excellent host, despite always being such a disruptive guest. Nevertheless, the depth of argument has now become suffocating, the two men unable to look at one another, embers of discord spreading an acrid smoke of deliberate small talk throughout the room. Meanwhile, Leonardo looks on benignly, with a half-smile.

They have only just finished their first course when Nicholas Rowe suddenly gets to his feet.

'I've just remembered I promised to let my wife back into the house,' he states lamely. 'I don't think she has a key.'

He turns to Bianca. 'I am most terribly sorry, but I shall have to leave.'

'Are you sure?' she asks gently, while accompanying him to the door, and expressing her sorrow.

In the distance behind her, she hears Byng say: 'I have heard some excuses in my time, but the story of the wife who doesn't have her own house key takes the biscuit...' followed by gales of laughter.

Having bowed formally to the table, Nicholas had retreated swiftly, without looking anyone in the eye. His departure leaves behind Solange, plus a vacuum of explosive comment that decorum dictates cannot be fully expressed. With his girlfriend still sitting there, the departed man cannot become a target for the abusive gossip uppermost in everyone's mind. As a method of recovery, Robin starts back on David Russell, taunting him like a recalcitrant schoolboy.

'You still haven't answered my question...'

Finally, Bianca is angry. 'No wonder you aren't married, Robin,' she complains. 'Living with you would be like living in a John Osborne play.'

It is the beautiful Giulietta Raine who eventually rescues things. 'Tell us about your new film, Leonardo,' she cajoles. 'We all long to know what it is you're doing?'

And so, Leonardo takes to the floor: 'I'm negotiating a film with Anglo-French backing, a collaboration,' he explains. 'I've just returned from Hong Kong and Singapore.'

'What's it about?'

'A love story, told against the backdrop of Tiananmen Square.'

'Isn't that difficult?' Beatrice asks. 'Surely the Chinese authorities are anxious to deny Tiananmen Square?'

'Yes, there will be a degree of censorship, but the love story is between a Frenchman and a Chinese student. In that sense, the story is not exclusively Chinese.'

53

As she serves the main course, Bianca suddenly notices Leonardo wearing a new watch. It sits glittering against the flourish of his pristine white cuffs, the formality of his double-breasted silk suit and inevitable Mickey Mouse flashiness of his tie. Timepieces fascinate Leonardo. He has a pathological fear of being late, preferring to arrive two hours early rather than one minute late. Often, when returning home from a long trip, he is wearing a new watch. But tonight's edition strikes Bianca as different. It sits heavily on his wrist, bulbously busy with multitude interrelated dials, their faces overlapping; a watch intended for deep-sea divers, except that it is wrought in facets of white on yellow gold, flirting with every nuance of light and responding to Leonardo's every distracted movement as he searches in his pocket for cigarettes, or merely spreads his elegant wolverine hands to make a point.

It is, Bianca realises, a watch he would never have chosen for himself. Was he wearing it earlier? She really can't remember. A gift, maybe? But from whom? Had Laetitia just given it to him?'

Experiencing a brief flutter of alarm, Bianca understands the significance of expensive watches as presents. Years earlier, a luxurious watch had been her own first gift to Stephen on finding him again.

Bianca carves the lamb herself, Leonardo too busy flirting with Solange to acknowledge his duties as host; their conversation with one another now greedy and exclusive. She has switched places with Beatrice to be next to him. Not even Laetitia's occasional references to him as 'Darling Leo' seem to dent their concentration on one another. The mood in the rest of the room is also one of fluent communication and never-ending debate. The magic of delicious food and good wine have gently worked their spell, Laetitia no longer trying to steal the show. Enhancement falls like a distinction on every single member of the table. It occurs to Bianca that not one of their guests now wishes to be elsewhere. It is as if the earlier squall has infected them all with renewed gaiety.

With certain people, Leonardo can be subdued; never actually bored by listening, rather than participating, but detached and abstracted back into the activity he loves most, that of plotting screenplays and constructing dialogue in his head. It is like a game he reverts to in moments of difficulty. Much as a clever child might lose himself in the pages of a book, Leonardo can absent himself from dinner parties by setting up sequences of thought that cannot be interrupted. Bianca frequently watches him run through patterns of thought, like the beads on a rosary, his features withdrawn, betraying nothing, except in their quality of constipated concentration.

But tonight, thought is left behind. In its place are glistening good humour and flirtatious fun; a face that opens unexpectedly into great beauty, combining formidable intellect with expansive good will.

This is Leonardo at his best, the moment when he unrolls the red carpet of his mind in effortless fun, reminding Bianca of her own early courtship conversations with him; the long lunches, his body suddenly turned squarely towards hers in undisguised attraction, the caressing teasing of his deliciously accented voice exploring the coolness of Western intellect from the point of view of Mediterranean manners. Even now, after twelve years of marriage, she is still impressed by the strong Presbyterian ethic that controls his Catholic heart.

Later in the evening, Leonardo, Byng and Robin start discussing politics. A subtle, understated criticism of America pervades the room, with which Robin, himself American, wholeheartedly agrees. Soon, everyone is joining in:

'Why does this nation of conspicuously untravelled people...' – Leonardo produces the statistic that only seven per cent of Americans hold passports – 'insist on policing the world?'

This same discussion is happening at dinner parties across London. The conversation rises and falls in undulations of agreement and dissent, until a single voice surfaces in furious contempt. Beatrice, although Swiss, had spent her youth in America. She suddenly erupts, appalled by the contempt expressed for her honorary countrymen, for British condescension and disdain towards American politicians and their mishandling of the Middle East. Thinking furiously of her duplicitous husband, she vents her spleen on 'the arrogant vacuity of the English'. Briefly, the table falls silent again, a slow flush travelling Byng's boyish features.

Hanan, the young Palestinian lawyer, diplomatically makes the point that the meanings of words are slipping between their translations from Arabic into English, and vice versa; that 'crusade' in English sounds notes of threat and antagonism to Arab ears that may not be implied by its English usage.

'Islam seems to have replaced Communism as the enemy of Western politics,' interjects Jocelyn Carpenter.

'And yet, can you, as a lawyer, conceive of religious and secular law being identical and enforceable as they are in Islam?' asks Hanan, a little less diplomatically, adding: 'I think such a concept is inconceivable to Western minds?'

Robin mentions the monstrous pain of those caught in the Middle Eastern conflict, and the room falls momentarily, respectfully ruminative.

Beatrice, again defending *Mayflower* probity, says: 'American presidents are at their best when speaking the simplistic down-home language most Americans understand.'

Giulietta Raine, known for her rebellious political stance, argues: 'Everyday Americans are like poor cripples, bereft of proper information, their minds reacting inappropriately to their impoverished diet of political rumour.'

Whereupon Hanan blushes in embarrassment.

David Russell, enunciating each word slowly, states: 'I think it wicked of the Saudi Arabians not to have rescued Palestine from its impoverishment by Israel, before things got out of hand.'

The Palestinian beauty murmurs: 'Surely there can be no greater indictment of society than when beautiful young people start committing suicide in the desperation of protest?'

At this point, Beatrice denounces the English as born snobs and counterfeiters of emotion, who turn a convenient blind eye on personal morality while simultaneously paying lip service to it.

'But aren't we becoming more like the French?' Bianca asks. 'Isn't morality becoming a code that each individual has to fashion and live by for himself, rather than one conceived in the light of either society or religion? God knows, not only the Church, but even modern faith in psychiatry is now debased.'

'Maybe?' Jocelyn counters, 'But there can still be no possibility of outwitting the residual lessons of history on patterns of thought and morality.'

'So, I did teach you something after all,' jokes Robin to Bianca.

Byng, finally roused from his stupor of shame, demurs. Looking directly at Beatrice, he says: 'Because morality is abandoned, it doesn't make it less valuable or true.'

The room falls silent, listening to this testimony, interrupted only by a school-girl snigger from Laetitia...

To break the silence, Leonardo tells a joke: 'A woman, happily married for forty years, goes up into the attic one day, where she discovers a box she neither remembers nor recognises. Inside are two eggs, plus a large quantity of money.

'That evening at supper she asks her husband what the box, the eggs and the money mean. At first, he is sheepishly reluctant to explain. Pressed further, he eventually admits that when they were first married, he made a pact with himself... Each time he was unfaithful, he would place an egg in the box, as a reminder of his transgression.

'His wife considers this for a moment, thinking: *Not bad, after forty years of marriage... Only two eggs.*

'Smiling indulgently, she leans across the table, to touch his hand affectionately, then suddenly remembers to ask: "But what about the money?"

'"Well, every time I had a dozen eggs, I sold them..."'

The whole room, except for Beatrice, collapses in laughter... all dissent vanished.

At 1 a.m., just as everyone is leaving, Giulietta Raine asks: 'Has anyone else seen Max Holland's new play yet?'

'Yes, we went last night.'

David glances at Adriana for confirmation.

'Quite fabulous, his best yet.'

For no particular reason, Leonardo suddenly notices Bianca looking anxious. His bright eyes steady into seriousness as he watches her. It is one of the moments when she perceives how well he knows her... yet, would never embarrass her by saying so. She smiles back sweetly.

He seems happy to be home, she thinks gratefully.

At that precise moment, nothing else matters.

CHAPTER 5

Hesketh's letter, addressed to 'Bianca Johnson', arrives the following morning, although she does not discover it until midday.

She had spent the entire morning rearranging furniture after the party. Leonardo had barely eaten breakfast before taking a taxi to his office, above a restaurant in Soho's Beak Street – an office which doubles as an apartment, where he can also bathe and shave. He is busy casting for his new film.

Still dressed in pyjamas at noon, Bianca scampers down to the front hall to rifle through the day's post. The envelope, with its stark, wide-spaced writing, lies like a rebuke to happiness among assorted bills and circulars. Recognising Hesketh's handwriting, some immediate wariness stirs in her. Picking it up gingerly, almost not wanting to touch it, she carries it upstairs. Slicing along the envelope's spine with a nail file, she removes two pages of writing, hands trembling; grateful to be alone, as she reads it.

Chelsea Embankment
  5 September 1998

Dear Bianca,

I had a strange dream. We were at some sort of country fair, with lots of stalls and bright lights, but not together. You were wearing a party dress, laughing and talking wittily to some of the stall holders. But I forced myself between them, so that you would have to speak to me. You looked elegant and slightly teasing, saying: 'We could do this, or maybe that.' You appeared floating and full of light. Then I asked if you would marry me, and you said: 'No, I've already tried that.' Then, everything in the dream got suddenly dark and I had a terrible, fearful presentiment of horror and dread.

Nothing specific, except that your life seemed to be threatened and losing control to some kind of trauma from a black source. I woke up at 4 a.m., feeling sick.

I'm very sorry, Bianca, that I didn't properly show you all the love that I felt. I should have protected you better, wish now that I knew that you were OK. Please phone me. I try to remember to keep my mobile switched on.

Love, Hesketh

P.S. The police were here today. I thought at first that you'd sent them.

Struck completely off balance by this letter, Bianca feels a sudden, escalating panic, yet is at a loss to know why. Over the years, she has received thousands of such letters, each one another throw in Hesketh's desperate game.

There were Hesketh's angry letters, smarting with subdued barbs... his kindly ones, dripping with entreaty... self-pitying letters, threatening his impending suicide... All twisted and turned about, flagellating themselves in looped disguise of the single ingredient they all share: his passionate need for control, his refusal to be locked out, his conviction that 'Hesketh knows best', plus menacing intimations of knowing more than he lets on.

Big Brother is watching YOU.

Denied ordinary vision, Hesketh seemingly watches through occult enhanced eyes. He refers constantly to his 'ESP' – extrasensory perception – as though it were a dog he holds on a leash.

Pathetic, disastrous fool, thinks Bianca. *Hideous, as always, with his incontinent emotions... He carries his selfishness around, like a ball and chain... But perhaps that's always the nature of low cunning*, she hisses within herself.

Her mind is infected by loathing.

Nevertheless, this letter strikes a depth of fear in her she has not felt for years... Until fifteen years ago, she had existed permanently in this fervour of panicked dread; her mind and body poisoned by the daily fight and flee doses of adrenaline pumping through her bloodstream. It was the roses that had finally brought her terror to a standstill; fifty dark red baccarat roses, delivered to a shabby, dust-ridden art-school staff room one summer afternoon. Even now, Bianca cannot see long-stemmed, blood-red roses without associating them with the death throes of her fear.

Years earlier, she had moved out of London in a deliberate attempt to escape from Hesketh. Her private life, by then, in tatters; the valiant love story between herself and Patrick ruined by the uglier moments of Hesketh's madness. Every day, for the previous ten years, the post had brought new letters of invective from him; the early hours of every morning interrupted by harassing phone calls. It became sensible not to go to sleep before 2 a.m. This was in a flat, off Kensington High Street, that she and Patrick had shared with others. These were their student days, when everything still felt flexible and free. Someone would pick up the phone late at night and a voice spitting ugly, halting cadences, would say: 'The next time you kiss Bianca, imagine her mouth against mine...'

Their friends, hers and Patrick's, had looked on these incidents with bemusement and ribaldry. It felt grown-up to be subjected to them, while, at the same time, reflective of a depth of passion as yet inconceivable. Laughter was the easiest way out. Nor were Hesketh's calls the only outrageous ones. There were the others, at more normal times of day, when the gang was enjoying a late breakfast or lunch. The phone would ring and a woman's distraught voice would hurl abuse, so painful, so noisy, that the whole room quietened to listen to it explode over the phone.

The thing Bianca could never forgive these calls, neither Hesketh's nor her mother's, was the way they changed everything; one minute, the innocence of happiness, the next total alienation, her world dissolved in embarrassment. Bianca could never rid herself of the intense isolation she felt in those moments, nor the sense that life had turned fatally slippery; her mother's vicious words distancing her from her friends.

'You... pitiful little tart. Unnatural daughter.'

Twenty-two years old, and already Bianca's hair had started to go grey. Those were the years of savage defeat, piled up on one another relentlessly, month by month, yet registered against a chorus of joy. When not bowing to the world's jealousy, Bianca was happy and in love – not yet fully aware of the canker nibbling at her soul. By the time joy had fallen apart into irreversible despair, her life smashed to pieces by Hesketh's blind, uncontrollable jealousy, and her futile attempts to escape to the seaside revealed in all their hollowness of pain, then it was that the incident of the baccarat roses had marked a turning point.

Bianca had gone home one lunchtime to her flat in the seaside town where she had a job lecturing at the local art school. By now frequently ill, her former delicate looks transformed into an image of stricken anxiety, she was learning to live without the crutches of family and old friends and finding the process painfully hard going. She had lost everything familiar in her life: her mother, father and sweet, darling Patrick. Her body was beginning to rebel on her with unpredictable maladies; urgent bouts of claustrophobia, coupled with precipitous tummy upsets. Her mind remained as sharp and raw as a razor, but it was no longer in control of her body.

Vainly attempting to heal herself, she came across a 1933 edition of Gayelord Hauser's *Eat and Grow Beautiful*. Reading it voraciously, and taking Hauser's recommendations at face value, she went home that lunchtime and mixed, for the first time, his cocktail of brewer's yeast and black strap molasses; the sudden excesses of Vitamin B on her bereaved body acting like a Mickey Finn. Unintentionally falling asleep, she failed to return to work, her 2 p.m. lecture dissolved in brown molasses oblivion. Not until 4 p.m. did she finally make her way shamefacedly back to work.

As she turned a corner to cross the road to the art school, she recognised Hesketh's blue Jaguar, parked clumsily half on, half off the sidewalk. Hesketh, his back to her, was striding towards some public lavatories next to tennis courts. Luckily, he had not seen her.

Moving quickly across the road into the building, Bianca apologised for missing her lecture and took her next two classes as normal. Eventually leaving work at 6.30 p.m., she knew Hesketh would still be there.

The minute he saw her, he ran towards her, dressed in tight, stone-coloured jeans and matching bomber jacket, a look of maddened desperation infiltrated his hyperthyroid eyes. Herself, poorly, almost shabbily dressed, her elegance and good looks vanishing in her increasing desire to conceal herself, she started to run. Twilight, by now...

Hesketh ran faster. As his arm reached out to touch her, her whole being froze in terror, indescribable panic and anger consuming her. For ten years, she and this man had exchanged nothing but bitter abuse, set against his violent attempts to outwit her evasions. She thought of the child she had lost to his threats and knew, with sudden clarity, there was nothing more to lose. Everything had turned to dust in her hands. What else could he do, other than kill her? In her own mind, he had already killed her child, the child Patrick had insisted she give up in the face of Hesketh's daily intimidation, the child whose invisible life she still recorded and held vigil over. His birthday would have been 7 May. At the time, he was just five years old. He would be twenty-three by now. Nor had she ever felt that another child could replace him. Even the miscarriage she had a few years ago had seemed a natural sacrifice to her first, beautiful unborn son.

Turning to face him, she found Hesketh did not look like anything she either recognised or knew, so final her loathing and hatred of the man standing in front of her that he more resembled a bestial contour than a human being.

Hesketh began to speak, his voice full of ugly presumption. Still, Bianca did not reply, simply observing this configuration of a human being, devoid of its humanity. Her mind was alert, the full volume of her intelligence undiluted by either sympathy, self-pity or even femininity – merely an instrument for assessing. And yet, something in her face struck Hesketh fearfully. Mid-sentence, his voice altered pitch. He took a step backward... Suddenly, Bianca found herself fascinated by details. She counted every stitch, the angles and intervals they made, on one of his buttonholes. Greedily scouring for more details, her interest in him was suddenly insatiably ravenous. Abstract, but voracious. One of his fingernails was rimed in black, the others scrupulously clean.

'Bianca,' he pleaded.

Continuing her relentless scrutiny, she witnessed him raise a hand to half cover his mouth; glimpsed in fascinated amazement his teeth, falling like tombstones within the beautiful bow of his mouth. He felt like no one, nor anything she had ever known. No intimacy, no recognition; nothing, except hatred and repugnance...

Then, to her amazement, he ran away; Hesketh retreated from her. She could scarcely believe it. At the time, it felt like some mysterious, significant victory.

Next day at tea time, fifty baccarat roses had arrived, without card or message. But Bianca knew perfectly well whom they were from. She also knew, at some fundamental level, she would never be quite so frightened of Hesketh again... That is, until today, fifteen years later.

* * *

Hands shaking still, she rereads the letter twice more, before refolding it in its envelope. Then, as with all Hesketh's letters, she throws it onto the floor of the airing cupboard, to be cooked in hell next to the hot water tank.

During the very early years, Bianca used to throw Hesketh's letters away directly on arrival, barely touched, often unread. Something she now regrets. It was Leonardo, when they first married, who advised her to start collecting and recording both the letters and his visits in her diary, in case she should need them one day as evidence against him. Reading somewhere of a people who contained the malign influence of their enemies by keeping any objects they had touched locked in a drawer, plus unwilling to countenance seeing Hesketh's letters lying about, Bianca chucks them onto the floor next to the water tank, much to the surprise of the plumbers, who occasionally come to service her boiler.

'I shan't be sending you any letters, if that's what you do with them.'

About to close the airing-cupboard door on this new letter, some instinct makes her pick it up and read it again. With the letter in her hand, she feels slightly breathless, her ribcage contracting in incipient panic. As in the old days, she feels her mind and body divide. With her intellect, she witnesses the flurry in her own emotions quite calmly, deriding them as abject nonsense, while simultaneously feeling her body submit physically to fear.

But why? Why give into fear now?

She runs through her thoughts like a checklist, searching for a key… Until suddenly, she happens upon a memory, almost twenty-five years old.

When she first knew him, Hesketh had bought a huge, grand, run-down mansion on Putney Common for a song. Outwardly Edwardian cricket pavilion in style, its interior was a four-tiered cake, with sumptuously proportioned rooms leading to a sequence of smaller attic rooms, rented out by the previous owner as a separate apartment.

The previous owner was a French woman from Marseilles, a pied noir, originally from Algeria, who had married an Englishman returning from Cairo after the war. She had that eternal, pouting coquettishness, typical of a certain type of French woman.

'I used to be vaary pritty,' she would say, teasing her permed, hennaed hairdo and wearing a cupid's bow of orange-fuchsia lipstick. She epitomised them all, from Colette to Edith Piaf; a spirited imp of a being, whose lean youthful beauty had, with age, become hamster-like, without her really noticing. Her English husband had set her up in Putney, then eventually deserted her, leaving her with a lumpen giant of a son, whose stolid silences were as extreme as his mother's incapacity to sit still. No longer married, she now had a browbeaten Indian friend living with her, whose cleverness as a lover she liked to hint at.

'Zees Eendiaans eire vaary cleveer inz bed,' she wheezed.

She was like a concierge in a country that still pretended belief in minding its own business.

Even then an astute businessman, Hesketh formed the habit of flirting with her, while simultaneously despising her. He bought her crumbling Edwardian palace for a mere £6,000, on the grounds, which were true, that it suffered subsidence. Plus the fact that in the attic were a couple of sitting tenants.

Hesketh's letter was incorrect in one small detail; Bianca had never actually lived with him, although she had stayed there often enough. She had also chosen the house's fashionable, mid-grey carpets. At the time, she kept rooms of her own in a mansion block in Barons Court, where there were always late-night scuffles at her ground-floor window, with Hesketh knocking on the panes of glass, begging her to come and spend the night with him.

The memory Hesketh's letter now revives occurred six months after he moved into the house. With the help of a friend, he had decorated all the rooms white, replacing peeling wallpaper and chipped cream gloss with gleaming, sanitised surfaces that began on the raised ground floor, ignored the basement, extended into the kitchen at the back of the house and travelled the stairs to the first floor, but stopped short of the sitting tenants' second-floor domain.

The tenants were a young Nigerian couple, expecting their first child. Every night, through the newly decorated hall of mid-grey carpets and clinical walls, flitted the handsome, dark-skinned figures and faces of Benin, with sculptural, long-limbed bodies. Every night, the happy babble of a private patois shed its ebullience from the second to the first and ground floors; every night the pervasively repugnant smell of boiled tripe emanated throughout the house. Meanwhile, the child was growing in its beautiful mother's belly, wrapped in sarongs and turbans of multi-coloured batik, evocative of some ancient tribal goddess.

And night after night, Hesketh's exasperation grew. He had taken over their tenancy knowingly. The French woman had insisted their rights were observed, leaving Hesketh no legal grounds whatsoever for asking them to leave. Once the child was born, his authority over them would diminish still further. One night, when they returned home, he had changed the locks.

He had left work deliberately early. In those days, before his success as entrepreneur, he still taught art, which was how Bianca first met him. He had brought his decorator friend with him as back-up. Together, they changed the locks on the front door. Bianca, who knew nothing of their plan, arrived shortly before the Nigerian couple came home. It was the wife, swaying her bulk elegantly along the tree-lined street, who arrived first. Bianca still remembers her piercing animal howls, matched by Hesketh's mad laughter, as he recklessly directed his glee at the sky.

The beautiful, dark-skinned Madonna sat rocking and keening on the doorstep in her private grief, waiting for her husband to return. When he did so, their high-pitched mutual babble of patois rose hysterically, punctuated by miniature shrieks and cries, like those of a tormented cat. Bianca remembers the subsequent long hours of their futile knocking at the house's glass-panelled front door, their dark, sculptural shapes darting closer and away again through the frosted glass; their litanies of complaint, followed by Hesketh's demonic laughter, and the increasing embarrassed dismay of both herself and his decorator friend. Then, at last, silence, and the exhausted hope that maybe, finally, the couple had given up.

Hesketh had calculated accurately that they would not choose to call the police in their own defence; that their visas and personal papers were perhaps not up to date or correct in some way. Silence built into fragile hope. Then came the moment Bianca could never expel from her memory. The tall, athletic husband had suddenly thrown himself bodily at the door, butting his handsome head so hard, the glass splintered and shattered; his head appearing through the jagged frame of glass, deeply cut on his proud forehead and spilling blood onto the new carpet. Bianca could still recall the gargoyle transformation of the man's beautiful face as panic countered fury... His terrifying realisation that he was trapped within the jagged star of shattered glass, that by any slight movement, forward or backward, he might cut his own throat. There he was, cruelly stranded in stocks of his own making, all set to the ugly music of Hesketh's laughter.

As Bianca scans the generous spacing in Hesketh's letter, describing the charms of his love for her, certain details continue to resurface inescapably in her mind. She remembers the bright red drops of the man's spilled blood retaining their shape, sitting unabsorbed on the tightly woven carpet, like scatterings of rosy beads.

Outside, the man's wife was now howling, rocking herself violently from side to side, like an animal in frenzy, her hurried patois escalating into a distraught language of tongues. She was seven months pregnant. At the bottom of the steps leading to the front door, a crowd of neighbours had gathered. Pretending to go to the lavatory, Bianca stole into the kitchen at the back of the house, dialled 999, and asked for an ambulance. Still, Hesketh laughed, never guessing it was she who had made the call. It was the first true evidence Bianca had of his unmitigated cruelty, his intense dislike of people with backgrounds different from his own. After she had parted from him, she was told his conversation became increasingly larded with terms like 'spics' and 'blacks'. But in her own presence, he had mostly remained circumspect and cunning. Only once had he used his prejudice openly, as a weapon to alienate her from some friends, whom he jealously feared, even then, might rescue her from him. She bows her head in shame and sorrow...

To think I was ever associated with such a man...

It is her greatest regret in life.

She thinks too of her estranged mother, the beautiful, extravagant Anya. This story had infected their relationship too.

Again, throwing Hesketh's letter to the floor in a fit of disgust, Bianca slams shut the airing cupboard door, her panicked heartbeat racing with palpitations. She tries to concentrate, forcing her mind to shake itself free of its brutal imagery.

Enough... she pleads. *Please God, let it be enough. Must I always, always be recalled to this ancient grief?*

Still breathless, she runs herself a bath and tries to contemplate the remainder of her day, setting about practising normality, as though it were a step-by-step recipe. Suddenly remembering that Leonardo won't be home until much later this evening, she thinks gratefully: *No need to cook, no need to explain.*

But still, her thoughts dart back and forth, spinning into panic before plummeting to again revolve around her mother.

It really is time, she decides, *to begin the stories I plan, based on my mother's old diaries.*

She had rediscovered them recently, hidden at the cottage where her father, William, still lives.

It's something I need to do... To take a forensic scalpel to this long-infected past – mine and Anya's.

She plans to trace it back to its beginnings, to 1936, the year her parents, William and Anya, first met...

CHAPTER 6

Two days later, Anya's diaries lie open before her on the polished walnut table. Bianca is correcting the text of a short story she had begun writing earlier. From her mother's notes, she is attempting to re-conjure her parents' wedding day.

* * *

At an address across town, quite unbeknown to Bianca, in a narrow street just beyond Trafalgar Square, an elegant woman, now elderly but still extraordinarily beautiful, sits in her student-like apartment, remembering the past; also remembering her wedding day.

* * *

It was London, October 1936, the year of the abdication. She wore a dress of shot green taffeta silk that circled her slender figure with continuous dances of light; over it the tight hug of an astrakhan jacket.

She had just crossed Waterloo Bridge in the fine rain and blustery winds of an autumn morning, laughingly clutching her hat, with its stiffened purple velvet bow, to her abundant copper curls. The old bridge was, by then, closed to traffic, the new temporary structure looming hideously alongside it. In the waters below, a carter had driven his horse into the Thames to help unload a barge.

She was barely eighteen years old, and the youngest of seven children. Her twin brother had died tragically at the age of four, falling from a window. In her face, as well as delicate beauty, was haughty defiance, as though any angry thought might threaten its symmetry. She was on her way to get married to a man she had met only six weeks earlier. Her mother had refused to accompany her, too busy skivvying for the family to make the journey across the river, too tired maybe to care. But her sister, Arlette, known as Lettie, had made the green silk taffeta dress for her. Their father had been a tailor with a shop of his own at Seven Dials, and Lettie too was a trained seamstress.

She had always preferred to be called by her second name, Anya. Only her family knew her as May. That morning in 1936 she was on her way from the steep, soot-coated family house on five floors in South Island Place to her new home in the heart of Fitzrovia. Marrying was her method of leaving home. None other would have been acceptable to the gang of older brothers who had brought her up in the absence of a father. Her father had died of a heart attack, eighteen years earlier, on his way to the hospital to greet the birth of his newborn twins – herself and her brother.

She was also a young woman very much in love. As she waited for her bus, it was early morning still. Men in homburg hats scurried along the Strand on their way to work, an animated picture of dark on dark; duskily clad people, set against darkened buildings.

Her wedding was due to take place later that day; 3 p.m. at Marylebone Registry Office. And her future parents-in-law, whom she had not yet met, expected to arrive from Sheffield, even though they disapproved. They had wanted their son to marry Mary Gimson, a local girl. Their journey south would take more than eight hours.

There was also the dilemma of where they would stay. Certainly not in Great Titchfield Street, where her future husband's two easels and accumulations of paintings, both oil and watercolours, occupied most of the space: one large room, plus small hallway, miniature kitchen and shared bathroom on the third floor of number 34. No one, in fact, was expected for certain, except their friends and witnesses, Rowland and Bunty Darblay.

A paper boy ran past her, shouting the question: 'Will Wallace Simpson be Queen?'

It was three months since the Spanish Civil War had begun and every day more Englishmen were leaving home to fight what was turning into Europe's most ideological battle. A double-decker bus arrived, its outdoor staircase wrapped like a protective arm around its bulk, the advice, 'Get it at Harrods', written boldly alongside. It took her to Oxford Circus, via Trafalgar Square, past the graceful, darkened silhouette of Eros in Piccadilly Circus.

Trafalgar Square was sombre in the early morning light, the top of Nelson's Column obscured in a light residue of fog, the National Gallery a proud, soot-ridden set of classically inspired intervals and indentations in the distance, against which the white-grey flurry of pigeons circled and flapped like the furies in a Greek chorus. And yet Anya loved the conspicuous ugliness of London, from which a more subtle beauty wrested itself. London, for her, was like a child's dream of finding a jewel around every squalid corner. She was eighteen years old, and she had already discovered the sometimes inherent dignity in ugliness; not only in the fatal juxtapositions of city grime, but in people too: her beautiful brother, Ernie, who had taken his bright flashing mind on the road, tramping, to relieve the family of financial pressure, then gone to the dogs, his bright intellect deficient in terms of personal hygiene and knowing how to look after himself. She would watch him probe at the diseased parts of his cancerous bones and then later bring them home from hospital in a jar. And yet, to her, he remained the most beautiful thing she knew and loved.

There was also Varinsky, with whom she had conducted a clandestine affair since she was sixteen, ugly with his vehement mane of black hair, his jowly features and big black overcoat, with its sable collar. And yet, the bright-flame glances from his eyes were more jewels in the dirt, as were the finesse and height of his smooth domed forehead, and, above all, the elegant tracery of line from the bridge of his nose, past the generosity and sensuality of his mouth, to the double dimple of his protuberant chin, whose precision dissolved into the forest of black stubble of his throat. How she had loved to happen upon his moments of beauty, delivered in their teaspoon measures among the generalities of his dark ugliness.

Exactly like London, *she thought.*

But that day in 1936 was different. Varinsky may have given her his signed copy of Ulysses, *first to read and then to keep. He was also a wonderful lover. But that morning, she was on her way to marry a man who had never read James Joyce, but whose magnificent handsomeness and youthful ambition matched hers. When she had met him six weeks earlier, he was, and still remained, a virgin. He was the Sheffield painter William Johnson.*

At Oxford Circus, Anya got off the bus and started to walk northwards, weaving her way through the lattice of streets north of Oxford Street, towards Great Titchfield Street. On the corner of Berners Street, a toothless flower seller called out her wares in high-pitched Cockney sing-song from a collection of vast wicker baskets set on the pavement. Anya took sixpence from her purse, a small fortune that would buy them a cheap meal at Bertorelli's in Charlotte Street, or a seat in the gods at the Old Vic and bought twenty-four bunches of violets at a farthing, each bunch set against a single viridian leaf. It felt like extravagance.

'For my wedding bouquet, and to match my hat,' she said, smiling at the flower seller.

The woman, who was middle-aged but looked older, was dressed in a pearly queen jacket and feathers, her face creased in patterns of avid longing, now tinged with despair. She glanced up at Anya.

'You'll need a rose at the heart of them violets,' she said.

She plucked a single long-stemmed red rose from one of her baskets and handed it to her. Anya fumbled in her purse for an extra coin, but the woman waved a clawed hand at her.

'My wedding gift to you, luv. Good luck to you, my beautiful. Gawd only knows, you'll need it.'

'Luck', good and bad, had emerged as the theme of the decade; the thirties, rushing from the disaster of one war to another, while alternating poverty with frivolous pleasure. 'More in luck than hope' had become a reversed truism. Since the psychological wounds of the First World War, hope had acquired a primitive ferocity, a passion for survival that excused anything and everything. Emotions had polarised into good and bad, rich and poor, and had done the same for the political and intellectual life of the country. To be 'intellectual' was a statement of association with left-wing ideas, much like being 'fashionable' was associated with the more aristocratic strata of society. Both operated their own hierarchies, in which, for the moment, everything was suspended in possibility and vain hope. Yet people existed at their most mentally alert, their most angry, most loving; perpetually at extremes, operating at the very edge of their dreams and respectability.

Anya had met William at the recently inaugurated Potato Marketing Board, where she worked. Winning a scholarship to grammar school, she had been refused permission by her busy, overflowing family to accept her place there. Like the others, she was obliged to find work to support that entity which was above the law, above education, and certainly above dreams, 'the family'. At its best, it had meant supporting the sweet frailty and dignity of her mother, denied a husband, but left with a robust, opinionated brood. The mother of seven children had grown into a curious asexuality.

At its worst, it meant running the gauntlet of her brother Arthur's gambling; the doubtful panic each week of whether he would arrive home on Friday evenings with his wages intact or have blown them in their entirety on the dogs. Arthur was himself the father of nine children, all of them with names ending in 'a' – Stella, Myrna, Vera etc. The trick was to conceal any gifts of money and deliver them straight into the hands of Violet, Arthur's wife, so the family could at least hope to eat for the following week.

There were also other sacrifices, more freely made; for poor, beautiful Ernie, caught in his slow pavane of death, but still in love with his mad wife and her son, a brilliant pianist, who, one day after a row with his maddened mother, cut off his thumbs with an axe and never played piano again.

For all these people, Anya had sacrificed her schooldays and taken the clerical jobs which eventually led to her being taken on by the new Potato Marketing Board.

The Board had arranged a promotional fair for themselves at Olympia and engaged a gifted young painter and puppeteer, recently arrived from Sheffield, an associate of Jan Bussell and Waldo Lanchester, who ran his own marionette theatre, using puppets hand carved by himself. That had been only six weeks earlier. For them both, it was love at first sight. Mary Gimson and Varinsky, for all their virtues, had never stood a chance.

Clutching her bouquet, Anya arrived at the dirt-spattered door of 34 Great Titchfield Street; the shop to its right a draper's. Climbing the dusty, linoleum-clad staircase to the third floor, she opened the door on to a bare, curtainless room with windows overlooking the street, directly into the sash windows of the house opposite. She glimpsed the shadowy shape of the old man who watched them from the other side of his grey net curtains.

William had not heard her arrive. He sat deeply absorbed in front of his easel, smoking woodbines and working on a landscape, based on St James' Park, where he had recently discovered a flock of sheep grazing.

Anya was both delighted and shocked to see him. She had imagined that, on this, his wedding day, his routine might change. A silent doubt threaded her mind: could a man marry and paint on the same day?

She threw her arms around his neck. As she did so, he carefully put down his brushes, held in his left hand like a fan. He could taste the cold air on her cheek. At the sight of her beauty, his mind rose in delight. He had discovered that just watching her was a joy beyond any he had previously known.

'How can you paint on your wedding day?' she asked breathlessly.

He stood up, towering above her, trying to rapidly shed the deep absorption of his previous mood.

'Easily,' he answered abstractly.

He stepped back from her embrace. Had he imagined that brief flash of anger in her eye? Yet he knew her to be proudly supportive of his painting.

How to explain? he pondered, still caught in the fog of painting.

'Do you not know that painting on my wedding day is the greatest compliment I could pay to the woman I love? What greater reflection is there of a painter's love and trust than his inspiration to work...?'

Anya glanced up at him quizzically. He took her in his arms, where she breathed in the heady, familiar fumes of turpentine and smoky Woodbines. He was about to kiss her when the doorbell rang. Abruptly, they stood apart...

* * *

Bianca puts down her pen.

Is that not enough for today?

She can feel her concentration flagging.

Would other writers force the prose on?

Pushing the papers away from her, almost in disgust, in the half-blank mood that follows mental exertion, she reaches for Aubrey Byng's new book, his dissertation on post-war politics. It is one of Stephen's handsome publications, under the imprint of his publishing firm, CERvello, although in no way represents his own political stance. Despite his wealth, Stephen is an ardent supporter of the Labour Party...

The truth is that Byng's recent work has disappointed Bianca. Not because of its political views, but because his writing has acquired a seamless intellectual superiority, which she finds vaguely offensive; his earlier writings, far less self-assured, were also more viscerally raw. She sighs. It is probably an easy mistake to make. Writers imagine themselves admired for their cleverness, whereas in reality...

I must ring Beatrice sometime soon.

Still in this cloud of rumination, when the phone rings half an hour later, she finds it is Matthew, her art dealer.

'Did you paint today, daarling?'

He knows she often works in her studio until lunchtime before returning home. Bianca is immediately apologetic: 'No, I'm afraid not... Leonardo is at home. Today seems to have vanished in chores.'

Even over the phone, Bianca can hear Matthew cracking his knuckles. She pauses. It is something he does when either nervous or excited. She listens carefully to his voice. In keeping with its guttural edge, the vowels either clip themselves precisely, like secateurs deadheading roses, or stretch elastically in some private ecstasy of sensual longing. The longing is not for herself, but for life in general and all its possibilities, hateful or otherwise. Matthew is her oldest friend, the one who engages with her most levelly; they were at school together. Nothing she can do would surprise him. He knew her long before her marriage to Leonardo, whom he treats as a necessitous condiment in her life, a little dash of pepper that enlivens the dish but in no way alters its consistency. It is he who had said hauntingly, many years earlier, 'You should take a lover, Biaancaa. It would suit you to go from one pair of arms to another.'

And when she had looked shocked and repelled by the idea, replying she could not begin to contemplate it: 'You would have no time to think, my love. The twin imperatives of being fair and loving would dictate your every move.'

Now, on the phone, he is speaking her name, drawing out the As.

'Biaaancaa.'

She detects his excitement.

'I have just spoken to Maaax Hollaaand, and he suggests meeting tomorrow at the gallery at 6 p.m., just as it closes.'

Bianca falls into a flurry of indecision. With Leonardo at home, she tends to over-elaborate her commitment to timetabling his desires.

'I'm not sure... Leonardo is here...'

'Do you want to bring him with you, Biaaancaa, daaarling?'

'No,' she replies, almost too quickly.

Still unable to gauge her encounter with Max, she is not yet sure what it would signify to meet him again, let alone to paint him. But she already senses she has no desire to introduce him to Leonardo. She recovers her poise.

'Let me ring Leonardo now at his office to discover his plans for tomorrow evening, then call you back immediately.'

Matthew laughs, a generous elastic sound full of amused knowing.

Bianca's telephone conversations with Leonardo are so brief as to almost end the same minute they begin; as though, even after twelve years of marriage, their familiarity with one another remains partly fabricated, revealing its fragility on the phone. And yet, his first notes of greeting are always warm and welcoming.

'Not yet sure... numerous meetings... someone coming to see me at 6.30... the possibility of a business dinner...'

It is a familiar litany, one she could have quoted off by heart, without bothering to pick up the phone.

'In any case, I'll be back home in an hour,' he ends stiffly.

Bianca glances at her watch, checking the time. He had not actually said, 'Was this call really necessary? You know how much I hate answering questions...' but he might as well have done. Bianca can hear him thinking it. She smiles as she replaces the receiver. She knows all Leonardo's tricks for keeping his life fluid until the very last moments. Nevertheless, she has obtained what she wanted from the call, the disclaimer, the busy man's brush-off, easily translatable by her into: 'I am free.'

She dials Matthew's number. 'Tomorrow at 6 p.m. will be just fine.'

Matthew pronounces her name on a smile. 'Biaancaa... how clever you are.'

* * *

The following evening Bianca makes her way to Cork Street. She had intended taking a bus, but she leaves her departure so late she has to call a taxi. She had worked on the Cavendish children's portrait all morning but made little progress. The children were overexcited, full of anticipation of a tea party they were going to that afternoon. They were accompanied by a nanny, who had even less control over them than Bianca, and because the double portrait had reached the delicate stage of moving from the broad plastic sweeps of acrylic to the delicate sable thinness of oil, Bianca had felt reluctant to commit herself to new marks on the canvas in the face of their uproar. She knows all too well the elusiveness of painting children; their faces hover between an abstract of innocence, almost an empty page, and nuanced knowing. By choosing to emphasise innocence, she could end up with featureless anonymity, but by emphasising personality there was also the danger of transforming childish delicacy into wizened dwarfishness.

By twelve o'clock Bianca had thrown down her brushes and asked the nanny to take the children home. The children hugged her legs with wide gestures of windmill arms and upturned smiles, then skipped off to the future, which in their immediate scheme of things was the party. She and the young nanny had exchanged indulgent smiles and agreed to 'try again next week'.

Then, at 12.30 p.m., Stephen had rung on spec. He is almost the only person to have her studio number. Not even Leonardo has it, although he had once arrived there unannounced.

'My business lunch has been cancelled. Could we not meet up?'

He arrived half an hour later, carrying a bunch of tall blue delphiniums. Unthinkingly laying the flowers across her still wet palette, he took her in his arms. In the warmth of her neck were traces of the perfume she had applied earlier that morning, but her fingers smelled of turpentine.

'Little painter,' he accused.

'I could always wipe my hands on your nice new suit?' she suggested in mock innocence.

As she disappeared along the long corridor to the bathroom to wash, Stephen chose a CD to play and kicked off his shoes.

'Are you planning on staying?' she teased on her return.

Bianca's studio, attached to one side of a late Victorian redbrick Gothic palace in Holland Park, is situated close to Leighton House. The house, although large, has a strange, narrow verticality with which the cottage dimensions of the studio appear in conflict. Its separate entrance leads to a long dark corridor, beyond which the light opens out into a magnificent, two-tiered space, dominated by a cusped Gothic window, thirty foot tall. Its farthest wall matches the window height in single operatic space. But to the right, as one enters, is a canopied, open-plan kitchen, dating from the 1950s; above it, reached by a wooden ladder, an improvised bedroom, consisting of a mattress thrown to the floor behind swags of diaphanous curtaining. In the main studio are accumulations of canvases, all leaning their faces to the wall, various easels and, behind a folding screen, some props useful for portraiture: ceramic pots, some lengths of rich curtaining, a variety of chairs and a plaster bust. Plus stranded in the centre of the room, a few isolated items of furniture, all looking like still-life objects: a Victorian button-backed chaise longue, covered in Schiaparelli pink, a tall brass candelabra on clawed feet and a moth-eaten oriental carpet, almost too typical in its jazz of reds, blues and greens.

As Bianca returned, Stephen smiled. 'It's getting to be vaguely Madame Récamier in here, don't you think?'

She grinned happily. He had also now removed his socks.

'I thought we were going out to lunch?'

'We are, but I thought we might have the beginnings of a cuddle first.'

This was one of Stephen's favourite things, to half make love before going out to eat; quickly, teasingly, coming close to fulfilment, then backing away. He loved the languorous desire it lent a meal, the impetus of a passion, barely controlled.

Moving about the vast space, giving one another a wide berth, they performed miniature last-minute chores. From the fridge,

Bianca fetched a half bottle of champagne and two glasses. Stephen turned the music up. Stretching out his arm towards her, she side-stepped him once more to half draw the diaphanous curtains against the magnificent window. They both knew the minute they touched, they would be caught up in one another, lost to the high-speed intimacy of their passion. Encircling her waist as he negotiated their path to the chaise longue, he arranged her like a piece of origami against the shocking pink canopy, the urgent warmth of his body transferring itself to hers. Beneath his touch, she felt her body melt.

They ate at a favourite local restaurant, where the Italian proprietor greeted them like old friends, their knees touching a reassuring warm promise beneath the table, their eyes dancing happiness in one another's. For them both, these snatched moments of joy were the very template of life, the standard of love and communication against which all else was measured. And yet, they both subscribed happily to the reality of their lives being lived mostly with other people. It was both their greatest strength and weakness with one another. They never wore each other out in tedium, their love forever renewed and enhancing. Day to day humdrum was no match for its ecstasy, in which every shared minute was a treat.

But in Bianca, it created a false sense of yearning, and in Stephen, a false sense of stability, which is what made her occasionally vulnerable to dreaming of the Max Hollands of this world. She yearned to enclose the beauty of her life with Stephen in another more continuous pattern – if not with him, with someone else, free of their duplicity with Leo and Sarah – whereas Stephen revelled in their duplicity and felt empowered by it. She also feared that there may not, in truth, be anyone else; that the joy she shared with Stephen was not transferable. She was like an insect caught in the finely woven web of her own desire and happiness.

For all these many layered reasons, she felt anxious in anticipation of her next meeting with Max. She liked him, had enjoyed their evening together, but she had no idea of her own intentions towards him.

Back at the studio, she and Stephen made love; a lovemaking that began gently and ended ferociously, with Bianca, stretched out naked on a sea of duvet. Afterwards they drank coffee and ate chocolates.

Draining the last dregs of his coffee, Stephen checked his watch. 'I need to be back at the office by 3 p.m.'

He started to dress. 'But first let me see what progress you're making with the painting?'

Wrapping a towel about her waist, Bianca started sifting through paintings, leaning one up against the wall. It was the painting of the Cavendish children; an enormous canvas, six-foot square, from which the two small children seemed to advance into spectator space, rather than remaining decorously behind the picture plane. Bianca's painting style was both descriptive and full of an abstract enjoyment of paint, like two distinct conventions, legible separately and simultaneously with one another. The little girl in the painting was dressed in a miniature red tartan kilt, suspended round her plump baby bottom between the neutral grey wool of her tights and jumper.

Bianca had caught the delicate play of light on the stretched rib of her tights, describing it with flecks of pale light that built up into sequences of marks that united with the jazz of her red-and-yellow kilt, then glanced adoringly on the ribbed neck and cuff of her jumper. In one miniature hand, for some strange reason, she carried a teapot, holding it at right angles to the picture plane, while she herself looked the other way, her face shown in profile glancing towards her brother. She was a plump, pretty child with a scattering of blonde curls, whereas her brother was fractionally taller and more fragile looking, his youthful face already fine drawing, in which plump curves had ceded to exquisite line. Everything in him was delineated, from the arch of his brow beneath his tangle of curls, to the intricate curve of his mouth set against pale, elongated cheeks.

'Isn't he beautiful?' Bianca asked.

Stephen nodded, hesitating slightly. 'He reminds me of Henry at that age.'

Bianca glanced up at him. The thought had depressed him momentarily. Putting her arms around his waist, she leant her head against his chest.

'I love you,' he whispered gently into her hair. It was said with a note of despair.

'I know,' she said soothingly. 'I love you too.'

She then broke free from his arms and turned other canvases to face the room: an unfinished portrait of Stephen, the nearly completed portrait of the Director of the National Gallery and a group portrait of the Patels, an Indian family grown wealthy on pre-packaged Indian food, their clothes falling from them in spangles.

'That's enough for today, don't you think?'

The moment of sorrow had passed. Smiling joyously again, Stephen kissed her goodbye.

'What are you doing this evening?' he asked, stepping through the doorway onto the street.

'I have to meet Matthew and Max Holland to discuss the possibility of doing his portrait.'

'Wow, how did you pull that one off?'

Bianca still hadn't admitted to her chance meeting with Max. She started to explain… but Stephen was now in a hurry. They had just made love, his mind on other things.

'If the portrait's a success, you should start charging higher prices.'

'It's *art*,' she replied teasingly. 'Don't you know that *art* has nothing to do with making money? That it's only ever done for *love*?'

Stephen laughed. 'Let's hope not…'

Out of the corner of his eye, catching sight of a taxi, he hailed it.

'Bye, my darling. Speak tomorrow…'

* * *

Each of these moments had been like a petal torn from Bianca's day. As her taxi turns into Cork Street, she no longer feels quite herself. While dutifully transporting her body to Cork Street, she herself feels left behind elsewhere; maybe on the doorstep of her studio, as she had kissed Stephen goodbye. In her current state the meeting with Max does not promise well. She feels mentally and emotionally fuddled, all passion spent. Normally, she would not care, but for some reason this meeting with Max Holland strikes her as important.

Bianca thinks of Matthew's Cork Street gallery as a rectangular box, stripped of all architectural detail and fronted from floor to ceiling by plate glass. There is neither cornice nor skirting board. Nothing divides the space proportionally; the fierce pitter-patter of inlaid halogen lighting strikes every surface with brash certainty. The eye is detained by nothing that does not pass for art. And in Matthew's current show, art comes on slender feet, fixing itself exactly midway on the walls between floor and ceiling. Ideally, it would remain there, small, unsmiling and isolated in its exquisite preciousness, like pieces of wayward jewellery, except for its unaesthetic need for electricity to make the art blink kinetically in some obscure, conceptual way. And so, small perfection is ruined by heavy black wires trailing discordantly to the floor.

Turning up at his gallery, Bianca always thinks, is much like stepping over the threshold of what one imagines to be a desirable dress shop, only to instantly discover there is nothing in the room to wear. And then, instead of backing out, forcing oneself to go through the motions of looking with interest at the empty contents of an empty room. Except that, in this case, the room is not empty but brimming with the presence of Max. He is standing in the distance furthest from the window, hands dug deep in his pockets, the red scarf slung about his neck in a mood of student abandon. He reacts to her arrival in silence but with a tremble of electricity passing through his body that makes the chip, chip, wink of the artwork look pathetically undernourished by their wire veins. Matthew stands equidistantly between the two of them, still unaware they have already met.

Matthew is shorter than Max, the same height as Bianca. He advances across the blonde parquet to greet her, holding out his arms.

'Biaaancaa.'

Submitting to his embrace, which, despite the warmth of his voice, is strangely impersonal, Bianca glances over his shoulder at Max.

'Biaaancaa, let me introduce you to Max Hollaaand.'

Shaking Max's hand, she sees he is as intent as she in maintaining the pretence of not having met before, although she can foresee no advantage to either of them in doing so. The sensuous, single-colour planes of Max's face break open in smiles.

'Nice to have a secret,' he remarks, apropos of nothing.

She looks up at him sharply... It might be Stephen talking.

Matthew disappears briefly into the bowels of the gallery, where rack upon rack of paintings reside behind sliding walls, in quest of a bottle of cheap wine. Matthew's private views are notorious for their unpalatable wines. When he returns, two people, presuming the gallery still open, have wandered in off the street.

'Please excuse me,' Matthew apologises, abandoning Bianca and Max to sip the distasteful wine.

They glance conspiratorially at one another, speaking little. Bianca notices that the unattractive mood of abstraction she so feared in herself has lifted. Matthew returns to explain that the visitors are serious clients, not just passers-by.

'Would you mind if I speak to them?' Matthew hesitates, his face full of remorse.

Taking hold of Bianca's arm, Max states decisively: 'We'll leave you to it... I'll discuss the portrait with Bianca and call you tomorrow.'

Matthew looks surprised, but also relieved.

Back on the street, so do Max and Bianca.

'Where shall we eat this time?'

Bianca smiles and begins to laugh. 'I don't much care, but it will have to be an early supper. I do need to get back. My husband is at home.'

They turn northwards towards Bond Street and Grosvenor Square.

'Let's go gastronomic... Let's go to Le Gavroche.'

At the corner of Bond Street, Max stops, turning to face her. 'Are you going to paint my portrait?'

She smiles. 'Only if you promise to sit still.'

Heading into Bruton Street, Bianca glances back along the rising slope of Conduit Street. With shops now closed, the street is almost deserted. In the middle distance, a tiny figure catches her eye. It is Nicholas Rowe's girlfriend, Solange, picking her way on high heels towards Regent Street. Her red miniskirt, black jumper and candyfloss wedge of over-bleached hair move against the grey buildings like the colours of a flag. She has not seen them. Yet a sudden troublesome doubt invades Bianca's happiness. Conduit Street emerges onto Regent Street, almost opposite Beak Street, where Leonardo's office is. Was that what Leonardo had meant, when he said: 'Someone coming to see me at 6.30... the possibility of a business dinner'?

* * *

The following morning, after Leo had left for the office, promising to be home by 6 p.m., Bianca returns to her desk, determined to finish the story of her mother's wedding day. Picking up her silver pen to write, all that happens are her obsessive doodles on the writing pad, as her thoughts revolve around her previous evening with Max. She remembers the expression on his face, as she told him how she had used his name as a mantra to ward off thoughts of Hesketh. His eyes had turned to dark stones.

CHAPTER 7

Hesketh wakes from a dream, knowing he has forgotten something important. His mind feels bruised and pleading, as though cradled in tenderness. He longs for forgiveness. Several days have passed, during which he had almost not thought about Bianca. Now, suddenly, the sensation of something mislaid. He cannot rid himself of the idea she needs his protection, cannot imagine how she will survive without the weight of his love.

It is a Saturday morning and he is lying alone, naked in bed. Without noticing it happen, his lean frame starts to rack with sobs, big tears quickly finding the ravines in his ravaged face. He can smell Chloe's perfume on the smooth sheets. She had got up at 6 a.m., to play with Bruno. Not that Bruno ever wants to play exactly, but he finds it soothing to be watched. Communication with him is rarely direct.

Bruno's room is directly opposite the lift. Ever since a baby, he had loved to sit in its doorway. Not in the expectation of people arriving; visitors to the flat are rare and mostly only the social workers, who come to check on him. Scattered around him, like marbles, are numerous screwed-up knots of paper.

Like a child preparing to be an adult, he dresses formally, in grey flannel shorts, long woollen socks and white shirt beneath his matching grey jumper. Chloe sits behind him, her slender figure wrapped in a pastel pink dress, over-printed with white feathers, her face resembling a pale flower that has drowned in too much emotion. She glances tenderly at her son. A certain adult formality infects Bruno's patterns of behaviour; refusing to look people in the eye, his face always classically turned away one quarter. Only his dancing fingers are never still. Everything about Bruno is elliptical. He likes people, even his parents, to keep a certain distance.

Whenever forced to submit to something childish, like being bathed, he maintains a haughty seigniorial detachment, implying that no aspect of what is being done is any part of himself.

Tearing another page from the old telephone directory in her lap, Chloe screws it into a ball and directs it softly at his back. It catches in the back of his collar. Shrugging slightly to dislodge it, Bruno smiles his secret smile. Chloe throws another, this time grazing his cheek. Picking it up, Bruno smooths it out and pretends to read it, as though it were a love letter.

It had taken Hesketh and Chloe years to puzzle out why Bruno always chose to sit opposite the lift; he likes listening to the soft wheezing music of the lift shaft, punctuated by the concertina cymbals of its doors, collapsing distantly open and shut from the floors below. It was one of their first clues to Bruno's obsession with detail. He grows angry whenever the sequence of the lift's music is broken, becomes agitated if people change their minds, opening the doors to get in, then shutting and opening them again without moving floors. Obsessive detail, they discovered, acted as graceful counterpoint to his clumsiness; Bruno's inelegant, lumbering way of placing his feet is juxtaposed by an extraordinary dexterity.

While listening to the music of the lift, clumsy feet folded beneath him, he would perform the most exquisite embroidery. Chloe prepares handkerchiefs and table mats, stretched taut on timbale frames, for him. Without once misjudging the length and evenness of his stitches, he dutifully fills in the transfer contours of flowers and mocking birds she irons onto their linen surfaces. So precise is his skill that it might almost be saleable, except for one small detail – his refusal to embroider in anything but shades of pink. Leaves, petals, the plumage of birds, it makes no difference; Bruno picks them all out in pinks and reds. Chloe had originally bought him rainbow skeins of silk, but he always selected the red shades, carrying on working until the last lengths of pink thread were finished, then stopping mid-leaf, like the mice in *The Tailor of Gloucester...*

'No more twist...'

The lift sighs and Bruno looks up briefly, smiling in some private swaddled understanding with himself, before bending his head intently over his embroidery again. Chloe sits behind him, never quite in view, addressing her comfortable Mummy conversation to his back. It soothes him to hear the gentle tones of her girlish voice, though he never replies. Best of all, he likes it if she is occupied too. He allows her to tidy his room, laying out his toys in orderly sequence on the floor, like a necklace; tidiness another of his passions. During the day, apart from his slender, pirouetting fingers, Bruno is mostly still, his pale face cocooned in silence. But at night, he fights his bedclothes in animal turmoil, making whimpering sounds as he kicks out, overturning the atlas globe lamp at his bedside. Although nine years old, he still sleeps in a high-sided cot, designed to prevent him falling.

Bruno also likes it when Chloe draws up the battered wicker chair, in which she nursed him as a baby, and takes up her knitting. That is their most serene communion, the fast exchange silence of thought as he embroiders and she knits.

Chloe is twenty-three years younger than Hesketh. She had first met him in Majorca, where, long before they married, they were distant neighbours; he owning a grand palace close to the central square of Valldemossa, and her parents renting a tiny cottage nearby. She had fallen in love with him at first sight. She was still a teenager at the time, although it was five more years before she got to know him. Against the backdrop of the Mediterranean, with the cicadas animating their sultry evenings, his offbeat energy had struck her as appealing. She knew there was something broken in him, that he had sustained some terrible emotional blow, but she liked the Heath Robinson construct of his gaiety as he repeatedly put his emotions back into some kind of disorderly order, determined to soldier on.

He had told her about his love for Bianca during their first evening together, and she had thought it sweet and rather romantic; a man betrayed, who nevertheless knew how to love; a man brave enough to express pain one moment, then throw back his head in laughter the next. She liked the yearning intensity in his eyes as they scrutinised her every move. Above all, she liked the sensuality of his beautiful mouth. And he was a generous and captivating host during their first summer together, driving her, in his battered bright-orange VW Beetle that he kept on the island, to all the best and most exclusive restaurants.

She did not notice at first the hesitation, the slight wariness with which the waiters greeted Hesketh's arrival, their wide smiles accompanied by eyes cast down as he pressed some generous note into their hands. It was not until their second summer together that she saw Hesketh get into a fight. A man at a bar, imagining her to be alone, paid her a compliment. Hesketh punched him and broke his nose. She had been appalled, but also secretly flattered. It had seemed to her, in all her girlish innocence, that she had finally seen off the spectre of Bianca.

Despite the testimony she was asked to give on Hesketh's behalf in his court case against Bianca and Patrick during their first winter in London, where she had briefly glimpsed Bianca, she still had no idea that she resembled her slightly. How, she argued, could a man be prepared to break another man's nose defending her and still love another woman? She had also, by then, begun to realise that she and Hesketh were at their best on their own, just the two of them. Hesketh did not mix well in company, unless it was to do with business.

By their fourth summer together in Majorca, she was pregnant and about to be married. She glances adoringly at Bruno's back. There is nothing she would not do, no sacrifice she would not perform, for her son… It occurs to her that, because of his disabilities, she loves him even more than she would an ordinary child; he is so exclusively theirs, hers and Hesketh's.

It was also Bruno's love of the sighing lift which first gave Hesketh and Chloe a clue to his delight in music. Hesketh bought him a piano, an old upright, offered for sale in the *Kensington and Chelsea Times*. Hesketh knew nothing of playing an instrument, his own tastes in music, despite his fifty-six years, fiercely modern: rock, electric. It was Chloe who had a limited knowledge of classical piano, having studied it up to Grade 4 at school. She could play 'Silent Night' and various practice pieces by Chopin.

When the piano first arrived, with its double-length stool and fascinating lid, in which musical scores were hidden, Chloe had sat down to play some scales. And that was the first, in a long time, that Bruno had chosen to sit next to her. He crept closer and closer until, unasked, he slipped onto the long stool beside her, never once removing his eyes from the performance of her hands, as though trying to remember the exact sequence of her fingers. Eventually, she took his long, slender hands in hers and placed them palm down on the keyboard. He left them there unmoving, silent for ten minutes, then stumblingly played 'Three Blind Mice', copying her musical fingerprints from a quarter of an hour earlier. Chloe had looked at him in amazement, while Hesketh, watching from the doorway, had wept. Within two weeks, Bruno could fluently copy everything Chloe could perform. She and Hesketh gave the old piano away and bought him a baby grand.

At first, Bruno was nervous of the new piano. The shape seemed wrong, alarming. He was frightened by the open mouth of its enormous raised lid, distracted by the depressed stops and visible coordination of the piano's frets with his own playing. But gradually the purity of the instrument's sound overcame him in intrigue. He began to revel in the separation of sound, like puffs of perfume, between each note. Hesketh and Chloe were delighted, yet at a loss to know how to encourage and teach him more. The prospect of hiring a music teacher seemed impossible. Bruno did not easily accept the presence of strangers. As a small child, he had attended day school briefly, but as his eccentricities grew, schooling had become increasingly difficult. It was progress enough that he allowed himself to be taught by Chloe.

Then, one day, Hesketh came home with a huge twenty-eight-inch television screen, installing it above the piano, where Bruno could watch while he played. He also bought videos of orchestral recordings, with long, close-up shots of celebrated pianists, such as Alfred Brendel, performing. Very quickly, Bruno was playing Brahms and Mozart with precision and ease, but always in snatches. Whenever the filming moved to the orchestra, following the movements of violinists and oboists, Bruno's capacity to imagine the music and reproduce it failed. Consequently, he could soon play whole concertos by memory from start to finish, but always with significant passages missing, those devoted on film to the conductor and orchestra... These days, it was the sweetness of music that filled Hesketh's reveries of Bianca. Loving Bianca and loving Bruno had become an indivisible activity in his mind.

It had taken Chloe ten years to realise Hesketh still loved Bianca, that her ghost was far from vanquished in their lives. She should, of course, have known. There had been the court case early in their relationship, in which the police had accused Hesketh of inflicting grievous bodily harm on Bianca's boyfriend, Patrick, at a rock concert, where they all happened to meet. She, herself, had testified on Hesketh's behalf, too much in love to notice her own perjury, while at the same time believing it represented the final bitter remnants of Hesketh's story with Bianca. Her disillusionment had finally come two years earlier, during one of their summers in Majorca.

Since the birth of Bruno, the Spanish waiters had again raised their eyes more respectfully to Hesketh. He still struck them as a jangled beast, with his extraordinary thirty-degree gait and his throwaway laughter, and they still feared the psychopathic speed of his moments of violence, but there was no mistaking his tenderness towards his son, nor his proud submission to the fates that had given him a child, whose cleverness was like a silent riddle.

At first, that morning, everything had seemed normal. Then, at midday, Hesketh had returned distraught from a simple expedition to buy bread from their local bakery. The bright, clownish Hawaiian shirt he wore seemed to do nothing to rescue his mood, all the jocular puppetry of his gait suddenly replaced by a volatile mixture of aggression and sorrow. While his hand stretched yearningly to cup his cheek, his feet, in their concertinas of white sock, even in the intense summer heat, kicked out viciously at the furniture, attacking the heavy Hispanic chests of drawers that adorned their vast sitting room. Sweeping precious pieces of antique Spanish pottery from a sideboard, he smashed them to smithereens on the decorative tiled floor. Bruno started to whimper, like an animal trapped in pain. But for the only time Chloe could ever remember, Hesketh ignored his son's distress.

Breathless, angry...

'I saw her... She's here in Majorca...' Hesketh repeated, again and again. 'I lost her in the crowd... Can you believe that? After all these years, she comes back to me... and I lose her in the crowd?'

'Who?' asked Chloe. '*Who?*'

'Bianca...' he replied distractedly.

As though it were the most natural thing in the world to reintroduce this name that for ten years had been suppressed, forbidden. Chloe had believed it forgotten. Now, she saw clearly, that the name had been there every day of her married life.

The realisation got worse. Hesketh improvised a crudely written banner, planting it outside their front door, like a primitive totem pole: 'BIANCA – PLEASE CONTACT ME', their telephone number proclaimed large to the crowd.

He also went to the local newspaper and placed an advert in both Spanish and English, alongside an old photograph of Bianca, aged nineteen, asking for anyone who had seen this woman to contact him.

A week later, hidden in a chest, Chloe found photocopies he had kept of the distraught letter he subsequently wrote to Bianca at her London address, plus photos of the totem pole and copies of the Spanish newspaper article.

Majorca, 27 June

Dear, dear Bianca,

So very angry with myself; devastated by what I have accidentally done. You probably thought that I saw you and deliberately blanked you. But it's not true. I would never, ever avoid you. I long to see you... Without my glasses, my eyes are a total blur. Only later, when I thought about it, did I realise that it was you.

At the time, I just wondered why such a beautiful woman would smile at an old fool like me. You looked so glamorous, sitting in the café in your dark glasses, that I assumed you must be smiling at someone else. What a fool I am.

I have since been everywhere trying to find you, my feet blistered from visiting every café in Valldemossa... Meanwhile, I have raised a banner everyone can see as they enter the square for the fiesta, with your name and my telephone number on it.

Ours was not some ordinary, meaningless affair. I fell completely, utterly in love with you, and know you felt the same. You loved me too… It felt inconceivable that we would ever part. Our destinies became inextricable. And yet, we did, and it was all my fault. Afterwards, everything I did only made things worse. In fact, I never knew that it was possible to feel so empty, unhappy and grief-stricken, yet still be alive. But in the end, no amount of pain and grief made any difference. Wherever you are, whatever you do, you belong to me.

There are so many more things I would like to say… to tell you and explain. Please let's meet. Please let me speak to you and hear your voice again. It would make me so very happy.

Perhaps you are back in London by now? I am not even sure you still live in Holland Park. But I am still here in Majorca. My phone numbers are below. I am always anxious about you.

All my love, Hesketh

As Chloe read this, she had felt part of herself die. Like watching her own execution. She could feel, second by second, her spirit dwindling away into a form of illness beyond recovery. For the first time in his life, she regretted having given birth to Bruno, aware suddenly of being caught in a vortex of need, love, and circumstance from which she could neither escape nor envisage any joy. She looked again at the newspaper article, with its blurred image of Bianca, aged nineteen.

Good God, he's even offered a reward for information on her: 500 euros… How could I have been so stupid?

She read the article carefully, half in Spanish, half in English; Bianca's slightly soulful photograph dividing the two languages.

GRATIFICARE con 500 E
A quien facilite informacion del paradero de la inglesa, senorita BIANCA JOHNSON.

Fue visita CIU... el pasado 11 de junio. Mide 1,70 cm, es delgada, guapa, rubia (?) y elegante.

Aunque la foto se hizo hace tiempo, no ha cambiado mucho.

MESSAGE FOR BIANCA

Should she read this notice

I am devastated, realising what I have accidentally done. You must think I saw you, and turned away deliberately to avoid you. That could never be true.

Without my glasses, I can't see properly; everything is a blur. Later I realised.

The penny dropped. PLEASE CALL. I would be so happy to see you.

HESKETH JAMES

Chloe felt humiliated. The Spanish waiters again knew that Hesketh was mad, rich and *malo*, once again casting their eyes to the floor as they accepted his money. Hesketh spent the rest of their summer holiday either driving around the island looking for Bianca or sitting in the central square, drinking Sangria, hoping she might chance by. It took almost two weeks before he rediscovered his love of Bruno. That was two years ago... Ever since, Hesketh and Chloe's marriage had been an uneasy truce, with Bruno the constant pawn of exchange.

* * *

Back in London, following the success of the piano, Hesketh bought Bruno an old battered Olivetti golf-ball typewriter, on which to tap out obsessive musical scores, composed of asterisks and private, uncodified sequences of letters with no meaning, except in the form of design. The only words to punctuate its riddles were repetitions of: 'Yes' and 'No'.

Now, lying in bed, distantly listening to Bruno and Chloe play, his face wet with tears, Hesketh feels no inclination to join them, but he does feel a momentary degree of peace and pride. Yet what was it he had forgotten? In his dream, before waking, he had been eating honey, dipping a silver spoon into a jar, when first a baby, then a giant alligator had escaped from the jar. He awoke, recoiling in fear... How he longs for the sweet reassurance of Bianca's touch, for just one more moment of her kindness.

Beyond the half-open curtains, on the opposite side of the river, he can see the Pagoda, with its golden Buddha addressing his beatitudes to Battersea Park.

Their bedroom is fifteen feet square. It was Chloe who had insisted on dragging their enormous double bed far out into the middle of the room, along with its improvised bed head of a seven-foot-long sideboard that serves simultaneously as bedside table and bookcase. It has the appearance of an altar, with its accumulations of decorative silverware brought home from Spain, plus a bronze sculpture that Chloe had never fully understood, but which Hesketh insists on keeping, of two people making love. She assumes Hesketh thinks it reminiscent of their own lovemaking, which like the sculpture is at times frenzied and angry. Chloe has the Dickensian idea that it is healthy to have the air circulating around one's head while one sleeps.

Why then, do I feel as though I am suffocating? Hesketh wonders.

But what was it I forgot?

Hesketh turns on his side. Extracting a pill from a packet, he places it, like a promise of oblivion, next to the glass of water on his side of the bed. He hesitates before taking it, yet can feel the urgency, the hurry beginning in his soul. There was something important he had meant to say to Bianca... in his dream...

Is it too late...?

He can feel a headache encroaching, the sweet sounds of piano failing to move him. His mind shuts fast on Bruno. Almost unconsciously, he picks up a pad of lined paper used for telephone messages. He had no intention of writing to Bianca. Here, in the bed he shares with Chloe, it would be an act of betrayal. He normally writes to her in his office, behind the panelled door next to the lift, or looking up at her painting in the wide sitting room. But the headache, his sense of loss, the urgency to communicate, plus the distant music and a sudden overwhelming sense of helplessness, urge him to recklessness. Almost unconsciously, he starts to compose a letter.

Tuesday, 8 October

Dear Bianca,

I remember the last time we made love. You didn't want to, but I insisted. I knew it was the only way to reach you. I couldn't find the right words… 'You, only you' is what I wanted to say.

Our bodies were so well matched, so completely in tune and harmony that our lovemaking surpassed the physical… But that was wonderful too. I deliberately put your pleasure first, only to find my pleasure strangely enhanced… both in and out of control. By being unselfish, without seeking pleasure, I received it in abundance. To make love to you made me feel complete…

Then you insisted you had to leave. Stupidly, I still could not find the right words. 'Don't go; please stay' is what I should have said. Instead, I hesitated, giving in to what I thought you wanted to do. How stupid of me not to know the truth. All I had to do was be honest and say what I felt: 'I love you; don't go. It is you I care about and want to be with. We are right for each other. I love you.'

But I let you go, assuming that Highbury was like the room you rented in Barons Court. I thought you would come back. There was also the fact that I had started to feel ill, worried what the doctors would say.

But so much time has passed that none of it matters anymore. What we have done since is irrelevant. All that matters is now. All you have to do is say where and when, and I'll be there. It's easy; just pick up the phone. I shall probably be nervous, but no matter. You might be nervous too? All that matters is that I would be pleased to see you…

I am now going to cycle around Battersea Park. It is such a lovely day. How I wish you were here with me.

All my love, Hesketh

* * *

Hesketh does not post this letter immediately; folding and sealing it, he hides it under his pillow. His hand reaches out for the pill. Sweet oblivion finally allowed... Later, when he wakes, he remembers Chloe and Bruno's plan to stay overnight the following Thursday with her mother in the Cotswolds. The next day, first photocopying his letter, he adds a postscript, enclosing a theatre ticket: 'Dear Bianca, come to Max Holland's new play with me – I shall be there.'

* * *

Bianca had spent her morning at the studio. Not painting but thinking... making herself endless cups of coffee, while drifting listlessly from the studio floor to the upper deck of her improvised bedroom, with its mattress thrown casually on the floor. Stephen often teases her about her need for 'thinking time', smiling one of his darling sideways grins and asking: 'Had a good ponder?'

Nevertheless, it represents an urgent need in her, this desire to uninterruptedly think something through; the fate perhaps of being an only child? When, eventually, thought had settled in her, and grown into optimism, she had turned the music up and danced wildly in front of the mirror, loving every sexy beat and nuance of her own movements. She had emerged from her studio feeling brand new, ready for anything... Back at home, Hesketh's letter was waiting for her.

It is only a week since Hesketh's last letter. She opens the new letter with trepidation. Plus a sense of relief that she and Stephen would soon be away in China. In fact, they will soon all be away; Leo, too, is returning to Singapore.

As the theatre ticket falls from the envelope, she gazes at it in horrified amazement.

Before having had time to read the letter, Bianca notices the word 'love' scattered liberally across its page. But instead of joy, it evokes nothing but fear and shame.

Why, she wonders, *does it feel so terrifying to be loved by someone one can't love in return?*

The shame is more transparent. It exists at the complex heart of the relationship between a stalker and his prey, feelings that no amount of logic can dispel... An overriding sense of repugnance towards herself for having inspired such hideous emotions in another human being, plus the relentless fear that she is herself the shameful, clandestine source of such ugliness, as opposed to merely its victim. Hesketh's letters, with their free bandying of the word 'love', leave her feeling anxious...

There is also yet another aspect to this shame... Bianca remembers the song her mother used to sing to her as a child: 'In Scarlet Town, where I was born, there lay a young man dying...'

Is it a crime to squander love? Any love?

Hesketh is coming closer, Bianca can feel it. This had always been the pattern. The madness builds in him, becoming more panicked and obsessive, then breaks for a brief while, in the numbness of disappointment and repeated rejection. There is then a period of recovery, wounds to be licked, before, Mount Sisyphus-like, he again rolls the heavy stone of his optimism back up the hill. For months before his last letter, everything Hesketh wrote had left Bianca unmoved. In her angrier moments, she had disparaged them as the 'innocuous bleating of a lost soul'. But just as his last letter had frightened her, so too does this one disturb her. It is as though Hesketh had overheard the tumultuous memories rack her being a few days earlier, and matched them with his own references to her room in Barons Court, veiled threats of danger from a black source, and his precise recollection of when she was about to leave him.

'The last time we made love...'

She cannot herself remember it. It was twenty-five years ago...

Yet he writes of it as though it were yesterday.

The immediacy, the assurance of his memory, confounds her. Too vivid to be dismissed.

How, she wonders, *has he kept this memory so distilled, so perfect?*

She tries to rediscover it in her own mind, but it is simply erased.

And his imbecile confidence that all he had to do was ask me to stay?

She grimaces furiously.

She may have erased her memory of their lovemaking, but not of those last months and weeks while she plotted her escape. She recalls perfectly the twin necessity for secrecy, while needing to appear transparent. Remembers the gradual, deliberate negotiation of her own being into a neutral that would neither attract nor arouse suspicion; remembers how, without being unpleasant, she had deliberately made herself into someone any man could afford to let go, and in whom the sparks of emotion were already blunted. All she had to do was get clear… Only then would his rage of twenty-twenty vision return. But by then it would be too late. Had Hesketh asked her to stay, she would have had to seemingly say 'Yes', while still succeeding in leaving. He was wrong to assume he was still part of the debate. By then, Hesketh was on the other side of a fogged screen. He had not yet said: 'Wherever you go… I shall find you.'

But she had already known they would wake up to trouble. To a certain extent, she was prepared. In her naivety, she had simply not known that 'trouble' could last twenty-five years. Twenty-five years! At the time, she was not yet that age herself, still four years to go.

In her scarred mind, Bianca searches again for their lovemaking and fails. She can only remember odd snatches of sex, coupled with tragedy, like the time he had tried to commit suicide after they had made love. That had been early on. He had taken a handful of barbiturates. She remembers being alerted to what he had done when he said: 'You'll have to find someone else to look after you now…'

By then, he was drifting into a coma. There was no phone, and she had gone next door at 3 a.m. to ask their neighbours to call an ambulance. She remembers the rain hard against the raspberry-pink walls of the little house he had bought near the art school. Pure suburbia… She knew nothing of first aid, yet instinct had dictated she keep him alive by talking. She made him cups of strong black coffee and insisted he get out of bed. She remembers him crawling like a naked sloth up the narrow staircase, trying to head back to bed; remembers the odd, impotent angles of his feet to his ankles as they struggled to grip the stairs.

Later, at the hospital, after they had pumped his stomach clean and he was sound asleep, they told her that her instincts had saved his life.

'Come back tomorrow... there's nothing more you can do here now.'

She had gone back the next day and there he was, sitting up in bed, making riotously provocative comments to the nurses, while laughing recklessly. Even then, young as she was, his behaviour struck her as dangerously unbalanced. She had perched on the side of his bed, and the matron, watching his body ease itself towards hers, had complained of his disgraceful gestures of intimacy – at which he became enraged and insisted on discharging himself, much to the nurses' dismay, as it was long before a psychiatrist had had time to talk to him.

Hesketh and Bianca had left the hospital together in another splash of his anger and resumed normality, but with a new blemish between them; the blemish of a suicide, never again mentioned, but treated like a day out at the races. Only many years later, did Bianca wonder whether all her subsequent troubles had stemmed from that single moment?

Did I, by saving Hesketh, make myself responsible for his soul?

Had she unwittingly accepted his own dreadful karma as her own?

As for their lovemaking, all she could rise to in her memory was the acknowledgement of a misspent passion. She knew that her crime with Hesketh had been a mad, headlong, lustful passion, yoked to a fatal youthful intrigue with the damage in him. But she could no longer either feel or recall it... Although she does remember, the first time she ever saw him, experiencing some involuntary reflex of recognition and warning. He had walked into an art-school studio, laughing recklessly and spilling boxes of paints and brushes onto the charcoal-stained floor. She also remembers that their relationship was powerful, sexual, addictive even... But it was like remembering a fact, learned by rote, without any visual memories attached, so obliterated are they by the acts of violence and destruction that followed. All of those she recalls perfectly... For her, memory had been replaced long ago by more rapturous loves. Yet the vividness of his descriptions was undeniable.

Perhaps at the time it was like that for me too? she puzzles.

Or had she instinctively known what Hesketh seemed never to

learn? That passion can drown itself in hideous behaviour, only to drain away, leaving nothing but sediments of shame and dismay?

By the time his letter mentions, she was already secretly in love with Patrick, who having befriended them both was a regular visitor to the house in Putney. Even though nothing had yet passed between them... no certainty, just an intimation of understanding... her only thoughts, by then, were of how to free herself from the devilishness of Hesketh.

Three months later, when it became clear that she and Patrick were a couple, and Hesketh's perfect vision was restored, the humiliation and betrayal that fuelled his hatred and persecution of them led to extremes of violence.

Bianca had moved into a new home, with friends, overlooking Primrose Hill. Patrick habitually parked his car in a Georgian square close by. One day Hesketh was waiting there for him. He had already frequently harangued him in the street, and once climbed the scaffolding outside his own house in Fulham to get in through a sash window and threaten him. Luckily, that time Patrick was rescued by the couple he lived with. But this time was different. One sunny afternoon, Hesketh came from behind and attacked Patrick viciously with a crowbar, just as he was locking his car. Not once did Hesketh laugh. Patrick only remembered the gravel of his voice, the soiled leaves of abuse falling about his ears; remembered the confetti of spring blossom falling against the daze of sunlight. Frenzy took over. Hesketh hit him savagely four times, twice on the head. Patrick fell to the ground bleeding, shouts for help stifled in his throat.

Someone, happening to look out from a daytime window, called the police, the sound of sirens approaching. At that point, Hesketh ran away. The police tried hard to trace the weapon. Only Bianca half guessed where it might be, believing Hesketh must have thrown it into the pond on Putney Common. Even if found, it would not have been traceable to him. At the time, Bianca still hoped this madness and fury of Hesketh's would die, be temporary...

She could not drum up one single image of lovemaking between herself and Hesketh, yet would never forget the mixture of love, resentment and fear on Patrick's bandaged face that evening when she visited him in hospital.

'Where are your clothes?'

'They had to be given to the police…'

He had soiled his trousers in fear. At the time, it had seemed to them both the greatest symbol of their humiliation and despair.

From that day onwards, Patrick had always both adored and occasionally hated her. Once, in front of friends, he had emptied a full ashtray over her head. Their friends had been angry and appalled, but Bianca was just very sad. She had loved him, but ever more despairingly against Hesketh's relentless patterns of persecution.

She looks again at the letter, the wide-spaced writing scribbled rapidly, then torn roughly from a block of lined paper.

Why has he photocopied it? Is he becoming his own connoisseur?

Everything else in Bianca's life, no matter how painful, had somehow been comprehensible and forgivable. But this ugly man, with his alert memory of lovemaking twenty-five years old? That she would never forgive. Too much had happened in the wake of his obsession… Too much hatred, masquerading as love… Too much harm… Too much loss… Her entire adult life seemed to have been played out against the twin loves, turned to possessive hatred, of both Hesketh and her own mother.

* * *

Just as she is folding the letter back in its envelope, Bianca hears the sound of Leonardo's key in the door. He is early. She drops the letter in her handbag.

'Dinner's not yet ready,' she apologises.

Leonardo studies her for a moment. *Has she been crying?* he wonders mildly, before picking up his evening paper and placing it as a deliberate screen between them.

Although, despite hiding behind his newspaper, Leonardo remains intensely aware of Bianca's every move. He peeks over the topmost edge of the news-sheet, rustling its pages loudly, before disappearing again.

She looks so very sad this evening...

He would never ask. He tracks her in his mind almost unconsciously. He has no idea of how she spends her time; no real desire to know. All that he cares about is the clear, good-willed gleam in her eyes as she turns her face concernedly towards his. He pretends indifference towards her, yet returns to her side, time and time again, like some homing pigeon. Mostly, he does not bother to analyse his own feelings and motives. The thought always uppermost in his mind is that he does not want to talk, does not want to explain. He just longs for Bianca to wait on him, hand and foot, for the brief times he is here, and then to let him burrow into the bedclothes beside her, to feel the silk of her warm skin next to his. It is not her conversation that he craves but her presence while he sleeps, breathing in the warmth of her perfumed body, being greeted by her teasing smile when he awakes; the way she eventually forgives his every transgression.

He knows she excites other men. He sees it occasionally in their eyes, in the way they take her arm, suddenly yearningly possessive. But 'excitement' is no longer the proper word for his feelings for Bianca. She is part of the sustenance he needs. He remembers her passion, knows that she now deliberately stifles it in his presence; that she eventually came to understand that he cannot and will not tolerate it. He had lost himself to passion just once, in his first marriage to Lisette; allowing the tumbril of jealousy to maul him. He had listened at doors, sniffed at her underwear for the scent of other men, then one day, returning home unexpectedly, had walked in on her delicious, naked body resting in the lap of a fully clothed man. She had shown no remorse, neither at the time nor later.

'What do you expect?' she had jibed.

As his mind had closed like a fist, on this image of pain, he had decided: *No more.*

At a stroke, his intellect had rebelled against his own disarray of emotion and denounced passion for ever. Henceforth, he wanted only the symbolism of passion, the play and courtesies of love; above all, the reckless, greedy stimulation of flirtation. But without any investment of passion. By the time he had walked in on Lisette a second time, this time in their bed, with a stockbroker they both knew, he had simply smiled, half bowed formally to them both and walked out again.

Yet Bianca had taken him by surprise, which is why he had married her. She had somehow contrived to love him, while not insisting on his loving her conventionally in return. In fact, the word 'love' was never mentioned between them. Unlike him, she was not a flirt. She relied instead on a kind of seamless sensuality that felt no need to primp itself in flirtation. He could successfully ignore her most of the time, yet still come home to relaxation and warmth. Only occasionally does he go too far. Then, in her rare moments of rebuke, amidst threats to leave him, his passion for her revives. He does not want to lose her.

Now glancing shyly from behind his newspaper, she strikes him as different in some way, upset maybe? He folds the paper carefully over his knees. Bianca recognises in this gesture an inarticulate signal he wishes to talk. As she gazes back at him from her preparations, he casts about blindly for something elusive to say. Taking the tumbler of whisky she had placed at his side, he balances it on his topmost knee. Bianca half smiles to herself. She would recognise his kneecaps anywhere. They are flat, like square saucers, his own inbuilt occasional tables.

Leonardo looks up at her, smiling hesitantly; his smile is always like sunshine after a storm, very beautiful.

'How are you?' he asks, casting his question into generalities.

'Okay.'

She is surprised; Leonardo never enquires how she is.

Sighing deeply, his eyes again search the room for something he fails to discover.

'We'll eat soon,' she reassures.

Turning away, her sleeve catches a glass, smashing it to the floor. She is not normally so clumsy. He watches her crouch down to sweep up the shards, noticing the slender, supple grace of her figure, then picks up the newspaper again. Why can't he say, 'I know you're upset. Tell me what's happened?'

He sighs again, deeply; the moment has passed… Soon, he will be returning to Singapore, Laetitia Norton joining him. Bianca does not know that yet.

What's the point of my asking what's upsetting her? What would I do, even if I knew... I shall be away for weeks.

In a few days' time, all that will concern him is his right to return; the reassurance that the fine fabric of his and Bianca's peculiar mix of understanding and misunderstanding has not been torn. He hopes that she, like him, will agree to live to fight another of their days together. And yet, he knows she will be angry when she learns that Laetitia is travelling with him, and angrier still if she knew he'd had lunch today with Solange, Nicholas Rowe's girlfriend. He takes a sip of whisky. Their marriage is one of irreconcilable differences.

Perhaps by tomorrow morning she'll no longer be upset?

The thought consoles him.

Bianca places plates, lavishly heaped with smoked salmon, on the table. 'Shall we eat?'

Standing up, he moves to the small table, her walnut desk, where they eat whenever it is just the two of them. Over the road, at the bus stop, a shadowy figure watches Bianca through field glasses, while Leonardo remains hidden from view. Hesketh continues to watch avidly, until Bianca suddenly remembers to close the silk curtains.

* * *

It is not Leonardo, but Stephen, to whom Bianca confesses her fears the following morning. Strangely, he has become the arbiter of all her actions and feelings of loathing towards Hesketh.

'He's sent me a ticket for Max Holland's new play...'

'When for?'

'Next Thursday.'

'You won't go?'

'No, of course not.'

'Perhaps you should donate the ticket to someone else?' he jokes.

'But to whom?' She sounds anxious. 'Hesketh might get violent if he thinks he's being made a fool of.'

'He's already a fool, already violent,' remarks Stephen grimly.

'Yes, but the whole point of this nightmare is that Hesketh has no concept of himself as we see him. He just wants things and seems to think that justification for getting them. He's like a brat, who won't be told *no*.'

'How much did the ticket cost?'

'£40.00.'

'Poor sod!'

'What I most resent is his insistence that the rest of us live our lives at the same bleak, emotional levels he does.'

'Probably doesn't feel bleak to him,' Stephen reminds her. 'To him, all this is the stuff of life, is it not?'

'Stuff' being the appropriate word.'

Stephen laughs, and she with him.

'Does he know how ridiculous he is?'

'No, I think he takes himself very seriously. In fact, I think he likes himself, which is about as ridiculous as it gets.'

'I suspect all monsters like themselves. They get used to their comfortable monster ways... Can't see anything wrong with them in the end.'

'It's like an advanced form of paranoia,' she adds. 'The whole focus of Hesketh's life is to persuade me that his point of view, no matter how wrong-headed, is justified.'

'So, what will you do with the ticket?'

'Just ignore it, probably.'

* * *

Half an hour later, the phone rings again. It is Max calling.

'When are we having our first sitting?'

'I could manage Thursday, during the day, if that suits you?' Bianca replies, consulting her diary.

'Excellent. You had better tell me the address of your studio?'

CHAPTER 8

That same morning, Bianca returns to her mother's diaries, hoping to conjure more truths from Anya's past.

* * *

Meanwhile, across town, in her student-like flat, caught between Trafalgar Square and the Strand, Anya is rising from her daily bath, as nimble and fleet-footed as any young girl. The flat is sparsely furnished, but immaculate, its only oddities the various flower arrangements, which sit next to lamps and pieces of blue-and-white pottery, in arrangements reminiscent of still lifes. Yet the flowers are all dead; the desiccated remnants of professional bouquets, allowed to stiffen and grow faint in colour, forming ghostly contrast with the strident Prussian blue and turquoise gaiety of her curtains and upholstery. Throughout her entire life, Anya had never been afraid of bold colour.

Sitting in her favourite raspberry-pink chair, enveloped in a bathrobe, she faces what she calls her 'altarpiece'; images of cherished paintings she has cut from various newspapers and journals to Blu-Tack to the wall above her television. Getting up briefly to fondly rearrange a branch of dead leaves, she sits back in her chair, preparing to dress; her clothes warming on the radiator. There is both anxiety and serenity in her face. They chase after one another, swapping ownership of her features. More and more these days, her thoughts turn to William and those early days and weeks of her marriage, haunting her still...

I was so very young... but perhaps if I had behaved differently...?

She still remembers every detail of her wedding day, as though it were yesterday...

They were about to kiss, when the doorbell rang... She and William stood apart abruptly.

'I'll go,' she offered.

William looked vaguely worried. 'It might be my parents...'

'But you're covered in paint,' she objected.

Discarding her hat on a chair, Anya left the tiny bunches of violets to scatter about its rim. Answering the door meant descending three flights; the bell ringing out shrilly in the stairwell a second time. Breathless, she flung the front door open wide. But instead of the two people she was expecting, there was only one: a tall wolf-like individual, exceptionally thin, with a face that might have been painted by El Greco. He was dressed in a shabby suit, over which the flourish of a dark opera cape revealed its red satin lining, his long, slender hands coated in nicotine. The bright yellow stain reached almost to the knuckles of his right hand.

Glancing down at Anya, traces of cruelty threaded his dark eyes, his smile sardonic. This was the celebrated poet, Paul Ottery, published regularly in The Listener.

'I heard you were throwing a party,' he said by way of explanation.

Anya returned his glance coolly. There was some element in Paul Ottery's face she neither liked nor trusted. Always that mask of superiority whenever he looked at her, as though knowing something she didn't. His presence aroused the fighter in her, quickly provoking her into abandoning feminine demure and going for the jugular.

'It's my wedding day,' she stated, with haughty dignity. 'Only our witnesses and William's parents have been invited.'

'Your wedding day?' he mocked. 'How very bourgeois.'

The word lay between them like a wound. No other word in the current pantheon of insults matched that of 'bourgeois'. It implied a blemish on the very fundaments of personality. Without the strength to outwit bourgeois morality, one had no right existing, let alone the right to be an artist, especially in Fitzrovia, where artists were considered aristocratically set apart from the fettered 'bourgeois' nonentities who renounced their life force to dreams of comfort and respectability.

Paul looked down on the diminutive, animated figure of Anya in malicious glee.

'What a little hell cat you are. Does William know yet about that little gift of fury you carry with you, or are you saving it up as a surprise for after you're married?'

Anya glanced back at him undaunted, her eyes appraising him slowly, full of disdain.

'I suppose marriage would seem unattractive to someone whom no one will deign to marry?'

Paul crossed his arms in amusement over the folds of his cape, his dark eyes sparkling in triumph. He had provoked her into revealing herself. There was nothing he enjoyed so much as a spat. He had recognised the firebrand in Anya the first time he met her. He also knew the story of her passionate liaison with Varinsky but had decided to hold that piece of information in reserve for another day.

'Why should I not marry, were I foolish enough to wish to do so?' he asked merrily.

'What woman is going to marry a man so vicious that he tours around London bragging about the number of women he has given a dose of the clap to?' she asked imperiously. 'We all know you're a disgrace.'

Momentarily, the poet looked shocked. But not for long, his natural aplomb reasserting itself almost immediately.

'Now that I'm here, I think I should like to come in,' he stated decisively. 'Let's see what kinds of old trout these Sheffield folk prove to be... Besides, I suppose dear William will stretch to a bottle or two to celebrate, will he not?'

Anya tried to bar his way, but Paul Ottery was too swift and strong for her. He swept past her, along the dingy, dust-laden hallway and hared up the stairs ahead of her. Anya, chasing after him, noticed that the soles of both his shoes flapped beneath his feet, almost adrift from their uppers.

'William, old chap. Congratulations! Your wedding day, I hear.'

William, again standing before his easel, lost in a dream of painting, almost jumped out of his skin. Recovering amiably, he combed back the dark, liquid tresses of his hair with a distraught hand.

'Paul, dear man, how are you?' He hugged the poet to him. 'I read your new poem in Tambimuttu's Poetry, just the other day. Excellent, quite excellent.'

Over his shoulder, the poet smirked triumphantly at Anya, who was *now pink and extra beautiful with suppressed rage. It occurred to him that he might one day seduce her himself, tear down that contempt and replace it with sensuality. But not today, clearly.*

'May I stay and celebrate with you, old chap?' he asked, his eyes twinkling naughtily.

'Of course, but of course.'

He glanced at Anya and saw her face turn away in a half scowl.

'Why don't you make Paul some tea while I wash and get changed?' he ordered his future wife.

Paul looked around him. Against the tongue-and-groove-clad walls of the threadbare room, suspended on hooks, were William's marionettes, each two and a half foot tall, hand carved in wood, then dressed like dolls by Anya. There was a clown in pale grey striped pantaloons, his face a wide grimace of happiness; an old man, his hook-nosed face benign and permanently smiling; a velvet-clad black cat with green eyes put in with the impasto of oil paint, and white whiskers made of unravelled string; and an unfinished and undressed cow, revealing its bare bones of manufacture, the way its individually carved limbs assembled in a jigsaw of clippity-clop movement. And finally, William's pièce de résistance: a dusky night-club singer, her dark hair carved at the nape of her neck into a smooth bun, her mouth lasciviously red and predatory, her eyes heavy lidded and enticing, and her body a sinuous construction of implied sexuality, dressed in strapless white satin and gold hoop earrings.

To one side, leaning against the wall, were the flats and frontispiece of the stage William had built for them, currently unassembled, its front panels hand-painted and decorated with harlequin figures teasingly drawing back the bold print swags of their curtains in a print that might easily have been the work of Sonia Delaunay. The marionettes hung from an upper ledge, where the tongue and groove formed a shelf with the wall immediately below the ceiling. Along this shelf, stored safely away from the assortment of easels, portfolios and heaped-up watercolour paintings and frames below, were numerous pieces of pottery, picked up in junk shops for a song and a farthing. Some of them were recognisable as the subjects of the various still-life paintings lying around, although mostly, William's paintings were either of figures or landscapes.

Having swept a connoisseur's eye through the tiny apartment, Paul threw his gaunt form into a ladder-backed rocking chair and rocked himself back and forth hilariously against the bare, paint-spattered floor-boards.

Returning with the tea, and making space for a red lacquer tray, Anya suddenly glanced out of the window. She saw the curtain move in the window opposite and, abandoning her fury towards Paul, transferred it instead to the old man spying on them from across the road. Positioning herself, arms akimbo, at the window, she glared furiously at him.

As William came back into the room, both he and Paul laughed.

'What a little firebrand you are marrying.'

'Absolutely,' William agreed.

Anya turned to glance at them both and, seeing their merriment, also started to laugh. Suddenly, all three laughed happily, joyfully and youthfully together, without really knowing why, all former animosity lost to the sheer delight of shared happiness.

'We mustn't leave things too late,' commented William. 'My parents, Rowland and Bunty will probably meet us at the registry office.'

* * *

Marylebone Registry Office stood, vaguely temple-like and forbidding, on the Marylebone Road, a little west of Baker Street, with a flight of broad steps leading to its colonnaded entrance. But inside, its corridors were a warren of officialdom, all former classical grace and sense of proportion lost to the red tape of its interior. The entire building had the appearance of having been wiped across by a dirty mop.

At the top of the steps, waiting for them, were the painter Rowland Darblay and his wife, Bunty. Rowland, who, like his father, had worked as a miner, before studying at the art school in Sheffield, was William's best friend. The two of them had made their adventurous journey from north to south together and were now locked in friendly rivalry in their efforts to attract the attention of dealers. The two galleries most interested in their work were Lefevre and Lucy Wertheim, whose gallery, at the back of the Albany, faced Savile Row.

Rowland and Bunty were more desperately poor than William. William had his occasional, slender moments of commercial success with his marionette theatre, and his father, a businessman in the steel industry, sent him a small allowance from time to time. Rowland, by comparison, had nothing except painting, and so the myth silently developed between the two friends that painting was more important to Rowland than to William. But this was not true. Rowland's situation was more desperate and therefore seemingly more deserving, but, of the two, William was the more intelligent and complex painter, also the more artistically ambitious, whereas Rowland was rightly known and respected for his stunningly beautiful 'wolf whistles' at landscapes.

Rowland, with his eager eyes and smiling, moustachioed face, wore cord trousers, lashed about his thin, undernourished body by a wide, tightly buckled belt. An anecdote currently circulating to considerable hilarity in the pubs of Charlotte Street was of how, at a recent private view of Lucy Wertheim's, for which she had, as always, baked a cake, Rowland, when offered the plate on which were some slices, had instead greedily taken the huge wedge of uncut cake...

'Why, Mr Darblay,' Madame Wertheim had said, in her shocked, tinkling flute of a voice. 'You seem to have taken the entire cake!'

At the top of the steps, as he greeted Rowland, William recounted the tale again to Paul. All of them, including Rowland, laughed hilariously; all except Bunty, whose normally smiling face remained a sombre mask. Rowland, handsome, tall and just a little desperate, was liked and admired by everyone, but Bunty was generally regarded as not quite 'the ticket'. She had been a nude model at the art school in Sheffield. Rowland, who always had a knowing eye for the ladies, had nevertheless married her. No one, except Rowland, quite knew why. She was neither beautiful nor clever. Her cheerful smile in its round, freckled face was vaguely clown-like. Her hair stood out in tufts of haphazardly applied henna, and her mouth was always a hit and miss gesture of bright orange lipstick, which seemed to float away from the contours of her face like a hieroglyph into free space. People thought of her as a kindly simpleton. And yet, Rowland, for all his infidelities, was passionately loyal towards her, and would cut any friend dead whom he overheard mocking her. Bunty, like William, was also a passionate collector of junk-shop trophies.

William, now dressed in a smart mole-coloured corduroy jacket over dark-blue, wide-cut trousers, and a rust-coloured open-necked shirt and waistcoat, surveyed the street below them. No evidence of his parents, the trains from Sheffield, habitually delayed, their time-tabled journey of seven hours often translated into a journey of as many as twelve.

Anya glanced up at him. He was six foot two and the most handsome man she had ever met. His dark chestnut hair swept back from a broad forehead, above intelligent blue-grey eyes.

They had fallen in love at first sight. She had no doubts, only a wonderful sense of truth and belonging. He glanced back at her, confirming her feelings in a look that swept over her in fierce delight.

William checked his watch, a Cartier, a gift from his father. As he did so, Paul observed him hungrily.

'I should pawn that if I were you.'

'I don't think we can wait any longer,' said William, deliberately ignoring him.

The five friends made their way upstairs to a large, dingy room on the first floor, with tall, proud windows overlooking the Marylebone Road. There, at three desks, the central one larger than the two flanking it, were the registrar and his two clerks, all three rendered threadbare and dismal by their daily duty of officiating at the optimistic ceremonials of strangers.

'These three are like the keepers at the Gates of Hell,' commented Paul.

The ceremony itself lasted no more than five minutes before Anya and William were declared man and wife. Anya's wedding ring of flattened, indented silver was one William had designed himself. The five of them then tumbled back down the steps to be absorbed into the humdrum of the Marylebone Road, still no evidence of William's parents.

'They have our address,' he remarked. 'Let's go back and celebrate.'

Back at the flat in Great Titchfield Street, William produced sardines on toast, some shortbread biscuits and parkin, sent in advance by his mother, plus a huge, nut-encrusted Dundee cake. Anya washed the dust from an old cracked tea set, and William produced three bottles of what he predicted would be a superior French red wine. The ornate label of black and gold, with lettering reminiscent of the Dukes of Burgundy, stated amid its curlicues 'Framboise'. But when they opened it, it turned out to be a rich, sweet raspberry liqueur, instead of the good Merlot they were expecting. They all laughed and drank it anyway. Rowland wound up the old gramophone, and suddenly the soft, sweet crooning of the Ink Spots invaded every corner. Rowland and Bunty started to dance. Within half an hour everyone was feeling tipsy and happy. Not until 7 p.m., as they were all about to make their way to

Bertorelli's for a one and sixpenny supper, did the doorbell ring and William's parents arrive.

Again, it was Anya who answered the door, skipping lightly down the three flights of stairs to throw open the door in tipsy abandon. She had, by now, discarded the formality of her hat and piercing violets of her wedding bouquet. Her long hair streamed about her shoulders in copper rivulets, her complexion pink and beautiful in tribute to some private ecstasy of her own, the delicious curves of her figure revealed beneath the electric folds of her green shot-silk dress. In the midst of this symphony of green, pink and gold, her eyes read as startling glances of blue from a face whose beauty was full of laughter.

Nevertheless, even as she registered the middle-aged couple confronting her, her laughter drained away to be replaced first by sobriety, and then by an intuition of haughtiness. Her new father-in-law's initial impression of immaculate formality quickly dissolved in a fond, teasing jocularity. But as she and William's mother studied one another, Anya detected an enemy, an enemy from whom she would never be free. The older woman was also formally dressed, her ample, big-bosomed figure wrapped in seemingly endless layers of buttery yellow wool crêpe, with elaborate embroideries of glass beads, masquerading as a necklace, at its neckline; over her shoulders, a camel-hair coat of the softest, finest quality, and over one arm, a huge portfolio of a handbag in shiny crocodile.

'More of a briefcase for carrying share certificates than a handbag,' Anya would later jibe to William.

In her hand was a cloche bonnet of beige felt, decorated with artificial pink roses. Her wedding outfit, Anya thought sadly.

As the older woman put out her hand to shake Anya's, Anya noticed the accumulation of gold bracelets she wore; one a delicately wrought chain secured by a heart-shaped locket, the other a thick, interlocking rope of gold, fashioned in a double knot, the gold a rich, undiluted chicken-egg yellow. Purest gold, thought Anya. Competing for attention with the glass beads was a large cameo brooch, framed in ovals of gold, profiling an elegant woman in eighteenth-century attire, her ivory presence set against amber.

Anya's mind flitted across these details, absorbing each one in miniature shock, but it was when she came to William's mother's face that she was most surprised. Despite her evidence of wealth and elegance, her face above them made no concessions. Neither to her own vanity nor to the beauty of the young woman standing opposite her. Unlike her pampered body, her face wore no embellishments — its heavy jowls floury with repeated dustings of loose powder; the mouth narrow lipped and unenhanced by any warmth of lipstick. Her hair lay like a thin crust of snow across her crown, to be caught in tight rolls of curls, protruding above her ears like the handles of a pot. Her face was unsmiling, her pale eyes unresponsively cold. It was a face that had found no use for charm; a plain-speaking face, used to getting its own way, which, in this case, would have been that nice girl next door, Mary Gimson. William's portrait of her still held pride of place in their parlour. The delicious creature confronting her was a mere piece of frippery, the least serious side of her darling son's devotion. As she had repeatedly reminded her husband on their long journey south,

'It won't last.'

Anya was equally unprepared for William's mother's voice — pure Yorkshire.

'Are ye wed then?' was all she wanted to know. Anya, now completely sober, nodded dumbly. Gallantly taking her arm, William's father kissed her on the cheek.

'Nor have I ever seen a prettier bride in all my life,' he stated.

'Enuff of that, Preston. Handsome is as handsome does… Shall we going oup?'

Anya looked at her in amazement. 'Yes, of course,' she said, offering to help carry her coat and bag.

'I like to keep hold of my bag,' stated the older woman firmly. 'Ye can carry me 'at if ye like.'

Preston's eyes twinkled merrily at her. William's voice isn't broad Yorkshire like this, thought Anya, still surprised by her new mother-in-law. Any minute now, she will say, 'Eee, by gum!'

At the top of the stairs waiting for them was William, looking faintly rakish.

'Eee, by gum, lad, it's good to see thee.'

For the first time, the older woman's cast-iron exterior dissolved in smiles and she hugged her tall son to her in pride. Her stern eyes began to weep.

'Come now, Mother, no tears,' he reminded her. 'It's my wedding day.'

'Aye, lad,' she replied sadly, 'it's thee wedding day.'

As Preston threaded his arm chivalrously through that of his new daughter-in-law, Edith glanced back at them blindly through her tears, and Anya, young as she was, knew that she had made one friend and one enemy. The whole experience left her feeling strangely uneasy. Up until now, hers and William's whirlwind courtship of just six weeks had seemed deeply romantic and great, good Bohemian fun. Now, suddenly, she was less sure. She saw the enormity of what they had done. And God knows, there was more to come. William had not yet been introduced to her own fearsome brood of older brothers; only to her gentle mother, too tired to be anything but indifferent to the passing, dancing show of passion in other people's lives, and her sweet-natured sister, Lettie, who secretly thought William a bit arrogant, his head too much in the clouds, but had, nevertheless, chuckled sympathetically and told her younger sister: 'If you love him that much, you'll make it work...'

For that was the one thing on which everyone agreed... William and Anya were very much in love.

With new additions to the party, the festive atmosphere in the dusty room suddenly died. Anya caught Edith running a finger along the mantelpiece before putting down her bag. Chairs were found and improvised. Anya perched on an upturned orange box. No one danced anymore... The gramophone drifted to forgotten silence.

Edith and Preston were understandably tired. Theirs had been a long day and journey, to reach this dusty room and these hilariously inappropriate people. Conversation dwindled. They decided not to come to Bertorelli's. They would just sit and have another cup of tea and a slice of parkin before going to bed. William had arranged for them to borrow their neighbour's spare room across the narrow hallway for a couple of nights.

'Perhaps we shouldn't go either?' suggested Anya, in deference to the older couple. Preston flashed her a smile of appreciation. But the indulgent mother and her indulged son understood one another perfectly.

'You won't mind, will you, Mother?' William asked unabashed.

'No, thee get thee sen gone, son,' she confirmed. 'Preston and me can make do.'

To Anya's ears the 'make do' sounded ominous.

Paul, bored now by all this bourgeois family debate, wondered whether to forego the pleasure of dinner at Bertorelli's and escape the *dismal atmosphere right now. While trying to decide, he busied himself casting a connoisseur's eye over the accumulations of pottery, mostly blue and white, that haunted the upper shelf of the tongue and groove.*

Rowland smiled knowingly but said little, drawing sideways on his thin reed of a red Rizla roll-up. He understood these people. They were part of his world; not only familiar because they were his best friend's parents, but because they were his people too, pure Yorkshire. As far as he was concerned, these were a few preliminary moments of necessary drama before freedom and Bertorelli fun beckoned again. It was Bunty who made the greatest efforts on Preston and Edith's behalf, giving up the single velvet armchair to Edith and fetching extra slices of cake for Preston, while settling him in the rocking chair and asking them in a troubled voice if they were sure they were comfortable. Rowland was proud of her, but neither William nor his mother were fooled. They both remembered Edith's pronouncements on Bunty when Rowland had first said he was marrying her.

'Common as muck, that one,' she had said, adding censoriously, 'I can't be doing with a woman who takes her clothes off for a living.'

Obliviously, the sweet-natured Bunty, her hieroglyph of orange lipstick dancing in haphazard judgement of where her mouth might be, continued her ministrations to the older couple. And Edith, self-styled queen that she was, accepted them ungraciously, as her due.

'I don't mooch like sardines,' she said sniffily, 'but put them down next to me anyway, so that I can decide for myself.'

* * *

Eventually, an hour and a half later than intended, the original five of the wedding party threaded their way through the streets of Bloomsbury to Charlotte Street, while Edith and Preston negotiated the narrow creaking bed and bare floorboards of their neighbour's spare room. Neither of them slept. The lavatory was down a half flight of unlit stairs. William had forgotten to give them the chamber pot.

'Tomorrow, Edith love, we'll check into a hotel,' Preston tried to soothe his troubled wife.

Silent now, she neither assented nor disagreed; he knew she was weeping. He also knew that if he said so, she would deny it.

At Bertorelli's there was the usual familiar crowd, plus those additional few whom no one had ever seen before. Most of these struck the familiar crowd indifferently, but occasionally a stranger stood out and was then treated to a joint process of speculation and wooing from the others. Paul dallied on his way to their table to chat to Dylan Thomas and Caitlin, who were dining with her former lover, Augustus John.

They were given a corner table, in one of the middle warren of interlocking rooms, a table just deserted by Ezra Pound and Dorothy Shakespear and some distinguished guests of theirs. The Italian waiters, in white sleeves and black waistcoats above trousers wrapped from waist to floor in the sheeting of long white aprons, re-laid the table with all the suavity and speed of toreadors, flapping the starched creases from a pristine white tablecloth before sending it out in a fast sail above the tabletop, as though at a bull, before smoothing it with caresses that any woman might envy, all the time shouting instructions at one another in a language they could mostly rely on their English guests to not understand. Although, occasionally, their bawdy, insulting banter was intercepted; then, and only then, did they stand momentarily still in abject, charming apology.

For one shilling and sixpence each, they ate dishes of zucchini fritti, a spaghetti al pomodoro, scaloppini di vitello al Marsala con verdure, and to follow, the warm, melting indulgence of zabaglione. To drink, they ordered the slightly spumante red Brancaccio, a wine that had become a favourite of theirs. As they sipped its uplifting notes, they all laughed and teased William, remembering how, the first time he ordered it, he had pompously sent it back, thinking the spumante taste meant it was fermented. Two waiters heard them and laughed, remembering it too.

With each new round of filled glasses, the toasts were repeated.

'To William and Anya. May they always be happy.'

Paul got to his feet to make a speech, but instead delivered a strangely clumsy poem:

'There was a young girl from Clapham
Who scrubbed the floors at Mappin.
Webb was delighted;
He was also far-sighted.
He gave her a potato

To take to the Board.
One day at Olympia
She met William Painter
And now she dresses his clowns.'

'*May they live happily ever after,' he concluded.*
'*Sit down, for God's sake,' said Rowland, embarrassed.*

Anya glanced darkly at Paul. But neither William nor Bunty seemed to notice. Instead, three of the waiters, finding a few minutes' lull in their programme of feeding people, joined shoulder to shoulder, and, in voices worthy of opera, serenaded them with Neapolitan love songs.

'*O sole mio.'*

By now the rest of the restaurant was aware that a wedding breakfast was in progress. A tall man, sitting unobserved in a corner, whispered to a waiter, just as he was leaving, pressing some money into the man's hand. The waiter bowed deeply, disappeared into the kitchen and returned with five champagne glasses, a bottle of chilled Bollinger and a huge cassata, decorated like a wedding cake.

'*With the compliments of the gentleman who just left,' he explained. He handed Anya a folded note.*

'*All the happiness in the world, my dear… and in anticipation of your return… Varinsky.'*

William took it from her and read it.

'*How very kind,' he commented. 'Who is he…? I wonder what he means, "in anticipation of your return"?'*

Anya blushed prettily. 'Another riddle,' she exclaimed.

'*Ah Varinsky, a riddle indeed,' breathed Paul, looking at her directly.*

At last Anya understood: Paul Ottery knew of her affair with Varinsky. That explained the gleam of contempt in his eye. But Anya was unmoved. What could he do? She looked at William, his innocent, handsome face spilling with undiluted, heady love for her. They were married. At eighteen years of age, she assumed marriage to be a state of immunity against the wayward comments of syphilitic humbugs like Paul Ottery. She glanced back at him defiantly. The pale-green pistachio heart of the cassata melted deliciously in their mouths.

By the time they left the restaurant, it was almost midnight. On the corner of Percy and Charlotte Street, they parted. Paul intended

walking back to Chelsea. Rowland and Bunty caught a bus to Ham-
mersmith, while William and Anya returned on foot to Great Titchfield
Street, to embark on their first night of lovemaking. Let the adventure
of marriage begin.

As they passed the door where his parents were sleeping, William
heard the springs on their bed creak. He guessed that his mother was
still awake. The thought sobered him. Together, from behind the stacks of
paintings, Anya and William pulled the mattress which was William's
bed into the centre of the room and spread it with sheets, pillows and
blankets. William turned off the two gaslights above the mantelpiece
and slowly they undressed. Moonlight streamed through the half-cur-
tained window, illuminating their every move. As always when he
looked at her, William was startled spellbound by her beauty. Never
before, even as a painter, had the delight in looking been so intense. It
was not a passion of possessiveness so much as a pure aestheticism that
Anya evoked in him. They lay down naked on the bed, not bothering to
cover themselves, shivering slightly from desire and expectation, rather
than from the chill air. They heard a door creak open nearby and someone
stumble in the dark as he tried to find his footing on the stairs.

Damn, *thought William.* I forgot to give them the chamber pot.

Taking Anya in his arms, she lay crouched expectantly in the protec-
tive curve of his chest. They kissed, first hesitantly, then greedily. Wil-
liam's body stirred between them. Anya waited for him. To her dismay,
he suddenly got up, fumbling in the dark.

'I forgot to get any French letters,' he explained. 'I thought perhaps this
might do instead?'

In the half-light, Anya made out a tasselled narrow sheath of oiled
American cloth, intended as a wash-bag for toothbrushes.

'I thought we might try this?'

She looked at him confused, unclear how to respond. Suddenly, she
saw that he was serious, that he really did not understand. She felt
momentarily frightened by his ignorance. What did it mean? She fled
into a mood of decorum.

'It doesn't have to be tonight,' she said gently. 'We can wait. I'm just
happy to be with you.'

William rolled onto his back, his handsome head and lean body sud-
denly relaxed. He was smiling. Anya watched his erection fade and

disappear. She sensed some note of failure between them but could not find any clue to it. They loved one another passionately, of that she was sure. She heard William's mother's heavy-slippered footsteps on the stairs. They pulled the blankets over them up to their chins and slept side by side, barely touching, like the stone effigies of husband and wife in a Romanesque church.

* * *

In the morning at breakfast, suddenly glancing up at their shelf of pots, Anya said: 'One or two of the smaller ones are missing.'

'Are you sure?' asked William.

'Yes, I think so. I remember seeing them yesterday.'

'How mystifying...'

* * *

Not until ten days later, in a pub off Charlotte Street, having just seen William's parents off at Euston Station, did they run into Paul Ottery again. Thanking them profusely for dinner at Bertorelli's, he handed them a flurry of pink tickets.

'If you really want all that bourgeois tat you insist on collecting,' he announced munificently, 'here are the pawn tickets.'

* * *

All these years later, Anya still remembers Paul Ottery with loathing.

What became of him? Probably dead, by now.

Dressed in black velvet trousers and a bright-pink mohair sweater, she rouses herself from her nostalgia and picks up yesterday's newspaper. Starting to read an article on immigration and its impact on the building trade, by Nicholas Rowe, she discards it abruptly.

'Right-wing fool,' she whispers.

Smiling gleefully, she remembers the time she and some of her friends had harangued him at one of his book signings at Hatchards... But later today she plans to attend a public lecture at the London School of Economics, given by another journalist whose writings she infinitely prefers: Aubrey Byng. She sometimes makes a point of reading his articles in *Le Figaro*, then translating them into English, to keep up with her French.

* * *

As the pill starts to work and the urgency, the hurry, begin to subside in Hesketh's tormented soul, Stephen is driving south, his wife, Sarah at his side. In the back seat are his sixteen-year-old son, Henry, and youngest daughter, Jessica, who is two years older. Their eldest child, Olivia, has stayed in London for a party. Also on the back seat, his nose resting between the two children, is an enormous chocolate-coloured poodle called Ruby. As Stephen drives recklessly fast, their tabby cat, Miska, perches watchfully on tightly bunched paws, gazing transfixed over his shoulder at the fast approaching stretches of motorway. This is the family's weekend ritual, to depart London for Gloucestershire, where, nestled in a village, with lanes sufficiently hidden by tall hedgerows to be reminiscent of Thomas Hardy, they own a country estate. It is on either Saturday mornings or Friday evenings, depending on how busy Stephen is at CERvello's Bloomsbury town-house offices, that Sarah reclaims the part of her life that most belongs to her. In two weeks, Stephen has just informed her, he will be in China, giving the keynote speech at a British Council conference in Shanghai on 'Modern Publishing and the Creative Industries'.

CHAPTER 9

When Thursday comes, Bianca feels nervous of spending time alone with Max. Too intimate. Yet countless men have visited her studio without causing her the least emotional tremor. Partly, it reflects the great mystery between painters and their subjects; the portrayed imagining themselves personalities to be explored emotionally in paint, and painters viewing them as a series of abstract forms, whose painterly investigation may lead to new perceptions of personality. Feeling too much emotion for a subject can be counterproductive.

Arriving on time, Bianca opens her studio door to find Max leaning against the door jamb. Tousle haired, his red scarf providing a ruff to his spiked curls, beneath a formal jacket, he is dressed in baggy white linen harem trousers, gathered at their ankles over stylish, black-and-white Prada running pumps. Smiling gently, Bianca asks: 'Is this how you want to be remembered? After all, it's the National Portrait Gallery, commissioning this.'

She dares not use the word 'scruffy'. Yet, examining him, she realises how contrived and expensive his scruffiness is; the beach trousers and jacket almost certainly by Armani.

'Do you mind if I smoke?'

Lighting a cigarette, he glances around the room, sweeping his gaze from the tall window to the Schiaparelli pink chaise; from the mirror leaning its angled reflections of them to the gauze-veiled bedroom, with its precarious wooden ladder above her old-fashioned kitchen.

'This place is magnificent,' he says admiringly.

'Yes, isn't it just?'

Finally, his dark eyes rest on Bianca. No longer the silent stones of the other evening as she admitted quoting his name to ward off the evil spirit of Hesketh, they are now shiny with intelligence; an intelligence so focused and all-seeing that even the strange handsomeness of his monochrome sensual face is left behind in passivity. Suddenly, she sees how little it matters how Max is dressed; that only the monochrome sloping planes in that passionate face, beneath bouffant fringes of curls and illuminated by the intensity of eyes with an inordinate hunger for engagement, matter. Max's head is an explosion, a complete landscape of intricate hills and hedgerows and glorious sunlight. And that is how she would paint him: a huge head, from the ruff of his scarf upwards, ignoring the anonymity of his clown-like garb. Just his head, hair and eyes, with nuances of intellect written in their every line. Talkative silence… That is how it would be.

Even as she contemplates him, she can feel the dialogue begin; not the laughter and repartee of their conversations at The Ivy and Le Gavroche, but another more profound dialogue, from which neither of them would easily disengage. She reaches out to touch his arm gently. 'I already know what to do. Shall we begin?'

Turning his silent scrutiny to the hand touching his sleeve, Max had already noticed her hands. They are light, gentle, automatically caressing; lying against his cuff, like a brooch, it flutters and is gone.

'Where shall I sit?'

From behind the screen, she produces an ornately carved, replica Chippendale armchair to place in front of the leaning mirror. She has no intention of including it in the finished painting, but it is comfortable to sit in; a chair into which all her sitters settle effortlessly. She also gathers some lengths of dark-blue velvet curtaining, draping them over the mirror to half eclipse Max's reflection.

'Intimations of theatre?'

She watches him nestle into the chair, fidgeting briefly, before his face stills into some internal debate with itself. Then, standing at her easel, she starts to draw directly in pencil onto a smoothly primed canvas, six feet square.

Unlike her use of the same sized canvas to frame the Cavendish children, their miniature beings skipping from the depths of it, ever closer, until their stub-nosed sandals seem to step into spectator space, she allows the landscape of Max's sensual features to fill the entire six-foot square, every capricious curve and indentation between his nose and upper lip explored and responded to rhythmically.

That's it, she thinks.

In Max's face there is some indefinable rhythm of forms with their own internal logic that spell a face lived lavishly, in both pleasure and pain; a face that has tried to forget, yet failed... one that knows its own value, yet remains modestly indifferent. A face, above all, that she might learn to love.

Forgetful of time, for two hours she and Max work in silence, like a mutual colloquy of thoughts tracked internally. Then, suddenly Max begins to move, to undo his pose. Bianca glances at her watch.

'Oh, Max, do forgive me, I completely lost track of time... You must be desperately uncomfortable remaining still for so long?'

'No, I was fine until a just few minutes ago.'

He stands up, stretching his arms, dissolving the image of compactness his body suggests beneath its Armani formalities.

'It's a comfortable chair... Shall I start again?'

'No, that's enough for today.'

She stands back, assessing her work. She has made good progress; the framework of her image of Max already established.

'May I see?'

Skirting the wide expanse of canvas, he stands behind her, one hand resting lightly on her shoulder. Scanning silently, he soberly traces every line.

'Just my head?'

She half turns her face to his, a look of anxiety in her eyes.

'Just my very big head?'

She laughs... His eyes are full of mischief and admiration.

'Come and see my new play,' he says with sudden urgency. 'Come this evening, if you like?'

Bianca's laughter vanishes instantly.

'You don't want to?' Max looks dismayed.

'No, of course I'd love to see your play.'

He looks strangely relieved, a slight twitch tugging the skin beneath his left eye. Bianca is amazed he should care one way or another. She explains how Hesketh had sent her a ticket for tonight's performance… how, therefore, she could not possibly accept. Max looks at her thoughtfully.

'Would you be free to come this evening otherwise?'

'Yes, I think so. Leonardo is having dinner with his producer.'

'Very well, show me the ticket.'

She fetches her bag; Hesketh's letter still in it. He glances at the seat number.

'Front row circle. My permanent ticket is back of stalls. Why don't you take my ticket and I take this one? Then I can report back.'

'Are you sure you want to do that? Hesketh can be unpredictable, violent even.'

'What can he possibly do, surrounded by an audience and finding himself next to the author? For me, it will be an intriguing encounter, and, for him, one of puzzlement.'

'Very well – if you're certain? But what if he recognises me in the foyer? He'll make a scene.'

'Wear a wig as disguise.'

'I don't have any wigs.'

'I'll get wardrobe to bike one over to you this afternoon.'

Bianca is too weak to demur further. As always, when emerging from two hours of concentrated work, she feels vaguely blank – certainly no match for Max's sudden enthusiasm for a prank. Besides, it involves perceiving Hesketh as a clown, something she is incapable of.

And yet, he is a sort of clown… A terrifying, dangerous joker… Scarcely funny.

The wig of long dark hair, heavily fringed, arrives later that afternoon. For safety, Bianca adds a pair of dark glasses.

* * *

At 7.15 p.m. she is waiting in the crowded foyer for Max, when Hesketh walks right past her. Converging on the box office in three separate queues, people pour onto Shaftesbury Avenue. This stampede for high culture both baffles and amuses Bianca; she witnesses urgency overcome good manners in well-dressed people fighting to be first in the queue, Max Holland's plays fast becoming a holy grail for the cultivated. Intricately plotted, written in a language rich in cadence, they are also, at their clever hearts, deeply compassionate. Bianca knows how rare that is; the capacity of an artist to transmit sympathy from his work to an audience. In painting, she thinks of it belonging almost exclusively to Masaccio and Velázquez. It is beyond aesthetics, almost beyond beauty. Yet, no matter how high the wire of intellectual erudition is set in Max's plays, his own emotional pledge to compassionate understanding is always greater. People flock to his plays, finding in them a mirror of both their sins and virtues.

Bianca cowers against a wall, watching Hesketh in a mood of horrified fascination. He looks like no one she ever knew; a man in his late fifties, his appearance almost anonymous, except for his energetic habit of ricocheting back and forth on his heels, then leaning impetuously forward to an angle of thirty degrees. His watery eyes, slightly hyperthyroid bulging, scan the crowd greedily. Yet he too is nervous. The paw of his right hand strays continuously to shield the carved oval of his cheek; his hair, although not receded, spikes thinly across his skull. For no obvious reason, he turns to the usherette at his side and laughs.

Yet he was such a handsome man...

At times, also very charming, in that reckless, throwaway manner of the emotional gambler. She remembers her fatal youthful confidence in dealing with so erratic and emotionally complex a character as Hesketh; she was fifteen years his junior. It was her mother, Anya, who initially encouraged his presence in their lives. Bianca's first instinct had been to avoid him. Later, when she became dependent on him, after her mother argued with them both and had thrown her out of the apartment they shared in Highbury, it was far too late.

Bianca tries to look at him disinterestedly.

What would I feel, meeting such a man now for the first time?

Wearing a lightweight linen jacket over a navy shirt, his body, she notices, is more youthful than his face. But his face is that of

Dorian Gray, every line of misery and violence written upon it in unmistakable code.

Corrupt, brutalised... the face of a man condemned to forage, like a pig snuffling for truffles, for things that don't belong to him...

Her loathing knows no bounds.

No, I don't find him attractive.

Yet even she has to admit... he is still a strangely compelling presence.

Suddenly, her view of Hesketh is blocked by the figure of Max struggling through the crowd to reach her. He greets her with a kiss on both cheeks, and when next she looks, Hesketh has disappeared.

'Is he already here?'

She nods.

'That wig suits you,' Max teases. 'Shades too – not taking any chances, I see?'

They laugh gently together, the inevitable scarf wound round Max's neck, this time silkily white and heavily fringed.

'Opera scarf?'

Disappearing briefly into the box office, he reappears with her ticket for the Stalls, the one sent by Hesketh in his hand.

'Rather than meet me in the foyer afterwards, let's go independently to the restaurant... I booked a table upstairs at the Groucho Club.'

'Is there no interval?'

'Yes, we'll meet in the Green Room. But I'll leave my seat five minutes early, so this Hesketh fellow can't follow.'

Glancing at the ticket she had given him, she says: 'As far as I remember, this is an end-of-row seat in the central aisle.'

'Very well...'

She looks momentarily ashamed. 'We're becoming as Machiavellian as Hesketh... That's what this kind of persecution does... forces you resort to the same low cunning tricks as the pursuer.'

Max lightly touches her hand. 'Don't worry. I won't let him hurt me.'

'My thought exactly,' she replies sadly.

From the front row of the Circle, Hesketh scans the crowd. He is like a tightly coiled spring, simultaneously fearful and optimistic, his hands clasped in angry conversation with one another, knees trembling. Looking down into the pit of the auditorium, something arrests his attention; a slender figure, elegantly dressed, her head a shiny crop of long dark hair. Briefly raising her face and eyes to his, before quickly looking away again, something stirs in his memory, but a rustle at his elbow distracts him. He turns as Max folds himself into the seat beside him. Blinking rapidly, and raising a hand to shield the fallen teeth occupying the bow of his beautiful mouth, Hesketh fails to recognise him.

'There must be some mistake...'

Pretending not to hear, Max focuses deliberately on the stage.

His voice, small and hesitant, almost the grizzled whine of a child, Hesketh plucks at the sleeve of Max's jacket. Noticing nails, nibbled raw to their quicks, Max turns gravely towards Hesketh.

'Can I help you?'

'Did Bianca send you?'

Stuttering breathlessly, Hesketh's hand hovers at his mouth, screening himself from Max's impending reply.

'No, I'm here to see my own play.'

Failing to hear the proprietary 'my', Hesketh continues, 'You must have the wrong seat... That's Bianca's seat.'

From the slender tones of his original whimper, Hesketh's voice is now hoarse with anger. Starting to notice, the audience glance in their direction, sensing a scene develop, Hesketh's last statement almost a shout. Meanwhile, Max continues to ignore him.

Suddenly prodding Max's shoulder with an aggressively accusatory finger, Hesketh cries: 'Where's Bianca?'

Chatter in the auditorium stills. Directly below them, Bianca hears Hesketh's desperate cry: 'Biaancaa.'

Max turns towards him with a demeanour of stone; in reply, Hesketh searches his face avidly, as though trying to decipher a map. Looking back serenely, Max detects only the bully in him. Then, something in Hesketh's face alters, a sudden movement of astonishment fluttering through it.

'You're Max Holland.'

'Yes, I believe I am...' Max's tone is indifferent.

Hissing now... Hesketh asks: 'So, where's Bianca?'

Neither notices the bell ring, surprising them as the auditorium suddenly falls dark. People compose themselves, coughing gently into the silence, as footlights reveal a revolving stage, against which a patina of dappled light falls on three characters assembled there.

Hesketh tries to remember to breathe deeply, finding the twilight auditorium, plus Bianca's absence, and his well-laid plans, yet again gone awry, oppressive. He cannot focus on what the actors are saying. Sounds of the sea consume his mind with confirmation of new humiliations. Max's clever, pun-ridden language spills into the darkness like jabberwocky. He detects no meanings.

Blindly pushing past Max, incapable of sitting still, he climbs the steep rake of the aisle to the exit.

Perhaps Bianca is late? He checks his watch. *Only ten minutes late... Probably caught in traffic.*

As always, he cannot conceive of her refusals. With this solace of thought, he descends the red velour cocoon of corridors leading back to the foyer to the now empty front steps to wait for her.

At the interval, joining Bianca in the Green Room, Max is called away by the theatre manager. Hesketh has positioned himself on the front steps and is refusing to move.

'Should I call the police?'

Max dissuades him, deciding not to tell Bianca Hesketh is outside, waiting for her. Feeling more rattled by his encounter with Hesketh than anticipated, he would try to analyse it later... There had been something deeply, unfathomably disturbing in Hesketh's face; not only aggression, but a dangerous, reckless fear... A face with nothing to lose.

As agreed, Max and Bianca leave the theatre separately. From his vigil across the street, Hesketh again notices the slender figure of the girl with straight dark hair, her eyes shaded by dark glasses. But it is now Max he is waiting for.

Glancing carefully around the foyer as he leaves, dodging the autograph seekers as brusquely as he can without causing offence, Max fails to spot Hesketh sheltering in a doorway opposite. Winding the white scarf more securely around his neck, he covers the short distance to the Groucho Club, pushing through its double doors on Dean Street, to where Bianca is waiting. Having signed in, he stretches an arm protectively towards her. She looks like herself again – soft, blonde curls tumbling about her delicate features.

'I loved the play.'

Max's face lights up. 'Did you?'

Bianca has visited this club numerous times; Stephen is also a member. Yet her first impression remains intact. It is like walking into a Vorticist painting by William Roberts. The room, the bar, the carpets and beaten-up sofas are all in the low key of burnt sienna and yellow ochre, with occasional flashes of bright blues and reds, the people who inhabit it all robust artist types, moving boldly from bar to sofas, gesticulating wildly, their faces, whether celebrated or anonymous, all lived in with a degree of pride.

Modern bohemia…

Bianca loves it too.

Scanning the sombrely lit room for spare sofas, Max is besieged by a couple of actresses, who desert their bar stools to surround him.

'*Max*, darling.'

Max's greeting of them is warm but curiously passive, refusing to feed the froth of their enthusiasm as he introduces Bianca. But 'Vescarro' is not her professional name; the actresses' faces remain blank, failing to recognise her as portrait painter to the rich and famous. A couple relinquish a crumpled stained sofa; in gratitude, Max and Bianca escape into its velvet depths, while Max asks the waiter to check on their table upstairs.

'What did you like most about the play?'

'The way style, cleverness and delicious language are all ultimately sacrificed in a submission to pain…' She pauses. 'That's your submission too, isn't it? Your creed in life?'

'Perhaps,' Max admits shyly. 'I'm glad you saw beyond the flourish of language to its pith of meaning.'

'They seemed like two separate conventions, fused in the same piece.'

'Yes!' he exclaims, delighted she had seen it.

Thoughtfully sipping their drinks in silence, Max suddenly remembers. 'But we're here to talk about that pitifully broken chap, Hesketh… rather than me.'

'Broken?' Bianca holds her breath. 'What did you really think of him?'

'I think he's a lost soul, desperately lonely probably, and caught up in some twilight of his own manufacture… like existing in a maze from which there's no escape.' He hesitates. 'I think his loneliness must be terrible, like doing violence to oneself daily.'

Bianca is aghast. 'You feel sorry for him?'

'Don't you?'

She shakes her head sadly. 'I'm incapable of it. He has inflicted too much harm… On me, and on others close to me.'

She recalls his violent attacks on Patrick. 'I think of him as evil, but with sufficient low cunning to primp it up in sorrowful demeanour.'

She too hesitates.

'I think this tussle between us is all about power… That, if ever I gave in to his demands, his sorrow would quickly vanish in jubilatory malice. I shall never ever forgive him. No matter what he does.' Her voice breaks slightly. 'He's the only person I'm incapable of feeling any sympathy for…'

'And yet the man is in torment,' Max rebukes her gently.

She gazes back at him quizzically.

'Just think what it must be like to be him?'

Something in her face changes. 'It's a self-inflicted torment. He chose it for himself.'

'No one ever chooses that for himself,' reproves Max. 'It's inconceivable anyone should elect such pain for himself. And even if he did, can you really not feel sorry for him?'

Bianca shakes her head slowly and sorrowfully. 'No, I really can't.' Her voice is devoid of energy.

Raising her downcast eyes to confront Max's dark, sparkling stones, it occurs to her that this moment will prove a barrier between them; that painting his portrait might never be so easy again. She is suddenly grateful there is only time for one more sitting before she and Stephen leave for China. Studying Max, she realises his opinion is reasonable… Yet she cannot accept his misunderstanding of what it feels like to be someone's quarry, hunted down like an animal, year in, year out. To her, it feels like a betrayal.

Observing Bianca closely, Max sees her rise in herself to enclose her hidden turbulence behind a facade of fragile beauty, not yet suspecting himself locked out from that calm. The waiter arrives – their table is ready.

'Shall we go up?'

Bianca nods politely. Smoothing her skirt over her thighs, she turns to retrieve her jacket and notices a face peering helplessly in from the street.

'Good God, Hesketh has followed us here...'

'What did you say?' asks Max above the hubbub.

'Nothing,' she replies.

When they get to the top of the stairs, Max turns towards her, taking her arm. 'What is it you feel Hesketh has taken from you?'

'My children...' she answers enigmatically.

Looking fleetingly serious, her face then breaks into a smile. She can afford to be gracious... Max has, for the moment, lost her completely.

* * *

Hesketh can feel the hurry in his heartbeat; a bravado sickness consuming him. The paranoia that guides him has not yet succeeded in uniting the dissonant elements of his evening.

Bianca was not at the theatre...

No reason, after twenty-five years, why she would be. Nevertheless, he had expected her. To him, her refusals feel ridiculous. An innate fondness for the lost goodness in himself rises in his own self-defence. It is at moments like this that he remembers his father.

Always, the same images haunt him... His father taking him camping near Cardiff... Waking in the middle of the night to find a rabid animal on the bed next to his. A violent, unidentifiable silhouette of a creature, rutting in the light of the moon against the canvas roof of the tent; his sense of shock and surprise as the animal had separated into two halves, the last-minute humiliation of realising that one half of the beast was his father, the other a beautiful, dark-skinned girl, her silhouette in the dark so firm, so precise in outline, that he never forgot it. Just as he also never forgot how she laughed at him, her big white smiling teeth jeering at him in the dark as she rode his father to oblivion. How he had hated her: for her beauty, for her possession of his father, but, above all, for her possession of some lost childish thing in himself. He was just nine years old, Bruno's age. His father had never known. Separated from Hesketh's mother, he died a few years later of cancer of the mouth. He smoked a pipe, always suckling it to one side of his mouth. After they operated to remove his jaw, he lived for three more years, his tongue permanently stuck out, like a naughty schoolboy's. Only in the final week before he died, and the last time Hesketh saw him, had he succeeded in withdrawing his protruding tongue into the haven of his mouth. The image of that closed mouth had broken Hesketh's heart.

Bianca should have come. By refusing, she had deprived herself of rightful joy. He thinks of how wonderfully happy he would have made her, how transparent his love for her would have been; her absence incomprehensible. As was the substitution of Max Holland for herself. What did it mean exactly?

Is Max Holland a friend of hers? He pauses in his thoughts. *Surely not...?*

Bianca lives alone, 'essentially solitary and deprived', he is certain of it. Maybe one or two smart friends, like the person whose car had collected her from her front steps recently, but no one as famous as Max Holland. It was unthinkable... He would have known...

After all, I know everything there is to know about her.

He has made it his business to know; her life, essentially like his, in stasis, waiting for the moment when they can be together again...

I know her better than she knows herself.

And never once, in all his 'out of body' experiences with her, had he happened upon the slightest intimation of a Max Holland in her life.

I would have known it through the ethers...

Nevertheless, the thought alarms him. His mind beats on, trying to organise the scramble in his brain into a smooth paste of presumption. Extracting a pill from his jacket pocket, he swallows it without water, gulping hard. Suddenly, he feels all the humiliation of peering through the windows of a club of which he is not a member; Max and Bianca, sitting on a sofa directly beneath the window, concealed from him. Nor did he see them get up to leave... Just a grown man, peering through a window, as though into a sweet shop...

He turns away in disgust. Not in self-loathing, but in distaste at the boisterous happiness of the Groucho crowd.

'Don't know they're born...' he mutters incoherently.

He has a sudden memory of Bianca dancing alone in one of the rooms in Putney to the sounds of Nina Simone, tears pricking his eyes. How innocent she had been. He had held that happiness in his fist and lost it. He feels momentarily dazed by grief.

But surely something lost can always be found again? he argues bleakly.

So, his scattered mind keeps debating with itself, sewing together the gaps the evening had torn in its fast-knit web.

Finally, turning away, he thinks: *Chloe will wonder where I am... What lie did I tell, to explain where I would be this evening?*

He scours his mind. *Did I tell her I'd be at a business meeting? Or was that the last time?*

He really cannot remember... She had said something about going to stay with her mother, then changed her mind...

Blindly turning back into Old Compton Street, someone reproaches him: 'Mind where you're going, mate.'

Stumbling on, he hails a taxi.

'Chelsea Embankment,' he says, slamming the door behind him.

'How was your meeting?' asks Chloe as he emerges from the rickety lift.

'Good. Very good. In fact, I think we've probably got the contract on that Lake District cottage I wanted to buy.'

* * *

Having completed the story of her mother's wedding day, Bianca decides to finish her portrait of the Cavendish children before writing another. China now looms very close; only ten more days to go. Leonardo is also about to leave for New York and Singapore. He is taking Laetitia Norton with him. Not telling Bianca himself, she had discovered it from something his secretary let slip, her heart missing a beat as she heard it.

Always that imbecile female, sitting predatorily on the touchline of my marriage.

Yet even she has the wit to mock her own inconsistencies. Her attitude is, she knows, ridiculous. She is about to spend ten days travelling with Stephen, of which Leonardo has no idea, and she no intention of telling him; gambling on the assumption that Leonardo will phone home so rarely that her absence should go unnoticed. If he rings, she hopes he will just assume her away, staying with one of her girlfriends. Nevertheless, as the day gets closer, Bianca's sense of living on the edge increases, a permanent buzz of anxiety infecting her mind.

She knows her jealousy of Laetitia Norton is ludicrous. It is also another of the paradoxes with which she lives. Loving Stephen does not prevent her from wanting to keep the triptych symmetry of their lives intact: Leonardo, herself and Stephen. Nor from preferring not to lose it to a nuisance harpy like Laetitia Norton.

Calling their nanny to arrange sittings, she spends the next two mornings working rapidly on the closing stages of the Cavendish children's double portrait. With no promise of exciting tea parties to go to, the children are gently, playfully quiescent; the older child, the boy, playing obsessively with an abacus, and the little girl fascinated by the roll of Sellotape Bianca hands her, amusing herself by wrapping her teddy bear in the clever sticky tape.

Bianca's mind, as she works, is fluid, making judgments with unselfconscious accuracy. Working in the melting, thin glazes of alkyd, a fast-drying oil paint, it allows her to perform the conjuring trick of preserving the children's sweet, fresh energy, while simultaneously rendering their faces memorable. She knows how easily the children's clothes might become their real portrait, and their faces some anonymous still life.

At the end of two days, she is exhausted but satisfied. The children hug her legs, submit to her kisses and chant their 'goodbyes' happily, with no melancholy sense they won't be seeing her again. The nanny, a buxom lass from Yorkshire, is more sensitively aware. She too kisses Bianca, shedding a momentary tear. Watching Bianca work, she had perceived a core of passion in her that explained some of her indefinable charm; had seen how beauty steals up on a face most pressingly when absorbed elsewhere. Bianca's face, as she concentrated on her painting, had been almost angelic.

Once they have left, Bianca calls Matthew.

'Biancaaa.' His deep throated growl of affection.

She trills breathlessly: 'It's finished, Matt... The Cavendish children's portrait is finally finished.'

'I'll call the parents right now and arrange for them to come and view it... Also to decide if they want us to frame it. Would sometime tomorrow suit you?'

Bianca smiles into the mouthpiece. It is part of what she loves about Matthew, this alacrity for business, alongside the sensualist and political revolutionary in his soul. He is the only West End dealer she knows who had once been a card-carrying member of the Communist Party.

The Cavendish parents arrive for their viewing four days later, the same day Leonardo departs for New York. His driver, Lily, arrives to pick him up, dressed as if on her way to deliver a strip-o-gram, in a well-cut black trouser suit, arrayed with gilt buttons, high glossy heels and peaked cap. From under its brim, extravagant nuggets of gilt jewellery swing freely with every tilt of her head. Arriving ridiculously early, Bianca knows that she will have been forewarned of the need to next drive to Chelsea to pick up Laetitia Norton. Yet Bianca says nothing, not letting slip what she knows of Leonardo's plans. It would only create some anxiety of shame and dissonance between them, the outcome of which would be pure resentment on Leonardo's part. He is about to be away for seven, maybe eight weeks... During that time, they will speak rarely, if at all. It is only the going away and the returning that are important to them both. As Leonardo smiles and says goodbye, he gives her a perfunctory kiss on the cheek, with no brooding sense of loss or regret.

Much like the Cavendish children, she reflects.

For eight weeks, they will lead separate lives, in which neither can share. Yet it is precisely this mood of parting, as though for just a few hours, that guarantees an equally smooth transition on his return. It is something at which they both excel. Meanwhile, they carry one another forgivingly in their minds, so as to pick up exactly where they left off. In eight weeks' time, Bianca will ask Leonardo only the most cursory questions about his trip, and he will probably ask her none at all... Two people, pretending that ignorance really is bliss.

The Cavendish couple, a banker and his more youthful, second wife, arrive at her studio an hour later. Bianca busies herself in the tiny kitchenette, making coffee, allowing the parents to assess her work without the embarrassment of feeling she is watching them. They are paying £20,000 for this portrait, of which, after Matthew's 40% commission, she will receive £12,000, the portrait having, at various times, occupied her for the past two months, as will Max's portrait for the next two. Leonardo thinks of it as her pocket money.

Reluctant to turn around, Bianca is as passionately perfectionist about her work now as she ever was. Leonardo's wealth has not altered that. She still pursues her visions of people as relentlessly as she did as a student. The only difference wealth has made is to afford her a certain immunity. Not from her own unforgiving judgement but from that of others. She hopes the Cavendish parents will like their children's portrait but is perfectly happy to forfeit the commission fee if they don't. It is one of the things she and Matthew argue about. He is used to the foibles of clients, who, in their absurd ignorance of art, not to mention shameful fear of it, try to take control by suggesting changes to a finished painting that no painter would dream of making; changes that only prove how little they understand the processes of painting.

Bianca waits... hearing the mother give way to pleasure: 'Oh, aren't they just darling!' she exclaims, as the image of her two favourite miniature people is unveiled.

But it is the father, the banker, who is paying. He feels there must be something more to be said. It is not in his nature to accept a deal without quibble. This is a matter of £20,000, yet there seems to be no tangible way of knowing whether he is getting good value for money. He thinks of value vaguely, in terms of endeavour, like a Victorian grocer.

Has she spent enough time on the portrait, this Bianca Turvey, to justify £20,000? Should I not ask her to do a bit more?

Surveying the image of his two youngest children, skipping from the depths of the canvas towards him, he has an imprecise memory of something seen at a corporate cocktail party one evening at the National Gallery.

By whom had it been that portrait?

He racks his brains, trying to remember. *Of course: Gainsborough, the portrait of his young daughters.*

'What about adding a butterfly or two?' he asks, without revealing his sources.

Suddenly, he feels better. He has taken charge again of the painting, and of the £20,000. He glances around the room, beaming.

'Don't you agree?' he asks grandly. 'A butterfly?'

Turning slowly, Bianca studies the husband, assessing his city looks. His suavity is so immaculate as to appear carved in soap. There are no surprises, no rough edges, just an ambitious man, with a surface so smooth one could swallow him like a pill.

'Perhaps a butterfly or two?' his wife agrees meekly.

Glancing from one to the other, Bianca's voice is honeyed with diplomacy. She speaks quietly, only Matthew recognising how angry she is. He hopes to God she won't ruin the sale.

'Wouldn't that make it ridiculously reminiscent of Gainsborough's two daughters chasing a butterfly?' she asks softly. 'Do you want the portrait of your children to read as pastiche? Wouldn't you rather it stood on its own, as an independent vision of two delightful children? *Your* children,' she reminds him.

The husband blushes deeply. He has been found out, finally realising that these decisions of value were never his to make. Conceding his defeat gallantly, he produces his chequebook with a flourish.

'We agreed £20,000, did we not?'

Matthew cracks his knuckles and smiles broadly, the young wife adding: 'An ornate frame in gold, don't you think? Could you please arrange it?'

Putting down a tray balancing four miniature polka-dot coffee cups, plus a plate of almond, sugar dusted croissants, Bianca smiles. 'Have some coffee...'

* * *

After the couple have left, Bianca and Matthew finish the croissants and open a bottle of wine to celebrate:

'Do you think it good for an artist, this immunity from financial difficulty that Leonardo affords you, Biancaaaa, my love?'

'Probably not,' she agrees, unwilling to discuss it.

Much as she loves Matthew, she will not let him become her conscience. He turns the elaborate pencil drawing of Max on the new six-foot canvas to face them.

'When is he coming next? This drawing for a first sitting is wonderfully complete.'

'Some time later this week, I think,' she replies distractedly.

Matthew glances slyly at her. 'Do you like him, Biancaaa?'

'Yes, I think so.' Her reply gives nothing away.

'Are you proposing to love three men, Biancaaa darling?' he asks mischievously.

Matthew had known Bianca when they were still at school. He was there when she and Stephen first met, long before the appearances of Leonardo and Sarah in their lives. In fact, it was he who arranged their engagement party, to coincide with Bianca's seventeenth birthday. He no longer quite knows how things play with the two of them, but he does know that Stephen is still there, hovering in the background; he occasionally accompanies her to one of his private views.

'No, I'm not polygamous like you...'

Following his divorce, Matthew had the reputation of running five different women concurrently for several years.

'I have always dreamed of loving just one man and being loved by him exclusively in return.'

Matthew watches her carefully, remarking, 'What a sad muddle we all make of life...'

'Yes, don't we just.'

Secretly, he wishes she would free herself from both Leonardo and Stephen. He knows more of Leonardo than he is prepared to admit to… And Stephen, charming though he is:

Let him be the past, for God's sake.

Nor is he the only one of her friends to think so, but to tell her would be fatal. Bianca had never willingly accepted unsolicited advice on her private affairs. Better to remain silent. Nevertheless, he cannot help noticing the look of sorrow that fleetingly lays siege to her features… A sudden horrified thought strikes him.

Might she, despite her extraordinarily busy life, be lonely?

CHAPTER 10

After the theatre, first silence. Then Hesketh again pouring out his dismay in letters: 'I suppose I have messed up again!'

This written sadly on a postcard; no mention of Max.

Three days later, reflecting on his previous letter: 'I remember the last time we made love; you didn't want to…':

Dear Bianca,

I shouldn't have sent that letter. I'm sorry. It was obtuse of me. I didn't mean to be emotionally manipulative. I know very well how bad it all feels… the butterflies, a mouth so dry that it's impossible to breathe… Feeling nauseous all the time, as well as desperate. As I wrote to you once, I never knew it was possible to be so unhappy and still stay alive. Nevertheless, we are both alive, and I still long to see you.

I went on a 'remote viewing' course recently. Not as good as some of the 'out-of-body' ones I've been on, but with my new extra psychic powers, I should be able to transmit my thoughts to you more directly. So, if you don't mind too much, I am planning to pay you a visit. With all your intuitive telepathy, you'll probably pick up the signals really easily.

I enclose the press cutting from the Daily Mail.

How busy you must be… so many congratulations.

Love, Hesketh X

Something different is happening…

It is not the chatty ending of this new letter that surprises Bianca; that had always been commonplace after a crisis, as though his ordinary mind would fight, last minute, to persuade him he is a nice person still, becoming almost old womanish in his loving nurture of himself. Bianca remembers Hesketh waking regularly from a dream in which his father had tied him to a railway track, telling him to prove himself a good boy before he could be released. What shocks her now is that he is reverting to type. No longer canny, the tone of this and his last letter are more akin to how she remembers his letters up until two years ago, when he had waited for her on her doorstep, and she had jibed: 'Year after year of writing about what *you* feel... *you* want... and *you* need? ... If you persist in subjecting me to these nauseating, incontinent emotions of yours, I shall again resort to calling the police.'

She remembers his keen look of fear, as her words had passed through his eyes like bullets. And finally she understands... For two years, Hesketh has been on his best behaviour, writing innocuous words, full of lame goodwill; words to which the police could take no exception, beyond perhaps issuing him with a warning.

And God knows he's used to those...

Despite his history of pestering her, and police records relating to their court cases, he knows the police are only ever truly galvanised by immediate threats of violence, whether written or recorded on the phone... And much as he has tried, Hesketh has still not succeeded in getting Bianca's telephone number... Yet suddenly, his confident, true nature is back. And what he really wants to write about are his feelings of loss, his memories of lovemaking, his sense that nothing between them either has, nor ever can be, changed. He wants to visit Bianca on some internal, star-strewn pathway and hitchhike a guide to her inner galaxies... to invade her mind from within, filling her thoughts not only with his passion for her but with the cosy minutiae of his life:

'I'm going for a bicycle ride in Battersea Park...'

'I went on a remote viewing course, hoping to meet you...'

For some ridiculous reason, the braggart image of Courbet's painting, *Bonjour Monsieur Courbet*, conjures in Bianca's mind.

That's what I've been missing these past two years. Letters, in which every new sentence begins with 'I':

'*I* love you...'

'*I* want to see you.'

'*I* never knew I could be so unhappy and stay alive...'

Also the domineering transference of his own emotional states to hers:

'I did not intend to be emotionally manipulative... did not want you to suffer butterflies in your stomach, like I do... I still want to make love to you, but, of course, I might be nervous...'

If it were not so fatally tragic, it would be hilarious...

As always, she throws this letter onto the floor of the airing cupboard to join the others there cooking in hell. Yet the wary side of her nature is concerned.

Hesketh is coming closer... I can feel it.

It is good that she and Stephen would soon be away. With any luck, the extraterrestrial highway will not stretch as far as China. And what had he meant by: 'How busy you must be... So many congratulations.'

Had he had trouble getting through on his telepathic intercom? Were the airwaves blocked? Congratulations for what exactly?

Bianca is completely mystified.

* * *

Three days later, Max returns to Bianca's studio for his second portrait sitting. But the mood between them is now very different. From having been enchanted by Max, Bianca suddenly feels less sure. Not having expected to meet him that evening in the hotel foyer, she had suddenly found herself enjoying his company, their meeting more like starting a friendship in the middle than at its very beginning, so seemingly easy was initial conversation between them. His request she paint his portrait had created further intimacy. But since their encounter with Hesketh, all the doubts missing from those early conversations had come crowding in vengefully. Bianca longs for some of the formality that has so far eluded them.

We know so little of one another...

From having felt happily at ease, she now feels rushed and slightly intruded upon, while reluctant to admit this might simply be the natural hostility felt towards someone threatening to dramatically change her life; the hostility that goes with incipient attraction. New meetings with men normally leave Bianca unruffled. But this meeting with Max, for some reason, is different. She thinks of her life with Leonardo and Stephen, her sense of responsibility to them both, realising, from the outside, that their crossfire of complex infidelities must seem lax, like some libertine code between them. But that is a misunderstanding. A rigorous morality, as formulaic as marriage, underpins them. To betray either feels unthinkable. It occurs to her that, while a woman might leave one man, she could never leave two. Too impractical to do so. It was as though the three of them had formed an unbreakable entity.

But am I missing the point? she wonders. *Perhaps someone whose emotions are divided always occasionally dreams of replacing them with a single devotion?*

Contradictory thoughts hurtle through her... As they do so, Max sorrowfully watches her beauty drain away in pained preoccupation and self-doubt.

Arriving at the studio on time, he was greeted by Bianca more formally than ever before. Almost immediately, she asked him to resume his pose in the comfortable chinoiserie chair; the six-foot canvas already on the easel, a wheelable trolley next to it, spread with a palette of colours, plus some long-stemmed brushes, which Bianca arranged aggressively in her hand like a fistful of chopsticks.

Speaking little, every new sentence stultified, as their session begins, they both feel grateful for the silence. Failing to understand the reason for her new mood, Max nevertheless follows it blindly.

Surveying her drawing of Max, Bianca knows she must not tamper with it; her mood is all wrong and she risks ruining her former good work. Busying herself instead with the neutral background areas to his huge head, she fills the four corners of canvas with flat passages of acrylic paint, which edge up to his unkempt halo of hair but dare not venture within to describe its tangle; the process of painting itself soothing, its repetitious movements providing a space in which to better discern the muddle of her thoughts. It occurs to her that she is furious with Max for becoming so important to her, so fast, while simultaneously offering no explanation for his invasion of her consciousness.

What exactly is it that he wants from me... if anything?

Unconsciously, she lets out a sigh.

Hearing her, Max shifts slightly in his pose, knowing he has upset her in some way, yet feeling incompetent to deal with it. He experiences a haunting, familiar mixture of panic and inevitable loss, as though, for all his qualities of intelligence, some raw element of emotion in other people's scheme of things eludes him; that same quality of visceral emotion his critics complain is too easily sacrificed to sympathy in his plays.

Perhaps I expect too much of people... Always relying on them to be their own exacting judges and organisers of their own passions?

Yet he feels sure his instincts about Bianca are correct; that, beneath her coverlet of distress, she matches him emotionally in some precious way. He settles himself more comfortably into the chinoiserie chair, resolving to play the long game.

After today, I shall leave her alone, he decides. *Suggest a break in our sittings, contrive a trip of my own... I need, in any case, to spend some time in Dublin... Perhaps by the time we get back from our respective trips, she'll know what it is she feels about me?*

As the sitting ends, he springs quickly from the chair, glancing at his watch.

'Sorry, but I have to rush... a meeting across town. Traffic, bad this time of day.'

Making no attempt to review his portrait, he kisses her lightly on both cheeks, then moves swiftly into the narrow dark of her corridor. Following him meekly to the door, as daylight streams over the landscape of his features, she notices nothing but the intensity of his dark eyes.

'See you when you get back from abroad... and I get back from Ireland.'

He has asked her no details of her trip, only knowing it to be China. She looks doubtful. 'Ireland?'

'Yes, I'll be at the Abbey Theatre for the next ten weeks or so.'

'Dublin... all that time?'

'No, I plan to stay mainly in the south, right on the coast, and commute to Dublin whenever I need to.'

'What about your portrait?'

He smiles smoothly. 'Won't it wait?'

Bianca is stunned. So far, everything about Max and his portrait had seemed urgent.

'Y-Yes, of course,' she stutters formally.

His final glance is ambiguously tender. Smiling wanly, she searches his face for explanation but finds none. Closing the door behind him, she feels strangely bereft but also curiously relieved, realising suddenly that she had been holding herself rigid against the expectation of needing to make some far-reaching decision. Max's departure is a sudden reprieve. Whatever the future holds, she can, for the moment at least, continue enjoying the sweet, peaceful pace of her life as it is… Leo is already abroad, working on his film and, in a few days, China… Stability has prevailed.

She recalls Max's play. Full of emotional subtleties and couched in the intricate cleverness of language, in which words were made to perform like fleas. Yet at its heart, a character who would more readily condemn his own actions than those of others.

That, she thinks fondly, *is Max. His own truth…*

CHAPTER 11

In the final few days before their departure for China, released suddenly from the duties of portraiture, Bianca turns back to her mother's diaries. To the days, weeks and months following her parents' wedding... to the story of William and Anya's indelible love for each other.

* * *

Across town, Anya Johnson is preparing to meet her friends and fellow members of a Humanist group known simply as The Society; their first talk arranged for 11 a.m., followed by lunch at the nearby student union. Then a return to Bloomsbury's Queen Square for further discussions at 3 p.m. Afterwards, some of them will catch a bus to Waterloo to take tea together at the Royal Festival Hall. This is their Sunday ritual.

Anya makes herself up carefully. Despite her age, she still performs all the old rituals of foundation, rouge and mascara, spitting into the miniature tray of black kohl to brush it onto sparse lashes, and finishing with a youthful dash of pale pink lipstick. It was only last year that she had finally admitted to the snowy whiteness of her hair; up until a year ago, still dying it blonde. She is a tiny, delicate individual, the youthful figure she once was still apparent in her elderly frame; still something girlish about her, even in the way she moves, like a swift, miniature sail crossing the room. In many ways, she has always chosen to live frugally, yet never at the expense of elegant clothes and good underwear. Her years in Paris had taught her the old French discipline of looking good outside the home, while living one's social life in restaurants and cafés, rather than the English idea of conducting society at home. Even now, she rarely invites people to her flat and dislikes it intensely if people turn up unannounced.

Pulling a pair of tailored black slacks and a vest, edged with white guipure lace, from her wardrobe, over them she shrugs a shimmering black silk blouse. Her few pieces of jewellery are expensive costume jewellery, mainly from Fior, and mostly presents, bought years earlier for her by William. She selects a pair of black jet earrings, cased in gold. He had also bought her elaborate bracelets. Around her wrist, she fastens a broad band of filigree silver, tarnished to gun-metal grey, and studded with miniature turquoise. Almost ready now, she glances around the room, standing momentarily still to bend tenderly over one of her many flower arrangements, the flowers all desiccated and dry. Nevertheless, lovingly tweaking their stiffened foliage into better arrangement, she is careful not to smash any of their brittleness.

'Who's speaking today?'

She glances at her copy of The Society's programme… it is the American philosopher, Robin Holderness.

Walking out into the late autumn sunshine of Bedfordbury, she steps behind St Martin-in-the-Fields, into the Strand. At the bus stop, another member of The Society is waiting for her. There was no arrangement to meet; he simply hoped she would be there. He is a swarthy, handsome man of forty-five or so. As he helps her onto the bus, he asks: 'Tell me the rest of your wedding-day story, the part you left unfinished last week.'

Anya looks up at him, surprised… Such a very long time ago. Why would he want to know?

Yet as she talks, she starts to wonder all over again what has happened to William? Is he dead? He no longer sends her any money.

* * *

Bianca, with her mother's diaries in front of her, starts jotting down ideas for a narrative…

William's parents, Preston and Edith, had decided to remain in London longer than originally planned. The morning after the wedding,

*William had produced the elusive chamber pot and there was no more
mention of their getting a hotel. They stayed in the borrowed room across
the hall for ten nights, during which time, William and Anya never
once made love. It was as if the proximity of his mother had put a jinx
on William's desire. Yet their days were busy. William's parents liked to
rise early. By 6 a.m. each morning, they were up, knocking at William
and Anya's door, begging to be let in, whereupon, the newlyweds scrambled to get themselves dressed and rearrange their makeshift bed behind
the leaning accumulations of canvases and portfolios. A rickety, square
table was ritualistically brought out into the middle of the room and laid
with a golden-yellow check tablecloth, plus William and Anya's junk-
shop accumulations of blue-and-white crockery; few matching but one
or two of the very finest porcelain, delicate and delicious to drink from.*

'I prefer Poole Pottery myself,' commented Edith.

'Too thick lipped,' shot back Anya.

Father and son smiled in complicity with one another: Women and
their territorial entanglements!

*Bacon had to be cooked on an old primus stove, eggs left to sizzle in
dripping, jam and marmalade produced, and chairs borrowed for them
all to sit on.*

*After breakfast on the second day, Edith could no longer conceal her
contempt for the dust. She produced a pinafore from her case and set
about her chores as though she were at home, washing windows and
curtains, much to Anya's dismay.*

*'All the better for that old fool across the way to spy on us,' she com-
plained to William when they were alone in bed.*

*Standing on the rickety table, one by one, Edith brought down every
trophy of blue and white pottery, washing it carefully in warm carbolic
soap suds before replacing it, careful not to break any against the cracked
china sink, which hid behind a curtain, hand-painted by William.*

*'I quite liked the graduated shadows of dust on those pots, Mother,'
teased William. 'It made them easier to paint as still-life objects.'*

'There'll be noon of that mucky doost whilst I'm around.'

Anya turned away in repugnance. She sounds like a character out
of the music hall.

*Meanwhile, Preston sat quietly in the corner, smoking his pipe and
reading the* Financial Times. *He was himself an accountant and*

Company Secretary to a Sheffield steel company, and privately liked to play the stock exchange. A subsidiary of the company he worked for was rumoured to manufacture mustard gas.

Breakfast and fettling seemed to occupy every morning from 6 a.m. until 10 a.m., by which time Anya felt exhausted. Edith had now started arriving for breakfast with her snowy hair in curlers, secured beneath a hairnet that encroached low on her forehead, emphasising the masculine cast of her features. Anya's spirit felt worn out by her mother-in-law's concerns. But not because she was lazy; far from it. Anya would gladly get up in the morning, lay out the carefully placed pieces of a paper pattern onto a new length of cloth, pin it carefully, then cut it out with big tailor's scissors, chopping their way through the cloth with wonderful accuracy, before performing the magic of raising her old Singer sewing machine from the wooden basket above its wrought-iron treadle and working ceaselessly all day until the garment was finished. As it was, she was beginning to look forward to going back to work. Anya had taken a few days' leave from the Potato Marketing Board in order to get married.

One of the things that shocked Anya most was William's parents' lack of curiosity about London. Despite making obvious her feelings of inadequacy about the rooms in Great Titchfield Street, Edith seemed reluctant to explore elsewhere. Anya asked in amazement: 'Wouldn't you like to go to the theatre, ballet or an opera?'

Anya and her family of older brothers had always listened to classical music in the dark on Sundays at home, with the gaslights dimmed. On weekdays, they were used to paying sixpence to sit in the gods at the Old Vic, listening to Ralph Richardson, Michael Redgrave and Lawrence Olivier deliver Shakespeare. Anya had also always read voraciously, by the age of sixteen, taunted by her brothers into reading James Joyce. Not only Ulysses, but Finnegan's Wake too.

'Oh nooo,' said Edith, 'We 'ave enuff of that fancy stoof with Preston in Sheffield.'

Preston sat quietly to one side, smoking his pipe, enjoying the gentle, lilting movement of the ladder-backed rocking chair, mostly contemplative. The times when he roused himself to conversation were rarely at home but when out shopping for the soft, sweet tobacco to feed his pipe. Then he liked to josh gently with the shop girls behind their counters.

'Which is heaviest, a pound of feathers or a pound of lead?'

He liked the frowns of perplexity on their faces, as they struggled to find the answer. He never went out without his soft brimmed hat.

But one rainy afternoon in Great Titchfield Street, when the rituals of breakfast seemed to have stretched into the eternity of a bleak afternoon, he had looked up from the financial pages of his newspaper, analysed the frown gathering on Anya's face and decided to tell a story – the story of his own youth.

When still a young boy of six or seven, and his sister, Emily, younger still, their father had left their home in Kendal one day and gone to live in Huddersfield. Work was scarce, and he got himself a job in a pub. He would come back on Sundays to see them all, and leave again on Monday morning, having first walked his children to school across the moors. At first, their mother was pleased to see him on Sundays, but as the weeks stretched into months, they began to quarrel. One Sunday morning he arrived to find his wife not at home, and both his children in bed. Their mother had told them that on no account were they to get up before their father arrived.

They had done as they were told and the little girl had wet the bed, too fearful to disobey, yet unable to wait. When he arrived, the father took both children in his arms and made them buttered toast with a toasting fork in front of an open fire, before putting clean sheets on Emily's bed.

By 5 p.m. it was getting dark, and their mother had still not returned. Dressing them in their coats, gloves and scarves, their father took them out to look for her. Knocking at all the neighbours' houses, women came to their doors dressed in hairpins – it was a Sunday – the men in their shirtsleeves. Most folded their arms, shaking their heads noncommittally, the children and their father turned away. But on one doorstep, after the door had closed in their faces, Preston's father stopped for a moment, using the light from a window to roll himself a cigarette. As he did so, he heard a sudden gust of laughter from within. Nothing else, just the laughter. But he knew what it meant. He searched no more.

He took the children's hands in his and walked them home. Making them some hot broth, he put them to bed, then sat in front of the blackened kitchen range to wait. He waited and waited, smoking his own thin roll-ups as he did so. At some point, he must have dozed off briefly, because he woke to find the fire died down to its embers and someone *moving around in the front room. He got up to look. The house was dark, but moonlight filtered silently through the lace curtaining of the front-room window. He had forgotten to draw the curtains.*

There, in the middle of the room, stood his wife. The light caught her upturned face and smile. She looked like the young girl he had married. Standing tall in front of her, his arms around her waist, was her brother. He must have made a noise. They turned simultaneously, searching the gloom.

'Is that you, Harry?'

Preston's father moved into the light. His wife's features hardened.

'You still here?'

Her brother kept his hands on her waist.

'Jack's moving in with us,' she explained noncommittally.

Preston and Emily's father put on his flat cap and walked out into the dark night. He never came back... Three months later, without telling anyone, the eight and six-year-old brother and sister set off across the Pennines to find him. Uncle Jack had left them tied to two chairs in the kitchen one Saturday, when he and their mother wanted to go to the races.

Edith, thinking it not quite nice to talk of such things, nevertheless remained silent, her bossiness finally stilled listening to her husband's tale.

The journey had taken the children four days. At night, they had cowered in doorways, their feet blistered. Emily could not stop crying. They only half remembered the name of the pub. But when, on the fourth day, their amazed father welcomed them with open arms, it had all been worth it. At the time, the owner landlady of the pub was nursing a very sick husband. Nevertheless, she allowed the children to sleep in a tiny room at the top of the pub, and the next morning, even made the journey herself to the local school to enrol the children in classes. Slowly, the dented expressions on the two children's faces began to smooth, first into peace and eventually happiness.

At school Preston began to flourish, and at the age of sixteen he became articled clerk to a firm of lawyers. In the evenings, he went to night school to study accountancy. Having learned both piano and clarinet, he started a musical quartet, who played in the pub on Saturday nights. Later, after he had married Edith and moved to Sheffield, he became conductor of a local orchestra.

The landlady's sick husband eventually died. Preston's father remained married to his children's mother. Outwardly, he and the landlady maintained the formality of their relationship as employer and employee; within the pub walls, they kept separate bedrooms, on separate floors. But the children grew up knowing that if, after a nightmare, they were not to be found in one room, they were in the other, alternating their favours with the rooms, but never with one another. They remained loyal and happy with one another for the rest of their lives, retiring eventually to a small cottage in Hebden Bridge.

The children only ever saw their mother twice more. She arrived unannounced in the pub one day, demanding money from their father, which he gave her. Her attitude to her two silent children, avidly fascinated by her every move, was strangely jocular, as though it had all been one big mistaken joke. The next time they saw her, she was in her coffin. Preston still remembered how pretty she looked. He, himself, had flourished, but Emily had never really recovered from her early experience of cruelty. It left her fearful of life, unable to decide. She never married. In middle age, her face grew a crop of moles as round as mushrooms, from which long grey hairs sprouted. They were like a manifestation of her loneliness. Meanwhile, Edith never really forgave her for her ugliness.

It was these stories of her new parents-in-law's youth that Anya loved best... What Edith loved best, it transpired, was operetta, by Gilbert & Sullivan, but more still, she adored the music hall. In her more relaxed moments after breakfast, she could be persuaded to sing...

'Lotte Lenya's got no drawers. Can you kindly lend her yours? Ta ra ra boom-de-ay, Ta ra ra boom-de-ay.'

Laughing, they all joined in with the chorus: 'TA RA RA BOOM-DE-AY – TA RA RA BOOM-DE-AY,' followed by the plaintive, trembling notes of...

'The boy I love is up in the Gallery. The boy I love is looking down on me. There he is, can't you see. Waving his handkerchief.'

The other thing Edith loved was afternoon tea. In fact, there were only two things she really wanted to do in London: to be taken out to tea and to visit the Changing of the Guard at Buckingham Palace. The abdication crisis was becoming crucial. George V had died on 6 May and it was already clear the Prince of Wales might never be crowned King.

Along with all the other matrons of Great Britain, Edith declared

Wallace Simpson: 'An American whore, daft enough to think she could be Queen.'

So, on the afternoon before Edith and Preston's departure for Sheffield, all four put on their smartest clothes and went to The Connaught for tea. It was the only time in their ten-day visit that Edith was perfectly happy. Everything was finally to her taste: the dark oak panelling, the liveried doormen, the number of doors deferentially held open for her to pass through, and the delicacy of the sandwiches and cakes she was brought on silver salvers. Not only was she fascinated by the snuffled rich silence of The Connaught, almost like being in church, something so still and sacred about its atmosphere, but also by the people flitting through its rooms; the elegant Mayfair set in their narrowly cut suits, with hats neatly cupped to their heads, the soft leather of the pale kid gloves they set aside to eat their sandwiches; the way they smiled with their mouths and not necessarily with their eyes. And their jewellery: the emeralds that sparkled on narrow, aristocratic fingers' the rubies that juxtaposed with cuffs and collars of diamonds at their wrists and throats. This for Edith was the potential heaven of London. And beneath its beatific spell she finally relaxed.

But later that evening, when they got back to Great Titchfield Street, they found Rowland and Bunty Darblay waiting for them, their baby daughter, Janna, crying in her mother's arms. They had been evicted from their rooms in Hammersmith for not being able to pay their rent. Both Preston and Edith looked shocked. The idea of not being able to pay one's rent was something they scarcely understood.

William and Anya were more understanding, their response more pragmatic. They had heard that the flat two floors above them might be available so William went in search of the landlord, while Anya took Janna from her mother's arms to soothe her. The baby girl stopped crying immediately. Edith sat down heavily on the rocking chair, this new drama a far cry from the glories of The Connaught, while Preston smoked his pipe in dignified silence.

William returned with the news that Rowland and Bunty could move into the new flat two days later. Until then, he had borrowed a second mattress, so that all five of them, the four adults and baby Janna, could sleep that night in William and Anya's room. Edith was appalled.

By the time William and Anya saw Preston and Edith off at Euston

Station, it was ten days since their wedding, and William and Anya had still not consummated their marriage. At the time, that small act of postponement seemed almost unimportant in the face of their affection for one another. Only later did it reveal its more sinister influence...

Throwing down her pen, Bianca is lost in nostalgia...

* * *

Stealing a glance at the handsome young man beside her, Anya's smile is a flash of gold, another remnant from her elegant Parisian days; a missing side tooth replaced by one of pure yellow-gold.

'Am I not boring you with all these reminiscences?'

'No, not at all.'

He has a way of looking at her directly, with such immediacy, that it creates its own unflinching intimacy.

Having travelled swiftly along the Strand, their bus had been held stationary at Aldwych for more than ten minutes. On the upper deck a commotion was developing, which the driver had left his cab to deal with, the air turning blue with extravagant exchanges of insults. Someone tried to intervene, only making things worse.

'But shouldn't we be talking about you, Andreas? Your dreams for the future are far more important than my past.'

Suddenly he looks embarrassed. 'Not much to tell...' he mutters.

CHAPTER 12

Hesketh is at home on Chelsea Embankment, hiding in his office by the lift, with the door firmly closed, but still able to hear the tip, tap, tap of Bruno's typewriter. Bruno's favourite key is the asterisk, almost rubbed blank from repeated use. Busily formulating another plan to gain Bianca's attention, a copy of *Vogue* lies open in front of him, devoted to fashion ideas for men. Hesketh studies it avidly. Tip, tap, tap, the old golf typewriter keeps up its staccato rhythms in the corridor behind him.

A memory has stirred in him. He had done something like this once before, twenty-five years earlier, just before she left him. Bianca had casually mentioned liking an outfit pictured in *Vogue*, of a man dressed in a black velvet suit, worn with a tank top, knitted in glistening, multi-coloured lurex wools, and accompanied by an enormous, floppy bow tie. It was 1973. Without telling her, he went out the next day and bought the exact same outfit. He can still recall the look on her face when he appeared wearing it; a mixture of surprise, plus something else, less easy to decipher? Contempt, maybe?

Had she already stopped loving me by then?

Patrick was, by then, a regular visitor to the house in Putney.

Perhaps even now, all these years later, she would like it if I were to dress more smartly? he argues desperately with himself.

Each new idea takes hold of his mind with distraught fervour. He remembers the expensively smooth, dark limousine that had collected Bianca from her front door two weeks earlier. Still it troubles him.

Abruptly swinging open his office door, he surprises Bruno into looking at him directly, before again swiftly turning his head away. Dashing into the room overlooking the river, Hesketh retrieves the invitation card, still propped up on the mantelpiece, to a formal dinner given by the local Conservative Party, at which the Chief Police Commissioner promises to speak. Studying it carefully, the wording is quite specific: 'Black Tie'.

What a laugh... Does the Police Commissioner know of his constabulary's occasional visits to my door? Not that I care... None of his business, for Christ's sake.

He glances again at the pages of *Vogue*. One photo shows a smoking jacket by Yves St Laurent.

Why not...? he thinks. *After all, I can afford it.*

Studying the invitation again, he sees that it is addressed to Mr & Mrs Hesketh James.

Would Chloe need a new dress? He quickly dismisses the idea. *Too busy looking after Bruno... Best, anyway, if I go on my own...*

He wonders vaguely where he can get a lurex tank top?

Hearing Chloe call, he does not reply, checking in his pocket for car keys: *She'll just think me busy...*

From the kitchen, where she is preparing lunch, Chloe hears the lift sigh, the grille doors open and shut. Bruno is making sing-song keening sounds, while rocking himself gently side to side.

Hesketh consults his watch. Noon. Even on a Sunday, the shops should be open in Knightsbridge...

I'll drive there right now.

Tucking the pages from *Vogue* into his breast pocket, he remembers how Bianca had always admired elegance. *Perhaps new clothes will bring her back to me?*

Not until he reaches Sloane Square does he remember he should have told Chloe where he is going. He calls her on his mobile, breezily explaining: 'Just going shopping, darling.'

'On a Sunday? Whatever for?' she asks tremulously.

'New clothes.'

'Oh.' Her mind skitters fast, trying to discern a motive... Yet she can think of none.

At the Yves St Laurent boutique in Sloane Street, Hesketh's purchase of the new clothes is dizzily swift. Barely allowing himself time to luxuriate in the sumptuous, silent depths of the shop's plush carpets, he remains perversely oblivious to the suave charms of the young Italian trying to persuade him to try on a second, longer cut jacket.

'No need,' he mutters fretfully. 'This one will do... Just a pity it's in silk, rather than velvet... I shall also need a bow tie.'

By now, the young Italian has realised that his inspirational sense of *la bella figura* is lost on this man, with his ugly habit of gesticulating aggressively, while cupping a hand over his mouth, in a gesture almost shy.

The bow ties he fetches are disappointingly narrow. Not at all how Hesketh remembers a bow tie should be.

'Don't you have any bigger, floppier ones?' he asks impatiently.

Concluding he is dealing with a peasant, the young Italian retreats into a mood of icy formality. Hesketh, barely noticing the implied rebuke, asks: 'Don't you have any tank tops? Preferably in lurex?'

Not understanding at first, the young man repeats the words mysteriously, rolling them around luxuriously on his tongue: 'Taank tops, taank tops...'

His feet flit swiftly over the acres of deep mushroom pile to consult with a colleague.

'Ah, tank tops,' he says, dancing back to Hesketh's side. 'Tank tops, no, we do not 'ave.' His face is full of practised sorrow. 'But we do 'ave ze waistcoats,' he reports triumphantly.

From behind his old-fashioned ladies' glasses, their flyaway style owing more to the 1950s than even to the 1970s, Hesketh glances myopically towards a distant cabinet. Having been empty, the boutique is now suddenly full of Sunday browsers. From the stylish vitrine, the young man extracts an array of silk waistcoats in multitude styles and colours, some discreetly sombre, others magically, beautifully colourful. Hesketh remarks doubtfully: 'Don't you have anything in Fair Isle?'

Racking his brains, Hesketh tries to remember precisely his outfit of twenty-five years ago. 'Fair Isle would be best.'

Then, noticing a waistcoat, whose front is an exotic tartan of bright mauves, pinks and yellows, he mutters hesitantly: 'Perhaps I'll try that one.'

Admiring himself in the mirror, Hesketh sees someone who is almost, not quite, familiar... Someone he had once wanted to be.

Still as lean as he was then, the image of his younger self dazzles before him… He thinks bravely: *That's who I really am.*

Encouraged by Hesketh's smile, the young Italian starts fussing over him again – tugging at the sleeves of the jacket, straightening the too-narrow bow tie and adjusting lapels.

'We also sell *occhilali…*' He searches for the English translation. 'Spectacles,' he dares to suggest.

Hesketh looks back at him blankly. The young man has failed to realise Hesketh has seen only the clothes and his lean figure. His distraught, ravaged face and thinly spiked greying hair, adorned by old-fashioned flyaway frames, have completely eluded the golden gaze of his adoring eyes.

'I'll take them,' he says.

He produces an American Express card from his jeans' pocket, neither enquiring nor glancing at the cost. Even as he scrawls his signature, he fails to notice the price. By now, the young Italian is both enchanted and mystified. In the space of just ten minutes, he has made a commission on a £3,000 sale, without having to use up any of his reserves of charm or time. For him, it is a novel experience. He is more used to devoting two persuasive hours to such a sale. Accompanying Hesketh to the door, he skips by his side like a young puppy.

'*Grazie, ciao, grazie,*' he says effusively. '*Ciao.*'

Fucking wop, thinks Hesketh.

'The alterations to the trousers… ready on Tuesday,' the young Italian reminds him, letting go of the heavy glass door. '*Ciao, ciao…*'

* * *

The following Wednesday, Bianca gets up deliberately early, intending to spend the day at her studio. Not to paint but to make further notes from her mother's diaries; something she usually does at home, sitting at her favourite walnut desk. But today she feels the need for grand operatic space in which to let her thoughts soar untrammelled. Staying all day, she waits for the pink of the evening sun to infiltrate her tall window.

When finally she arrives home, one of her newer neighbours

meets her outside on the street. 'There's been a man here since early morning, dressed in black tie and a colourful waistcoat, asking for you.'

'Really? Did he leave his name?'

'No.'

'How very odd...'

So odd, in fact, that it does not occur to Bianca that it may have been Hesketh. For the past twenty-five years, whenever she has seen him, he has always been dressed casually, in nothing more elaborate than jeans and anoraks.

* * *

The quarrel on the upper deck is finally resolved. As their bus moves off again, Anya turns to Andreas, resuming her story of the weeks following her marriage...

* * *

With Rowland and Bunty living upstairs, a new routine had developed between the two couples, not least between the two men. William and Rowland still went out hunting in the late afternoons and early evenings for painterly success and galleries together, their mornings spent at home, working independently on their canvases and thick sheets of Whatman watercolour paper. But their afternoons were now spiced with extra rivalry as they daily, jealously reviewed each other's work, trying to assess who had achieved the most. Camaraderie remained intact, yet they watched one another like hawks for new moves, for fresh signs of advancement in the business of painterly understanding. And frequently it seemed to them both that Rowland had succeeded best. There was an edge of urgency to his work, perhaps that of a man running away from the coal pit, which, without the benediction of painting, might still claim him. It lent his paintings a quality of dash.

William's work, by comparison, was more contemplative, less impetuous. He allowed himself to dwell on complication and complexity before resolving it into a hum of nuanced, pitter-patter painting steps. William had looked at Cézanne to greater effect than Rowland, who was more in the school of early Vlaminck. They both made sharp-noted wolf whistles at landscapes. But it was Rowland's wolf whistles that were loudest, and most clamorous.

Most conspicuously different between them at this stage of their careers was their sensibility towards colour. Rowland's palette was devoted to the brown shades of raw sienna and burnt umber, which he enlivened with surprise dashes of pale pinks and baby blues, whereas William's palette was a never-ending symphony of blues and greens, from which he extracted an array of subtle, nuanced tones, fixed in thoughtful, premiere tache sable brushwork.

William's paintings at this point were like gentle rain, a happy glance at English landscape that turned it almost tropical. Rowland's paintings, by comparison, were more like the wind that roared across the moors of his Yorkshire childhood, bending everything in its path.

In the late afternoons and early evenings, painting done, and the solemn moments of mutual assessment forgotten, a kind of joyous hilarity infected their camaraderie. Together they went out on the prowl; for galleries and people to admire, and others to heap scorn upon. By late afternoon, their thoughts had polarised into love and hate, their world sharply divided between those worthy of consideration and those not. Yet even then, love was not constant. A firm friendship, forged in the Wheatsheaf Pub on the corner of Charlotte Street with Rathbone Place, could be sent fleeing by a perceived slight or small moment of criticism. As a result, William and Rowland's emotions and intellects were in constant ferment and often indistinguishable from one another. They made no distinction between emotional and intellectual truth. And the people whose help they needed most, that of dealers and potential patrons, were often those who ended up seemingly most deserving of their contempt. For them both, to sell a painting was a minor reprieve, an optimistic moment of food and rent. But once satiated their joy was swiftly replaced by contempt for the person who had paid so little for a gem that he was almost certainly too philistine to appreciate. Lucy Wertheim arranged a show of Rowland's paintings in which every painting was sold in advance, each dignified by a spot of red at the Vernissage, someone gloomily exclaiming: 'Patrons leave behind little spots of their blood...'

But Rowland's happiness at his success was short-lived. The promises proved empty. People who had wanted something desperately when in *the shop window of competition no longer wanted it when it was theirs to have and to hold. They made their excuses, never turning up to collect the paintings they had stained with their little spots of blood; others simply neglected to pay. Those that did paid in dribs and drabs, so that the trophy of a large, useful sum of money dangled before the hungry eyes of Rowland and Bunty never quite materialised. In the end, it was more fun dealing with Mendelssohn, who, at the time, kept a shop opposite the Wheatsheaf, across whose frontage was printed: 'ENGLISH PAINTINGS BOUGHT HERE.'*

William and Rowland would visit it together. Inside, was a dark Aladdin's cave of bric-a-brac; canvases and portfolios of drawings piled high. Initially, the shop always seemed deserted. But at the back, out of sight, was a woman employed as a pair of eyes. Whenever a customer arrived, she rang a bell, and the owner, Mendelssohn, would uncurl himself from beneath the long wooden counter, where he had been asleep like a cat.

He was a tall, imposing man, six foot four in height. In both winter and summer, he always dressed the same, in a heavy black overcoat with astrakhan collar. Having woken up, he always first put on his homburg hat before getting down to business; as he spoke, he picked at his teeth with a gold toothpick, kept in his lapel. He had a catchphrase, which the rival friends came to recognise and love: 'Without looking, I give you £5...'

So, William and Rowland got into the habit of turning up at his shop with portfolios of paintings and drawings interleaved with newspaper to make them appear bulkier. Nevertheless, Mendelssohn had a good eye, and William later regretted not having bought from him works by other artists he saw there for sale cheaply. Also, Mendelssohn was, in his own way, completely honourable; whatever sums he quoted, he paid promptly in cash. And this cash was like freedom – the freedom to breathe, the freedom to live.

The developing relationship between the two wives, Anya and Bunty, was different, although no less fond. Anya was out at work during the day, at the Potato Marketing Board, doing any domestic chores she considered necessary in the mornings, before leaving. But in the evenings, she simply wanted life to be fun.

Also, she and William were in agreement: although their possessions were modest, each one was deliberately chosen for its particular visual charm, whether a pot, a table, a chair or cracked mirror. Within the studio atmosphere of easels and paintings turned to the wall, everything in their tiny apartment had its place, each the result of some sensibility of arrangement – from the sequential juxtaposition of blue-and-white pots along the upper shelf of their tongue and groove, to the careful placing of a chair in relationship to the decorative threadbare Persian rug on which it stood, or the shape a vase of flowers made above the mantelpiece, flanked either side by the elegant silhouettes of battered candelabra. Everywhere, a sense of beauty and order... of still life. One evening at Bertorelli's, Paul Ottery was overheard commenting that Anya too was just another of William's aesthetically chosen possessions.

But upstairs, in the rooms kept by Rowland and Bunty, chaos reigned. Janna's potty was always left un-emptied, infecting the air with acrid smells, despite Bunty being at home all day, sitting quietly, watching Rowland paint. They too, Bunty in particular, accumulated trophy junk; more extravagantly so than either William or Anya. But the things, once acquired, simply had to exist alongside one another. With no special place to occupy, they were simply possessions, jumbled higgledy-piggledy on a shelf or tabletop, accumulating dust.

One of these possessions was a handsome oak refectory table Bunty had picked up for a song and had transported back to Great Titchfield Street for a few extra pence. Rowland, wraith thin beneath his clothes, having found that he constantly knocked his hip as he advanced and retreated from work on a painting, took a saw one day and chopped the offensive corner off. William and Anya were both appalled at such blatant desecration of an object's proportions.

Occasionally, one of the smaller objects submitted to baby Janna's curiosity, smashing to the floor, but otherwise remaining untouched, like the objects in a catacomb, shrouded in dust. It was as if Rowland needed to be surrounded by disorder in order to find the breeze in his paintings.

In the evenings, the two women liked to dress up a little and go out; Anya much better at this than Bunty. Like her homemaking, Bunty's sense of style was a bit haphazard, whereas Anya had an innate sense of dress. William loved the details of Anya's clothes – the miniature ruffs of lace at neck and wrist, the pearl button fastenings of her bodice. He came home one day, having bought a length of raw gold silk, as heavy as hessian, and hand-painted a design on it for her to make into a skirt. He frequently bought her unusual pieces of jewellery; never tiring of revelling in her beauty. A final dab of lipstick and she and Bunty were ready to go out. Bunty's lipstick, for some reason, was always bright orange.

The mood in the country, the talk in the pubs of Fitzrovia and Charlotte Street, was preoccupied by the Spanish Civil War, which had begun in July, plus the possibility of another war with Germany. On the abdication crisis, like Dreyfus, everyone had an opinion. Some sided with true love and whoredom, others with the Constitution and the great sacrificing responsibilities of kingship. No one knew how things would turn out. There was a sense of frenzied excitement in the air. Evenings in Charlotte Street were like the mood after a funeral, when grief gives way to hilarity and daring, and even promiscuity. People felt abandoned to the urgency of their passions. Eyes, skin and smiles were alive with the talkative promise of happiness.

But at home, sleeping on the pulled-out mattress, things were far quieter. Passion had become a conversation. The postponed urgency of William and Anya's lovemaking throughout those first nights of married life had taken their toll. Their marriage was now consummated, but it was as though, in those first important nights together, a mood of reason had crept in, to stealthily argue that, despite loving one another, they did not always need to make love in order to prove it. William was hesitant. In a sense, his delight in Anya's looks was, as Paul Ottery had guessed, more aesthetic than sensual. Having made love to her, he had also made the difficult discovery that, although their intimacy seemed to make her happy, it made strangely little difference to him. He felt curiously uninvolved in his own actions, some central core of the overwhelming importance of sex gone missing. He could not feel whatever it was she felt when they made love. He preferred painting. Those, for him, were the moments that held authority.

Anya consoled herself with the thought it was still early days. Unlike herself, William was a virgin when they'd first made love, and she had been anxious not to alarm him by revealing the true ferocity of her passions. She loved him. They must take things at his pace. Nevertheless, she could not help remembering the seamless, thoughtless lovemaking she had shared with big bear Varinsky.

Two months later, in December 1936, the abdication crisis was resolved in a grand moment of public suicide, the rumblings of war

164

ever closer. With spring in sight, Anya decided they should briefly get away from London for a postponed honeymoon. William had received an invitation to teach at Langford Grove in Essex; invited there by a Mrs Diamond, a relative of Roger Fry, who ran an artistic finishing school for young ladies. They cycled out of London, into East Anglia, on two ancient bicycles, bought in a junk shop on Tottenham Court Road for three pence each.

They had no precise plan, beyond that of a pilgrimage to Dedham Vale and Willy Lott's Cottage, on the Suffolk–Essex borders, to pay their respects to William Constable. Langford Grove was closer to London, not far from Maldon. They would return there, in time for the teaching commitment, on their homeward journey.

* * *

Negotiating the rapaciously busy East End, William and Anya felt happy to be back in the isolated joy of sharing exclusively with one another. They cycled until the remnants of city gave way to patchwork fields of bright yellow rapeseed and maize, alternating with orchards of apple and pear, until arterial roads were replaced by steep-sided lanes, more familiar to horses and cattle than motorcars.

The brakes on Anya's bike were lazy, sometimes responding to pressure, sometimes not bothering to react at all. The moment when they failed completely was on the long, steep winding hill that descended through the Dedham Vale to the miniature Georgian village of Dedham, nestling next to the river Stour in the fist of the valley below.

The bike started its decline slowly, then took wing, speeding faster and faster, nothing to stop it. At first, exhilarated with the wind and sun in her face, the steep bushes either side turning the descent into a fast-moving green tunnel, its acceleration started to outmatch Anya's hold on the bike. Trembling under its own momentum, its front wheel threatened to go slower than its freer-wheeling twin; Anya's outstretched arms on the handlebar, rigid with the effort of control. William, whose brakes worked, watched in dismay as she flew past him, his shouts of concern lost to the rush of air in her ears. Reaching the bottom of the hill, her front wheel struck a clod of earth, thrown from the mighty hoof of a dray horse, delivering wooden barrels of beer to the village pub.

Bucking like a kicking horse, the bike skidded, still violent with its own build-up of momentum, throwing Anya sideways and impaling her on the tall hedgerow that rose like a wall above their heads; a wall composed of densely spiky hawthorn, interlaced with long, predatory succulents of brambles. The hawthorn received her delicate figure in a fierce embrace, the brambles welcoming her hair and clothes with greedy thorns.

William, throwing his bicycle to one side and rushing to rescue her, was distraught. Never before had Anya seemed so fragile and helpless. With the help of a motherly woman from the pub who had witnessed the accident and hurried over to help him, he extricated Anya from the tangled briars, the kindly woman offering to wash the bleeding scratches on her face, legs and arms before making up a bed for them with pristine clean sheets in the upper rooms of the pub. That night, for the first time, William and Anya truly made love, with a ferocity and abandon that had so far eluded them. William had sensed Anya's fragility and capacity for fear – something he had not associated with her before. And she had witnessed the desperate urgency of his love for her.

Thereafter, conjugal happiness for them both was associated with those delicious pre-war days in the Eastern Counties. The following morning, they took a punt along the river to visit the unchanging legend of Willy Lott's Cottage, before returning to thank the woman from the pub for her great kindness. She had even had the brakes on Anya's bike mended overnight and her tyres newly pumped with air. They asked if they might pay her and stay another night. Such was the spell of those days, they resolved to find themselves a new home in this orchard of God's making, a home that would also be a studio, and cast their lives and love into happy isolation.

Two days later, fifteen miles closer to London and five miles short of Langford Grove, they found 'the cottage', which ran like a leitmotif through all the subsequent years of their lives; the cottage that became like a personality in its own right.

* * *

Anya glances at Andreas, listening enraptured beside her, his eyes half closed, suddenly shocked to notice the fleeting undertows of weariness in his handsome face.

Who is he? she ponders doubtfully. *Where, and to whom, does he belong?*

Sensing her gaze upon him, he opens his eyes, smiling happily. 'Have we arrived?'

His image of tiredness immediately dissolved, he seems all light again, a flash of brilliance from his dark, caressing eyes.

* * *

Later that evening, Bianca gets a surprise call from Max.

'Might you have time to meet up for a last-minute coffee before you leave?'

He pauses, holding his breath. She is unable to erase her smile at the sound of his voice.

'I thought you'd already left for Ireland?'

'No, not yet... Although soon.'

She arrives first. They meet in the Sainsbury wing of the National Gallery. On the distant wall, Paula Rego's mysterious grotesques spell out their menacing truths about human nature, while at café tables grey-haired art worthies chatter earnestly in their smock-clad bodies. Bianca thinks of her father, William, ruminating at the cottage: 'What can you hope for from people who think *art* is nice?'

Spinning on her heels, the hem of her long dark coat skims the floor as she scans the room for Max. He is not there. She feels a stab of panic, almost of loss... Then, suddenly, he is before her, his wonderful tousled head wearing a half-smile, and dressed unlike any way she has yet seen him, in a navy Barbour jacket above grey pantaloons. She feels momentarily startled, as if her familiarity with him were again mistaken. Then, glancing into the jewelled prisms of his eyes, as they settle on her in a mood of joyful amusement, she feels her entire being relax beneath their spell.

'Where shall we sit?'

Small knots of people cluster unevenly throughout the empty spaciousness. They decide to sit apart. Detecting a fleeting look of impatience in Max's demeanour as he fetches their drinks from the counter, Bianca puzzles: *Is Max secretly capable of an anger I've not yet anticipated?*

Unpredictable tempers remind her too much of childhood, creating immediate feelings of foreboding and panic in her. Both Stephen and Leonardo are capable of behaving outrageously, but never unkindly.

When Max's eyes next settle on her, the look has vanished. Instead, tracking her every expression, he scrutinises every small gesture, while pouring an avalanche of amusing, clever words about her ears. In the early morning light, there is a bruised, brooding feeling to Max's monochrome features she had not previously noticed.

And yet, he is beautiful...

Glancing at her, his eyes appear to refract the light. How she loves the greedy directness of his gaze. Yet his features remain impassive. Her own blue eyes meet his unwaveringly, the corners of her mouth upturned in smiles as his exchanges of energy pass through her, her former anger towards him now completely dissolved.

Even in repose, she appears to dance, thinks Max.

Hesketh, their visit to the theatre, has momentarily vanished from her thoughts, her mind focused exclusively on this moment. A horrifying possibility occurs to her: *Am I falling in love with this man?*

Intrigued by the stories she has published under a pseudonym, he asks her to describe their plots. She mentions her mother's diaries.

'Are those the stories already published?'

They talk about the business of writing, versus portraiture, with Max quoting Picasso: 'When I start a painting, it feels as though someone is working with me, but later feels as though I have been working alone – without a collaborator.'

'That's how it feels to me too,' Max explains, 'when working on new ideas for a play.'

'Where do those new ideas come from?' Bianca asks.

'Sometimes from nowhere, or, at least, nowhere tangible. At others, I just see or hear something that intrigues me, usually hinging on some personal tragedy, which I can elaborate on and subject to veiled threads of history. Tragedy works best, played out against time.'

Unthinkingly explaining that most of her stories are romantic, erotic even, about a married woman and her lover, Max, who had been leaning ever more intimately across the table, suddenly draws back, like a man sharply reining in a horse. So far, she has only mentioned her husband, Leonardo, yet sees in his eyes that Max has immediately guessed the truth. That Stephen had always been there too, a phantom flitting implicitly between the pages of their dialogue. And now suddenly centre stage.

Max turns away, his eyes no longer searching hers. Without their electric gaze, Bianca feels an immediate lonely panic. She has disappointed him.

Glancing back opaquely, impassively observing the plaintive anxiety in Bianca's face, her sensitivity to his every thought, Max wonders whether he has ever known such responsiveness in a woman. Yet there is still scepticism, resistance to her in his gaze. Although not for long. Despite their dissonant mood, neither is yet prepared to let go... both, despite their mutual warnings, sufficiently intrigued to want to go on.

Eventually remembering to check her watch, they have been talking for more than an hour. It had felt more like ten minutes, Max still holding her spellbound in a tumultuous net of words. Yet she had promised to meet Stephen for lunch nearby.

'I have to go,' she explains sadly.

'I'll walk with you.'

She shakes her head. 'No need.'

Looking momentarily embarrassed, Max stands, watching her walk away from him... Bianca, meanwhile, carrying her mood of excitable elation to the fifth floor of the National Portrait Gallery, where she spreads it like an unwelcome coverlet between herself and Stephen. Now late, Stephen is already waiting for her, struggling to hide his dismay. Bianca had lost all sense of time, something he is incapable of.

It could be weeks before she and Max meet again, yet the emotional charge between them feels so fierce, she thinks it must be tomorrow...

* * *

'So, tell me about the cottage.'

Anya gazes back at Andreas, delighted but also wondrous at his curiosity.

Is he flirting with me…? If only I were thirty years younger…

His handsome, swarthy looks appeal to her. She glances at his clothes. Beneath the fire in his eyes, his lean, athletic body is almost threadbare, clad in garments grown grey and lifeless from repeated washes.

Their bus has arrived in Red Lion Square.

'Later,' Anya says with a smile. 'Should we not go and see what this fellow Robin Holderness has to say for himself first?'

She steps daintily from the bus.

'Do you need me to carry your bag for you?'

Ahead of them, on their way to the meeting room in Queen Square, are other members of The Society. Anya is fond of them; there was a time when these Sunday meetings rescued her from despair. But as a group, they are a motley crowd, far easier to identify in terms of temperament than background. There is some melancholy mood in which they all share. So used to it, Anya no longer notices precisely, although occasionally she can still recall her first impression of them years earlier. Some are formidably bright, loudly opinionated; others, less well read and gentler in manner. But each has suffered some indefinable cruelty and wears that suffering like a badge. Anya likens them to 'courageous dogs, subjected to years of torment and neglect'. It has left their personalities a little proud, a little belligerent, never quite subdued, yet seething with resentment… They come here on Sundays to reclaim the memory of the person they had once been, before life flung its disappointments in their faces. Not only are they attracted by the desire for freedom of thought, but also to the spirit of anger they find in each another. It provides a framework from which to forgive their own uncontrollable outbursts of fury. They come here for a fight, albeit in the guise of angry debate.

Their meeting room is not the main auditorium but a smaller room lurking half concealed on the first floor. As the group settle, its younger members stretch out languidly, while the elderly struggle to remove unwieldy anoraks from arms grown stiff with age. A subtle dress code appears, less in terms of stylishness than in expense. Everyone has made some concession to economy. Gaily subverting her own elegance, Anya has chosen to carry a lightweight plastic Tesco bag, instead of a handbag. Another woman, in her fifties, throws off her good woollen coat to reveal a fatally short rah-rah skirt from the 1970s, beneath which knee-high striped stockings leave her exposed thighs mottled and bare. The men, all dressed anonymously in muddied tones of tweed, look like aspirant gardeners.

Into this melee of expectant faces and dented ambition, the gaunt figure of Robin Holderness suddenly makes its appearance, treading carefully, like a camel placing his gigantic hooves very deliberately beneath his long, corduroy legs as he makes his way to the podium, his angular height and sandy-coloured body, as always, a mismatch for his head, with its angry gaze and chrysanthemum hairdo. Anya regards him with a mixture of admiration and contempt; the look she adopts when anticipating a fight with a worthy opponent.

The subject of Robin's talk is: 'Freedom – Can the Morality of Freedom Ever Be Anything More Than a Purely Emotional Response?'

Allowing his gaze to sweep the room, Robin balances half-moon spectacles on his nose. 'Good morning.'

He glances myopically at his notes. *Why, oh why,* he wonders, *did I agree to this? What a way to spend my Sunday, lecturing to this nonsensical ship of fools.*

He has long since forgotten the moment of addictive pleasure when the invitation to talk first arrived six months earlier, and he had thought: *Why not?*

Appraising his audience, he now thinks he knows why... Not that he underestimates their intelligence, but he could almost reach out and touch the lack of intellectual discipline in the room. It means their response will be uneven. An audience of students or academics might violently disagree, but they would follow certain rules in doing so. *Whereas, who knows what this little lot will do? Erupt in glorious mutiny, probably...*

The door to the meeting hall rattles suddenly, struggling to be opened. Everyone turns to see who is causing the disturbance, no one more surprised than Robin when the glamorous, perfumed figure of Beatrice Byng, wrapped in a lavender pashmina, smiles and waves gracefully to him from the back of the room before taking a seat.

Raising his head, looking directly at her, he nods, then addresses his audience: 'Most of us would agree that it is our moral sentiments which distinguish us from animals,' he begins. 'Beasts do evil, because it is their nature to do so, whereas men aspire to do good, even as they commit evil.'

A wave of emotion passes through the room, like a wind ruffling open the pages of a book. People hug their arms and thoughts more closely to their chests, not yet ready to speak. Someone stage whispers: 'I most certainly don't agree...'

Robin pretends not to hear. He too is not yet inclined to speak; not yet prepared, that is, to speak as Robin. For the moment, he is still Professor Holderness, the well-known philosopher.

'So, what do we think of Christianity?' he asks. 'Do we expect God to protect us, both from the evil done to us and that which we do to others?'

Robin glares at them.

'Haven't seen much evidence of God recently,' someone jibes.

'Does he understand he's lecturing to a group of Humanists?' asks a large, imperious woman, dressed in a vast wrap of a dress overprinted with blue roses.

Christ, she looks like she's just walked through a bedroom wall, thinks Robin.

He feigns deafness, but at the back of his mind, a second, private voice is starting to make itself heard. *Actually, I prefer dogs to human beings.*

Looking directly at his audience, he nevertheless struggles to convey the party line: 'The orthodox Christian view is that the tendency in human beings to moral imperatives is always the result of divine intervention. What we must ask ourselves is if a moral framework, ignorant of any concept of God, would perform identically to the one we are already familiar with? That is to say, can an instinctive morality be the same as one based on either religious teaching or historical reasoning?'

He pauses. 'Put differently, can morality be purely intuitive? That is to say, a matter of feeling, rather than calculation?'

Silence.

Got you, thinks Robin jubilantly, surveying the sea of baffled faces. The intricacies of argument have defeated them.

Although, probably not for long, he reflects sadly. *Still, it's a small victory...*

He relaxes briefly, revelling in the sensation of his own authority. He knows it is his 'authority' that an audience like this both craves and yet plots to overturn. He fully expects to have to slog it out later. But for the moment, his audience is stunned.

Excellent!

'Until very recently, the Catholic Church presumed evil to exist outside ourselves, in the form of temptation. It has since reversed this to assert that evil can also come from within, despite the purification of baptism. Different cultures have different concepts of right and wrong, but the framework of polarising good with evil seems to be a human constant, and one to which Christianity adheres. The opposing view, that of the atheist, sociologist and biologist, would be that the "moral choices" we make are polarised between "aversion and desire", rather than between "good and evil". For example, most cultures have an instinctive aversion for incest, and for the abuse of the young. Most cultures also reflect a desire for comfort, peace and well-being, naming them "goodness". Although, this may be more because of their capacity to promote happiness than because of any intrinsic worth.'

'When did the Church say that?' asks a distraught-looking young man with a caste in one eye, his agitated frame bent almost double like a hairpin.

'Say what?'

'That evil is inside us?'

Chewing violently on his thumb, the young man rocks himself to and fro in his seat.

'In the early 1990s, I think, in a Papal bull,' replies Robin.

'They kept that fairly quiet, didn't they?' ruminates the young man, rocking more wildly. 'After all, it changes things quite a lot, doesn't it?'

'Yes,' agrees Robin, 'It certainly does; it means all the difference between personal and divine responsibility.'

'How bloody dare they?' erupts the young man.

Robin looks at him in surprise, his reaction so fast as to be like a flame emanating from him. Worse still, his comment immediately mobilises the rest of the audience into more unruly gear.

'Here, here...'

'Is that seriously the best you can do, Professor Holderness?' asks an elderly woman condescendingly, her querulous body shrouded in a gigantic paisley shawl, over which amber beads as big as birds' eggs string from her neck.

Robin thinks grimly: *In good tailoring, she would probably look like a man.*

The haughty lines of the woman's outrage open deep crevices in her thickly powdered face.

'How you have the indecency to come here, putting everything into simplistic terms of "this and that", I simply don't know,' she complains. 'Everything seems to be "either... or" with you. What, may I ask, do you yourself believe in... if anything at all?' she adds contemptuously.

Robin can feel his 'authority' slipping. He had hoped to hold on to it a few minutes longer. But instead of panic, his naughty second voice rises gleefully to the challenge, the old lady's defiance feeling more like a sudden reprieve than a rebuke. *Let battle commence...*

Robin, rather than Professor Holderness, now feels set free to answer her.

'I think it's probably a waste of my time talking to any of you,' he flings back at her. 'Your inability to listen properly makes you intellectually fretful. You seem to think ideas are some form of coconut shy, set up especially for you to knock down again.'

'Well,' quavers the old lady, 'I don't know when I was last so insulted.'

'That, madam, I have difficulty in believing... Your entire manner is one that invites ridicule,' asserts the newly naughty Robin.

A flurry of disturbance passes through the room. Suddenly riding to her defence, a greying man, with a Home Counties accent, says: 'We shall need the name of your superior.'

'He should be made to return the fee for his talk,' adds a plump, confident young woman, in a long grey smock over footless black leggings, beneath which sprout fetlock clumps of hair from her unshaven legs.

Robin replies triumphantly. 'There is no fee. I'm doing this of my own free will.'

'Even so, there must be someone to whom we could complain?'

Robin surveys his audience knowingly. *Not quite on the boil yet.*

He forces himself to think professorially again. 'Would you like me to go on, or shall we call it a day?'

'No, go on, of course,' orders the Home Counties man. 'Finish what you came to do, young man.'

I came to assassinate you all, thinks second-voice Robin.

'Let's see how much further we can advance these arguments before we next disagree,' states Professor Holderness firmly.

Nevertheless, he is secretly pleased, thinking brightly: *This is going to turn into a bun fight.*

His own temperament is not so dissimilar to theirs; he too lives to do battle.

'So, we have to ask ourselves whether the tendency of fathers not to sleep with their daughters is an instinct for the good, or merely an aversion mechanism that operates between parents and children, brothers and sisters; an aversion based on familiarity, rather than on any concept of right and wrong?'

Again, a tremor of suppressed feeling passes through the room.

'A distinct moral framework,' he continues, 'whether Christian or belonging to some other faith, is always in part designed to resist temptation. However, if something is not recognised as temptation, are there other constraints that will cause someone to either not want to, or choose not to do it? In which case, an individual's morality may be choices based purely on intuition and feeling... Temptation is only an issue when we have a desire to do something forbidden.'

Robin has his audience's attention again.

'Perhaps the real truth is that we all, as human beings, have a tendency to dramatise our personal feelings into storytelling exercises about our own emotions, then use them to create a reliable progression of ideas, both for and about ourselves, which allows each of us to become the hero or heroine of our own life story?'

'It's true that it is very difficult for someone to dislike himself, no matter how evil he might be,' murmurs Anya.

Robin beams at her. 'Absolutely.'

She has spoken the first sensible thing he has heard since entering the room. He senses an ally.

'In other words, we use our feelings of like and dislike to create a story that we tell about ourselves, which, once formulated, we evolve into a series of "moralising" strategies by which we reliably tackle the world. That is to say, we first turn human desire into daily ritual, then dignify it by the term "morality". The instincts that inspire these strategies may be purely instinctive, but the dogma we derive from them is the result of prolonged meditative thought. That which we call our "morality" is always the result of time spent in recollection.'

Robin glances around him; the room is now perfectly still.

'In other words, we use the man-made tool of logic to construct a story, called "morality", about the usefulness of the emotions that serve us instinctively, as they do animals... We too share an animal's instinct to withdraw from pain, flee from danger. But at those levels, emotions are kept simple, and their usefulness obvious. It is only when our instinctive or emotional responses become complex that human difficulties of morality arise. Depression, for example, can distort a man's attitude to pain. In such instances, a psychological appreciation of the virtues of pain and suffering tend to come with hindsight, rather than with the immediacy of instinct.

'We must also remember that instinct or emotion, at its strongest, can feel like an irresistible force whose appeal is entirely emotional, but which, nevertheless, allows for the sensation of knowing overwhelmingly within ourselves when something is either good or evil. It is because of this incommunicable, unanswerably strong sense of "knowing" that it can also feel in some way divine. That is to say, God given. Yielding to this highly evolved process of emotion becomes our imperative for making decisions. And so evolved, clever and complex is it, that it seems to exist outside ourselves in the form of God.

'Formalised religion would prefer to keep us forever in this suspense of our own emotions, calling it "faith"... But it too has its opponent force; not just the easily anticipated one of dogma, with its gradual brutalisation of both emotion and ideas, but the altogether unemotional one of pragmatism. Because the story we tell is ours, these highly evolved emotions and strategies, called "morality", persist only so long as they still strike us as true. If our perceptions change, we start to use our instinctive emotions all over again, to evolve new stories about ourselves.'

Robin reshuffles his notes and looks up. 'Thank you... I think, for the moment, that is all I have to say. Perhaps someone else would like to add something? I am happy to take questions.'

'Surely tea and coffee first?' someone suggests cheerfully from the back of the room.

Robin lets out a sigh. That suits him perfectly. Stepping down from the podium to hesitantly join the queue for tea and biscuits, he is immediately besieged; a knot of people surrounding him, each anxious to have his say.

'That point you made?'

'Are you sure your information is correct?' demands another.

'Have you considered this alternative view? Can you clarify your terms?'

Finally, a small, withered man of fifty asks: 'What about the Muslim threat?'

Robin knows this is his cue to disengage. Dealing with people's need to assert themselves, whether wrong-headedly or not, is one thing; dealing with their secret bigotry is another entirely. Not in the mood to tolerate a rant on Islam, his height allows him to see over the heads of his Lilliputian gang of captors. Beatrice Byng is standing nearby, talking animatedly to the young man with a caste in one eye.

'Excuse me... There's a friend of mine here to whom I must say hello.

'Beatrice... I wouldn't have thought this was your kind of thing?'

Her smile at his approach is like sunshine.

Good God, she's the only person here who looks truly happy... Although, that can't be true? Otherwise, why would she be here, in this room?

Whatever the state of Beatrice and Aubrey Byng's marriage, Robin never before having given it much thought, he does know they live a relentlessly glamorous life. Byng is famous for his willingness to accept party invitations; during weekdays, whether in Paris or London, they rarely eat at home. Beatrice, looking directly up at him, intercepts his doubts.

'Byng is in Paris, chairing some conference or other... I saw you were speaking and decided to come. I haven't heard you talk before.'

Robin looks surprised. 'I had no idea that you wanted to hear me talk.'

'Nor I, until the other evening at Bianca Johnson's dinner party. You were superb...'

Robin looks startled. 'I was extremely rude. I wrote to Bianca the following day to apologise.'

'Well, no need to apologise to me. I found you a breath of fresh air.'

Robin feels both mystified and pleased. *What is it that she wants from me?*

He had never really looked at her before. He knows, of course, that she is beautiful, but that is almost all he knows. She is Aubrey Byng's wife, yet she seems to be taking some special interest in him, as if she were suddenly intent on claiming him as her specific friend. He starts to wonder: *Where does Byng fit into all this?*

A hungry, brooding look settles on his craggy features, his eyes scanning her face remorselessly for clues.

'Are you staying for the afternoon session? I believe they have another speaker arranged for later.'

'No, it's you I came to hear.'

'Would you like to have lunch with me in that case?'

Glancing around him at the motley sea of faces, queuing for coffee and biscuits, he checks his watch: 12.15 p.m. A careless, Robin-style rapture catches up with him suddenly.

'We could leave now, if you like?'

'Don't you have to take questions first?'

Smiling slowly, his Cheshire cat grin, he says, 'Yes, unanswerable ones.'

He looks at her as if for the first time, seeing her beauty, her courage and her frailty, all in one sweeping glance.

'Why don't we go and get drunk together instead?' he suggests.

Glancing up at him painfully, a wavering look of indecision on her features, she hesitates, then raises her face to his. 'I want you to make love to me.'

'Yes, I know,' he says quietly. 'I know.'

They turn, as if in one synchronised movement, towards the door. Stretching their necks, the tea drinkers start to gobble their dismay. But Robin barely notices them. It is only the diminutive figure of Anya, who registers with him at all. She had been standing close by, listening. Her face is wet with tears. Hovering nearby, she had heard him mention a name: 'Bianca Johnson'.

As Robin and Beatrice walk out, Andreas reappears at Anya's side to comfort her. He puts his arm around her narrow shoulders, hugging her to him. He has no idea why she is so upset. Nor why he should care so. Still mystified, he says: 'Come and sit down… Maybe tell me the story of how you found the cottage? Sometimes, it helps to think of other things…'

Anya runs her hands distractedly through her hair. 'They mentioned a name I haven't heard for many years,' she half explains. 'It took me by surprise.'

Andreas looks at her astonished. 'Why didn't you say? I'll run after them, if you like? They can't have got far.'

'No, best to leave it,' she says sadly. 'It's too long ago. Another lifetime; someone I used to love.'

'A man?' There is jealousy in Andreas's voice.

Anya smiles through her tears. 'No, a girl I used to know…' She is incapable of saying, 'My daughter.'

Sitting close, Andreas watches her intently, insisting: 'Tell me about the cottage instead…'

Sluggishly, Anya makes the effort to remember. 'It was on our return journey from Dedham to Langford Grove that we first found the cottage…'

* * *

Bianca has already packed her suitcase for China. There is little more she can do, everything in the flat tidy. Picking up her mother's diary, she starts to read…

From Dedham, William and Anya had cycled to Colchester. William, already fascinated by archaeology, was intrigued by the town's origins as a Roman settlement. It excited him to think he was journeying along the same straight road from Colchester to London once marched upon by men in Roman uniform. Whereas Anya preferred pedalling slowly along the winding side roads, their intricate design fashioned from dirt tracks, intended for horse and cart. It was spring, and the landscape a never-ending celebration of ebullience. All the dwellings, whether haughtily grand houses or small cottages, hid behind hedgerows grown tipsy with their own formidable energy; all decorated with scatterings of green buds. Everywhere were new depths of green.

In the moss-cradled ditches, beneath towering hedges, grew pink campion and the swaying, filigree branches of cow parsley. Peeping above these hedgerow parapets, the blossom hairdos of apple trees seemed to laugh and wave their candelabra arms amidst storms of confetti. To cycle along these fortified pathways, meandering lazily through fields, following the direction of a stream, was like going to a party where all living things had learned to be happy. Lizards basked in the sun, their lungs expanding and contracting like a heartbeat. Field mice performed with the gentle inquisitiveness of Beatrix Potter characters. Slow worms crossed their path with silvery sluggishness, and in the woodland distance, a cuckoo sang his usurping hymn.

William and Anya deviated from the straight Roman road, along a narrow pathway, with a rotted, fallen stump of a signpost at its head, pointing towards Maldon. Initially, the path wound predictably through flat fields, until reaching a makeshift bridge across a fast-flowing stream, in which the waters were clear and reeds submerged, like hair streaming beneath its fast-running current. The flash of a trout briefly divided the waters; a kingfisher sent his shock of turquoise, darting low. At the bottom of the stream could be seen gudgeons, looking like untidy, slow-moving leaves and, above their heads, the spirited hairnet dance of minnows, spiking the water with flashes of silver. Beyond, were a mill and mill house, the first a tall clapboard structure, painted white, with gigantic wheel and sunken floors, the second, Regency red-brick;

both handsome, and with that purity of design that is at once pragmatic and beautiful.

William and Anya dismounted their bikes to dawdle over the bridge, throwing stray buttercups into the fast-running stream and delightedly watching them carried swiftly away. They then pushed their bikes up the steep hill, rising almost vertically from the mill to a miniature Gothic church and rectory, the church set back snugly from the road, amidst green arms of yew and a higgledy-piggledy graveyard of tumbling, listing stones.

They remounted their bicycles to wind their way past more fields, canopies of patchwork each shielded by leafy hedges and deep ditches; past comfortable-looking farm houses and more modest tithe cottages, disappearing behind bowers of pink cabbage roses. In the fields, silhouetted against the sun, stood men with long scythes, caps on their heads and rough tweed trousers tied at their ankles with string. They cycled past a deserted school and schoolhouse, set in a triangle of land, and up another steep hill to the Green Man pub, where happiness was a slow, silent sup of stout, imbibed beneath the watchful eye of the landlady, Mrs Perry – a woman who spread her ample, un-corseted bosom over the narrow, dark-stained counter of her snug, like fluid dough, below her severe, mask-like face. Either side of the bar, the same dark silhouettes of farm labourers as in the fields, with weather-beaten, impassive faces, drank silently, supping the dark brown liquid contemplatively. No need for speech when there was the animated chatter of the hedgerows outside?

For a few pennies, Mrs Perry agreed to put William and Anya up for the night in a creaking, badly sprung bed, its horse-hair mattress imbued with the smells of stale beer and tobacco from the bar below. At lunchtime the next day, before cycling to Langford Grove, William asked if she knew of anywhere locally to rent. She turned her masculine head towards one of the silent farm labourers, like someone consulting a dial, the process of communication between them inscrutable. No speech was swapped, yet she turned back to William with the information that the Victorian schoolhouse was empty.

'You must have passed it on your way here...'

Later that day, they met Jack Briscoe, the local vicar. The disused schoolhouse belonged to the church, or rather to a trust administered by the church. Happily, it turned out that Jack Briscoe was himself *interested in painting. Not only would he rent them the two-up two-down smaller schoolhouse but also one of its two enormous, high-raftered schoolrooms as a studio. At the farthest end of the building stood a handsome campanile, its massive iron school bell still intact.*

The key they were given to the enormous wooden school door, with its gigantic metal lock, was eighteen inches long... The house and schoolroom, set in its acre triangle of garden, at whose apex two roads met, was marked for miles around by its three tall, evenly spaced, sentinel poplar trees.

A week later, having given up their rooms in Great Titchfield Street, William and Anya moved in; delighted, but not yet really knowing the indelible significance of their new home.

This was 'the cottage'.

In future moments of thrift, Jack Briscoe often gladly accepted William's paintings in lieu of rent...

CHAPTER 13

Last minute, before locking the apartment, Bianca closes the tall wooden shutters over their front windows; a decision that takes her twenty minutes. She had even phoned Stephen on his mobile.

'Should I close them or leave them open?'

'I don't do miniature decisions,' he had replied tersely. 'I'm with the driver now; we'll be with you in five minutes.'

Putting down the receiver, she thinks crossly: *I'm drowning in busy, self-important men.*

Pale and anxious, she has not slept for days, holding her breath against the sound of the phone, worrying that Leonardo might yet call to say he is coming home early; the impossibility of explaining in detail. She sighs deeply. These are the moments she loathes her fractured life. The image of Max flits across her mind, like a promise of reprieve...

Is that seriously how I think of Max? she reproaches herself disdainfully. *As a solution to my own problems?*

She dismisses the thought. *Max is his own bundle of complexity and intrigue.*

She forces him to the back of her mind.

Waiting downstairs is a hire limousine. The driver, a debonair thug, takes her case, while Stephen glances fondly at her.

'We're on our way,' he murmurs happily.

It is the evening of their departure for China.

Only Stephen's ticket is business class, paid for by the British Council. He has agreed to be keynote speaker at a conference they are organising in Shanghai on 'Publishing and the Media'. At Heathrow, he enquires about the possibility of an upgrade for Bianca, but it is a Thursday, and their evening flight to Hong Kong is already full.

'Take my seat on the way out, and I'll travel business class on our return. By then, I'll be surrounded by British Council folk, so more complicated to explain my sitting elsewhere…' He smiles. 'That way, we get to share the luxuries.'

Looking into his amused, benevolent smiling face, the face that always seems ready to indulge her, Bianca's irritation and anxiety begin to dissolve. Although capable of a ferocious, scornful anger, designed to humiliate all that cross his path, never once has he directed that anger at her.

Gradually, over the past fifteen years, Bianca has accepted that no one ever has nor ever would love her better than Stephen does. He is forever thinking ahead, feeling in anticipation what she must feel. Despite their marriages to other people, there is a purity of certainty between them that nothing can dent. How can two people sleep in the arms of other people most nights and still keep the sensation of their love so pure and without misunderstanding? It is the question that has haunted and fascinated them to the point of wonderment. Even as he turns his head towards her, the familiar scent of his breath causes her instantly to relax.

'Has anyone told you today how handsome you are?' she asks.

His eyes crease in happiness. He threads his arm possessively about her waist.

Perhaps it was the fact that she had been at school when they first met; first love for them both? Yet he worries about her. Bianca has no idea how much. She seems so strangely far away at times; no less loving, no less passionate, but as though needing to be brought back into focus. He is depending on this trip to China.

Flirtatiously, she stretches out her left hand. 'Doesn't my ring look pretty?'

Whenever they are together, Bianca exchanges Leonardo's wedding band for the diamond eternity ring Stephen had given her for their tenth anniversary of meeting again. Then, glancing at him a little more soberly, she says, 'That business-class ticket is yours, darling, your privilege. It represents work. You should enjoy it.'

But he insists: 'No, you have it.'

Too tired to argue further, she gives in gratefully.

Their flight, through the night, takes eleven hours. The soft reclining seat cradles Bianca like a big hand. Sleeping soundly for ten hours, all her anxieties have finally reached crescendo. There is nothing more she can do but to live this moment to the full. By the time she awakens, their flight is already in descent and she feels brand new with the mystery of travel. The man sitting next to her smiles.

'You slept well.'

They have arrived at the tail end of a typhoon. As their taxi drives along the causeway and bridge into Hong Kong, visibility is poor. Palm trees bend against the boisterous wind, like hairdos unravelling. Disappearing distantly behind veils of white chiffon cloud are lines of undulating hills, gun-metal grey. Local time is now 4 p.m., eight hours ahead of London.

Their hotel overlooks the bay at Tsim Sha Tsui, their fourth-floor room luxuriously dressed in toffee-coloured silks, sufficiently low-rise to feel almost on level with the water. Leaving the curtains open, they watch the scrolled hills across the bay disappear into navy shadow, to be replaced by Hong Kong Island's night-time dance of neon.

Having showered, Stephen throws himself naked onto the bed, the elegant lengths of his tall body suddenly pale and isolated against the caramel bedspread. Holding out his arms, he asks: 'Coming for a cuddle?'

Simultaneously switching on the television, CNN's bright graphics appear.

'TV and cuddles?' she teases, joining him.

'Have you decided yet where you want to go this evening?'

Bianca smiles. He is far more tired and travelled than she is, yet it wouldn't occur to him to rest. Mock seriously, she states: 'I thought we'd just stay in and reserve all sightseeing for tomorrow...'

He looks at her askance. Bianca laughs.

'I know you... You're the man who'd rather open tins than do nothing at all.'

He smiles into the curve of her neck, his hands starting to explore her.

'That happens to be true,' he whispers, kissing her nipples into life. 'Raspberries.' He smiles, pinching her.

A voice causes Bianca to glance at the screen; the French president. Watching the wonderful mobility of his face, listening to the perfect diction and poise of his aristocratic French, she asks: 'How can a man be so very handsome, yet strangely unattractive?'

Stephen laughs.

'Don't you think him too handsome? All that harmony leaves the mind at a standstill.'

'Goodness, I'll never get used to all these sweeping generalisations of yours.'

'One likes a bit of grit,' says Bianca, smiling happily at him.

Looking shocked, he asks: 'So, where do I keep mine?'

'In your nose, mainly. There is also, of course, your big toe.'

'What's wrong with my nose?'

'Nothing, it's a little crooked, and just so beautifully imperfect.'

She glances the length of his body. His erection is like a wand, listening to every beat of her voice. She stretches out her hand to stroke its velvet skin. She knows that he wants to half make love before sailing out onto the town in a mood of sensual stupefaction. Switching off the television, his kisses become suddenly rough and urgent.

Later, starting to dress, Bianca remembers their taxi having passed the grandiosely luxurious Peninsula Hotel.

'We could go there for drinks before dinner?'

Stephen regards her a little more soberly. 'Little sybarite… Only ever the best for you. Is that not so?'

She smiles gently. 'It wouldn't be the best if I weren't with you.'

Stephen grins, but onto the screen of Bianca's mind suddenly walks Max, it feeling almost as though she might have just betrayed him. Shivering, shaking herself free of the nonsensical thought, she chides herself angrily: *What possible reason do I have for feeling any emotional responsibility towards Max?*

Threading her arm through Stephen's, she half curtseys to him. 'I'm ready to leave, darling.'

* * *

The following morning, at breakfast, the waiter delivers a copy of the *South China Morning Post*. Stephen, wearing a loosely tied bathrobe, is idly forking slices of omelette into one side of his mouth, while casually flicking through its pages. Suddenly, his expression changes to one of contempt, a strange half-smile on his face.

'Did you know about this?'

Wrestling violently with the unwieldy newspaper, he throws it down open at her feet. Dominating its centre page is a huge photo of Leonardo, accompanied by an article celebrating his new film. Bianca scans the image of her husband in dumb amazement.

'So, he's followed us to China, after all?'

The photograph shows him in classic, ponderous pose. *Poor Leonardo – how badly he photographs...*

No photographic image ever seems to match his real-life presence. Suddenly aware Stephen is watching her closely, Bianca turns the page abruptly.

'At least you can't be accused of liking a man just for his looks,' he comments disdainfully.

Bianca looks up in dismay; even after fifteen years, she has never yet been subjected to the torment of seeing photographs of Stephen's wife, Sarah, whereas photographs of Leonardo are inescapable.

She sighs, taking in Stephen's own delicious handsomeness. It is true, Leonardo is not exactly handsome, although strangely he thinks he is. But her instinct not to lie, to be fair to them both, prevents her from allowing Stephen to crow.

'No, but he can be very charming and amusing,' she says musingly. Then, observing the quick change shuttering through Stephen's glance, regrets her own honesty.

Why can't I just say what he wants to hear – that Leonardo is a vain, ridiculous braggart...

All of which would be true. But only half true... And that is the point about Leonardo. Whereas Stephen has all the qualities that go with being handsome: equable, relaxed, self-assured and eternally good-willed, plus used to charming his own way, for Leonardo life is more mysterious and therefore more polarised. With him, everything comes in pairs: very beautiful and very ugly; very intelligent and very stupid; very vain, yet also very shy. And at the centre of these paradoxes is a gem of magnificent brilliance, visible sometimes in the brown depths of his currant-bun eyes. Even with women, thinks Bianca, it is the same; for every beautiful woman in Leonardo's life, there is an ugly one lurking and plotting somewhere in the shadows. Suddenly, she remembers: *What was it, Leonardo had said the other day? Ugly women are so much more grateful.*

Bianca discards the paper beneath her chair and takes another sip of coffee, without bothering to read the article or scrutinise the smaller photographs displayed alongside the main one.

Stephen, meanwhile, starts to collect the remainder of the magazines and stray business documents he had brought with him from London. His chairmanship of five subsidiary companies, plus the running of his own successful publishing company, CERvello, means he is always drowning in paper. Bianca had never forgotten her surprise the first time they travelled to New York together. Having read each page of business documents, magazines, and even occasionally books, he tears them out, discarding them on the floor, until, by the end of a flight, there is a sea of paper beneath his feet. The few documents that survived their flight to Hong Kong, he now dumps in the hotel waste basket, adding the *South China Morning Post* to the pile.

Bianca makes no comment, but later, while Stephen takes his shower, she retrieves the article and reads it quickly. It is mostly devoted to Leonardo's current film being made with Anglo-French backing; the love story of two students, one French, one Chinese, set against the backdrop of Tiananmen Square. It goes on to list a history of his previous films, and the books he has written, mainly on the process of film-making; books which are partly technical and partly ruminative – at times, so it is claimed by his greatest fans, almost philosophical. It explores his childhood in Venice and mentions the miniature palazzo close to Siena that he and Bianca had bought early in their marriage, and where they traditionally spend the month of June. Also, the annual international master-class in script-writing and development that Leonardo runs at the palazzo against a backdrop of much entertaining of local mayors and politicians. It fails to mention the long weeks and weekends, scattered throughout the year, that Leonardo and Bianca spend more privately in Siena, catching up with Italian friends and bickering with the Mazettis, the couple who act as guardians of the palazzo whenever they are away; not to mention dealing with all the inevitable cheating that goes with absentee land-lordship.

Only in the very last paragraph does Bianca learn anything new about her husband: 'Leonardo Vescarro has recently bought a French chateau in the Loire, close to Saumur. His assistant, Mrs Laetitia Norton, is busy organising its interior design, as well as helping him on set with his current film.'

Feeling a sudden breathlessness consume her, as she gets up from her chair, Bianca knocks over her cup of coffee.

'Damn!'

She is only ever this clumsy when upset. Fury and hatred mount in her throat, catching at her breath and her thoughts in a moment of obsessive loathing; simultaneously, she remembers how inappropriately and extravagantly indulgent such emotions are right now. Stephen would any minute reappear.

With a massive act of will, she swallows hard, quelling her feelings, forcing them back down, and leaving herself momentarily blank with exhaustion. She recalls how frequently Leonardo had travelled to France recently; how, rather than join him, she had chosen to stay in London with Stephen. She has no excuse. She knows perfectly well that it is on such miniature moments of decision-making that the fates always turn. Suddenly, she feels frightened.

She glances more closely at the strip of smaller photographs, set alongside the large, main photograph in the article. One shows Leonardo in a Singapore restaurant, smiling happily, surrounded by twelve women of assorted nationality, plus just one other man, his long hair tied in a ponytail. In another, he and Laetitia shake hands with the chairman of the Bank of Hong Kong. These images just serve to confirm Bianca's irritation with Laetitia. But it is the final photograph which perplexes her most and causes her greatest alarm. In a small, postage-stamp-sized photograph at the bottom of the page, Leonardo is dancing with Solange, Nicholas Rowe's girlfriend.

Where, she wonders, *was that taken? In England or the Far East? Has he flown Solange out to join him in Singapore?*

She scrutinises the photo once more... There they are, just as she had seen them at her dinner party a few weeks earlier, locked eye to eye in intense, exclusive conversation, even as they dance. Looking closely at the photo of the twelve women in a Singapore restaurant, she tries to recognise their faces, checking to see if Solange is amongst them, but the only person she knows is Laetitia. Nor does she recognise the other man at the table, his dark, unsmiling figure next to Leonardo.

She refolds the newspaper and returns it to the bin, just as Stephen emerges from his shower. Grinning happily, the troublesome fact of Leonardo already forgotten, he starts busily planning their day; consulting guide books, checking for facts. Bianca smiles back at him, her turn to bathe, as she fights to regain her composure, wondering: *Was Leonardo ever intending to tell me about his acquisition of a chateau?*

An hour later, she and Stephen are on a fast-moving hovercraft, travelling to Hong Kong Island, over turbulent deep swell in the windblown water. Following the guide books' advice, they visit a Chinese temple, heavily fogged with the perfume of joss sticks, from whose vertiginous ceiling, spiralling almost to the floor, hangs a forest of white paper lanterns, each dangling its tail of bright red prayer label.

In quest of change, they lunch at the waterfront Western Market, opposite the Macao ferry, the only Europeans there. Waitresses circle the room, barking flat vowel commentaries and offering trays of identical dishes. Someone dumps a pot of tea unceremoniously on their table. At a separate counter, three young chefs, looking like caricatures, cook dim sum to order, the dim-sum pastry stretched and folded like sheets of muslin, before being chopped into bite-size pieces with the violent blades of hatchets.

Stephen and Bianca are lost in this fray. No one speaks English. No one cares. Yet instead of annoyed, they feel strangely peaceful; grateful, both for their own ignorance and that of the Chinese. Eventually pointing to one of the dishes on the menu, it takes another forty-five minutes to arrive, during which time they sip their tea, feeling restored by the aggressive cool of the air conditioning.

Barn-like spacious, and gaudily swaged in red and gold, the restaurant is like an English village hall, preparing for a Christmas party. A Chinese woman approaches them, placing her round, flat face two inches from theirs, then goes away giggling. Stephen smiles. 'I expect she sees us as we truly are.'

He watches Bianca carefully. She is looking a little pale. He knows she is upset about something and trying to hide it. He too has moments when he wonders why he loves her so very much. There are always things nagging at her emotionally. Not that she is ever any less loving because of them, but they seem to hold her back in some obscure way. She is like someone waiting for real life to begin, while determined to live every day at full tilt.

But what could that extra thing be?

He secretly supposes it to have something to do with her mother, Anya; the mother who has refused to speak to her for the past twenty years. Bianca was sixteen, and still at school, when he first met and fell in love with her; introduced to her by some of his fellow university students at the London School of Economics. For him, essentially, nothing has changed. He is still enchanted by her, still as attracted to her now as he was then...

It is true that, for both of them, there had been other relationships, other commitments, other loves even. For all of which he accepts full responsibility, as does she. It had been Bianca's decision, even more than his, to realise they could never build their own happiness on the embers of other people's distress; particularly not that of his own children... Yet nothing else was ever like this, equally serene and passionate; nothing else, like looking at someone and knowing it's where you finally belong. He had pretended not to notice her reaction earlier to that article on Leonardo, guessing that something in it has infuriated her.

Yet why does she care?

She is certainly not in love with her husband; there are no children of the marriage. No longer any great sexual relationship between them, as far as he knows. Yet it is as though she and he were locked in some elaborate game of romantic warfare, from which neither agrees to retreat; a game, called 'Betrayal'.

Their food arrives, interrupting his thoughts; an exquisite dish of asparagus with prawns, floating in a white glutinous sauce. More adept than Bianca at using chopsticks, observing her difficulties, Stephen thinks it unlikely, while in China, she will ever overeat. Too much like hard work.

Glancing at their watches in amazement, they prepare to leave; they have been there for two and a half hours. Outside, a towering, old-fashioned tram sways to a halt, on its way to the Star Ferry. They run to catch it.

* * *

Early that evening, Stephen has agreed to return to Hong Kong Island on his own, to meet a famous Chinese businessman. Archly, over the phone, the man had asked: 'Are you here with your wife, mistress or boyfriend?'

Stephen is reluctant, the arrangement not his but that of his sister-in-law, anxious to show off her international connections. Considering the scheme annoyingly intrusive, Stephen has refused an invitation to dinner but felt obliged to go for a drink.

Bianca, meanwhile, falls back on her London habits, putting on a dress that is a sliver of black velvet, edged with satin. On his way out, she had overheard Stephen call home on his mobile phone; a conversation full of laughter, followed by: 'Goodbye, my love.'

It was the same tone of voice in which he speaks to her.

Feeling a stab of dismay, Bianca's own feelings towards Stephen's wife had changed. Originally, she had felt guilty concern for another woman's fate; shame at her own trespass on someone else's happiness. She had tried several times to leave Stephen. But the whole thing between them was too strong, the compass of their emotions always circling back towards one another. Eventually, guilt had given way to the sensation of dealing with something beyond herself. She had shown responsibility towards the children, but Sarah was a woman too, who must either look after herself, or be looked after by Stephen. Just as she herself is committed to looking after Leonardo. Only recently, while listening to Beatrice's distress at Byng's infidelity, had some of her original guilt started to return.

As she makes herself up in the mirror, the distraught expression on Max's face as he had left her at the door of her studio, plus the more quizzical gaze he levelled at her as they parted outside the National Gallery, engulf her thoughts. She stands very still, watching the movement of her own emotions, then deliberately shakes herself free, like a spaniel emerging from water.

That night, after dining luxuriously in a room of extravagant flower arrangements and formal red lacquer, reminiscent of a David Lynch film, Stephen and Bianca switch off the lights in their hotel room, leaving the curtains open to the view. The night sky is now clear, Hong Kong Island dropping before them like a spangled counterpane. It is to the joy of this panorama that they make love. All day long, they have been peacefully companionable, absorbing, side by side, every new view, every new impression. But now, after an evening that has felt celebratory, both elegantly dressed, they are in their more familiar London mode.

The mood between them alters, accelerating fast, escalating in a matter of seconds. A sudden, urgent, passionate ferocity consumes them. Their lovemaking propels them from the bed, to the sofa, to the floor; the carpet burning beneath Bianca's back ignored. Pleasure becomes a race against time, their faces turned first to the view, then dissolved hard against one another... devouring, straining and exciting every inch of skin and touch, until they ache with one another... Sighing, they shout their ecstasy... A helicopter passes nearby, glancing in on them.

Afterwards, they fall into a deep sleep, during which Bianca dreams of her parents' cottage, of furniture left outside and men collecting it prematurely. Recognising no one, yet in a state of fury, she pushes at someone unfamiliar, who unbalances, tripping down steps into deep water. A female voice asks: 'Are you seriously going to let go of two irreplaceable men?'

At which point, Bianca wakes in a state of dread, unable to remember more. With no idea how the dream resolves, she panics... Middle of the night still. Stephen stirs in his sleep, stretching out his arm. Huddling closer, she curls herself around his back, his warmth pacifying her and persuading her back to sleep.

They awaken at 8 a.m. to find sunlight sparkling on the water; a newscaster predicting temperatures in Hong Kong reaching 90°F. After yesterday's rain, grateful for the change, they plan to spend their afternoon visiting the Peak, before catching their evening flight to Guilin.

Later, relaxing at a balcony café, overlooking the crowded airport floor, having already checked in, they are served exquisitely elaborate cakes, embroidered in pink, filigree icing. It is only forty-eight hours since their arrival in Hong Kong, yet already London begins to feel left far behind, both physically and emotionally.

* * *

As Blanca and Stephen board their Dragon Air flight to Guilin, night begins to fall. In London, it is Sunday morning. Normally, Hesketh would be at home with Bruno and Chloe on Chelsea Embankment. Instead, he is again waiting outside Bianca and Leonardo's apartment, having just discovered that, by standing a little to the left of the bus shelter, he can get an unobstructed view of Bianca's neighbours emerging from their flats onto the central staircase.

He has no specific plan in mind... He had got up early, woken by the sound of Bruno tapping out rhythms on his typewriter. Refusing Chloe's offer of breakfast, he said: 'I'm going to fetch the papers... Probably have a coffee on the way.'

But once outside, instead of walking to the King's Road, he had got into his car and started to drive. With no clear idea of where or why, he drove slowly along the Embankment, in the direction of Tate Britain. Having left his watch by the side of the bed, he has no idea of the time. Parking briefly in front of the Tate, it was early still. Instead of people streaming up and down its steps, there was only the erratic flurry of pigeons.

Filthy fucking birds... He is angry suddenly at being thwarted.

Driving on slowly towards Parliament Square, at that point unable to decide, he had driven round and round the square at a snail's pace, circling it ten times. Two policemen, standing chatting, while monitoring the gates to Westminster, tracked him lazily with their eyes; first out of amusement, then with a growing sense of alarm. Other drivers, exasperated by his slow crawl, loudly honked their horns.

Suddenly lurching the car sideways into Birdcage Walk, having driven too slowly, he accelerated dangerously fast, causing some tourists to scatter in a helter-skelter of red and blue anoraks. Driving recklessly fast now, with St James's Park to his right, he looped his way past Buckingham Palace, still with no particular plan. All this while, a distant buzzing sounded in his ears. Or perhaps his mind. He was unsure which. It was like a mild tinnitus, humming to the tune of his thoughts. And then, he remembered a voice: 'Do you imagine we've all spent our time becoming more unintelligent like you?'

Bianca... Of course, Bianca. That was what the background noise was all about. She's calling to me, pretending to be angry, so that I can hear her better...

Suddenly, his tinnitus was gone, his mind in sharp focus.

He started to drive neither too slowly nor too fast, at Hyde Park Corner stopping courteously to allow other drivers right of way before turning up Park Lane, then left along the Bayswater Road.

Parking in Kensington Garden Square, a square still bearing the scars of its bedsitter days, he then walked his thirty-degree-angled gait along Westbourne Grove. Passing a Kentucky Fried Chicken place, he remembered suddenly that he was hungry; no breakfast. Hesitating, unable to decide, he bought himself a bucket of fried chicken nuggets and sat at the bus shelter, opposite Bianca's apartment, eating them unselfconsciously, like a child with a bag of sweets, his mind again a blank. He wasn't even thinking of Bianca particularly. He had arrived at his destination and felt hungry. Everything felt simple, uninvolved. He did not even see the other people at the bus stop.

Only now, no longer hungry, does he finally raise his head to look around him, thinking: *It's nice here...*

Even the bus stop feels like home.

Bianca is just across the road...

As though they were in the same room together, he feels almost happy. Wiping his greasy fingers on the knees of his trousers, he gets up to stretch his legs. By standing to the left of the bus shelter, he can see right to the top of her building, although, only the staircase is visible. He had left his binoculars at home.

What a nice day.

Bruno and Chloe are forgotten.

I think I'll stay here for a bit.

He looks up at Bianca's windows, half expecting to see her shadow move beyond the white silk curtains. But nothing... He looks away again, neither surprised nor disappointed. Then, suddenly, as if on a timed loop, his head swings back violently. Something is different. The windows are blind, their surfaces white facades. No light enters the rooms. No one flits behind the curtains. The windows are blanked by wooden panelling, Bianca's apartment deserted. Propped at the gated entrance to the steps leading to her front door is an estate agent's hoarding, marked SOLD.

From mindless comfort, Hesketh advances into a psychopathic rage of panic. Bianca has left, sold her flat...

Without telling me...

He has no way of knowing how to find her. Knowing where Bianca lives is crucial to Hesketh's stability of mind. The sweet comfort of being near her, of standing at a bus stop and breathing in the same air, is suddenly lost. The thought burns into his mind unbearably. He starts to look around him, increasingly distraught, distractedly searching the faces of every passer-by for a clue to the truth in their eyes. They glance back in embarrassment before looking away, the steep angle of his torso ever more exaggerated. He shouts her name: 'BIANCA! COME OUT PLEASE!'

The buzzing is back in his ears, getting louder... The last thing he remembers before he falls is a leaf, as big as a hand, blowing against his face, as if to blind him.

When he comes round, a group of people is standing over him. Someone asks: 'Has he hurt himself?'

'No, I think he just fainted.'

'I've seen him before,' remarks another.

'He often hangs around this bus stop.'

'Are you alright, mate?'

Rocking himself into a sitting position, two men help him up. Yet he does not even stop to thank them. Disengaging his arms from theirs, with one last scandalised look at the blank shutters, Hesketh stumbles away in the direction of his car.

It takes another forty minutes to find; of his walking bewilderedly around the streets, pointing his automatic key at each car, waiting for one to respond. He cannot remember where he left it. Even when he finds it, he just sits vacantly for half an hour.

Will I need to resort to private detectives again in order to find her?

He does not yet have a plan.

Might one of her neighbours know where she is?

He can't think, can't decide.

Suddenly, the shrill sound of his mobile phone interrupts him – Chloe, asking, 'Where are you?'

'I'm here,' he replies unthinkingly, 'where I always am…'

Chloe can hear the sob in his throat. 'Come home,' she orders, adding almost sternly. 'Get back here now…'

Hesketh hears her voice as if from miles away.

'Where is home? I can't remember where we live?'

'For God's sake, Hesketh, Bruno needs you.'

'Bruno!' It is the magic word. Hesketh remembers everything; all is bright focus again. He starts the engine.

'I'll be right there…'

* * *

Max is no longer in Dublin. Having spent a few indulgent days in the magnificent opulence of the Grafton Hotel, while overseeing last-minute rehearsals for his play at the Abbey Theatre, it had opened the previous night to glorious reviews. He is now escaping luxury and celebrity for the more rugged truths of the south, around Bantry Bay, its coastline as unpredictable as torn lace. For a month, maybe two, he has borrowed Wessex Island from a friend, who, having bought it as a retreat, uses it little.

Flying from Dublin to Cork, he was met by Sinead, the island's caretaker, for the further two and a half hours' drive to Skibbereen.

'Sinead,' his friend had warned him, 'is a sports-loving, daredevil young woman with abundant energy, who treats momentary flirts with danger as necessary affirmations of the life force.'

'I don't really know the south,' confides Max.

'Do ye not?'

Smiling privately, she registers his eclectic get-up of red baggy trousers, green-and-gold leather trainers and the white double-breasted jacket around which he has wrapped a Hermès shawl. Plus, of course, his head – that explosion of contradictory planes, the violent landscape of Bianca's portrait of him.

Nevertheless, he's attractive, she thinks.

'Did you think to bring Wellington boots?'

Max looks astonished. 'No, I'm afraid not.'

'We'll get you some in Skibbereen.'

They drive south in her four-by-four, the vast car swaying along the curves in the road like an overweight beast of burden.

'I miss the speed of my previous car,' she says, apropos of nothing.

Max smiles, taking in her lack of ceremony, her indifference to his fame. *I shall like her...*

He is already beginning to like Ireland. Every small town, every village they pass through is a masterpiece of intimacy. Stone cottages, offset by brightly painted doors, jostle next to the idiosyncrasy of individual shops – some old-fashioned drapers' stores; others, butchers and bakers. But all independent, private businesses, with the pride and optimism such enterprise entails; all simultaneously declaring their cosy indifference to big-time society, their preference for life in miniature. As they pass through Kinsale, Sinead asks: 'Do we stop for lunch?'

Parking, they enter the low-beamed interior of a pub, advertising hot dishes, such as steak and kidney pie and fish and chips; a country pub like any other, except that their entrance is met with such warm interest; in every face, turned in their direction, is genial welcome.

'Don't be looking at the menu, now,' says the landlord. 'We've got some fine, fresh sardines. Have them fried and ready for you in just a tic of a minute.'

Sinead and Max both smile their assent.

'Will it be bread and butter or chips you'll be wanting?'

They sit in the corner by the fire, nursing their drinks.

'How long have you worked for Peter?'

'Three years… although now only part-time. When we were setting up the island, there was much more to do. In the winter, we now mostly close it down.'

'October soon… Doesn't that count as winter?'

'We'll see. There's been plenty of sunshine these past two weeks… What is it you do?'

'I'm a playwright.'

'Comedies?'

Max smiles. 'No, not exactly.'

Their sardines arrive with a newly baked brown loaf, still warm from the oven, and lashings of pale butter. Changing the subject, Max smiles again, relishing her indifference and remembering last night's opening party; the schmoozing actresses fawning over his every word, desperate glints of ambition in their eyes.

What a relief not to have to explain myself.

'Let's eat,' he says enthusiastically. 'These look delicious.'

'They are so.'

Sinead bites into a slice of bread, leaving an imprint of her front teeth in the generous spread of butter. For no reason, Max laughs… This is what he was hoping for – freedom from sophistication. At least for a while. Thinking of Bianca, as he does each day, he wishes he could speak to her, wishes he knew exactly where she was. But in her absence, he is glad to be as inaccessible to her as she is to him. It feels more equal. Plus he knows that absences between two people need to be lived to the full. That otherwise true reunion is impossible. And that, more than anything, is what he wants – to again witness the adorable flight of passion and uncertainty across Bianca's face.

CHAPTER 14

Still distraught when he gets back to Chelsea Embankment, the morning has left Hesketh feeling wounded.

How dare Bianca humiliate me like that. By moving away without warning?

He considers it an abuse of some abstract code of rules between them, as though she were no longer playing their game fairly.

Waiting anxiously, Chloe is sitting on the floor by the lift next to Bruno, who, with his face turned from hers, is knitting furiously.

Why, she wonders, *is Bruno happy to knit in bright blue wool, yet refuses to embroider in anything but shades of pink?*

Her world is one of impenetrable mysteries; the mystery of a son who won't communicate and the mystery of a husband whose mind is falling into disrepair from attempting to communicate too much. Yet instead of more fragile, with each new disappointment, her world feels ever more certain, as though sheer complexity were welding it for all time into a dense pattern of need. Nor does it ever seriously occur to her to leave Hesketh. She glances tenderly at Bruno, his hands locked in a delirious rhapsody with the knitting needles.

It's because of Bruno that I stay.

Yet secretly even she knows that not to be true. Really, it is because of Hesketh. She cannot give up their relentless, dizzy lovemaking. It is her daily spoonful of happy oblivion. The rest is all hard work, but punctuated by the blissful rhythmic reassurance of orgasm; her last and first thoughts in an otherwise busy day.

Raising his head to listen, Bruno has heard the collapsing wheeze of the lift doors, five floors below. He smiles in secret pleasure. His father is coming home. Chloe watches him in profile.

Will he always be this beautiful, my clever son? How, she wonders wistfully, *to capture those special looks of his for all time?*

Bruno refuses to be photographed.

The lift gets closer, its dumb-waiter interior creaking breathlessly to the top. As the grille doors open, Hesketh stumbles and sprawls at their feet. It has taken all his strength just to arrive. The speed of Bruno's knitting slows, his head turned briefly towards the fallen figure, struggling incapable on the floor.

Startled, Chloe asks: 'Have you been drinking?'

Suddenly, Bruno's small frame starts to hyperventilate wildly, whimpering, animal sounds choking his throat. He cannot breathe.

Chloe scrambles to her feet. Lifting Bruno bodily, she deposits him at the door to his room, with his back to them. Emitting a prolonged, desperate cry, his body nevertheless grows quiet beneath her touch... It is important Bruno does not witness his father in this state. Being close by, even listening to him sob, are more or less okay. But forcing him to watch Hesketh in physical disarray can only bring chaos.

Hesketh appears to have aged at least twenty years since breakfast. Kneeling beside him, Chloe asks: 'What on earth has happened to you?'

There is a trickle of blood from his left ear to his collar. Looking at her blankly, silent tears streak his cheeks. The planes of his face have rearranged themselves into a distraught crazy paving. Only his beautiful mouth is strangely composed over its graveyard of fallen teeth, the whites of his eyes shot with bulbous veins of yellow. Chloe places a finger tenderly in the hollow of one eye to wipe away a tear. Still he cannot see her properly. Words yawn incoherently in his throat.

'Let's get you to bed,' she says gently. 'You can tell me later.'

He allows her to lead him stumbling through their large square room, past Bianca's painting, into their bedroom. The golden Buddha flashes a semaphore at him in the afternoon sun. Behind them, music suddenly plays fast and loud, snatches of Rachmaninoff engulfing them.

'Bruno?' asks Hesketh breathlessly, his eyes immediately more focused.

Chloe nods in reply. 'He's so very beautiful... our son. I wish he'd let us photograph him. I want to always be able to remember how handsome he is... He's like you,' she adds gently.

Still trembling, Hesketh reaches to undo the top button of her blouse. She glances at him. He is suddenly her creature again. So swift, the change, she could not have tracked its movement. The music plays louder, and she and Hesketh are suddenly that knot of ecstatic sculpture which haunts their bedhead, the bronze of the sculpture made flesh in the fierce sprint of their lovemaking. Briefly, they belong to one another. No doubts, no Bianca, not even Bruno; just the joy, the music and the urgency to race one another, she always slightly ahead of him. As she waits for him, feeling his body speed and strengthen against hers, hearing him shout her name, feeling him dissolve, a sudden thought occurs to her of how to capture Bruno's beauty for all time...

Hesketh rolls onto his back besides her.

'Feeling better?'

He smiles. 'Much better.'

He looks around the room, noting all the familiar objects, glancing fondly from their great platform of a bed towards the golden Buddha. He feels spent, peaceful.

'I wonder where Bianca's hiding,' he murmurs, as he falls into a deep, deep sleep.

* * *

The Sunday following Robin Holderness's talk, Andreas is again at the bus stop, waiting to accompany Anya to Queen Square. Looking into the eyes of this young man, she feels both flattered and mystified. He reminds her of someone she once knew.

But who, exactly?

Something familiar in the long, lean lengths of his body? She hesitates. *How much should I tell him of my past?*

A memory hovers elusively at the edge of her mind. She knows he is attracted to her in some obscure way; to her personality most probably, her vivacity and looks maybe. But could it also be sexually?

Surely not? Why would so young a man be interested in such an old lady?

Nevertheless, his eyes settle on her in undisguised hunger. Despite the great difference in their ages, it is a look she recognises only too well. She has provoked it in the faces of men all her life. She turns away from the intimacy of his scrutiny, trying to remember...

Should I tell him everything?

'At the beginning of the war, William and I remained at the cottage. William had declared himself a conscientious objector and was sent before a tribunal in Cambridge, where they asked him what he would do if he saw a German fornicating with his wife?

'"Nothing," he replied.

'Perhaps foolishly, he dreamed of being allowed to stay at home. Painting was already everything. Not just pleasure, but a deeply felt private mantra, far beyond any concept of either pacifism or patriotism... Instead, he was sent to Liverpool, where fast asleep one night in a school requisitioned for barracks, a bomb exploded nearby, causing a railway sleeper to erupt from the ground and come hurtling through the school roof, crashing to the ground in the narrow space between himself and the conscript next to him; the other man, a brave, bullish, elegant homosexual called Tanderelle, who simply turned over in his bunk, declaring, "What a perfect fucking nuisance," before going straight back to sleep again.

'But for William the threat had seemed real. He recanted his objections and joined the Royal Scots Engineers, initially as a private and later as corporal.

'Soon after that, he was put on a troop ship, bound for Cairo, where he entered a world he expected to hate. Yet the reverse turned out to be true; instead, finding himself part of a richly jumbled camaraderie of men from every stratum of society, all set to the hilarious background cabaret of a rebellious troop of Southern and Gordon Highlanders...

'"I hope you appreciated the eggs and bacon at breakfast this morning, chaps?" an officer would enquire politely.

'"Fuck off," they chorused in unison.

'The Highlanders hadn't seen any bacon and eggs.

'Among his fellow English recruits were Christopher Robin, A.A. Milne's son, plus a tall, haunted skinny man who could take the poetic rhythms of Thomas Wyatt and transform them into a poetry of his own. William quickly forgot the man's name but kept the drawing he made of him, and always remembered every single line of his poetry, learned on that troop ship.

'Once in Cairo, there were further unexpected joys. William was assigned to the British Embassy under the banner of Camouflage. With his knowledge of typography and painting, he was employed to create posters for the Ministry of Information. So, instead of the nightmare of battle, he was granted the luxury of time to make friends and, above all, to paint. And like so many Englishmen before him, he found himself falling in love with the life, beauty, and gentle manners of Arabia. Stationed in Maadi, a district of elegant villas, embassy buildings and avenues of pepper trees, from there he would cycle along the banks of the Nile and cross by ferry to Sakkara. In fact, only once throughout the entire war did he use his rifle. He fired at a jeep that failed to stop at a checkpoint. No one was hurt. But, ridiculously, it was one of the army's own jeeps, and for that he was put on a charge.'

Pausing in her tale, Anya looks sad suddenly. A wave of nostalgia engulfs her. She can still remember how it felt to be left alone and lonely at the cottage, plus the moment she had never forgotten of having to say goodbye to William at Rivenhall Station. Even now, all these years later, she can still feel the fear, the terrifying, distraught joy of holding that love in her hands so completely and never wanting to let go.

She looks up, surprised, into the probing eyes of the young man sitting beside her.

Perhaps it's doing me good to talk?

She continues: 'After William left for the Middle East, I joined the Land Army and was given just two lessons before being left on my own to drive a milk float. Getting up early to deliver the milk, I often drove the float straight into a ditch. I become a connoisseur of apples: Golden Russet, Cox, Grieves and Bramleys... I could recognise them all. In those days, East Anglia was a land of orchards, the blossom blowing over the hedgerows into our garden like confetti.

'I deliberately kept myself busy. George, one of my brothers, brought his wife and daughter to stay at the cottage as evacuees, and I ran up whole wardrobes of clothes for them on my treadle sewing machine. But I was still desperately lonely for William. He sent me letter cards from Cairo, beautifully decorated with pressed flowers, and maybe including a small painting or sketch he had done, along with sweet words of "Missing You". But they took weeks to arrive and were never frequent. My life felt at a standstill; emotionally, I began to feel like an amputee. I had been a Londoner and now suddenly my life was in miniature; that of a tiny, sparsely populated village, set in farmland, against a Constable sky. I remember, in one of my letters to William, inventing having seen an adder, just to make my letter seem more interesting. Then, a few days later, having posted it, actually seeing one, exactly as I had described – as though I had conjured the creature into life.

'Whenever I could, despite the bombing, I visited my mother, sister and brothers, in London. And a year later, almost on a whim, applied for my services to the war effort to be used elsewhere. I was interviewed for the job of warden, but instead my form was marked: "VGT".

'"What does it mean?" I asked.

'"Very good type," the interviewer replied.

'As a result, in 1944, I was asked if I would be willing to fly to Paris, to work for the American forces, following the Liberation. They needed someone to interview people in Paris for jobs with the Americans. It was a wonderful, extraordinary opportunity. France, after the occupation, had been left desperately poor, the Americans the only people in Paris with any money. Everyone wanted to work for them. They flew me to Le Bourget in a military aircraft without seats, only straps to hang on to, and set me up in a flat on the Left Bank, in the rue de l'Université.

'At work, I began the task of sifting through endless queues of applicants, people of all types, my days spent interviewing writers, entrepreneurs, businessmen, refugees and members of the French aristocracy. At night, I would go dancing with colleagues at Le Boeuf sur le Toit or join friends at the Folies Bergère. The French were still smarting from the humiliations they had suffered at the hands of the Germans. But I watched them also now suffer differently from some of the thoughtless, boisterous arrogance of my Americans colleagues. At the Folies Bergère, American soldiers, high on Jack Daniel's, would use their cigarette lighters to set fire to the scanty costumes of the waitresses, which, due to post-occupation scarcity, were made mostly from paper.

'And just once I saw an American GI empty his lavish pack of Lucky Strikes onto a pavement and laugh cruelly as desperate Parisians scrabbled in the dirt to pick them up. How one proud beauty of a girl spat in his face, grinding the cigarettes into the dust with her heel. The look of shock on the GI's face…'

Anya glances out of the bus window, then into Andreas's brown eyes. That same intense look, watching her still.

'We have almost arrived.'

'Will you tell me the rest of the story, later at tea…?'

She nods, looking dazed and a little shy.

'I wonder what this fellow, Aubrey Byng, will have to say for himself? I often read his articles in *Le Figaro*.'

He smiles. 'Surely anyone would be an improvement on Robin Holderness last Sunday…'

Looking stricken suddenly, Anya turns her face away. She still remembers the familiar ease with which he had mentioned the name Bianca Johnson.

* * *

At that precise moment, Bianca and Stephen are disembarking from their Dragon Air flight to the southern China town of Guilin. It is already evening.

The following morning, at Mopanshan Pier, a flotilla of decorative, charmingly old-fashioned, double-decker river buses await their daily quotas of tourists at the start of the famous Li River cruise. Stephen and Bianca step nimbly from the stern of one to another, until reaching the seventh, which is theirs.

The four-hour cruise to Yangshuo unfurls itself in drifting linear repetition, its lingering rhythms broken only by small moments of theatre, as in a Chinese scroll painting. The first of these that of the tethered cormorants, flapping over their prey like disabled umbrellas. The day is cool and a bit misty; ideal for this landscape of 'karsts', the sugar-loaf mountains of Chinese legend, which require qualities of fogged, misted light, and the low-lying chiffon clouds that obscure their summits to render them identical with the language of Chinese painting.

Stephen and Bianca stand on the upper deck, silently, not touching, conscious of the offence displays of physical affection between couples can cause. Yet relishing sharing the discovery that a landscape of such superimposed depths upon depth of diffuse shadow and stillness should exist. They glance at one another and smile. These are the moments in a relationship that cannot be undone. Taking out a sketch pad and small palette, Bianca prepares to sketch in watercolour. She had not anticipated the sheer abundance of it – of hills developing from other hills, like twins, while others rise from the ground independently, tall and solitary, their sides so steep that the delicate lattice of river-walk pathways, interlacing them, are no longer navigable. Bianca's watercolour technique, rapidly suggestive and delicate, swiftly conjures views as monochrome pale and elusive as breath, very different from the slow investigative drama of her portraits.

Stephen watches her work, admiring the deft authority with which she wields her brush, the way she works from light to dark, allowing the white of the paper to illuminate her sketch. Moving from one page to the next, she performs conjuring acts as light as soufflés. He marvels at the accuracy of her eye, her capacity to see and respond in the immediacy of a breath. It is the same concentrated quality that he loves in her lovemaking – her capacity to make every minute count in the accumulated brushstrokes of their shared sensuality.

Yet why do I currently feel alarm? he wonders. *Why does she feel both so wonderfully present, and absent, all at the same time?*

He cannot fathom it, but, nevertheless, interprets it as a threat. *Almost as though I were jealous. But of what? Certainly not of Leonardo.*

Sensing his gaze upon her, Bianca looks up and smiles. 'Are you alright, darling?' she asks.

'I am, if you are.'

'One more sketch, and then we'll have lunch.'

'Is Matthew planning to show these at the gallery?'

'He might, if he likes them enough.'

Bianca shrugs. She barely cares what Matthew does with them. Her thoughts return to Max.

I seem to be carrying him like surplus luggage, she thinks moodily. *Yet, more than anything, I simply want to forget him.*

At 1 p.m. they land at Yangshuo, to be presented at the quayside with carnival gifts of brightly coloured silk balls... It feels like enchantment.

* * *

Max's first glimpse of Wessex Island is in the late afternoon sunshine. Stopping in Skibbereen to shop for Wellington boots, and offered a choice between old-fashioned black and bright sunshine yellow, Max had chosen the yellow ones, Sinead and the shopkeeper exchanging secret smiles as he tried them on over his red harem pants.

'Sure they'll do now?'

Max nodded unselfconsciously, like a child absorbed in the act of just being. In another shop, Sinead bought local cheeses to add to the hamper of provisions already in the boot of her four-wheel drive.

Driving the short distance to Bantry Bay, Sinead's big beast of a car seems to tumble down the narrow, high-hedged, winding track to the torn lace edge of the coastline. As the afternoon sun turns pink-gold, she parks beside a nondescript white bungalow and toots her horn. From it emerges a fisherman of thirty-five or so, his movements as lean and agile as a cat's, but with the face of a seventy-year-old, the skin on his face flayed to toughened leather by its daily punishments of wind and surf.

'How are ye, Jack? Will ye be coming down to help me launch the boat now?'

The young man nods shyly. Max watches him with interest, the man's fleet body movements suddenly overcome by sluggish uncertainty.

He's attracted to her...

Max notes the way Jack has pulled the southwester from his crown and stands holding it crumpled into a fist at his chest.

In fact, it's worse – the poor man's in love with her...

He turns his attention to Sinead, who is doing her best to act as an honorary man. No physical task beyond her.

She has no idea of his feelings, Max observes delightedly.

A new drama unfolding before his very eyes, he starts to watch them both more sharply.

Agreeing to follow them in his car, Jack tows the large pneumatic dinghy that is Sinead's only access to the island behind him. At the water's edge, a small gang of locals gather to watch them ease it into the surf and secure it with ropes.

They all know each other. Yet they couldn't be more different, thinks Max. *It must be the sea that unites them.*

His own glance searches out the distances across the bay, the pink sun slipping lower, painting the sky red, as it falls. Jack stands next to him knowingly.

'Early sunshine tomorrow... But there's a sinful breeze about. Could be a storm,' he declares emphatically.

'Would you rather put up in a bed and breakfast for tonight and see how the weather is in the morning?' asks Sinead, looking directly at Max.

Max has no idea how to answer; there is nothing beyond the charm of the journey to guide him. As his eyes scan the horizon, he longs to be there, but has no clear idea of the conditions. Nor of what they will find. Sinead smiles broadly. She thinks he is like her, in love with danger.

She's almost beautiful when she smiles...

Max interprets her look as though she had spoken out loud.

'No, I'm not particularly brave, but I like the business of arriving... never wanting the momentum of a journey to be broken.'

'If we hurry,' she says, 'we might just get there before the wind.'

She and Jack busily load the boat, then help settle Max in the front, next to her. Jack starts up the powerful motor.

'Now, will ye be coming to dine with us tomorrow evening, Jack?' shouts Sinead above the wind.

Jack nods, looking both eager and shy.

'Come for tea, and we'll walk the island first,' she says, waving him goodbye.

Settling herself squarely, Sinead starts the engine. Max is amazed by the springing speed of the dinghy as it leaps forward to challenge the water, before raising its nose to ride the spray. Tacking from side to side to avoid the shallows, they are then in open water, and Max experiences the sheer exhilaration of skimming the waves. He looks at Sinead in surprise; her smile matches his. This is the excitement she craves, throwing the dice of her energies in the face of nature.

God, how different all this is from the refined suffocation of London...

He has come here to write... But for the first time, it occurs to Max that maybe he had come here to live.

They disembark in the half-light. Sinead secures the boat to the island's narrow shelf of a jetty and throws a complex net of red ropes over the slanting rocks, with their bank upon bank of slippery teeth. Skidding against the mud and stones of the pathway leading to the island's three dwellings, they need several journeys to collect all their belongings.

Using a torch, Sinead runs around the exterior of the buildings, opening shutters and igniting the boiler. Stepping into a kitchen with red flagged floor tiles, the warmth is almost instantaneous. As Sinead prepares a log fire, Max looks around him, feeling, for the first time that day, at a loss; aware, suddenly, of their isolation, of the impenetrable, alien darkness beyond the windows, of the sheer unfamiliarity of the place. From having been so certain of his destination, he cannot now find his place in it.

Appraising him, Sinead says vaguely: 'Don't worry. Tomorrow all will be clear.'

What can she mean?

The following morning, as he draws his curtains, Max sees, for the first time, the white crests of waves dancing towards the island, beneath a sky that hurries after them with a coverlet of grey cloud; outside the window, against the roar of the wind, the faint, soft bleating of goats, congregating in shelter. They sense a storm brewing. Their soft muzzles jostle one another, blowing patterns of breath on the glass.

The island's three dwellings are single-storey, stone-built crofter's cottages, arranged in three arms of a quadrangle. After a supper of toast and pate, in the kitchen of the main building, Sinead had shown Max into the second dwelling, consisting of a large white-washed bedroom, and beyond it, a Spartan bathroom and shower, its only window a wide letterbox rectangle, placed low on the wall. Having drawn the curtains, Max retreats back to bed, snuggling beneath the heavy blue-green patchwork quilt to enjoy the view; the window's glorious framing of the sea, plus the soft, soothing bleating of the goats. As he looks around the sparsely furnished room, his earlier panicked sense of dislocation dissolves. Noticing a rudimentary pine writing desk, tilting precariously in one corner, he begins to know what he must do. Showering, getting dressed and pulling on an old moth-eaten, cable-knit sweater, he crosses the courtyard to the main house and knocks timidly on the door.

But Sinead is already up, a fire blazing in the kitchen as she cooks their breakfast of bacon and eggs.

'Did ye sleep beautiful and well now?'

'Dreamlessly.'

'Will it be just two eggs or three?'

Max laughs happily. 'I think perhaps just one is enough, don't you?'

* * *

They have been given a first-floor room in the Dujia Fandian, Yangshuo's most luxurious hotel, nestling at the base of the tall karst that dominates the town. Perched at its summit, like a forgotten Christmas decoration, is a miniature temple. Built around a courtyard garden, the hotel is spaciously serene, its sweeping foyer boasting life-size photos of the many world leaders who had stayed there: Nixon, Clinton, Mao Tse Tung, Mitterrand... Kissinger too.

Only from their bathroom window is the actual street life of Yangshuo revealed. An old man, his features as crumpled as tissue paper, fishes from his narrow balcony into the stream below; swags of laundry, incapable of drying in the monsoon humidity, drape from every surface. Yet Stephen and Bianca watch fascinated as, from these hovels of dwellings, a man emerges, pristinely smart, in pressed white shirt and black slacks.

'This is like Italy… the creed of *la bella figura*,' Bianca says, smiling.

They are still only three days into their trip, three days from the familiarity of London, but already the strangeness and joys of difference are stretching their consciousness of time. London has ceased to exist. Only its people remain: Sarah, the children, Leonardo and Max. But even they at a blurred distance. Bianca and Stephen are increasingly in their own separate cocoon of togetherness; less romantically fierce than in London, maybe, yet enthusiastically side by side, observing it all.

They even start to look different; younger, less *soigné*. Stephen wrestles a navy jumper over his jeans, this his weekend uniform that Bianca normally never witnesses, his smart city clothes all chosen by her. The jumper writhes in corkscrews about his arms.

She laughs. 'Would you like me to unstring you?'

His eyes dance in amusement. 'I chose this jumper myself.'

'Yes, I can see that,' she remarks flatly.

He catches her in his arms, kissing her greedily. 'I'm still me,' he breathes into the dab of perfume at her neck. 'Shall we go back to bed?'

Bianca laughs, glancing frowningly over her shoulder at the twin hardboard cots they had slept on beneath clouds of spun-silk duvet.

'Good for backs,' the woman at reception had said. Although, it had hardly felt so.

Glimpsing herself in the mirror, she hardly recognises herself, her long blonde curls crimped into a riot of frizz in the monsoon damp.

'I look like a ragamuffin.'

Stephen rests his arm about her shoulders, sharing her reflection. 'More like a slightly chaotic, beautiful teenager,' he comments. 'Let's go.'

They hire two bikes for 80p; years since Bianca last cycled. She feels nervous of the traffic, fanning randomly from every junction in great billowing drifts. But suddenly the town is left behind for open countryside, and all the joys of cycling return. It starts to rain; a light mist, soon a gently penetrating downpour. But it only adds to their exhilaration as they ride past scenery similar to that seen from the boat. Although now, on either side, are paddy fields, the rice yellow and ripe, some of it already harvested into dollies.

Reaching the Banyan Tree Bridge, they rest a few minutes. Immediately, as if from nowhere, a swarm of nut-brown women surrounds them, smiling toothless grins and imploring them to buy bangles and postcards. Bianca and Stephen smile and say: 'Buha.'

The women laugh happily.

Riding on further towards their destination, Moon Hill Mountain, they are again greeted by a flurry of women, eager to make money.

As Stephen and Bianca begin the hill's steep climb, four of the women follow, the younger two prancing energetically back and forth before them, practicing their staccato English.

'What is your name? How Do YOU DO?'

Their enthusiasm, combined with the steep climb, proves exhausting. Eventually, Stephen turns on them more viciously, insisting: 'Buha... Buha... BUHA.'

Startled, they retreat, but the two older ladies are both more tactful and tenacious. Diplomatically dropping behind and speaking more quietly, they nevertheless keep coming. The mountain steps are well made but very steep. Bianca stops for breath. The two older ladies stop too, monitoring her progress with practised eyes. Turning to smile at them, they grin widely in reply. This is not an activity for conversation but one for intense concentration. Stage by stage, they almost reach the top; hotly perspiring now, out of breath, but elated. A great arc of stone rises above their heads, while the landscape stretches far below them in a miniaturised patchwork of yellow and green fields, many thousands of feet below. They look back, astonished at how far they have climbed.

As always, Stephen is ambitious to go higher still, to squeeze every last drop from every experience, the path, at this final stage, almost vertically steep and muddy. Bianca's shoes fail to grip, and she slips uncontrollably from stone to stone. The younger of the two ladies advances to help her, taking her elbow, Bianca immediately struck by the implicit strength and grace of her touch. Stephen, ahead of her, stretches out his hand to help.

'Come along, darling. It'll be worth it. Just a few steps more.'

But Bianca skids helplessly onto her knees in the mud, whose colour, until now, she had not really noticed. It is bright brick red.

With one last effort, they find themselves at the top of the world, with nothing but pearl-coloured air above them. Bianca and Stephen pant joyously, waiting for their breathing to subside, while the Chinese ladies, not remotely out of breath, busily pick fronds of leaves and, softly cooing, all laughing now, scrape the mud from Bianca's palms as though she were a baby.

The landscape unfolds beneath their feet like a map. As the Chinese ladies build cushions of leaves for them to sit on, Bianca takes a miniature sketchbook from her pocket, preparing to paint... For no reason, she suddenly remembers a sliver of dream she had last night, of Hesketh walking right past her, his face full of laughter – his presence so graphically clear it had been like watching a film; her own limbs sluggish with panic.

'What's wrong, darling?' Stephen has noticed her sudden change of expression. 'What is it?'

'Hesketh appeared in my dream last night.'

Stephen looks out distantly across the landscape, his eyes suddenly as pale as ice.

'That shabby bastard... Forget about him.'

'This is the second cinematic dream I've had since we arrived. I don't normally dream this often,' she says, remembering her dream in Hong Kong.

'It's the Malarone,' replies Stephen. 'The side effects of our malaria pills.'

Bianca sighs, forcing herself to concentrate. Thoughts of Hesketh are like a disease, requiring quarantine. Picking up her brush, she dips it in a puddle, her hands still shaking, while the Chinese ladies laugh delightedly to see the muddy water turn Prussian blue.

For half an hour, silently, almost reverently, they watch Bianca paint, occasionally tiptoeing to glance over her shoulder; Bianca working rapidly, until four small sketches are completed. As she puts down her brushes, negotiations begin.

Would they like to buy a canned drink for £1.50?

'Buha.'

Do they have any spare English coins to give them?

The two women hold their breath, beneath Stephen's disapproving eye, as Bianca awards them each £5 in single coins.

'All you're doing is wrecking their economy by making begging more attractive than work,' he objects.

'Don't you consider this work, clambering up and down mountains all day? Besides, what jobs, or fractions of jobs, are available to them?'

Whenever she and Stephen travel, they always quarrel over this business of tipping. She thinks being generous the least they can do. He dislikes the low cunning expectations of it; the sense of being taken for a fool. Sensing his disapproval, the older Chinese lady delivers a bitter stream of invective. But the younger one, in the purple jumper, is happy. She and Bianca smile, already good friends.

'Do you want to go to the Dragon Caves?'

'Buha.'

Descending the mountain together, as they say goodbye, the women's eyes are already distantly focused on a busload of tourists just arriving.

Retracing the eight kilometres to Yangshuo, by which time the rain has stopped and their clothes, although mud-caked, more or less dry, instead of returning to the hotel, they decide to cycle straight on to the village of Fuli; this new direction more uphill, the landscape less beautiful, both soon starting to feel saddle-sore.

* * *

Straggling behind Stephen, fifty yards ahead of her, Bianca finds herself remembering the ostentatious watch, with its multitude of dials and facets of gold, that had glistened on Leonardo's wrist the evening of their dinner party in London.

Are the watch and the chateau connected in some way? she wonders.

Switching thoughts to La Casa, the home in Siena, where she and Leonardo had always been happiest, she asks herself: *Will owning a chateau unbalance that happiness in some way? Is Leonardo planning to sell the house in Siena?*

It is not fear she feels exactly. Being in China with Stephen, and so distant from their everyday lives, is itself a form of immunity. But she does feel alarmed.

Are our lives finally starting to unravel?

For years, she has lived daily with the half expectation of change, the sense that their lives might eventually prove untenable. But only now does its harsh reality strike her.

With Stephen cycling ahead, Bianca is grateful to linger behind with her thoughts. Something is nagging at her, something beyond her occasional, annoying preoccupation with Max.

Suddenly, she recalls an incident in London ten days earlier, just before Leonardo left for Singapore. They had met at his office in Beak Street, on their way out to dinner together; one of Leonardo's favourite amusements, to discover forlorn, empty restaurants and sit in their windows, gleefully watching the place fill up around them, while giggling at his own charismatic effect.

'We must look especially respectable.'

That night, they were planning to eat at a restaurant just off Piccadilly.

Walking arm in arm past the tall, wrought-iron gates of the Royal Academy, the pavement was suddenly crowded, forcing them to separate into single file. Bianca walked ahead, turning a few paces later to check on Leonardo's progress, only to find that he had been accosted by a squat, heavily made-up woman, dressed in a lavish fur coat.

A friend, someone from abroad maybe? she mused, happy to wait.

She is used to people accosting Leonardo in the street. The woman, waving her cigarette in Leonardo's face, was smiling teasingly at him.

Surely only an Italian woman would dare wear such a fur coat in Piccadilly?

Leonardo, meanwhile, was smiling and bowing deferentially.

Noticing he had shrugged on his overcoat so casually that it sat right back off his shoulders, as though still containing a coat hanger, Bianca smiled in secret pleasure; these, the ridiculous details she so loved in her husband.

Just as she had decided to retrace her steps and join him, a young Slavic woman with platinum hair intercepted her, demanding to know the way to Green Park. Turning from her view of Leonardo, Bianca responded graciously, pointing the way further west along Piccadilly. At first, appearing not to understand, the young woman engaged her in ever more elaborate directions, asking increasingly nonsensical flurries of questions, while gesticulating wildly, seemingly determined to deter her every attempt to turn back towards Leonardo. Initially responding with cool politeness, suddenly exasperated, Bianca pushed past her. To her complete amazement, the young woman followed her.

By now, Leonardo was no longer in sight. Bianca found him and the middle-aged woman nestling in the shadows of the Royal Academy archway, with Leonardo impaled against the wall and the little middle-aged woman pressed tightly up against him, one arm around his neck. They looked like two middle-aged people who had decided to embark on sex standing in the street in plain daylight.

Talk about don't frighten the horses...

Bianca was appalled. Not only because of the stark image of intimacy, but the speed with which it had happened – the only oddity that, even as she snuggled up to him, the woman still held a cigarette in her mouth.

As Bianca appeared, Leonardo looked deeply embarrassed, almost scared, like a little boy caught out in naughtiness.

'We're trying to light her cigarette, but the match keeps blowing out,' he explained.

'But you don't carry any matches with you,' Bianca objected.

Although Leonardo likes to smoke obsessively at home, especially in the mornings, he attempts to cut down the rest of the day by never carrying either cigarettes or a lighter with him. That way, if he craves a cigarette, he is forced to cadge.

'She has her own matches...'

'Are you telling me she asked you for a light, then provided her own box of matches? Who the hell is she?'

Bianca surveyed them both with contempt.

'I-I don't know,' he stuttered.

By now, the whites of Leonardo's eyes were showing too conspicuously, the dark brown pupils swivelling in their sockets like marbles. The woman, meanwhile, continued to smile knowingly, still certain of her own allure.

Stretching out an arm, Leonardo suddenly handed the matches to Bianca. 'You try.'

A bead of perspiration, like dirty rain water, trickled slowly from his sideburns past the five o'clock shadow of his jowls.

Good God, has he started dying his hair?

She really didn't know... Glancing from Leonardo's panicked face to that of the woman still leaning her purring bulk, one arm clutching his neck, Bianca's gaze swept over her in disdain, noticing the gaudy bric-a-brac of her earrings, gleaming through the bubble curls of her hennaed hairdo; the deft, dramatic sweep of black eyeliner to mark the naughty brilliance of her sparkling eyes, and the way she had chosen a lipstick to match the fur of her collar. Her hand, resting possessively on Leonardo's shoulder, was like a little brown paw, with chipped jewels of bright-red nail polish. Bianca recognised her instantly as a type – a type whom Leonardo seemed to attract wherever he went. There were times when these aggressive women seemed to come up through the floorboards.

Is it a Mediterranean thing? she had often wondered.

Behind them, abandoning all pretence of not belonging in the same drama, the young Slavic woman watched them in anxious silence.

'Can't you see what's happening?' asked Bianca. 'They're a double act.'

Leonardo looked startled... Undaunted, the older woman smiled her cat-like grin.

Hesitating briefly, Bianca was still unsure.

Does Leonardo know these women? But pretending otherwise? she puzzled.

'Is this what you actually want, Leo?' she asked.

'No, of course not.'

A second dark tear of perspiration stained the blue of his collar. She waved the box of matches.

'You try lighting her cigarette,' he said.

Almost imperceptibly, the woman's face altered slightly. Striking a match, Bianca held it deliberately high into the wind gusting along Piccadilly, before moving it back into the embrace between them, glancing scornfully at the woman as she did so. Dutifully, yet curiously unbowed, the woman placed her cigarette in the flame. It lit immediately. With one final look of contempt, Bianca handed her back the matches, whereupon the over-made-up woman finally released Leonardo from her grasp. As she did so, he shook himself free, like a Labrador puppy, the younger Slavic woman looking on distraught.

Reclaiming Leonardo's arm in hers, they walked away without another word.

'Each time I tried to light it, she must have been blowing into the cigarette, rather than inhaling.'

'You looked like you were having sex in a doorway.' Bianca laughed. 'Isn't that what they call a "knee-trembler"?'

A sudden sinister thought occurring to her, she asked: 'Have you checked your wallet and credit cards?'

Leonardo grimaced, suddenly aghast. He frequently carries vast quantities of cash with him, dollars mostly. They halted mid-pavement while he rummaged in his breast pocket. Everything was there. By the time they reached the empty restaurant, they were both laughing hilariously at the sheer absurdity of it all.

'Walking with you is like becoming involved in street theatre,' she said, giggling.

Nevertheless, remembering it now, it occurs to Bianca that this incident, with all its hidden audacities, presages something she does not always fully acknowledge in her marriage to Leonardo; something in the way he so readily gets caught up in these impetuous scrapes, from which she, or others, have to rescue him.

Like a wayward child, she thinks despairingly.

The fact that Leonardo often appears to be smiling, even when he isn't, only makes things worse.

Simply encouraging the idiots all the more, she thinks fondly.

In a more sober mood, she acknowledges that it reflects the kernel of ignorance they share in not quite knowing enough of each other's lives. Although they laugh about it, recklessly at times, is it really so amusing to half love one another the way they do, without ever really knowing the truth?

Perhaps lots of marriages are as elliptical as ours?

Secretly, she fears it a sign of something else; something not yet fully acknowledged and worryingly out of control, like the photograph of a smiling Leonardo dining in a Singapore restaurant, with just himself and one other man enjoying the company of twelve smiling, greedy-faced women.

* * *

The village of Fuli is further than they anticipated. At one point stopping, too tired to go on, they suddenly arrive at a hotchpotch village, its deeply rutted mud tracks running inland from the main street. Haphazard scatterings of white buildings, children and bicycles are everywhere. They find themselves in a food market, where mountainous varieties of apple juxtapose with vegetables, emerald green and fresh. Weaving their bikes carefully, Bianca and Stephen dismount occasionally to admire tanks of squirming, primeval-looking fish.

The furrowed village paths initially dictate their route. Then, suddenly, they are lost. Fluffy, miniature pet dogs run everywhere, like a parallel village population of baby Alsatians. Stephen and Bianca arouse neither curiosity nor hostility. Only the schoolchildren, their features flecked in black ink, acknowledge them, chorusing, 'Hello, how are you?' before running away giggling.

About to turn back, they happen on the riverbank. A restaurant, cool and welcoming, settles by the water's edge, a sign in English advertising 'Good Food & Clean Toilet'.

As Bianca and Stephen relax, grateful for views glimpsed between overhung branches, framing the river and shading them from the sun, Stephen's mobile suddenly rings. He looks at it in amazement. He had almost forgotten having it with him.

'Hello?'

From within the tiny device, a stream of urgent business talk penetrates the Chinese sunshine. Bianca can hear the frantic pace of its communication, a look of bored tolerance settling on Stephen's handsome features. He attempts to parry the call.

'Can't this wait, Piers? You do know that I'm in China?' he asks testily.

The voice carries on undeterred. Draping himself a little more languidly, Stephen pulls funny, mocking faces at Bianca. Capturing her hand in his own, his index finger softly traces designs in her palm. Smiling, she glances across the river to where a herd of water buffalo graze peacefully. In the distance, two peasants in coolie hats work the paddy fields; beyond, more sugar-loaf karsts.

Suddenly, Stephen's mood alters. He stands up, more business-like, speaking and pacing rapidly, his great height ducking in and out beneath the banyan tree's weeping curtains of black roots. From having been indifferent to the call, he now dictates it, Bianca recognising one of the things she loves most: his sudden, volte-face moves from languor to high-flown determination.

Having read Stephen a list of potential candidates for Chief Executive of a division of one of his publishing companies, the voice on the phone pauses. Stephen, who normally hesitates to make any kind of psychological judgment, dismissive or otherwise, suddenly reverses position… Usually it is only Bianca who analyses every nuance of personality, until he begs her to stop: 'Must we – all this girly stuff…'

But now revealing his own capacity for devastating shrewd discernment, one by one, he goes through the list of candidates, giving fast but thorough résumés of their merits and failings, until all but one is left unscathed. The rumbling voice of the man on the phone falls silent in the face of this onslaught, Stephen, meanwhile, hugging one arm about his chest and smiling boyishly. Finally, he agrees. The interviews can go ahead in his absence.

Why not…? Their conclusion is already foretold…

Stephen is all gentle charm again. Having made his decision, he lazily sloughs off the conversation like an unwanted skin, reverting to genial jokiness, the timbre of his voice again resuming its conversational mumble, in which the listener is left forever chasing for missing words.

'Thank you for your call, Piers… Good speaking to you.'

Putting down the miniature phone, he smiles and picks up the menu. 'Sorry about that… Have you decided yet what you want for lunch?'

Appraising him coolly, she says, 'You're a bit like the Red Queen. Off with their heads… Those poor people have toiled away, elaborately filling in application forms, and you've just reduced their hopes to ashes in a twenty-minute call, even before interviews take place.'

He laughs.

'Yet the interviews will still go ahead?'

'Yes, of course.' Stephen smiles. 'But only as a formality.'

'Won't the candidates be annoyed if they find out it's already a done deal?'

'Yes, probably,' he replies equably. 'At that level of business, people don't apply for jobs unless they realistically expect to get them.'

'So, how can you know who to reject, before having interviewed them?'

'I've already asked around… spoken to people who've either worked with them or for them. Lots of people who interview well are absolute shits to work for.'

Draping his elegant frame still more languidly, Stephen grins his happy-go-lucky smile, then frowns, looking mock cross. 'So, what are we having for lunch? I'm starving, aren't you?'

Bianca smiles too. Despite her teasing, she has just witnessed one of the things she most admires: Stephen's absence of doubt, once a decision is made, followed by his capacity to shrug the whole thing off, ready to move on to the next problem. That decisiveness sustains her too. Yet she also sees its occasional edge of cruelty, its absence of sympathy, not for the first time reminding herself how lucky she is that Stephen perceives herself and her faults so generously, while still adoring her for them. He has all the qualities of a practised éminence grise; of knowing how to conceal power until ready to use it. It can take people by surprise. Yet far more than her marriage to Leonardo, he is the most reliable anchor in her life. She smiles, reflecting proudly: *No one, absolutely no one, can quite match Stephen.*

It suddenly occurs to her that he would never have chosen to retreat or let her go of her as easily as Max had; would, instead, have stayed doggedly, benignly in place. Stephen, in any game, is always dependably two moves ahead. No wonder his formidable reputation for business, even though right now, in his jeans and Marks & Spencer's sweater, he looks more like a student than a high-powered businessman.

'You really are a piece of work, my darling.'

He grins naughtily. 'I shall take that as a compliment.'

They both burst out laughing.

After lunch, Stephen enquires about the possibility of their returning to Yangshuo by boat. But in no hurry to depart, Bianca takes out her notebook and performs six miniature sketches. Her watercolours from the boat yesterday had been essentially topographical, reliant on her ability to draw. But the aerial perspective, imposed by this morning's landscape, viewed from the top of Moon Hill, along with the day's rain-misted atmosphere, had dissolved all sense of distance, reducing her little paintings to flat cartographic images, spread outwards from their centres in translucent pools of coloured light. She has no idea whether Matthew will want to exhibit these little five-finger exercises of hers. Either way, she foresees no reason not to enjoy experimenting. Besides, Matthew's taste is frequently unpredictable and reflective of two quite separate strands of interest. Although liking to represent commercial portrait painters like herself, he rarely shows their work at the gallery, preferring to mostly rely on private commissions for sales. But whenever yielding to personal taste, he likes to put on shows that are 'conceptual', 'political' or 'kinetic' in some way, much of which Bianca despises for its lack of craftsmanship.

Matthew had once overheard her say, 'Absolute tripe.'

'Biaancaaa...' his elongated vowels had remonstrated, without rancour.

What Matthew has come to love most is the thing he once hated: the business itself, the art of deal-making. Curating shows, attempting to coincide his tastes with those of clients, has started to bore him. He now mostly leaves that to assistants. There is also the added complication that his interest in politics deters him from feeling overly possessive of either his own tastes or opinions about art: 'Far too bourgeois.'

As she contemplates the river views of bamboo, water buffalo and coolie hats from beneath tangled canopies of Banyan tree roots, Bianca realises how very different Chinese colour values are. Even this afternoon, with everything tenderly glanced over by sunshine and the earlier mists burned off, the colours are still vastly different from any she associates with Western landscapes. Here the distances are never Prussian blue, but subdued tones of Payne's grey, sepia or khaki. She decides, in her next few studies, to concentrate exclusively on colour, isolating it from any need to be descriptive; treating it as a language in its own right. She wants these Chinese miniatures to be about something deeper than simply conjuring topographical views on a page and so does several even smaller paintings, framing them within the already constrained frame of her sketchbook, to create small windows of light, colour and patina that aim to be abstractly beautiful.

'If Matthew does decide to show these, I'll call the exhibition "Small Essences of China".

Stephen smiles. 'How very pretentious.'

He is reading a book on the workings of the human brain. Glancing over her shoulder, he comments: 'Ah, China in Miniature...'

Bianca looks up delightedly. 'Oh yes, that's perfect... Much better idea for a title. I shall tell Matthew.'

Turning over another page, she asks doubtfully: 'You don't think I'm pandering to Matthew's interest in minimalism, do you?'

She pauses, as if caught out in calculations of modishness.

'Yes, I think you've finally succumbed to the idea of making money,' teases Stephen.

He stretches out his hand, fondly touching the curls which gather in corkscrews at the nape of her neck, whenever she wears her hair up.

'Actually, I hope so.' He smiles. 'Make some money... What, a very good idea. Besides, I've never known anyone with a talent for selling things so distinguished by their vacuity as Matthew. He's an absolute genius at selling the Emperor's clothes.'

Bianca peers back at him, slightly troubled and anxious. 'You do still like Matthew, don't you?'

'Yes, of course I like him. We've both known him for so long, I wouldn't know how to dislike him. He's just Matthew.'

When they finally make a move, two boats stand waiting for them, both lying low and flat against the water, the more substantial of the two a canopied boat with a straggle of Chinese waiting alongside. The smaller, independent boat, resting as lightly on the water as an upturned leaf, is a sampan.

As they gather up their belongings and step onto the jetty with their bikes, Bianca notices the carcasses of two beautiful ducks, with golden polished skin, lying on the steps closest to the water's edge. Unperturbed, she turns away briefly, then immediately swivels her head to look again. Horrified, she realises that the ducks have long tails... At their sides, lie two neatly severed heads, their serrated muzzles pulled back in a last-minute rictus of agony. Not ducks after all... Shockingly, she recognises them as two of the darling puppies she had noticed earlier and assumed to be village pets. A man descends the steps close behind her and begins washing their entrails in the river. Bianca shivers in repugnance, their livers and hearts still fresh and bloody...

CHAPTER 15

As they fly from Guilin to their next destination, Xian, Bianca begins writing the central drama of her mother's time in Paris... First, she reads one of Anya's letters to her father, dated Paris 1945. She is carrying all she could find of their wartime correspondence in her handbag. Like the diaries, these too she had discovered lying forgotten at the cottage, tucked between the mildew pages of one of William's numerous black-and-white Phaidon editions in his library.

Mrs Anya Johnson,
AG Civ.Pers.
HQ Com Z. ETOUSA. APO 887.
US Army.
Tuesday, 20 February 1945

My dearest, dearest William,

I have just received your letter dated 16 January and I'm very unhappy. How could you write such a letter? I could weep my eyes out! You say 'I feel that you no longer care for me' and you are all resigned to it! William, could you be resigned to that? Please, my darling, never be resigned to being without me, because I could never be resigned to being without you. You are my man, first, last and always. I love you. Always I am thinking of you. When I am unhappy, it is because of you – and when I am happy, it is the same. Always, it is you. My happiness I identify with those wonderful years when we were together – my unhappiness with these bad past years of separation. Please, William, do return soon! And meanwhile write and reassure me that you will never become resigned to being away and without me.

William, perhaps now you can appreciate how badly I felt in those past days, waiting and waiting for mail from you. I also had the same misgivings. But I'm hoping now that they were wrong – that I put the wrong interpretation to your silence as you do towards mine.

These letters – they are crossing or arriving late – or never even arriving at all. Only the bad letters arrive, it would seem. One other particular letter of yours which hurt so much was that one in which you stated that I must now loathe the cottage and the country. William, have we become so estranged that you could believe that?

I cannot write more – I'm too sick at heart. But please remember that I love you and will always love you. That I love you, the man and the artist.

Yours always,
Anya

Startled by her mother's evident passion, Bianca glances through her father's letters, trying to find one that might have elicited such a response. But his are all dated earlier, from 1941 to 1942, with nothing in them to match Anya's impassioned vehemence.

Her father's letters, in comparison, all evoke a numbing, mainly descriptive impartiality: 'Every day we do fatigues. Last night I was on guard. The moon was full, and the desert looked like snow. Very peaceful, until the sirens went.'

Alternatively, much preoccupied with himself and painting:

Things around here are difficult, and I have not written to you for some time. It will take me ages to rid myself of these strange feelings of frustration which the army gives one. Can you imagine what it is like for me, doing drawings to please others, rather than myself? Also, the front line is quite close in a way. I have been busy, and I hope you will understand.

They are, Bianca thinks, the naively presumptuous letters of someone who goes on an adventure called 'war', lasting more than four years, and fondly imagines that the person left behind will stay exactly in place, like Sleeping Beauty, waiting for her prince to come and wake her with a kiss.

But what must that letter of her father's, dated January 1945, have been to elicit so distraught a response in her mother? Bianca reads a few lines from another letter, sent from Cairo:

The sun strengthens throughout the day. At night it is cold, and the mosquitoes fly about frantically, while frogs croak like old men along the side of the water. The date palms have lovely golden fronds where their fruit will form in the autumn, and many of the views are just like Van Gogh paintings. There are trees that have no leaves, yet are covered in flowers, and in the gutters, along the roads, magenta petals everywhere... How I wish you could see this country. Everything is dirty and broken-down, but the people have a strange grace, with clear eyes that look you straight in the face. The women don't have much of a time of it though... They wear black robes and black veils. But their deportment is superb, because they carry water jars and baskets on their heads, and the balance of their walk is lovely. The men often carry baskets of brightly coloured flowers, and their little skull caps are bright with embroidery... Do you mind me writing such long descriptions and not talking of home?

* * *

Back in London, sitting in her raspberry-pink chair, Anya is also thinking of William, wondering if he is still alive. It is now six months since she received his last cheque through the bank. Neither he nor Bianca have her address, only a bank account number by which to contact her. She presumes he no longer lives at the cottage.

Should I tell Andreas the truth about Paris...? Why is he so curious about me? she wonders.

Last Sunday, the talk by Aubrey Byng, English political correspondent of *Le Figaro*, was cancelled and given instead by the youthful vicar of St James's in Piccadilly. His pious views had clashed with the group's humanist beliefs and they had dispersed early, so she had not finished telling him her story of Paris. She leans back in her chair, facing her altarpiece images, cut from magazines, mostly by Cézanne and Picasso, but juxtaposed with favourites from the Renaissance: a *Madonna and Child* by Raphael, *The Baptism of Christ* by Piero della Francesca. Her hair is white now, thick and long. Yet her features still have the delicacy of a young girl. She is, despite her age, very beautiful. The light from the window catches the cornflower blue of her eyes.

* * *

She can still remember the exact moment of her first meeting with the Vicomte. She had, that Monday morning, already interviewed several people at American HQ ETOUSA: a bearded white Russian, a French provincial manufacturer of porcelain and a disappointed poet. Just before lunch, she had looked up from the papers piled on her desk to find a man in his early thirties, with swarthy good looks, smiling at her. He half bowed and offered her his hand as he introduced himself.

'Madame, je suis le Vicomte de Courcelles.'

His English was better than her French. He had friends in England and had spent the inter-war summer holidays of his youth with the Astors and the influential political group surrounding them at Cliveden. Early during the war, he had joined de Gaulle in London with the Free French and lived in the Albany, opposite Fortnum & Mason's. His straight dark hair swept back from the high crown of his forehead to reveal the perfect symmetry of eyes that were quick and discerning. Anya had the feeling that he already knew her, or perhaps knew something of her, so intensely familiar was his scrutiny. But below the austere perfection of his brow was the mobility of a lean face whose features were as elastic as clay; a nose that was slightly bulbous and too long above a mouth that widened and charmed in generous smiles, yet pursed into miniature pouts whenever he wished to emphasise a point. He wore an immaculately tailored double-breasted suit, its silken threads fraying slightly at the cuffs. He had not come for a job; that would have been inappropriate for someone in his position. He had come to offer his services.

Three days later, he returned with a bunch of blue and red anemones and invited her out to lunch. Anya accepted the flowers, but graciously refused the invitation.

'Je dois refuser, monsieur. Je suis mariée,' she explained.

'Où est votre mari?'

'Au Caire,' she had replied.

'Alors, vous n'avez pas le droit d'avoir des amis?' he asked teasingly.

And Anya had blushed. Yes, of course she was allowed friends, but not special friends, not friends who might try to make her forget William, the husband she still loved but who wrote to her so very rarely.

Her love for William was still intact, but her sense of his presence in her life was diminishing daily. Just as he had fallen in love with Arabia, and found it new inspiration for painting, so too was she falling in love with Paris. There was so much in the city to admire: the handsome boulevards, the women with their inevitable sense of chic. Above all, she loved the way the French had retained immense pride in themselves, despite the deprivations inflicted by the Occupation. In it, she found a match for her own pride, which, in England, had been deemed her greatest flaw, whereas in Paris it was considered a virtue. And everywhere, in cafés, on street corners, was lively debate, and impassioned exchanges of idea and purpose. It was similar to how she remembered her pre-war London days, the sensation of being at the hub of something, only now with the additional difference that she was affluent enough to enjoy it.

When, some weeks later, le Vicomte first brought her violets, reminding her of her wedding bouquet and the little flat in Great Titchfield Street, they had sat at a table at Les Deux Magots, sharing their first lunch together. It was then that he told her how she had appeared to him that day of his first interview with her. He had marvelled at the unruly copper abundance of her hair, which now fell almost to her waist, its rough curls barely secured by the two tortoiseshell combs either side of her temples. Beneath this halo, the features of her face were all delicacy of movement and expression. He loved the way every new comment initiated some new response in the blue of her eyes and in the set of her mouth and jaw. At that first meeting, he felt he had experienced with a light touch the full range of her emotions: her tenderness, her cruelty, her pride and her great longing for the essence of things. He was captivated by her. But more importantly still, he had felt his own being capture hers. Despite her fierce resistance to him, he had felt from the start an overwhelming sense of ownership over her.

He had also noticed every detail of her dress as it clung to her slender frame: the dark blue wool crepe, with its squared puffed sleeves, edged with broderie anglaise to match its inset bib of white lace and interlaced with ribbons to match the blue velvet bow at her throat. He recounted the joy of her beautiful face and head thrown back haughtily on the delicate length of her throat, the proud set to her jaw dissolved by the shy feminine softness of her mouth and the clear blue of her eyes, which looked at him with equal measures of reproach and joy.

That same evening, she had danced in his arms at 'Le Boeuf sur le Toit', and two weeks later, after William had carelessly selected the wrongly numbered automated message to insert into the telegram he sent for her birthday, she and Charles de Courcelles became lovers. The telegram had read, 'Congratulations on the birth of twins.' It had felt like a gesture of mockery and contempt, reminding her not only of how much she had longed for William's child in those Eastern County days before the war but also of the tragic story of her own twin brother, who had fallen to his death at the age of four from a casement window, the never quite remembered, nor properly resolved agony in her own mind that it might have been she who pushed him.

But now, all that torment was forced to the back of her mind, and the exhilaration and fluency of her early love affair with big bear Varinsky came back to her, but even more so. She and the Frenchman were still better matched, in age, temperament and desire. Their lovemaking was, from the start, self-assured and free of inhibition. As they looked at one another, they knew that something had begun; some profound exchange between them that could not be halted.

Three weeks later, so intense and possessive was Charles's love, that he jealously locked her in his apartment in Neuilly to prevent her from joining her friends, the Volkoffs, for dinner. And she, furious and ferocious in response, had fought and bitten and insulted him in her efforts to rescue the key and enforce her own will against his. But he already knew her too well.

'Ma petite chatte,' he taunted her.

He had held her small fighting frame firmly but at a distance, imprisoning her shoulders as her limbs flailed out, kicking against his; and, *finally, when she was tired, crushed her in his arms and made love to her there and then on the bare floorboards of his hallway. By then, he knew how to read her face well. He had seen her last-minute fleeting look of triumph as she finally submitted to him.*

Not that he had completely stolen her love for William, but he had robbed her of any future desire for him. She now knew for certain how tentative hers and William's lovemaking was in comparison. This new lovemaking was like equal combat, whereas William, she realised, would always limp behind her somewhat in innocence. For him, she would always have to make allowances, but with Charles there were no allowances to be made, nor room for manoeuvre even. There was only the fierce, undeniable truth of their union, and, no matter how they abused it, it would never let either of them go. It was as though a force had entered their lives, and with a mighty turn of the wrist, turned the kaleidoscope cascading into new patterns. 'For better or worse' – what a useless concept that proved to be. Thereafter, there was only the truth of passion, no matter how cruel and fateful that truth might be.

* * *

Bianca's silver pen skids off the narrow, melamine aircraft table onto the floor beneath her seat. The impassive Chinese businessman in the seat behind picks it up, handing it back to her disdainfully, without comment.

In London, meanwhile, Anya tries to shrug off her memories… *Too painful.*

She glances at her reproduction of *The Baptism of Christ* by Piero della Francesca. *To think he was only sixteen, when he painted it.*

Suddenly, a quote from Frank Lloyd Wright occurs to her: 'In my youth, I believed that the Renaissance was a sunrise. It has taken me all my life to realise it was a sunset.'

* * *

After making love to Chloe, Hesketh had fallen into a deep, brief sleep but an hour and a half later was already back in his study by the lift door, fervently writing letters and making ten phone calls, in quick succession, to Directory Enquiries; trying, yet again, to trick the various operators into revealing Bianca's telephone number. He knows perfectly well that she is ex-directory yet feigns angry surprise when they refuse to give it to him.

His mind buzzes with questions: *How to account for Bianca's disappearance...? How could she sell her flat without my knowing?*

He rings the estate agents whose boards were outside her house.

'Sorry, sir. We're not aware of that flat being sold. Although we do represent flats four and six, if you care to arrange a viewing?'

The image of those closed shutters had been so emphatic, so final, that Hesketh refuses to believe them, remaining convinced Bianca has escaped him. His voice, as he speaks to telephone operators and various anonymous agents, pretends geniality, before slowly degenerating into gravels of menace; each call ending sarcastically on notes of threat, as they refuse to divulge the information he craves. Plus all the carefully cultivated goodwill in his feelings towards Bianca – 'Don't be such a silly-billy...' – suddenly revealing its underbelly of brutality.

This is no longer a wistfully seductive game with someone who needs to be gently coaxed into realising her best interests, but the temerity of someone who has dared walk away; of someone who may even have outwitted him forever. Hesketh's response is one of pure outrage. Although capable of expressing a jokey tenderness in his letters to Bianca, whilst believing her always in place, and available to the storms of his nature, this is a different truth. That of a woman prepared to walk offstage without leaving any trace of herself... And that he finds unendurable. Hesketh feels murderous towards everyone he speaks to.

He decides to drive straight back to Bianca's apartment and demand that her neighbours tell him where she is.

Sensing a dangerous edge to his mood, Chloe stretches her arms plaintively across the lift doors, attempting to debar him from leaving. But in her struggle to restrain him, he throws her to the floor, their lovemaking of two hours earlier not only forgotten but no longer registered, as though leaving nothing indelible on either his body or mind.

Back on the street, he mocks some poor individual, sweeping leaves from the pavement. It doesn't help that he is dark-skinned, Hesketh blindly ranting: 'Get back to where you came from.'

'Brixton,' replies the man, an insolent gleam in his eye.

To him, the Heskeths of this world are commonplace. Nevertheless, he picks up his broom, holding it defensively across his chest like a weapon... But Hesketh just stumbles on.

No longer content with the bus stop opposite, Hesketh now huddles at the top of the steps leading to Bianca's front door, questioning everyone who arrives.

'Have you seen Bianca?'

But they have all been warned numerous times about answering questions about Bianca, no matter how innocuous-seeming. Her neighbours peer carefully into his face, intrigued to know what madness looks like close to. But all they see is a face distraught with grief. It is his voice and mannerisms which alarm them most; the ugly, insinuating tones of someone barely able to maintain control over the hideous anger that propels the rasp in his voice, the threats, laced with sarcasm, as they declare their ignorance of Bianca. They turn away, mystified, slamming the door in his face, incapable of associating this broken, distraught creature with the elegant, carefree personality that is Bianca, and briefly wondering: *How did she become tied up with someone like that?*

Then they forget, swiftly returning to their own, more pressing concerns.

A tall, dark-suited man, Bianca's neighbour from the floor above, whom Hesketh had attempted to interview on his way indoors, re-emerges, dressed in jeans and sweater.

'You still here?' he asks, reaching for his mobile phone. 'I'm calling the police.'

Hesketh looks up at him dazed, the young man even taller than himself. Attempting a knowing smile before performing one of his volte-faces, Hesketh shifts seamlessly from aggression to maudlin self-pity, pleading: 'I need to know where Bianca is.'

His voice is now an insistent whine.

'I'm a barrister,' announces the man, unimpressed. 'You may decide for yourself... Either clear off right now, or I'll call the police. You're already well known around here. I've often seen you lurking at that bus stop opposite and am more than prepared to testify to the fact.'

Attempting a jaunty tone, Hesketh explains: 'You don't understand who I am... I have rights... Bianca Johnson is my wife, you know.'

'Really?' replies the young man with contempt. 'I somehow doubt that.'

He is about to add, 'She already has a husband,' but his promise to Bianca of circumspection in all things kicks in last minute, and he remains silent.

Recognising something obdurate and uncompromising in the young man's demeanour, Hesketh acknowledges defeat. Nothing more he can do today. With one backward glance at the tantalising blindness of Bianca's shuttered windows, he slinks away. Nor, now the decision is made, does he hesitate, his mind sharp, no longer befuddled. He has no problem remembering where he left his car. He gets in and drives off smoothly, for momentary comfort playing Bianca's tape:

'Do you imagine we've all spent our time becoming more unintelligent like you?'

But her voice, so often enchanting, now simply annoys him.

'Haven't done with you yet, lady,' he threatens out loud. 'I'll show you, once and for all, just what I'm capable of, Bianca, my poor, poor love... Remember my vow? Wherever you are, whatever you do, I shall find you. Even if I destroy both of us in doing so.'

He takes a deep breath. 'No one gets the better of me... no one. Do you hear me?'

He switches off the tape, no longer interested in anything she has to say.

'What does she know anyway, the poor wretched innocent? I have emotion big enough for both of us,' he spits out loud. 'Everything you do and think will turn out to be just whim, my darling Bianca,' he threatens darkly.

Reaching Sloane Square, he glances at his watch. There is a woman he knows and visits occasionally who holds Sunday teatime séances with a Ouija board in her flat off the King's Road.

They aren't exactly serious occasions, even Hesketh acknowledging them to be a bit hit and miss. But she, and the slightly disturbed characters who collect about her, throw up some interesting perceptions from time to time. Unable yet to face going home to Chloe, Hesketh has just remembered wrestling with her and throwing her to the floor, Bruno's terrified howl of dismay as he had done so. Perhaps a session with the hippie, tea-time madame and her Ouija board would settle his mood and provide him with a nugget of an idea of how to reach Bianca?

Parking his Saab by the flower seller in Sloane Square, he buys an enormous bunch of long-stemmed Madonna lilies to give to Chloe later, leaving them in the boot before making his way towards the promise of a cup of tea and a séance.

After tea and slices of angel cake with six strangers, Hesketh asks the Ouija board: 'Where is Bianca?'

The board spells out the reply: 'A I R.'

'I don't understand,' objects Hesketh.

His hostess regards him coolly, her voice haughtily vague: 'No, nor I.'

She knows Hesketh of old; knows he can be charming, albeit in a slightly dislocated way, but also knows there is a psychopathic strain to his nature, not always immediately apparent or active, but always there, bubbling beneath the surface. She had spotted it in him that afternoon, even as he walked through the door. She has her own ideas of how to interpret Hesketh's reply from the Ouija board. In the air… hiding high-up somewhere… up in the air. Uncertainty, maybe? Or perhaps in an aeroplane?

But she decides to share none of these ideas with Hesketh. The name Bianca had surfaced before in his questions for the board. She has no idea who Bianca is, yet knows for certain that no woman deserves to be visited by Hesketh in his current mood.

'Have another piece of angel cake, darling,' she recommends sweetly.

Later, surveying Hesketh's enormous bouquet of bouncy, sheath-like heads of unopened lilies, Chloe thinks only how funereal they look. Dutifully placing them in water, she deposits them on the mantelpiece in front of Bianca's painting, their beauty bringing her no joy. She knows them to be merely an inarticulate apology for an action, in any case, inexcusable. Recently reading an article explaining the tragedy of people who find themselves loving someone whom it is impossible to like, she had thought sadly: *That's what's happening to me... I no longer like the father of my child. In fact, he repels me... Yet I can't stop loving him.*

She turns towards Hesketh, who is watching carefully, trying to discern her reaction. From next door come the sounds of Bruno playing Vivaldi. They smile shyly at one another in sudden pride.

* * *

Whilst in Singapore, and about to start filming, Leonardo and his film crew learn of a dispute with the Chinese authorities over their rights to film in Beijing's Tiananmen Square. Much of their filming can be done in Suzhou and Shanghai, but certain sequences in Tiananmen Square are essential to the heart of the plot. The Chinese are prepared to tolerate the idea of a Franco–Chinese love story set against the Cultural Revolution, but fail to see why its setting in Tiananmen Square should be necessary. They are as busy denying the connotations of Tiananmen Square, as the rest of the world is busy recording its tragedy – 1989, the year when troops and tanks were mobilised against their own people, a year the Chinese prefer to forget.

Leonardo plans to tell the story of a Catholic French girl who falls in love with a student political leader from Beijing University, whom she first meets in Suzhou and Shanghai. It is less a story of their union than of their long separation and loss. The story, in two parts, details their haunting moments of first love, followed by twenty years apart: he in prison, and she returned to Paris, dutifully locked in a cruel marriage with her cousin. Then the effects on them both, as they meet twenty years later.

'How does the story end?' someone asks.

'Don't know yet,' Leonardo replies.

Leonardo flies first to Beijing to resolve the problem, and then on to Paris to meet with his French producers, most of his film crew remaining in Singapore, awaiting new instructions. But

Laetitia Norton travels with him. Leonardo wants to also visit his new chateau while in France.

Just one other of their entourage flies directly from Singapore to Paris. This tall figure, with a ponytail of lank, dark hair, is waiting for Leonardo and Laetitia at Charles de Gaulle airport. Moving towards them swiftly, the masculine figure effortlessly picks up both their bags before leading the way to the exit. Laetitia greets the tall figure with 'Haiii', one of her sing-song Strine-inflected greetings, which succeed in conveying contempt at the same time as implying courtesy. Leonardo just smiles. The statuesque figure walks between them, turning first to one then the other, voicing concern: 'How was your flight? You must be very tired?' – all lisped in a high-pitched little girl's voice, while addressing Laetitia as 'Madame' and Leonardo as 'Master'.

Like witnessing a cocoon of words being spun, thinks Laetitia, glancing sceptically at the unsmiling face bearing down on her. Leonardo, meanwhile, looks up at the figure with benign acceptance, asking: 'How are you, Maria?'

The tall figure blushes, feigning the unimportance of answering any question as trivial as one about herself.

My God, thinks Laetitia. *What a performance it is, when the servants start taking control.*

Feeling a moment of repugnance, Maria reminds her of one of those monstrous, sixteenth-century Mannerist figures from a painting by Parmigianino, in which graceful gestures of femininity are applied to figures of overwhelming masculine proportions.

Her hands are twice the length of mine, she notices.

Depositing their bags heftily in the boot of her elegant Citroen car, Maria unfolds a copy of the *South China Morning Post*, pointing to the postage-stamp photograph taken in a Singapore restaurant.

'There we all are,' she lisps.

How completely wrong Bianca had been; Leonardo was not surrounded by twelve women in the photo but by thirteen. The grim-looking figure sitting next to him is Maria, and not another man, as Bianca had supposed.

She drives them from the airport to the Georges V Hotel in the 16eme Arrondissement, a short stroll from L'Etoile. It is a part of

Paris that Leonardo considers best at night, the intervals of street lighting and their '*son et lumière*' focus on dark, imposing buildings conveying a sense of luxury and drama. But during the day, the ornate facades on relatively empty streets, along with the district's exclusive fashion boutiques, bestow a mood of suffocation and solemnity.

The least attractive side of all that was ever meant by 'bourgeois', ruminates Leonardo.

Old friends that they are, Leonardo and Laetitia share a suite with two bedrooms.

'I'll take this one,' says Leonardo, unhesitatingly choosing the grander of the two.

His meeting the following morning with his French producers is amiable but not particularly productive. Someone talks of creating an artificial film set of Tiananmen Square.

'That would cost a fortune,' objects Leonardo. 'We're already hugely over budget with these delays. Having a film crew holed up in one of the most expensive hotels in Singapore, awaiting instructions, doesn't help.'

As speculation mounts, the meeting becomes increasingly animated, with much gesticulating and shrugging by the French.

'How are we going to show the tanks and soldiers firing on the students?' someone asks.

'By 3 June 1989, Beijing belonged to its people,' says another.

'There were no buses, no ordinary police... Millions of people were camping out, blockading the Square,' remembers a third.

Despite his Italianate background, Leonardo remains impassive, only one remark reminding him of the greatest difficulty he faces.

'Beware of false sentiment,' someone shouts angrily. 'This is a French film, after all. No Hollywood schmaltz, I implore you.'

Three hours later, nothing is much closer to being resolved, except for the all-important kernel of the matter. No one, Leonardo suddenly realises, has mentioned pulling out. The project, no matter how difficult to achieve, is a commitment none of them is prepared to abandon. Leonardo emerges from the meeting feeling jubilant. He had begun to fear having to use his own private funds to finance the thing.

Later that day, after an expensive lunch at Fouquet's in the Champs-Élysées, Maria drives them south towards Tours. Although Leonardo has seen numerous photographs and plans of the building, plus a DVD showing aerial shots of the house and grounds, this is his first actual visit to the chateau. He had bought it blind. It was Laetitia who had found it, and Maria who had negotiated its purchase on his behalf.

Close to Saumur, and set in eighty acres of forestry and grounds, not since the First World War had it been a family home. Its more recent use was as a hotel, which was part of its attraction for Leonardo. He plans to run an international film school there, teaching groups of up to thirty; the house, with its numerous bedrooms, many already converted into the modern idiom of en-suite bathrooms ideal both for work and entertaining. In addition to which, by some quirk of fate, arranged by one of its earlier inhabitants, two of its vast ground-floor salons had been converted into a theatre, with a proper stage, curtains and wings... Leonardo had bought it all for a song, just a few hundred thousand pounds, not the millions its imposing size might suggest. Nevertheless, there is considerable work to be done: a new roof, the general repairs and modernisation of its interior and bathrooms, plus the cost of new furnishings. Formerly run as a hotel, it already has an old-fashioned but nevertheless adequate kitchen, capable of catering for large numbers.

'We could probably even run our own restaurant,' jokes Leonardo. 'I could design new dishes, exclusive to us, with unorthodox combinations of ingredients.'

Laetitia glances unenthusiastically out of the window.

It is only as Maria's car turns in between tall, wrought-iron gates, making its way along an avenue of trees leading to a circular gritted courtyard, at the centre of which is the bowl of a fountain with its statue missing, that Leonardo realises the chateau he has bought is not beautiful. It has all the attributes of fairy tale: walls eighteen inches deep, a roof full of turrets as ornate as jewellery. But its bulk is not handsomely distributed between welcoming circular towers and elegant wings. Instead, it is constructed, as one might build a funeral pyre for burning at the stake, the struts of the pyre soaring stone buttresses, with neither play nor enjoyment in the intervals of their design. It is a fortress, designed exclusively to protect.

Leonardo gets out of the car, and remarks: 'How ugly it is.'

Laetitia looks at him in disbelief. Maria, more circumspect, turns away, hiding her feelings. About to joke and make light of his remark, something in Leonardo's face silences Laetitia, his disappointment almost palpable. She turns towards him: 'Work on it is almost finished...'

'Good... That means we can sell it again. Put it straight back on the market.'

'You can't possibly mean that? Anyway, you haven't seen inside yet.'

'Nor do I want to,' he replies decisively, instructing Maria: 'Take us back to Paris.' He glances at his watch. 'We can stop to eat somewhere on the way.'

'You refuse to even go in and see what I've done?' Laetitia asks incredulously.

He replies indifferently. 'You go in, if you like. In fact, stay if you want to... Make your own arrangements to return, whenever the work's finished, if that's what you prefer?'

She gasps. 'Won't you need me?'

'No, not particularly; Maria can handle everything in your absence.'

Laetitia has known Leonardo for many years. He is rarely this obdurate. Nevertheless, she knows no amount of argument will change his mind, at least not right away.

'Okay,' she agrees. 'There are still things I need to do.'

Reluctantly getting out of the car, with Maria's simpering help, Laetitia retrieves her case from the boot. The gravel crunching beneath its wheels, the car moves off almost immediately, leaving her standing alone, not even time to open the chateau's vast fortress-like door. She watches the car disappear, waiting to see if Leonardo will turn to wave, but not once does he look back. It is as though both she and the house were written off in a single glance.

* * *

Instead of returning to the Georges V, Leonardo stays with Maria in her flat in St Germain and, the following morning, takes the Eurostar to London. Bianca is not expecting him, but he does not phone her, reflecting: *Even if she's out when I arrive, she's bound to be at home later.*

As he lets himself into their apartment, it is the absolute stillness of the rooms and their immaculate tidiness which strikes him first, and then the unusual twilight of their sitting room. Only as his eyes grow accustomed to the gloom does he realise the panelled wooden shutters have been folded over the windows, Bianca clearly away.

Sinking heavily into an armchair, Leonardo thinks fast and furiously while deciding what to do. The phone at his elbow is alight with the winking semaphore indicating accumulated messages.

Should I listen to them? he wonders.

As he hesitates, the phone starts to ring. Automatically stretching out an arm, a last-minute thought stops him. It might be Laetitia trying to track him down again, as she had the night before in Paris, and again this morning on his mobile. For the moment, he doesn't want to speak to her.

I'll deal with both her and the chateau later.

Whoever has rung hangs up without leaving a message.

Leonardo sinks back in the chair and into the mellow half-light. Bianca had not mentioned going away, but nor had she any reason to do so. She is not expecting him home for another five weeks and might easily be in the country, staying with girlfriends. It is not her absence that alarms him particularly but the strange finality of her absence, signalled by her closure of the shutters.

There is something else in this scenario that worries Leonardo, but he cannot fathom what it is. Standing up, he makes his way to the kitchen to make coffee. Again, everything is neat and tidy, nothing out of place. It is then that he remembers. Suddenly, he feels transported back, all those years ago, when he had returned home to find Lisette, his first wife, in the arms of another man. It was not the fact of her infidelity that had hurt so indelibly, but the irreversibility of his moment of discovery.

Replacing the cup and saucer, he suddenly knows clearly what to do. Acting like a thief in his own home, he retraces his steps to the sitting room, smooths away his imprint on the armchair cushions and picks up his bag. Resetting the alarm, he shuts and locks the door behind him.

No one will ever know I've been here...

It is not that he automatically suspects Bianca of infidelity, nor even duplicity. That is not the point. The point is that whatever the truth of her absence, innocent or otherwise, he does not want to know it. Had she known of his arrival, she would have been there, good-willed and happy to see him. It is that which he does not want to disturb, the contract of faith between himself and his wife. Whatever freedoms they afford themselves when apart, he does not want to lose Bianca to some casual, unimportant discovery.

Hesitating and listening carefully before descending the stairs, he encounters none of their neighbours. No one would be able to report his having been there. Once in the street, he hails a taxi, and directs it to Beak Street. He has decided to spend the night sleeping on his office sofa bed.

Later that afternoon, after he has showered and found time to look through his post, he picks up the phone and calls the one person whom he can trust to never tell Bianca of his presence in London.

'Solange,' he says, as a husky voice answers. 'I'm in London for one night. Come and have dinner with me?'

* * *

Chloe senses new storms brewing in Hesketh, his attempts to maintain normal daily routines starting to break down. Increasingly erratic, he now stays out late at night, something he only did rarely before. He also keeps losing things – simple things, such as his keys and glasses.

He continues to make love to her, but in ways ever more frenzied and detached. And Chloe, from having relied on the bond of their lovemaking, now finds it strangely lonely. His attitude to Bruno is also increasingly abstract and watchful, as though no longer expecting to participate in the drama of his own son's life. Chloe begins to fear Bruno is becoming more of a fascinating phenomenon than a complete personality in Hesketh's eyes...

She has no idea where he goes when he stays out late at night. He says he is at meetings but returns home distraught and drenched to the skin. How should she guess that his meeting place is a bus stop opposite a house in Holland Park?

She hears him whispering on the phone, and once when he was out, a young man rang, asking to speak to him. She is both mystified and anxious. There had been numerous incidents in the past of Hesketh's distraught behaviour, but they normally broke after a couple of days. This one is lasting longer.

One night, he arrives home slightly earlier, soaked to the skin, but jubilantly clutching a fistful of letters. So crumpled are they that Chloe cannot see to whom they are addressed. Before she can begin to decipher their envelopes, Hesketh vanishes into the sanctity of his private office and locks them in his filing cabinet. On re-emerging, he smiles at both herself and Bruno for the first time in days.

Sensing now is not a good time to challenge him, Chloe refrains from harassing him with questions of where he has been. Wherever it is, she knows it has brought him no happiness. Instead, she affectionately resorts to wifely tricks, providing him with lashings of comfort food.

'A young man phoned while you were out.'

'Probably just ringing to get his instructions,' remarks Hesketh mysteriously.

She silently places a plate of stew and dumplings before him, and Hesketh eats ravenously, followed by servings of apple crumble, swimming in custard. Chloe glances at the time.

'Good God, it's after eleven. Didn't you think of getting yourself something to eat?'

But it is as if he hadn't heard... Bruno, who should be in bed, is standing at a typical elliptical distance from them both, he, too, unusually quiet, as though sensing a new change of mood in the household.

'Let's get to bed, everyone,' suggests Chloe, as she washes up the few remaining dishes.

'I'll follow you shortly… There's something I need to do first.'

He disappears into his office. Bruno attempts to follow, Hesketh shutting the door in his face. The unusual gesture confuses Bruno. He is more used to being petitioned by Hesketh than forbidden access to him. It leaves him momentarily at a loss. Sensing her son's dismay, Chloe leads him gently to his high sided cot, preparing him for bed.

Behind the closed door of his study, Hesketh unlocks the filing cabinet and removes the letters. One is addressed to Bianca Johnson, another to Bianca Vescarro-Johnson, the third to L. Vescarro. Picking up the phone, he makes a call. A sleepy voice asks: 'What time is it?'

Hesketh does not bother to tell him. 'I need you to watch her house all day tomorrow…'

'Okay. Do you know it's almost midnight?' a young man's voice asks.

Hesketh ignores the attempt at complaint. 'I'll pay you at the usual rate of £10 per hour,' he says, replacing the receiver.

Before opening the letters, Hesketh first examines them closely, turning them over slowly in his hands, sensing their weight, smoothing their creases, and scrutinising their postmarks. The one addressed to Signore L. Vescarro has an Italian stamp. Hesketh reflects on his good luck in getting the letters at all. He had spent the entire day waiting outside Bianca's shuttered apartment – for what he hardly knew. She was clearly not there. From the other side of the road, he had watched her neighbours, some of whom he now recognises, coming and going. At one point, a man with grey ringlets, swarthy complexion and dressed very formally, whom he had never seen before, emerged and immediately hailed a taxi. Later, he watched the postman climb the steps to deliver the days post.

It was when the Marks & Spencer's van had arrived to deliver food to one of the other flats that he sensed his chance. Needing to make several trips, the deliveryman had put the Yale lock on its latch, so as not to keep ringing the doorbell. On one of his trips upstairs, Hesketh had dashed across the road and let himself into the communal hallway. There, without thinking, he did the only conceivable thing that might increase his chance of intimacy with Bianca – he stole the three letters from the box marked with her flat number, filching them blindly, without checking to see if they were addressed to her. He wanted information, any information that might lead him to her, and felt vaguely surprised there were only three in total. He had no idea that Leonardo had collected the earlier accumulations of post and taken them to Beak Street with him. Most of the letters were, in any case, for him; the odd one, addressed to Bianca, Leonardo had known that he could easily re-post, without Bianca realising he had visited the flat in her absence.

Hesketh carefully examines the letter addressed to Signore L. Vescarro, postmarked Siena, something familiar about the name 'Vescarro'.

Where have I heard it before?

Taking a nail file from a jar of pens on his desk, he slits the letter along its spine. Inside, a sheaf of blue airmail paper crinkles, like a present wrapped in tissue. The letter, handwritten in Italian, seems to be some kind of informal inventory and invoice, plus a note, imparting news. Using his pidgin-Spanish, Hesketh attempts to tease out its meanings, but the letter defeats him. Even the address from which it is sent is incomplete, written simply as: 'La Casa, Siena'.

The signature at the bottom: '*Ciao e baci*, Giovanna.'

Folding the tender leaves of paper back into their original creases, he returns them to their envelope.

The next two letters look more promising. He regards them with expectancy and excitement, as something to savour; almost hesitating to open them, so sure is he of being about to discover all that is, so far, missing.

The first, addressed to Bianca Johnson, is from an old colleague of hers; a newsy letter, detailing his career as university lecturer, with barely any mention of hers.

'What's the matter with these people?' Hesketh asks out loud.

Once again, the address is incomplete – '2 October, Dorchester' and signed 'Robert'. No surname.

Hesketh rereads the letter. *Perhaps there's something I missed?*

But nothing.

It is the final letter that intrigues him most.

How is the surname of the first letter, 'Vescarro', included with 'Bianca' and 'Johnson' in the third? Why would anyone address Bianca as 'Bianca Vescarro-Johnson?

The letter is postmarked London, its envelope an imposing, stiff white vellum. Even in its current crumpled state, there is something pristine and self-important about it. Using the nail file, Hesketh slices open its spine. Inside is a contractual letter from Matthew's Cork Street Gallery to Bianca, containing neither personal information, nor any kind of informal message. It is simply a renewal of contract, to be signed in triplicate and returned to the gallery, signed 'Matthew Dancer'.

Hesketh turns the letter over, searching for clues. Bianca clearly has some working connection with the famous Cork Street gallery, but even the nature of that work is unclear from the contract's wording, which simply refers to a continuance of the terms of some former document. He presumes it refers to a show of Bianca's paintings; up until now, he was uncertain she still painted. As for the double barrel of her name with 'Vescarro', that remains a mystery.

Why adopt a second name when she's not married? he argues bitterly. *Perhaps she requires some kind of anonymity for her work?*

He would certainly know if Bianca had ever married... He has had teams of private detectives regularly check the registers of births, marriages and deaths for her name.

In fact, Bianca and Leonardo had married in Siena.

But he now has the name of a gallery, plus a telephone number, and a 'Matthew Dancer' to apply to for information about her. Refolding the letter, he restores all three to his filing cabinet, making sure to lock it again. Nothing more to be done tonight...

Switching off the hallway light, he makes his way to bed, past the panels of Bianca's triptych; forgetting to take his normal pill, he nevertheless sleeps soundly for the first time in days.

The following morning Chloe is delighted to find Hesketh more cheerful.

Perhaps the bleakness of his mood has finally broken?

Bruno, too, seems less agitated. Chloe watches her two men eat breakfast together, noting again the reflection of what was once Hesketh's beauty in the pure lines of her nine-year-old son's face and loving them both for it. She remembers her thoughts a few days earlier: *How to capture Bruno's fleeting beauty?*

Later that day, when Hesketh is out, genuinely occupied at a meeting about a property on Ibiza that he is hoping to sell, Chloe rings The Royal Society of Portrait Painters to ask if they could recommend a painter with a good reputation for capturing the likenesses of children.

'We can recommend one or two names now, over the phone. Or, if you prefer, you can visit our office in the Mall and view some slides from our various portrait painters' portfolios, to choose for yourself,' explains the woman answering her call.

Chloe agrees. She calls in at the Mall Galleries a few days later. Shown the work of four painters whom the Society considers particularly successful at having captured portraits of younger children, each approach very different, it is when Chloe is shown the slide of Bianca's portrait of the Cavendish children that she finally decides. She likes the combination of isolation and intimacy the artist has conjured. Plus the painting is on a vast scale, six-foot square. Chloe wants a portrait of Bruno large enough to supplant the triptych hanging above the mantelpiece in their sitting room.

'The painting would need to be kept secret,' she explains. 'It's a surprise birthday present for my husband.'

'That particular artist, B. Turvey, is abroad right now but will be back in a week or so. However, you may have to wait. She's currently in the middle of another commission, I believe. Probably best if we speak to her dealer on your behalf, and you then contact him yourself, once she's back.'

She writes down a name and telephone number. 'Insist on speaking to Matthew Dancer himself, rather than to one of his assistants,' she advises.

So, within ten days of each other, Matthew receives phone calls from both Hesketh and Chloe, enquiring about Bianca. In Hesketh's case, soon guessing who he is dealing with, he instructs his secretary to screen all calls, only putting people through if she is sure they are already known to the gallery.

'We represent no artist named Bianca Vescarro-Johnson,' he states abruptly, replacing the receiver.

But with Chloe, Matthew fails to make the connection. Chloe also still uses her maiden name from time to time, especially when organising something intended as a surprise for Hesketh. Agreeing to take a call from a gentle-sounding voice announcing herself as Chloe Smythe, Matthew promises to arrange a meeting with B. Turvey as soon as she gets back from China.

* * *

The following day, Leonardo flies to Siena... Last night, Solange had stayed with him in Beak Street. Replaying over and over in his mind the way her pale, miniature figure had fitted so perfectly against his own olive-skinned bulk, he does not feel guilt, only amazement. This is not remotely his first infidelity, but he more typically reserves such indiscretions for when he is abroad. Some woman detaches herself from the international audience at one of his film talks and spends the night at his hotel. He always enjoys the hours of flirtation leading to these one-night stands but has few memories of the sex that follows. To him, it almost always feels like a bothersome, last-minute duty and, whenever he wakes up next to one of these casual sirens, he feels grumpy, treating them to an immaculate but cold formality. A sort of self-disgust takes over, causing him to react angrily if they expect him to share either his toothpaste or breakfast with them.

He had always found conversation with Solange exciting but without it ever occurring to him to translate that excitement into sex.

Perhaps I should have realised?

The last time they met, before he left for Singapore, he had taken her with him to a reception at the Chinese Embassy, where officials and journalists had assumed she was his wife, and he had done nothing to correct that impression. Afterwards, they and some of the same crowd had wound up at Annabel's, where Leonardo had been quizzed by a particularly eager student enrolee to one of his film courses. In between drinks, this young man had also insisted on taking photographs of himself and Solange dancing on the postage-stamp dance floor. When Leonardo turned up several days later with his film crew in Singapore, this same student had arrived at their hotel, now smartly dressed and revealing himself to be the chief features writer for the *South China Morning Post*.

After dinner at a nearby Italian restaurant, Leonardo and Solange had returned to the clutter of his rooms in Beak Street, where she had laughed at his piles of paper, scattered on the floor and resting in the laps of armchairs, leaving nowhere to sit. And laughed again in the morning as ten different alarm clocks, sitting up next to the narrow sofa bed in his study, like circus poodles, all went off at more or less the same time, making it impossible to tell which one to switch off next.

'You must be pathologically anxious about time,' she had teased.

But it was the time in between that had surprised him most and taken him by storm – the sheer intensity of their lovemaking. He had not anticipated it. He felt both woken up and alarmed by it. Nor had she dissembled in any way. Even as she pleasured him, she had made it quite clear she would leave neither her husband, nor her lover, the tub-thumping architect Nicholas Rowe.

'They are my life.'

Arriving in Siena several hours later, he can still taste and feel her perfume on his body, in his hair, and in his mind. Despite her protests, he knew they would make love again.

At the miniature palazzo which he and Bianca had simply named 'La Casa', he experiences rapturously the very thing missing two days earlier at the chateau in France – the sheer, spellbinding beauty of the place, plus the joyous, hullabaloo welcomes of Roberto and Giovanna Mazetti. They are a couple after his own heart. Although cheating him regularly over money, their invoices for *benzina* to run the generators at La Casa astronomical, they are also genuinely fond of him. So happy and relieved is he to feel 'at home' again, that Leonardo decides to remain in Siena for the rest of the week, before rebooking his return flight to Singapore from Rome. In his absence, the Chinese authorities have reluctantly agreed to a limited film schedule in the streets close to Tiananmen

Square. But Leonardo has by now, in any case, decided to outwit them by splicing old news footage of the Tiananmen Square massacre with new film, in order to better reflect the politics at the heart of his story.

CHAPTER 16

Flying north from Guilin to Xian, Stephen and Bianca discover a change of mood in this vast country of China, and their own mood changes with it. In Yangshuo the atmosphere had been relaxed, almost permissive, Guilin County too close to its southern border with Vietnam, someone explained, not to be infected by some of its louche Francophile ways. Xian, in comparison, wears its pall of Communist loyalty heavily; the mood of its people brow-beaten, yet obdurate. Added to which, the weather is bitterly cold.

They are booked into the Bell Tower Hotel, where a brash foyer of shiny Formica surfaces acts as a deceptive prelude to the long, Soviet-like, plum-coloured corridors above, leading to Spartan cells, whose only luxury is an abundance of hot water. Breakfast in the morning is like a scene from Fritz Lang's *Metropolis*, the elaborate machinery of a previous industrial age translated into gigantic toasting machines and samovars, designed to miniaturise men and their banal desire for food and drink. The kitchen staff each have a sliver of a job: 'Dispenser of sugar-buns'; 'Maker of omelettes...'

Tables are communal. Innocently joining one, almost empty, Stephen and Bianca experience the immediate rebuff of the two Chinese people occupying it, who pick up their plates to escape from them in repugnance. It leaves them feeling bewildered. Unlike the pretty smiles of the faces in Guilin, here the features of the Chinese are darkened in gloom, the monochrome of their complexions as though carved in wood. A persistent joylessness pervades the room.

But for Stephen and Bianca, there is work to be done: the ornate cruciform structure of the town, with its massively built walls and drum towers to be understood; the Muslim quarter of the town, with its surprise medina of narrow streets and magical mosque to be explored, and, on their second day, the Goose Pagoda and Xian warriors to be visited.

The warriors, beneath their duvets of red mud, gaze back impassively, without surprise, at the tourist hoards who come to revere them. Their features, like their modern equivalents in the bowels of the Bell Tower Hotel, are curiously swaddled and inexpressive, like people who remember duty but have long relinquished feeling. But the moments which enchant Bianca most are sudden, fleeting moments of perception, rather than any great sense of holiday. She too feels duty bound: to the Bell Tower, the warriors, the endless meals of chicken with peanuts and boiled rice, and to the cabaret dancing of pretty, acrobatic young girls, as supple as bamboo, who interweave and animate their Chinese minuets with calligraphies of jewel-coloured silk sashes, all set to a music that is like hysterical rain.

Passing incidents of paradox also delight her: the elegance of a young, handsome Chinese man in the Bell Tower foyer, his Italian-suited suavity compromised by still having its designer label lightly stitched to the outer cuff of his jacket; the breathtaking reversals from prudery to immodesty in the lavatorial habits of Chinese women. How they begin their undress in the public corridors leading to toilets then leave the doors of their stalls open and flapping, while loudly performing their ablutions, all the time chatting to one another in the blunted vowels of Chinese.

Best of all about Xian, Bianca loves hers and Stephen's lovemaking. At night, in their warm, crimson cell, they find each other out and fight against the cold in a pavane that is both sweet and desperate.

Bianca does not forget Max. On the contrary, she misses him. But the importance of her love for Stephen is too indelible. She cannot imagine turning to him, to say: 'Last night I made love with someone else.'

She realises part of her confusion over Max is her own persistent feeling that he expects something from her; something imperative, yet impossible to understand. He has become a feverish buzzing in her mind, as though travelling with them and breeding an excitable anticipation in her. Yet expectation of what exactly eludes her.

She is again the dutiful child, trying to make sense of adult emotions, in codes she does not fully understand... And always there alongside her, the only man whom she actually trusts and loves, Stephen. Whatever the truth of her feelings for Max, she knows he is to be treated as a chimera in their lives. For if not, all else in their world would be made suspect. Not only are her emotions under attack but the very fundaments of her life. She refuses to apply the word 'love' to her feelings for Max. Too extravagant. It is also a word that already belongs to Stephen.

Stretching out her hand, she whispers: 'I do love you, you know.'

Stephen sighs, turning away and looking into the distance... That is the point – he does know, better than she at times, just how much she loves him. But for him, things are infinitely simple. He had always loved her; he still does. And because of that passion, it has had to be accommodated in lives that had no expectation of ever making room for such a love. Whereas Bianca seems, at times, to be waiting still for something more definitive, some extra sign of truthfulness.

I blame her mother.

Losing her mother's love at so young an age had taught Bianca unthinkable, instantaneous loss, leaving her unsure of her bearings. Alongside her natural optimism was always her expectation of things going irretrievably wrong.

He recalls William and Anya Johnson, as they were, when he first met them... At the time, Bianca was seventeen, and he three years older and about to leave the London School of Economics with a first-class degree in Political Science; politics had already started to interest him. Anya's fundamental anarchy, combined with her glamorous beauty and surprising Bolshevik snobberies, had both alarmed and intrigued him. Better read than anyone else he had so far met, she was also passionate about theatre. Whenever he stayed at the cottage, they would travel to Colchester, where a fast-paced exchange of repertory would replace Chekhov's *The Seagull* one week with Ugo Betti's *The Burnt Flower-Bed* the next.

William Johnson was suave, driven and cruel with angry regret. Elegantly witty, he was nevertheless brutal in his criticism of others. In fact, they both were. Suppressed anger informed his every mood and gesture; even the energy which impelled him across a room was imbued with ferocity. He railed against the tragedy of his own self-imposed choices. At the time, Stephen knew little of art but enough to recognise the graceful integrity in William's paintings, which were littered everywhere... on the walls, stacked behind bookcases and hidden behind curtains. Despite masquerading as a home, the cottage, with its modernist G-plan sofas, marble-topped coffee tables and Swedish glass ashtrays remained one giant studio... William's studio.

As a couple, they seemed to vacillate between stormy hilarity and violent loathing of all things... including each other. Although not knowing it at the time, he was witnessing a marriage in crisis, a crisis whose roots in the war were again simmering to a boil. Bianca, meanwhile, was both little diplomat and chief pawn in their game, as well as their most precious possession. They both, in their different ways, adored her and resented Stephen's intrusion into their little triumvirate, while grudgingly recognising his every right to do so. It was clear, even to them, that Stephen loved her very much too.

* * *

Several years after William had returned belatedly post-war from the Middle East, eventually coming to live with Anya in Paris and bringing with him a high pram, 'une carosse Anglaise' – much to the admiration of the impoverished French, who had never seen anything so luxurious – he and Anya went to the Mairie together to register the birth of their daughter, Bianca.

Standing in the shadows, unnoticed by William, was a tall, handsome man in a double-breasted suit. He had tried to persuade his father, le Comte de Courcelles, to agree to Anya's divorce so that he could marry her, but the Count had refused. The family owned a mansion in Neuilly, and an estate in Les Landes but was in every other way impoverished. His normally charming father was adamant: Charles must either marry an aristocrat like himself, or the daughter of a wealthy industrialist who, in exchange for a title, could be expected to reverse the family fortunes. Le Comte had always welcomed Anya gladly into both his homes, had greatly enjoyed her company, her intelligence and her beauty, but he would not let his son marry her. And Anya's sweet-natured, diminutive mother, suddenly arriving unannounced from London, had persuaded her daughter that she must therefore maintain her marriage to William. Anya and Charles had both given in, but their affair was never renounced. And when the name 'Johnson' was added to Bianca's two birth certificates, one in French and one in English, the man in the shadows had silently wept. To witness his child given over into the care of this Englishman, William Johnson, was a task almost beyond him.

It was not until shortly after this ceremony, at which, much to William's surprise, the Maire himself had presented them with dragées, the sweet, sugar-coated, nursery-coloured almonds used to celebrate a new birth in France, that William finally realised Anya's affair with the Frenchman was continuing behind his back – even as he painted in the studio Anya had found for him in the rue Jacob. He left Paris immediately, returning to England and the cottage, so wretched at the time that he almost threw himself overboard on the Channel crossing – only prevented from doing so by a Yorkshire friend, Walter Greenhale, who just happened to be travelling on the same steamer.

Anya had eventually resigned herself to coming home to 1950s Britain, persuaded to do so by her own mother's concerns for her daughter's respectability. She and Bianca arrived at the cottage without warning one morning to find that William, in her absence, had set up home with a girl of gypsy extraction, known locally as 'Bubbles'. Bubbles was asked to leave. But thereafter Anya always made particular efforts of kindness towards both her and her subsequent family of three children, all boys, whom she and her farm-labourer husband housed in an old-fashioned, decoratively painted gypsy caravan, tucked into a narrow village lane lined with moss.

When Bianca was five years old and on her way to Sunday school, William had sat her down, explaining that neither he nor Anya believed in God, but that she could, if she wanted to… And just six years old when, following a particularly brutal fight between herself and William, Anya first told her that she had no way of knowing whether Bianca was William's or Charles's child, while adding: 'You look like the Frenchman…'

The rows got worse and worse. Now deprived of American funds, and attempting to live on William's painting, they were, despite his regular exhibitions at the Redfern Gallery, increasingly poor, even resorting to smoking the dried filigree leaves of poplar trees whenever tobacco was scarce. At the village shop, they lived increasingly on tick. They also fought frequently and viciously, and periodically Anya would return on her own to Paris. Bianca had never forgotten her mother's distraught fury when, as a child, she had one day spilled Anya's last bottle of Arpege perfume. It was that delicious scent, along with the sweet smell of Pond's face cream, that she most nostalgically associated with childhood. Not until years later did she realise the significance of her mother's anger; she had spilt Charles's last, precious gift to her.

Eventually, Charles had married the industrialist's daughter his father had hopefully predicted for him. Anya and Charles met only once more, in London, during one of his visits to the Astors; their love, by then, tired and worn out. Their eyes, which had once sought each other's greedily, now flickered with uncertainty. But the grief they both felt at their loss had never healed. It expressed itself throughout both their lives in bouts of infidelity and fury. They no longer sought what they had lost in each other but searched for it constantly outside their marriages. And in their relationship with their two daughters (Charles also had a daughter with his French wife), tried to recapture some of that passion with life that they had lost, treating their daughters like miniature adults, who must grow up quickly and learn how to respond to adult emotion; not sexually in any way, but with that fierce emotional purity and finality of an undeniable love. It was rich cake and for both Anya's daughter, Bianca, and Charles's daughter, Marie-Therese, there was the perpetual bruising tempo of unadulterated passion and growing up with the imperative race of always needing to catch up with the understanding of others.

* * *

The following day in Bantry Bay, a violent storm prevents Sinead's fisherman friend, Jack, from reaching the island. Blackened cloud chases early morning sunlight. Rain lashes the island in furious diagonals of energy, tall waves exploding in spray against the narrow jetty landing… By midday, all is twilight.

After humdrum breakfast chatter, Max feels himself longing

for silence. Making fitful apology, he returns to bed, lying fully clothed beneath the patchwork quilt, his arms supporting his tangled halo of curls like a pillow. He waits... Once or twice, he gets to his feet, restlessly pacing the room. From the low-slung, letter-box window, there is little to see; sleet and rain creating a river of its surfaces.

His thoughts are of Bianca, his features shot through with grief. Memories of smiles chasing tantalisingly across her face haunt him.

What did I do wrong?

He feels trapped in a familiar scenario of giddy optimism, all too suddenly stifled.

And why was she so reticent about her trip to China? Is some secret attached to it?

Despite their patched-together truce at the National Gallery café, their real misunderstanding, he now realises, had originated at the theatre, the night he played Hesketh James for a fool. Although reluctant to admit it, Hesketh's presence had shocked him deeply. Even now, he was unable to rid himself of the impression made on him by that poor, blight of a creature; the bloodshot eyes, the distraught, haggard face and intense loneliness of a man who, no matter how unlovable, waits desperately, year after year, for the salvation of one kind, familiar word saying: 'I remember you.'

It was heart-breaking stuff, yet Bianca had resented him for saying so. He wonders just how damaged she is by it all. Up until that evening, she had seemed so very poised.

Perhaps beyond that facade is someone altogether more fragile?

Restlessly throwing back the quilt, Bianca continues to preside, hawk like, over his thoughts, but she is not the only focus of his reverie. Feeling as though Bianca already exists inescapably within himself, there is something else, still more elusive, which he awaits to inhabit his mind... It might be a memory, a fragile seam of thought or a single line of poetry – his only certainty knowing that it trembles there, at the very edge of his mind, and all he needs do is wait.

The isolated joy of this island is that there is no one to chide him while he waits; no phone calls to parry, not even his agent to placate. Above all, no one demanding witty, sophisticated conversation from him. In that sense, Sinead does not count; he expects her to be neither alarmed nor intrigued by his silences. She is simply part of the blessedness of solitude. He starts to read, then falls asleep, fully clothed, only waking several hours later to her gentle knock on the door, telling him supper is ready. Feeling momentarily drugged, he sips the cup of tea she brought him, checking for the missing thought. But no, still not there.

The following day, the storm is worse. Venturing outside, the wind whips the door viciously from Sinead's grasp, inviting in a whirlwind breeze, which lifts books and papers into the air and causes plates from the pine dresser to smash to the floor. The log fire belches acrid smoke, and lightweight broom handles scatter like nine-pins. Only with Max's help does she close the door against the fierce gale. To her great dismay, her mobile phone fails to work.

With the day darkening to menace, Sinead and Max settle into the womb-like seclusion of the warm kitchen, a hesitant solidarity playing between them... But it is a false intimacy, based more on insularity and need than any true sympathy of knowing. Max tells anecdotes from theatre life, designed to amuse, while revealing nothing of himself; the same stories he dines out on whenever forced to endure expensive dinners with the Hollywood producers who love his screenplays but remain sceptical of his bohemian personality. Once or twice, he notices Sinead glance quizzically at him. He turns away, refusing the questions in her eyes.

But he too surveys her windswept looks, guessing her to be in her late twenties, surreptitiously tracking the strands of unkempt blonde hair plastering her brow, her tiny figure, heavily disguised beneath androgynous jogging clothes, the neat, fleet rhythm of her movements and feet encased in rubberised trainers, with the moulded wings of Pegasus at their heels.

'What about you?' he asks reluctantly. 'Is this job temporary or have you other ambitions?'

Thinking she detects a note of scorn in his question, her dark eyes study him carefully. Max again finds himself thinking: *She's almost beautiful at times.*

His mind turns away in agony, missing Bianca. It occurs to him this was an odd choice, agreeing to be locked in such isolation with a perfect stranger. His mind somersaults between loneliness and a yearning for intimacy.

'I'd like to sail the Atlantic single-handedly,' she announces thoughtfully.

Astonished, Max smiles brightly. 'You could start right here. Just turn right out of Bantry Bay and keep going.' He pauses. 'Will you ever do it, do you think?'

'I don't know...'

Reluctant to discuss it further, she suddenly asks: 'Are you married?'

Max flinches. Initially intending to lie, the question catches him off guard, and he answers truthfully: 'No longer... Although, I used to be.'

This was the very conversation he was most hoping to avoid.

'What happened?'

Max hesitates. 'I'd rather not talk about it,' he begins.

Witnessing Sinead's doubtful expression, he reflects scathingly: *Perhaps she's one of those women who require all personal details to be discussed openly? The gentle art of coaxing familiarity through confession*, he speculates viciously. Then, changing tack: *What does it actually matter what I tell her? She's a stranger... someone I'll never see again after this trip.*

Taking a deep breath, in a sudden swift tumble of words, he admits: 'My wife fell in love with my best friend, and I divorced her so she could marry him.'

'Good God, weren't you angry?' asks Sinead, aghast.

'No, not really... That was partly the problem; I think she needed me to be angry. But I've an annoying habit of always seeing things from the other person's point of view.'

Everything was now beginning to sound throwaway and meaningless to Max.

'Have you remained friends with them?' she asks, puzzled.

'Yes, although more for their sakes than mine. The spark in their relationship seems to depend on my still being there to cuckold.'

Starting to enjoy himself, the whole situation suddenly strikes

Max as hilarious, while Sinead remarks uncomprehendingly: 'How dreadfully sad...'

Whereupon, Max's mood reverses yet again. 'At your age, I would probably have thought so too,' he replies dismissively. 'But now I just think of it as one of the more unlikely truths. People are far more complicated than they even know themselves to be. It's part of what makes them so fascinating.'

He pauses, still vaguely irritated by Sinead's conventional display of innocence. There is nothing he despises more than emotional naivety.

'Actually, it's one of the things I love most about people – their occasional, inevitable bouts of perversity.'

Stammering, Sinead's Irish brogue is shocked into a caricature of itself: 'Heavens, what... can... you... possibly mean now?'

'I mean that I love people for all the idiosyncratic, paradoxical ways they turn out to be, despite themselves. It's what makes me want to write. Had my ex-wife deliberately set out to hurt me, I might never have forgiven her. But it wasn't like that. We were all three often together, my wife, my best friend and myself. He too works in the theatre, and one day she discovered she loved him more than she loved me.'

He glances away, hiding a momentary blush of shame. 'Yet even that,' he adds pensively, 'turned out not to be strictly true.'

Sinead gazes at him, wide-eyed.

Can she really be this innocent, so easily shockable?

Max feels oddly annoyed. In his catalogue of values, a lack of emotional complexity rates as one of the world's most guilty sins.

Turning towards her squarely, refusing to be charmed, he asks: 'What makes you so sure you're capable of loving just one person forever?'

She pales, recoiling from the raw contempt in his voice. Witnessing her dismay, Max suddenly remembers that they are strangers... his anger deserting him.

'Please forgive me. I didn't mean to be so unforgivably rude.'

Gazing back steadily, Sinead admits: 'I really don't know...' the honesty of her reply causing her to blush. 'But I hope so... The trouble is, I like to take risks.'

'But why?'

She hesitates, searching for the right words. 'Flirting with danger makes me feel alive.' She struggles to be more exact. 'I just seem to need it in some way. To me, risk feels like ecstasy.'

Again, she blushes at her own revelation.

'You must mean physical danger?' pursues Max, following his line of thought to the bitter end. 'But perhaps what you really need is emotional risk? If you haven't yet met your match emotionally, when you do, the need to prove yourself physically will feel less urgent.'

It is now Sinead's turn to feel contempt. She glances at him quizzically, as if seeing him for the first time, his eyes half closed in thought. Propelling himself to and fro in the battered rocking chair, his tousled head of curls attractively to one side, he is again dressed like a clown, in red pantaloons caught halfway up his calves in thick woollen socks and a moth-eaten jumper trailing almost to his knees. Yet there is no mistaking the intensity and handsome intelligence in the lines of his face, nor the sensitivity in his expressive hands. It occurs to Sinead that he is dangerous in some inexplicable way.

Lowering her gaze, she asks in a subdued voice: 'Have you met your match?'

'Good God, yes,' Max replies unhesitatingly, thinking of Bianca.

Sinead blushes deep scarlet, before turning away in embarrassment.

Like two creatures who have ventured too far, they both now retreat. As the storm battles, they play Scrabble, to cover the long silences hovering between them. After lunch, exhausted, they fall asleep; Max, stretched out on the tartan blanket covering the sofa in front of the open log fire and Sinead now curled in the rocking chair.

Not until their third morning does the storm finally abate and the sun begin to shine. Sinead's mobile rings merrily again, just as they are finishing breakfast. It is Jack! Now that the storm has passed, he plans to 'walk the island' with them after lunch, bringing some of his morning's catch with him for their supper.

Back in London, Robin Holderness and Beatrice Byng had met twice more since the afternoon of Robin's talk at The Society's headquarters in Bloomsbury.

Unbeknown to Leonardo, Robin had recently moved from the elegant expanse of his Highgate home to a tiny flat in the West End, at the top of a tall town house in Soho's Golden Square. Often spotting Leonardo out and about in adjoining Beak Street, he had never yet gone out of his way to say hello. Nor had he the impression that Leonardo had seen him and was avoiding him. Attending Leonardo and Bianca's dinner parties was one thing; making small talk in the street quite another. Plus Robin has the sombre mentality of the academic who considers it vulgar to make money from intellectual ideas, not sure that he approves of Leonardo's reputation as philosopher film maker and the vast sums of money he makes running his international film school. Robin suspects him of being a plagiarist and charlatan, rather than an inspired originator. Whereas, Robin considers himself a purist, with the wit not to confuse philosophy with other disciplines, the way European philosophers do, with their all-inclusive emphasis on psychology and literature.

Leonardo is Italian, for pity's sake... Besides, what can philosophy possibly have to do with film?

Recently, Robin had also spotted Leonardo early one morning at a café in Old Compton Street having breakfast with Solange, the wife of one of his most respected colleagues and girlfriend to that 'nauseating dolt' Nicholas Rowe. But the only person he mentions this to is Beatrice, insisting she repeat his discovery to no one.

That first, heady afternoon spent with Beatrice, after his fiasco of a talk to The Society's 'crowd of misfits' as he now thinks of them, had graduated from drunken flirtation over tapas in Lamb's Conduit Street to an afternoon showing of an early Bellocchio film *I pugni in tasca*, followed by tea in his Soho Square eyrie.

Despite Beatrice's extraordinary confession at The Society lecture, he was still unsure what to do. He felt shy. Partly of her beauty but also of her glamorous marriage to the celebrated Byng.

Glancing at her heavily bejewelled fingers, their dazzle of ruby and gold, he wondered what he possibly had to offer her, feeling inhibited in ways that never affected him when seducing students. They, after all, were his own creatures… at least for a while. Although, it always eventually transpired that they too were only on loan.

Settling Beatrice on the battered leather sofa that had witnessed some of the most important moments of his life to get a good look at her, the late afternoon sun from one of his tall windows streaming unhindered over her pale face, he took up position opposite her on a high-backed chair, with the light behind him. Gently, he encouraged her to talk.

A look of lightning panic crossed her features, like a dam breaking; her voice at first tentative, strangled by its sense of shame, was laced with insult. The skin on her face was heavily drawn and almost blue in pallor, the dying afternoon light revealing networks of fine lines beneath its surfaces of beauty. All of a sudden, Robin noticed a strange, rancid smell infecting the room… the smell of fear. She spoke of love and hate, in equal measure; the love Byng owed her, the hate she felt for him and his former mistress for humiliating her so publicly with their passionate indiscretions, adding triumphantly: 'Yet he insists he loathes her now.'

She talked and talked, like a river bursting its banks, incapable of stopping. Occasionally looking up, she searched the room bewildered, unclear to Robin whether she still knew he was there. And yet, he managed to stay still. He, the arch academic inquisitor, managed to stay silent. Perhaps she had already forgotten saying 'I want you to make love to me.'

Robin, himself, no longer knew what he wanted to do.

Then, suddenly, a violent cracking sound broke the stillness of the room as a London pigeon, a great beast of a bird, flung itself against the tall window. Robin flinched in alarm, but Beatrice rose to her feet, trembling. Robin turned to look at her – all beauty spent. No longer the glamorous odalisque of Bianca's dinner party, she resembled a frightened little girl, her focus solely on him, looking up beseechingly at his great height. To them both, it seemed as if the distance between them might last forever.

Robin witnessed her frailty, her slenderness, the pale violet pashmina now crumpled to shabbiness about her narrow shoulders. Above all, he witnessed her new ugliness and fell in love with her. In one big stride, he crossed the room, looking long into her tear-stained eyes before kissing her tenderly. At first, she seemed not to know what to do, how to respond. Then, suddenly, a shudder of joy possessed her, and her stricken body became soft and sensuous in his arms. All doubts falling away, he lifted her in his arms and carried her effortlessly, kicking open the panelled French doors behind the old leather sofa to reveal an alcove bedroom, its space taken up entirely by a vast bed, dressed in tobacco-brown sheets. His bachelor pad.

Laying her down gently, he arranged her against the counterpane. 'Do nothing... I want to undress you myself.'

She lay obediently still, observing his every move, while slowly, piece by piece, he removed her clothing, every stolen piece another small revelation of joy. Motionless, she lay looking up at him watchfully but unafraid. He expected her underwear to be coquettishly feminine, to match the elegance of her expensive skirt and blouse. Instead, her plain black panties had panels of torn lace at their sides, her bra discoloured and frayed. Yet instead of disappointment, her rags of panties delighted Robin. After all the crushed luxury of her outer clothes, it seemed to confirm something he needed to know. No longer unsure, no longer afraid, nor was he fooled. As he took her in his arms, she responded joyously. A fierce desire consumed him. In the morning, she looked more beautiful than he had ever known her.

* * *

So affected with renewed gaiety are Max and Sinead by the afternoon sunshine and warm breeze in Bantry Bay, they fail to notice Jack's fishing boat slide silently into dock against the island's narrow jetty of serrated rocks. He walks in abruptly, to the tune of their laughter.

Max is telling an anecdote about an actress who had sent him a photograph of a different part of her naked body every day for a week, in the hope of being given a part in one of his plays; Sinead is giggling helplessly. A dark shadow suddenly blocks the light from their open kitchen door... With the sun behind him, Jack appears a featureless, threatening silhouette. Startled, they both jump, Max simultaneously registering the younger man's dismay.

The poor fool is jealous!

Laughter now dying in her throat, Sinead throws herself into a profuse pantomime of welcome.

'How are ye, Jack? Come indoors, won't you now?' she insists, relaxing into her sing-song Irish lilt.

Obeying, the fisherman steps into the room's warmth, standing hesitantly, midway on the red flagstones, his weather-beaten cheeks nodding formally, speechlessly to them both; his sharp, animal eyes watching them carefully. Undeterred, Sinead takes charge.

This is the kind of familiarity she's best at, thinks Max admiringly.

He watches as she weaves a web of diplomacy between all three of them, until the upright solemnity of the fisherman's ruffled soul is transformed into happy well-being. He holds out two plastic bags, the smaller one containing silver crescents of whitebait, caught earlier that morning, the other a black bin liner.

'These two haven't eaten, so they're a bit sleepy... Put them in the fridge and have them tomorrow.'

Sinead peers into the depths of the bag. 'What are they?'

The bag moves suddenly, and she drops it in alarm.

Jack laughs, a breathless, skittish snort of a laugh. Onto the red flagstones crawls first one, then a second, lobster, their shells the lustre and colour of blue-black bruises. Sinead backs away from the primeval creatures in horror.

'Just what am I supposed to do with those now?' she asks aghast.

Jack chuckles hysterically.

He laughs like a young girl, thinks Max grimly.

'Put them in a deep pan of tepid water and bring it gently to the boil.'

'I don't know how to pick them up,' she states doubtfully, observing the lobsters' blind progress across the kitchen floor.

With practised expertise, Jack picks them up midway, leaving their claws flailing impotently. Depositing them in the lower compartment of the fridge, the lobsters arrange themselves slug-gishly, like unstrung marionettes. Max suddenly notices their claws, bound tight with rubber bands. Watching the play of this scene, he relishes every moment of its drama.

As Jack shuts the fridge door, the lobsters' long pincers wave optimistically one last time; Sinead, emerging from this encounter with the primitive world a little pale, whereas Jack is back in his element. He starts to look younger, almost boyish. Max asks about his morning's fishing?

'Prawns mainly… We sell several tons a day to Spain.'

Gambas alla Plancha, thinks Max gloomily, remembering the ubiquity of this dish on every Spanish holiday menu.

They drink coffee, accompanied by thick slices of Dundee cake, heavily encrusted with almonds, before setting off 'to walk the island'. Max had noted this peculiar turn of phrase two days ear-lier but not really understood it, imagining it Irish shorthand for 'going for a walk'. Not until they have walked for more than twenty minutes, the crofter's cottages no longer in sight, does he finally begin to appreciate its accuracy.

Beyond the quadrangle of dwellings, overlooking the cove and jetty, by which all visitors to the island must arrive – the rest of its coastline too impenetrably steep with teeth-like rocks – the land rises magisterially above the buildings in a protective hug of sculpted land before stretching out into long, sweeping pla-teaus of grassland, whose only interruption is a ragged pond, with a tall look-out shelf of land to one side. This is where they find the goats congregated, their gentle faces turned benignly out to sea, in dreamy contemplation of Sinead's ambition to sail the Atlantic. In the turbulent waters far below, there is nothing but a rough gun-metal sea and the miniature flecked sail of an occasional vessel, while, above their heads, stretch canopies of sweet-scented emptiness – a panoramic sky with baroque land-scapes of gigantic scudding clouds. Unfolding beneath their feet are luxurious mattresses of supple, springy green grass, which ferocious island winds have persuaded to lie sideways and long, creating surfaces surprisingly easy to walk on. Max is completely spellbound.

Most enthralling of all is the unexpected, greedy sensation of private ownership. Owning property had never held more than casual appeal for Max. His town house in Islington and his weekend cottage outside Bath, both overflowing with books, affect him with a despairing, neglectful indifference. So much so, he occasionally books himself into a hotel to get away from their clutter. But this new sensation of owning one's own miniature, private world, too vast to walk in a single day and surrounded by water, with its connotations of inviolability, exclusivity and privilege, feels suddenly headily addictive. It is something Max would neither have sought nor anticipated for himself. Yet it suits his temperament perfectly. He begins to understand his London friend's pleasure in owning the island, no matter how infrequently he visits. There it remains, a sort of innocent presence, forever wild, forever unchangeable, yet patiently waiting to bestow its silent blessings of freedom and unspoiled nature.

After two and a half hours exploring, with the wind stealing the words and laughter from their mouths, they return exhilarated to the warmth of the kitchen, where, in addition to boiled chicken with rice, Sinead tosses the freshly caught whitebait in seasoned flour and fries them quickly in butter, before deliciously squeezing lemon juice over them.

Max shares a celebratory bottle of Chablis with Sinead, while Jack sticks to the cans of lager he had brought with him, all three finally happy and at ease. After the tensions of the past two days, Max and Sinead are grateful to relax in the company of a third person. It feels more normal, less claustrophobic, Jack's jealousy finally dissolved. Sinead enquires solicitously after his father, who had recently died, a fisherman before him, knowing that Jack is grieving still.

'Tell us about your childhood, Jack...'

Which is when Max's little miracle happens.

'I never properly understood or appreciated my father until after he died,' Jack replies sadly. 'Always a hard task-master, he never explained why it was just the two of us while I was growing up; never spoke of my mother, except to say she had left us when I was a baby. Then, after he died, I found some letters exchanged over the years with my aunt, his brother's wife, hidden in an old suitcase and secured with padlock and chain… My uncle refused to make the journey, but his wife came back from America for his funeral and, at long last, told me the truth…'

Max raises his head to observe Jack more closely; his eyes are bloodshot and threaded with pain.

'You see, not only was she my aunt but my mother too. The two brothers had jointly inherited the cottage belonging to my grandfather. Early in her marriage to his brother, she and my father had an affair. It was my uncle who insisted she abandon me in the care of my father, rather than face the shame of discovery. She used to write, begging news of me, and every birthday, my father would send her a photograph, addressed to a PO Box, so my uncle wouldn't suspect… I still remember those Box Brownies of his, the endless care he always took in setting up my portrait…'

Sinead gently stretches out a hand, instinctively touching Jack's sleeve in a gesture of sympathy. Whereas, for Max, this is the elusive moment he was patiently waiting for; a slender kernel of an idea for his next play. Fleetingly thinking of his ex-wife, now married to his best friend, he resolves: *But I'll base the aunt's character on Bianca, rather than my ex-wife.*

'Why are you smiling?' asks Sinead, shocked by Max's sudden elation in the face of Jack's grief.

'Nothing,' he replies, wrapping the arms of his moth-eaten jumper about himself in a close hug. 'Nothing at all… Just the joy of this island, that's all.'

Wiping away a rough tear, in his simple good nature Jack has misunderstood, presuming Max to have kindly, diplomatically changed the subject on his behalf. He glances appreciatively across the table, raising the can of lager to his flayed, weather-beaten lips.

'Cheers…'

'*Santé,*' answers Max more soberly, sipping from his wine glass.

'Shall I be dishing the trifle now?' asks Sinead.

Inexplicably, all three burst out laughing.

* * *

The following morning, Jack having sailed back to the mainland late at night, and Max already busily working on ideas for his new play, Sinead opens the fridge door to find the two lobsters still sluggishly waving their long, tired pincers at her. Picking them up gingerly in rubber-gloved hands, she carries them down to the water's edge. Any idea of cooking them strikes her as unthinkable. The tide is out in the little cove as she places them in the shallows, before snipping the elastic bands binding their claws, then watches in wonder as their blue-black shells take on the patina of pebbles beneath the gently lapping waves. Briefly, the two creatures hesitate before moving forward more confidently to become dark shadows beneath the ruffle of waves as they take to their element, the sea.

CHAPTER 17

From the barren corridors of the Bell Tower, Stephen and Bianca now fly to five-star luxury in Hangzhou, a city built on the borders of the gigantic lake where Chairman Mao kept his summer house. In the late afternoon of their arrival, both the lake and their hotel are shrouded in dense, cotton-wool mists, the Shangri-La's elegant foyer and extravagant flower arrangements displaying the same details of comfort and chintzy good taste as any English country-house hotel. But by next morning, with the mists burned off, the views from their room reveal an interlace of delicate walkways, stretching out across the lake's vast, peaceful surfaces. They might just as easily be in Geneva; everything here reflective of familiar middle-class comfort. Not just the hotel, but the entire town, with its modern, turreted Tyrolean-style villas, plus the obvious affluence of its people. Yet all interpreted through a veil of sensibility that is purely Chinese.

* * *

On the day of Chloe's secret visit to the Society of Portrait Painters, Hesketh is at home with Bruno. As always, Bruno is sitting on the floor by the lift, with Hesketh nearby, gazing fixedly at Bianca's triptych, something he refrains from doing whenever Chloe is at home for fear of offending her. He is practicing a new discipline of (e)xtra (s)ensory (p)erception, suggested by an article in the same newspaper that publishes an anonymous, weekly column of erotica, signed tantalisingly 'Miss Dior'.

The sweet floral, little-girl scent of Miss Dior had been Bianca's favourite perfume twenty-five years earlier, and there are days when Hesketh believes the column is written by her and secretly intended for him; Bianca's ingenious, extrasensory way of communicating with him.

Foraging recently in the basement, where all the flats keep extra storage space, he had opened an ancient trunk full of Bianca's things. As he did so, the sweet scent of Miss Dior had escaped into the dank air, filling him with nostalgia. It was like letting a genie out of a bottle. Greedily plunging his fists into the feminine tangle of her clothes, he had buried his face in the delicious scent emanating from an outfit she had seldom worn.

Concentrating hard on her painting, attempting to empty his mind of all thought other than a fierce meditation on the painting itself, according to the upbeat wording of the article, having successfully eliminated the ceaseless jabberwocky of his 'ordinary' mind, the miniature figures of a man and woman in each panel should step from their frames and start to speak, yielding up the riddle of their message for him. Still believing the figures in the miniature paintings to represent himself and Bianca, there is no one to observe the sensuous rapture invading his features.

His reverie is broken by the sound of the doorbell. Not expecting anyone, he decides to ignore it. But the bell chimes again, this time more insistently. Bruno starts to make dangerous humming noises. Reluctantly tearing himself away from the painting, the ill grace in his voice sounds almost vicious, whereas the voice greeting his is gentle, carefree and innocent. It is the voice of a young American social worker, newly appointed to check on Bruno. Buzzing her in, Hesketh waits by the lift; Bruno, silent now, concentrates on the music of the lift.

Five minutes later, a young, pretty Californian, with bubbly blonde curls framing a freckled, sun-kissed face above a curvaceous body steps from the lift, draped in hippy-style cheesecloth, her manner nonetheless formal as she explains, 'I've come to see Bruno.'

She glances fondly at his averted face.

The greater surprise is that, tucked invisibly into a shawl, in the curve of her arm, is a brand-new baby; no more than a few weeks old. Hesketh, fresh from the miasma of his attempt to contact Bianca through the ethers, looks at her in disorientated amazement.

She, in turn, blushes prettily, explaining that she hopes he doesn't mind her turning up a day early, but she had found herself in the neighbourhood, visiting another patient, and thought she would try her luck with their doorbell, particularly since her baby needs feeding quite urgently.

'Would you mind if I were to feed the baby first, before examining Bruno?' she asks sweetly.

All this information, accompanied by the mysterious appearance of a beautiful young woman, acts like a somnolent drug on Hesketh's mind. Had she stepped from the painting to speak to him, instead of Bianca? Nodding blankly, he clumsily asks: 'Would you like to use one of the bedrooms?'

She smiles. 'Please, if it's not too much trouble?'

Hesketh hesitates. *Should I offer her mine and Chloe's bedroom?*

Probably not, he decides. Nor would Bruno tolerate any invasion of his. Instead, he offers her a little-used room, which, like his study, is concealed behind a panel in the zigzag of the corridor; the room itself small, containing no more than a spare bed for the visitors who never arrive and a few lesser known works from Hesketh's collection of post-war paintings. Poorly lit and a little dusty, it has a small bathroom attached to it.

'Perfect,' sighs the young woman gratefully.

Sinking down onto the soft bed, she lays the chortling baby on his back beside her as she prepares to feed him.

Hesketh remains in the doorway, still mesmerised, and waiting to hear Bianca's message to him. Smiling, she glances up at him, while unselfconsciously adjusting her numerous layers of clothing to reveal the milky ripeness of her beautiful breasts. Still, Hesketh remains standing. Continuing to smile at him, she picks up the baby and places him greedily, contentedly to the wonderful ripe bruise of her nipple. Nor does she complain as Hesketh draws up a low armchair, the door closing to behind him, and his knees now almost touching hers, as they both bend their heads over the suckling babe; a moment of pure intimacy. Occasionally looking up, they exchange glances of inflamed understanding with one another.

Meanwhile, Bruno is left alone, with no noise to comfort him. At first, silent, he starts to hum again; a sound that starts gentle and low before escalating into a high-pitched keen. He starts to rock himself violently side to side. Ignoring him, Hesketh and the young woman crouch absorbedly over the soporific suckling baby in her lap, their eyes meeting in secret, shared smiles.

Hearing the familiar wheeze of the lift start to ruminate several floors below, Bruno falls silent for a moment before again murmuring his distress call. It is into these two mutually exclusive scenes that Chloe suddenly steps, unheard.

Witnessing Bruno's distress, she asks: 'Where's Daddy?'

Bruno does not reply. From further along the corridor, she hears faint sounds she cannot quite identify; greedy suckling noises, punctuated by sighs. Following the corridor towards the kitchen, she notices a panel in the wall to her right slightly ajar. Neither light nor sound emerging through the crack in the door.

Must have opened of its own accord.

About to pull the door firmly shut, some instinct prompts her to push it wide open.

And there they are, lost in the gloom, her husband and the pretty young girl, the gorged baby now fast asleep in her lap, her beautiful breasts still exposed from beneath the strictures of her clothes, and Hesketh, one hand outstretched fondling one breast, while his tongue licks the other with gentle kisses; the young woman leaning back ecstatically on splayed arms, her eyes tightly closed against the rapturous sensation. It takes several seconds for either of them to notice Chloe. Behind her, watching carefully from the corridor, his face no longer averted, is Bruno.

Hesketh turns suddenly, Bruno's presence, rather than Chloe's, bringing him back to reality. Part of him still believes this moment meant; a gift from Bianca's painting to himself. Only the distraught expression on Bruno's face causes him to doubt. Getting up clumsily, backing away abruptly, he almost falls over in confusion. Startled, the young woman opens her eyes, blushing bright crimson, her freckles disappearing into the warmth of her skin.

'I-I'm so very, very sorry,' she stutters pleadingly. 'I just got carried away... The baby needed feeding.'

Chloe backs away, saying nothing, her face eloquent with sorrow and contempt. Not much older than the American girl, yet, in the space of minutes, she has been transformed into an old woman. It feels as though some new, inescapable thud of anger has lodged in her brain. For years, her jealousy had concentrated on outwitting the ghost of Bianca, until, at times, it had felt like a familiar game, with each player holding a specific role. Now, suddenly seeing how easily Hesketh would betray both herself and Bruno, even with a stranger, all her brave efforts at family life feel reduced to nil. She realises that she always has, and always would, in some indefinable way, play catch-up with the emotional frenzy devouring Hesketh. Like witnessing a new canker enter her brain, outwardly she does not react immediately. Yet slowly, slowly, she feels the new infection take hold, promising herself vengefully: *Next time police come looking for confirmation of an alibi, I shall tell the truth...*

Unresistingly for once, Bruno allows her to hug him.

'Let's go and play the piano,' she says gently.

So loudly does Bruno strike the piano keys that neither of them hears the lift doors open and Hesketh saying a confused goodbye to the now tearful young mother. Returning to the room overlooking the river, he stares hopefully, miserably at Bianca's painting again.

What does it mean?

* * *

Robin Holderness's talk in Queen Square, his casual mention of Bianca's name, have unsettled Anya badly, the bravado certainty with which she had faced the past twenty years, since she and her daughter last spoke, finally crumbling. Nor does she remember why she and Bianca had quarrelled so viciously; only that Charles de Courcelles's most enduring gift to her, her own precious baby daughter, had chosen to side with William, the father who may have treated her as his own but had never really deserved her. There was also something else, some more elusive stain of unresolved anger between them... but she no longer recalls what it was. These days, she only remembers her battles with William.

Although age has deprived Anya of none of her elegance and charm, nor has it sweetened her capacity for anger. She is as feminine and graceful as many women half her age, yet her opinions remain the same violent denunciations of her youth. Many aspects of modern life strike her as malevolent – rotten even. She is as capable of showing enthusiastic enchantment one minute, only to turn scornfully dismissive the next, as she ever was. At heart, she is still the beautiful firebrand of her youth, forever standing up to authority and the overbearing baiting of older brothers. That which the French so admired in her, her imperious mixture of righteous indignation and pride, remains intact. Even now, she would not flinch from a fight. In her own mind, her fights with William have continued unabated, despite their long absence; in many ways, just as they always were, still supremely good fuel for life. Which is why, more than any question of money, it so worries her that he might be dead.

Can one fight with the dead?

Charm may have been something she and William shared in abundance, yet they both condemned it as the language of fools, reserved mainly for dealing with life's idiots. *Il faut epater la bourgeoisie...* Whereas, in her own relationship with William, things had been more proudly, truthfully, fierce; both emotionally and intellectually. A sudden submission to sorrow sweeps over her.

How was it we lost the thread to our own darling labyrinth? she wonders despairingly.

They used to joke about it. William had known the sculptor Michael Ayrton during his East Anglia, Wivenhoe Park days. Whenever seeing yet another of his bronze Minotaur colossuses, Anya would laugh gleefully. 'That's us... blind, blundering and passionate.'

However, escalating laughter, no matter how hilarious, had never prevented them fighting. Anya still remembers how, during their most bitter rows, furniture would be thrown, crockery smashed and knives produced. Anything, but anything, to win an argument.

She remembers how once, when Bianca was little, William had hit her while in the bath; the old zinc bath at the cottage that needed filling with endless kettles of hot water, while forever spilling its suds over the kitchen floor. Meanwhile, Bianca, a pretty child with a ponytail, and dressed in one of the numerous dresses she ran up for her on her old treadle Singer sewing machine, had bounced scissor kicks up and down beside them, chanting: 'God can hear you wherever you are.'

Sometimes they stopped mid-fight, just long enough to glance at her in abashed amazement, asking: 'Who are you? Where did you come from?'

Questions that left Bianca feeling simultaneously special and lonely.

There had been something unbelievably raw and terrible about those post-war years at the cottage. Yet, to all three, they had felt like real life, devoid of either falsehood or sentiment, in those days, neither William nor Anya hesitating to tell the truth. Anya had famously gone to a party in Belsize Park and suddenly announced: 'You people have no idea how vulgar you are.'

At the village shop, she had mocked the villagers for their mealy-mouthed purchases of 'half pounds of tomatoes and quarters of Spam'.

'You're not in Great Titchfield Street now,' William reproached her.

Yet he too laughed uproariously, later reflecting that it was amusing to witness Anya on the warpath with someone else, but a little bit of hell when directed at oneself.

Whenever their battle was not with the outside world, it was with each other. They fought over the obscure meanings of words, such as 'prehensile' or 'oneirodynia', the argument so delicious that the first to reach the dictionary would lie, rather than admit defeat. Anya remembers how critical she often was of William's painting, jibing: 'Rowland was always a far better painter than you.'

After a particularly vicious row, she was not above tearing his paintings in half. Yet William too, in a white fog of rage, could also be dangerous. Even Bianca, by the time she was five years old, had learned that the trick was to always step forward into the arms of his fury; never to retreat. Retreat meant a huge, heavy arm would lift high above one's head, like a club, and come falling with a crushing blow. With the white mist of anger in his eyes, only a pace forward could restore them to their baby blue. Whereupon, William would retreat like a wounded animal.

277

The truth was, William had never forgiven Anya for her affair with Charles de Courcelles, and she was incapable of forgiving him for his failure to do so.

What was marriage for, if only to make such deadly mockery of life's passions?

William had spent his own four, absentee years of the war remaining faithful; like all cheated lovers, counting his fidelity his most virtuous and precious gift. The fact that, one night in Damascus, he had fallen in love with a beautiful Polish girl called Christine de Meinska, who had later committed suicide, didn't really count, as they had never actually been lovers – no matter how much he may have wished them to be. Confronted by his army pals' regular visits to the brothels of Cairo, he had remained sexually timid, also pathologically wary of infection. Nor had he forgotten the lascivious debauchery of his former friend, the poet Paul Ottery, with his braggart reputation for passing on the clap to unsuspecting females he encountered in the pubs of Charlotte Street, and who, along with some lesser pieces of blue-and-white pottery, had eventually stolen a valuable porcelain Chinese vase from their tongue and groove shelf in Great Titchfield Street, and, for once, failed to present them with the redeeming pawn ticket. As the years passed, Anya felt less and less convinced by the great worth of William's great prize of fidelity.

What was his relationship with the gypsy girl, Bubbles, if not infidelity?

It depended entirely on one's point of view. William, meanwhile, silently promised revenge.

But it was also true that Anya had never really forgotten her love affair with Charles de Courcelles and had perhaps inflicted its memory on her marriage in ways William could neither forgive nor forget. Occasionally, even now, she still finds herself reliving some of her more precious moments with Charles...

She remembers the celebratory, hysterical mood marking the end of war: VE Day in Paris, 8 May 1945. By then Charles's handsome face was disfigured to one side by a stray bullet from a German sniper, during one of his forays liaising with the local Bordeaux Maquis, close to where his family kept their country estate. The bullet had caught his cheek, smashing the bone and permanently blurring his vision in that eye. None of which had caused Anya to love him any less passionately; if anything, her tenderness towards him enhanced. But for him, this German insult to his good looks mattered shamefully. He started wanting to be seen less often in public, again locking Anya in his apartment to prevent her from spending evenings with colleagues and friends. Nevertheless, going out to dine the night before, on 7 May, they had ended up dancing into the smoky small hours of their favourite nightclub, 'Le Boeuf sur le Toit', surrounded by tables alternating between joyous laughter and accusatory fights; the accusatory stain of collaboration never far away.

The following morning, Paris had seemed numb, reluctant at first to react to the news war was over, a strange lassitude infecting the city. People slept late. Nothing matched the riotous euphoria that had accompanied the Liberation eight months earlier. Not until mid-afternoon, with the sun shining brightly, did crowds gradually swarm the streets. Everywhere, the tri-colour fluttered, draped from buildings and the jeeps of triumphant GIs, accompanied by raucous, hysterical women. General de Gaulle broadcast solemnly to the nation, while the full-dress Napoleonic uniform of the Garde Républicaine was rendered farcical by screaming girls clinging to every rider and horse. But not until after dark did Anya and Charles witness the incoherent, frenzied joy of the crowds at full throttle as they danced in the street against buildings, illuminated for the first time since war began, the fountains again allowed to play.

And yet, there had remained an underlying cloudy mood of sorrow in the city. Did rescue really count as victory? Was a return to everyday life truly to be looked forward to?

Many were desperately poor. Others had little notion of how to contemplate life beyond the passionate urgency of war. The freedoms they had fought for felt tainted. Anya and Charles were not the only couple in Paris that night to fear change.

William, meanwhile, was detained in the Middle East, still working for the Ministry of Information, while suffering prolonged bouts of malaria that precluded travel. So it was that, initially, Anya and Charles's dread of imminent separation proved unfounded. Anya continued working for the American army, and not until two years later did she dutifully travel back to England and the cottage to be reunited with William, as he was finally, belatedly demobbed from the army.

Arriving at the cottage in advance of him, she stepped into the chill, damp still of the place, where spiders, field mice and immense daddy-long-legs had enjoyed uninterrupted freedom. Mice ran giggling uninhibitedly through the wainscots with the authority of Beatrix Potter characters. Spiders had woven delicate networks of diaphanous threads from ceiling to mantelpiece, from windowsill to picture frame. Talcum powders of dust settled on William and Anya's still-life arrangements of pottery and furniture, each piece still in place, exactly as left years earlier. On the tall, soaring walls of the studio, reaching high into the rafters, the spiders and daddy-long-legs had had a field day, leaving long swags of webs grown heavy with dust, until they resembled dirty rags attached to the white-washed walls, the furniture standing curiously formal, as though knowing it deserved better.

Standing watchfully at the windows of the cottage, Anya witnessed William's arrival long before he could see her. He was on foot, having walked the two and a half miles from the Rivenhall Station. Instead of rushing to greet him, she mutely observed his progress and her emotions, coming ever closer, along the winding, familiar road; empty of cars, but busy with tractors and horses, leading to the two steep, landmark hills of the Mill and Green Man Pub. Through the diamond-pane windows, the pink of late afternoon sun shed dancing shadows of horse chestnut leaves onto the peeling distemper walls, colouring and reinvigorating one of William's pre-war paintings, left to mildew above the mantelpiece. Seeing him first from a distance, then close to, tall, gaunt and travelled, a dark beret on his head, his features marked by malaria, she instantly knew she no longer loved him.

Nevertheless, that night, beneath damp army blankets, they made love. She allowed him no precautions, still having the residue of her period. Not for one moment did it occur to her she might get pregnant... Two days later, during which they had rowed incessantly about the money he had been secretly hoarding from sales of his paintings in the Middle East and stealthily sending home to his parents 'for investment and safe-keeping', she again left for Paris, reminding him that it was her salary from the Potato Marketing Board that had supported the early years of their marriage and allowed him to paint.

Their rows during those two days were incendiary, spiteful and vicious – no criticism, no denunciation, no insult too severe. They railed ferociously at one another across the bruised landscape of their love, like two animals for whom pain is preferable to silent dismay... if not the capacity to love, better to inflict hurt than retreat into a torpor of sorrow. When, a few days later, a letter arrived at the cottage with a Parisian postmark, William did not hesitate to open it. Unable to decipher much of its French, he nevertheless managed to translate its opening line:

'Ma tres chere petite chatte.'

Six weeks later, Anya discovered she was pregnant. Not strictly knowing who the father was, she assumed it to be Charles de Courcelles. That first night of her return to Paris, he was waiting for her in the café on the corner below her apartment in the rue de l'Université, alerted by the telegram she had sent in advance. As she walked through the frosted door of the bar, he noticed some difference in her. She was smiling, beautiful and glowing, yet strangely hesitant; reminding him of how she had seemed when they first met, simultaneously proud and shy. He had found it a compelling mixture. Watching her cross the café floor to his side, while nimbly negotiating the tables and chairs blocking her path, he realised that he still did. The unruly copper curls of her hair tumbled to her waist, barely held in check by the tortoiseshell combs at her temples. He stood up, uncertain of himself, then sat down again abruptly. Her detour with the tables led her to the bar, where she stopped briefly to shake hands with her friend, the patron.

Has he noticed the difference in her too?

Charles found the wait insufferable.

Why waste time talking to someone else?

He got to his feet. 'Anya?' he rasped.

Turning, recognising the note of desperation in his call, as her eyes met his, she made her decision: *No need to explain… Never tell.*

Suddenly clumsily overturning a chair in her way, she rushed into his arms, allowing her small frame to become enwrapped in the folds of the pale mackintosh he wore over his double-breasted suit. Despite their many layers of clothing, she could feel the heat and speed of his erection rise to greet her. Nor would he let go. Still wrapping her close, he lifted her in his arms like a child, past the raised eyebrows of the amused patron, carrying her through the door leading to the staircase immediately below her flat. Then got no further. By now, their bodies were enmeshed in a fight; tenderness replaced by anger, absence by possession. There seemed to be no distinction between where his body began and hers ended; to Charles, she felt like an extension of all that he ever was, his limbs and his desire.

Leaning her against the closed door, her face jammed against its scuffed, peeling panels of blistered paint, his hands lifted the many yards of her wide skirts, bunching them impatiently into fists, while feeling for the delicate, strained elastic of her suspenders, tugging at her corset, desperate for the softness in her. Vaguely, her body protested, then relented. This violence was hers too.

As he entered her, he let out a cry, followed by a deep sigh; his again, to have and to hold. His body raced his pleasure against hers, just stopping in time. Nearly, not quite. Turning her towards him, his mouth and tongue angrily devouring, he lifted her in his arms, now positioning her mid-flight on the stairs, raising her skirts and lifting her narrow pelvis towards him, hands cupped beneath her buttocks, tenderly now, as if to drink from a cup. Her hands interlacing the dark ringlets of his hair, her cry of pleasure rang out unimpeded on the unlit stairs. She had come home. He waited for the sobs that racked her body to subside, then lifted her into position against him and rode her small frame to oblivion; both equal now.

Glancing up at him sleepily afterwards, she smiled, her confidence returned. He lit a Gitanes. They remained there for another half hour, just sitting on the stairs, an elderly neighbour complaining as he struggled to step past them; happily leaning against one another, her head on his shoulder, occasionally exchanging titbits of news but mostly silent, just remembering and exploring the vast mood of their love. As Charles turned to look at her, she seemed familiar again, the impression of shyness vanished.

Her first instinct was to not tell William, so sure was she the baby must be Charles's. It was her own mother who eventually persuaded her. Charles, much as he loved her, much as he rampaged and threatened revenge, failed to persuade his father to grant him permission to marry her. There were numerous objections; he was Catholic, she would be a divorcee. More importantly, he refused on pragmatic grounds. Despite their chateau in Les Landes, where she and Charles had spent carefree days bare-back riding against the sand dunes and long pampas grasses, plus the Paris house in Boulevard Lanes, the family was relatively poor. Charles's duty, his father insisted, was to marry wealth, so as to invigorate the fortunes of his aristocratic family.

Eventually, still working for the American bureau, Anya had followed her mother's advice, telling William of her pregnancy and inviting him to join her in Paris, just as she had originally dreamed of doing when they were apart. But now doing so joylessly. Still wealthy enough, she rented a studio for him in the rue Jacob, as well as maintaining her apartment in the rue de l'Université. She had not admitted to Charles her night at the cottage with William; perhaps he had guessed. She continued to insist the baby was his, with William nevertheless prepared to forgive the single night of fluke passion she had described, in exchange for the promise that it would not, could not, ever happen again. To all of which, Anya had agreed.

Consequently, William arrived in France in celebratory mode, a few weeks later... Bianca, born in a clinic in the unfashionable 13th arrondissement, where the nurse who attended Anya, a young woman called Marie, was so impressed by William's now restored handsome good looks, she first flirted with him, then tried to seduce him, suggesting he must be lonely, 'n'est ce pas', with his wife so heavily pregnant?

William, only vaguely aware of his own good looks and feeling baffled, haughtily rejected her.

For the first three weeks of her miniature life, according to French custom, Bianca was kept swaddled in bandages and picked up, like a parcel, from the bow around her baby waist.

Tentatively, back at home in the rue de l'Université, William and Anya set about making a new life for themselves. Still arguing vehemently, they also gloried happily in the galleries, restaurants and freedoms of their Parisian post-war existence, their painful memories of those two vicious nights at the cottage deflected by the daily cabaret provided by their baby daughter.

William's painting, at this time, was still imbued with the English watercolourist tradition of his contemporaries, Sutherland and Piper, but overlaid by his memories of the ill-lit interiors of Cairo; the dark nights of Egypt, illuminated by the glare of a single light bulb swinging on a hangman's noose, above the heads of wraith-thin British soldiers, caught between light and shadow, feverishly playing cards around a crowded table. Or a decorous Baghdad prostitute caught in a backlit doorway. Nothing he encountered in Paris quite matched the sensibility he had forged for himself. At times, fearing losing his way, he also saw that the challenges were irrefutable, irresistible even in some obscure way, and that he had to meet them with courage.

But when eventually discovering Anya was still seeing Charles de Courcelles behind his back, William left immediately for England and the cottage, crossing the Channel in despair, only to be rescued by his old Yorkshire pal, Walter Greenhale, who chanced to be travelling on the same boat, on his return from Marseilles. It was the French midwife Marie who had finally revealed the truth to William, happening upon him in the Tuileries Gardens one day, dutifully pushing Bianca in her high pram, and jealously provoked into revenge by his smug rejection of her. She had encountered Charles and Anya leaving a hotel together, *cinq a sept*, a few days earlier, close to La Coupole.

And it was true... Anya and Charles had dined that lunchtime at La Coupole, half shielded from prying eyes by the high-backed banquettes, their hands resting on each other's knees beneath the starched white napery of the tablecloths, theirs and everyone else's view intercepted by the turreted towers, on which oysters lay obscene and glistening on their beds of ice and lemon; the very delicacy and food of love.

They had formed the habit of meeting twice a week. Occasionally, as a special treat, Anya brought Bianca with her. Mostly, she just slept, with Charles adoring to watch her, his eyes drinking in her slumbers greedily. If ever Bianca was looking pasty-faced, Anya dabbed some rouge onto her baby cheeks to make her bonnier.

After lunch, they would repair to his apartment in Neuilly or, if time were short, to a hotel. If Bianca was with them, they laid her sleeping in an empty chest of drawers, cushioned with pillows, to prevent her falling, while they made love; the familiar pavane, which, each time, felt miraculously, deliriously reinvented.

The relationship between them had grown more tender since Bianca's birth, although a tenderness tinged with sorrow, Charles reminding himself proudly: *Anya is the mother of my child.*

But physically it remained as fiercely passionate as ever. They played out their desire for each other against the green and gold counterpanes of high-packed, old-fashioned beds, almost too steep to climb onto, yet, once reached, of delicious feather-bed softness. During these sessions, they deliberately avoided mentioning William, avoided discussing anything that might get in the way of their exclusive concentration on one another; love never in doubt.

Since becoming a father, Charles had felt less ashamed of his broken cheekbone and misted vision in one eye. He again faced the world squarely, proudly, the broken surprise in his formerly regular handsomeness now lending his looks a blemish more distinctive than repulsive. The only thing missing from their afternoons was the finality of possession. No longer was it possible for Charles to angrily lock the door against Anya's departures. By not marrying her, he had renounced all such rights; obliged now to allow her to return to William, who, at seven in the evening, would be returning home, still lost in that day's painting; still debating with himself abstraction versus figuration, oil versus watercolour...

Racing up the stairs to their flat in the rue de l'Université, he would burst through the door to greet Anya and Bianca, feeling exhausted, yet happy... Right up until the day Marie told him the unhappy truth.

Looking up at her altarpiece, Anya sighs. The past has overtaken her again; her memories now more passionate than the present, except maybe for that strange young man, Andreas, and his determination to spend time with her. The other day she had gone to a public lecture at the London School of Economics, only to find him in the audience, waiting for her and having saved her a seat. Amazed, she asked him: 'Don't you need to be at work?'

'Afternoon off,' he replied dismissively.

His brown eyes scanned her clothes. 'That outfit really suits you.'

She was wearing a primrose-yellow dress, scattered with white polka dots.

'Thank you,' she said in wonderment. 'Thank you very much.'

His eyes, creased deeply in smiles, scrutinised her closely.

* * *

Leonardo and his film crew had spent only a few more days in Singapore before leaving for Beijing. Despite assurances from the Chinese authorities, numerous obstructions had been placed in their way, until eventually Leonardo had felt vindicated by his secret plan to outwit them by splicing his new film with old newsreel footage of Tiananmen Square. In Beijing, he contents himself with shooting short, innocuous sequences of dialogue between the film's two main protagonists, the famous French film star and her less famous Chinese male counterpart, deliberately setting them against either heavily traditional interiors, with elaborate Chinese motifs of red lacquer and fire-eating dragons, or at the corners of busy modern streets, where rickshaws jostle with bicycles and everything is pell-mell. The outdoor sequences he conducts almost as filmed interviews, to pretend the less odious implications of documentary film-making, rather than evoke the altogether more subversive implications of ART.

After Beijing, he plans brief spells of filming in Suzhou and Shanghai, before returning to Paris to complete more footage, followed by the lengthy process of editing. He had originally intended editing his new film in London, but because of the planned sale of the chateau has decided to do so in Paris, further delaying his return home to London and Bianca.

Laetitia Norton is no longer travelling with him. When, eventually, she had tracked him down on the phone, Leonardo had agreed that rather than immediately put the chateau up for sale, she should finish work on its restoration, hopefully getting a good price; she, in that same call, making it clear she expected a commission from its sale, in recognition of her hard work.

Sighing, Leonardo replaces the receiver. *All these people with their endless expectation of money.*

There are days when he feels tired of being the goose, forever expected to lay everyone a golden egg. Maria, standing next to him, composes her masculine features into a mask of deference, but remains silent.

'I need to make a personal call,' he states abruptly.

Lowering her head in a gesture of simpering acquiescence before striding heavily to the door and closing it behind her, Maria listens from the other side. Hearing Leonardo pick up the phone and dial a lengthy number, she wonders: *Who can he be calling?*

She hears the former curt gravel in his voice replaced by sensuous, self-indulgent chortles of delight. 'Have you missed me?'

Maria's masculine features darken into a scowl.

'Yes, I have, quite,' replies a husky voice, before laughing hesitantly.

Who can it be?

Smiling, Leonardo asks: 'If I got my secretary to send you a ticket, would you come and spend a weekend with me? Could you get away?'

'Yes, why not?' answers the fragile voice, before adding: 'Is your secretary discreet?'

'Yes, very.'

The tremulous voice, more tentatively assertive now: 'I don't want to come and spend time with your film crew.'

'No, of course not; we don't have to meet here. I can take off for the weekend. Is there somewhere you particularly long to see – Paris, Singapore, New York? I'll tell the crew I need to talk to the film distributors and have arranged to meet them elsewhere.'

'I've always wanted to visit Victoria Falls,' Solange whispers.

Leonardo gasps in surprise... The very last place that would have occurred to him. Recovering his balance, he, nevertheless, agrees: 'Perfect... My secretary can arrange your ticket. I'll meet you in Johannesburg, and we'll take the short flight on to Livingstone together. My secretary will have booked us into a good hotel.'

As in all Leonardo's telephone conversations, there suddenly seems nothing more to say; they share a moment of embarrassed silence.

'See you, then,' murmurs Solange, her breath catching.

'Yes, see you,' he replies, excited now.

Having replaced the receiver, he turns, opening the door so swiftly that he surprises Maria, still listening behind it.

'What on earth are you doing?'

The harsh tone is back in his voice. Although noting her thunderous expression, he is too happy to care.

'I was about to knock,' she simpers.

Regarding her peasant scowl in unfettered contempt, he replies: 'Whatever! I shan't be needing you this weekend, by the way – I'm taking a few days off.'

'Where will you be, Master?' she asks in her little girl's voice, lisping to disguise her sullen mood.

'Haven't yet decided,' he replies breezily.

He is damned if he will admit to Victoria Falls... Planning to be unreachable, only his London secretary will know how to contact him.

Remembering herself suddenly, Maria smiles deferentially. 'Have a pleasant time, Master.'

* * *

While Leonardo and Solange are in Victoria Falls, Stephen and Bianca complete the last few days of their trip to China, moving swiftly from Hangzhou to Suzhou and Shanghai.

In Hangzhou, they gaze at the gigantic golden, fairground effigy of Buddha, with his sleepy smile and platoon of dwarfed monks, robed in rough brown hessian, performing modest rituals of obeisance at his enormous folded feet. Joining the crowds of tourist Chinese, they dice the slippery path of rocks, punctuated by miniature waterfalls, against the sacred wall of Fei Lai Feng, famous for its tenth-century Buddhist carvings, some still intact, others demolished by zealots of the Cultural Revolution.

* * *

In Bantry Bay, Max and Sinead quickly develop a daily routine. Max wakes at 6 a.m., hungry for the lavish breakfasts Sinead prepares... yet eats them in defensive silence, as if the exchange of a single word might chase away his writing. Initially, his early morning silences had caused her dismay, but she has gradually adapted to them, occasionally detecting gratitude in his oblique gaze. After breakfast, he retreats, hunched shouldered, to the solitude of the second dwelling, taking a mug of coffee with him. There, at the rickety pine desk, he spends his entire morning writing. At 11 a.m. Sinead brings him more coffee, which he barely acknowledges. He writes in long, or rather miniature hand.

How can such a large man have such tiny writing? she wonders.

She sidesteps the sea of A4 papers at his feet, all carefully numbered, but with numerous crossings out. No precise time is ever set for lunch. It depends entirely on his day's progress.

Meanwhile, Sinead busies herself in the main house, occasionally scrambling up the high grass banks to look down precipitously at the mesmerising, white-crested surfaces of the Atlantic, while waiting for her lunchtime theatre to begin. By midday, the table is laid, with soup warming on the stove and a salad of seafood to follow. When Max finally bursts through the kitchen door, his face and mood are blank, wiped clean of all expression; his tangled hair plastered in dark kiss-curls against the perspiration of his brow. Undaunted, Sinead pours him a glass of Chablis and places a bowl of steaming soup before him. Smiling, as if from a great distance, he sups the first three mouthfuls in silence. Then, slowly, some small hint of colour invades his monochrome cheeks, and his dark, inquisitive eyes start to unpick her carefully, noting the unfashionable Arran sweater, her windswept hair and pale, unmade-up face.

Playing a silent game with himself, he counts the numerous pockets sewn to the legs of her cargo jeans, all stuffed with handyman oddments of string and wire, which serve to further disguise her tiny, slender figure, and suddenly he longs for her smile; his voice a whisper, as he starts to tell his first joke of the day, at which point her face opens to his in a sunshine of delight.

After lunch, whenever they can, they walk the island, of which Max never tires. But if the weather defies them, they stay indoors reading and playing Scrabble. If sunny, they sometimes unhook the rubberised dinghy from its anchor of spiteful rocks and skim back over the waves to the mainland, collecting Sinead's big beast of a car from Jack's forecourt and driving to Skibbereen, either to shop for provisions or simply to mooch about, glancing in shop windows and happening on strangely old-fashioned garments to buy. If back from his day's fishing, Jack joins them; perhaps visiting a wine bar to sup Guinness, before retreating back to the solitude of the island in hilarious moods of delight with their trophy purchases. Within just a few days, Skibbereen has become Max's idea of a good day out.

Yet during the mornings, as he obsessively writes, he is aware of an underlying unhappiness stalking him. In fact, he cultivates it, knowing it is precisely this kernel of empathy and despair, battling within himself, that drives him on, lending both anguished impetus and elegance to his words. Happiness can wait. He has the writer's ability to postpone pleasure; even the ability to postpone grief, should it threaten his progress.

Please God, let it feed the work, rather than infect life here on the island, he pleads secretly to himself. *I'll deal with my misery later.*

Instead of resisting Bianca's patrol of his thoughts, he allows it to grow. Daily, re-conjuring her moods, her fleeting gestures, the hesitant cadence of her speech, until she is no longer simply 'Bianca' but 'Dorothea', the main character in his new play, based loosely on Jack's story of his aunt. Yet looming so large in the plot that it is unclear, even to him, which is fact and fiction. Not only has Bianca become Max's version of the truth but also increasingly his own invention, his new drama altogether a love letter to her. When during their evenings together, in front of an open log fire,

Sinead asks him to tell her about the characters in his play, he pretends to not yet know them well enough… While happy to regale Sinead with his fund of amusing anecdotes, he will not risk her laughter dwelling on Bianca.

Then, one lunchtime, he giddily announces: 'I've almost finished the first draft.'

It is the first time Sinead has seen him completely elated; his monochrome complexion divided in a foolish smile of even dentistry, above his red clown's pantaloons. Running his hands impatiently through his tangled hair, he persuades his fringe from his eyes.

'I'll be flying back to London soon, to show it to my agent.'

Sinead looks up, startled; Max is looking at her fiercely now, drinking in every detail, his handsome, tousled head emerging from the frayed knitting of his neckline, his dark eyes challenging her gaze.

'When?' she asks breathlessly.

'Next week probably. I'll spend a couple of days in Dublin, then fly back from there. Come with me, if you like? We can drive back to Dublin together.'

Sinead turns away, her attention focused on the soup warming on the stove. Max has noticed her occasional moments of proud silence before, yet finds them indecipherable. Besides, he has no use for her solemnities, only for her laughter.

Perhaps she's more ordinary than I imagined? he thinks disaffectedly.

His mind hurries on, not really caring.

'Did I ever tell you about the time I went to Rome to meet an American film producer?'

Sinead hesitates, holding herself more erect. 'No, I don't think so.'

'It was about ten years ago, when I was still married. This American film producer and myself were walking on the Via Veneto one evening, when a car drove up beside us and two elegantly dressed Italian guys got out and asked us, in fluent English, if we'd like to go to a party? I was immediately suspicious, about to say no. But Ray, my American colleague, was intrigued.

'"What the heck?" he said. "Let's do it. Let's have some fun. We're in Rome, for Christ's sake."

'So, they drove us to a private villa and garden, halfway between Rome and Ostia on the coast, and introduced us to two of the most beautiful women I've ever seen; both straight from central casting. There was a bar, with several couples dancing in sultry clinches, and lots of well-dressed people lounging on vast, opulent sofas. The two women immediately joined us at the bar, flirtatiously touching and moving ever closer, until eventually they were perched on our laps, kissing us on the cheek and telling us how handsome we were. Someone behind the bar produced an ice bucket with two bottles of champagne in it. We were enjoying ourselves. In the distance, up a short flight of stairs, other couples were jiving on a tiny dance floor, its illuminated panels responding to every beat of the music... Eventually, we moved to the sofas to continue our flirting and canoodling in the arms of these two beauties more comfortably.

'Then, much, much later, both of us, by then fairly drunk, got up to leave and were presented with a bill for the equivalent of £3,000 in lira. Recklessly tipsy by then, I refused to pay, whereupon my exquisite dark-haired beauty, who'd spent the entire evening explaining how attractive and sexy I was, took off her stiletto-heeled shoe and hammered me repeatedly over the head with it. Blood streamed down my shirtfront, but I still refused to pay... However, my friend and colleague, whose new "friend" was not hitting him but screaming violent abuse, became suddenly afraid of what would happen if his wife, back in New York, ever got to hear of it. So he offered to pay... I still refused. By now, I was angry and far less drunk. Suddenly, the police arrived. Driving us to some unknown police station, they left us in separate cells all night, having first taken away our jackets and passports.

'I must have slept fitfully, at least for a while, because suddenly woken by the dawn, I noticed in the half-light my cell door slightly ajar and my passport lying on the table just outside. So I took my chance... Stealthily pushing open the door, I grabbed my passport and ran out into the street, abandoning my jacket. No one followed. It was barely daylight. With no idea where I was, I just kept walking, until two hours later I got back to our hotel, in time for breakfast. I later learned my American friend had paid both our bills in full.'

Max laughs…

'You would think that was the end of the story. But months later, it was my turn to visit New York. A play of mine had transferred from the West End to Broadway. Contacting my producer friend to see if we could meet for a drink, he explained that he had to be in Los Angeles that week. However, his wife would be glad to show me around.

"'Anything special you want to see?"

"'Yes, the Frick Collection."

'Meeting me in the foyer of the Algonquin, I recognised his wife immediately from some photographs Ray had shown me in Rome. She was one of those beautiful, greedy, anorexic-looking American women who always seem to know, at any given moment, precisely what they want and how to get it. Shaking hands with her, she insisted on a kiss. Suggesting we visit the Frick first, then have lunch in the Russian Tea Rooms, she replied casually: "Why bother? Ray's out of town. Let's go straight up to your room… If we're hungry, we can call room service…"'

Smiling in secret amusement, Max hugs the unravelled knitting of his moth-eaten arms about himself in glee while glancing surreptitiously at Sinead for her reaction.

'That was the wife he so feared hearing about our little escapade in Rome.'

He starts to giggle jubilantly at the thought of yet another nonsensical jewel from life's inexhaustible catalogue of paradoxical nature, expecting Sinead to laugh with him. Instead, she looks strangely sad and embarrassed, whereupon his own laughter dies in his throat.

'Why are you angry?' he asks bleakly.

* * *

Nervous in the face of Chloe's silent anger following the incident with the American social worker, Hesketh decides to escape on his own for a few days to Majorca. He needs time to think, time to plan his next move. Still feeling distraught at the thought of Bianca's disappearance, although acknowledging her absence with his anger, sentimentally he simply cannot accept it. His need to communicate with her: to write, speak, make contact with her, even if through a fog of ethers, is so urgent that it casts out all logic.

Sitting outside the café in the square close to his house, covertly observed by the Spanish waiters, forever wary of what he will do next, Hesketh starts to write Bianca a new letter. Once again, resurrecting a memory from their distant past, he separates it like a plum from a rich pudding. With no sense of real time where Bianca is concerned, the plum might just as easily belong to today as to yesterday; therefore, eternally ripe for interpretation as a perpetual truth between them. In fact, this new incident, still so alive in his memory, is more than twenty-five years old.

Wondering where to address it, he has not forgotten the insult of Bianca's recent behaviour; her casual indecency in daring to sell up without having the least courtesy to let him know how to find her. He thinks her behaviour a complete disgrace; still very angry.

Nevertheless… Nevertheless… How not to love and forgive her?

His face relaxes into a sloppy grin. *I'll send it c/o Matthew Dancer in Cork Street.*

Although not having a written note of the address with him, he can recall it by heart – even the postcode.

The incident which has suddenly, dramatically distinguished itself from the unravelled threads of his mind dates from when he and Bianca were still a couple, more than twenty-five years ago, when she had once stood up for him in public.

Is she still protecting me now?

The very thought astonishes him, spurring him on. The brash presumption of his 'love' for Bianca normally guards against such self-consciousness, but the movement of his mind accelerates forward, as though the machinery of love and its exclusivity were suddenly, magically restored.

Why has she never yet gone back to the police?

Even he is surprised by her refusal to be provoked. Picking up his blue Bic pen, he starts to write…

Dear Bianca, Valldemossa, 31.10.98

I remember being in a West End pub when someone started a vicious fight. Some man punched me in the face, almost knocking me off my feet, leaving me seeing stars. As I reeled backward, he went to grab me again, but you were so brave. You placed yourself between him and me, putting yourself at risk of his fists. You fended him off heroically and saved me that night. How could I ever forget?

I have been desperately trying to reach you at home… Naughty Bianca, to tease me like this. You must know how much I worry about you? And yet, my instincts tell me you are protecting me all over again. I just don't know from what. But thank you anyway. I only wish I could reciprocate in some way, although you probably wouldn't ask – always so proud. Even though it would be you helping me… But please don't say that's the very reason why you would never ask.

I am staying at my house in Majorca for a few days, but I leave here tomorrow. I am meeting someone in London who I hope can tell me where you've gone. I worry about you all the time. But I will find you, Bianca. You can never get away from me for long… I expect you know that after all these years. I wish you would phone me. I'll try to keep my mobile on and in my pocket. By the time you get this, I shall be back in London looking for you. I have to know you're okay.

All my love,
Hesketh xx

Throwing down his pen, he causes it to skit onto paving stones, where a stray dog sniffs at it gingerly. That had not been the only brawl in public… So very many in those days. Any slight misunderstanding and he would go in with lacerating tongue and fists flying. In that sense, nothing much had changed.

He shudders, picturing the scene in court during the case the police had brought against him in Knightsbridge, more than twenty years ago... He stares balefully at the dog, lost in unhappy thought.

Then, raising his head, he laughs mirthlessly and asks for the bill. '*La cuenta, por favor.*'

The waiter responds immediately, delivering the chit to his table with a toreador flourish, barely concealing the contempt in his eyes. Ever watchful, the waiter has already made his assessment... Hesketh is heading for one of his '*episodes di loca...*' The extra steep angle of his torso, as he dodges the shade in favour of bright, dappled sunlight gives him away.

CHAPTER 18

In one of those strange moments of coincidence Hesketh interprets as extrasensory magic, Bianca also finds herself remembering that day at Knightsbridge Magistrates' Court twenty years earlier. Perhaps his thoughts had successfully travelled the ethers, reminding her, after all? For long years afterwards, her mind was irresistibly redrawn to those four desperate days of high emotional drama and savage humiliation in Knightsbridge; above all, to remembering the vicious attacks on her character by Hesketh's defence barrister. She had not known such unfair denunciations were legally possible, had simply not expected it, later realising: *How naïve I was...*

Hesketh's roly-poly barrister, in a baritone more suited to opera, had portrayed her as a tart and a liar, accusing her, amongst other things, of using language unsuitable for a Victorian young lady.

Baffled, she had replied: 'Queen Victoria died in 1901. I may have sounded a bit shrill, but that is all... I was extremely frightened.'

But he did not stop there, producing a magazine of erotic nudes to show to the jury, arguing that Bianca had posed for its centre-fold. She had no idea what he was talking about. Even the jury, comparing her solemn image in the witness box with the photos in the magazine, looked nonplussed. She can still visualise Hesketh in the dock: lean and distraught, his tie loosened around the collar of his shirt, a grey check jacket forming a trapeze shape about his torso, as he lifted his arms, gesticulating wildly; his index finger stabbing the air furiously while laughing recklessly and lying under oath. She remembers his threatening, toothsome smile leering at her from the dock, cruelly ridiculing her every claim, while simultaneously insisting on his right to love and be loved by her – even in court, unable to resist hinting at his supreme ownership of her. He looked frenzied and mad, the memory filling her with revulsion.

Hoping to dispel it, she takes one of Anya's Parisian wartime letters from her bag, to read...

Darling,

I am delighted with the paintings of Baghdad you sent me, or 'sketches' as you, surprisingly enough, insist on calling them (a term I never associated with your work). But one thing piques me, William. Why do you always make these things impersonal by signing them? In doing this, I feel you are intentionally putting a monetary value on them, which I object to. Surely you do not have to send signed copies to me? It is the same with the photographs you have sent at various times. It makes me feel I am just one of many on your mailing list...

Bianca sighs. *How complicated thing always were between them, even before I was born...*

No amount of intelligence ever seeming to alter that.

Luckily, the judge had not believed Hesketh. Unlike the jury, he had access to Hesketh's police file and was able to perceive the patterned incidents of pestering and previous numerous incidents settled out of court. This was Jocelyn Carpenter, many years before Bianca met him. Jocelyn Carpenter, QC, the gentle, handsome giant of a man whose amputated arm flapped beneath his judge's robe like a broken crow's wing, striking violent contrast with the otherwise smooth urbanity of his manner. No one knew how his arm had been lost; no one dared ask. Nor when she was introduced to him many years later by Leonardo was she sure if he recognised her, deciding not to embarrass him by mentioning it herself. Just occasionally, at some dinner party, she would turn to find his fond, thoughtful gaze upon her, at which point, rather than turn away, he always smiled.

William,

How I wish you were here. I love this Paris, and know that you would also. I seriously hope it will be possible for us to come and live here after the war. I want so much to watch you enjoy this place – to see those keen blue eyes of yours absorbing everything. The beautiful avenues, and houses and windows, AND the women. They are the most attractive women I have ever seen. Their dress sense is superb. Every woman, young and old, has 'something'. Such poise and charm, and always the inevitable and enviable good taste of the French. When they dress, they do more than that. They produce themselves and never slip up on any detail. Their dress is sometimes obvious, in fact theatrical, but never vulgar. They would be a never-ending source of delight to you – they are to me…

Bianca smiles. Her childhood and teenage years had been a never-ending conspiracy to pursue and preserve that sense of French chic, for both herself and her mother. Even though the next person most likely to knock at the door of the cottage was either a farmhand offering to set rabbit traps, or Jack Briscoe, the vicar, asking William to produce painted replicas of heraldic shields with which to decorate the village hall for a jubilee barn dance… Anya would see a photograph of a chic, bold, black-and-white dogs-tooth outfit with shawl collar in the pages of *The Daily Telegraph* and send away for it, amazing the villagers by her elegance.

Hesketh was charged with causing GBH, grievous bodily harm, to Patrick, the boyfriend who had rescued her from him – the man she had loved and left him for.

That particular incident had followed yet another confrontational attack in public, of which there were already many, all hastily settled out of court. Another moment of vicious harassment, although this one more violent than most, which is why the police were involved. Deciding to prosecute, they called Patrick and herself as witnesses; this a different prosecution from the one five years earlier, when Hesketh had attacked Patrick with a crowbar and almost killed him. This court appearance related to a lesser incident, following a concert, where Bianca, Patrick and some friends had gone to hear Lou Reed play his nonchalant brand of rock cabaret.

The audience was already starting to disperse, Bianca descending the sweep of staircase from the Circle to the foyer. Patrick, slightly ahead of her, turned as he reached the bottom step to glance back at her. It was the change of expression in her eyes that alerted him. He spun round, just as Hesketh landed his first blow, the metal clasp of his watch sliding across Patrick's jaw, tearing viciously at the corner of his mouth. Blood everywhere. Yet Hesketh continued to brawl, indifferent even to Patrick's blood also staining his own shirt. The concert bouncers, blunt faced and pneumatic, were soon upon them, breaking up the scuffle and calling the police, with Bianca screaming at the top of her voice, and Patrick's eyes again looking at her in a misery of resentment, love and confusion.

The remainder of that night, for them all, was spent at a police station, where, after taking statements, Hesketh was formally charged with GBH.

Apropos savings, William!

In a recent letter, you mentioned sending home £300. I have never received any such sum from you. Perhaps you did not send it to me but to your people. I suspect this to be the case, and I am not very happy about it. Perhaps my attitude is unreasonable, but I feel it shows a lack of faith on your part, which in itself leaves me feeling very anxious about our future together...

Bianca remembers only too well the antagonism that had festered unabated between Anya and William's mother, Edith. The two never reconciled. Christmases in Sheffield were a minefield of favouritisms, set against a backdrop of unbelievable cold; the bathroom tiles freeze burning beneath their feet. She remembers the cosy opulence of the pink satin eiderdown under which she snuggled at night, her mother's expression, having begged William for a sip of his late-night warm milk, only to find it heavily laced with whisky. She, herself, had been offered none. At family dinners, Edith made a point, before everyone sat down, of limping arthritically around the table to remove slices of ham from everyone else's plate and heap them onto William's. Always either gammon or ham; this was Yorkshire.

Two months later, when the case came to court, Hesketh's legal team, as always, begged to settle out of court. It was Bianca's insistence, more than Patrick's, that the case must be heard. By then, she was distraught with Hesketh's ceaseless, daily persecutions; his endless threats and regular accosting of them in the street, his twice-daily abusive letters and phone calls. Not once had it occurred to her that she and Patrick were anything but innocent, nor Hesketh anything but guilty. Which is why she failed to anticipate Hesketh's barrister's attempt to discredit her in the eyes of the jury; the sheer injustice of it taking her by surprise. There was only one moment of respite…

Already pent up and debilitated by the ordeal, on their fourth day in court, Bianca had suddenly, uncontrollably, doubled up on a bench in the marble, polished wood corridors outside the courtroom and started to sob. Patrick was still in court, giving evidence. A young policeman came to her rescue. Having witnessed the entire case, he sat quietly beside her, speaking soothing words, gently reassuring her that no one, but no one, could imagine those things said of her to be true. Offering her his perfectly laundered handkerchief to dry her tears, as she held it to her face, she discovered it drenched in lavender cologne. Eventually stifling her sobs long enough to raise her face to his, she discovered eyes the colour of violets, the deep cleft in his chin making his face instantly fascinating and memorable, even though she never saw him again.

One thing I am disappointed in myself is that I am not making much headway with the language. This limits my pleasure here. Especially as regards the theatre, and I am unhappy about it… But one thing I have accomplished of which I am proud and think you will agree is something is that I have met Picasso.

I managed, through some friends of mine, to get an invitation to a formal gathering at his studio. What a man he is – dynamic! Little – five feet or thereabouts, sturdy and with the vitality of a bull. His studio – even on this occasion (a social one) – still looked like a studio, with that old familiar smell of turps and odds and ends that every artist seems to collect. Pebbles – smooth, round, patinated, shapely; frail, wispy sere leaves; twisted pieces of wire! How nostalgic it made me, Darling, how I long for us to be together again. To smell turps, to clear away those odds and ends you always accumulate. Please forgive me if I am being a trifle offensive and sentimental.

Picasso apparently lives very simply but has a weakness for animals about the place. He has quite a menagerie! I purposely avoid mentioning his work, because frankly I do not feel up to writing about it sensibly. The most I could say is that some I liked and others I did not. What I am most definite about is a large etching that was in the process of being finished. A lovely thing. About 30" by 24", steel plate of the Guernica period. An absolute masterpiece. His studio was neat, with its stretchers and canvases neatly piled according to their size, against the wall, or hung upon nails. Paints packed away in cupboards; palettes adorning the walls, still caked with hard old paint (remember this was a social occasion).

There was, apart from his own work, a number of paintings of other artists. A recent Matisse – a most pathetic achievement, the inevitable flower piece against the inevitable patterned curtain, etc., etc. There was also a Modigliani (Cocteau's portrait). The thing I most enjoyed in Picasso's studio was a large-scale reproduction (a detail only) of a painting by Cranach, of the 'Diane' subject. A most wonderful painting, which I have never seen before.

There is so much more I could tell you about this visit, which I could not do justice to in writing, but I will tell you about that happy day when we are together again…

Bianca remembers the fiercely fought arguments about painters and paintings as she grew up, also the rows and Anya throwing her wedding ring out of a bedroom window into their overgrown garden; William patiently sifting through the dirt to retrieve it several distraught days later. The letter ends with mention of their old friends, Rowland and Bunty.

You ask me about Rowland. I'm afraid I know nothing. I wrote to him several times, when in England, but he never replied, and I concluded that they had moved from Great Titchfield Street. When I was last in London, I went to see the Kersleys. They told me that Rowland had recently held a show at the Leger Gallery, which was not very successful, and that as far as they knew he had moved to Suffolk. Do hope that we shall get to pick up with them again when we return… I have never sent you any photographs of myself because I am frankly a little nervous of sending one. I feel in myself that I may have altered considerably in the past four years. I can only hope that it is for the better. You will have to decide that when we meet again. Until then, William, keep all the good memories of me…

Bianca smiles; after all the posturing anger and resentment, the letter ends with the anxiety of a woman still in love with her husband, despite having taken a lover, plus that eternal feminine preoccupation: *Will he still love me and think me beautiful?*

The jury returned a verdict of: 'Not guilty.'

But Jocelyn Carpenter, having read Hesketh's legal history, remained sceptical of their judgement. Obliged, nevertheless, to set Hesketh free, he refused him costs. Paying a barrister for four days in court, plus the travel arrangements of two witnesses, flown in especially from Germany to testify on his behalf, a deterrent of a sum had finally been settled against him. Although never ceasing to persecute Bianca with his unwanted attentions, Hesketh was never again quite so overtly, rapturously violent, the idea of settling out of court having lost its appeal.

* * *

The city of Suzhou is famous for its ancient canals and production of shimmering lengths of fine silk, but, most of all, for its ornamental gardens. The modern town is low-rise concrete. But behind tall secretive walls are hidden ancient gardens of such careful aesthetic that life within them is distilled into a series of frames within frames, in which moments of exquisite beauty and the beholder briefly become one; even their names reading like fragments of poetry:

The Joyous Garden
The Lingering Garden
The Master-of the-Nets Garden
The Humble Administrator's Garden

The Lion Forest Garden

The Garden of Couple's Retreat

Walking past empty restaurants, with multi-coloured lanterns swaying in the breeze against the bright red and gold of their exteriors, Bianca and Stephen turn right beside a fetid canal.

This is suburban Suzhou; a lazy mixture of apartment blocks, shops and occasional houses. Beyond a bridge are lock-up shops of single-room breadth, where Chinese youths exchange their smooth sculptures of dark hair for razor-cuts, with shaggy tips dyed citrus blonde, next to putty-coloured skin.

To their right, a muddy passageway, lined with paltry tourist stalls, opens unexpectedly into the courtyard entrance of The Master-of-the-Nets Garden, its tall walls concealing an ambitious structure of interlocking pavilions encircling a miniature lake, linked by lattice walkways and humpback bridges, as in a willow pattern plate. Still early, few tourists disturb its pallid colour scheme with their bright red and blue anoraks. The garden itself, like a prism, forever turns this way and that to refract and steal yet another view from itself. Ahead of them, the cameras of a small group of French whirr like crickets: '*Qu'est qu'il est beau... Qu'est qu'il est beau.*'

Bianca and Stephen move inside to avoid them, enjoying the sparsely furnished rooms of dark wood, set against pale, shadowy surfaces, the wood intricately fretted and polished. Bianca is especially intrigued by the lattice window frames, each weaving a unique decorative spell, in endless nuances of pattern making.

Behind a wall pierced by rhomboid windows, mimicking the rake of twin staircases leading to a central pagoda, is a garden of miniature karsts, as cotton-wool cloudy as the sky above them, all set with lacy orange blossom; each garden a separate room, momentarily divorced from the others by its singular invitation to meditate.

The pavilion interiors also turn in on one another, like Chinese boxes, forcing open secret spaces before abruptly closing them again; decorated one moment sparsely, the next intricately. And all the while, the sky lying above them is as dense as a Suzhou spun-silk duvet. By the time they leave, Bianca and Stephen feel exhilarated, almost drunk on its beauty. Their day starts to feel optimistic.

Walking on further than intended, chattering delightedly and involuntarily linking arms, Stephen suddenly remembers the impropriety in China of couples touching. They release one another into the distance. By now, the Suzhou roads are broad intersections, as wide as rivers. They keep walking, their steps interlacing with the vast, slow-moving drifts of cyclists and cars, ever willing to stutter and stall at the feet of pedestrians. Hesitantly counting the intersections on their map, Stephen spots a signpost, indicating 'The Lion Forest Garden', its complexities more to do with landscape gardening than any interlocking battle of exterior with interior.

Their exhilaration does not last. Having walked and walked, they tire themselves out, attempting to cram two days' sightseeing into just a few hours. Their train for Shanghai leaves at 5 p.m. Unknowingly, they have already experienced the best.

'In a few hours, we shall be in Shanghai.'

'Yes, but that means work...' Stephen recalls sadly. 'Delivering keynote speeches on British publishing, plus heaven knows what other networking duties the British Council will expect of me... My time will be much taken up.'

Bianca sighs, slipping her hand into his. 'I had almost forgotten,' she murmurs. 'How I have adored having you to myself these past two weeks.'

* * *

Having deliberately arranged an early flight, in order to meet Solange's plane from Heathrow, Leonardo's flight from Beijing is delayed. Stranded, alone and terrified at Johannesburg airport for four long hours, with neither a mobile phone nor any information to pacify her, Solange starts to panic. She is unused to travel. Although place names attract her, they are like the seminars she gives at London University – reliant on abstract concepts, with no basis in practicalities. What Solange loves most is ideas; the upside-down performance of them, the way they mould themselves into truths one minute, only to flee in tatters of disbelief the next. She thinks of herself as sophisticated, but her worldliness depends on the safety of that exploded village which is central London.

When Leonardo's flight finally arrives, she is no longer at the barrier, waiting for him, but huddled forlornly in a distant corner. The airport desk pages her seven times before she makes her way to Information. Greeting her bedraggled little figure, Leonardo asks: 'Where were you hiding?'

Glancing in surprise at the enormous suitcase she drags behind her, he says: 'You do know we're only here for three nights?'

His own luggage is miniature, containing two newly laundered shirts, some clean pants and a clutch of ties. Unsmilingly reluctant to raise her face to Leonardo's kiss, her eyes dart in silent fury.

'Have you missed me?' he asks boisterously.

Noticing a faint trace of moustache on her upper lip, he feels a sudden stab of pity. She nods distantly, too preoccupied to speak. Nor does she speak during their short flight to Livingstone. From their taxi, she stares out glumly at the yellow parched earth, the scrub and dirt of poverty; above all, at the ebony darkness of skin.

Only as they arrive does a gleam of wonderment ignite in her eyes, the hotel's extravagance a rebuke to the squalor they have just passed through. They are staying almost directly on top of Victoria Falls, on the Zambian side, in a magnificent adobe building, with blonde curtains flapping from high ceiling to floor in the light breeze from the rapids, the roar from the rushing waters of the Zambezi audible across the luxuriantly manicured lawns.

Shown into a suite of rooms on the ground floor, its windows opening onto a private patio, leading to elegantly landscaped gardens and a vast swimming pool, Leonardo asks anxiously: 'Does it please you?'

Fishing a red rubber band from her pocket, Solange sweeps her peroxide hair into a chignon, while glancing around imperiously. Leonardo draws in his breath, observing the delicate, slender length of her neck. He is impatient for their familiar, fast-paced conversation to begin; for the mixture of insult with flirtatiousness that he finds so exciting at London dinner parties to resurface. He keeps expecting a thought, an idea, to seize her attention and not be let go, until allowed to roll around in the intellectual dust of their minds for at least an hour or so. That is what he is used to. Nor does he expect their recent night as lovers to have altered it in any way, having even begun to wonder if fierce conversation were not Solange's version of sexual foreplay. Looking her directly in the eye, he invites her to challenge him, first with a smile, and then with a concept.

But her gaze continues to flee his, leaving him unsure what to do. To introduce a brief note of normality, he rings his secretary in London, suddenly grateful for the fluency of her everyday chatter. Throwing the windows open wide to let in sunlight, he reveals the full elegance of their rooms, while Solange sits curled like a kitten, filing her nails. Startled by a knock on the door, a tall, graceful black man in red waistcoat asks them if there is anything they need? Unhesitatingly removing her dusty trainers, still warm with perspiration, Solange hands them to him. 'These could do with a clean.'

Only Leonardo notices the discreet blink of revulsion in the man's eye.

'May I also call home?'

'Of course,' responds Leonardo. 'In fact, why don't I leave you to it while I go to the bathroom.'

Sitting on the lavatory, Leonardo nevertheless hears Solange's halting, breathless phrases being relayed to her husband in London; the husband who rejoices rather than resents her desirousness in the eyes of other men.

Leonardo reflects miserably: *Perhaps this was a mistake?*

He starts to question his wisdom at having transported the carrion of one of his extra-marital affairs abroad, rather than conveniently leaving it behind somewhere, as usual. He hears her throaty laughter rise on the gleeful comment that 'someone is looking pretty ancient these days' and his pride reasserts itself: *Surely she doesn't mean me?*

'Why don't we order tea?' she remarks as he emerges from the bathroom, her dark eyes meeting his for the first time. She has sprayed herself with heavy perfume.

'Yes, of course; let's unpack later.'

Perhaps now, at last, we can talk? he thinks optimistically.

Making their way to a sumptuous lounge beyond the hotel foyer, they order tea and cakes. Weaving her way elegantly towards them, hips swaying voluptuously between tables and sofas, is the most beautiful African woman Leonardo has ever seen. Lifting his face to hers in a bright flash of smile, unable to conceal his delight in her, he asks flirtatiously: 'Are you a Zambian princess?'

Like all powerful men, Leonardo feels vaguely sorry for all the women he has not yet found time to make love to. She smiles demurely in reply. But Solange, whose sullen cool had been about to relent, looks crestfallen, fierce contempt brewing in her eye.

Noticing her scowl, Leonardo rejoices in her jealousy, suddenly feeling less afraid and neglected. He looks deeply, merrily into her eyes. But he has gone too far, embarrassing her by so transparently acknowledging her jealousy.

'This room reminds me of your sitting room in London,' she remarks as if trying to slough off the skin of him.

Mystified, Leonardo glances about him: at the deep sofas, with plumped cushions covered in subdued, elegant African prints, set next to gleaming mahogany furniture, and tall silhouettes of lamps with their memories of voodoo sculpture. He really cannot remember.

Is this what home looks like?

So used is he to staying in this degree of luxury around the world that he no longer notices nor particularly remembers any interior, including that of his own London home, once he leaves it. The exception is La Casa in Siena – the only place to have truly stolen his heart. The thing that affects him most while travelling is his own degree of comfort; the same being true of his relationships with people. Working hard for so much of the time, 'home' is a constant seeking out of transitory teaspoonfuls of comfort, in both places and people. Remaining eternally loyal to those who provide it, he is equally forgetful of those who don't.

Glancing at Solange, her miniature form almost vanishing between two enormous cushions, her upswept blonde hair uncombed since early morning, her slick of make-up rubbing thin to reveal the freckles she is always anxious to hide, her dark eyes darting everywhere, without settling, he sighs deeply. No playful ideas surface from behind her doleful countenance. Beginning to suffer doubt again, he nevertheless refuses to be utterly dismayed, their night of shared passion still uppermost in his mind. He cannot erase its memory...

Where is the laughing, teasing girl I made love to in Beak Street?

It is as the waitress returns with more tea and cakes, swaying prettily between the tables, that he first notices Solange's instinct to be rude to waiters. It takes him by surprise.

Solange surfaces from her moroseness to comment: 'You should have brought them sooner. We've been waiting at least ten minutes. Plus there's insufficient butter.'

Solange's husky, haughty, querulous tone leaves the waitress suddenly fearful for her job; she bows her head in abject apology. Leonardo is furious. Witnessing Solange regain some of her self-assurance, he feels both repelled and a curious tenderness: *Why does ineptitude in women excite me? It's not as though I were fooled by it. Surely she can't still be jealous?*

He hears his own voice, as if from a great distance, ask, 'Might you be suffering from depression?'

Solange's pained eyes meet his, before quickly escaping again.

'Perhaps you only feel secure when enacting superiority over others?' he whispers.

Luckily, she doesn't hear. 'Did you say something?'

'No, nothing.'

What would Bianca do if she knew I were here with Solange? he wonders.

It suddenly feels urgent she should never find out. Unexpectedly finding himself missing her, the very thought astonishes him. Whatever else he feels for Bianca, he rarely misses her, if only because he always carries her silently, dependably within himself.

After all, she's my wife.

* * *

Back in London, Robin Holderness and Beatrice continue to spend time together. Unlike Byng, whose affair had rampaged through fashionable London, dividing society like Dreyfus, they conduct theirs discreetly. This less at Beatrice's insistence than Robin's, even though it is she who has most to lose. With Byng, she leads a glamorous, wealthy, international lifestyle, whereas life with Robin is pared down into miniature celebrations of frugality: the inexpressible delight of finding a cheap restaurant serving excellent food; the rowdy, roller-coaster pleasures of late-night buses rather than taking taxis. Robin, having wilfully turned his back on wealth, shunning every opportunity to make serious money, believes too completely in his status as philosopher to be detained by considerations of wealth. Although some of his colleagues would disagree. Not that they consider his work inconsequential, merely stalled. He is like the father in *To the Lighthouse*, incapable of getting past 'R' in order to reach 'S' and 'T' in the philosophical alphabet. Robin imperiously attributes their attitude to jealousy, Beatrice, meanwhile, thinking his simple tastes deliciously quaint.

Whenever possible, Beatrice now opts to stay in London, only joining Byng in Paris when absolutely necessary. Yet Byng appears not to have noticed. Her encounters with Robin follow a reliable pattern. They begin formally, an hour or so before lunch, with them both greeting one another slightly awkwardly, like distant acquaintances. Robin likes their day to start with something educational, his mind currently focused on China: 'I want to understand both the society and political philosophy that inspired it… Above all, why the forbidden philosophy of Confucius has continued to have such clandestine hold on the Chinese people, despite its brutal outlawing by their political leadership.'

They spend an hour or so in the Oriental Galleries at either the V&A or British Museum, with Robin treating Beatrice much as he would one of his students, haranguing and quizzing her with endless ideas and information.

He then takes her out to lunch, during which they share a bottle of red wine and their mood becomes more playful. Finally, they retire to his eyrie, high up in the rooftops of Golden Square, where the prim orderliness with which their day began ends in a glorious chaos of lovemaking, all formality shed, their lovemaking increasingly violent.

'Don't mark me, in case Byng notices,' she whispers.

Although, secretly, she longs to show off the purple stains around her nipples, the necklace of bruises to her errant husband. It would serve him right.

But Robin has forbidden it. This is the point in the day when Robin simultaneously loses and reveals himself. Realising he is both hugely proud and deeply insecure, Beatrice loves him for it, relieved, finally, to be with a man whose flaws defeat rather than promote him… as Byng's do.

* * *

Bianca and Stephen's journey to Shanghai takes less than an hour. As the train pulls out of Suzhou, it is 5 p.m. But in this continent-sized country with its single time zone, night is already closing in around them, the carriage windows turning black, behind their diminutive frocks of stiff white lace.

Bianca's mood is infected by romantic excitement, fuelled by stories half remembered from childhood: 'Shanghai Rose'… the opium-funded 'Peace Hotel', where Noel Coward wrote *Private Lives* against its backdrop of high ceilings, ornate woodwork and art deco ballroom; the city's scandalous reputation throughout the 1930s for more prostitutes per capita than either Paris or New York; its division into International Concessions, both architectural and cultural, with France, England and America competing to leave their distinct versions of elegance, sophistication and depravity on the city, only to desert it abruptly in 1949 with the establishment of the Communist Party. Thereafter, all elegance superseded by the ruthless, prudish austerities of the People's Revolution. Also, more recent, contemporary speculations as to whether Shanghai's former louche ways might yet again revive, against its high-rise, Disney skyline of investment banking Pudong, where, for the past ten years, forty per cent of all the world's cranes had been kept permanently busy.

Their train is met by an unusually tall guide, calling herself 'Jackie', her black hair burnished with henna, her handbag a Louis Vuitton copy, her manner one of Americanised super efficiency and charm.

'Whatever can her name be to have arrived at Jackie?' whispers Bianca.

Moving swiftly ahead of them through the crowds, Stephen and Bianca run at her heels like desperate schoolchildren.

Outside the station is an agitated throng, moving rapidly in different directions, crisscrossing each other's paths like some fast-moving diagrammatic puzzle. This is something new. Stephen and Bianca have grown used to the uniform drifts of Chinese pedestrians and cyclists, moving like untidy dust clouds, in slow motion. Bianca is reminded of Boccioni's Futurist drawings, condemning 'those that stay' to linear aspic, while celebrating 'those that go' in fast-forward diagonals of energy.

They are led to a taxi, a nicotine-stained wrap of fibreglass protecting the driver from his passengers. He and Jackie exchange an indecipherable bark of flattened vowels, followed by an opening and slamming of doors. Once settled, Jackie asks them to confirm the name of their hotel.

'Holiday Inn,' they chorus.

She shakes her head reprovingly: 'Wrong reply... Naughty children... There are several Holiday Inns. You must specify which before getting into any taxi... The Holiday Inn, Pudong,' she reiterates in her Americanised twang.

Meanwhile, the driver hurtles into the rush of traffic. Unfazed by his aggressive manoeuvring, Jackie attempts polite conversation, asking Stephen endless questions: 'You are here on business?'

'Yes,' he replies, barely admitting his British Council connections.

She perseveres inquisitively: 'In London, you are a businessman?'

He nods distantly, refraining from saying anything that might identify him as an aristocrat of British publishing. Bianca remains silent, listening to his blunt evasions. Not only do his monosyllabic replies register an indifference bordering on insolence but also his youthful, jean-clad frame and obdurate expression. He glances, conspicuously bored, from the car window, refusing to engage with her questions.

Although often bored by chit-chat, Stephen is usually more forgiving and affably disposed. The truth is that only now that they have reached Shanghai do the complexities of their private situation

312

finally begin to reveal their ugly heartbeat. It is only Bianca, who is actually staying at the Holiday Inn, whereas Stephen is double booked; at the Holiday Inn, but also, far more glamorously, at the Shangri-La, overlooking the Bund, where the British Council conference is being held. Other colleagues will join him there later that evening, one of whom knows Stephen's wife, Sarah, well, and yet another is a good friend of Leonardo's; both men with reputations as flamboyant gossips.

As the taxi speeds into the city, diving on flyovers between tall skyscrapers, Jackie points out landmarks: the new opera house, with its modern interpretation of flying roofs above an interlace of steel frame engineering, announcing proudly: *'Les Misérables* is about to open there.'

Stephen and Bianca exchange secret smiles.

Beyond the opera house is the squat, flying-saucer-like structure of the new Oriental Museum; glowing rose pink against the dark night sky, the Oriental Pearl, as they cross the river into Pudong; the old city's proud, turn-of-the-century British buildings and elegant French Art Nouveau town houses, now overshadowed by skyscrapers. Their arrival feels both fearful and full of intrigue. Bianca asks: 'How far is the Holiday Inn from the Shangri-La? Is it within walking distance?'

Jackie gazes at her in amazement, replying tersely: 'At least twenty minutes by taxi, depending on the traffic...'

Feeling a sudden rush of loneliness, Bianca begins to regret not having chosen to fly straight back to London.

Now on a dual carriageway, rushing ever further from the bright city lights, their driver suddenly performs a pirouette of complex right turns to accelerate up an industrialised ramp, straddling one side of an anonymous, monolith building; the ramp, it turns out, the Holiday Inn's main entrance. As a bellboy takes their luggage, Jackie checks them in. Bianca fretfully absorbs the disappointing code of polished brass and brown-spattered marble decorating the foyer; the typically vast, exuberant flower arrangements in bright orange and yellow.

Jackie hands them each a card, stating in both Chinese and English: 'Please take me to the Holiday Inn, Pudong.'

'For the taxi drivers,' she explains.

Bianca accepts hers gratefully, aware how urgently she will need it.

Bidding them goodbye, Jackie mentions: 'You won't see me again.'

She, nevertheless, leaves them her telephone number. Stephen shakes her hand, affable again now free from her prying.

A porter conducts them to a room on the twenty-sixth floor, where beige and toffee upholstery are dominated by a widescreen television and a cloudy view, stretching out towards suburbia.

Immediately consulting the handbook, Stephen attempts to decipher the hotel's selection of restaurants, while Bianca hangs up one or two desultory garments. They decide to return to the safety of the ground-floor twenty-four-hour restaurant, where Bianca's breakfasts will be served; supper to be something of a test. Not only is the hotel booked in Stephen's name, but on his Barclaycard. Although carrying large quantities of cash, Bianca has no credit card with her. Clearly inappropriate to pay in cash, Stephen has devised a plan. Bianca will first print his name in block capitals on any bill, before scrawling her own signature below it. Presuming Chinese waiters find English handwriting as indecipherable as he and Bianca find Chinese characters, he also assumes they will have been instructed to check that the capital letters match the name registered to the room.

Having eaten a bland meal of soup and pasta, Stephen defers signing the bill to Bianca, who prints 'MARCHANT', before scribbling 'Bianca Johnson' but omitting the more tell-tale 'Vescarro'. They wait anxiously... but all is well. The waitress returns with a smile.

Returning upstairs, Stephen collects his luggage. He now plans on taking a taxi to the Shangri-La, to check in for a second time, where he will also eat another supper with British Council colleagues, promising to phone Bianca later: 'I'll probably stay the night at the Shangri-La, so as to be visible at breakfast,' he states in the plain, undecorated manner he adopts whenever imparting distasteful news.

Bianca glances up at him quizzically. 'You still look deliciously handsome.'

He stands extra tall, his body turned fully towards hers, lightly assessing her nervousness and thinking sadly: *Her fear is almost palpable. I could reach out and touch it...*

In moments of distress, her eyes lose their colour. Her manner, he notices, is suddenly hesitant – almost shy. Blonde curls corkscrew about her face... He shrugs helplessly: *Nevertheless... Nevertheless...*

As Bianca kisses him goodbye, an immense mood of disquiet settles on her. There is, she realises, something deep within this subterfuge that offends her... even though knowing it to be what she has, herself, chosen.

CHAPTER 19

Arriving in London from Shanghai, Bianca buys newspapers to read on the Heathrow Express. On the front page of the *Evening Standard*, a strange byline catches her eye: 'Man accosts owner of the *Daily Mail* outside his London club, demanding to be told the name of the columnist who writes under the soubriquet "Miss Dior".'

'I'm not sure I ever knew it,' he replied urbanely.

There was a scuffle in the street, the police called, and the man led away for questioning. Briefly detained, he was later cautioned and released.

'The man's name: Hesketh James.'

Inside, was an article by Solange's boyfriend, the architect and occasional journalist, Nicholas Rowe, debating the incident, entitled: 'Remembering a woman by her perfume?' Secretly, all women are whores seemed to be the essence of his view.

Bianca looks up, startled. 'Miss Dior' was the scent she wore in the days when she and Hesketh had first known one another.

Perhaps he thinks of it as some kind of talisman between us...?

Although she and Stephen had returned on the same flight, they are no longer travelling together. They had taken separate taxis to Shanghai airport, where Stephen was immediately closeted in the business-class lounge with his British Council pals, while Bianca, whose turn it was to fly economy, was left to patrol the airport shopping malls. Nor had they met up again at Heathrow, Stephen collected luxuriously by the same thuggish driver who had delivered them to Heathrow two weeks ago.

'It's what we agreed,' Stephen had stated briskly, with Bianca willingly nodding her assent.

Nevertheless, after long days and nights together, it felt bleak, almost cruel. More worryingly, it had brought her suppressed thoughts of Max back into focus.

Is he in Ireland still? Will there be a message waiting for me in London?

Turning the key to her apartment, she experiences the same shocked surprise that had struck Leonardo ten days earlier. The rooms feel unaccountably dark, no light flooding in from their tall French windows.

Why on earth did I bother closing the shutters? she scolds herself. *As though any thief could get in without being seen?*

Refolding the tall, cumbersome panels flush with the wall, she looks about her, immediately falling in love again with its familiar beauty. Suddenly, she is glad to be back home, the telephone busily winking messages at her. Flopping down into a plump armchair, she lazily promises herself: *I'll unpack later.*

With Leonardo not due back for several weeks, she has the place to herself.

By then, I'll be fully ensconced back in London mode, she reflects gratefully, *China a fascinating, secret memory.*

Nevertheless, she is glad Leonardo is not here to witness her make the transition between travel and home, the same discomfiting transition she has often witnessed in him.

Making herself some porridge and a pot of English Breakfast tea, she sits at the kitchen table, listening to telephone messages and reading post, many of the calls business related and intended for Leonardo, all of which she carefully saves. There are also messages from various girlfriends, hoping to meet for lunch, plus a breathlessly agitated one from Matthew: 'Biaaancaa, daaarling, I've a new portrait commission waiting for you... We also need to talk urgently.'

'Drama queen,' sighs Bianca. 'Everything with Matthew always *urgent.*'

But not a single word from Max.

Perhaps he wouldn't choose to leave messages on this phone in any case? she consoles herself.

Nevertheless, she feels disappointed.

Poor Leonardo – this is how he must feel, returning home from a long trip. Always longing for parties and the razzmatazz of a hero's welcome.

She too feels strangely deflated.

Exhausted suddenly, the long flight catching up with her, she switches off the phones and goes to bed to sleep it off, waking four hours later to the buzz of the doorbell.

'Hello,' she answers sleepily.

'Flowers for Bianca Vescarro-Johnson.'

She releases the street door and a young man bounds up the stairs, bearing an enormous bunch of blood-red baccarat roses. Bianca stares at them in horror. They are the flowers she associates with Hesketh; the same roses he had had delivered all those years ago to the art college, where he tracked her down. Some of the outer petals, she notices, are already turning black.

Like dried blood, she thinks grimly.

About to refuse their delivery, she notices a card pinned to their cellophane, the young man, gazing in dismay as her trembling hands struggle to open it.

Thank you, my perfect darling, for all the wonderful days of China. All my love, Stephen xx

* * *

'I think you'll like her,' Matthew is saying in his guttural tongue, allowing the emphasis to rest unnaturally long on the vowels. She envisages him standing at his desk, rifling through papers, while crouched in the hollow of his neck is a miniature telephone, as though about to play the violin.

'She's fairly shy, a bit depressed maybe, with the air of someone faintly embarrassed by life. Yet her intentions are quite clear… She wants you to paint a large-scale portrait of her son, the same size as the Cavendish children's portrait, as a surprise birthday present for her husband.' He pauses. 'She says her name's Chloe Smythe, but for some reason I don't believe her… Sounded a bit rehearsed, as she said it.'

Bianca hears him take a deep breath.

'What possible reason would she have to lie?'

'I don't know,' he says, laughing scornfully. 'You trade under three separate names yourself. Remind me, what they are now…?

318

The artist B. Turvey; the original, uncomplicated Bianca Johnson, daughter of the painter William Johnson; and, more recently, the celebrity housewife Bianca Vescarro-Johnson.'

'You think she also has a stalker?' Bianca asks, amazed.

Matthew gives another brief snort of a laugh. 'Perhaps her husband is famous and she doesn't want us to know who he is? In this business, nothing surprises me… But I'm just guessing. I also got the impression there's some difficulty with the son, although she didn't say what exactly. Actually, everything she said was a bit elliptical, apart from the certainty of her wanting the portrait.'

'So, what was so pressing you wanted to tell me?'

Matthew's voice, in full-flight sceptical mode, falters suddenly into a stutter: 'I-I don't remember…'

'In your phone message, you said that you needed to speak to me urgently?'

A brief silence.

'But you haven't yet told me about China?' he says, changing the subject. 'Have you lots of new paintings to show me?'

Bianca sighs. 'Yes, quite a few, although I've no idea whether you'll like them? They're a bit ethereal. I call them five-finger exercises.'

The pause has given Matthew time to think. He starts to dissemble. 'No, nothing especially urgent, my dear. I just wanted to know if you would have time to accept a new commission, to so short a deadline, while still having Max Holland's portrait to finish? Chloe Smythe's husband's birthday is only four weeks away; not long in which to finish a large-scale portrait.'

He lets out a breath so heavily into the mouthpiece that Bianca feels repulsed, taking the phone from her ear.

He is glad to have got away with it. At the time he left his message, he was feeling panicked and under siege, anxious to communicate the news that that ridiculous madman, Hesketh James, had somehow managed to infiltrate her connection to his gallery. But the wretched fool had not rung for several days now, and Matthew had begun to think better of it, arguing to himself: *Why worry Bianca when she has so much new work in the offing?*

As well as being his friend from schooldays, she is also one of his geese, capable of laying the most golden of eggs.

Why disrupt her now?

'So, what do you think?' he asks cautiously, cracking his knuckles again. 'Could you handle this new commission in good time, as well as finish Max Holland's portrait?'

It is now Bianca's turn to dissemble: 'Actually, I haven't heard from Max. There were no messages waiting from him on my return… so I assume he's still in Ireland? Perhaps you should make an appointment with this Chloe Smythe and her son to meet me at my studio later this week. That way, I can assess what it is she wants exactly?'

'Perfeeect, Biaaancaa, darling. I'll call you tomorrow, after I've spoken to her.'

They talk a little longer, swapping gossip and arranging for Bianca to give him his first glimpse of the watercolours she had done in China, when suddenly she remembers: 'By the way, those papers you wanted me to sign haven't arrived yet. Did you send them?'

Matthew hesitates. 'Yes, I'm sure I did… But you know how muddled I get. I'll get my secretary to check and let you know tomorrow. Otherwise, I'll ask her to send them again.'

A sudden, discomfiting apprehension assails him, which he struggles to suppress. 'Perhaps they went missing in the post?' he says lamely. 'Lots of things do.'

* * *

Arriving at the door of Bianca's Holland Park studio a few days later, Chloe is anxious and overwrought. She would have much preferred to come alone for this advance chat with the artist, but Matthew Dancer had insisted, with time so short, that she bring Bruno.

She had forgotten what an ordeal it is to transport Bruno anywhere from the safety of Chelsea Embankment, mostly only happening when visiting her mother in the Cotswolds, in which case she straps him in and drives. Or whenever she and Hesketh share family journeys to Majorca. Bruno had not minded travelling down in the lift but had rebelled at negotiating the short flight of stairs leading to the dusty hallway, offended by its untidy accumulations of post. There was also the difficulty of Hesketh finding out and objecting. Right now, he is in Majorca, having returned briefly to London a few days earlier, his clothes crumpled and torn, only to leave again, saying that he had spotted a rundown property on the other side of the island which he wanted to investigate and buy.

In the taxi, Bruno had hummed in falsetto, while rocking himself energetically side to side for the entire journey, the driver eventually stopping to help Chloe strap him in more securely. As she thanked him for his kindness, Bruno, hating to be touched by strangers, had squealed in loud fury. Arriving at Holland Park, he appeared more lame than ever, his clumsy feet refusing to walk properly.

Opening the door of her studio, Bianca discovers an ashen-faced young woman with mauve circles beneath tired, grey-green eyes, pleading messages of apology and fear, dressed in a feather-print dress and accompanied by a savagely disturbed young boy. As Bianca shakes Chloe's hand, Bruno swings his head away. No expression in his eyes, Bianca notices.

'May I not shake your hand too?' Bianca asks him gently.

Turning his back on her and huddling against the door jamb, he starts kicking at the rotten stump of her door frame. Bewildered, Bianca hears the wood splinter beneath his toe. Yet Matthew had mentioned none of this. What was it he said?

Some difficulty with the son?

She turns to the mother, scrutinising her face for clues. But Chloe is almost as inaccessible as her son.

'Come in,' says Bianca despairingly.

Determined to stay optimistically facing the receding light of the door, Bruno stumbles backward along the narrow, dark length of corridor leading to Bianca's studio. Putting out her hand to steady him, he flinches, mewing like a kitten. Only when suddenly finding himself beneath its high ceiling, with sunlight streaming in from the thirty-foot-tall window, caressing every surface, does he turn around; from somewhere next door, the faint sounds of a piano playing Debussy. Bruno visibly relaxes.

'What a good idea,' says Chloe. 'Do you have any classical CDs we could play? It might pacify him.'

It is her first admission there might be anything wrong.

Bianca is at a loss what to think. Registering Chloe's pained mix of self-effacing timidity with ferocious motherly protection, she feels simultaneously both sympathy and repugnance towards her. Wordlessly opening the small CD player perched on the counter of her 1950s booth of a kitchen, she plays Vivaldi's *Four Seasons*. The delicious music soars high into the rafters, becoming part of the ecstasy of dappled sunshine invading the room.

'I understand you want a portrait on the same scale as the one I did of the Cavendish children?' Bianca asks, determined to establish some slender formality to this meeting.

'Y-Yes, please,' stutters Chloe. 'It needs to be at least that scale, to replace a large painting belonging to my husband that we currently have in our sitting room.'

I wonder which poor fool of an artist they are planning to demote with my portrait? Bianca thinks, saying nothing.

She has inherited some of her father's scepticism towards patrons and collectors of art. William was forever giving away virtuoso paintings only to realise how underappreciated they were when he discovered them hanging in a stairwell or someone's back bedroom. At the same time, it occurs to her to that Chloe is exhausted. Mulling over various possibilities fast, she dives behind a screen, dragging the fake Chippendale armchair into the centre of the room.

'Why don't you sit here, while I decide how best to approach Bruno's portrait.'

A six-foot-square canvas, already prepared, she now manhandles it onto her easel. Bruno, his head no longer averted, watches in astonishment. Next, she climbs the ladder to the makeshift bedroom above her kitchen and drags a duvet and some cushions onto the studio floor. Spreading the duvet in the middle of the room, she covers it with a length of Prussian blue velvet curtaining, the same length she had used to lend theatricality to Max's portrait, before scattering the cushions on top of it. The cushions are all brightly coloured tapestry images of fruit and vegetables, analysed with pointillist precision. Picking one up, Bruno runs his long, delicate fingers over it inquisitively.

'He likes to embroider,' remarks Chloe mysteriously.

'Would Bruno prefer to sit or stand?'

Business-like, Bianca feels a desperate urge to get on; to already finish a project not yet begun. She glances at Bruno, lying slumped on a pile of Persian rugs, hugging one of the cushions to him.

'He likes sitting on the floor,' Chloe volunteers.

'Very well, get him to take up any position on the duvet that suits him, and I'll start to make some tentative drawings.'

Suddenly remembering the abacus with which she had kept the Cavendish boy absorbed, she dives into a drawer, but instead of handing it to him directly leaves it lying diplomatically at the edge of the duvet, waiting to see if he picks it up. She also takes a role of Sellotape and hands it to Chloe.

'This might intrigue Bruno and stop him worrying.'

She does not add that it is the sort of ruse she would only normally use with a much younger child.

Bianca watches carefully as Bruno stands, initially stork-like, in a sea of blue velvet, before slowly, slowly sinking to his knees, his soft-boned feet folding uselessly beneath him. As he does so, he raises his face to hers in a flash of scrutiny; Bianca thinking she perceives a brief look of ecstasy, before he rapidly withdraws into himself again, his face again raised inexpressively to the window and the music. But it has given her a clue how to proceed.

Hoisting the canvas as high as it will go on the easel, she fetches some kitchen steps. Climbing to their second rung, she immediately begins work. Now able to look down on Bruno, it is as though the shape of his face and body form the central stem in the wide spread of a bouquet. She sketches rapidly in pencil, directly onto the primed cotton duck of the canvas, as she had with her portrait of Max. The circular, centralised design of her composition forms fast, flattering the square format of the canvas by allowing her to make decorative play of the folds of velvet as they stray into its difficult empty corners.

Having begun to resolve an idea for a composition, she pins some Cartridge paper to the canvas and makes numerous detailed sketches with the same pencil, constantly catching Bruno unawares as he glances up towards the window, in thrall to the combination of light and music. In his nimble hands, whenever he looks down, is the all-absorbing sticky tape; his dancing fingers forever binding themselves close, only to fight acrobatically to free themselves again. Unable to see Bianca's face watching him, except as an occasional flicker of movement, over the tall upper edge of the canvas, he is unaware of being intimately scrutinised. It allows Bianca great freedom. Finally, she fishes in the pocket of her painting smock for a miniature camera, so tiny it might almost be a lipstick. She had bought it from the spy shop near Lowndes Square, especially for capturing unselfconscious photos of children; with it taking numerous surreptitious shots, without either Bruno or Chloe noticing, the light in the studio so bright, there is no need for flash.

Meanwhile, Chloe sits obliquely to one side, happy to relax while still anxiously monitoring Bruno for signs of distress. Unable to observe Bianca directly, nor to see what she has drawn, she nevertheless begins to register some mystery in her. Even the mood of her studio seems imbued with it; a strange combination of serenity and excitement. Chloe finds it strangely restful. Despite her modest charm, Bianca strikes her as a woman who is supremely confident but in ways Chloe cannot quite identify. There is her obvious gentleness, her sympathetic handling of Bruno; yet, beyond that, another quality, a sort of accentuated self-containment, which Chloe envies and finds puzzling.

She's probably also beautiful, thinks Chloe, not good at judging the secret attractions of other women. *Yet it's none of these things.*

Suddenly, the ugly, unwelcome truth dawns on her. Bianca is loved. She has the looks and bearing of a woman who is very much loved. As the miserable thought forces itself to the surface, Chloe feels herself recoil. From having started to like Bianca, she feels suddenly repulsed, as though witnessing something unnatural, beyond the scope of her comprehension. It is the very thing she fears most in her own marriage: *'Am I truly loved…?'* – the question that daily haunts her marriage to Hesketh.

She glances at her son. Bruno has found the abacus and is busily arranging its colourful beads into elaborate patterns, as complex as any musical score. Bianca too has noticed his sudden obsessive interest.

Perhaps that's another toy we should get him at home? Yet how is it, she wonders sadly, *that this stranger, this unknown woman, has known how to anticipate my son so well?*

Instead of gratitude, she feels a darkening flood of resentment.

I am his mother. Only myself and Hesketh should know how to fore-cast his needs, she thinks unhappily.

As the final chords of Vivaldi reach their ecstatic conclusion, Bianca steps back onto the paint-spattered floor, her blonde hair tumbling untidily about her shoulders; the sharp blue of her eyes focused in smiles, her face prettily flushed from her past hour of concentrated drawing, not having once thought about herself.

'That's probably enough for today, don't you agree?' she asks, a jubilant, joyous energy spilling from her. 'Although, we do need to discuss how to proceed next,' she adds a little more soberly. 'Have you time for a cup of tea before you leave?'

Chloe looks up, startled out of her reverie by the question. 'You mean go to a café?' she asks shyly.

Bianca notices she is looking pained and anxious again. 'No, I can make tea here... Or coffee, if you prefer?'

Chloe hesitates, the fast tumult of unhappy thoughts making her feel claustrophobic.

'Perhaps another day,' she says diffidently. 'We should probably be getting home.'

'Where do you live?'

Chloe wavers, Bianca meanwhile remembering what Matthew had said about giving a false name.

'Chelsea Embankment,' she finally, grudgingly admits.

'That's quite a journey, especially in rush-hour traffic,' reflects Bianca, deciding to tackle the problem head-on. 'I don't normally suggest this method of work, but in Bruno's case I think it might be best. I already have the design of the painting, plus some sketches and photographs to remind me of Bruno's correct colouring...'

Chloe looks at her in shocked dismay.

'Photographs of Bruno?' she asks resentfully. 'But how? Bruno never allows either my husband or myself to photograph him.'

Bianca shrugs, unable to see why it matters.

'I doubt he even noticed me take them,' she replies indifferently. 'Wouldn't it be best,' she perseveres, more determined than ever to place the meeting on a business footing, 'if I were to complete the bulk of Bruno's portrait in his absence, then invite you and Bruno to return here just once more, for last-minute touching up?'

Turning to face Chloe squarely, she notices her extreme pallor again, the dark, mauve circles, like bruises, beneath her confused eyes, plus her slender, young girl's figure.

She should be extraordinarily beautiful, Bianca thinks. *How I would prefer to be painting her portrait, rather than Bruno's... But what is making her so depressed? It can't simply be Bruno's disabilities; she so clearly adores him. Is proud of him too, in some obscure way... What is it that so fills her with shame?*

'I imagine that arrangement would be altogether less stressful, for both you and Bruno?' she argues pointedly.

Chloe stares back at her, helpless and embarrassed, like a child found out. But before she has time to reply, Bruno lets out a terrified cry. Scrambling awkwardly to his feet, he had tripped on the rough terrain of blue velvet while still gazing rapturously up at the window. Without warning, his boyish frame, in its school-boy formalities of grey woollen shorts and jumper, starts to shake. Bianca glances at him in alarm, while Chloe moves swiftly, her outstretched arms imploring him to stop. But it all happens too quickly, and she fails to reach him in time. Seized first by violent tremors, his boyish frame stiffens suddenly, then falls rigidly forward, striking hard and heavily straight onto his face, making no attempts to save himself. Missing the soft cushioning of the duvet, he hits the studio floorboards, like a lumberjack's log, cruelly slicing open his mouth on grimaced teeth. On the ground, he continues to shake, convulsing violently.

'He's having a fit,' Bianca exclaims in desperation.

Chloe looks at her in stunned amazement, followed by a cry of anguish. So it was true, after all – the very thing Bruno's doctors had warned her of and which she had always refused to believe. And that it should happen here, in the studio of a stranger, not even in the privacy of their own home...

Bruno's first bout of epilepsy... How will I explain it to Hesketh? I should never have agreed to bring him here...

Unfairly, her resentment towards Bianca grows. She watches, mesmerised in misery, as Bianca bends lovingly over her own darling son, turning him expertly on his side before gently gagging him with a clean paint rag to prevent him from biting his tongue; delicately wiping the foam forming at his mouth while holding his fragile body tenderly close to still the sobs racking his small frame. Peering anxiously into his bleeding face for signs of recovery, Bianca notices how the throes of seizure have robbed Bruno of both age and introversion. Instead of nine years old, he has the open face of a baby.

Sluggishly, Chloe starts to react, her hands stretched impotently towards her injured child. She begins to sob primitively, like an animal in pain.

'I'll call an ambulance,' says Bianca.

'No, please don't,' implores Chloe through her tears. 'They'll keep him in hospital if you do, maybe even take him away from us. My husband and I couldn't bear to lose him. Besides, Bruno would find hospital intolerable. He can't bear strangers touching him.'

The image of his compliance in the hands of this painter, bent solicitously over her son still jealously uppermost in her hysterical mind, she blows hard into her handkerchief, willing herself to regain control.

'We love Bruno very much,' she explains bitterly. 'He's what's holding my husband and myself together.'

Bianca looks at her in alarm. After all her former evasiveness, it is an extraordinary admission. And in that very moment of Bianca's shocked countenance, something stirs distantly in Chloe's memory, some fleeting sense of having met Bianca before, although she has no idea where. Many years earlier perhaps?

'Let me at least put some antiseptic on his cuts,' says Bianca, scrambling to her feet to search for a bottle of Dettol. 'Then I'll call you a taxi... That is, if you're really sure?' she adds doubtfully.

Chloe nods mutely, unable to tear her eyes away from Bruno's bloodstained face.

The taxi arrives almost immediately. As the ravages of his epileptic fit start to subside, Bruno appears calmer. Sharing his weight between them, Bianca and Chloe carry him unresistingly to the taxi, his young body now completely malleable in their arms.

'I'll call his doctor as soon as we get home,' promises Chloe emptily.

Not believing her, Bianca helps settle him and is about to close the taxi door, when Chloe suddenly remembers: 'Yes, do please finish the painting in the way you described. Perhaps you could come to us in Chelsea for the final sitting rather than our making the journey here again?' she adds hopefully.

Bianca does not know what to say. 'I'm not sure that would work,' she starts to explain.

A note of authority intervenes.

'I do understand this is a difficult commission for you,' pursues Chloe, mustering all her scattered dignity. 'But I do very much want a record of my son, while he is still young and beautiful, whatever the cost.'

Bianca starts to say: 'Cost is not really an issue…'

But Chloe appears not to have heard, hurrying on: 'After all that's happened today, a portrait of Bruno seems more urgent than ever. I intend it as a birthday present for my husband… but really it's a present for me.'

She blushes bright pink, as if making some sinful confession. Bianca smiles sadly.

'Yes, of course; I'll do whatever I can. I'm just so very sorry about today…' Her voice trails to an uneasy silence.

Chloe lifts her hand in a limp, inadequate gesture of goodbye, Bruno, for once, lolling against his mother, his head cradled unresistingly in her lap.

Standing watching the lights of their taxi disappear, Bianca wonders if she will ever see either of them again. Part of her hopes not; she feels exhausted.

With her house keys still in her smock pocket, she locks the door of the studio without bothering to go back inside, instead hailing the next taxi home. As she walks in, the phone is ringing, but she doesn't reach it in time, the caller leaving no message. She sinks wearily into a chair.

What a day…

Suddenly tearful, she longs desperately for Stephen; for the sweet comfort and reassurance of his strong body enveloping hers. He is the only person who would truly understand.

* * *

Bianca leaves the duvet, the cushions and her easel, with its sketches of Bruno, exactly in place to continue work on his portrait. Three days later and she has still not heard from Max. Nor, apart from Stephen and Matthew, has she spoken to anyone since her return from China; Leonardo still away. Although, she isn't sure where exactly, his secretary would know.

'Did you know that young boy was disabled?' she asks Matthew the following day at his gallery.

'No, only that he was nine years old. His mother said something about his being highly strung, but that's exactly how she struck me, so I thought little of it... Why, what's he really like?'

Bianca lets out a sigh. 'He's a sadly enfeebled, desperately closeted little being. He may even be crippled... It's hard to judge how much of his condition is psychological as opposed to physical.'

She pauses, searching for the right words. 'It's a bit like witnessing a young animal, bred for sacrifice... almost as though he were designed to be broken. And yet it's impossible to guess at the process destroying him, despite its outward effects being so very conspicuous... and probably destined to become more so. I think that's what his mother most fears, and why she's so anxious to have a portrait of him. She sees it as an opportunity to hold on to him, to fix his beauty for all time, and remember him as he is now, before the mysterious destruction devours his handsome exterior.'

She pauses, again searching for words. 'Yet there's also a strange intensity in him which defies the destruction and makes him strangely beautiful... I suspect Chloe Smythe knows that the years ahead can only hope to steal more and more of the person she loves, that the beauty of a broken child can only be replaced by ugly ravages of adulthood. It is very sad. Plus I don't really know how to proceed with his portrait. I can't subject him to any further sittings; they are simply too stressful for him.'

She glances seriously at Matthew. 'Perhaps you should ring Mrs Smythe and either persuade her to cancel the commission, or explain, as diplomatically as you can, that I have agreed to make a portrait of her son based purely on the material I already have, right up to the point immediately preceding any finishing touches, at which point she can review the portrait, just herself alone, at the studio... If she likes it enough, you can charge her for it, but otherwise I think we'll just write it off as a failed experiment. That way, there'll be no further need to subject her son to another sitting.'

Matthew watches Bianca carefully during this speech, thinking, *What an enigma she is... Perhaps she always was, even at school?*

There is no doubt in his mind that she is deeply wounded in some obscure way that never seems to heal. He sees it in her face sometimes, especially in repose, and he can hear it now in the tremble of her voice as she struggles to identify with this unknown woman's pain.

Perhaps that's why people are so drawn to her, he speculates. *Although never confessing to any distress of her own, it always seems to be there, subtly implicit in her understanding of others?*

It occurs to Matthew that it is only her compassion for others holding Bianca together; that the only thing preventing the open wound in her from turning sour are memories of her glorious childhood, when she still felt secure in her mother's love. As it is, the discreet silences she carries with her create a sort of attractive mirror effect, causing others to long to see reflections of themselves in her eyes while basking in the balm of her sympathy and attention. Along with her technical skill, it is what had made her into such a good painter. She truly wants to understand the people she paints. He despairs, however, of her attitude to money.

'For heaven's sake, Bianca, can you really afford to paint a six-foot-square canvas and not get paid? Think of all the work it entails. I have queues of people waiting for portraits by you. If this woman and her son are such a bad bet, just let them go and begin work on something else... These are good, by the way.'

Spread before him are the watercolours Bianca had done in China. Many more of them than she had remembered.

'I didn't expect you to like them. They seem so lightweight and experimental to me,' she whispers hesitantly.

'No, you're wrong; they're just different from your normal studio work, but that's what makes them interesting. I think we should plan an exhibition at the gallery, exclusively of these. Broadly framed, they will look most handsome… Of course, I'll need to check the gallery calendar. As far as I remember, these next few months are choc-a-block, but I do have one artist dragging his feet over a show meant to open in a few weeks' time. If he really can't come up with the requisite number of canvases for a convincing show, I'll postpone his exhibition and show these instead.'

Bianca laughs. 'Poor chap. I feel sorry for him already.'

Matthew glances slyly at her. 'When is Leonardo due back?'

'I don't really know,' she replies casually, her expression suddenly obdurate.

'What a strange creature you are, my Biaancaaa…' he says, cracking his knuckles in glee.

'Me strange?' she replies. 'What about you, scuttling off to left-wing meetings having made a capitalist killing on some deal here in the West End. Not to mention that feverish love life of yours. How is that club, Les Chandelles, that you frequent in Paris, by the way?'

Matthew laughs, used to her teasing. 'But seriously, what shall I tell this Chloe Smythe person about her son's portrait?'

'That I will work on it daily for these next three weeks, then let her see it… After all, the only other piece of work that's remotely urgent is Max Holland's portrait, and I haven't heard from him. Has he been in touch with you?'

'No, but I called his agent yesterday. He's in Ireland still, working on a new play.'

Bianca turns her head, hiding her disappointment.

'Very well, Mrs Smythe's son it is,' she says brightly.

Later that evening, while making herself supper, the phone rings, Bianca taking it in the kitchen.

'Hello?'

There is a long silence.

'Hello?' she repeats. 'Hello, hello?'

The line crackles, and a slurred, accented voice that might be Mediterranean or Eastern European breathes slowly, harshly, almost snorting down the line: 'Arrh, you're Bianca... You're that Bianca... the Bianca that sleeps with the old man... that WOMAN.'

The broken vowels continue to pursue her fiendishly, the voice revving up more forcefully, savouring the kill.

'Well, I want you to know I have his SON... his baby son.'

The voice starts to giggle... followed by a long pause.

Bianca is stunned, sluggishly asking: 'Who are you? You must have the wrong number.'

From having been baffled into silent listening, Bianca's fury suddenly erupts, accelerating and spilling into the phone: 'What the hell is this...?' Her voice seethes with disdain.

The voice at the other end gasps, as if taken by surprise, followed by a muffled sound of doorbells, the connection broken. Bianca sinks back, deflated into a chair, her mind racing, wondering how to interpret the call. She dials 1471, but the caller had withheld her number.

How did this person even get our number when it's ex-directory?

She feels strangely dumfounded, invaded, unsure of both herself and the caller.

What kind of mother of a newborn would first jealously inflict pain, then refer to the father so deprecatingly as 'the old man'? She feels shocked, unable to think.

What does it mean exactly?

Yet nor does she stop to pretend with herself... She knows, without the slightest doubt, that the caller was referring to Leonardo, even though she had no reason whatsoever to suspect him.

Perhaps I should ring him?

It is something she rarely does, when he is away. If ever she needs to get in touch with him when abroad, she rings his secretary to learn where he is; he never answers his mobile phone. Besides, she has no idea whether he is currently in the Far East or Paris... And this isn't the sort of conversation to attempt over the phone.

Perhaps the woman stole our number from his phone?

She sits down, breathless and afraid. Yet all she can think of, beyond her anger, is how cruel and unloving it was to have described Leonardo as 'old'.

Why would she call a man in his late fifties old? Is that how a woman would describe the father of her child, even if true?

'Ignore it,' advises Stephen, when they speak the following morning. 'You don't know for certain it wasn't a crank call, and what can you hope to achieve either by confronting him or by knowing? He'll only be embarrassed and think you don't trust him.'

'The truth? I could achieve the truth,' she replies bleakly, whispering hoarsely.

Stephen laughs. 'Oh, the truth... Far too late for that... Besides, even if what the woman said is true, he's bound to lie.'

Embarrass him? thinks Bianca exasperatedly.

What with this and the unexplained purchase of a chateau, 'embarrassment' strikes her as the least of it. Nevertheless, feeling forestalled, she accepts Stephen's advice and refrains from calling Leonardo's secretary.

* * *

Max plans returning to London within the next few days. But first Dublin, he and Sinead deciding to drive the entire distance back to Dublin together, deliberately timing their journey one day early so that Max isn't tempted to argue he is too tired to attend the gala performance the following night of his play, already performing at the Abbey Theatre. Politicians, film stars and local dignitaries have been invited. Max had hoped to avoid it, but his agent insisted.

Dropping him off at the Fitzwilliam Hotel on her way to visit her parents in Little Rock, Sinead offers to collect him two days later and drive him to the airport. Max's gaze sweeps over her like a lamp, detecting neither moodiness nor guile. She means just that: 'I'll pick you up in two days' time and drive you to the airport to catch your plane.'

He is unused to such straightforwardness, such lack of curiosity. *Yet why does she look at me so intently?* he wonders.

There are moments when her eyes feel on fire, puzzling him. Throughout their long car journey, she had chatted easily, inconsequentially, laughing happily at his jokes. Best of all, she had remained silent for long, comfortable hours at a time, without the slightest need to speak or even to listen to the radio. So why had those silences felt like good conversation?

Yet now, dropping him off at his hotel and not even bothering to switch off the engine, she simply remarks: 'Arrgh, the boot's properly open now… for you to collect your luggage.'

Max suddenly hears himself say: 'Might you like to accompany me to the gala tomorrow night?'

A few seconds earlier, he had no intention of inviting her, the whole 'gala' thing striking him as a bore – a spurious social occasion that happens to have adopted a performance of one of his plays as its vehicle.

Surveying her dishevelled hair, her dark eyes in her pale, travel-worn face, the numerous familiar pockets sewn to the legs of her cargo jeans, he remarks: 'Your trousers remind me of a chest of drawers, like in one of those paintings of female nudes by Salvador Dali.'

She looks confused. Ashamed for even mentioning it, he adds: 'You would have to dress smartly.'

Turning towards him in surprise, she switches off the engine. 'Surely is it not your grand occasion now? Would you not be best going off on your lonesome?' she asks shyly.

Max shocks himself by admitting: 'No, I don't think I would.'

He is about to ask: 'Do you have a dress? Would you let me buy you one?' but thinks better of it. Her smile is suddenly radiant, her pale hair lit into a halo by the last-minute gold of the evening sun; all tiredness banished.

Let her come in cargo pants, if she wants, he thinks aggressively. *What do I care how people dress?*

Disappointed in himself for even thinking it, he had imagined himself beyond such bourgeois etiquette nonsense.

'What time tomorrow?'

'If you pick me up here at a quarter to seven,' he estimates, 'that should give me plenty of time to say hello to one or two people, before the performance starts at 7.30 p.m. There's also a formal dinner afterwards we're invited to.'

'We?' she asks, dismayed. 'Will I be after coming to dinner with you too?'

'No.' He laughs. 'We'll drop you off at McDonald's on the way.'

The following evening the Fitzwilliam lobby is densely crowded; people in evening dress throng its foyer. Sinead had rung to say it probably best if they went to the theatre by taxi, in case of parking difficulties.

'I'll leave my car in the hotel car park and meet you in the foyer.'

Arriving downstairs early, Max cowers, slightly hidden, hoping to avoid the central hubbub. He is elegantly dressed in a dark suit and white, tasselled opera scarf, wound too tightly, throttling his neck; his hair a delicious tangle of kiss curls. A couple he vaguely recognises sail up to him – the woman, effusively cupping his face in her hands before kissing him, bird-like, with a peck on his mouth; her husband, seemingly unperturbed by her indiscretion. Yet anxious, nevertheless, to shake his hand in vigorous bonhomie. Max sighs.

Why do these people irritate me so much?

Instinctively, he searches for a handkerchief to wipe fleetingly across his mouth.

I hope Sinead does decide to come in cargo pants, he thinks rebelliously.

These people, with their air of well-bred presumption and charm, strike him as suffocating. He turns away abruptly from their elaborate goodbyes, the wife still blowing him kisses as she is swallowed by the hotel's revolving doors, only to find yet another person blocking his path.

'Excuse me,' he says with immaculate coldness, his eyes hardening to black stones.

Then, as if from a great distance, hearing a familiar voice: 'I waited, until they left...'

The slender, miniature creature in front of him is Sinead. Failing to recognise her, he had never before seen or imagined her like this. She is dressed in a pale, floating shift of blue silk, darting shafts of silver one minute and Prussian Blue the next, while encompassing a tiny figure, balanced on silver heels. A pink rose, tied to an elaborate black satin bow, nestles at her neck, her pallid, anxious face of two days ago glowing blushingly beneath her smooth coif of ash-blonde hair. Max cannot conceal his delight.

'You look wonderful,' he gasps.

'So do you,' she replies, her eyes creasing in happy smiles.

* * *

The following Sunday, Anya wakes feeling strangely faint. Unlike her usual nimble self, she struggles to get out of bed, her head swimming with dizziness. She sinks back onto the pillows, willing her equilibrium to mend itself. Nor does she feel like having her usual early morning bath. Without noticing herself, she drifts back to sleep, only to be woken several hours later by the shrill call of her doorbell. Struggling, shuffling to the door, still feeling feeble, her voice on the answer machine is a whisper.

'Hello?'

The familiar, accented voice of Andreas answers: 'Anya, I worry about you. You not at the bus stop… I wait for you.'

It is the first time she has noticed the incompleteness of his sentences, the bright scrutiny of his dark eyes usually disguising their absence. Feeling disoriented, she can see her clothes warming on the radiator, next to her raspberry-pink chair.

'But I haven't yet had my bath.'

She doesn't like surprises. Weak as she feels, she doesn't like him turning up uninvited, her voice suddenly haughty and stern. 'How did you get my address?'

Turning up at her door, is not the same as waiting serendipitously at a bus stop.

'The Society's list of addresses,' he replies logically. 'I come to see you?'

Anya hesitates, anger starting to make her feel better.

'I'm not yet dressed,' she replies more gently. 'I wasn't well earlier. I think I'll leave The Society for today but hope to see you next Sunday instead.'

She replaces the answerphone without waiting for his reply. Andreas, standing in the street, looks nonplussed.

Perhaps she drop receiver by mistake?

He rings the bell again. 'Something I can get for you, Anya?'

Anya's voice softens. 'No, nothing, thank you. I just need to stay warm. I'll see you next Sunday.'

'Okay,' the accented voice reluctantly replies.

Negotiating her way unsteadily to the warmth of the radiator, where her clothes are cooking before her altarpiece, Anya glances up at her reproduction of Piero della Francesca's *Baptism of Christ*, smiling secret joy in acknowledgement of its reassuring presence. She feels a little better, although still not strong enough for a bath. Nor, despite not having eaten, is she hungry. Automatically stretching out an arm, she lovingly tweaks the crisp brown leaves of one of her dead flower arrangements displayed on the coffee table at her elbow.

How very odd everything is… What is he hoping for, that strange young man?

Still not satisfied, she carefully rearranges the branches of dead leaves again. Then, letting out a deep sigh, falls into reverie… Recalling the past with clarity is becoming ever easier. It is only the present that feels increasingly muddled and elusive.

In her thoughts, she is suddenly back on a London street, many years earlier. She and Bianca, having returned from Paris by then, were living at the cottage with William. Yet barely happy. As often as she could, she escaped back to London to stay with her sister, Lettie, in the pretty house she shared with her circumspect husband, set in a sunken garden in Highbury, its quaint Victorian architecture hidden beneath bowers of heavy-headed cabbage roses. It had been her husband's extreme circumspection that led to their fear of depositing their savings in a bank. Instead, he had encouraged Lettie to use her dressmaking skills to sew ever larger sums of cash into the cushioned tops of their kitchen stools, right up until the moment Hesketh arrived to steal their £25,000.

Bianca always accompanied Anya on these excursions, even if it meant missing a day or two of school. Family trips abroad often meant missing a week or two. William and Anya may have resorted to the frugality of smoking dried poplar leaves and buying food on tick from the village shop, but nothing had ever prevented them from spending their slender means on travel.

Bianca also always accompanied Anya on visits to her own mother. Anya can remember being on a street in Kennington on her way to visit her mother in South Island Place...

Scanning the broad, busy Brixton Road, for a gap in the traffic to cross, she had suddenly tugged extra hard at Bianca's small hand in hers, propelling the protesting five-year-old into the onslaught of traffic, forcing cars to skid, before braking violently. Trembling with fear, Bianca was unused to the rough and tumble of London streets. Anya nevertheless sped her daughter on, ignoring her distress.

In the distance, a burly figure in a big black overcoat was fast receding from view, walking with hasty, miniature steps, Anya tugging all the more desperately at Bianca's hand.

'Mummy, you're hurting me.'

'We need to hurry,' replied Anya.

Just then, the man in the distance paused, standing still, before crossing to the next street. Removing his homburg hat to retrieve something from its crown, he replaced it carefully on his head.; By now, Anya's voice was so hoarse that even Bianca could not hear her shouts above the roar of traffic. All she saw was the distraught, ever open mouth of her mother, miming desperate, impotent calls on a busy London street.

Suddenly, for no apparent reason, the burly man hesitated, glancing back in their direction, Anya waving frantically. At first, he looked unsure, peering into the distance almost timidly. Then, at last, hearing his name, he took a step forward. Bianca heard him say: 'My dear child...'

She assumed he had meant herself... but it was to Anya that his arms were held out wide.

Even to Bianca's childish gaze, Anya looked dishevelled and distraught. Yet big bear Varinsky appeared not to notice, his smile not missing a beat.

'My darling child...'

His glad arms folded around Anya's small frame, breathing in the familiar scent of her hair.

'How I have missed you,' he whispered.

He seemed to not count the absent years, nor need to know, remarking only: 'I heard you were back in the country.'

Turning to smile broadly at Bianca, he revealed a gleam of gold tooth to match the one illuminating Anya's Parisian smile, tousling her hair as though both she and her presence were the most natural thing in all the world. Without stopping to enquire whether they had the time, he stepped into the traffic to hail a cab, declaring that they must come and have tea with him at his hotel right now. His shoes, Bianca noticed, were shiny, black patent leather. He explained: 'I'm living temporarily in a hotel while searching for a new London base... Did you know that, until recently, I was living in America?'

'But we're on our way to Grandmamma's,' objected Bianca, having, until now, remained watchfully silent.

'She doesn't know we're coming. I forgot to send the telegram,' Anya explained breezily. 'We'll come back later.'

'The Savoy please,' Varinsky instructed the cab driver.

The taxi immediately filled with the sweet musk of his aftershave. Twenty minutes later, they were all three perched on deeply upholstered armchairs, with blonde wooden armrests, sipping delicate Orange Pekoe in front of mountainous plates of miniature sandwiches and cakes in the stylish art deco interior of the Savoy Hotel.

Even now, Anya can remember how Varinsky's eyes never once left hers; the feelings of warmth and authority evoked in her by those heavy-lidded eyes above the delicate aquiline of his nose and the soft, sensuous beauty of his voluptuous mouth; the dark forest of his five o'clock shadow disappearing into his throat of chins. Those same jewels 'flashing in the dirt' that had enthralled her at the age of sixteen.

'Darling, would you be alright here on your own, just for ten minutes, with the waiter looking after you? You can order an ice-cream sundae if you like?'

Feeling shy and frightened at the prospect of being left alone in this vast, unfamiliar room with a frock-coated waiter, looking more like the rooks who scavenged the ploughed fields behind the cottage than a human being, Bianca dared not say no. Anya and Varinsky were gone for more than half an hour; an eternity for a frightened five-year-old... But when she returned, Anya looked happier and more beautiful than Bianca could remember her being for a long time. By then, neither her mood nor her clothes were in disarray.

Thereafter, whenever Anya travelled to London to visit either Lettie or her mother, Bianca was mostly left at home, with William instructed to collect her from the village school on his bicycle after the day's painting. It was on those cycle rides from the school to the cottage that William and Bianca forged their friendship. Stopping to admire a view, William would take out a sketchbook and make rough drawings, while Bianca picked posies of primrose and velvet-leaved pink campion, growing on verges next to willowy, swaying branches of cow parsley.

Cycling back from school with William became miniature adventures that Bianca never forgot. They forged an unbreakable bond, albeit one not entirely immune to anger and disappointment. There were still days when William looked at her uncertainly, remarking wistfully: 'I think you have my eyes.'

And Bianca, in adult life, having finally understood the implication of all the stories she had been told as a child, would know he was thinking of the Frenchman, who stood like a resolute, unspoken grievance between them.

Nevertheless, it remained a bond exclusive to them; one that Anya had failed to anticipate and came to resent. Not once had it occurred to her that a father could become so very important to a child, let alone to her own *enfant unique*. Nothing in her own experience helped her to understand. Instead, she argued vociferously with herself: *After all, Bianca isn't really William's child, so why would she love him?*

It struck her as unnatural, almost ugly in some secret, perverse way. Even now, all these years later, resurfacing from her reverie, she still resents it.

* * *

'I'll be after driving back to the island now.'

Dropping Max off at Dublin airport to catch his flight to London, Sinead is again dressed in her favourite cargo jeans. Suddenly concerned, Max asks: 'What will you do there, all on your own?'

His mind summons up the weather-beaten features of Jack; his stilted shyness and strange undertows of aggression. *Will he make his move now?*

'I'll get everything nice and tidy, ready to shut down the island for winter,' she replies indifferently. 'We've been fairly lucky with the weather. But November storms can be mighty cruel... And I doubt Peter will come here again, much before the spring...'

Max cannot resist asking: 'Will Jack help you?'

But she appears not to hear. 'I'll probably just stay on shortly, until the weather gets the better of me.'

'What then?'

'Come back to Dublin and help my father run his accountancy business. Did I not mention I've a law degree?'

Max looks at her aghast. 'Why did you never say?'

'I presumed you knew... I imagined Peter would have told you?'

'And what about your dreams of sailing the Atlantic?'

'They're probably just that – dreams,' she replies evasively, adding: 'But thank you for inviting me last night... It was a grand evening.'

Almost formal again now, Max feels suddenly disoriented, wondering unhappily: *Was it my play or the evening she so enjoyed?*

In fact, they had both enjoyed the gala. Even Max, far more than he'd anticipated. Yet they are both now reluctant to talk about it. Sitting together in the front-row stalls, surrounded by local dignitaries and politicians, all Max could think of was the sweetness of her perfume, reminding him of Bianca. Then, after the conviviality of an evening in which everyone had welcomed Sinead, and conversation at the formal dinner afterwards had been easy and relaxed, Max had made a joke in the taxi about his desolation at returning to his untidy house in Islington, with Sinead, for the first time that evening, failing to smile, an uneasy silence again settling between them. Asking her if she would like one last drink at the hotel bar, she had replied that since she was driving back to Little Rock, she preferred not to.

Strangely at a loss for words, anxious his intentions may have been misinterpreted, Max had bowed extra formally to her on the hotel steps before retreating quickly beyond the swing doors; she, meanwhile, observing him solemnly before disappearing. All the false intimacy of their time on the island had, in those few minutes, suddenly fallen apart, leaving them embarrassed and exposed as strangers. Yet up until those final moments in the taxi, the evening had been a success.

A residue of embarrassment remains now, as they prepare to say goodbye. Once again, Sinead neglects to switch off the car's ignition, leaving her burdensome beast of a car to purr loudly beneath its sumptuous leather seats. Attempting to shake hands, Max states over-formally: 'Thank you for all your help.'

She responds by putting the car into first gear. 'You're most welcome.'

Max smiles hesitantly. 'Goodbye then...'

He feels there is something more he should say but cannot think what it is. Neither of them mentions the possibility of meeting again. Holding open the car door, still searching for the elusive phrase, he is unusually at a loss for words. Sinead surveys him one last time; dressed in his red harem pants and gold Prada trainers.

Breezily, her foot already on the accelerator, she replies: 'See you...'

Max peers in through the passenger window, but she is already looking straight ahead.

As he makes his way to Departures, Max feels a mixture of troubled nostalgia and relief.

When I get to London, I'll phone Bianca... The Unfinished Portrait, he thinks gratefully. *I could probably use that as the title of my new play.*

How he longs to hear Bianca's voice, witness her smile, reflecting: *How right I was to keep faith with her.*

CHAPTER 20

On his return from Majorca, Hesketh senses a change of mood in the Chelsea Embankment apartment, even the Buddha in Battersea Park seeming to wink at him less brightly. Incapable of analysing it precisely, he longs to ask Chloe if something had happened while he was away but feels too shamefaced.

Still not knowing whether she had been told or seen mention of his brief arrest in the *Evening Standard*, he hopes not to have to tell her. After the incident with the American social worker, it feels enough just to be tolerated, let alone loved. Negotiating his position within the family warily, smiling solicitously at every turn, he feels like an interloper in his own home. The only thing he can put his finger on is that Bruno seems more nervous of getting to his feet, of walking unaided, always seeming to want to trail one hand along a wall to steady himself.

Terrified by the deep cuts disfiguring Bruno's mouth, he is preempted from querying them by Chloe saying she had forgotten to raise the side of his cot one night and he had fallen out of bed. Disbelieving her, for once, he would have liked a second opinion. But since Chloe's complaint, no social worker had come to inspect Bruno, the authorities now searching for someone new, preferably a man. In the meantime, the mood on Chelsea Embankment is distantly sombre, with Hesketh ingratiatingly grateful for any small crumb of affection.

But away from the apartment, his existence is altogether more baroque. Just as he formerly spent hours outside Bianca's address, he now spends those same hours waiting outside Matthew's art gallery, except that, in Cork Street, there is no bus stop to shelter from the rain and cold. Matthew has noticed this bedraggled figure but failed to recognise him. It is only the messages he leaves late at night on the gallery answerphone that he recognises: that distraught, ugly menace of a voice.

How could one ever forget?

Nevertheless, Matthew still delays announcing these anxieties to Bianca; her painting currently so profitable, he does not want her disturbed. Besides, Matthew has his own worries: the extravagant rents, plus salaries, of running a West End gallery. Bianca is a friend he has no desire to deceive, but the fluency and speed with which she completes her increasingly fashionable portraits is offsetting some of his worst financial worries. For that reason alone, he does not want her distracted. He hopes, like the police, that Hesketh will give up and go away.

In fact, Hesketh has developed a new habit. He takes photographs of everyone going in and out of the gallery with his battered Leica, which has languished in a drawer, untouched for years, though for his bus-stop vigils of Bianca's apartment, he prefers relying on his fierce new binoculars. Meanwhile, having entirely given up trying to photograph Bruno, who became too agitated, he is suddenly rediscovering the joys of black-and-white photography. At night in his office, with the tap-tap of Bruno's typewriter as background music, he pores over black-and-white images of strangers, searching for clues, believing Bianca's whereabouts to be hidden in the nuance of a smile, in the expensive cut of a jacket. Somewhere, somehow, these were the people who were shielding her.

He tries to remain cheerful, but one evening, locked in his study, he starts to weep. Big, involuntary tears and gulped air invade his being; tears of frustration and grief. Frustration at not being able to find Bianca; inconsolable grief at not being able to undo the past. Bianca had slipped out of his grasp, without his noticing properly at the time, his mind ever since racing to catch up. He could not forgive himself. More to the point, he could not forgive Bianca.

Meanwhile, Matthew has decided to show Bianca's watercolours of China sooner rather than later. Plus Matthew has discovered, serendipitously, that Bianca's friend Robin Holderness is planning a talk at the Royal Geographical Society around that time, on the clandestine hold Confucianism continues to have on modern China.

What could be more apt than to make the two events coincide...? By advertising Bianca's show alongside Robin's talk, perhaps I can steal some of Robin's audience to come and buy her pictures?

Picking up the phone, he asks his secretary to arrange for their framer to visit him. Although Bianca's watercolours are minute in scale, he has decided to surround them with vast mounts of dove grey, so their muted colours flourish more jewel-like against their neutral ground. The frames themselves, he resolves, will be in pale wood, lightly dusted in gold, so turning Bianca's miniature five-finger exercises into objects of luxury. He will entitle the show 'China in Miniature', just as Bianca had jokingly suggested.

* * *

Later that evening, Leonardo rings Bianca to say his return to London will be delayed; he now plans to edit his new film in Paris.

'Have you finished filming?' she asks, surprised.

'No, still most of the Parisian sequences to complete.'

'Are you hoping I might join you?' she asks hesitantly.

He pauses... She can hear the smile in his voice, swiftly followed by a more severe note: 'Probably not; I shall be working most of the time...'

He feels a stab of guilt. 'But we could plan a weekend in Siena, if you like... whenever suits you?'

'Okay...' Bianca agrees slowly, her mind racing.

La Casa was where they had always been happiest together.

'Of course, I'll have to check my schedule and get back to you with some dates...' He is suddenly anxious to terminate the call, even though it is now several weeks since they last spoke.

Used to his abrupt manner on the phone, Bianca replaces the receiver, only to immediately remember he hadn't once mentioned the chateau. Nor, following Stephen's advice, had she mentioned the strange call from the woman, claiming him as the father of her child. She sighs. What a mess they all feel at times, these sophisticated games of relationship...

Yet the truth is she hadn't really wanted to join Leonardo in Paris and was simply being dutiful in suggesting it. Equally, she had forgotten to tell him about the opening of her exhibition, wondering cagily: *Will he be back by then?*

Perhaps best if he's not... That way he'll assume any references to China in my work as pure fiction and 'China in Miniature' some abstruse, fanciful title, designed to make the work seem more exotic. By not having seen them, he will feel no curiosity.

Bianca knows it is only ever direct evidence that upsets Leonardo.

If he arrives back in London after the show, he may not even recall there had been an exhibition...

She should be angry, but what she actually feels is tenderness; tenderness for Leonardo, plus a little for herself. She remembers a conversation she had had with her mother when still a little girl: 'People have a habit of missing one another... that is the great tragedy of life.'

At the time, still too young to understand, she now understands perfectly. Stephen might irrefutably be the love of her life... Nonetheless, she is full of sorrow for the blight Stephen's presence has cast over her marriage to Leonardo.

The following day, she gets a call from Matthew. 'I hear Max Holland is due back.'

'Really, who told you?'

'I rang his agent again,' he admits sheepishly.

'Goodness, he must think we're harassing him,' she exclaims, feeling annoyed.

In fact, Bianca had done exactly as promised, working briskly on her portrait of Bruno. The ground of the picture, with its spread of blue velvet and scattering of petit-point tapestry cushions is almost complete, as is the upward exploding figure of the boy, viewed from above and dressed in his schoolboy formalities of grey flannel shorts, socks and jumper.

Has he ever actually been to school? wonders Bianca, as she works on the ribbing of his socks and jumper, discovering the subtle patina of elusive colour: blues, greens and mauves, lurking in their grey shadows, and flecking them in with light touches of a sable brush, so deft they set up fast-paced rhythms of their own, creating miniature, painterly storms of abstraction. She has also already completed the under painting of the boy's face and hands, but that is where she now proceeds more circumspectly, anxious not to deaden the fleeting moments of beauty in his uncommunicative face, nor to betray the furious, animated dance of his long-fingered hands. The photographs she stealthily took of him are good, as are the sketches, but she now needs his mother's sanction before applying the final touches.

'I've almost finished the boy's portrait,' she explains. 'But until it's done, I really don't want to resume work on Max Holland's portrait.'

Hearing Matthew's stifled gasp of admonition, she tries to explain 'Because I have had to work so very fast and differently on this portrait, I want to keep it separate from my normal working methods. Also, I'm finding doing the boy's portrait hugely depressing and sad, and just want to get it over with as soon as possible.'

'So how do you want to play it?' asks Matthew. 'Should I arrange for the mother to visit your studio again, either on her own or with the boy?'

'Definitely not with the boy,' Bianca replies crisply. 'Too stressful for him... Nor do I particularly want to see the mother again before the painting is complete. Despite all her efforts at cheerful concealment, she seems so crushed and miserable somehow, and might succeed in hindering me.'

'So what do you suggest?'

Matthew, feeling increasingly exasperated listening to all this suffocated emotion, thinking, *What emotional claptrap.*

'I was wondering if you might make a detailed video of the work, so far, and show it to her at the gallery? If she gives the go-ahead, I can probably finish the painting within the next ten days, certainly in time for her to have it framed before her husband's birthday.'

Matthew sighs. 'Okay, let's do that.'

Artists are like babies, he thinks bitterly, *with their endless plea for special attention.*

Nevertheless agreeing, he adds: 'Perhaps I'll also make one or two slides, so I can project the painting exactly to scale for her.'

'Perfect,' says Bianca. 'Then, if Max Holland gets in touch and still wants his portrait done, I'll work around the clock to get that finished too,' she adds on a sigh, failing to admit just how much she both dreads and longs to see Max again. If only she could, she would postpone doing so forever.

* * *

Stephen and Bianca are now back in their London routine of meetings planned around restaurants, theatre and lovemaking, neither of them ever demurring or saying: 'I don't really feel like it today.'

Instead, it is like an imperative between them, a promise that cannot be undone; the minute they are alone, an instantaneous sensuality consuming them. There is also Stephen's unquenchable thirst for new experience.

Shortly after their return from China, he had rung Bianca with a new idea: 'Supper in a restaurant in Charlotte Street, rather than one of our more usual haunts?'

In nearby Tottenham Court Road, a glamorous new nightclub had opened with a 'decorous' cabaret of naked pole dancers.

'Won't that just be seedy and exclusively for men?' Bianca asks, feeling perturbed.

'I don't see why. According to the press, it's all very upmarket. Besides, we'll be there just for the spectacle and to enjoy the theatre of it all...', adding: 'Although, we should probably dress up.'

Feeling slightly nonplussed at the prospect of pole dancers, the very thought of Charlotte Street fills Bianca with nostalgia. It seems to have contained so many threads of her youth: *scallopine al limone* with her parents at Bertorelli's, purees of spinach with green noodles at Schmidt's, plus the nostalgic lore of her parents' tumultuous Fitzrovian youth, handed down in the form of familiar anecdote. It seems to have been where all the ferocity between William and Anya first began.

Dressed in a black silk velvet shift, which roams about Bianca's slender, shapely hips like liquid treacle, matching her elegance, Stephen is dressed in one of the many dark suits she had chosen for him. As they approach the doors of the new club, she is precipitated into another memory.

Years earlier, while still at school, the frugal, painterly years of her parents' bohemian existence already replaced by exorbitant wealth and Diners Club suppers, bought at the expense of William having exchanged his precarious, uplifting career as painter for the well-paid tedium of an advertising agency, she had been called out of class one day to take a phone call. She still remembers the ominous, slowed tempo of her father's voice as he delivered his carefully chosen words: 'I've some bad news for you...'

The leap in her heart, as she heard them.

'Your mother has had an accident...'

Working on the Simcar account at the time, they were running two of these miniature cars as replacement for the handsome, sage-green Alvis of their bohemian years, with its proud coach work, polished walnut dashboard and low slung, policier-style running boards. So low that they regularly caught on the high clotted grass verges of country lanes, dislodging its big-end. These two miniature Simcars were like biscuit tins on wheels. Driving the bronze-coloured one, Anya had turned suddenly without looking and collided with a lorry in Tottenham Court Road, the miniature car propelled unresistingly first onto the pavement, scattering terrified pedestrians, then through not only one but two sets of double glass doors before finally coming to a precarious halt at the top of a broad flight of stairs.

'They've taken her to University College Hospital... She's badly shaken, but it looks like she's got away with just cuts and bruises,' her father had eventually admitted, deflating the suspenseful drama of his earlier tone. It was difficult to judge whether he was pleased or disappointed by her survival, adding scornfully: 'But the car's a write-off.'

Now, all these years later, Bianca finds herself poised above that same flight of stairs, remembering the exact foreboding in her father's voice that dreadful day. But instead of fragmented glass, she and Stephen find themselves surrounded by a small gang of suave bouncers; men whose tall bulk and pneumatic bodies belie a subtext of violence. But first of all there are the club's outrageous entrance fees to negotiate.

At the bottom of the stairs, still more nostalgia awaits. The interior of the club is large and spectacularly beautiful, bypassing thirty years of disco interiors to recover an earlier nightclub age of pure elegance, with comfortable sofas, low tables and discreet lighting surrounding a raised dance floor, on which beautiful young women, with delicious figures, wrap themselves sinuously, sexily, in strangely introverted dance routines around a gleaming pole; simultaneously demanding the attention of their audience, yet never once soliciting it with flirtatious looks.

These were the interiors of Bianca's adolescence, identical to the nightclubs William and Anya had first acquired a taste for during their time in Paris, 'Le Boeuf sur le Toit' forever on their minds, later to be replaced by 'The River' and 'White Elephant' clubs – the only difference that the smoky cabarets of sweetly plaintive saxophone, with husky singers performing what Anya used to call 'jazz *intellectuel*', had been replaced by pole dancers. Bianca had spent much of her childhood and adolescence sitting in the plush alcoves of smart boîtes, watching adults at play. It had been just one way to grow up fast, not physically but in terms of perception; her natural shyness teaching her to be extra observant. It had also taught her to think visually, to interpret all experience as tableaux vivants – a way of seeing that had proved invaluable when she, copying William before her, had trained to become a painter.

She can visualise them now, her clever, conflicted, good-looking parents: William, in a well-cut, navy pin-stripe, bought from the shop he always referred to as 'Foreskin Reed' and Anya in a cocktail dress of ridged black silk, her tiny waist encircled in broad sashes of shiny satin, the bold costume jewellery from Fior William chose for her sparkling at her ears and wrists; her tiny, size-four feet, clad in precariously high suede stilettos by Pinet. Despite no longer being 'successful lovers', as Anya's occasional whispered comments to Bianca throughout her childhood years regularly hinted, they still knew how to dance well in each other's arms, relaxing easily, responsively to the music. They also knew how to laugh well, except whenever fighting. Later, when she had become better able to snuffle out the paradoxes, Bianca began to wonder if fights were not her parents' version of lovemaking.

Sometimes they would conjure nightclub moods at the cottage, throwing endless parties, with William doing serious cooking and furniture pushed back against the wall for everyone to dance to the Mighty King Sparrow's naughty Calypso lyrics, while drinking lethal 'gin and Italians'. Any excuse for a party would do...

Bianca remembers her seventh birthday. William had invited Dicky, a photographer friend he met in the Middle East during the war, along with his wife and children. Anya had invited various village schoolchildren. She had also made a cake, sunk in the middle, but which she had levelled with chocolate icing, before scattering with hundreds and thousands. The party started at four thirty. They danced that day to Bob Azzam and his orchestra, children and adults alike. By five thirty the adults were tipsy; by six thirty dead drunk and all laid out on the floor like corpses. Bianca never quite forgot the grown-up strangeness of finding the tallest people in the room to be children, and herself, at the grand age of seven, responsible for it all.

The huge expense not stopping at entrance fees, even though she and Stephen have merely come to observe, they order some drinks and position themselves together on one of the club's deep sofas. But this fails to correspond with house rules. Dotted around the room are other close-knit groups, equally elegantly dressed, but mostly men. No sooner have their drinks appeared than Stephen is accosted by one of the beautiful girls, now descended to earth from her dance-floor gyrations, skimpily dressed and asking if she can perform a dance exclusively for him?

'No, I'm here with Bianca,' he explains amiably, placing a possessive hand on Bianca's knee.

The girl retreats, only to be replaced a few minutes later by two more beautiful girls, one asking if she can dance for Bianca while the other dances for Stephen. Again, Stephen refuses but agrees to order more drinks. Intrigued, the two new beauties stop to chat. They are students at nearby University College, one studying philosophy, the other German, pole dancing, their way to make ends meet. They compliment Bianca on her dress and jewellery, eager to talk fashion. But pressure is mounting...

As the two girls finish their drinks and depart, one of the bulky men whispers in Stephen's ear. It seems they cannot be left alone.

'House rules,' he explains. 'Either participate or leave.'

He calls a young sliver of a girl to their table, who offers to take Stephen to a side room to dance for him.

'Shall I find another girl to dance for you?' she asks Bianca, in a bored, listless voice. 'What are your tastes?'

Bianca is horrified, her devotion to elegance in serious jeopardy, the prospect of another woman dancing exclusively for herself simply repellent. Yet Stephen is reluctant to leave Bianca on her own. Despite the immaculate luxury and beauty of the place, its mood feels increasingly predatory.

'No, you can dance for me, but Bianca must be allowed to watch,' he decides.

The girl, who is a pale, translucent, blonde imp of a creature, shrugs indifferently. Why should she care? Despite her youth, her world is fast becoming just 'people'; horrible, unpredictable people, with unfathomable erotic 'tastes' and the money to pay for them.

She leads them to a plush curtained alcove, inviting Stephen and Bianca to sit side by side on red velour banquettes. At a secret signal, music begins to play and the girl begins a writhing, strip-tease dance in time to its beat, her impish body gyrating slowly, teasingly from the silky confines of her Emilio Pucci palazzo pants to reveal a translucent body, tightly crisscrossed and bound by thinly strapped bra and thong, while simultaneously tottering on heavy platform-heeled shoes that turn her feet into miniature hooves. Not once, as she dances, does she remove her eyes from Stephen's and, although never quite touching, gyrates ever closer between his splayed legs. Taking her discarded Pucci pants, she slides them silkily around his neck, drawing him to her. Much to Bianca's surprise, he starts to respond. His eyes develop an alert, glassy brightness, while never deserting those of the girl. Unembarrassed, Bianca watches, fascinated.

As soon as the music stops, the little blonde imp resumes her everyday character, with its intimations of ennui, while waiting for Stephen to pay her. Bianca then watches in startled admiration as she seamlessly pulls on the tight Pucci pants again without bothering to remove the cloven feet of her built-up shoes.

'What wonderful skill,' whispers Bianca, smiling.

Glancing at Stephen's flushed face, she asks: 'Did you enjoy that, darling?'

'Yes, I did rather...'

He smiles a strange lop-sided grin of pleasure.

They both laugh softly in their throats, the impish girl leaving them with a tight, bored smile.

As they make their way back to the main floor of the club, the two girls they spoke to earlier are now writhing sinuously onstage. Stephen asks: 'Do you want to stay for more?'

'Only if you do.'

'I think the same thing will happen... More pressure to pay for drinks and dances... Let's go home instead.'

Bianca glances at her watch; they have been here less than an hour. By 'home' Stephen means Bianca and Leonardo's apartment. It often feels like his home too. So much so that Bianca has let him have his own key.

At the top of the stairs, passing by the posse of suavely suited bouncers with their rakish air of calculation, they hail a taxi. Twenty minutes later they are wrapped in a storm of their own lovemaking, while giggling at the absurdity of Stephen's latest experiment.

* * *

It is late one night, when Max finally gets in touch. Not expecting anyone to ring so late, Bianca is in bed, watching television. She assumes it to be Leonardo, who occasionally miscalculates the difference in time zones, counting incorrectly either backward or forward. That last time they spoke, he had been in Paris, but he could easily be anywhere now between Paris and Beijing. She does not always keep track.

Engrossed in watching a film, she is tempted not to answer, only reaching the phone just before it switches to Message: 'Hello?'

A pause on the line, then a familiar voice, full of laughter says: 'Bianca, this is Max Holland. Have I rung too late? I just got back from Ireland.'

It is almost as though nothing had happened. All the intervening weeks of abstract promises to herself, of carefully constructed indifference, fall away. She had started to cultivate the idea of Max as an aberration, briefly belonging but now relegated to the past; someone who had cast an audacious spell over her emotions while claiming priorities for himself she neither felt nor matched, let alone wanted. But just the sound of his voice immediately places him back in the present. She feels her own smile rise to match his.

He recounts very little of his time in Ireland, concentrating mainly on minor difficulties his play had encountered in Dublin, while also explaining he had begun work on a new play. He mentions nothing of Bantry Bay, neither the island nor even the goats, his voice betraying him by a rise of several octaves as he asks: 'How was China?'

'Fine,' she replies, equally non-committal.

'Just fine?'

Suddenly, they both laugh. Inexplicably, she says: 'It doesn't matter.'

Yet he completely understands. 'Are we going to meet?'

He sounds both eager and shy. She pauses, asking timorously: 'Do you still want me to finish your portrait?'

'Yes, of course; I want to see myself through your eyes.'

'Oh dear,' she teases. 'Are you quite sure that's what you want?

'I've just had the go-ahead for the last stages of a rushed portrait of a nine-year-old boy,' she explains. 'Matthew called me earlier to confirm the mother's approval. But I still need another week to finish it. Then, at some point, the mother wants Matthew and I to deliver it personally to her flat on Chelsea Embankment, to oversee its hanging. All of which I can probably do by the Friday after next. So why don't we meet at my studio that weekend?'

'Perfect... Which day do you prefer?'

'Let's make it Sunday... but come to the studio whatever time suits you.'

Max stops to consider. 'Let's make an early start on the portrait, then I can take you out for a gastronomic lunch.'

She laughs. 'Ah, food again... How wonderful...'

Having chatted a little longer, they agree to meet at 10.30 a.m.

* * *

Given Chloe's full permission to finish Bruno's portrait from her sketches and photographs, Bianca proceeds swiftly, with confidence. She has already completed the flat underpainting in acrylic, and now, as with the Cavendish portrait, resorts to thinly veiled, fast-drying alkyd paints, which allow her all the broken-brush excitement of oil colour without the need to wait overnight for it to dry. Applying the paint in thin glazes, she again uses fine sable brushes to tenderly conjure the perfect oval of Bruno's face, plus the pained, delicate introversion of his elusive gaze, while faithfully recording the energetic pirouetting of his hands, and thinking: *It's almost as though his hands have stolen his mind and greedily kept it for themselves.*

After long days, during which she barely speaks to anyone, apart from Stephen, the portrait is finally finished. It had felt somehow imperative, right from the start, to execute the work hastily, in order to be free, as though she were running away from some unidentified threat, without knowing why. Not simply the pressured deadline of Bruno's father's birthday but something else; a mixture of pity and terror maybe at having witnessed the stern solitude in that brittle young boy rendered helplessly broken, as she watched him fall under the cosh of his epilepsy. She would have preferred to leave the hanging of his portrait to Matthew, but Chloe had insisted she come too. Plus Bianca is feeling a measure of guilt, secretly daunted her portrait may have trespassed indecently on that poor child's soul.

Matthew keeps a tall white van, specially customised with wooden racks, for occasions such as this, when clients demand he deliver a painting personally, although it is part of his job he doesn't care for. Despite his everyday frugality and allegiance to socialist values, he affords himself one secret, self-indulgent luxury: a liking for fast cars. To be seen beetling around London in a white van, as opposed to driving one of the two low-slung Ferraris, one in flaming red, the other bright blue, that he keeps in a lock-up garage close to his home in Kensington offends his finer sensibilities.

Collecting both Bianca and the painting en route to Chelsea, he is already in a bad mood. Throughout the drive, his mobile phone rings incessantly; every time he answers it, he launches into a volatile tirade against the foolish vagaries of clients.

'I hope you're going to switch that wretched thing off when we arrive,' objects Bianca. 'I don't think you have any idea just how sensitively difficult this encounter is likely to be. You and your mobile phone might just be enough to precipitate another bout of epilepsy in the boy.'

'I thought you said he likes music?'

'Yes, I did, but that raucous scream you keep on your phone hardly counts.'

By now, both fretful and ill-tempered, Bianca is also feeling nervous about the reception of her painting, which is odd. Normally, she couldn't care less what clients think, equally happy for them to either take or leave it.

Parking the van in a side street, alongside Chelsea Physic Garden, together they manhandle the six-foot canvas to Chloe's front door. As Matthew rings the top bell, a distant buzz and click is followed by silence. He rings again, pressing more heavily. This time, the door opens, and they find themselves in a dusty pentagonal hallway, at the centre of which is a refectory table, overflowing with uncollected mail. Up a short curve of steps, they discover a narrow lift.

'This won't do,' complains Matthew despairingly. 'The painting won't fit.'

'There must be stairs somewhere... Beyond that tapestry curtain maybe?'

'You go ahead in the lift, if you like, and I'll carry the painting up by myself... It's not particularly heavy.'

'No, but it's unwieldy. So let's carry it together,' says Bianca, wondering why she begins to feel so afraid of Chloe Smythe and her son.

Fighting their way past the tapestry curtain, huge clouds of dust envelop them, causing Matthew to choke and rub his eyes. 'What I won't do for bloody clients,' he exclaims furiously.

'Calm down,' Bianca reminds him. 'There's already sufficient drama waiting for us at the top of these stairs without your adding to it.'

Matthew sighs. 'Okay, I'll go first.'

Lifting one side of the canvas, he starts to climb, Bianca commenting: 'It's pitch dark in here… Don't they run to light bulbs?'

Feeling their way carefully to the top, they arrive at a scuffed, peeling door, which Chloe opens, wearing the same feather-print dress in which Bianca had last seen her. From behind her, a sudden dazzle of daylight streams down the darkened stairwell towards them. A few feet away, sitting on the floor, embroidering neatly in skeins of pink silks, is Bruno.

'We've brought the painting,' Matthew states unnecessarily.

'Come in.'

Chloe's welcome immediately striking him as charming, he begins to wonder what the fuss was all about. Lifting the painting over the final step, he leans it gently against the lift doors, whereupon Bruno starts to hum dangerously.

Chloe remarks anxiously: 'Maybe not put it there… My son likes to hear the music of the lift.'

Matthew rests it further along the corridor wall, the painting itself concealed beneath heavy wraps of bubble wrap and brown paper.

'Would you like a drink, some coffee maybe, before we start?'

Matthew has begun noticing how unnaturally pale Chloe is; her face almost translucent, while still hauntingly beautiful. She strikes him as an enigma. He stalls, cracking his knuckles, while ostentatiously consulting his watch. Instinctively liking her, he is tempted to say yes but replies with charming regret: 'Alas, no time… Best to press on.'

Chloe looks confused, while Bianca regards Matthew grimly. Sometimes, in professional mode, she finds him unbearable. She knows he has no further appointments throughout the day; in fact, after this, he plans taking her out to lunch.

He looks Chloe directly in the eye. 'I take it your husband isn't at home?'

Whereupon, a strange dance of emotions, ending in dismay, flit across her pale features.

'No, he's at our other home in Majorca, on business, but back on Monday, in time for his birthday,' her gentle voice flutters hastily. 'The thing is we first need to dismantle the other painting over the mantelpiece. I tried to do it earlier, but it's too heavy and thought maybe we could do it together?' She adds shyly, 'That's if you wouldn't mind?'

Matthew recovers his equilibrium: 'Certainly.'

Following Chloe into the vast sitting room overlooking the river, with Buddha gleaming gold in the distance, he stops in his tracks to gaze about him in shocked disbelief. Not for years has he happened upon such a superb cache of post-war British paintings. He turns to Chloe in wonderment. 'Are all these yours?'

'No, they belong to my husband. He had a travel agency, which he sold to Thomas Cook… Collecting paintings… is one of his hobbies.'

'Would he be willing to sell any? He clearly has a connoisseur's eye.'

Max turns back towards the corridor, where Bruno has abandoned his embroidery and is now knitting furiously, calling out enthusiastically: 'Biaancaaa… Come and see this exquisite collection of paintings. They're quite extraordinary, you'll love them… some Graham Sutherlands, even a Christopher Wood.'

Bianca is still in the hallway, patiently stripping brown paper and bubble wrap from Bruno's portrait, while wrapping masking tape into small sticky balls to drop playfully at Bruno's feet. Picking one up, he examines it closely.

'Biaancaaa, come here,' Matthew insists again. 'Come and see these paintings by Paul Nash and Ben Nicholson.'

Hearing the familiar elongation of the vowels in her name, Bianca realises Matthew has recovered his good spirits and is starting to enjoy himself. She calls out happily: 'Just coming…'

Vaguely, as if from a very long distance, she hears Chloe's troubled voice ask: 'I didn't know the "B" in your name stood for Bianca.'

Half nodding her assent, she walks into the handsome room, turning to glance sweepingly around the walls then towards the mantelpiece. It takes her a few minutes to realise why the painting seems so familiar. Where had she seen it before…? In a sudden volte-face of desperation and fear, she recognises her own lost painting; the triptych she had believed destroyed by fire, twenty-five years earlier. It is what Hesketh told her had happened…

Chloe's eyes follow hers in a mood of contempt. 'Yes, that's the painting I want replaced...' she states dismissively. 'I've always hated it.'

* * *

'So, what happened next?' asks Max the following Sunday.

Having spent the entire morning at her studio, with Bianca working on his portrait and Max again posed comfortably in the fake Chippendale chair, they are now enjoying a boisterous restaurant lunch with all the other late Sunday diners.

Max had arrived promptly at 10.30 a.m., to find her studio door wide open. Hearing him knock, Bianca had called: 'Come in.'

Rather than rush to greet him, she was standing mid-studio, dressed in black jeans and sweater, nervously waiting for him to appear, meanwhile, busily dismantling the velvet bed and scatter cushions of Bruno's portrait.

She's even more slender than I remembered... Max had thought.

Glancing anxiously at him, neither of them moving, they had stood ten feet apart, his eyes greedily searching hers before he eventually said, 'You're looking well.'

He says it again now, as they sit side by side in a windowed alcove, waiting to order lunch.

'You look well...'

Their table is formally decked out in white napery, the restaurant, although in central London, resembling a country-house hotel. Bianca glances tenderly at Max, refamiliarising herself with his presence, his monochrome complexion extra pale from the strain of a sitting that had lasted more than two and a half hours, during which he had sat silently with his thoughts, Bianca, meanwhile, losing herself in the intricate landscape of his face. Her earlier drawing, directly onto canvas, still held good, and she was able to proceed swiftly and fluently, blocking in the planes of his face in the nursery colours of Naples yellow and flesh pink, before repudiating their brash chalkiness with subtle glazes of terra verde, in preparation for the final, intricate stages of warm oil colour, floated thinly across her careful structural underpinning. Remembering her recent success with photography, she had also sneakily taken one or two portrait shots of him, in case Max should disappear back to Ireland again.

As the session ended, he'd asked: 'Why have you painted me green?'

'Because you've turned into a leprechaun,' she'd teased... before relenting... and explaining: 'Beneath the pink warmth of skin tones, there are always cool, translucent depths. Terra verde is a better ground on which to float those top notes of warmth... It will ensure the portrait looks more like you, rather than thick, chalky paint.'

He had blinked in surprise, unsure what she meant. But they are now chatter-box companionable again. After those first renewed moments of encounter, all their anxieties had fallen away again, leaving only familiarity. Just as it had that very first evening, when they had chanced upon one another in the hotel foyer.

Now, talking voraciously over lunch, they might easily be old friends, except in one small detail: their eyes never stop searching for the hidden truth in each other. Despite sitting side by side, they barely glance at their food. Constantly turning towards one another, the spirited interlocking dance of their eyes matches the fierce flight of their conversation, as though each were recklessly yearning for communication with the other while remaining oblivious of the impression they made on other diners. A waiter approaches to pour them more wine, but Max brushes him aside: 'Just leave the bottle on the table. I'll pour it myself.'

'So, what happened next?'

Until now, they have talked only books, plays and London gossip, deliberately skirting around Ireland and China, while failing to mention Hesketh. Hearing the question, Bianca's laughter dies in her throat. Max had never seen her so transformed. Starting to tremble, she repeatedly clasps and unclasps her hands while acrobatically bending her fingers with cruel pressure, something she only does in moments of extreme anxiety.

'I-It was difficult,' she stutters. 'While still confusedly recognising my own triptych, after twenty-five years of believing it lost, there was also the sudden, unexpected hostility of the boy's mother

to deal with... While I was experiencing the wonderment of rediscovering my lost painting, Chloe Smythe was spitting abuse at it.
Apparently, she hates it... She had also reacted badly to hearing my
name. At the time, I neither understood why she should so suddenly dislike me and my name, nor why she should want a painting
she so loathes to be replaced by another by the same artist... I
had imagined she and I understood one another, the incident with
Bruno at my studio establishing some sort of sympathy between
us. I felt confused, and a little afraid, without knowing why. It was
Matthew who eventually put two and two together. Turning to her
suddenly, with one of those low growls of his, he asked:

"'Would you mind telling me what your husband's name is?"

'She looked mesmerised, as though not quite understanding the
question.

"'No, not 'Smythe'... your husband's name?"

'By now, sneering imperiously, almost taunting her, she gazed
back at him in torment, stammering: "W-Why do you want to
know?"

'Matthew insisted: "Just tell me..."

'By now, his arm was gripped tightly about my shoulders. Partly
to shield me but also to prevent her noticing how badly I was shaking... My instinct was to flee, but the fate of my own lost painting
kept me rooted.

"'James," she whispered. "My husband's name is Hesketh James."

'I then wrenched free from Matthew in panic, almost sick, as
though a volt of electricity had passed through me. Starting to retch,
my diaphragm heaving in shock, I again made to leave. Whereupon, Chloe looked suddenly startled and afraid; also, strangely
young, like an adolescent girl. She still only half understood. In
fact, only Matthew truly understood. But he had the advantage of
knowing that which he had been putting off telling me: that while
I was in China, Hesketh had managed to infiltrate my connection
to his gallery and has been repeatedly hanging around outside, and
leaving sinister messages on the gallery's answerphone ever since.
He was reluctant to tell me in case I decided to break my contract
with him... Matthew says he's feeling the pinch financially at the
moment.'

Max watches Bianca intently. Her face has turned forlornly pale, her blonde curls lifeless. It is as though her beauty were retreating from him, minute by minute. Even her voice sounds dull and strangulated, yet curiously hurried, as if to get the worst over soon. Briefly disengaging her eyes from his, whispering angrily, she revisits the scene…

'Having guessed the connection, Matthew turned to Chloe, saying that if she really hated the triptych that much, he would gladly swap it for Bruno's portrait and waive the portraiture fee… He then lied, saying that, while he was well acquainted with the work of Bianca Johnson, who had painted the triptych, she was in no way to be confused with Bianca Turvey, her son's portraitist.

'"I think I saw you once," replied Chloe mysteriously, clearly unconvinced.

'Then, starting to look hostile again, she announced disdainfully: "That woman has made our lives a misery."

'By this time, I was shivering with cold. Matthew, nevertheless, held my arm tight still, to prevent me from bolting. Meanwhile, poor Chloe Smythe looked more like a scared adolescent than a grown woman, so desperately unsettled and confused was she. In the end, I simply felt an overwhelming sorrow for us both. We are both, in our different ways, Hesketh's victims. I had liked her, but there was nothing more I could do, except to go along with Matthew's lies…'

Pausing in her thoughts, staring into the middle distance, as though to discern some new unthinkable truth, Bianca asks: 'What must it be like to be married to a man who relentlessly stalks another woman year after year? We're still not absolutely sure, but we presume Bruno to be Hesketh's son. How strange that he should have this elaborate family life yet still find time to pursue me… I feel sorry for her in so very many ways. To leave a mother and her disabled son at home, to come chasing after me, seems almost more disloyal than if he were actually conducting an affair… How does she bear it?'

Max's glance is suddenly sceptical, a flash of anger darkening his eyes. 'Maybe she loves him?'

But Bianca appears not to hear, the thought too outrageous. So long is it since she had stopped thinking of Hesketh as a human being, let alone as someone attractive and lovable, that in her mind he is more of a phenomenon; an aberrated, loathsome, filthy piece of malevolence and evil. Yet Max could still ask: *Maybe she loves him?*

Bianca feels shocked and slightly repulsed. Nevertheless, blundering on, still wrapped in her cocoon of self-concern, she continues: 'Thank God he was away from home... Bad as this encounter was, imagine my horror if I had come face to face with Hesketh in his own home? It's unthinkable... Plus we would have been on his territory, within his control... the very thing he desires most.'

Shuddering in fascinated fear at the very thought, her voice starts to ruminate more slowly, shedding some of its outrage: 'Perhaps I should have recognised something familiar in the boy while I was painting him; the same oval face? It simply didn't occur to me.'

'And the fate of the two paintings?' Max asks in a clipped, neutral voice, his dark eyes hooded from scrutiny. Bianca gazes blankly at him, only half registering his change in tone.

'Yes, we dismantled the triptych and replaced it with my portrait of Bruno, just as Chloe Smythe wished. The effect on her of seeing her son suddenly rear up prominently, in replacement of the older painting, was astonishing. She transformed before our very eyes into a figure of happiness... it clearly giving her immense pleasure. She then started to weep. In my painting, Bruno looks quite proud; a little distant maybe, but almost focused, and certainly very handsome. She went to fetch him, shepherding him into the room, so that he could see for himself.'

Max, immediately more curious, the abstraction in his gaze vanishing, asks: 'What did the boy do?'

'He turned away, refusing to look, Chloe only eventually persuading him to turn around. It was unclear, at first, whether or not he even recognised himself; his mouth is still very badly scarred, poor kid.' She pauses. 'Then, with all of us gazing up at the newly installed painting, the dismantled one now blocking the corridor, where Bruno apparently likes to sit, Matthew suddenly asked: "Where should I store the other painting, while you decide if you want to swap it for Bruno's portrait?"

'I was still shaking uncontrollably but deliberately staying silent, pretending indifference to the fate of my rediscovered painting. It was Bruno who forced the issue. Clearly torn between ridding herself of a painting she hates, while worrying how Hesketh would react when he got back to find it missing, Chloe simply could not decide. Busily arguing the pros and cons of all this with Matthew, I meanwhile scrutinised the other paintings in the room; some of them extraordinary beauties, just as Matthew had said... Yet Hesketh did always have a good eye for paintings, even when I knew him. He used to buy up the more prestigious works at students' end-of-year shows, long before he had the funds to put together his current, wondrous collection. Then, suddenly, in the middle of all this debate, Bruno started violently kicking his toe against the lower edge of the triptych's tall central panel, damaging it slightly. Matthew and I turned in alarm... Matthew even stretched out his hand to restrain him, remembering just in time to hesitate.

'"Stop it, Bruno," pleaded his mother.

'But he simply refused, kicking even harder, until having torn a corner of the canvas... whereupon Matthew adopted his most suave, art-dealer manner, haughtily explaining that if the painting were damaged any further, he would be unable to make the exchange he had so generously suggested half an hour earlier...'

A little colour returning to Bianca's cheeks, her hands twist less viciously in her lap. But Max has seen how fragile her buoyancy is; that the ghost of Hesketh has robbed her of far more than he imagined. Watching the words bubble up again in her throat, it suddenly feels to him like watching a stranger.

'Chloe Smythe then whispered that Bruno had always been jealous of my painting, because his father spent such long hours looking at it, instead of focusing on his son... At which point, I was seized by uncontrollable tremors, and on the point of collapse. Realising, finally, the extreme state I was in, Matthew said: "Mrs Turvey is clearly unwell. I need to get her home."

'Then, turning formally towards Chloe Smythe, almost clicking his heels, he said: "Tomorrow morning, Mrs James, I intend invoicing you for the full fee of £20,000 for Bruno's portrait."

'At his use of her married name, she flinched. Then, her inde-cisiveness immediately vanishing, she asked: "Could you not take the painting away with you now?"'

'We were both flabbergasted… Yet that is exactly what hap-pened. We packed up the painting as hurriedly as we could, dis-mantling each panel separately and wrapping it in bubble wrap discarded from Bruno's portrait, before bringing it away with us in Matthew's van, having again braved their ill-lit staircase.'

'So where's the painting now?'

'At Matthew's gallery. He's arranging for it to be cleaned, and the damage Bruno inflicted to be repaired.'

'Good God,' says Max, astonished. 'Although, presumably, once Hesketh gets back, you won't have heard the end of it? What do you think he'll do?'

Bianca sighs despairingly. 'I really don't know… Something ter-rible, I expect. The painting is, of course, rightfully mine, not his in the first place… But Matthew is bound to regret having effec-tively had to buy it in exchange for the portrait… I really had no idea he was in such poor financial straits.'

Unexpectedly, Max replies: 'You look tired…'

They had not yet ordered dessert, their bottle of wine only half drunk.

'I'm going to ring for a taxi and deliver you home. We'll talk about this another day.'

His eyes, as he looks at her, are again affectionate and full of desire.

But once at her door, having graciously helped her from the taxi and kissed her lightly on both cheeks, Max instructs the driver to take him straight home to Islington. Partly intrigued by their day together, by the strange, mesmerising intoxication of the por-trait sitting, followed by the ugly, dramatic stories told over lunch, another part of him feels violent distaste. He recalls the unsettling experience of having sat, pretending to watch his own play, while the seething, distraught animation of Hesketh's desperation had played out alongside him, followed by Bianca's ambivalent coolness towards his attempts at sympathetic understanding of the poor man's feelings.

'What a spectacular mess,' he thinks out loud.

For all his careerist love and commitment to drama, this feels beyond even his elastic code of understanding. That such fatal false hope should be allowed to proliferate in a man's maddened mind like this, for twenty-five years and more… to him it feels like an act of cruel inhumanity. Nor can he begin to encompass the depths of despair it must entail, either for Bianca or that poor benighted creature, Hesketh. No matter how skilfully veiled, he sees clearly how damaged Bianca is, yet also feels critical of her for allowing it to happen. For the first time in his life, having made it his profession to revel in the absurdities and complexities of character, he feels like an outsider, as though suddenly, inexplicably debarred from other peoples' emotions. Although witnessing Bianca's distress, he no longer feels it… He longs for simplicity… All this complexity and spite feels repellent.

But why should that be?

He is normally engrossed to the point of intrigue by other people's entanglements; that, after all, what the many-layered nature of good drama relies on. Certainly, it is what is starting to formulate in the text of his new play.

Perhaps, he slowly ruminates, *I'm not yet back up to speed with the emotional rough and tumble of London but still languishing in the warmth of a red-tiled kitchen, while walking the island in my mind?*

CHAPTER 21

Having forgotten the chateau for several weeks, it starts to prey on Leonardo's conscience. Back in Shanghai for a few days' extra filming, he rings Laetitia to find out what progress she is making with its refurbishment.

'Haiii, Leo,' she says, giggling, in her sing-song Strine. 'Heoew's the weather in Shanghaiiii? I hear it's vairee muggy...'

She has just come in from the meadows around the chateau, where she and some of the French gilders had been playing badminton; one of them having woven a daisy chain to wear in her hair. Looking flushed and beautiful, she stalls for time.

'The farmer, who uses our laind for pasture, says this good weather's gonna hold.'

'*Our land?*' he questions sternly. 'I was ringing to find out how soon I can put the chateau back on the market?'

Her voice descends into uncertainty. 'Shall we discuss it when yer next in Paris?' she delays.

'Sure, I'll be there towards the end of next week.'

She struggles to find a reply, having imagined him away several more weeks.

Briefly, he muffles the phone; distantly, she hears him speak to someone else.

'The maid,' he explains, uncovering the mouthpiece.

At which Laetitia sniggers mischievously. 'It's me, you're talking to Leo, not that gullible woife of yours. I know what you're really laike, oddment babies and all, down't forget.'

Leonardo mildly wonders: *Is that some sort of threat...?*

'So, when will you be coming deown here? Don't you at least whant to see the chateau agaain?'

She pauses, waiting for his reply, before finally admitting: 'The work's almost finished.'

Relenting, although reluctantly, he says, 'I suppose I should try and find the time... I still have film to shoot in Paris. So I'll ring you when I've had a chance to review my schedule.'

Sensing a chink of hesitation, she reverts to a more syrupy tone of voice, preparing to make her move: 'You haven't forgotten, Leo darling, that we agreed I'd get a commission on the sale of the chateau, for all the work I've done?'

'Really? I don't remember that?' he replies stiffly. 'Aren't you already paid as my assistant?'

'But, Leo honey, this is a little bit different, deown't you think?'

'No, not particularly.'

'But I've worked so haard on getting this reight, Leo. Deown't I deserve a break?' she whines.

Leonardo sighs. How he loathes these absurd, greedy confrontations that pepper his every day. It is easier sometimes just to give in. Hoping to abdicate from the whole wretched debate, he murmurs: 'We'll talk about it when I'm back.'

'Once you've seen the chateau properly finished, you might not want to sell,' she suggests hopefully. 'Think of all the wonderful parties you and I could hold here.'

Again, he sighs. Never any mention of Bianca, whenever Laetitia and parties were concerned. The truth is she regrets not having inveigled him into marriage herself and now, not having done so, likes to pretend that his marriage to Bianca had never really happened.

'We'll see, we'll see... I'll be in touch... Okay?'

Leonardo puts the phone down, staring at it in disgust.

Standing a few paces away, watching him carefully through heavy-lidded eyes, is Maria, her dark hair scraped back from her sallow, unmade-up face into a lank ponytail.

Lisping her little girl voice, she says, 'Who was that, Master?'

'Laetitia,' he replies, without further discussion. He picks up his jacket. 'Let's get going, while there's still some light left out there.'

Glancing up at her, she vaguely reminds him of an Easter Island sculpture.

Christ, the pair of them, he thinks bitterly. *This is what Bianca means when she talks about the 'dance of the sycophants'.*

He glances out of the hotel foyer window. *Hardly any light left in the gun-metal sky, yet I need to get that last shot of the couple arguing in the street.*

Planning to film it directly outside the Peace Hotel, on the corner of Nanjing Lu with the Bund, this is what more truly concerns him – getting his film exactly right.

Effortlessly picking up the two heavy bags loaded with cameras and equipment, Maria strides mannishly towards the minibus, where the rest of his crew are waiting.

Yet it is neither the chateau nor even finishing his film which haunts Leonardo most. His greatest torment is Solange. Their weekend at Victoria Falls had been less successful than he hoped; even now, he is still unable to shake off his distaste at her insolence towards the hotel staff.

What possible reason had she for such behaviour?

Nor had he been able to pacify her, following her ordeal at Johannesburg airport, her same ugly, dislocated mood persisting throughout breakfast outdoors their first morning, with sunshine prettily dappling the hotel lawns stretched before them, and sable-skinned monkeys, with clownish, chattering smiles and obscene pink bottoms, racing athletically across the grass to steal croissants from their table.

'Oh, go awaaay,' Solange had wailed.

Flapping her napkin in frustration, she had glowered disdainfully at one of the willowy, dark-skinned waitresses, complaining: 'You would have thought they might have found a way to stop them...'

'You sound like Eliza Doolittle,' Leonardo remarked, surprising both her and himself with his rudeness. Tossing several small packets across the table at her, he said: 'Have some extra sugar why don't you? It might make you a little sweeter...'

Her fretful mood had persisted throughout dinner that evening, both now elegantly dressed: she in a dress of caramel silk, adorned by shimmering beads of turquoise, and Leonardo in an immaculate white shirt, to set off his tan, plus the flourish of a bold silk tie.

Suddenly, a group of twenty or so pneumatically inflated men with enormous legs, bulbous arms and tiny pin heads had lumbered past, their legs competing uncomfortably for space with one another and all looking like exaggerated versions of a child's toy, to seat themselves with immense difficulty at an adjacent table. Their weekend visit had coincided with the World's Strongest Man Championship finals, also being held at the hotel. Leonardo thought these physical grotesques, reminiscent of the Michelin man, delightfully quaint, while Solange dismissed them as hideous freaks, Leonardo again looking at her askance.

'Can't you see,' he pleaded. 'They are like the monkeys... they too have a right to exist. You can't go about switching people off, you know?'

On their first and second nights at the hotel, Solange had not wanted to make love, Leonardo neither demurring nor minding particularly. He half understood that her lonely vigil at Johannesburg airport had frightened her so fundamentally as to make her inaccessible. Not everyone shared his stamina, even if he sometimes had difficulty remembering so. Instead, turning over uncomplainingly, he clung to his side of the bed all night but in the morning was resentful when she helped herself to his toothpaste, enquiring indignantly: 'Did you not bring any of your own?'

'Sorry, I forgot,' she replied indifferently.

Perhaps what mystified and disappointed Leonardo most was that his Mediterranean charm seemed not to be working. It was not simply that he missed sex... He had, in any case, started to have serious misgivings about its great importance, once remarking to Bianca: 'Too much bother.'

But the thing he did miss, and which he loved more seriously than sex, was flirtation. At London dinner parties, Solange had always been so exceptionally good at it, and throughout those first days of their long weekend together, it almost felt as though she were wilfully denying him its exquisite pleasure, while punishing him for something he had not actually done. Nor could he equate her current behaviour with his memory of their passionate night in Beak Street, only a few weeks earlier.

Why did she agree to come?

The moment of change came on the narrow bridge, suspended perilously high above Victoria Falls. Unexpectedly cut off from other visitors by a dense cloud of mist, the slats of the bridge dangerously wet and slippery underfoot, the views precipitous, they suddenly found themselves caught in the colourful arc of a rainbow, transcending the exhilarating, headlong spray of the Zambesi like a hologram, their own beings driven to respond to its fierce, violent energies. Suddenly, Solange became her loquacious London self again, ideas and enthusiasms pouring from her. They talked voraciously all the way back to the hotel and into the evening, discussing the nature of light, the transparency of colour. They recalled the theories of Goethe and Chevreul, competing with one another for better understanding. Then, late in their hotel room, with the jalousie blinds drawn against the dark African night, they finally made love, her small frame again fitting perfectly against his olive-skinned bulk and restoring to Leonardo his joyful sense of being Italian.

But now, having returned to the relentless treadmill of work and travel, he begins to worry how to proceed with Solange. Their affair represents a serious breach in his promise to himself to restrict any sexual exploits to travel, rather than allowing them to complicate his London life with Bianca… Yet he is determined to spend more time with Solange. Despite her fractious temper and often ill-judged social manner, she continues to fascinate him; despite her moments of cool rejection, he is plagued by desire for her, unable to let go…

Perhaps editing my film in Paris will provide the perfect opportunity?

He had already agreed with Bianca that she would not be joining him in Paris.

But perhaps Solange might? It would certainly be one in the eye for that dreadful, jobbing architect boyfriend of hers, Nicholas Rowe, Leonardo thinks, chuckling to himself.

Deciding to suggest it the next time they speak, his mind races on, eagerly wondering: *Perhaps Maria would agree to put her up in her flat, rather than at a hotel? Maybe even move out for a bit, so we could be together?* he envisages longingly.

He would have to ask her.

In any case, Maria could always stay at the chateau and help Laetitia finish her work there... Or perhaps I should delay the sale of the chateau, after all? Maybe Solange would rather stay there with me instead?

His mind is abuzz with possibilities.

Meanwhile, he intends stepping up pressure on his crew, so as not to risk going too dangerously over budget. Picking up the phone, it barely rings, before Maria simpers: 'Yes, Master?'

'Can you organise the final shoot here in Shanghai, then arrange to get us all, including the crew, back to Paris by the end of next week?' he instructs her.

It has begun to occur to him that Solange, unlike Bianca, is not a woman he can afford to leave alone for too long. That despite her complicated private life of quiescent husband and boisterously opinionated boyfriend, if he wants her to continue pleasuring him, he may have to work a little harder than usual to ensure it happens. There is some strange, quixotic volatility in Solange that might lead to her capriciously saying no. And that, right now, whatever the threat to his marriage, he simply could not bear...

As for the chateau, he decides to wait and see whatever transformations Laetitia has achieved before making a final decision, reminding himself to be neither too critical nor bored by the whole project. Nevertheless, his private assessment remains: that, ultimately, the chateau will not do. Having struck him as ugly on his first visit, he knows that so forceful an impression is unlikely to dissolve. Unlike La Casa, which he fell in love with from the start, and would never dream of selling, he views the chateau as something of a white elephant.

*　*　*

Bianca too is full of strange misgivings. Her portrait sitting with Max had been a success, her painting of him advancing well. So why, as she climbs the stairs after he had dropped her off by taxi, does she suddenly feel so numb? It's not as though she had secretly hoped he would sweep her off her feet.

Far from it...

Max had been right to point out how tired she was; the dramas of the past week have left her exhausted.

372

No, it was something else, far more elusive and disconsolate. The only way she can describe it to herself is as a 'failure of nerve'. It equates with the same feeling that had haunted her in China; a sense of dismay at Max's willingness to take a step back. Plus her realisation that Stephen would never make so arid a choice on their behalf. Whatever Stephen might feel – whether doubt, irritation or dismay – he would never leave their relationship to chance like that. In Bianca's mind, only fierce, needful emotion ever truly signifies. She has an addiction to passion which rarely shows on the tranquil surfaces of her daily demeanour, yet is always there. Growing up against the backdrop of her parents' volatile marriage had taught her that anything less than ardour was just passing show. It was what had misled her, as a young girl, to feel intrigued by Hesketh's passionate, unbalanced nature; his capacity to use up emotion, to fill minutes and days with feverish desire, while she was still too innocent to suspect its corrosive nature. To survive Anya and William's bouts of anger, she had, from an early age, become a keen connoisseur of rows, quickly realising that any emotion left open to interpretation was irrelevant; that only urgency counts.

Before she left for China, Max's emotional need of her had seemed overwhelming. In fact, far more than his attractive looks and intelligence, it was that depth of emotion in him to which she had found herself irresistibly drawn. Anything in a lesser key would have simply been playful decorum and good taste. But if that urgency in him no longer exists, then there is no further reason for her to be haunted by his desire.

And yet she is left feeling oddly dejected and mournful, as though suffering a sudden, bereft awareness of having lost something significant, while, simultaneously, no longer feeling any impending imperative towards change. The status quo of her life can remain intact. Of that she is finally both sure and grateful. It was as though she and Max had waited patiently, desperately for one another, in order to dance joyously one last time in each other's eyes... but then instinctively, perversely, both turn away. Perhaps Anya had been right all those years ago, when she said: 'People have a habit of missing one another...'

***

Hesketh returns to London early the following Monday. It is his birthday. But arriving at Gatwick, he feels no anticipatory sense of celebration. Chloe has been so very cool towards him since the incident with the social worker that he wonders whether she will have even remembered his birthday at all?

Opening the lift doors, he is surprised not to find Bruno sitting on the floor, waiting for him. The apartment feels strangely empty, although it is unthinkable that Chloe would go out, taking Bruno with her. Apart from anything else, he is becoming increasingly difficult to handle in unfamiliar circumstances.

Putting down his bag, he strolls into their room overlooking the river, the golden Buddha seeming to radiate a personal greeting to him. Still no voices. Turning on his heels to look up at Bianca's triptych, he takes two steps back in amazement. Instead of the familiar miniature figures of a man and woman disporting themselves across twelve panels, figures he has always firmly believed represent himself and Bianca, confronting him is a towering portrait of Bruno. Observing the painting's obvious skill, he is surprised not to know the artist's work.

After all, I'm familiar with most modern painting…

Searching for a signature at the bottom-right corner, he finds 'B. Turvey', the name meaning nothing to him.

How did the painting get here?

Slightly breathless and faint, he sits down heavily in one of the white leather swivel chairs, feeling mesmerised by the new portrait.

How was it achieved?

His connoisseur's gaze traces every line, every brush mark, its huge scale dominating the other paintings in the room; no matter by more famous artists. Depicting Bruno as the central motif in a decorative design, his boyish figure rears up soberly against a sea of bright colour, his head and upper torso emerging ever closer to the picture plane, as if threatening to pierce it, while the lower part of his body dwindles telescopically, to dissolve in a frenzy of pointillist cushions. His acrobatic hands flirt, like ballerinas' tutus, against the colourful beads of a child's

374

abacus. But that which strikes Hesketh most, both delighting him yet filling him with despair, is how the artist has captured one of those fleeting moments in Bruno's face whose existence Hesketh has always suspected and desperately sought but never yet found for himself. A moment of heightened intelligence and pure focus, revealing the perceptive eye which explains Bruno's skill as a pianist, his delicacy of touch at embroidery. All that has so far baffled and eluded Hesketh about the son he adores is suddenly revealed by this unknown artist. It is both a relief to see it depicted so clearly, yet repugnant to discover its revelation in the hands of a total stranger. It feels punitive – a moment of gross unfairness which should have belonged exclusively to himself and Chloe.

So absorbed is he that he does not hear them arrive; they were waiting for him on the back roof terrace, with its views over Chelsea Physic Garden.

'Happy Birthday,' they chorus.

Even Bruno, managing to mumble the words. Hesketh turns towards them speechlessly.

Does this mean I have been forgiven?

He strides the room, tousling Bruno's hair and putting his arms around Chloe, his whole being flooded with relief. He glances up at the painting.

'It's magnificent, but how did you manage it?'

For the moment, not remotely anxious about Bianca's missing painting, he presumes it hidden next door somewhere. Chloe plants a timid kiss on his cheek.

'Welcome home, darling. We're having birthday lunch on the terrace, followed by birthday cake, exquisitely decorated by Bruno.'

* * *

Bianca and Matthew are at Matthew Dancer & Co., his gallery on Cork Street. Displayed at their feet, in correct sequence, are the twelve smaller panels of Bianca's lost triptych. Stripped from their rigid ply-board backing, they skid on the shiny parquet like loose stepping stones.

'Did you never see these at the time I painted them?'

Matthew shakes his head, looking unusually solemn. It is ten days since their installation of Bruno's portrait on Chelsea Embankment and he has opened the gallery specially, confident that on that on a Sunday at least, no one is likely to turn up. Daily expecting to hear from Hesketh, he braces himself each morning against a madman's potential litany of complaints, interlaced with legal threats about the absent painting and insistent badgering for information about Bianca. Yet so far, nothing. He has even consulted a lawyer on how to proceed, should Hesketh appear.

Adjusting his glasses, he suddenly notices how extraordinarily pale Bianca is looking. Like someone in shock, yet she has mentioned nothing out of the ordinary.

'How did your session with Max Holland go?'

'Fine,' she answers indifferently.

'When's your next sitting?'

She shrugs. 'I don't really know... We didn't discuss it... Whenever he can afford the time, I expect?'

Matthew looks at her strangely. It is unlike Bianca to be so apathetic, her manner mostly one of full-on engagement. In fact, her enthusiasm is one of the things he most cherishes about her. He hesitates, still doubtful, yet cannot resist asking: 'Are you worrying about what Hesketh will do next?'

Speaking slowly, like someone reciting a familiar creed, she sighs. 'I'm always a little bit preoccupied by what Hesketh will do next. It's one of the things I live with...'

Her voice sounds dull, as if on automatic pilot. Then, picking up a note, she adds: 'But yes, I'll have to be extra wary now that he's discovered my connection to you. Also some of his recent letters have been strangely off-balance, which is never a good sign. It seems to go in waves, this madness of his. Sometimes, he writes slap-happy, jolly little messages, like a teenage girl – "How are you? Lots of love, Hesketh" – at others, sinister little notes that are way beyond adult, and always pulsating with threats.'

Matthew cracks his knuckles noisily, not knowing how to reply. He feels guilty for not having been more circumspect, as though it were his fault Hesketh had succeeded in infiltrating her connection to the gallery. Although difficult to see how exactly?

Bianca glances at him, trying to assess what he's thinking, realising that he's deeply troubled. Not a look that suits him. For all his intelligence, Matthew is at his best when life strikes him as some absurdist joke, played like a Feydeau farce. Big, maddened passion of the Hesketh variety strikes him as shamefully self-indulgent. Bianca tries to reassure him.

'Don't worry. I've been through all this before. The trick is to keep one's nerve and not do anything too precipitous or provocative.'

She places her hand gently on his arm, smiling bravely. 'Cheer up.'

Wanly, he smiles back at her. Matthew has known her since adolescence. Knowing her too well, he can feel the sorrow in her; could almost reach out and touch it. He gets up briskly, determined to break the gloom.

'Let's have a cup of coffee, then get down to work... First, we need to decide what to do about these paintings. How best to restore them, and whether or not you want to sell them. That's if you even have the legal right to do so... I've asked my solicitor to check if Hesketh can claim legal ownership after twenty-five years. Possession being nine tenths of the law and all that,' he reminds her. 'Plus we need to go over the selection I've made of your Chinese watercolours to see whether you agree? I've had a couple provisionally framed, just to give us an idea of how best to present them at your exhibition.'

Bianca is only too glad to turn her attention to work. It is true that she feels sad, but that has less to do with Hesketh than with Max. She doesn't want Max restored to her emotionally but is suffering withdrawal symptoms from the depths of feeling she had invested in him. More, perhaps, than she had realised at the time. She also feels cross with herself, fearing she may have inadvertently let Stephen down, a thought more alien and unbearable than any other. The hollowness of it all is making her ill and dragging her into a flu of displaced emotion. How she longs for it to pass...

In the meantime, she is enthralled to be reunited with these lost works from her youth. The tiny naked figures, which animate the twelve smaller panels of the triptych are not representations of herself and Hesketh, as he so fervently believes, but of her parents, William and Anya, reunited in the miniature panels as they no longer were, even then, in real life. Yet it is not simply the personal history of these paintings that fascinates her, but the work itself. Twenty-five years ago, she realises, she had been a far better painter than she ever believed at the time. She recalls her own difficulties when starting the painting: how many false tries before finding the key to its success by studying Duccio's *Maestà* in Siena Cathedral. How she had failed, at first, to spot the device unifying its ambitious, storytelling composition, with each background to the figures seemingly advancing and receding haphazardly in scale, while dependent on guesswork perspective.

Then, suddenly, she had seen it. Despite the fluid changes in backdrop, the figures themselves were all identical in scale and played out uniformly on the immediate picture plane of each panel, providing both consistency and readability. Once discovered, she had not looked back, operating the same device in her own panels, and working confidently. Picking up one of the tiny panels, she holds it lovingly up to the light. Although it lacks the virtuoso complexity of her recent work, its graceful simplicity and sensitively delineated little figures, filled in almost blankly in rich, fat paint, enchant her. Turning to Matthew, her eyes bright and shiny again, she asks hopefully: 'What do you think we should do with them?'

'Sell them,' he answers a little too quickly. 'I'll get a good price for them, far more than the fee for Bruno's portrait... We've made a good exchange.'

Bianca turns away, concealing her disappointment. Having rescued these precious relics from her past, she is reluctant to lose them again. She glances surreptitiously at Matthew, knowing he is worrying about money, wondering: *Perhaps I could persuade either Stephen or Leonardo to pay the commission on Bruno's portrait, so he's not left out of pocket?*

Matthew, beginning to suspect her reluctance, adds quickly: 'But let's not decide now. In any case, I need to consult the lawyers some more, before we think of selling.'

Bianca stares blankly at him. 'Surely Hesketh can't seriously claim the paintings as his?'

Matthew turns away. 'I'm not so sure… Meanwhile, I think we should have them cleaned and arrange for the corner on that big, central panel Bruno kicked in to be restored.'

Bianca nods slowly, looking mystified. 'Very well.'

Leaving the paintings to skid on the slippery parquet, they retire to Matthew's private office, a windowless bunker to the rear of the building, where he opens two small portfolios – one containing the watercolours he has chosen for her forthcoming show, the other those he has put aside for the future.

'Feel free to change my mind,' he states grandly, his arms spread disarmingly wide.

Bianca smiles, knowing that any 'change' would involve far more of a fight than his breezy tone suggests. In fact, she is perfectly happy to let him decide. She feels far less possessive of these little five-finger exercises, than she ever does of her major portraits. To some extent, she is both baffled and charmed that he wants to show them at all. It is only when he pulls out the two framed paintings, lying hidden behind his vast slab of a marble desk, that she finally sees what he has already foreseen in them. Her face suddenly lights up, and she looks her animated, joyous self again.

Matthew had arranged for one of the little watercolours to be surrounded by a vast mount of dove grey and set in a simple gold frame, the other in an equally expansive mount of pale pink but surrounded by a six-inch depth of frame, sculpted from honeyed polished oak, and divided from its mount by a delicate white beading. Bianca is astonished what perfect taste Matthew had shown. She would not have guessed it of him. Yet he has transformed her little painterly experiments into magnificent jewels. Glancing gratefully at him, she exclaims: 'Matt, how wonderful they look. Extraordinary…'

'But which frame do you prefer?' he insists doubtfully.

Pondering, glancing from one to the other, she concludes: 'Neither… Could we not simply alternate the two around the gallery walls, with one painting floated against gold, the next against honeyed oak?'

He looks startled. Such variety had not occurred to him. In the world of modern gallery presentation, uniformity is key. Nevertheless, the idea pleases him.

'Okay,' he agrees slowly. 'Perhaps you're right...'

Her expression turns suddenly serious. 'But do you really think the exhibition can still go ahead with all this fuss from Hesketh about to break over our heads?'

She pauses, her mind chasing down every avenue of possibility, in quest of what Hesketh might do next, then laments, sighing: 'I've no idea what he will do, only that he will do something. With every new piece of information, Hesketh always does something. In fact, the only certainty in all this is his incapacity to do nothing. Nor is there any point in pretending otherwise.'

'I suppose he wouldn't be a stalker if he could persuade himself to do nothing,' Matthew ruminates.

Bianca notices him start to look worried again, cracking his knuckles anxiously rather than in glee.

* * *

Leonardo and his entire crew have now arrived back in Paris, their travel arranged by Maria, who is never less than efficient – attention to detail her greatest strength and the principal reason Leonardo employs her. She also has an uncanny, anticipatory instinct for other people's needs, detecting their nascent desires for comfort and ease, even before they do, then willingly providing it. The people who find her simpering laughably cloying are those who match her capabilities, therefore finding her endless offers of assistance almost insulting.

Their first few days in Paris are spent filming, while in the evenings Leonardo meets with his producers. They are a quarrelsome crowd whom Leonardo secretly dubs philistine, but since he needs their help and consensus to complete the project, he treats them like the seasoned diplomat he is, not letting his contempt show.

On the fourth day, after filming in oppressively blustery winds on the Île de la Cité, Leonardo decides to give both actors and crew a day off, while asking Maria to chauffeur him to the chateau.

He has decided not to tell Laetitia in advance of his visit, but just to turn up.

Much to Leonardo's astonishment, Maria seems reluctant to accompany him. He cannot remember her ever refusing a request before. She invents one excuse after another: 'I need to visit my mother in the Parisian banlieue... Would it not be best to wait until all the work on the chateau is completed? Is it fair to Laetitia to turn up unannounced?'

Leonardo observes her carefully, this last excuse giving lie to the rest. He knows perfectly well there is nothing but veiled animosity between his two assistants. Deciding to parry her objections with blank looks of incomprehension, he adopts what Bianca refers to as 'one of his twenty faces', Bianca often heard laughingly explaining to their London friends that Leonardo has twenty faces, all of them eloquent, impassive and utterly irresistible. Finally Maria admits defeat. Nevertheless, she is strangely fidgety throughout their journey south, her driving oddly erratic. Mystified, Leonardo had presumed she would be pleased to be spending a day in the country.

They set off early, arriving at the chateau before lunch. The massively ornate wrought-iron gates have now been painted, the potholed drive newly spread with gravel and the missing sculpture of a youthful hunter blowing his horn rediscovered in the basement and restored to the empty bowl of the fountain, whose waters now play like the tinkle of girlish laughter. From the open door to the chateau, voices can be heard calling to one another, like children playing hide and seek.

Leonardo pulls heavily on the metal door pull, whereupon the sounds of laughter cease. Silence. Removing his dark glasses, he peers into the gloom of the vast entrance hall, everything perfectly still. Leonardo's eyes busily scan the walls and ceiling, attempting to focus, a small, distant movement suddenly distracting him. There is someone watching him, from behind a half-open cupboard door. He senses a mood of fear... Unperturbed, he crosses the threshold and vast flagged floor to wrench open the cupboard door, Maria following a few paces behind him. To his absolute amazement, cowering against some faded Toile de Jouy wallpaper the builders have not yet found time to strip bare and replace, is the naked figure of Laetitia Norton, the look on her face at recognising Leonardo one of shocked dismay.

'How did you get here?' she gasps, her arms folded impotently over her bare breasts.

Over his shoulder, she witnesses Maria's look of disdain, coupled with something else, triumph maybe, thinking: *I wonder what that peasant upstart has got to feel smug about?*

She refocuses her alarmed gaze on Leonardo.

At that very moment, softly calling, 'Cuckoo… Cuckoo,' an athletic-looking man, dressed in boxer shorts and wearing a tall white chef's hat, strides into the hall. Laetitia squeals in further dismay, while both Leonardo and the new arrival look baffled. The man bows to Leonardo. 'Monsieur.'

Then, turning suavely towards Laetitia, he says: *'Je t'ai trouve, alors.'*

He stretches out his arm to her as she emerges, blinking, into a brash beam of sunlight cast from the open door. Still not understanding, he assumes Leonardo and Maria strangers who happen to have walked in on their secret world. Languidly picking up a dust sheet draped over a chair, he hands it to Laetitia, then selects another to wrap, sarong-like, around his own waist, clearly unembarrassed.

'Monsieur,' he says again, stretching out his hand to Leonardo.

Producing one of his twenty faces, the one with the naughty, mischievous smile, Leonardo takes his hand gleefully.

'Mademoiselle?'

The man turns towards Maria with a bow, looking momentarily startled. He too, suddenly wondering whether she is a man.

'What exactly is going on?' Leonardo asks Laetitia.

His manner towards her is far sterner than towards her companion. She explains lamely: 'We weren't expecting you.'

'Clearly not.'

Maria is wearing a strange, tight, inscrutable expression; no one would guess she is jealous. She starts to speak, lisping her little-girl words, provoking in the man's face sudden relief. Not a man, after all.

'Est'ce que vous avez mange,' he suddenly asks. Turning to Laetitia, he orders: *'Explique pour moi.'*

'He wants to know if you've already eaten?' she asks meekly. 'He's just prepared lunch.'

Leonardo laughs outright. Never has he seen Laetitia so completely cowed.

Having correctly assessed the situation, Leonardo immediately starts to forget it, his mind already on other things. What does he care what games people get up to? Looking around, his eyes newly accustomed to the gloom, he realises the hallway with its magnificent panelling has been lovingly, impressively restored. From the ceiling, twenty feet above him, hang two massive brass chandeliers, their gleaming, octopus tentacles extending in a wide diameter. Against one wall hangs a threadbare tapestry, fifteen feet wide, some of the faces of its seventeenth-century milkmaids now bleached down to the pale warp and weft of its weave, while others retain the lapis-lazuli blues and deep rose pinks of its original. Leonardo glances at it approvingly.

Laetitia, who had taken the opportunity to sidle away briefly, reappears wearing a dress of white broderie anglaise, her make-up and hair now immaculately redone. Leonardo glances at her acidly. 'Cast yourself in the role of modern shepherdess, I see?'

'A *table?*' suggests the tall man.

Although not exactly handsome, he is superbly masculine, his movements spare and agile. Now dressed again, Laetitia feels free to ignore him, leaving him standing in the hallway, while instructing Leonardo: 'Come upstairs… Let me show you the bedrooms.'

She leads the way, nodding to Maria, with whom she has not yet exchanged a single direct word, to follow.

They pass through room after room, each meticulously finished in the grand style, only their en-suite bathrooms conspicuously modern. The larger bedrooms on the first floor all have views overlooking the parkland and formal gardens to the back and sides of the house, leading to meadows beyond, where sheep and cattle graze. There is no mistaking its beauty.

'We thought of this room for you.'

Laetitia flings open double doors, painted eau de nil, and embellished with graceful mouldings picked out in gold leaf. Inside its generous spaces are bow-fronted chests of drawers, a cheval mirror, imposingly ornate desk and wide bed, festooned from a rose in the ceiling with powder-blue drapes to match the billowing curtains. Delighted, Leonardo begins to appreciate the chateau's possibilities again. On the floor above are still more bedrooms, smaller in scale, but equally charming.

They return to the ground floor, where immense, panelled, pastel-painted sitting rooms lead from one to another, interrupted occasionally by smaller, more intimate vestibules, acting like the punctuation stops in a well-constructed sentence, until they eventually arrive at the chateau's pièce de résistance, that which had first recommended the chateau to Leonardo, its theatre.

Laetitia explains: 'Its restoration is not yet complete. Today is the gilders' day off.'

The stage, although minus curtains, already evokes foretastes of future magnificence; Leonardo begins to imagine himself lecturing here to a group of devoted fans.

They proceed below to the vast basement kitchens, empty apart from the formerly déshabillé chef, now dressed in pale trousers and a white linen shirt. Having already passed through a dining room where no table was laid, Leonardo looks around expectantly. No table laid in the kitchen either. He is beginning to feel hungry.

As if able to read his thoughts, the man says: '*J'ai nous avons prepare une table au dehors, sur la terrasse.*'

Leonardo throws Laetitia a look of contempt as she translates unnecessarily.

'He has prepared a table outside,' he mocks.

They pass through a narrow corridor with an alcove built into its thick outer wall, where an old-fashioned, bow-fronted desk sits, loaded down with papers. Almost too casually, Maria places her scarf and bag on top of them. Watching her do so, Laetitia is reminded of something. She takes Leonardo's arm cajolingly.

'I've been going over some of the contract papers, Leo darling. Some of its pages are missing; they must still be with the lawyers. Nevertheless, there seem to be some anomalies in the wording. You'd better get them to check.'

'We'll talk about it after lunch... Aren't you going to introduce us properly?' he asks genially, as they emerge onto the sunlit terrace.

'This is the architect, Bertrand Delvaux. He owns the building company responsible for all these changes.'

The man smiles, bowing from his waist. Leonardo laughs happily. *I thought he was a chef…*

'Try some pate, monsieur,' says Bertrand Delvaux, switching effortlessly from French to English and revealing the typical reluctant disdain of the French to speak anything but their own language, except when absolutely necessary. Suddenly remembering, Leonardo produces another of his twenty faces: *I won't ask you what you were doing when we arrived.*

He pulls out a chair to sit at the exquisitely laid table.

Bertrand Delvaux opens a bottle of vintage champagne.

'*Santé,*' he toasts.

Laetitia looks up at him and blushes.

CHAPTER 22

For the first two weeks following his return from Majorca, Hesketh basks in his return to family life. He appears forgiven; no need to tread on eggshells. Chloe had even confessed to the disastrous portrait sitting at R. Turvey's studio that had precipitated Bruno's first epileptic fit, explaining the cruel scars defacing his mouth – also his fear of walking and constant need to cling to walls. Discussing his injuries without rancour, equally heartbroken for their beautiful son, they are both anxious to do whatever they can to help. Nor has Hesketh yet started to miss Bianca's painting, still assuming it to be in their basement or stacked in the room where Chloe had discovered him with the American social worker.

For two weeks, the family are never apart. Not since their early courting days in Majorca had Chloe known Hesketh so amorously attentive. They even go shopping together in the King's Road and take Bruno with them, walking either side of him to prevent a fall. Hesketh is reluctant to break the spell of this new intimacy by rummaging too conspicuously for the missing painting. Nor does he want to remind Chloe of the incident with the social worker by rifling through their spare room. But he also simply adores the newly installed portrait of Bruno. To him, it feels like a miracle of healing, plus at first almost a relief to be free of Bianca's triptych, with its constant reminders and infuriating riddles.

Not until Chloe decides to drive with Bruno to the Cotswolds to visit her mother, where, Chloe gently explains, Hesketh is no longer welcome, does he start to remember the painting.

* * *

Meanwhile, the various pressures on Bianca begin to take their toll, her resilience starting to unravel. Not only is there her puzzled ignorance about the chateau and the mystery caller claiming Leonardo as the father of her son, but also her dismay at what had and had not passed between Max and herself. She feels enveloped in emotional fog, asking herself distractedly: *Has all this just been vanity on my part?*

More unnerving still are her tenterhooks of fear, as she anticipates Hesketh's next move, knowing it inevitable that he will do something extreme, something for which no amount of wariness can prepare. Providing Hesketh with new information had always been much like throwing meat into a ring, provoking a feeding frenzy. But what exactly? She remembers the past depths of violence he was capable of, dreads him discovering, from Chloe, her studio address and destroying that last bolthole of serenity too. But she also feels deeply embarrassed, recalling the way Matthew had effectively bullied her long-lost painting from Chloe's grasp, a deed she now considers underhand and one they may yet come to regret. Above all, she feels shocked and guilty at having unwittingly trespassed on Hesketh's home turf, imagining how terrifying it would have been, had he been there. Fear roams about her mind, like looped film.

Over lunch, she discusses these anxieties with Stephen. Looking deliciously handsome, he bites the head off a long spear of asparagus, smiling a little automatically before trying to reassure her, part of him bored by the soap opera that is Hesketh, although contriving to conceal it. He carefully wipes melted butter from his chin.

'Won't taking the painting by stealth only have inflamed Hesketh's self-righteousness all the more viciously?' she asks.

'Only if he has the wit to make the connection between "Bianca Johnson" and "B. Turvey",' Stephen replies sceptically, 'which I very much doubt.'

His long lashes, shading the icy disdain in his eyes, flutter furiously against his cheekbones in a dissemblance of the contempt he feels for this never-ending destructive force in their lives, his famous laser-beam focus in dealing with problems currently a little deflected by a tricky publishing deal of his own, making him react dismissively to any adjacent problems. Plus it suits him to think of Hesketh as a fool, whereas Bianca is less sure that 'fool' is the correct term. She sighs despairingly, keeping her thoughts to herself, while Stephen rapidly recovers his equilibrium, fast sloughing off the reptilian worry of Hesketh to smile his disarming, lop-sided grin at her, his long arms hugging her knees beneath the table in the promise of the afternoon's lovemaking they have planned. His face is flushed, still lightly tanned from China, his eyes a bright cornflower blue again.

She glances out of the window, away from his eager smile. It is always the same; in moments of extreme distress, she missed her mother, wondering dejectedly: *Will we ever be mother and daughter again? Or will I get a phone call one day, telling me my mother has died, without ever speaking to me again?*

As her poise deserts her, thoughts of Anya become too painful. Only half listening, she drifts into reverie.

She recalls her childhood and teenage years, when she, Anya and William were a family still, living within the protective hug of 'the cottage', that fourth member of their little clan, with its ravishing, run-down personality of unevenly raked floors and crumbling red-brick, interlaced with long fingers of ivy, and carpets of wild violets sewn into its lawns; the graceful laburnum tree which greeted visitors at its front gate with its golden chandelier blossoms and lime hedge, flourishing its flutter of pale leaves, referred to always by William as 'the block of flats' because of the nesting birds who flew in and out of its doors all day. She remembers the high-banked brambles, interwoven with pink dog roses and mauve lilac, whose long suckers caught greedily at her clothes while producing lavish yields of blackberries. Imbedded in the vast back lawns were greengage, cherry-plum and apple trees whose fruit fell faster than Anya could bottle it against the ravages of winter, when the cottage revealed itself to be little more than an attractive sieve through which the East wind whistled relentlessly.

She remembers the rhubarb growing sub-tropically, with the contents of the Elsan lavatory spread around its roots, until both it and the old zinc bath were replaced by an ugly modern bathroom extension and septic tank, buried deep at the bottom of the garden; the creeping tendrils of nasturtium Anya always chose to grow, their graceful cadmium heads threaded jauntily across every pathway. Plus the three sentinel poplar trees, spaced evenly along one side of their triangular acre of garden, while magnificently spreading horse chestnut trees occupied each of its three corners, their big hand leaves and abundant candles stealthily disrupting the cottage's early Victorian foundations with their octopus roots, energetically nourished by the rich, elastic clay of the Eastern Counties to produce resplendent mahogany conkers in fresh nests of white and green, like pristine jewels, soon to curl and yellow like ingrown toenails. How the village children used to dare one another to dash past their lower garden gate to collect them before Anya could reprimand them.

She also remembers the families of preening cats, draped purring on every windowsill and fence, ever watchful, always self-contained and so numerous that strangers would leave an extra kitten on their doorstep overnight; how Anya, as her marriage crumbled, felt unable to cope and drove all thirteen cats in the silver Simcar one night to a farm four miles away, leaving them in a nearby ditch, only to be so racked with guilt that she returned faithfully each night at dusk to feed them. How the cats recognised the Simcar's familiar throttle engine and rose up out of the ditch to greet her, their pricked ears and cats' eyes caught eagerly in the beam of her headlights. She returned every night with tinned food and bowls of milk, until no trace of them was left. Later that night she broke down in angry tears.

These were William's advertising years, years of opulence and dismay, with Anya again finding her days spent alone in the too-miniature world of village life, just as she had during the early years of the war, before her escape to Paris. William, conscious of having sold his talent as painter for thirty pieces of silver to the hollow, greedy values of an industry he half admired and half despised, made his own sacrifice bearable by becoming a connoisseur of food, becoming almost as passionate about cuisine as he was about painting. Replacing his former favourite readings from *The Arabian Nights* and dissertations on archaeology were now the recipe books he devoured to turn himself into a skilful cook who insisted on cooking every night on his return from his London office, buoyed into renewed energy after a long day's work by the lethal delusions of gin and martini; by the time the food was ready, often too tired and drunk to eat it.

Manhandling the food with his fists onto Bianca and Anya's plates, he would then slide unconscious to the floor in drunken stupor. Every evening, Anya, prettily made-up and dressed for dinner, despaired at finding herself washing-up saucepans at midnight, frustrated and furious that while William thought nothing of spending £100 on food from Harrods for a single weekend, at a time when the most expensive pair of kid leather shoes in Elliot's window cost no more than £7, he nevertheless refused to countenance investing in a house of their own, his love and attachment to their irreplaceable dream of a cottage too complete. Since the installation of a new bathroom, their rent had risen to £45 a year. William would, nevertheless, send Anya out, generously armed with blank cheques, to shop for new clothes, which she returned home without having spent, in a mood of disgust.

As well as inhabiting London's nightclubs, they ate weekly at the city's most fashionable restaurants: Trattoria Terrazza... Meridiana... Mario's & Franco's.

Anya would gleefully drive one of the biscuit-tin Simcars to London in time to meet William after work, starting her evening in high spirits, immaculately coiffed, elegantly dressed, looking stunningly beautiful, then drink one glass of wine too many, whereupon a brief respite warning, lasting no more than three or four minutes, followed, with William and Bianca watching knowingly, fearfully, as the telltale corners of her mouth turned down. Thereafter, the evening would escalate into Jacobean drama.

First, Anya would enter into flirtatious political arguments with one of the handsome, busy waiters.

'Permesso, signora?'

Before then picking a more fractious political fight with his suave patron, followed by aggressive, denunciatory attacks on William and any adjacent diner bold or foolish enough to intervene. Within half an hour, the convivial atmosphere of the restaurant would deteriorate into a scandal of exchanged insults, many of them abusively insulting of William's parents, Preston and Edith, whose years of hard work had flourished into great wealth, but with whom, despite the long years since their first fatal encounter on her wedding day, Anya had never become properly reconciled. Most annoying of all, Edith had never bothered to conceal her niggling uncertainty as to whether Bianca was truly William's child and therefore rightful heir to their considerable fortune, Anya, meanwhile, sneering: 'What does your mother need with all those expensive crocodile handbags? Are they for carrying her portfolio of shares?'

At her most destructive, Anya would lean across the table and accuse William of being... 'No good in bed.'

As things went from bad to worse, the previously happy-go-lucky waiters slowed their toreador waltzes around the restaurant, to stand sorrowfully wringing their hands, and murmuring: '*Peccato, peccato...*'

William, nevertheless business sleek and handsome in his navy pin-striped suit from Austin Reed, would then pay the restaurant's extravagant bill and drive doggedly back to the cottage, no matter how late at night, travelling the dreary, blackened silhouettes of the Mile End Road, past the suburban dolls' houses of Eastern Avenue, to the anonymous roundabout at Gants Hill. With Bianca sitting silent in the back, their row rumbled on, its embers refusing to die, accompanied by Anya flinging herself theatrically back and forth in the front passenger seat to emphasise how bad a driver William was.

'Can't you learn to change gears without relying on your brakes?' she scoffed.

'Sarah Bernhardt, all over again...' he jibed.

Occasionally, the row would escalate so viciously that Anya would insist on being dropped off in the dark, by the side of the road, sometimes as many as four or five miles from home. William would then restart the car, crash the gears and drive on, cursing and worrying about her in equal measure, while Bianca remained trembling and afraid for her mother in the back seat. Yet Anya always eventually turned up, sometimes as many as two or three hours later, with blistered feet, no longer beautiful, bedraggled and angry but with a strange, imperious look of triumph on her face.

During those adolescent years, Bianca remembers feeling a permanent sense of conflict and unease, of which she now feels bitterly ashamed. She was young, impatient for her own life's dramas to begin, while prudishly, fatally embarrassed by these wayward emotions of her volatile parents. At times, her mother's anger felt like a permanent running sore... And yet, there were also still those weekend mornings when she found William and Anya in bed, wrapped in each other's arms and laughing hilariously at some joke he had just told, too young, at that point, to understand the consoling sweetness of warm flesh on warm skin. Whatever her parents' moods, they were always extreme, never remotely middling, always see-sawing between love and hatred.

Only now, in retrospect, does she remember and understand her mother's anguish more perfectly and the grief that must have maddened her beyond endurance.

Tragedy can belong to a single day. One afternoon, in her early teens, Anya had collected herself and two of her friends from school. Having almost arrived home, Anya suddenly announced that she needed to stop briefly in the village, to use the phone box. Despite his new wealth and new bathroom extension, William still refused to install either a telephone or television at the cottage, too jealous of either intervening in the brief, precious moments of painting he still insisted on snatching from the manacles of commerce at weekends. A few hours earlier, Anya had received a telegram from her sister, Lettie, asking her to phone London urgently.

Bianca still remembers how her mother was dressed that afternoon: in a bold black-and-white dog-tooth skirt beneath a swing-back jacket of bright canary yellow. Never afraid of colour, Anya had always dressed with panache, often shocking the villagers by the outré stylishness of her get-ups. She wore her copper hair shoulder length, her face prettily made-up and lightly touched with rouge. While Bianca and her school friends waited patiently in the back of the car, swapping adolescent secrets, Anya, in four-inch heels, dashed across the sluggish country crossroads, with its accumulated excess of golden gravel, from which moist, black eyes of tar glistened, to reach the solitary phone box, positioned like a red beacon next to the dilapidated village hall, with its amateurish announcements of the local operatic society and jumble sales flapping pathetically in the wind. Bianca still remembers how marvellously light on her feet her mother had looked that late afternoon, with the sun shining radiantly on her face. No shadows, no ill temper. She was simply very beautiful...

She was gone for more than twenty minutes, and, when she returned, she was broken, her bright-pink lipstick smeared haphazardly across her face by her own distraught hand, her lovely face haggard and drenched in tears. She could not stop sobbing; furiously gulping in air, she retched as if about to be sick. Nevertheless, putting the car into gear, she started to drive, her speech slurred and incoherent. At one point, she stopped the car to open the door and be sick, then drove on without explanation. For one shameful moment of adolescent prissiness, Bianca wondered whether her mother was drunk. She glanced with amused, raised eyebrows at her by-now-subdued school friends, while Anya lurched the car forward, repeatedly stalling, in exactly the way she criticised William for doing. Still without explanation, she dropped off the other two startled schoolchildren at their garden gates before lurching the car forward again, her frame still racked by violent sobs. Bianca sat stock-still in the back, terrified now, yet still unable to decipher whether her mother was angry or sad.

Only when they had made it back to the cottage, haphazardly clinging together and stumbling against the clotted, mole-disrupted earth of the lawns – slipping against the steep rake of the sitting-room floorboards, where big hand reflections of horse-chestnut leaves joined in dance with those of the diamond-pane windows to filter the dying gold of the sun, casting a dazzle of moving shadows against one of William's paintings, in which a frieze of characters walked centre stage, as in a Ravenna mosaic, infusing it with light and colour – did Anya double up in pain, and Bianca finally learn the shocking truth...

Anya's gentle, modest, self-effacing, widowed mother, the solitary, diminutive matriarch of seven unruly children, had fallen from an upstairs window to her death, exactly as Anya's four-year-old twin had done all those many lonely years earlier.

Later that same evening, Anya, still barely composed, dutifully drove one of the Simcars to their local rail station to meet William from work, before catching a train of her own to London. Sobbing uncontrollably the entire journey, first by train, then crossing London by Tube, she went straight to the steep house on five floors in South Island Place, the scene of the tragedy, then directly to the morgue, insisting on being allowed to see her mother's body, even though Lettie and her gang of older brothers tried to dissuade her.

As they lifted the sheet from her mother's body, Anya recognised with a jolt just how fragile and tiny she had been... She remembered how her mother had always dressed in modest combinations of clerical grey and navy, how she liked to spend her afternoons sitting in the soot-ridden graveyard of her local church, clutching at saccharine images of Christ and his disciples... But the thing Anya could never erase from her troubled mind was how completely her poor, gentle mother's face was smashed to smithereens on one side, like an egg, while the other half remained perfectly intact, like the raised profile on a coin, her eyes squeezed tight against the impact of her own death. Later, when she and Lettie had looked out the window from which she had fallen, they found her slippery, desperate fingermarks, traced against the London filth of a drainpipe.

Afterwards, for many years, Anya was beyond recovery. Little mattered to her, little was worth saving, least of all her fractious marriage to William. She would demand imperiously: 'Why aren't you like other husbands? Why don't you go and find yourself a girlfriend?'

Fatal words. Anya could never forgive herself for not having been there when her mother died; she had last seen her three weeks earlier, cheerfully waving goodbye to her from a red London bus. Now every inconsequential detail mattered. She longed to share in her poor mother's pain, to smash her own life against those paving stones of memory.

'Why have I been spared this fate meted down so symmetrically to both my mother and twin brother?' she groaned.

It was a senseless agony, leading to unanswerable questions. Had her own darling, much neglected mother been concealing her grief for her youngest baby son throughout all these years of missing him? Was it for him that constant vigilance in blackened graveyards? No one dared mention the word 'suicide', yet had she finally elected to join him by dying in exactly the same way? And did the urgent, slender fingermarks on the drainpipe mean she had tried, last minute, to save herself? Or frail and elderly as she was, had she simply been trying to clean her own windows and accidentally lost her grip? No one knew.

Equally terrible, and finally admitted to, was the unspoken fear that had silently stalked Anya since childhood. Had it been herself, all along, playing with her four-year-old twin, all those many years earlier, who had innocently pushed him from that upstairs sash window to his death? And had her own sweet-natured, overburdened mother always known the truth and discreetly concealed it from her? The pain of wondering became unendurable. Was it she who, as a four-year-old, had innocently inflicted this monstrous grief on her recently widowed mother by killing the baby son who was her own feckless husband's last gift to her, before he himself had collapsed and died on his way to the hospital to greet his newborn twins? And had William been right in his assessment throughout their marriage, when he taunted her that the fatal, ugly schism between anger and charm in her personality was the direct result of losing her twin at so early an age; that she had never become reconciled to his loss? Was it true that she always had been, and always would be, incomplete without him?

For several years afterwards, Anya's anger of grief knew no bounds. Now finding herself even more repelled than usual by the petty-fogging trivia of village folk peacefully going about their business, she declared their amoeba-like ignorance beneath contempt.

'What do they know, these simpleton peasants, of life or love?'

As for the village 'aristos', with their mealy-mouthed, church-going morality, to Anya, they all looked like Breughel peasants inexorably leading the blind from one muddy ditch into the next.

'I want nothing from people except their intelligence,' she declared rather grandly, three weeks after her mother's funeral, to a startled congregation of gossips in the village shop.

'Let's go?' says Stephen, smiling and picking up the bill.

Bianca sighs, forcing her mind back to the present, realising that there will always be a part of herself too that is trying either to become or to imitate her mother; she, too, forever imagining her absent mother's life and longing to share in her suffering. She imagines her mother lonely and unhappy, the thought striking her like a fist. She had watched her mother's love die, their family life together disintegrate, wanting ever since to become her, to experience whatever her mother experienced, in order to again share life, love and living with her.

* * *

Following the unfettered silences of Ireland, Max is finding London loathsomely busy, even his clothes seeming to fit him less well. Endless business meetings detain him. Visiting Americans arrive, commissioning new screenplays. There are play readings and auditions to fit in, not to mention the inevitable drinks parties that pepper every evening. In his current frame of mind, they feel more of an assault than a pleasure.

He has deliberately refrained from ringing Bianca, still too unsure of his feelings to know what to say. Nor has she contacted him. Only Matthew, fretfully anxious as ever, has repeatedly rung his agent, asking whether further portrait sittings were timetabled, Max instructing his agent to parry making any immediate arrangements. He needs time to think, quizzing himself sternly: *Do I really want to become involved with a woman married to a famous man and targeted by a jealous stalker, along with myriad other complications? No matter how charmingly she conceals them?*

He remembers his own secret, inadmissible heartbreak at witnessing his ex-wife choose another man over himself – his best friend, no less – while simultaneously expecting him to gallantly pick up the pieces for all three of them.

Is that what Bianca expects of me too?

At the time, he had carried it off with a certain elegant bluster. Being in the world of theatre, and knowing how to act, had helped.

But never again, he had promised himself. *Yet in comparison with Bianca's potential dramas, that little episode was mere sideshow.*

It occurs to him that, had he and Bianca retained the innocence of their initial meeting in the hotel foyer, followed by the passionate encounter of their first portrait sitting, perhaps all might have been well. They might even have made a gloriously clean sweep of it, into careless rapture. But absence had sewn irreversible doubts in them both. The opaque distances of China and the morning cries of seagulls over Bantry Bay had intervened between their happiness and reality. Plus that other great doubt...

While Bianca's presence excites him, leaving him feeling breathless and exhilarated at times, as if dancing on a precipice, whenever she mentions Hesketh and he hears that disturbed, brittle note invade her laughter, or witnesses the inadvertent smiles that play about her mouth, whenever discussing that poor, wretched, broken clown of a creature that is Hesketh, he is filled with dismay. In her fierce loathing of him, she is never less than convinced she is right... It is that which alarms him most – Bianca's certainty in hating him. Although perhaps justified in her hatred of him, he nevertheless finds it intimidating, mistrusting its undivided antipathy, its refusal to recognise the elemental struggle in every human being to find something resembling happiness for himself. At such moments, she reminds him all too completely of his ex-wife.

Would Bianca, too, he wonders, *ultimately turn against those who love her? Or am I simply concocting my own poisonous cabal of thoughts?*

He sighs. How he longs for simplicity, for something untainted... Yet where had this recent nausea for all things sophisticated come from?

Perhaps it's been creeping up on me, for some time?

He is used to feeling numbed by the braying, braggart, world-weariness in certain people, but to suddenly find himself enervated by it, when sophistication and worldliness had always been his great strength...

Yet another paradox? he thinks sadly.

Nevertheless, feeling weary of all the social jousting expected of him, he muses: *Maybe it's me, in the end, who's even more fatally damaged than Bianca?*

It occurs to him suddenly that his ex-wife had perhaps made an even bigger fool of him than he ever realised, the full impact of her revenge only revealing itself now that he has had the temerity to try and fall in love again. Glancing down at his black-and-gold trainers, he unbuttons his double-breasted jacket, tucking his shirt into the waistband of his red harem pants and adjusting the paisley shawl at his throat, before distractedly running his hands through the romantic tangle of his hair, suddenly stating out loud: 'God, what an effort it is, to remain bohemian in this modern world?' his voice sounding hoarse, almost bitter.

The truth is he has begun to fear the disruptive way Bianca's presence exhilarates him, only to later depress him into self-doubt by her absence, everything between them a series of contradictions. He longs for a return to certainty. All his life, until his divorce, he had been in love with complexity. But now his thoughts zigzag. He, too, had found Hesketh's presence strangely repellent, that night at the theatre...

Nevertheless, how not to feel sorry for him...?

Hesketh is like a marionette character who has got under Max's skin. Whenever he visualises Sinead's fisherman friend, on whose story his new play is loosely based, Jack strikes Max as an embryo Hesketh, albeit one still slumbering beneath his coverlet of potential slavery to madness. He recalls Jack's loose-mouthed expression, as he sat in the red-tiled kitchen, mawkishly observing Sinead, while stumbling through inarticulate memories of his aberrant childhood. He remembers the strange, obsessive look in Jack's eye, evoking a certain stubborn malaise as he tracked Sinead going about her chores. In some extraordinary way, the two characters of Jack and Hesketh have fused into one in Max's mind, thereby creating something still more riveting and intriguing for the purposes of his new play than his principal character, based on Bianca. His love letter of a play to Bianca is slowly transforming into a love letter to Hesketh. He has begun to relish the riotous contagion of Hesketh's madness in his new play, more than he welcomes Bianca's haughty repudiation of it.

Also, while Bianca has managed to retain something of herself intact, in the midst of all her difficulties, Hesketh appears to have lost everything knowable about himself; all his actions have become reactions, as though someone, other than himself, were pulling his heart strings. Max suspects the identical propensity in Jack. As the melded characters of Hesketh and Jack gain more and more empathetic ground in his authorial mind, so the character, based on Bianca, strikes him as less and less lovable.

So far, Max has only written a first draft. Perhaps if the play were already finished, his attitude to Bianca and Hesketh might reverse yet again? But for the moment, there is little he can do; he is in thrall to the unfinished narrative of a script which plays over his mind in waves of imperative. Making a success of the play has become more important than turning his relationship with Bianca into victory. As for her unfinished portrait of him, he barely cares. Obtaining the National Portrait Gallery commission had simply been a ruse to ensure spending more time with her.

While allowing all these contradictory thoughts to ebb and flow, he realises there is still something else – something more deeply rooted and emotionally layered than he is yet prepared to admit to. He looks around him. It is early morning in the Green Room of the Shaftesbury Lane theatre, where his most recent play is still playing to sold-out audiences. One of the stagehands has busily skipped out into the narrow streets of Soho in quest of newly baked croissants and, on a scuffed chest of drawers spilling with brightly coloured scarves and discarded wigs, an old-fashioned electric percolator is blowing thick bubbles of bitter, overstewed coffee into its glass lid. In one corner, two young actors bicker theatrically, pretending to quarrel. Max smiles appreciatively. How he loves this world of theatre; the way its participants, while remaining indelibly riveted by a sense of their own uniqueness, nevertheless willingly collaborate in putting on a show. He consults his watch: 9.30 a.m.

Turning to the breathless young actress he has been auditioning for the past half hour, he remarks affably: 'I think we're probably done for the moment?'

He likes her but already knows she is not right for the part of Bianca. The role he has in mind requires greater sensual range. Smiling sweetly, she squints up at him through long lashes.

At least she didn't try to flirt with me in order to get the part, he thinks gratefully.

Picking up a shabby canvas bag containing his unfinished manuscript and an old, battered computer, he walks out into the sharp November sunshine.

He has no precise plans for the rest of the day, just a vague memory of meetings agreed to by his agent. Ambling along Piccadilly, he hesitates, looking earnestly in Hatchards window before passing through the swing doors of Fortnum & Mason's. Putting on glasses, he studies the curlicue labels on elegant canisters of tea.

Just as he contemplates choosing one to try at home, a middle-aged man of faintly military bearing, dressed in ostentatious tweeds, accosts him; initially, with effusive, grovelling, compliments then increasingly with an abusive expose of what he had most disliked about Max's latest play. Accustomed to such gaffes, Max shakes the man's hand genially, preparing to move on. But the stranger is not to be fobbed off so easily. Carefully replacing the green-tea caddy back on the shelf where he found it, Max starts to move, crab-like, towards the door. But the stranger pursues him, talking animatedly, his face brightly flushed with this sudden proximity to fame. As the doors swing open onto Piccadilly, Max raises his hand and, with a brief wave, disappears into the back of a black cab, the stranger peering in disconsolately after him, while Max leans back, sighing relief, and thinking disaffectedly: *Perhaps I should be used to this by now?*

'Where to, guv?' asks the taxi driver.

'Islington…' Max replies automatically, despite having had no real intention of returning home this early in the day. His London house has begun to depress him again. He nervously checks the canvas bag for his unfinished manuscript and computer; both are safe. As the taxi performs a U-turn to crawl along Piccadilly, before turning left into Regent Street, another thought occurs him: *Why not go to my cottage near Bath? To hell with business meetings… Perhaps I can finish the play there, more easily than in Islington?*

Several months since he was last there, he has no idea what state the cottage is in. He taps on the driver's window.

'Sorry, but I've changed my mind. Would you mind just driving west for a bit, while I decide what I want to do?'

The driver swerves last minute, descending into the Haymarket, before turning up St James, then left towards Knightsbridge. Max's mobile rings; his agent. He decides not to answer. They pass the V&A, and onto the Cromwell Road, with its signs indicating Heathrow straight ahead, then beyond Gloucester Road to Earl's Court. Suddenly, Max knows exactly where he wants to go. He taps on the driver's window...

* * *

Robin Holderness has already completed most of his research in preparation for his forthcoming lecture to the Royal Geographical Society on 'The Role of Confucius's Teachings in Modern China'.

The same talk whose lavish publicity Matthew is hoping to profit from by inserting more modest notices of Bianca's exhibition alongside them.

Meanwhile, Robin and Beatrice Byng continue their affair, but discreetly. As scathing as Beatrice now feels towards her marriage, her contempt falls short of wanting to humiliate Byng too openly. Besides, Robin forbids it. If anyone questions how often she has been seen with Robin recently, she merely confirms they are friends and that she often goes to his lectures whenever Byng is in Paris. All of which is true. Yet they are a strange couple: he, tall, taciturn and forbidding in his sandy-coloured corduroy suit, hanks of lank grey hair shading the ferocious, challenging stare in his intemperate eyes – 'the corduroy ghost', as one of his colleagues describes him. And she, the self-styled 'odalisque', her slender, elegant figure wrapped in bohemian layers of turquoise damask silk, a pale lilac pashmina about her shoulders to keep her warm, her wrists, neck and ears dripping with heavy goblet jewels, fashioned from precious stones fretted in gold, even for a simple lunch at a neighbourhood bistro. Her glorious cascade of red-gold hair, if not set free, hidden beneath a matching toque, and her mellifluous voice, with its soft intimations of German Swiss floating deliciously on the air, making an impression of grand theatrical beauty.

No one seeing them together would guess either the depth of their intimacy, nor their addiction to one another. Not even Byng. Plus, in public, they always seem strangely disconnected and turned away one from another, even when sitting side by side, barely speaking or exchanging glances for two or three hours at a time. The only outward clues to their affair are in the way Beatrice's former talkativeness, and the graceful cover it supplied for the fretful undercurrents in her nature, has been replaced by day-dreaming trances, while Robin's restless quest for hectoring debate has been overtaken by a new reluctance, now seeming less immediately drawn to the abrasive feuding of intellectual quarrel.

'Where did those two disappear to?' one of Beatrice's more perceptive girlfriends asked one day.

'Oh, they're both still in London,' came the obtuse reply.

But in reality, things were very different. In private, their relationship had become one of ever deepening frenzy. They might reach the foyer of Robin's Soho building looking abstractly bemused, but they surface from its lift onto his top-floor lynx-like, brief enclosure having transformed them. Neither of them had known before what they lacked. Robin, despite his purist notions of philosophy and routine sexual pursuit of students, had never quite lost himself intellectually in the concepts he sought to elucidate, nor lost himself physically in the flirtatiously intelligent young women he seduced. As a set of ideas about life, his were intellectually attractive but, in practice, as arid as stale bread, Robin's zest for life relying mainly on the stuff of quarrel. Anything to make the sentences spin and the juices in his gaunt body flow faster. Meanwhile, Beatrice had been devoutly fashioning herself in the role of paradigm wife, while failing to notice that her principal audience, Byng, had long ago absconded from her performances. Bit by bit, she had forgotten how it felt to be loved.

Despite his initial aggressive pursuit of them, Robin had never treated any of his student conquests less than tenderly; always, beneath his gaunt, adversarial exterior, the gentle giant. And

Beatrice, with her endless sense of the exquisite, coupled with her prissy, histrionic demands for respect, had no idea she might need the pristine shell of her beauty trampled on for it to rise again, phoenix-like. They had stumbled upon these truths almost by accident. Robin had found himself lost in a frenzy of lovemaking more profound than any he had previously known and clumsily underestimated his own strength. She had cried out in pain, then immediately racked in orgasm, loudly calling his name like an invocation. Recognising freedom in her cry, and finding himself more excited, more centred and less preoccupied by himself than ever before, his own body abandoned its clumsy manoeuvrings and raced to catch up with hers, like an athlete finally reaching his stride. Afterwards, they lay in one another's arms, gazing in speechless wonder, all words irrelevant.

In Beatrice's complicit company, Robin finally discovered that thought only truly held the purity he always envisaged for it when he abandoned his attempts to control it. And Beatrice discovered that femininity was not just about the smooth, pristine surfaces of soigné beauty, but in the rough and tumble secret codes shared with a trusted lover. In many ways, they were identical; they had both invested too much in the surface of things – he intellectually and she physically. Now whenever they emerge beneath the skylight ecstasy of Robin's tall garret window, with its anthem to the vacant sky above them, they submit ravenously and without decorum to one another, as though at a banquet.

Now, at long last, Robin has also started to believe his mind will stretch further into the philosophical alphabet, beyond the full stops of R & S, while Beatrice believes the love between them indelible, and that it will not be long before Robin asks Byng to grant her a divorce, so that he can marry her. Meanwhile, Robin's understanding of Confucianism, in which the concept of how the superior 'gentleman' is perceived in public far outweighs any considerations of his behaviour in private, is developing in leaps and bounds. Laughing triumphantly, while planting a kiss on her thigh, Robin explains: 'Confucius's central message seems to be: "Don't frighten the horses."'

The morning Chloe leaves for the Cotswolds to visit her mother, taking Bruno with her, Hesketh is as attentive as ever, helping Chloe load the car, before gently coaxing Bruno into the lift. Much as Bruno loves the music of the lift, he often detests travelling in it. Whenever forced to share the miniature space with one of his parents, he huddles, quivering, his nose pressed flat against the lift's mahogany shell, with his back to whoever accompanies him. Only if Hesketh and Chloe are both at home can things be handled differently, with one parent installing him, then leaving him to ride on his own, in the sure knowledge the other parent is waiting solicitously below. Only in those brief moments of independence does Bruno ride the lift joyously, his youthful, swaddled features leaning ecstatically against the open grille doors to watch the lift and its shadows shudder from floor to floor.

Having waved them goodbye, Hesketh retreats upstairs to make a cup of coffee. There are one or two urgent business calls he needs to make. The run-down cottage he recently discovered on Majorca is now his but needs restoring, before anything else can be done requiring a new roof. He nevertheless hopes to have it ready in time for the following summer's rentals.

Why does Buddha look so lonely today? he wonders idly.

Placing the coffee cup on a low table, he leans back luxuriously in one of the sumptuous swivel chairs. Life feels good, almost normal. Glancing up at the portrait of Bruno, everything about it delights him. Not only the depiction of Bruno, but the painting itself.

How clever of Chloe to find someone whose work I'd not yet discovered.

Although hoping to discover more about the artist and her technique, he is amazed to have never heard of B. Turvey. But his selection of paintings for his private collection had rarely focusing on portraiture.

Maybe that's why? Portraiture, perhaps, belonging to a separate world?

The phone rings twice, then cuts off – a missed call. Glancing at the phone in a sudden flare of annoyance, he mutters: 'Stupid buggers...'

Stretching out languidly in the padded chair, he feels no urgency to be anywhere. The past two weeks of family life had been like a balm on his ragged soul; there is nowhere he would rather be. Lazily picking up his copy of the *Daily Mail*, it falls opens on an article by the mysterious Miss Dior. Which is when he starts to remember: *I wonder what Chloe did with Bianca's painting?*

Still trailing the *Daily Mail*, he shuffles his concertinas of white sock along the corridor, past the lift, to the concealed panel door, just as it veers left towards the kitchen. Struggling to open it, the door appears stuck. This is the first time he has entered the room since that fatal afternoon with the social worker. The light inside is gloomy, its window too adjacently close to the bathroom wall to catch much sun. Motes of dust hover in the air above the little-used roly-poly bed, shrouding the rejects from his grander collection of paintings displayed next door.

Although fully expecting to find the panels of Bianca's painting stacked neatly along one wall, he is not particularly alarmed when they are not there.

Chloe must have taken them to the basement. I'll check after lunch.

Unwilling right now to face all the grime and dirt it would entail, he reminds himself: *I'll need to change out of my good clothes.*

Half an hour later, the phone rings again; this time, Chloe, letting him know she and Bruno have arrived safely.

'Give my love to your mother,' Hesketh jokes spitefully, only remembering the painting as he replaces the receiver.

Perhaps best not to have mentioned it anyway?

Preparing himself a steak and salad for lunch while devouring an entire small, crusty loaf, lavishly spread with Hellman's mayonnaise, he then makes a second cup of coffee and changes into some paint-stained overalls, first grabbing a long-handled torch from the glove box of his car before descending into their allotted portion of the dungeon basement.

Opening the padlocked door, the cluttered disorder of the room strikes him tumultuously; depending on the mood of his most recent visit, boxes either hurled disruptively or piled methodically.

It was on his last visit that he had discovered the trunk containing Bianca's old clothes, emanating the genie, residue sweetness of Miss Dior. As a result, the room was left in chaos. It is almost impossible to see where anything might be, arguing slightly feverishly to himself: *The paintings must be here? Surely Chloe wouldn't have bothered to hide them at the back of all this mess?*

He doubts whether she could even lift some of the heavier boxes. The lighting is poor, and mainly reliant on a single sixty-watt bulb, suspended in a hangman's noose of long flex from the ceiling. Using the fierce beam of his torch to delve into corners, Hesketh swings its focus ever more frantically, his search starting to feel desperate. Trembling with sudden intimations of despair, he groans sorrowfully and sinks to his knees.

The paintings are gone...

Only now, remembering how much Chloe disliked Bianca's painting; how when they first married she had implored him to get rid of it, he argues: *But would she be so vindictive as to destroy it without telling me?*

He begins to feel afraid, his mind pleading pathetically: *She must know how much it means to me?*

By now, his senses begin to dissolve, overtaking him in frenzy, his mind in a rage. Madness is upon him.

Deep breaths; deep, deep breaths, he falters, remembering his doctor's advice.

Getting up off the floor, his body automatically lurches at thirty degrees. Kicking his heavy loafer shoes in frustration, he overturns an unused set of porcelain cups and saucers belonging to Chloe's mother, stacked neatly by the door, a delicate china jug rolling broken at his feet.

How, he wants to know, *could she have been so vindictively stupid?*

Retreating upstairs, he forgets to padlock the door, by now utterly distraught.

What am I to do?

Absentmindedly picking up his half-finished cup of coffee, he takes a sip. The cup slips clumsily from his grasp, spreading an ugly stain on their expensive Indian rug. Making no attempt to clean it up, still dressed in paint-spattered overalls, he instead grabs his car keys from the mantelpiece. Not occurring to him to phone Chloe, to ask what she had done with the painting, he curses furiously: 'That bloody interfering mother of hers...'

Too angry to do anything logical, he descends, sighing and fuming, to his car and drives automatically, unthinkingly to his current default point of contact with all things Bianca: Matthew's gallery in Cork Street.

Traffic in the West End is at a standstill. Having spent longer in the basement than he realised, he reaches Cork Street, just as Fortnum & Mason's clock strikes 6 p.m., barely missing Matthew, who had decided to close the gallery a few minutes early to attend a private view where he anticipates doing business; the lights in the gallery turned down low. Hesketh presses his face to the glass, shielding the last remnants of daylight from his eyes to peer in. But there is little to see, the gallery appearing to be in a state of transition, as though preparing for a new exhibition. He is just about to turn away when something distantly catches his eye. Still, he cannot quite see. He strains his eyes, staring hard, causing the glutinous yellow streaks in their whites to bulge ominously. He takes off his flyaway lenses, cleaning them desperately on the sleeve of his spattered overalls.

That's better... his mind gasps. *There... there... right at the back of the gallery...*

Leaning against a distant wall, he can just make out a familiar image, a miniature of two grown-ups on a bed, conceived almost as a flat, heraldic design, with a child lying between them. It is one of the smaller panels from Bianca's triptych. He would recognise it anywhere. Hesketh bangs desperately on the plate glass, as though to break it, causing an alarm to sound from within, its clamorous, piercing shriek bringing him to his senses. Turning away, glancing at his watch, he suddenly remembers something else. Although not a Sunday, the woman who holds Sunday teatime séances in the King's Road occasionally also keeps open house in the early mid-week evenings.

Ages since I last visited her, but worth a try.

Reaching his car just as a traffic warden is approaching, he throws back his head, laughing jeeringly at her as he edges himself back into the onslaught of rush-hour traffic. Knowing where the painting is, he begins to know what to do.

Plus the Ouija board should give me some extra clues... At least I've found the painting, he thinks menacingly.

CHAPTER 23

At first, not recognising him, it is just the shape of his body against the light that she responds to; something familiar, something forgotten. He is wearing some type of uniform. Having only ever seen him looking threadbare in his faded Sunday clothes at The Society's gatherings, she finds herself admiring the well-cut blue serge of his trousers, the crisp, dazzling white of his shirt, until her gaze reaches epaulettes, punched with metal numbers, only to fade with dismay. Not until she meets the intense brown eyes devouring her does she fully recognise him as Andreas. He breathes deeply, an immense sigh of relief. 'Thank goodness. You're well again...'

'Are you a policeman?' Anya asks, horrified.

'No, a security guard for a jeweller's in Hatton Garden... I've been giving evidence at the law courts.'

He gestures to the Gothic Fleet Street archway behind him.

'We aren't exactly close to Hatton Garden here,' she remarks illogically.

Feeling flustered suddenly, while hoping to conceal her repugnance, a lifelong distrust of authority has made uniforms repellent to her. His manner is jovial, almost carnival-like: 'I have the rest of the afternoon off and am on my way to a talk Aubrey Byng is giving on French politics at the London School of Economics,' he remarks casually. 'Why not come with me? It's a public lecture, open to everyone.'

Her blue eyes engage with his, instilling a moment of silence between them.

Why are you so fond of me? she wants to ask, remembering, just in time, to stay silent.

Although reluctant to admit it, Anya is still feeling slightly unwell, her recent health scare having shocked and reminded her of her own mortality. Not that she fears death exactly. It is more the idea of not existing that she so dislikes. She is tempted to join Andreas at the talk, Aubrey Byng's articles in *Le Figaro* those she admires and still takes the trouble to translate to keep up with her French. But it would mean abandoning her own arrangements for the afternoon; plans that represent a potentially fractious return to her youth. She hesitates. *I suppose I could just plead illness and not turn up?*

Andreas watches her carefully, his brown-eyed gaze caressing her face softly, the white of his shirt matched by the flash of his smile.

'It's very enticing,' she says, blushing

Yet some small instinct of decorum detains her. *The person I'm meeting has travelled all the way from Suffolk... How can I possibly let her down?*

She takes Andreas's arm, relishing the sinewy strength beneath his shirtsleeve, yet resting deliberately lightly. Andreas glances down, welcoming her touch, like the soft fluttering of a bird's wing.

'I truly mustn't,' she concludes sadly. 'I've arranged to meet an old friend I haven't seen for thirty years. But I'll walk with you as far as the London School of Economics. We're meeting in Lincoln's Inn Fields.'

He laughs happily. 'Yes, of course.'

Walking slowly, in companionable silence, having rediscovered the intensity of his gaze, her mind starts to forgive the blemish of his uniform. *Besides, it lends him a certain elegance...*

He is that familiar, Sunday-afternoon puzzle of a person, Andreas, again. As they part at the university steps, he promises to wait for her at the bus stop in the Strand the following Sunday. She turns away reluctantly, with a smile, thinking how wonderfully lean and handsome he looks. *Why isn't he married... Perhaps he is?*

It suddenly occurs to her that she knows nothing about him.

As she enters the corner of Lincoln's Inn, a clock chimes 1 p.m. She hurries her pace, already fifteen minutes late. Students wearing donkey jackets and long knitted scarves brush past her on their way to seminars. Yet she finds herself loving the impact of their loose-limbed bodies rushing towards her, reminding her of how eager she too had once been for life to begin.

At Lincoln's Inn Fields' café, little more than a dirt clearing between trees, against which rusting tables and chairs sprawl next to a kiosk selling iced buns and stained teacups, sloshing with dark brown tea, Anya surveys the crowds carefully. *Will I recognise her after all this time?*

A boucle coat of vibrant orange catches her eye, suddenly reminding her of the nasturtiums she used to grow at the cottage. As the hunched figure turns, her smile is equally orange, Anya's instincts correct. It is her old friend, Bunty, Rowland Darblay's wife, from hers and William's Charlotte Street days... But the once familiar, floating hieroglyph of orange lipstick now emanates from a withered, weather-beaten face, deeply crisscrossed with wrinkles. Struggling clumsily to feet clad in Clark's bright red sandals for children, Bunty plants dry kisses on Anya's cheek. Her face feels like sandpaper. The two women stand back from their embrace, assessing carefully.

'How are you, after all these years?' Bunty's voice, still a little-girl trill.

Anya remembers sadly: *It's more than thirty years... So much has happened since...*

Throughout the war, Bunty and Rowland had remained fearlessly in the top-floor flat in Great Titchfield Street that William had negotiated for them in the days following his and Anya's wedding, with Rowland shouting daily, blistering defiance at the bombs raining down on them. Unlike William, Rowland had proved exempt from the army. As a very young man, before enrolling at Sheffield Art School, he had followed his father down the pit; in adult life, he had never renounced smoking. His lungs too badly damaged to enlist, he was allowed the coveted luxury of remaining at home to paint his wolf-whistle landscapes, while exhibiting occasionally with Lucy Wertheim and Leger Galleries. But immediately after the war, Rowland and Bunty had copied William and Anya's idyllic flight to East Anglia by renting a tumbledown farmhouse in Suffolk, allowing the two couples to meet from time to time. Once a month, they contrived to spend a day together, laughing, drinking and reminiscing hilariously about their Charlotte Street days; the two men still eagerly, jealously checking, praising and mocking each other's work, while telling venomous tales of mutual friends, such as that 'syphilitic humbug' Paul Ottery.

After the war, Paul Ottery's poetry had attained a certain celebrity, featuring often in *Horizon*, before publishing three slim volumes of verse, running to several Faber editions. Having swept most of the maidens of Charlotte Street off their feet, he had eventually married a white Russian aristocrat and experienced the luxury of being able to afford hand-stitched shoes, whose shiny leather soles no longer flapped furiously beneath his feet.

'Wonder what happened to that moth-eaten black cape, with the red silk lining, he used to swank about in?' William had said, laughing.

He and Rowland were both still unanimous in their commitment to painting, but since the war Rowland's paintings were less stylistically changed than William's. Whereas Rowland's vision remained transfixed by English landscape, William's paintings had undergone the transformative experience of the Middle East, with shadowy figures emerging from the spangled night lights of Cairo and Baghdad. Of the two, Rowland exhibited more frequently, although they were both, by now, showing at the Redfern Gallery. Unlike William, Rowland had not had to remake his reputation following four years absence of war.

Of the two wives, Anya was still the more glamorous, using her dressmaking skills to run up fashionably wide skirts, onto which William hand-painted bold designs. Bunty, meanwhile, continuing to dress haphazardly from jumble sales. She also still obsessively collected junk-shop trophies of china, glass and broken furniture for a penny here, a farthing there, from the lavish antique shops buried like treasure in every Suffolk village. As their day wore on, the two couples becoming increasingly drunk, Bianca and Bunty's daughter, Janna, increasingly sidelined by their fun. As their hilarity escalated, Anya always particularly enjoyed listening to Rowland's wry jokes, amid his passionate declarations of artistic creed, all emanating from a body as thin as a rake, his dark-moustached face a pleasure of smiles as he bent over his red Rizla machine to fashion the slender, soft roll-ups he maintained permanently to one corner of his mouth, even as he talked. They were all four the best of friends; only much later, in vicious moments of rows with William, did Anya reveal she had always thought Rowland the better painter. In those immediate post-war years, despite living frugally, they had all felt purposeful and happy.

The change in mood between them developed insidiously, almost imperceptibly at first, with William's abdication from painting into the brand-new world of advertising, prompted partly by Anya's increasing dismay at having to live on tick at the village shop. The brutal contrast with her recent, luxurious Parisian days had begun to feel humiliating, penury no longer optimistic fun. Now suddenly awash with money, William and Anya embarked on their favourite high-life of nightclubs, restaurants and ever more luxurious travel, none of which Rowland and Bunty could afford, except whenever exhibitions of his were sponsored abroad by the British Council and their tickets paid. Now, whenever they met at the cottage, the food and drink William provided was lavish beyond words.

Yet increasingly, indisputably, it was Rowland, who held the moral high ground. He might be the lesser intellectual painter of the two, but he had not committed the sin of desertion. Also Rowland still relied exclusively on the traditional techniques of watercolour and oil. Not for him the quick, flirtatious flash of magic markers that began to infiltrate William's painting throughout those early advertising years. While jealous of his friend's new affluence, Rowland was full of contempt for the simplistic, money-loving horizons of publicity. Nor did it help matters that William, at times, felt precisely the same contempt as his friend for the industry he now inhabited. Giving up the narcotic of wealth, however, was proving far harder than he imagined. There was so much about it to enjoy: the camaraderie of the office, daily laughter and fun. Also the sense of riding a gigantic wave attached to the pioneering world of advertising. Plus William was actually very good at what he did, already hugely successful at this new trade, which relied on his skill as painter, while simultaneously outlawing it from his everyday existence and thereby creating a well of sorrowful yearning in him.

The crunch came late one summer, when William, Anya and Bianca had driven to the Suffolk farmhouse one Sunday in their proud new acquisition of a pale-green Alvis – the suave, coach-built car, with Maigret-style running boards and pig-skin canopy roof. Bianca was seven years old at the time. They arrived bearing gifts: a whole salami from Camisa's in Old Compton Street and three bottles of Chianti, looking touristic jolly in their fat-bottomed raffia baskets, Rowland asking: 'What are these for?'

William looked nonplussed, only Anya detecting the concealed jibe.

'They're for holding candles or making lamps out of,' she responded swiftly.

'I can remember the days when you thought Framboise a good Merlot,' mocked Rowland.

Each time they visited the farmhouse, it seemed to have sunk further into the landscape. Grasses grew, flowering waist high, only a narrow path of flagstones carving a corridor to their front door. Crab-apple trees, as gaunt and gnarled as old men, surfaced from a wasteland which had once been lawn to shake their fists furiously at a sky which fled above them in pale-grey washes of cloud, tinged mauve, pink and vulnerable. From the back of the house, extending as far as the eye could see, were deep-ditched, pocket-handkerchief fields, elaborately fringed and divided by fat hedges, full of wildlife. These the subjects of Rowland's paintings. He seemed to follow the advice of the Pre-Raphaelites: 'Paint whatever you find directly outside your window.'

The house stretched horizontally, with ribbons of rooms traipsing one after another over two low-ceilinged floors. Having for years suffered neglect, birds nested happily in its thatch, a hornets' nest buzzing sleepily in its rafters throughout the night. The bright-blue paintwork of its outer doors and windows had peeled, leaving their warped frames to rot. Plaster fell in large chunks, to reveal the delicate scaffold of the house below – moments of wounded nakedness that felt strangely moving. Only the two robust chimneys rose tall, proud and unaffected by the silent, destructive burrowing of time.

Despite its ample space, the same higgledy-piggledy disorder that had prevailed within the tiny constraints of Great Titchfield

Street was here spread throughout an entire house, room after room, piled high with junk that Bunty had bought on a whim, with no particular purpose in mind. The things just had to get along with one another as best they could. In the main sitting room, the magnificent refectory table Rowland had cut the corner from, so as not to knock his hip as he painted, had been transported from London, its surface piled high with streaked bottles of turpentine, linseed oil and dirty paint rags, balanced on inadequate scraps of newspaper, next to the oddments of glass and china from which they daily ate and drank.

That particular day, William, Anya and Bianca arrived later than planned, although still in good time for lunch. But right from the start, even as Rowland emerged from the swaying field of grass to greet them, he appeared strangely out of sorts, talking rapidly, diving restlessly in and out of rooms while never quite looking anyone in the eye, except for Bianca, whom he welcomed with dancing smiles.

Anya noticed his fretful mood immediately, while William remained oblivious; too steeped in office politics these days to readily respond to another man's passing moods.

'You seem to be acquiring all the immunities of wealth,' accused Rowland.

Taking the gigantic salami, he laid it with a look of puzzlement on the vandalised tabletop, remarking with disgust: 'Can't see that featuring in a still life any time soon… Might advertising be turning you into a socialist Mycenas, given over to sybaritic pleasures?' he asked bitterly.

William let out a great guffaw of laughter, as though paid a compliment. Only Bunty remained composed and wary, while Anya's mood perked up a little. There was something about the hidden violence of impending argument that never failed to excite her.

The conversation centred on Picasso's painting of *Guernica*. William had discovered in Schwemmers a book showing black-and-white photographs of the dramatic, evolving stages the painting had been subjected to, in order to reach the extraordinary tension of its final design. While William was full of enthusiasm and admiration for the painting, Rowland was less convinced.

'You can't expect a giant such as Picasso to confine himself to the pedestrian habit of landscape,' William started to explain earnestly. 'For him, painting is both political and philosophical; it requires greater scope. Can't you see that he uses aesthetics to take a moral stand, as well as to create beauty?'

The reference to landscape was unfortunate. Rowland flushed dark, glancing furiously at Bunty, who gazed back reassuringly at him.

'Besides, Picasso made a point of visiting Sheffield when he came to England... If nothing else, doesn't that, as a Yorkshire man, persuade you?' ribbed William.

Cherishing the memory of her own Parisian encounter with Picasso, Anya sided with William. Meeting Picasso was part of the glamour of life. Tenderly, William turned his handsome forehead and clear blue eyes towards her. No matter how bitterly they fought at home, the dangerous spectre of Charles de Courcelles still hovering chaotically between them, William never ceased to respond to Anya's beauty. It was he, rather than Charles de Courcelles, who now afforded the delicious scent of Arpege with which she perfumed herself daily. Whereas, Bunty's scrubbed face and vigorous little body, as she moved about their farmhouse kitchen, still smelled of pink carbolic soap.

'Anya wrote to me during the war, describing Picasso as powerful as a bull,' William remarked proudly, as if to trump Rowland's objections with the first-hand authority of his beautiful wife.

Nevertheless, these arguments of taste held a dangerous political edge. It was not simply individual opinion that was at stake here. What one read or thought, which paintings one admired, promised the ever-serious threat of denunciation. The atmosphere in the farmhouse fizzled with insults not yet voiced. That dangerous word 'bourgeois' again hung menacingly in the air. From so injurious a claim, there could be no return.

'You seem to have come a long way from that "Nation of Shopkeepers" speech you gave in support of Tom Driberg,' jibed Rowland, his brow suddenly furiously stormy. 'In fact, you seem to now be immersed in the very industry that supports shopkeepers and their bourgeois ambitions.'

Anya gave a sharp intake of breath. It was true, she and William were frequent visitors to Tom Driberg's beautiful Georgian pepper pot of a house at Bradwell-on-Sea.

Startled and surprised by the sheer vociferousness of this rebuke from his old friend, William nevertheless gazed back at him quizzically, as if almost amused by his outburst, his carapace of new wealth holding him in good stead, just as Rowland had feared it would, William's refusal to rise to the bait only making Rowland more angry. Beside himself with indignation, he translated the impervious gleam in William's eye as contempt, and bristling with hostility, he snorted: 'I suppose you think I've a chip on my shoulder?'

'No, no, not at all...' William replied laughing. 'More like a log.'

A look of violent distress invaded Rowland's features... Feeling suddenly ashamed, William remembered he had not yet asked to see Rowland's latest work. Smiling a little more diplomatically, he asked gently: 'Why don't you show me what you've been working on?'

'Come through,' said Rowland, his gaze still unable to meet William's.

Having ducked beneath the lintels of doors too low for their twin heights, Rowland led them to the back of the house, where a former scullery of cracked concrete served as his main studio.

He had just completed a sequence of ten paintings of the fields surrounding the farmhouse, all identical in scale but differing in composition. Painted on different days, they recorded the ever-changing turbulent weather sweeping through the Suffolk fields, causing the hedgerows to tremble, yet with the unrelenting insistence of the Eastern counties that the bigger drama of sky should prevail over the more miniature incidents of land. The paintings were in oil, yet had a watercolourist's instinct for broad washes, making use of their primed canvas backgrounds to illuminate the white of the sky. Although painted in colour, they were curiously monochrome, with burnt umber and sienna substituting for black. Against this light to dark scudding melancholy, the details of landscape: trees, hedgerows and distant buildings, were half drawn, half painted; the skeletons of windswept

417

trees, conveyed by hasty filigrees, conjured in burnt umber, and clouded last minute in bravado washes of pinks and purples, surprise moments of intense colour made all the more poignant by their pallid backdrops. And this is where their magic lay – in the sudden perceptive insight of a trained eye; in the artist's instinct for making a transient movement of the wind count for permanent joy.

As he surveyed his old friend's work, William recognised both its limitations and strengths. His earlier absence of diplomacy was not without some truth. The paintings were pedestrian, parochial even. And yet they dared to dream most gloriously. There was something thrilling about them... As well as admiration, William felt a stab of self-pity. He had quit painting at the point his own work was becoming more complex, more intriguingly interesting. He hardly knew how to forgive himself. He glanced at Bianca, who, although only seven years old, was looking at the paintings with the same intense absorption as himself. He had fallen in love with this child, whom he too often reminded himself might not be his.

'You look just like me,' he said, apropos of nothing, smiling sweetly at her, while consoling himself: *At least her future will be made secure by my sacrifice.*

Anya and Rowland both glanced up at him in alarm, with Anya turning away to conceal her embarrassment.

For lunch, Bunty had stewed some lamb and carrots in a thin-bottomed aluminium saucepan on top of the farmhouse's blackened range.

'At least she didn't cook it in their daughter's chamber pot,' as in the old Great Titchfield days they laughed hilariously on their way home.

The lamb had been reduced to a dried-out, blackened scaffold, resembling some of the bruised hulks of boats, sunk in estuary mud, in one of Rowland's seascapes, the carrots caramelised to black. Rehearsing his newfound enthusiasm for cuisine, William spoke knowingly of Escoffier, while dutifully eating his share of the charred meat, but not without Rowland suspecting his repugnance in doing so. Although not always himself perfectly loyal to his long-suffering wife, Rowland nevertheless refused

to countenance a single slight against Bunty. As the meal pro-
gressed, his temper developed a rollicking, scantily concealed
fury. It was only Bianca who now dared smile openly at Rowland.

Their daughter, Janna, now sixteen years of age and full of insou-
ciant beauty, arrived late at the table, flopping down heavily in
her chair, and glancing at everyone with studied contempt. Woven
into her long, blonde tresses were strands of hay. Noticing them
stoked Rowland's rage all the more brashly.

'You've been cavorting with that great lummox of a farmhand
again,' he accused.

She glanced back, rapturously indifferent, while insolently
holding out her plate to be served. William and Anya watched in
astonishment.

*How very different her behaviour is from that of our own shy, seven-
year-old.*

To complete their meal, Bunty made cups of tea, selecting a
delicate Japanese porcelain tea set, eggshell thin, from the back
reaches of the vandalised table. Into these fragile cups, she poured
a pallid stream, which they all chokingly drank… The tea service
had been languishing unused on the injured tabletop for months.
Floating densely on the cup's surfaces were thick films of dust, tast-
ing like waddings of top notes, against the delicate, smoky perfume of Earl Grey.

That Sunday, William, Anya and Bianca left the farmhouse
unusually early, their day feeling strangely truncated and unresolved. Nevertheless, they drove home in only slightly troubled
mood, joking hilariously about burned carrots and dusty tea. A
month later, Rowland wrote inviting them to lunch the following
Sunday, to which William gladly replied, all difficulties forgotten… But last minute, a crisis at the agency over securing a new
account obliged William to bring home graphic work, urgently
needed for presentation the following Monday. Unable to phone
Rowland, William sent a telegram, which never arrived. Two days
later, Rowland wrote a furiously accusatory letter, the last line of
which, Anya suddenly remembers, Bianca had never forgotten:
'Still endeavouring to finish the cream cakes…'

To Bianca's young ears, it had seemed to hold the same intriguing pathos as: 'No more twist...' in *The Tailor of Gloucester.*

But for Rowland it was the last straw. The rewards of advertising had finally won over the value of friendship. He and Bunty never spoke to William and Anya again, nor responded to their letters.

Now, assessing the resolute little figure of Bunty standing before her, Anya feels an overwhelming sorrow for their lost, precious years. She would never again see Rowland's smile or hear him laugh. He had died just a few weeks earlier, one night in his sleep, with Bunty waking up next to his stiffened corpse. She had not thought of him especially for years but now feels all the wretchedness of living in a world bereft of his extraordinary vitality. He had left Bunty a large collection of unsold paintings but no cash, and no hope of continuing to live in the Georgian mansion that housed the local museum, where, in recent years, Rowland had been curator. Like a farm labourer's tithe cottage, the house belonged with the job. Bunty's reason for being in London, as well as to meet Anya, is to conclude her negotiations with Sotheby's. They had sent down a man in a Savile Row suit to review the contents of her old Suffolk home, stored for years in a dilapidated barn, under green tarpaulin. Amidst all the useless bric-a-brac, collected obsessively throughout fifty years of marriage, were some real gems, as well as dross. Sales of her collection of rare Chinese pottery, antique Venetian glass and ruined Georgian furniture had raised enough money for her to finally buy a home of her own, she announced jubilantly: 'The first I ever owned in my entire life...'

She chose a miniature cottage in Stoke-by-Nayland, the village in whose antique shops she had unearthed some of her best treasures, while leaving sufficient income to keep herself comfortable for the rest of her life.

As she and Anya sit sorrowfully reminiscing in the cool November breeze of Lincoln's Inn Fields, with London pigeons circling fearlessly overhead, Anya detects a new quality of confidence and serene detachment in her old friend; almost of indifference.

Had Rowland needed to die for Bunty to reveal this new inner strength? she wonders.

Bunty's glance across the scarred tabletop conveys an abstract, uncritical kindness. Yet her manner is strangely cool and unimpressed, leaving Anya feeling baffled. She has the distinct, unsettling feeling that Bunty may even feel pity for her.

Rowland may not have been the perfectly faithful husband, allowing himself all sorts of exotic, philandering adventures, especially whenever in pursuit of new patrons. Pleasuring strident, wealthy women with his thin, alert, joyous body, while successfully courting their commissions for paintings, was something he knew how to do well. But he would never have abandoned Bunty, as William did Anya, for his secretary, a woman barely older than Bianca...

Five years after dashing up to Sheffield one winter to watch Edith's severe white-powdered countenance suffuse last-minute pretty with the encroaching deathbed, rosy warmth of pneumonia, William had finally succumbed to her cherished dream of 'the girl next door', just as she had always hoped. That 'girl' was no longer Mary Gimson of his youth, but her equivalent... a woman who cared nothing for painting, who had never once reached for a dictionary to settle a quarrel over the precise meaning of a word; someone whose most fervent topics of conversation were sport and the Royal Family; a woman who wore twinkling gold buckles on her navy leather moccasins and headscarves with motifs of bridle and tackle over her helmet of heavily backcombed hair. She was neither beautiful nor cultivated; at thirty, far less alluring than Anya at sixty. But in comparison, she had one single major virtue: she was unstintingly kind. No more humiliating outbursts of mockery to be endured. No more dismissive taunts, publicly accusing him of being hopeless in bed. In William's world, the word 'bourgeois' had finally become an epithet no longer to be avoided.

'How's Bianca?' asks Bunty, her eyes steely grey and curious.

'I don't really know...' Anya is forced to admit, her breath catching in her throat. 'We haven't spoken for twenty years.'

* * *

The following morning, Hesketh notices a small insert in the *Daily Mail*'s arts pages:

'China in Miniature'
Watercolours by B. Turvey
at
Matthew Dancer & Co., Cork Street,
opening on 10 November,
to coincide with
'The Teachings of Confucius in Modern China'
A talk by
Robin Holderness
at
The Royal Geographical Society

Worth going to...? he reflects, still not making the connection with Bianca but eager to see more work by his son's portraitist.

How odd, this sudden focus on Matthew Dancer in my life? Perhaps that accounts for the gallery's empty walls last night?

A vengeful thought strikes him. *As the new owner of a B. Turvey portrait, they won't be able to refuse me admission.*

Last night, after leaving Cork Street, he had driven to the King's Road, where, having drunk two cups of tea and eaten three slices of angel cake, followed by several thimble-sized glasses of sweet sherry, he had joined a motley crew around the Ouija board. A disconsolate-looking solicitor, his face like a squeezed lemon, his tie stained with bacon fat, lolled on a miniature sofa next to a middle-aged woman with a sweetly dimpled face above an overflowing fleshy body. Two dainty, elderly spinsters sniffled and gossiped like hamsters, and a young, fresh-faced workman, still dressed in his workaday dungarees, carried a heavy metal toolbox, which he insisted on moving obsessively from chair to chair as he chatted with the others. Finally, there was the madame of the establishment: a willowy former hippie, swathed in butterfly layers of silk, strung with beads, an early confection by Zandra Rhodes, her flowing, waist-long locks threaded with grey, her eyes dark with kohl. Despite the carnival frivolity of her dress, her highfaluting

English vowels indicated steely reserve, giving little away. Bitterly disappointed as she was to see Hesketh, she nevertheless welcomed him with a kiss.

The sherry loosening their tongues, the two elderly spinsters confessed their hope of making contact with their dead; one with her brother, the other her father, both of whom had died suddenly, with no time to say goodbye. As the party atmosphere developed, the hippie madame performed her most elegant sleight of hand, passing around a purple velvet beret, left over from her Biba days, upturning it like a soft paw to receive the evening's contributions from her guests.

'How much?' asked the young workman.

'Darling, far too vulgar,' she whispered. 'Whatever you think appropriate.'

Embarrassed, he fished a £20 note from the depths of his dungarees and laid it, fluttering like a blue petal, in the bowl of the hat, everyone else feeling bound to follow suit, with Hesketh flamboyantly adding a pink £50 note, before making their way to a round table, curtained off from the main sitting room by lavishly embroidered lengths of Indian fabric, winking with tiny mirrors. The young man heaved his toolbox one last time, storing it under the table, the hippie madame airily commenting: 'I do hope all that metal won't chase away the spirits, darling.'

The young man looked up at her in sudden alarm.

The two elderly ladies' turns came first, both reassuringly rewarded by anodyne messages from the other side, tears silently streaking their poor consoled faces.

The melancholy solicitor wanted a clue as to where the last will and testament of a recently deceased client was hiding, and the plump, middle-aged woman wanted to know if her first husband was still alive. The young workman's questioning of the spirit was rather more complex. He wanted to know if he would ever father a son? Only Hesketh wanted to know what had happened to a missing painting.

The Ouija board spun and deliberated, taking its time, before spelling out: 'S O L D.'

'Who sold it?'

Hesketh's desperate mind is now in overdrive, his eyes behind the flyaway lenses betraying panic and menace. The board hesitated, the atmosphere in the room raw with electricity.

'Breathe,' whispered the hippie madame. 'Breathe.'

'Do you know my doctor?' asked Hesketh, looking at her confusedly, the distraught, glutinous whites of his eyes now over amplified in the flamboyant flyaway lenses of his spectacles.

'Just leave it, mate,' came the muffled comment from the young workman. 'What's it matter? Only a painting... Not like real life, is it?'

Hesketh's glance swerved towards him, wildly scornful and immediately threatening. The Eastern promise serenity of the madame suddenly faltered, remembering the last time Hesketh had come to one of her soirees. Why she had regretted letting him in.

Haltingly, the board began to speak. 'W I F,' it spelled out, before skittering helter-skelter into shocked disarray.

'Enough,' said the madame, her dreamily floating English vowels suddenly clipped and bellicose.

'But what does it mean?'

Distraught, Hesketh peered into each of their faces, searching for clues, the two neatly dressed spinsters refusing to meet the madness in his eyes.

'Sounds to me like your wife sold the painting, mate,' stated the pragmatic young man. 'That's if you've even got a wife?' he added suddenly, as though seeing Hesketh for the first time.

Hesketh struggled to remember.

'Bianca,' he stated in a strangulated voice, his eyes clouded with tears. 'Bianca's my wife,' he whispered brokenly.

'Best go home and ask her then...' advised the practical young man.

Ignoring the hippie madame's gasp of disbelief, Hesketh looked at him with ruthless pity, his anger surfacing dangerously close. He had not invited anyone's advice, only the TRUTH.

'How dare you?' he choked.

Thoughts of his recent days with Chloe washed clean from his mind. Lumbering clumsily to his feet, he first hovered menacingly over the young man's shoulder, before stumbling myopically towards the door, his frame automatically retrieving its favourite angle of thirty degrees, and making no attempt to say goodbye.

Letting himself into the apartment on Chelsea Embankment, he expected to hear voices, but Chloe and Bruno were not yet back. Sitting in the kitchen, grimly waiting and plotting what to say once they arrived, not until an hour later did it occur to him to check the phone for messages. Pressing the button, he heard Chloe's girlish voice explain: 'I hope you don't mind, darling, but we've decided to stay on a couple days more. I'll ring when we're about to return... Hope your business meeting went well today.'

What business meeting? Damn...

He was supposed to meet a client at 4 p.m. Pressing the button again, he hears a man's disdainful voice.

'I waited half an hour in the foyer of Claridge's before giving up on you. Another day, no doubt?' sneered the voice. 'You're someone who always seems to need another day... wouldn't you say?'

Hesketh smiles a sudden idiotic grin. The man's derisory tone has had the reverse effect of restoring faith in himself. He has succeeded in annoying someone, after all.

* * *

Leonardo delays returning to Paris for several days, Maria staying just one night at the chateau before reluctantly driving back to the city alone.

'She was in a strange mood,' remarks Laetitia after she had gone.

Leonardo nods, vaguely acknowledging the truth of her observation, while unprepared to discuss it. He would never admit to barely caring what Maria does or doesn't feel. She is useful to him, supremely efficient at organising his affairs, but that is all. He sends her back to Paris with lists of instructions, in the meantime planning a leisurely few days at the chateau while deciding whether to resell it.

'She looks like a man in drag,' complains Laetitia vehemently.

'Yes, I know she does,' he replies absentmindedly.

For an entire week, he relaxes, living the Arcadian spirit of the chateau. There is so much to enjoy. He still finds its exterior unpardonably ugly, with stone buttresses supporting its massive bulk like a funeral pyre, but the expansive spaces of its interior delight him.

'If only the buttresses had been flying, and perforated with filigree quatrefoils, how handsome the building would have been,' he laments.

No matter, he thinks, as he sits relishing an early morning coffee and his first cigarette of the day on the broad terrace, overlooking the ornamental gardens at the back of the chateau. Thinking vaguely of Versailles, he remarks: 'They look as if designed by Le Notre...'

'Hardly,' rejoinders Bertrand Delvaux. 'Far less extensive for one. Nevertheless, a certain grandeur.'

Leonardo had never known Laetitia so relaxed, so self-evidently happy, the inevitable competitive edge to her personality seemingly at bay. He had seen her with various men but never quite this relaxed and passive, almost gentle. Even as he thinks it of her, the word surprises him. He sits tinkering with his film script, watching the chateau's various goings-on: the arrival of the gilders, singing Jacques Brel songs; at lunchtimes, challenging Bertrand and Laetitia to games of badminton.

'Come and join us,' invites Bertrand, handing him a racket.

Much to his own surprise, Leonardo finds himself remembering his more athletic youth, when tennis and horse-riding were the norm. The chateau has its own stables. *Maybe even a horse or two?* he dreams.

He also dreams of Solange. He is tempted to ask his London secretary to send her a ticket to join him. But then thinks better of it. *Perhaps not yet?*

Besides, he does not want to add to the advantages Laetitia already holds over Bianca; of knowing more of his secrets than he has any intention of admitting to.

In the evening, as he dresses for dinner, he looks out from his magnificent bedroom to the vast acres of woodland beyond and finds himself falling in love. Not with the chateau's beauty, as he had so immediately with La Casa, his Sienese palazzo, but with its undeniable possibilities, its comfort and sense of luxury. He glances down into the courtyard at the comings and goings of the young village women, drummed in to cook and clean, rejoicing in the sounds of their giddy laughter on the evening breeze and smiling secretly to himself. *Success had made all this possible... And to think my own father wanted me to remain a schoolmaster in the Veneto.*

Laetitia calls up to him: 'Come and see how the theatre is looking... The gilders have finished embellishing the mouldings, and we're about to hang the curtains.'

Finishing the glass of champagne she brought him earlier, he slowly descends the magnificent curved sweep of staircase to the ground floor. Passing through two of the grander reception rooms, threaded with bursts of early evening light, he reaches the theatre, the aspect of the building which had attracted him in the first place, to find Bertrand and two of the workmen balancing on tall stepladders, fixing last-minute touches to the curtains, which, as Leonardo enters, they suddenly let fall in a cascade of silver cloth, sprigged with gold, and tied with fat, plaited ropes of silver, finished in tassels of gold. The effect is breathtaking.

That night, at dinner, they eat foie gras, followed by choucroute, which they celebrate with a bottle of Minervois, the softly delicious red wine stroking their throats with promises of happiness. Leonardo raises his glass: 'To the chateau.'

'To the chateau,' chorus Bertrand and Laetitia, joined for the evening by the local mayor and his wife, whom Laetitia has invited as witness to this special evening.

'I have decided...' Leonardo hesitates, smiling broadly the smile no one can resist – the smile of a naughty child and powerfully influential man. 'I shan't be selling the chateau, after all. It's ours to keep. We'll run our international film school here, as originally planned.'

'Hurray,' shouts Laetitia, adding, 'I must arrange a house-warming party.'

'Bravo, monsieur,' the mayor and his wife join in.

'Felicitations,' says Bertrand, producing a bottle of sweet Sauternes and some miniature glasses with which to make a toast.

They invite the two village girls, acting as scullery maids, to join them and Bertrand retrieves a dusty box. Concealed in its lid, are some ancient 78 rpm records. Winding up the old dinosaur gramophone, discovered in the attic, he provokes it back into life. The muffled, cracked but still beautiful voice of Gigli penetrates the balmy night air, causing them all to sigh… followed by Edith Piaf's plaintive singing of: *'Non, je ne regrette rien.'*

'Moi, non plus,' they shout in unison, the evening already transformed into a party.

The following morning, Bertrand drives Leonardo to the local station. Having stayed longer than intended, he must reluctantly get back to Paris to finish filming. As she hugs him goodbye, outside the chateau's massive wooden doors, the fountain playing especially for him, Laetitia presses an unruly bundle of papers into his hands.

'If you can find the time, read these for me, will you? I no longer quite understand them. They are the papers relating to the deeds of the chateau,' she explains. 'All mostly there, but I think there's an extra document missing. Maybe it's with the lawyers still, or maybe I've misunderstood the terminology? In any case, there seems to be some anomaly in the wording of the contract. So please can you look at them yourself, just to be sure?'

Smiling reassuringly, before kissing her on the cheek, he thanks her almost formally. 'Thank you for your magnificent job of restoration.'

She answers with a quick, gratified smile. Then, levering himself into Bertrand's Citroen, he waves goodbye.

Two hours later, as his train eases into the Gare de Lyon, Leonardo has uncovered the truth. He had forgotten doing so but while negotiating the purchase of the chateau over the phone from Singapore, he had arranged for Maria to fly to Paris briefly to conclude the deal for him, giving her brief power of attorney. The chateau belongs neither to him nor to Laetitia. At the very last minute, Maria had changed the name on the title deeds from 'Leonardo Vescarro' to that of her own name, 'Maria Chandos', while, in a separate document, all the costs of both the repair and upkeep of the chateau were assigned to Leonardo. Short of a lengthy court case, there is probably little he can do. The chateau cannot now be sold without Maria's consent. Furiously, he crosses Paris by taxi, intent on the one thing that he can do.

He can sack her.

* * *

There is that bruised, brooding feeling about him, yet he is beautiful still. As he glances at her from the open door, the prisms in his eyes refract the light. How she loves the directness of his gaze. His features remain impassive, yet his eyes track her greedily, her dark eyes meeting his, the corners of her mouth upturned in smiles, with the constant exchanges of energy passing through her.

Even in repose, she appears to dance... he thinks gladly.

He had bought himself a ticket to Cork and been able to board almost immediately.

'No luggage, sir?' the flight attendant queried suspiciously.

At Cork, a thick fog threatened to make it impossible to land, the plane circling for half an hour before finally given clearance. But it was early morning still, and he was in no hurry. Instead of taking a taxi, he waited for a bus to Kinsale, where he bought himself lunch, before taking another to Skibbereen. Calling in at the baker's to ask where he could find a taxi to take him to Bantry Bay, the baker emerged from the back of the shop, rosy faced, his hands covered in flour, saying, 'Sure, I'll take you myself,' meanwhile wiping his hands on his dark blue apron.

'I couldn't possibly put you to so much trouble,' replied Max, embarrassed.

'Sure, you could. Where would we be without neighbours, now? Tell me that?'

The jovial man picked up his car keys, nodding acknowledgement of his wife's laughter. He then drove down the steep tumble of lanes to the sea, as though the wind were at his back, tantalising glimpses of the torn-lace coastline appearing and disappearing above its tall hedgerows. Without stopping to ask where Max was going, he already knew. He drove fast past Jack's prim white bungalow, too fast for him to spot their arrival, then straight onto the jetty. Nodding at the sky, he remarked: 'Picked a fine day for it...'

At the jetty, there was the usual gaggle of people: some arriving, some leaving, while others simply stared out to sea. He hailed an ominous-looking figure in a knitted balaclava, resembling some ancient Celtic warrior, carefully recoiling ropes around lobster pots.

'There's a fella here that needs you to hop him a lift to Wessex Island,' the genial baker instructed him.

The man with the lobster pots reacted unhesitatingly. He got to his feet, hauling a drowning rope which slowly, invisibly awoke a bright-blue dinghy, bobbing twenty yards from shore, propelling it, like one of Coppélia's dolls, into negotiating a phantom path across the water, gently bumping and curtseying its passage between the other boats.

Turning gratefully to the baker, Max shook his hand. 'What do I owe you? I really can't thank you enough...'

'Don't insult me now. You owe me nothing, absolutely nothing... Paraic here will take good care of you.'

He grasped Max's hand in both of his as he helped him into the dinghy and Max noticed how unusually soft they were from kneading dough. The amiable baker then breezed off back to his parked car with a parting wave.

It's not even as though he really knows who I am... To him, I'm simply the man in the red pants and yellow Wellington boots.

The owner of the little blue dinghy negotiates the shallows carefully, first allowing it to find its stride, followed by their exhilarating race across the bay, the salt spray in their hair and on their cheeks as they share the sea's magical zest for life. Max tries hard to compose himself. Despite the long journey, he has no real plan of what to say.

Just the truth maybe?

As always for him, the journey – and getting there – is everything.

Released from the boat, he clambers up the slippery teeth of diagonal rocks rising almost vertically from the narrow jetty, wondering whether he has been seen, the little dinghy already no more than a blue speck in the distance. He slips to his knees in a pool of mud, struggling to wipe clean his black-and-gold trainers on a clump of grass. Turning the corner of the main dwelling, he sees the kitchen door left open to the late afternoon sun. Standing with her back to him on the far side of the room, she turns towards him startled, her sudden fear instantly replaced by joy. No speech is needed. He recognises her reply in her smile. He crosses the room to her side, enfolding her slender frame in his arms. Her kiss tastes sweet, a hint of violets on her breath.

'Sorry,' he murmurs. 'Sorry not to have understood sooner.'

Her body moulds to his, feeling the quick pace of its response. They do not even close the door.

Who would come calling at this time of day?

They make love there and then on the tartan blanket, before the open fire, gently peeling the clothes from one another's bodies to reveal the skin and bone and warmth of the true garment below.

Afterwards, as Max sprawls luxuriously, with Sinead tucked naked against his chest: 'Home?' she whispers, laughing.

'Yes, home...' He kisses her. 'Will you cross the Atlantic with me?' he asks, deadpan... 'But in an aeroplane – I have to be back in New York towards the end of this month.'

* * *

With no one at home to quiz him, Hesketh leaves Chelsea Embankment very early the morning after the séance. By 6.30 a.m., he is already outside Matthew's gallery in Cork Street. Half shielding his face, he stands in the doorway opposite, witnessing the street wake up. At the Bond Street end of Cork Street, a narrow, steamy cubbyhole of a café is doing a brisk trade in cappuccinos and almond croissants; not yet daylight, the rest of the street slumbering still.

As it starts to get light, he crosses the street just once, positioning himself outside Matthew's vast plate-glass window. He wants to check that he had not been imagining it, that it really was one of the panels from Bianca's triptych he had spied in the half-light the night before. He peers in carefully, this time with the aid of some miniature opera glasses, needing to be sure. With the enhanced lenses, he scours back and forth along the depths of the gallery at floor level. No, not mistaken. There, in the distance, is Bianca's small painting of a man and a woman in bed, a girl-child of seven or eight asleep between them. He strains his eyes some more; as yet, nothing more he can do. Wary of setting off the alarm again by trying to break in, he retreats circumspectly to the opposite side of the street to look through his collection of black-and-white photos of people entering and leaving the gallery, taken several weeks earlier. The gallery does not open until 10 a.m.

By 7.30 a.m., the street is more awake. People rush past on their way to work, the street beginning to acquire its sense of purpose. But still no activity in the gallery. At 7.45 a.m., from the far end of the street, a siren sounds. Momentarily distracted, Hesketh turns, straining to see what the trouble is. When he looks back again, the lights in the gallery have been switched on. His heart starts to pound, although he still can't detect any movement.

Perhaps the lights are timed to switch on automatically?

He raises the miniature binoculars to his eyes, hoping to penetrate the gallery's thick glass frontage, suddenly spying movement. There is someone inside, after all. He waits nervously, biding his time. He cannot afford that someone to be either Matthew or his secretary, both rigorously programmed to turn him away at the door, maybe even call the police.

That's always been Bianca's threat... the police... Damn her.

He feels outraged.

If only she'd speak to me, none of this would be necessary.

The thought that B. Turvey and Bianca Johnson might be one and the same has still not occurred to him.

He crosses the road obliquely, stationing himself to one side of the gallery's main door, daring to peep in. He can hear the distant growl of a vacuum cleaner, shrinking from the window in alarm as a man in overalls, carrying a bucket of water, approaches. He starts to wash the windows in broad, acrobatic sweeps of his arms. There are two of them. Hesketh breathes a sigh of relief; only the office cleaners. He contemplates rushing the door and fighting both men for possession of the painting. But just as he is working out the choreography of his moves, the man with the bucket disappears towards the back of the gallery. From inside, still the distant drone of the vacuum cleaner.

Deciding to take his chance, Hesketh leans against the plate-glass door. To his surprise, it yields, opening easily beneath his weight.

The stupid bastards have left it unlocked, he thinks gleefully.

Removing his leather brogues, anticipating the heavy clatter they would make on parquet, he tucks them into his jacket pockets. In white stocking feet, he races, slipping harum-scarum across the polished floor. Grabbing the miniature panel, he looks about him wildly.

Where are the other panels? he wonders frantically.

His flyaway lenses askew on his nose, he hears a voice close by say: 'I'm about to wash the outside of the windows.'

No time to think, Hesketh retreats, slippery footed, out of the door, carrying the miniature panel with him, hugging it jealously to his chest. Half walking, half running, he reaches the far end of Cork Street without stopping to put on his shoes, avoiding last night's puddles as best he can. He turns into Burlington Gardens, past Cecconi's, already serving breakfast, before stopping breathlessly on the corner of Savile Row to put on his shoes and tie his laces. No one is following him. He begins to laugh, directing the distraught, chaotic sound at the wind, a woman passer-by glancing at him in contempt. He meets her look full-on.

'Old boot,' he says and laughs jeeringly.

She doesn't deign to turn around and the ugly, jubilant laughter dies in Hesketh's throat. Suddenly he realises how paltry his victory is; little more than a despoiler. All that he has done is to retrieve a single fragment of Bianca's much bigger, more ambitious composition. Not even his favourite among the panels and, on its own, little more than a bargaining chip.

But a bargain with whom? To whom does the painting now belong?

Returning to his parked car, he drives slowly back towards Chelsea Embankment, feeling relief that Chloe and Bruno will be away for the next few days, not sure he could face them in his current mood. He feels angry and betrayed.

* * *

Later that morning, Matthew has everyone desperately searching the gallery, insisting: 'It must be here somewhere.'

He calls the cleaners, asking what they have done with the painting? 'Do either of you remember moving it?'

But they have no idea what he's talking about. The day develops into a frenzy of search and phone calls, only Bianca convinced that its disappearance must have something to do with Hesketh.

No matter how improbable that might seem...

CHAPTER 24

The morning of his talk at the Royal Geographical Society, Robin wakes early, and alone. Byng is currently back in London, and Beatrice is with him at their home in Little Venice. He feels nervous. Not of lecturing, which he does regularly to his students at London University, but of lecturing to an audience largely comprising friends and colleagues, certain to judge him less kindly.

Confucius had proved a more intriguing subject than he first anticipated: his *Analects* like perfumed riddles, provocative of thought and sensation, while mysteriously open to interpretation. Also delightfully free of dogma. Despite his western caste of mind, Robin finds himself responding to the purity of a philosophy stripped bare of cant. For him, philosophy has always been adversarial. Confucius is neither argumentative nor combative but instead that rare thing, intriguingly elusive to a personality like Robin's, merely 'persuasive'.

The phone rings, startling him – Beatrice, whispering, so as not to awaken Byng. Robin would have preferred her not to ring at all. He has fallen in love with her, deeply in love, but that is not the point. Today is about him, his work and professional standing, and he does not want it infected by the ordinary squalor of life, either his own or anyone else's. Today he wants to be the lone philosopher prince he has always imagined himself to be.

'You sound a bit gruff.'

'I feel a bit gruff,' he replies bluntly. 'Let's talk later.'

Replacing the receiver abruptly, he feels a stab of dismay, knowing he has hurt her, while thinking exasperatedly: *I must stay clear-headed.*

The phone rings again. 'Don't be jealous of Byng; there's really no need,' she whispers imploringly.

Robin smiles, caught suddenly in the act of loving her. 'I know,' he says gently, 'I do know. Don't worry, I'll see you later. I'll expect to find you in the front row right under my nose.'

* * *

Touting untidy bundles of paper and a laptop in a scuffed Gladstone bag, Robin arrives so early at the Royal Geographical Society on Kensington Gore that the doors are still locked and he has difficulty getting in, his lecture not due to start until 1 p.m. Already set up in advance is an overhead projector. To Robin, the atmosphere in the empty hall feels almost sepulchral. Dust motes catch in shafts of November sunlight; distantly, from outside, the puff and wheeze of London's red buses slowing to a halt in front of the Royal Albert Hall.

One of the organisers approaches, mincing her steps tenderly, betraying her flattering deference. Inwardly, he laughs, doubting whether his performance can hope to satisfy such reverence. The phone call with Beatrice has upset him. He can feel his old rebellious self, resurfacing.

Why do people come to lectures? he wonders disaffectedly.

Despite public speaking being at the very core of his profession, it suddenly strikes him as ridiculous: *Why can't they just get by with thoughts of their own...?*

'*They went to sea in a Sieve...*' For the past few days that phrase of Lear's has haunted him.

What, he wonders, *would Edward Lear have said about Confucius? A bit earnest, maybe... forever chasing the superior gentleman in oneself?*

He pauses. *Yet how closely do any of us match up to poor Confucius's expectations?*

Anxiously, he checks his watch... *People will start arriving soon.*

He makes a precautionary dash to the lavatory. Examining himself in the washbasin mirror, his face is haggard and grey, his eyes crazily bloodshot. He is wearing one of several corduroy suits, ranging from English mustard to pale silvery gold.

I should have had a haircut, he thinks belligerently, angrily forging a parting between curtains of lank grey locks with his big-knuck-led hands.

Taking a broken comb from his breast pocket, he tries to make sense of their disarray. *Now I just look like a Russian anarchist*, he thinks grimly. *Well... that's who I want to be – an anarchist philosopher.*

Shaking his head, he restores its spiked, chrysanthemum disor-der. *That will have to do*, he decides carelessly.

Nevertheless, the escalating quarrel inside his head refuses to abate. He wanders back, prepared for a fight, only to find the hall still empty.

The sound of doors opening and shutting, the scraping of feet on concrete... As his audience start to trickle in, he looks at them in surprise. *Who on earth are they?*

He recognises no one. Studying their faces and moods carefully, he notices some of the women have come dressed as if for a cock-tail party.

Perhaps this is a good pick-up place? he hazards. *A sort of dating agency for the cognoscenti?*

He chuckles. *To hell with Confucius, just find me a good mate...*

A couple wave to him. Robin readjusts his glasses. It is those two plump pigeons, David and Adriana Russell, the merchant banker and his wife whom he had hectored so insultingly at Bian-ca's dinner party a few weeks earlier.

Yet they look pleased to see me? Perhaps people like being insulted more than I realise? he ruminates. *Perhaps it invigorates them... preferable to being ignored? I should probably revise my way of treating people*, he thinks hilariously. *Insults are clearly too good for them.*

There is a sudden surge at the door. More people arrive, many jockeying for front-row seats. He sees Solange arrive with her architect lover, Nicholas Rowe, her face turned towards him in a blank, cold stare of contempt. Finding a seat, she stands longer than quite necessary, fussing with her coat, allowing time for people to notice her, her miniature frame wrapped in a semi-trans-parent sheath of black lace. Nevertheless, her strategy works; by now everyone is looking at her. At her side, Nicholas Rowe's huge, hunched frame, beams proudly. Robin, meanwhile, muttering vengefully: 'Disastrous, wretched female...'

437

But where's Beatrice? he wonders anxiously.

Scanning the front two rows, he glances sweepingly around the hall, only to look away again in swift dismay. It had not occurred to him she might bring Byng with her. Instead of sitting directly in front of him, as promised, they are seated a little to his right, high up in the second tier of oak seating. Robin feels suddenly humiliated; found out, like a naughty schoolboy. He shudders, wondering: *Did our lovemaking mean so little?*

He had almost forgotten about the actual presence of Byng. Glancing down, studying his fingernails, hoping to disguise the slow barometer flush infusing his distraught face, he finds his friend, Sir Jocelyn Carpenter, QC, and his diminutive wife Laura peering amiably over the edge of the podium at him. Bending courteously to shake their hands, their plain-faced affability restores his mood a little.

Thank God for unpretentious people...

Nevertheless, things are not looking good, the quiet sobriety instilled in him by Beatrice faltering badly, his old abrasive self rising to the challenge – adversity, the impetus to fight, upon him again. Strangely, it feels almost a relief, like greeting an old friend. Stepping onto the podium, one of the organisers passes him a note. Immediately recognising the handwriting, he sighs. 'Love you,' Beatrice had written in her backward-leaning scrawl.

But will that be enough? his tortured mind asks.

Byng has risen to his feet and is glad-handing large swathes of the audience, every move of his tall, blonde, boyish grace demonstrating his impeccable urbanity and Parisian chic while leaving Beatrice abandoned in her seat.

Perhaps Byng suffers from the same vanity as that futile little trollop Solange? reflects Robin bitterly.

Nevertheless, he dares not glance directly at Beatrice.

The hall now full, an anticipatory hush of excitement invades the room. As he gets to his feet, Bianca walks in, with Leonardo in tow. Looking deathly pale, almost unwell, she nevertheless waves brightly, blowing him a kiss, before taking her seat high up at the far end of a row and ushering Leonardo ahead of her.

Good God, Leonardo Vescarro... the very last person I expected to see, thinks Robin, greatly amused. *Poor fellow must have been bamboozled into it by Bianca.*

Seated immediately below him, eagerly occupying most of the two front rows, are his daily gang of students.

Almost time to begin, he thinks grimly. *What was I thinking agreeing to this?*

The last time he had suffered this degree of reckless claustrophobia was that morning at The Society when he had first encountered Beatrice on her own. When lecturing to undergraduates, no such doubts afflict him.

A small scuffle erupts outside the main door. Hearing voices raised, then muffled, the door opens with a bang and a distraught-looking man in black tie and a colourful waistcoat enters. Hesitating briefly by the door before making an agile monkey scramble to the uppermost tier, he flings himself recklessly into the aisle seat of the same row as Bianca and Leonardo, twenty people between him and them. Following him at a discreet, watchful distance is a policeman. Only Jocelyn Carpenter tracks the man's progress in silent alarm. From all his many days in court, he has never forgotten either a name or face.

Hesketh James, he thinks anxiously.

His glance searches out Bianca, but she is too preoccupied talking to Leonardo to have noticed the man's arrival.

Standing now, and pausing in what he is about to say, Robin is suddenly struck by the intense violet of the policeman's eyes.

Joining him on the podium, the diminutive, sycophantic organiser announces: 'We are exceptionally lucky to be joined today by the well-known writer and philosopher, Professor Robin Holderness, who will explain the significance of the ancient teachings of Confucius on modern-day China.'

Polite applause, followed by an artillery of coughs... as Robin steps up to the lectern.

'You probably find the concept of Confucianism having fostered the greed of modern capitalism alien,' he begins.

A soft flutter of alarm rifles through the room, disrupting their acquiescent mood.

'Yet,' he continues deprecatingly, 'this is a modern fairy tale of greed, akin to *The Bonfire of the Vanities* comes to China.'

Starting to fidget uneasily in their seats, this was not what the audience was expecting, nor what they have come to hear... They have come in a mood of supplication, and with 'open minds'. But they are not prepared to listen to the ancient world being insulted.

Robin is too practised a lecturer not to register their disaffection. As for their minds, he thinks he knows precisely how 'open' they are. He starts again, a little more formally: 'Born in 551 BC, Confucius was the son of a nobleman and officer in the elite Lu military, who, dying when Confucius was three years old, left him to be brought up by a destitute mother...'

Robin scrutinises the audience over the top of his glasses. They have settled down again.

This is what they were hoping for, he thinks disdainfully. *Nice, cosy, biographical data... Yet who in this room has any real concept of 551 BC? Not even myself, having studied it... That is the essential problem: how to make ancient history feel intimate?*

Nor, he suspects despairingly, will many of them have any real concept of morality, whether ancient or modern. In the light of their ignorance, he wonders why they don't just dispense with all this irrelevant biographical stuff and jump straight to the bigger questions?

But perhaps that's too harsh? he sighs, admonishing himself. *Confucius preached benevolence, happiness to all...* 'Of neighbourhoods, benevolence is the most beautiful...'

Taking a deep breath, he presses on, dutifully relaying the facts: 'As a boy, despite his impoverished upbringing, Confucius was assiduously studious, his early career as cowherd followed by a later, superlative one as diplomat... his core beliefs always devoted to valuing meritocracy over those of aristocratic birth... his graduation to the newly established bourgeoisie of *Shi*, suspended, just as he himself was, between commoner and aristocrat... *Shi* introducing a process whereby China's warrior elite were eventually replaced by an equally elite coterie of civil servants.'

Listening, Bianca recalls her instinctive repugnance, confronted by the unyielding, swaddled features of Xian's terracotta warriors beneath their duvets of red mud.

Robin's voice drawls on…

'Confucius's appointment as police commissioner of Lu, at the age of thirty-five, by the Duke of Ting… How, in negotiations with the Duke's arch rival, he initially distinguished himself as skilful diplomat, followed by an abortive plot to destroy the city strongholds of three rival aristocratic families, the failure of which earned him such bitter enmity that, rather than suffer the humiliation of banishment, Confucius chose to live in exile for thirteen years… Nevertheless, it was during this hectic period of fierce diplomacy that he first developed his nimble dealings in political matters, as well as the strong insights into human character that formed the basis of his philosophy.'

By now, Robin's audience has that mesmerised quality of daydream, half listening.

How loathsomely passive they all are, he reflects angrily. *Sitting there, waiting to be spoon-fed, like intellectually bereft babies…*

Meanwhile, he himself begins to feel stupendously bored. Attempting to get a grip on his rebellious thoughts, he steals a surreptitious glance at Beatrice.

How beautiful she looks, he thinks wistfully. *Will I, too, be forced into exile?*

His voice lifts into a bark. 'Arguments continue, even today, in academic circles, as to whether Confucianism may properly be considered a religion or a philosophy… Nor without a certain amount of good reason,' he adds stiffly.

'While Confucius acknowledged his belief in Heaven and an afterlife, he nevertheless remained strangely nonchalant about the existence of soul… his far greater emphasis on the importance of study and cultivation of moral character. Yet without ever wishing to debate the ethical merits of an individual's acts of morality. To Confucius, "Heaven" represented a divine but impersonal harmony. But in pragmatic everyday terms, he was more urgently preoccupied by understanding what exactly constituted the perfect "gentleman", whose success, he believed, depended entirely on his discovery of "the Way", that elusive, essentially poetic concept for which there were, even at the time, numerous rival versions, each boasting vastly different conclusions.'

Robin glances up from his notes. For the moment, he seems to have captured his audience's attention. Yet he knows it cannot last. Distress is creating a barrier around his mind. He is beginning to not correctly gauge the sounds he is making.

If only I could talk to Beatrice for a minute or two, his mind whimpers.

Raising his voice above its normal low gravel of lazy American intonation, the blood beats feverishly in his ears.

'With their emphasis on self-cultivation over explicit rules of behaviour, Confucius's moral teachings represent a defiance of logic. His ethics, based purely on notions of virtue, rather than on rational argument, are conveyed indirectly, through a subtle process of allusion and innuendo, more akin to poetry than to logic, and one that relies heavily on intuition for discernment of its meanings. Confucius's interpretation of "the Way" is therefore riddled with mystery and high emotion... its actual meanings blowing on the wind as fugitively as perfume...'

At this, a startled ripple of laughter runs through the hall, causing others to look up from their daydreaming stupors.

'In Western terms,' Robin adds naughtily, 'Confucius's concept of "the Way" equates with that equally elusive riddle we in the West are so very fond of: "the Truth".'

Unable to stop himself, he starts to giggle, his audience, although mystified, laughing with him. Only Beatrice observes him in sober alarm.

* * *

Matthew Dancer had slipped in late. Sitting surrounded by Robin's boisterous gang of students, he is grateful for their abundant energy and enthusiasm.

Most of this audience might just as well be dead, he thinks morosely, as he warily tries to assess their potential as patrons of art.

He has brought with him catalogues to Bianca's exhibition, plus pinned posters to the noticeboard by the entrance. Sebastian, his new intern, recently graduated from the Courtauld, will arrive later to hand out leaflets. As always, Matthew is despairing of his finances, although not for himself particularly. Like Confucius, he would be happy to retreat into exile and live frugally for the next thirteen years; all he would require is an endless supply of books on politics, and an occasional spin in one of his Ferraris. It is the gallery staff he worries about most. How to continue paying their salaries? Plus he feels anxious for the good name and reputation of a gallery he has built successfully over many years.

The far sadder truth is that the artists he represents have started to bore him. Not all of them, of course, but in general. Their endless self-importance, their seemingly bottomless need for reassurance, has begun to repel him. As a young man, it fascinated him. The exultation, the occasional bouts of petulant bossiness, the flights of brilliance and amusing anecdote, interlaced with terrible periods of despond, had struck him as the height of good drama and the very pulse of life. Theirs was a deliciously fierce impetus, in which he both longed to share and profit by. But lately, he found he could scarcely care less. These days, he much prefers the company of businessmen, whose emotional needs were less intimately on show.

Are business men whom Confucius meant, by the 'perfect gentlemen'? he speculates idly. Probably not. *And yet it would mean sacrificing a lot to give up my gallery*, he reflects unhappily.

He had spent the earlier part of today again chasing after Bianca's missing painting. He and his staff had scoured every inch of the gallery, Bianca, meanwhile, remaining annoyingly convinced the missing panel is, in some way, Hesketh's fault.

But how exactly?

Even she has no convincing explanation for how Hesketh might have stolen it.

At her insistence, he had phoned Chloe to ask whether they might have mistakenly left the painting behind, even knowing it not to be true. He distinctly remembers handling the little panel the day before it went missing. The whole thing is a mystery.

Despite supreme efforts at diplomacy, Chloe had been offended by his call, strangely tongue-tied and evasive, while making it clear she never wanted to hear mention of Bianca or the painting ever again.

What she failed to admit was that she was looking at the missing panel right then, propped up in their hallway... Nor did she reveal how Hesketh had accused her outright of selling a painting that was 'his', nor how they had ended up screaming viciously at each other, against a backdrop of Bruno's increasingly frantic sobs. As Chloe shrieked her loathing of the painting, and Hesketh his irreplaceable loss of it, Bruno had suddenly fallen headlong into another violent fit.

'Can't you see... it was the only thing I had left of her...' Hesketh kept saying brokenly, bending solicitously over the quivering body of his young son... 'The only thing... and YOU dared to steal it from me... The painting used to talk to me and tell me things!' he shouted furiously.

The honesty of this speech shocked them both.

'So, you are finally MAD,' Chloe screamed, as she tenderly wiped the foam and blood from Bruno's injured mouth.

Her mood, instantly deflating, she then reverted to the gentle, ashamed manner of her normal self, sorrow again overwhelming her. It was the first time she had ever defied Hesketh so openly, let alone voiced so cruel a word as 'mad'.

Yet Hesketh had simply laughed, the word 'mad' holding no threat at all.

For his own part, Matthew is still unclear what to do. Without the missing panel, Bianca's triptych is worth less than he anticipated. He even wonders whether to belatedly invoice Chloe for the price of Bruno's portrait, after all. Without consulting her, he has decided to exhibit Bianca's incomplete triptych alongside her miniature Chinese watercolours, when her exhibition opens in ten days' time, although now with little idea how to price it. He too had been astonished to see her arrive for Robin's talk with Leonardo in tow, wondering slightly whether his presence in London might not disrupt their plans in some way. Bianca is far too discreet to have said so, but he suspects Leonardo knows nothing of her recent trip to China.

She relies far too heavily on that divine ignorance of his...

Shaking his mind free of such thoughts, he rouses himself to concentrate on the lecture...

Robin, now quoting from the *Analects*, is stringing out Confucian sayings, like disembodied verse:

"Although a man's virtue might be a gift from Heaven... it is more assuredly something cultivated within."

Robin's mood, altering pitch, displays a sudden lazy hauteur, the next point of particular interest to him and seeming to affirm his own teaching methods.

"'Led by law, and threats of punishment, people will try to avoid punishment, without feeling shame... Whereas, led by virtue and rules of propriety, they anticipate shame, and cultivate goodness."

'Confucius believed absolutely in the power of shame,' he drawls.

Standing extra tall, he joyously waves his corduroy arms about in order to deliver this angry rebuke.

'He believed that if a ruler led by correct action, orders in the imposed, legal sense would become redundant... and men would willingly follow the propriety and actions of their rulers without needing to be coerced.'

Robin waits for the full implication of this to sink in, knowing that for many of his audience, such ideas spell either fantasy or anarchy. Certainly nothing resembling reality. Flashing the quotations up large on the overhead projector, he adds: 'Confucius's point was not only personal but political... He was registering opposition to the routine punishments recommended by the alternative political system of his time, that of "legalism".'

Robin is notorious in academic circles for taunting the best from his students. Relentlessly shaming them during seminars, with mocking denunciations of their 'impoverished intellects and slow-coach minds', young women are frequently reduced to tears; several of Robin's colleagues have threatened to report him. Yet the great mystery is how much his students seem to love him for it and to flourish academically under his tutelage.

Relaxing a little, Robin's distraught features now reveal an immense tiredness.

'If only I could hear Beatrice's voice,' he whispers unhappily to himself.

His own voice sounds strange... even to his own ears.

'Confucius insisted that man's two most fundamental goals, those of "goodness" and "benevolence" should be cultivated purely for the sake of virtue,' he announces operatically. 'That is, in sublime, stoical indifference to either their success or failure.'

Onto the screen flashes: *Although inconceivable that a gentleman should seek to stay alive at the expense of benevolence, it may occasionally happen that he has to accept death, in order for benevolence to be accomplished.*

By now, Robin is laughing hilariously, a wild recklessness possessing him.

'Yes, every bit as bad as that,' he brays.

But his audience seem less amused, jokes about death not striking them as remotely funny.

Prim-minded, pedestrian fools, he thinks angrily. *Kidding themselves they want the truth, when all they really want is palatable sweeties of idea...*

He grins madly, utterly failing to detect his own absence of benevolence, his eyes, beneath his chrysanthemum mop of hair, steely and unforgiving. Wearily, he battles on: 'Confucian "goodness", therefore, describes a "morality" to be pursued intuitively, yet in ways that allow different counsel for different situations, while always based on sincerity and knowledge... Hence, the importance of study.

'"*Virtuous dispositions without knowledge are susceptible to corruption. Virtuous actions without sincerity are never truthfully righteous.*"

'Confucius thought it important for the truth to be represented, even in facial expression.

'"*How, if a gentleman forsakes benevolence, can he hope to make a name for himself?*"'

Robin glances up naughtily from his notes.

'The perceptive among you may begin to notice an increasing emphasis on the importance of what others think in Confucius's moral teachings; a constant preoccupation with how an individual is viewed in society... The following, his most famous quote: "*Do not impose on others what you do not wish for yourself.*"

'You will recognise this as mirrored in our own later Christian orthodoxy: "*Do unto others as you would be done by.*" Both versions serving as a reminder that, in its inception, most religious thinking is essentially philosophical. Only as it develops into dogma does speculative thought transform into rigid cant... It is also precisely this emphasis on "benevolence" and "reciprocity" which so distinguishes Confucius's teachings from other schools of Chinese thought.'

* * *

I wonder... ponders Bianca doubtfully.

She remembers Robin's slavish devotion to truth tables and the idiosyncrasies of logical positivism twenty-five years earlier.

Surely he can't have abandoned all his former rigid thinking quite so easily?

Nor does she remember him as a doyen of speculative thought. In her own student days, he was mostly driven by a constant, almost paranoid need for certainty.

The audience starts to betray its rebellious mood again; one or two people shoot their hands in the air, hoping to interrupt him. Robin pretends not to see them, his mind silently shouting: *Shut up. Shut up... SHUT UP!*

Yet he is finally beginning to enjoy himself. Having got his audience riled, he feels glad, the atmosphere in the hall brewing nicely, his own energy levels rising, ready for a fight.

Staring out menacingly at the crowd, the intellectual braggart in him starts to plot their shame.

'What do any of you really know of morality?' he banters.

But he has gone too far. Gulping down the statement in a panic, he suddenly remembers... *Am I not myself a recent recruit to that loathsome gang of London adulterers I so despise?*

He feels stricken, wondering: *What is the morality of adultery exactly? Did Confucius justify his actions with intuition when he abandoned his young wife and baby son?*

Surveying his audience grimly, Robin spreads his corduroy arms like some gigantic, golden eagle.

Just look at you... he thinks disdainfully. *All dressed up in your peacock finery, hoping for a date.*

447

He counts at least thirty Georgina von Etzdorf scarves, with their shimmering, jewel-coloured silk velvets casting notes of bohemian gaiety over otherwise sober-suited necks and shoulders.

Who would ever have thought a velvet shawl would become the mark of intellectual respectability?

His mind is a riot, battling on, barely in control.

And what does my own sense of being a 'superior gentleman' come down to? he reminds himself, suddenly painfully aware of his own myriad contradictions. *Would Confucius have shamed me for it too?*

Byng had been one of the crowd to raise his hand, Robin having ignored him while continuing, unabashed, his indolent monologue of American, gravel vowels. Studying him with autocratic contempt, and unaccustomed to being treated as invisible, Byng feels angry, both with himself and Robin.

Bad form, of course, to interrupt a speaker, regardless of whether or not one agrees with him. Nevertheless...

Byng's journalistic, opinion-seeking self, of whom he occasionally feels secretly ashamed, had briefly got the better of him. Having always admired Robin, and rather coveted his friendship, he now finds himself surreptitiously edging back the crisp blue of his shirt cuff to consult his watch; thinking exasperatedly: *How much longer is this nonsense going on?*

Turning conspiratorially towards his wife, to his amazement, he finds Beatrice is listening raptly to Robin's every word, a look of dazed, greedy concentration in her darkly sparkling eyes. A sudden horrific doubt assails him, which he immediately puts to one side.

No, too ludicrous to contemplate, he thinks dismissively.

Robin, looking more and more like an animated scarecrow, embarks on his next point – explaining the superior gentleman's dependence on the rites. That body of rules culled from ancient repositories of insight into morality...

'Despite its emphasis on intuitive judgement, it's another paradox of Confucius's teaching to simultaneously insist on respect for one's superiors, thereby reviving the ghosts of feudalism and evoking accusations of conservatism...'

Robin stares bleakly at the crowd. If only he dared, he would walk off stage right now.

Just the touch of Beatrice's hand...

His sigh seems to reach the rafters.

'Confucius also famously proposed the relationship between a leader and his followers should mimic the structure of family life: *"Being a good and obedient son is at the core of a man's character."'*

Robin's voice lowers pitch, sounding momentarily gentle. 'Now compare that statement with the following from *Liji*, the Book of Rites: *"Kindness in the father, filial piety in the son... Good behaviour in the father, obedience in the wife... Benevolence in the ruler, loyalty in the ministers."'*

Robin's voice has turned into a solemn sing-song. 'If being a good son makes one a good citizen, does it automatically follow that being a good father could make one a good ruler?'

Glancing up mischievously from his notes, he says: 'Please hold on to that thought for later...'

Bianca listens to Robin with increasing dismay. Not because she disagrees with anything he has said but because it strikes her as too ordinary. He has outlined a certain set of attitudes, many well known, and delivered them with a certain bravura, neurotic elegance. It is precisely what she remembers of him from her own student days. The things he had to say were always correct but essentially anodyne. The difficulty, the excitement in Robin's personality is something separate, something within himself, just as Confucius had seemed to predict; an unorthodox, unpredictable quirk of personality. It is Robin's ever fermenting, adversarial code of unhappiness and disquiet that makes him so fascinating. At its height, his emotional turbulence can bring the house down. She remembers how easily he had disrupted her own dinner party just a few weeks earlier. Whereas his intellect, somewhere in its flawed depths, she suspects of being timid...

She stops listening and turns her attention on Leonardo.

He had arrived home, without warning, late last night, on Eurostar. Luckily, she was at home and in bed. Hearing his key fumble in the lock, she had panicked briefly, fretting: *Has Hesketh finally found a way to get through our front door?*

Huddling beneath the covers, trembling and distraught, she remembered, as if from nowhere, that Hesketh had once owned a set of skeleton keys.

But surely they would be out of date by now?

She then crouched low, holding her breath, trying to hide... adrenaline pumping... Yet the minute Leonardo pushed open their bedroom door, everything changed. Immediately registering his unhappiness, he, with perfect symmetry, failed to recognise her fear.

'Hello.'

His voice sounded muffled and strangely over amplified. Her own first shocked thought: *How aged and dissolute he looks...*

His silk tie was askew, his hair rumpled, too much white showing in the frightened corners of dark eyes, which danced skittishly around the room, refusing to settle. He said very little, the shadows on his pocked cheeks like bruises. As always, after one of their long absences, there were certain rituals to be observed. No questions allowed, let alone one as intrusive as: 'What has happened to upset you?'

As always, her own dismay is immediately dismissed by Leonardo's ability to commandeer the emotional space in whichever room he happened to find himself.

Without further comment, he started to undress, folding his clothes neatly, laboriously onto a chair, despite the immense fatigue enveloping him, then climbing straight into bed, still without really looking at her. They lay there briefly, the two of them, like Romanesque effigies in a parish church, not quite touching, the bedclothes shrouded evenly over their sculptural forms.

'Should I get you something to eat?' she eventually asked, her voice staccato, almost embarrassed.

'No thanks; I had something on the train,' he mumbled.

With his sonorous, formal voice and Italian inflexions more than usually accented, he might have been talking to a stranger.

Perhaps that's what I've become... a perfect stranger whose bed he expects to share?

Then, rolling abruptly onto his side, he presented her with the stubborn curve of a back, breathing defensiveness towards her, and started to snore. She should have felt angry, but all she felt was a yearning tenderness towards him, plus a little puzzled, meanwhile chiding herself hopelessly: *By now I ought to be used to this awkwardness whenever he returns from a long trip?*

She lay there thinking for five minutes, her mind now as busily, skittishly dancing as his eyes had been when he first arrived. Then, on a sigh, she turned out the light, and threaded her arms around his waist, hugging the familiar baked-bread warmth of him, drinking in his sweet, idiosyncratic perfume. In his half-sleepy state, he snuffled a loud sob of contentment, and she felt his rigid body relax, snuggling heavily against hers, to let out a deep sigh. It was the only language, as man and wife, they truly understood; the soporific language of skin on skin, the deep sigh of uninterrupted sleep.

Not until this morning, after making his favourite breakfast of scrambled eggs with smoked salmon, followed by endless cups of fierce black coffee to accompany the perfumed Gitanes Parisian life had imposed on him, did she learn his real reason for hurrying back to London. It was to consult lawyers. Full of indignant anguish at having been so mercilessly cheated and made a fool of, he unthinkingly blurted out the whole wretched tale... of how Maria Chandos, an assistant, whose name Bianca neither knew nor recognised had had the bravura effrontery to effectively steal a newly acquired chateau from right under his nose.

'Tomorrow, I'm meeting a specialist in international property law, recommended by Jocelyn Carpenter,' he explained. 'I rang Jocelyn from Paris. We're hoping he'll know how to force her to restore the property to me... But nothing is certain. The lawyers I consulted in Paris seem to think the chateau may already have acquired the status of a gift, made voluntarily by me to her, and therefore legally irretrievable.'

In his pent-up resentment and distress, Leonardo, normally so guarded, had finally talked openly, like a child unburdening himself, apparently forgetting that Bianca supposedly knew nothing of the chateau in the first place, having instructed his London secretary to keep it secret from her.

Bianca said little, betraying nothing, simply intent on listening. Watching the busy traffic of moods clouding his face with furious dismay, turning his tan sallow and aged, she realised it was not the potential loss of vast sums of money that had so upset Leonardo but the dishonourable reversal of roles between master and servant. Maria Chandos had deceived him, played him for an imbecile. It was that which wounded most. It also confirmed Bianca's estimation of him as someone who remained sublimely indifferent to any form of humiliation, except whenever its details were exposed: 'Don't frighten the horses' not only Confucius's motto but Leonardo's too.

Emboldened by this rare moment of confession, Bianca eventually stood up, disarmingly poised in her jeans and soft, angora plume of a jumper, to clear away the breakfast things, careful not to break the spell of intimacy between them, the tone of her voice tender and unchanged. Summoning up her courage and smiling sweetly, she began on a slight lisp...

'Imagine it... ridiculous really... a few weeks ago a woman... a total stranger... rang here to tell me you were the father of her child... A baby boy, I think she said?'

Through veiled eyes, she had watched the effect of these feather-light words, expecting Leonardo to pout and look affronted. Maybe even to murmur one of his rare pantomime castigations of other people's stupidity... followed by a joke or two, while blustering: 'What now the price of celebrity?'

Instead, blinking fast, he raised his dark, perceptive eyes to hers in a fierce jazz of alarm, before sinking back, babyish and trusting, into the affectionate warmth of her uncritical gaze. She had seduced him into telling the truth.

Now, listening to Robin's vaunting salutation of Confucius's faith in the power of shame, she remembers how little remorse Leonardo had shown as they talked after breakfast. Replacing the broken figure of despond, it was as though a hero from Italian opera had suddenly stepped, centre-stage, into their London kitchen. Leaning back expansively in his chair and adopting what Bianca always laughingly called his 'dripping with ermine pose', he casually announced, 'Actually, I have two other children besides the new baby boy...'

A smug, naughty little boy's self-congratulatory smile, elongating the wide mauve of his mouth against his broad, tanned cheeks, played mischievously across his face. It was like watching a man throw down the gauntlet of his virility.

An appalled, numbing paralysis invaded her. Fleetingly, she felt as though she had always known what he was going to say. But that was not true.

So why does this news feel so inevitable? she wonders.

She is at a loss to explain. Leonardo is self-confident and smiling again.

'I have a son of twelve, and a seven-year-old daughter, as well as the new baby boy.'

He listed them breezily on knuckles stroked with dark silky hair, as though nothing in the world were more natural. Bianca blanched, about to be sick. Feeling her stomach convulse, she swallowed hard.

Stephen was right... Better not to have known.

This was worse, far worse than anything she could have either imagined or invented for herself; all three children, she realised in shock, conceived in the years since she and Leonardo had married. It was like being told she had fallen desperately ill, many years earlier, only to learn the morbid truth, when far too late to do anything. There was, she saw perfectly clearly, no possible remedy. Aghast, her voice choking, eyes pricking with the stormy heat of suppressed tears, she asked: 'Are all three by the same woman?'

'Good God, no... Absolutely not,' he replied in disgust, the very idea of any kind of constancy seeming to affront him.

Her voice dwindled to a frightened whisper: 'But were you in love with these women?'

'Never,' he answered unhesitatingly.

'Then WHY? Just tell me why, Leo?' she suddenly exploded. 'WHY would you do this to us?'

He looked up at her through bright, shiny eyes, suddenly enjoying the uncertainty of her mood, while announcing indifferently: 'Out of pity, mostly.'

'PITY?' she replied uncomprehendingly. 'Yet you must have known that I would have liked to have had a child?' she whispered plaintively.

'Really?' he replied, looking genuinely surprised. 'You never asked,' he objected, utterly unrepentant.

It was the perfectly aimed rebuke: *You never asked...*

Bianca felt the full weight of her own childlessness like an insult... plus all the impotent sorrow of having fallen irreversibly, irreplaceably in love with a child who would never be born but who still lived vividly in her imagination.

The morning, their conversation, with the light filtering through Venetian blinds onto their kitchen table, had felt all too extraordinary. They might have been discussing the weather, Bianca meanwhile asking herself: *What's wrong with me? Why aren't I like other wives? Why don't I weep and lash out... tear the place down, like any normal wife would?*

Yet secretly, she knows why not... As well as being rapturously in love with Stephen, she had always felt partially guilty and ashamed. She had taken all the single-mindedness of her passion from Leonardo and awarded it to Stephen. There was no point in imagining he had not sensed its loss, no matter how obscurely.

Yet how very different we are... she ruminates. *All these long years of my constancy towards a single lover, while Leonardo has been going about the globe, indiscriminately sowing his seed like a man throwing gold coins at the peasantry.*

Now, exactly as Robin is attempting to explain, a tiny part of her almost welcomes the shame her own failure is inflicting on her conscience... plus something else, far deeper than either guilt or anger. She has always felt indelibly protected by the finality of hers and Stephen's love for each other. Not once, in all their years of unorthodox living, had Stephen ever left her, even momentarily, in any doubt as to how very much he loves her. He is and always would be the greatest gift of her life; impossible to repudiate. Without him, her life would feel bereft.

But there was also that other, more intimate truth, running still deeper. It wasn't that she had ever actively disliked her lovemaking with Leonardo; far from it. But its sweet, cosy, soporific languor was no match for the rapturous ecstasies she and Stephen were capable of. All his life, Leonardo had relied on his extraordinary stamina and a natural, happy buoyancy in his relations with women but had never bothered to learn to make love in all the complex, intricate ways people who are really interested in sex do. It is this which now makes her feel most guilty of all – her inability to love

Leonardo with the same intensity and abandon she had always felt for Stephen. Her actions strike her as unfair, unjust even.

As different as Leonardo and Stephen are, would a more skilful wife have created equal happiness for them both? she wonders unhappily.

It is one of the conundrums that haunts her.

Perhaps, she muses, *that is always the true tragedy of sexual relationships... the inability to forget what one already knows... the inevitability of comparisons.*

As always, in moments of distress, Bianca's thoughts dash, lizard-like, to Anya: *Where is she? How is she? Is she suffering in any way?*

It was sexual comparison that had ruined hers and William's marriage too.

'How old is your baby son?' she had asked sorrowfully, thinking of her own lost child, still unshakably sure he too would have been a boy.

'Ten weeks old last Wednesday,' Leonardo replied crisply. 'He was born at the beginning of September.'

At last, the sting of deep shock reached Bianca. She felt tears streak her cheeks; her imminent loss of control. She wanted to ask: 'Are you sure the baby's yours?' but dared not sound so spiteful. Instead, she asked tremulously: 'Where's the baby now?'

Leonardo looked at her hard. 'With his mother... in Hungary.'

Of course, Hungarian – that had been the woman's indecipherable accent.

Suddenly she remembers how Budapest, with its pioneering film history, had always been one of Leonardo's annual film-teaching destinations, realising: *Leonardo could have known the mother of this child for years.*

Baffled, she asked: 'But weren't you in Singapore and China these past ten weeks? Have you even seen the baby yet?'

'Yes, I took a weekend off from filming and flew to Hungary from Singapore.'

He glanced about him suddenly, as if searching for something. 'She gave me a watch to commemorate the baby's birth. But I think I must have left it in some hotel bedroom or other. You didn't happen to find it, did you?'

He glanced at her searchingly, his dark eyes accusatory, as if expecting her to lie.

'Was it a bulky watch, with lots of dials, like a deep-sea diver's, but on a bracelet of white and yellow gold?'

'Yes, that's it,' he agreed triumphantly. 'Did you find it?'

'No, but I remember you wearing it at our last dinner party... I thought at the time that it wasn't your normal style.'

'No, it was hideous, vulgar really,' he agreed, relaxing again. 'A relief, in many ways, to have lost it...'

Then, as though enough were enough, swerving dismissively away from their topic of conversation, he asked abruptly: 'What have you got on today?'

Bianca stared at him in surprise. Leonardo rarely showed any interest in her daytime activities. It was only ever their evenings in London that they shared.

'I'm going to a lunchtime talk Robin Holderness is giving at the Royal Geographical Society.'

'Then I'll come with you,' he said decisively.

It was the only sign he gave of his anxiety about what she might do next, determined, for once, not to let her out of his sight.

Astonished, she said: 'But I thought you considered Robin Holderness a bit of a clown intellectually.'

'Yes, I do... He's like all those tedious English logical positivist philosophers, incapable of relieving himself of the god of logic.'

'But he's American.'

'That only makes it worse. Same difference, same brand of silliness.'

Bianca remembers this with amusement now as she listens to Robin explain Confucius's disdain of logic. According to Leonardo, it was Robin's love of logic that had kept him intellectually tethered, as though to a ball and chain. Although reluctantly, she agrees with him... In fact, on the rare occasions she and Leonardo ever discuss anything, they always agree. It is just that they mostly shun serious conversation. Leonardo had looked at her, suddenly piercingly, smiling the wide magic of his delicious bruise of a mouth, the radiant eyes like moist, dark currants in his fleshy bun of a face, pomaded, curled ringlets of grey above the dashing turquoise of his starched collar. Now that he had finally told the truth, the shadows had disappeared, and he looked breathtakingly handsome again. He looked as he had when she first met him.

'Robin will probably expect them to put a blue plaque on the wall of the Royal Geographical Society now he has graced them with his presence.'

As full of doubts and dismay as she was, Bianca could never resist Leonardo's hilarity. They had ended up laughing ridiculously, deliciously together.

Now, sitting dutifully husband-like beside her, he scrutinises her every move. Alarmed by her extreme pallor, belatedly conscious of having hurt her, he feels unsure whether she can cope with his morning's terrifying cascade of home truths. Meanwhile, he makes every effort to concentrate on the meandering claptrap of that fool, Holderness.

Why did I ask him if he had loved those women? puzzles Bianca.

'Love' had never been one of Leonardo's words. In all the years of their marriage, he had only mentioned it once. It was 'respect' that interested him far more.

And what, she wonders, *is this mysterious tendency in women to give their lovers expensive watches?*

She too had given Stephen a luxurious watch on rediscovering him again, the only difference that he still proudly wears his, fifteen years later.

* * *

Robin lets out a deep sigh.

'Before I move on to the second part of my talk, revealing the renaissance Confucius's ideas are currently experiencing in modern China, and the reasons why, I should like to remind you of Confucius's belief in the importance of not making false promises. The superior man may only boast of his successes in retrospect, once a deed is done: *"A gentleman acts silently, before allowing his words to follow. Quick to act, slow to speak... Only trustworthiness in word and deed allows his words to be repeated..."*

'But now for the present day... while Confucius appeared to tiptoe carefully between ambition and morality, admiring social refinement, yet scathing of it, whenever at the cost of sincerity and morality, modern China appears to rejoice in it, to the point of greedy cultivation...'

* * *

Lounging untidily in his seat, one lean knee supporting an ankle, one arm extended intrusively along the back of the seat next to his, where an ancient professor sits huddled, Hesketh lazily surveys the lecture hall, taking in its lofty ceiling and air of high seriousness. He is feeling unusually optimistic and composed, despite still a little enervated from his past weeks of pent-up emotion, recently brought to a head in his furious row with Chloe, his mood now almost touching acquiescence. Looking about him, he recognises no one. This moment of silent quietude in the depths of his being feels like pure pleasure. His mind tracks everything Robin is saying but as if from a great distance. Other than the gravelled, broken cadences of Robin's American vowels, and the audience's occasional coughs, the hall is quiet. Yet to Hesketh, the room seems full of background noise, with Robin's voice faint against the din.

The loudness of thought? he reflects, relying on his connoisseurship of ESP.

He has come to Robin's talk in the vague hope of meeting B. Turvey.

Although how would I recognise her in all this crowd?

Partly, also, to gain insight into the opaque business practices of modern China. Hesketh is sufficiently astute to know that China will play an increasingly important role in the economy. He may have sold his original travel business to Thomas Cook and bought some valuable paintings with the proceeds, but he is not above plotting to start another travel agency, devoted exclusively to serving the Chinese, whenever their current visa restrictions should finally relax. It is one of the grand contradictions in Hesketh's nature, that the clever, business side of his brain remains miraculously unimpaired by the distraught scenarios infecting his private life. Plus neither side of his nature seems capable of acting as solace to the other.

He is dressed deliberately smartly in his new Yves St Laurent smoking jacket and trousers, and dazzling silk waistcoat, which he still regrets not being a lurex tank top. As a miniature concession to casualness, he has left the velvet bow tic at home. His stiff white dress shirt, open at the collar, reveals the tender meeting point of his lean torso with the ravaged, corrugated skin of his neck and jaw. Although exhausted, his mood is almost sober, the madness temporarily vanished from both his mind and body, his gait almost upright. Chloe and Bruno are back home again, the rituals of family life tentatively re-established, despite his and Chloe's recent row over the missing painting and the increasing worry of Bruno's epilepsy.

Nevertheless, the vicious lines carving the Brancusi oval of Hesketh's cheeks remain deeply indented, an air of plundered sorrow never quite deserting him. He listens sympathetically to Robin's attempts to decipher the enigmas of Confucian thought. His own obsessive interest in the occult has left him open to every new nuance of telepathy or mysticism. Without the riddle of Bianca in his life, he might have retained the brash pragmatism of his youth, but Bianca had become his education... his finishing school.

She taught me complex meaning, the need to transgress physical isolation with the power of thought... I should probably feel grateful to her, he reflects peacefully.

He knows she has changed him. In rare moments of acceptance, he also knows there is no way back. It is just that 'madness' was never his word for it. To him, his elevated state of mind feels more like a superb extra reality, soaring high above the norm; a privilege, despite its excruciating pain. Listening to Robin, Hesketh's whole being rejoinders effortlessly in the affirmation that he too has found 'the Way', promising to follow it faithfully to the grave. To him, in as much as he has ever consciously thought about it, fierce passion feels identical with morality, morality without passion striking him as mere primness. Yet he still has no conscious perception of having trespassed on Bianca. Perhaps because he had never been capable of acknowledging any division between them in the first place? To him, he and Bianca are, and always would be, one and the same; mere extensions of each other. Nor does he call his malicious acts of revenge ugly names, such as 'jealousy', 'lust' or 'pride'. He calls them 'LOVE'.

What else could they be?

For him, there is no debasement between thought and action where Bianca is concerned. 'LOVE' is possession. The compass of his emotions forces him to act like a pointer dog. Only rarely does he admit to himself that the goal he strives for so rigorously is not so much the certainty of being loved by Bianca as sexual possession of her. He wants the right to make love to her again. In fact, he demands it.

After all, isn't that what 'possession' means?

'Although I expect you would probably like to talk a bit first… and we might both feel a bit nervous…' These were the thoughts he had written to her in his letters. Not to mention: 'I remember the last time we made love…'

What Hesketh believes in, above all, is sex. Nothing else spells such eternal truth for him. And 'love' is a useful word with which to set about achieving it: 'All my love… Hesketh.'

Poor, sad, deluded Bianca. Who could ever have imagined she would so foolishly lose her way as to forget the magnificent truth of sex? Only to need persuading of it all over again?

Oh well, he thinks brokenly, *I live to fight another day*.

Yet despite his proud, high-wire performances at ESP, he has still not sensed Bianca, sitting further along the same row as himself… nor she him. Her back is turned, her entire being watchfully, almost protectively, focused on the suavely suited figure of Leonardo sitting next to her. Plus she is wearing a Russian-style coat, discreetly fringed with fur, and a vast black Cossack hat that crowds her blonde curls beneath a halo of spiked black fur. There is nothing familiar about her.

Hesketh strains to listen more closely as Robin starts to outline modern China's opportunistic rediscovery of Confucius's ideas.

* * *

More surprisingly still, Leonardo has not yet noticed Solange sitting distantly to his right. Nor had it occurred to him she might be there. Before discovering Maria Chandos's sleight of hand in stealing the chateau, his mind had been a palpitating bruise of anticipatory passion for her. But since reading the documents pressed upon him by Laetitia on his fatal journey back to Paris, he has barely thought of her. His mind, usually so forgiving, is full of anger. Rearranging his bulk in the too-narrow seat, impatiently following Robin's minuet of thoughts, he longs to be released.

What is it about academics? he ponders. *Why must they always talk in parentheses? Why not state their meanings straightforwardly, instead of this vested interest in obfuscation?*

Nevertheless, he is prepared to put up with the tedium, at least until he is certain his marriage remains intact. Until then, he is determined not to let Bianca out of his sight.

They had spent their entire morning together, something which only normally happens at La Casa, all his immediate thoughts focused on her, neither the chateau, his unfinished film, nor even Solange counting for much on his current mental screen. In fact, not until breakfast this morning had he known how deeply he cared for his wife, so used is he to enjoying a marriage he can afford to forget about for weeks on end, yet not risk losing; Bianca always there whenever he returns. Forever busily working and travelling, their marriage is simply another part of life's heady rush; one of the things he takes for granted, neither stopping to weigh either its pleasures or disappointments. Certainly he had never contemplated either separation or divorce. It is simply that, against the vast panorama of endless hard work, he craves the occasional freedom to do whatever he feels like doing: on that day, at that hour. But never with any malicious intent of inflicting actual damage on his marriage.

When, earlier that morning, he had self-indulgently treated her to the very confidences he had for many years kept elaborately hidden, she had said so very little. Yet as he watched the pink slowly drain from her cheeks, he had seen a fierce mixture of independence and resignation ignite in her eyes. And it was that look which had frightened him and fast-forwarded his thoughts more than any hysterical outrage she might have rained down on his head. In those few bleak moments, he had understood with perfect clarity that she was capable of leaving him. There was something disturbing, terrifying in her ready acquiescence to pain, as though not quite knowing who she was while simultaneously realising divorce the very last thing he wanted.

I married her, for God's sake, his mind suddenly raged.

Not that he thinks of Bianca as a possession exactly, in the way Hesketh does. But he does think of her as belonging to him, not to mention paid for.

Plus hasn't she always been the perfect playmate to return home to?

And now, rashly, in a fatal moment of adolescent boast, he had delivered these devastating blows, only to feel their backlash in his sudden, desperate fear she might leave him.

Normally, Bianca copes so effortlessly with just about everything I do...

He feels that deep well of panic the fondly unfaithful always feel.

Can't you see I'm still me? Nothing has really changed! he wants to plead, shouting it to the rafters.

Gauging Robin's audience, Leonardo knowingly compares it with his own audiences, yet observing from a strictly Italian point of view: *No* bella figura, he thinks disdainfully. *Just randomly respectable London bourgeoisie attempting contemplations of morality at the behest of that fool, Robin Holderness.*

It strikes him as laughable, his troubled mood momentarily replacing benign indifference. As for Solange, she currently belongs to another life, one which may or may not resurface later. Right now, his thoughts of her are tepid. All that concerns him is his marriage and his potential loss of the chateau to that duplicitous nonentity Maria Chandos...

I should never have trusted so masculine a female, he reminds himself, remembering some of the venomous things Laetitia had said about Maria looking like a man in drag. He has entirely forgotten having once boasted: 'Plain women are more grateful.'

Composing himself, forcing himself to listen a little more attentively, he suddenly realises: *If true, the things Robin is starting to say about modern China sound more intriguing... Perhaps there's still time for me to weave some of his ideas into my film?* serendipitously taking possession of every useful new idea that comes his way, while remaining scornful of the man delivering it.

* * *

Solange, on the other hand, had noticed Leonardo the minute he arrived, sending her tiny frame into alert. Her furtive gaze, constantly redrawn to him, pretends simultaneously to haughtily ignore him. She is annoyed, resolved to play hard to get, yet cannot resist peeking, to gauge the effect of her strategy on him. Her hand movements become ever more extravagantly attention-seeking. Draping one slender arm amorously around the bully-boy shoulders of Nicholas Rowe, she distracts her immediate neighbours by ostentatiously tickling his ears and running her hand through his thatch of dark hair.

'Treating him like a dog,' she overhears someone complain.

Undaunted, she is furious that Leonardo is here with Bianca.

Why didn't he tell me he would be in London? she seethes, beneath the spitfire of her strategy, starting to feel lonely and dejected.

Have I overestimated my power over him? she wonders tremblingly, remembering Victoria Falls.

It is too humiliating a thought to be tolerated. Although not having seen him since their weekend in South Africa, up until a week ago, he had rung her frequently from Paris. Then silence. Making the mistake of phoning his London secretary to ask for his number, she had been met with the immaculate courtesy of an exquisitely polite refusal.

'I'll pass on your message,' the secretary reassured her. But that was a week ago.

Perhaps he's met someone else…?

Tormented by paranoia and jealousy, there was the added impediment of having Nicholas Rowe in tow. To distract herself, she insists on retying his club tie, come loose at his throat, whereupon he looks up at her, both surprised and pleased, through watery eyes, betraying his age. Tucking her arm cosily in his, she savagely pulls away from this sudden intimacy.

'Shush,' people whisper.

Momentarily distracted by the raised arc of Solange's arm, Robin thinks: *Christ, that woman again.*

He turns away, so she is no longer in view.

'Let's now consider the legacy of Confucius in modern times,' he states carefully.

Almost back in his stride again, the lecture is now taxing him less gloomily, despite his feverish anguish over Beatrice.

Not long now... he thinks gratefully, his voice lifting as he embarks on his next point.

'Confucius had numerous students... of whom the most famous were Mencius in the fourth century BC and Xunzi in the third, each promoting vastly opposed aspects of his philosophy: Mencius keeping faith with Confucius's trust in the innate goodness of man and its capacity to guide ethically, while Xunzi extolled the pragmatic, materialistic aspects of Confucianism, celebrating a morality based on tradition and devout submission to rigid bouts of training, intended to act in parallel with the contradictions of 'legalism', things coming to a head in 223 BC with the Qin state's conquering of China... Confucius's ideas, subsequently abandoned, Confucian scholars were brutally murdered, and their books publicly burned...

'But in the succeeding Han and Tang dynasties, Confucius's ideas resurfaced again... the *Analects*, from 140 BC, faithfully acknowledged as representing official imperial Chinese philosophy, became required preparatory reading for all civil-service examinations, initiating a tradition which would endure until the end of the nineteenth century... Confucius is known as "the civil servant's philosopher..."'

Pausing, Robin judges the mood of his audience to be tired. Like him, they are anxious for his talk to end. Soon, for better or worse, he would know his fate with Beatrice.

On a sudden shrill note of euphoria, he asks: 'So, how did Confucius's ideas first come to influence the West?'

Bianca glances at him in alarm, wondering briefly: *What can be the matter?*

'It was Jesuit monks, stationed in China, who first translated

Confucius's philosophy into European languages,' he explains. 'In 1687, Father Prospero Intorcetta translated his life and works into Latin... Subsequently, the deists and enlightenment groups of the seventeenth and eighteenth centuries were sufficiently intrigued to attempt to integrate Confucian ideas with their own thinking.

'Even in recent, revolutionary times, despite being outlawed by the Communist Party, whose anti-intellectual leaders viewed them as a threat to modernisation, Confucius's ideas have revealed a curious, seemingly indelible durability... continuing to be studied secretly throughout the Cultural Revolution.'

Looking up from the lectern, Robin sees Byng whisper something to Beatrice, his mouth pressed close to her ear, and starts to lose the thread of what he is saying. *Is Byng kissing her?*

His mind reacts in panic, fighting to regain control. The audience cough, fidgeting uneasily in their seats.

'And now, finally, the story of Confucius's ideas in modern China...'

Robin chokes on a sigh. 'Chinese infants, as young as three years old, are being taught to learn and recite Confucius's sayings by heart.'

Bianca recalls the miniature schoolchildren of Fuli, with their features flecked in with black ink, calling out to Stephen and herself: 'Hello, how are you?'

'Modern Chinese parents,' Robin explains, 'again extol Confucius as the philosopher best known for promoting filial piety, wistfully believing that, even should these tiny scholars misunderstand Confucius's words, they will become imbued with his ideas and subsequently treat their parents with greater respect, this modern form of Confucianism sadly representing a last-ditch attempt to rectify a society whose values are fast spiralling out of control. A society in which corruption is rife, and all sense of familial and social unity increasingly abandoned to the greed of consumerism... Perversely, China's rapid economic growth, instead of bestowing freedom and emancipation, has left many feeling fearful and still less in control. Many cherish their memories of former authoritarian stability, even at the risk of reviving the ghosts of revolution and feudalism... The ancient rites again arrived to claim the soul of China.

'Yet the dispiriting truth is that, having lost the previously unbroken threads of Confucius's ideas to the brutalisation of revolution, few of these newly enthusiastic apostles are able to describe, let alone follow the philosophical core of his ideas... Instead, Confucianism has become a reckless mishmash of self-help proverbs that people tailor to their immediate needs... Nor does it help that the communist government having performed the sly volte-face of reversing their original antagonism to Confucius's ideas by now appropriating them serendipitously as a way of enforcing social order, meanwhile lending greater historical legitimacy to Communist Party rule.

'As for the parents of these miniature Confucian scholars, the seduction is obvious. They hope to raise a generation of obedient children who will neither neglect nor disgrace their parents. Plus something else... In a time of blatant consumerism, Confucian ideas have started to appeal to the new, fast growing class of "*Chi*", the very same middle class to which Confucius himself belonged... At last finding themselves with increased leisure, they beg to resurrect their long-neglected spiritual values, stolen by revolution.

'With Confucius's birthday now celebrated ever more lavishly each year in his birthplace of Qufu, his traditional values of filial piety and paternal authority have again turned full circle to become the foundation of a successful career, as well as the most successful method of rapid self-promotion... just as Confucius always predicted they should.'

Robin gives a shout of a laugh. 'As in ancient times, Confucianism still represents the perfect mantra for the ambitious civil servant...

'That's all. Thank you for listening...'

He nods formally to his audience, with a half bow. 'Thank you.'

Having reshuffled his dishevelled notes, he collapses his long corduroy limbs into a chair. Meanwhile, the chairwoman minces on to the podium to invite questions, a forest of eager hands shooting in the air.

'The gentleman at the back,' she says, pointing decorously.

One of her keen assistants scrambles upstairs, leaning across rows, to deliver a microphone to a diplomat from the Chinese Embassy.

Initially, the man's diplomatic effusiveness and waist-deep bows towards the podium disguise his resentment of Robin's irreverent tone, but it slowly becomes clear he suspects Robin of having made fun of Chinese politics, both ancient and modern. Yet his knowledge of English is insufficiently colloquial to be sure. Caught between anger and a diplomatic resolve not to show it, he resorts to ever more flowery politeness, in barely correct English but with those same disastrous flat vowels, like plates smashing, which Bianca remembers so well from her own trip to China. Leonardo also recognises the sound, but to him it feels more familiar, less alien.

At first haltingly, before suddenly hitting his stride, the Chinese embassy official delivers an opaque, ambassadorial defence of China's modern political system, the gist of which reveals his own subtext contempt for Western values over those of the upwardly mobile Chinese.

'In Shanghai...' he keeps reiterating. 'In Shanghai...'

Yes, in Shanghai, thinks Robin, *the buildings are taller, tallest...*

The man is now talking unstoppably. After ten tedious minutes, Robin offends him anew by asking: 'What was the question again?'

He had never before seen a Chinese man blush. The diplomat sits down abruptly, with a strange over-boiled look on his face, only to be immediately replaced by the next questioner, and the next; all seemingly representative of some society or organisation, giving them the illusion of privileged authority over all things Chinese. It soon becomes clear they had only sat through Robin's speech in anticipation of delivering their own lengthily prepared speeches immediately afterwards. Performing with the erratic rhetoric and desperate vanity of an out-of-work actor, one man sneeringly asks Robin: 'Have you ever even been to China?'

To which Robin is obliged to confess, 'No.'

Whereupon, a flurry of commotion invades the hall, as though Robin had just, himself, denounced any authority he may have had on Confucius, let alone China, even the timid, formerly admiring organiser looking at him askance.

'But I'm planning to travel there soon,' Robin offers lamely, his gaze now boldly directed at Beatrice.

'Well, if there're no further questions...?' the organiser suggests, embarrassed. 'It only befalls me to thank Professor Holderness profusely for his fascinating talk.'

Her voice in the microphone is a whisper.

The audience respond by clapping half-heartedly. Only Robin's robust gang of students clap loudly; some standing to gustily whistle cat-calls, while the more sedate among the audience look on surprised, fearful they may, after all, have missed some precious point in his talk.

Robin, laughing broadly at his unruly brood, thinks: *Thank God for students.... At least their minds are not yet tainted by respectability. Why on earth did I ever bother coming to this country in the first place?*

He is suddenly, disaffectedly furious with himself... even though it is now thirty years too late to do anything about it.

Getting to their feet, people start slowly collecting their belongings. Turning swiftly towards Beatrice, Byng says: 'Let's beat the crowds and get out of here fast.'

'Shouldn't we at least have a word with Robin... to congratulate him?' she demurs.

'Congratulate him? On what exactly?' Byng looks at her aghast. 'Good God, it would be too embarrassing.'

Undaunted, Beatrice holds her ground, Byng, meanwhile, taking a step back and regarding her with a stern amazement. Finally, shrugging Parisian style, he turns his mouth into an elegant moue and says: 'You talk to him, if you must. I've an editorial meeting, so I'll catch you later at home.'

Nodding automatically, she allows him to plant perfunctory kisses on her cheek, then watches him thread his way nimbly through the crowds; taller, blonder, more handsome than most, speedily greeting people with a handshake here and a kiss there, without once breaking his stride. Nor does he glance back, his mind already on other things. Eventually swallowed up by the crowds nearest the door, at that point she turns her face expectantly towards the podium, where Robin is deep in conversation with Jocelyn Carpenter.

Jocelyn had both loved and admired Robin's talk, particularly his unravelling of the laws of benevolence, to which, in legal terms, his entire career had been devoted to implementing. He is intrigued by any clue to justice that spells forgiveness. Robin is equally admiring of Jocelyn. Like himself, Jocelyn still believes in a successful welfare state, even if doing so was becoming harder by the day.

That was the principal reason I came to England thirty years ago, he suddenly remembers.

Plus the autocratic Robin had never yet felt bored by anything his friend had to say. So it is despite his absolute absorption in listening to Jocelyn that he nevertheless feels the sudden warmth of Beatrice's gaze upon him and glances away to meet it. Jocelyn, sensing his sudden distraction, looks up amazed to find Robin's haughty, haggard demeanour miraculously transformed, his gaunt features lit with pleasure. Following the trajectory of his gaze, he watches it fall fully on Beatrice, her expression matching his.

So, the recent rumours are true... Those two are in love.

Performing a rapid calculation in his head, having known Byng for more than twenty years and understanding both his strengths and various peccadilloes, he nevertheless estimates that Byng won't take kindly to the humiliation of being revealed a cuckold by Robin. Turning away to smile at his wife, he links his good arm with hers.

Thank goodness for Laura.

Their marriage had been a success. Never once had he felt tempted to stray from her side, as he so often had with his first wife.

* * *

Having abandoned her plan of playing hard to get, Solange is now pushing her way roughly through the crowd, desperate to reach Leonardo's side, while insisting that Nicholas Rowe tag along behind her. Leonardo has still not spotted her. It is Bianca who sees her in the distance and gives a friendly wave. But

Solange tosses her head, ignoring her, all her energies focused on reaching Leonardo. It occurs to her fleetingly that he looks unwell.

Is that why he's come back to London without telling me?

Bianca and Leonardo have risen to their feet but are unable to move. Bianca has exchanged places with Leonardo, to allow him to push ahead of her. But the people in front, many of them elderly, show signs of lingering, reluctant to join the turmoil fray in the busy aisles. For long minutes on end, the crowd is held in a static crush, unable to budge.

Hesketh, meanwhile, sprawls indolently in the aisle seat of their row. He, too, is reluctant to move but obligingly swings his long legs outwards, making it easier for people to pass. In no hurry, he relaxes back into his seat, enjoying the bustle and spectacle of it all. His and Chloe's long years of devotion to Bruno's needs have meant they rarely find themselves in crowds as large and spectacularly varied as this. The commotion alone would defeat Bruno. Nevertheless, one or two people squeeze past him, leaving only ten or twelve more, before a confrontation with Leonardo and Bianca becomes inevitable, Leonardo's pin-stripe bulk still concealing Bianca from his view.

It is the jazzy flourish of Leonardo's tie that first catches Hesketh's eye, its bright medley of colours matching those of his waistcoat. *Kindred spirits*, he thinks ironically without bothering to scrutinise Leonardo's face.

Suddenly spotting Jocelyn in the distance, Leonardo turns to wave at him. Too far away to make himself heard, he mimes an elaborate semaphore, confirming their meeting with the lawyers, the two men's operatic waving of arms starting to attract attention.

'Isn't that Leonardo Vescarro, the film director?' Bianca hears someone whisper.

'And that must be the famous QC, Sir Jocelyn Carpenter?' says another.

Unaware of the impression they are making, it is only as Jocelyn's gaze turns to greet someone calling from elsewhere in the crowd that his gaze finally alights on Hesketh again. Previously hidden by people bypassing him, Jocelyn had assumed Hesketh had already left. Now, foreseeing that Leonardo and Bianca are about to stumble on him, he panics. Reaching for his mobile phone, he wonders whether to call the police. Looking long and searchingly at Bianca, he hopes to attract her attention, but she remains oblivious. Plus she is too far away. It is Leonardo who notices Jocelyn's exuberant expression turn to one of dismay without being able to guess the reason why. Meanwhile, the crowds continue to shuffle slowly forward. Feeling increasingly helpless, Jocelyn decides, at the very least, to act as witness to whatever happens next. Turning to Laura, he instructs her: 'Have a pen and paper ready... I'll explain later.'

The earlier pantomime of air-born exchanges between the two men has also sluggishly aroused Hesketh's curiosity. He studies Leonardo's face a little more earnestly. *Who is he? Something familiar, but I can't remember why...*

He gets to his feet, half standing, only to fall back again from the pressure of the crowd.

Where have I seen that man before?

Slowly, slowly, a memory starts to flicker and surface.

Wasn't he one of Bianca's neighbours? That day I stole the letters from the postbox in her hallway? Isn't that the man I saw leaving?

An urgent thought filters his mind. *He must know where Bianca is!*

A sudden hurly-burly optimism invades his frame, invigorating him intravenously, like a drug. A few minutes earlier, he had been wearily, gently peaceful, that mood now instantly replaced by the madcap, rollicking hurry in his soul, with its vicious power to make nonsense of reason. As Hesketh scrambles to his feet, Jocelyn notices his torso slant to thirty degrees. It is what he remembers of him in court twenty years earlier. Clumsily catching his foot in a trailing coat hem, he is again tumbled back into his seat, his right hand straying tremulously to his mouth, concealing a sloppy grin. With this strange cocktail of desperation and heady optimism upon him, he is incapable of proper thought, his mind on fire. Every instinct dictates he must confront Leonardo and ask him where Bianca is hiding. Nothing else matters. Yet he deliberately bides his time, his distraught gaze never once deserting Leonardo's face, as he advances slowly, inexorably towards him.

Who is this man? he thinks furiously. *Why is he famous?*

Looking around briefly, people everywhere seem to recognise him. Leonardo's popularity starts to annoy him.

From the opposite side of the hall, Jocelyn watches mesmerised as the inevitable encounter between the three of them moves ever closer; only two more people to go. While Jocelyn holds his breath, Hesketh trembles from head to toe.

What if this man refuses to speak to me? he thinks blindly.

Blood thunders like music in his brain.

Peeking over Leonardo's immaculately tailored shoulders, Bianca has finally recognised Hesketh too. Instinctively, she turns on her heels, seeking an escape route. But there is none, their end of the row blocked, with neither access to an aisle nor stairs. The only possible exit is past Hesketh, the seating too high backed to clamber over. Even in her panic, Bianca recognises the distraught, familiar gesture from years earlier, Hesketh's tender nursing of his cheek whenever agitated, knowing it to be a bad sign. Leonardo is now almost level with him. It occurs to Bianca that not once have Hesketh's eyes left Leonardo's face, thinking chaotically: *He must know that Leonardo's my husband.*

Fearing a sudden attack, one of Hesketh's unpredictable bouts of viciousness about to be visited on her poor, unsuspecting husband, she has no idea how to stop it. Hesketh's lean body is tightly coiled, like an animal about to spring. She casts a distraught glance about her, dizzily wondering whose help she should call.

Would it be best to make a scene? Would the crowds protect us... the police get involved?

Suddenly, her distraught glance falls on Jocelyn Carpenter, only to find his look of fear matches hers. Intently, their eyes lock, and she sees that he too has sensed danger. After long years of careful dissemblance between them, there is finally only room for the truth. Despite the impossibility of speech, their faces eloquently acknowledge all that delicacy and diplomacy had so far forbidden them. Exactly as she had always suspected and feared, Jocelyn remembered her perfectly from those four disastrous days in his courtroom more than twenty years earlier. And now they are both in this vast lecture hall, where he can do nothing to help, other than watch impotently.

Things start to happen in slow motion… Gripped by terror, she watches the hand cupping Hesketh's cheek suddenly form into an aggressive claw, plucking at the cuff of Leonardo's jacket, her mind silently begging: *Please, please don't hurt him.*

Yet Leonardo appears not to have noticed. He moves on unperturbed, Bianca hearing a strangulated, half cry: Hesketh.

'Excuse me… Excuse me…' he croaks.

His fist now bunches the hem of Leonardo's jacket in a tug of desperation, his jaw opening and shutting on gobbled words.

'Please wait…' he pleads. 'Will YOU please WAIT? Speak to ME. Speak to me…'

His strangulated cries are an odd mixture of timid whine and pure aggression. He makes a stab at throwaway laughter, the ugly sound causing people to turn their heads… But not Leonardo.

Trembling from head to foot, scarcely able to maintain control, Bianca too is now almost abreast of Hesketh. Making one final, monstrous effort at calm, holding herself very still and erect, she forces her gaze away from Hesketh, out towards the crowded hall, hoping against hope he will not recognise her as she stealthily edges past him. Jocelyn, watching in the distance, continues to champion her with the sympathetic beam of his kind, unrelenting gaze.

Just as she is finally immediately upon him, with Hesketh still sprawled in his seat, Leonardo turns and smiles. Bianca witnesses the slow, sensuous elongation of his mauve mouth, followed by the familiar, happy shower of golden warmth from his eyes. He has assumed Hesketh is a fan, someone hoping for an autograph maybe. He is being gracious; a moment of pure distraction. With her face still deliberately turned from his, she edges past Hesketh's splayed knees, almost reaching the relative safety of the crowded aisle. Pale-faced, distraught, she holds her breath… at the very last minute of escape, her curiosity nevertheless too great. She cannot resist turning back. Despite her good intentions, she half turns, gazing at Hesketh in fascinated awe, despite everything, needing to know and confront with her own eyes the ugly truth of her hatred of him...

Suddenly, it is identical with that moment many years earlier, when Hesketh had accosted her outside the art college where she worked, every detail of him again appearing over amplified and exaggerated. That last time, she had witnessed each individual stitch of his clothing. Now it is as if only his face submits to the powerful magnifying glass of her scrutiny, every detail of hair, skin and texture precisely etched. Seeing beyond the spiked thinness of his dark, greying hair to his skull below, she witnesses each hair separately. She examines the sharply boned points of his Persil white collar, next to the grey, lunar wasteland of his throat and jaw, scarred with emotional decay; the papery folds of rough skin crumpled like layers of soiled tissue paper, curiously pinpricked by shaving blood; the grim, sculptural lines carving his cheeks, making sad mockery of the once handsome oval of his head.

Like a disfigured bust by Brancusi, she cannot help thinking.

She notices the thickened, pugilist distortions of his Roman nose, peppered with blackheads, contrasting with the terse, pretty moment of his rosebud mouth, opening before her fascinated gaze to reveal its chaotic tumble of tombstone teeth; the glutinous yellow streaks criss-crossing the bloodshot whites of his eyes, all too cruelly magnified by the outmoded, flyaway lenses of his glasses, providing an unlikely setting for the hysterical gaze of his golden eyes. His entire face strikes her as something as rugged and unyielding as pitted stone, yet somehow left to dissolve in floods of tears. She feels breathless with fear and repulsion. Yet throughout her leisurely scrutiny, Hesketh's eyes never once reach hers, his mind too obsessively in pursuit of Leonardo. Nor does he sense her presence. It is all too fantastic; all lines of telepathy finally broken.

Just as Leonardo turns back again, about to speak to her, breaking the spell, a swift, forceful disturbance disrupts the nearby crowd, creating turmoil. Someone pushes through, calling out: 'Leonardo... LEONARDO.'

He turns away again, Hesketh's eyes still pursuing him greedily.

As Hesketh starts to his feet, Bianca takes her chance to brush past him, this time not looking back. The crowd, formerly so static, jostles kaleidoscopically to alter its pattern, as a miniature figure, dressed in beguiling black lace, squeezes through the crowd to Leonardo's side.

For one full minute, he does not recognise her; she just seems vaguely, distantly familiar. Struggling to remember from where, all of a sudden he looks at her in amazement. Following fast on her heels is the boisterous, dark-haired giant, Nicholas Rowe. The whole dynamic of the situation is abruptly changed. The crowd surges forward, leaving Hesketh behind.

In his embarrassment, Leonardo barely knows what to say, either to Solange or Nicholas. Resorting to antiquated Italianate formalities, he bows deeply to them both. Meanwhile, Solange takes the opportunity to jealously manoeuvre herself into the already tight space between Leonardo and Bianca. Hesketh, now several people away, glares resentfully over Leonardo's shoulder at Solange. Catching his furious look and interpreting it as desire, she rewards him with a naughty, half smirk of flirtatious smile before again turning her attention fully on Leonardo, while haughtily flicking her wedge of peroxide hair in Bianca's face. Briefly, Bianca can taste her shampoo on her own saliva. Leonardo, having given another formal half bow, turns diplomatically towards Nicholas Rowe, effusively shaking his hand, with all the deference traditionally owed to a man one has recently cuckolded. But to Solange herself, he does not utter a word. Instead, his anxious gaze follows Bianca as she wriggles past him, placing her hand briefly in the small of his back and whispering hoarsely: 'I'll see you outside.'

He nods agreement. She then turns away, having just spotted the possibility of a faster escape route by going against the general downward movement of the crowd to climb upwards instead. Out of the corner of her eye, she sees Hesketh on his feet again, trying to force a path towards Leonardo. But he is too late; too many people now intervene, the crowd in turmoil. Following Solange's disruption, Leonardo is now surrounded by a seething knot of fans, some begging autographs, others anxious to engage him in conversation; some simply trying to push past.

Bianca wonders what Hesketh's interest in Leonardo can mean. Desperately fearful for her husband's safety, she nevertheless feels an overwhelming need to flee, to separate herself as fast as possible from the contagion that is Hesketh. She pushes on determinedly, annoying people with her ruthless, upward progress to the uppermost tier of the hall, where a brief, narrow corridor allows her to rejoin the crowd's slow shuffle downward by yet another staircase, promising to emerge closer to the main exit – one that Hesketh, by now, cannot hope to reach. Almost home free, she half turns; to her amazement, Leonardo is directly behind her. She had presumed him still with Solange and his gang of fans... No sign of Hesketh. Shielded by Leonardo's great bulk, they fight their way together to the bottom of the stairs, where the crush is greatest, converging in a scrum towards the main exit.

Waiting for them is Matthew, with his new gallery intern, Sebastian, who has arrived just in time to hand out leaflets advertising Bianca's exhibition to the departing crowd; her show due to open in ten days. Neither knowing, nor particularly interested in, either Matthew or his assistant, Leonardo turns instead to greet Jocelyn and Laura, who have deliberately hung back from the crowds to wait for them.

Jocelyn and Bianca exchange a long look of mutual understanding, Jocelyn placing his good hand reassuringly in hers. It feels like a benediction. His half arm is folded snugly out of sight, within the pinned sleeve of his jacket, rather than being allowed to flap freely, as she so vividly remembers it doing beneath his judge's silks in court all those years ago. Leaving them to talk, she turns smilingly towards Matthew and his new assistant.

'I need to rush off,' Matthew states impatiently, cracking his knuckles loudly and kissing the air either side of her cheeks. 'I'll leave you in the capable hands of Sebastian... He has lots of your leaflets to hand out.'

With a wave, he too starts pushing towards the door. Not one of them has, so far, mentioned Robin's talk, it seemingly having left no trace on any of them.

As they watch Matthew's compact figure bustle through the crowds, Bianca and the handsome young man smile conspiratorially, both amused by Matthew as well as immensely fond of him. Sebastian is a recent graduate from the Courtauld Institute, having studied medieval manuscripts before becoming an intern at the gallery. His father, a Nigerian diplomat, and Japanese mother are both anxious he should experience having dealt with the modern art market before seeking a museum post as curator. Still a little breathless with fear but unable to see Hesketh, Bianca assumes him, by now, to have reached the exit ahead of them. Nevertheless, as a precaution, she draws the young man a little to one side, into the shadow of a column, to stay out of sight.

'But what about the leaflets?' he objects.

'Oh, don't worry... I never much care whether people buy my work or not.'

'Matthew appears to care,' he rebukes her.

Bianca smiles. 'Yes, you're right, he does.'

Looking up into Sebastian's innocent features, full of youthful laughter, she finally starts to relax. Her hurried breathing stills as she deliberately sloughs the reptilian skin of Hesketh's madness from her mind, just as she has done numerous times before.

From their vantage point in the shadows, she sees Solange again approach Leonardo, this time more timidly, yet still with that strange, secretive smile on her lips, suddenly remembering Robin once having said: 'She has a cruel mouth.'

She then watches amusedly as Jocelyn politely but decisively rebuffs her on Leonardo's behalf, he and Leonardo now locked in earnest debate about the chateau, with Jocelyn refusing to be interrupted by small talk. For his own part, Leonardo remains silent and embarrassed, making no attempt to lighten the blow. In fact, anyone watching might guess that Leonardo was meeting Solange for the first time, so completely ruthless his strategy of extreme politeness. But Bianca is not fooled. She has seen Leonardo resort to this form of polite rebuff before; usually a last resort. She sees Leonardo turn anxiously, searching for her in the crowd, checking that she is still close by. And as his gaze finds her, Bianca's face responds with a dazzling smile, directed forgivingly at

Leonardo, before swinging joyously back to encompass Matthew's handsome young recruit at her side. All three of them, for different reasons, suddenly laugh happily. In Bianca's case, it is sheer nervous relief.

'You have an eyelash on your cheek… May I?' Sebastian smiles, leaning over her with his hand to tenderly brush it away.

It is at that precise moment, with Hesketh still caught, jostling distantly through the crowds, that he finally recognises her.

At first, he cannot quite believe it, so used is he to the deceiving chimeras of his own myopia. In certain distraught moods, he sees Bianca everywhere. Removing his glasses, breathing hard, before rubbing them vigorously with a crumpled handkerchief, he replaces them on the bridge of his nose. Yet it is impossibly, wonderfully true. Despite the disguise of her blonde curls beneath her wide-brimmed Cossack hat, her smile had given her away; that same smile he has dreamt of for years.

How could I ever forget?

He raises his hand in friendly greeting over the heads of the crowd, expecting, as always, that she will be pleased to see him. But she has already turned away to talk to the young man, who, with the robust height of his father and the delicately drawn features of his Japanese mother, is a distinctive, intriguing presence. To Hesketh's myopic gaze, the young black man appears to be drawing Bianca tantalisingly out of sight, into a darkly secretive corner. A pulse starts to throb visibly on his forehead. Racked by irrational jealousy, he immediately assumes the young student to be her lover. Anger floods his entire being, his chest convulsing violently in a sudden effort to breathe. He starts to feel nauseous, dizzily forcing his way through the turbulent crowds to reach her.

Bianca and Sebastian do not linger long in the shadows. Instead of handing out leaflets, as Matthew had expressly wished, he leaves them lying provocatively by the door, Leonardo, Jocelyn and Laura following them out into the street. By the time Hesketh reaches the exit, Bianca is nowhere to be seen, a surge of people preventing him from seeing in which direction they left.

Having said goodbye to Jocelyn and Laura, Leonardo and

Bianca hail a taxi… and by the time Hesketh fights his way onto Exhibition Road, they have all disappeared. Only Sebastian is just visible in the far distance, fifty or more yards away on the corner of Kensington Gore, standing hesitantly by the kerb, as if undecided which way to go. As the traffic lights change, he crosses the road, heading towards the Serpentine. He is now Hesketh's only lead.

* * *

As he had spotted him, Hesketh was opening the door to his car, parked untidily, illegally, directly across the road from the Royal Geographical Society and preparing to drive off. Ignoring the reprimand ticket flapping threateningly on his windscreen, he scrambles in the glove compartment, trying to decide whether to follow Sebastian by car or on foot. Unthinkingly relocking the car door, he chases after him, tracking his every move, while allowing his hatred to build up with each new step, every new glimpse of his dark complexion. He starts to imagine him making love to Bianca, teasing his mind with familiar, over rehearsed misery; the ever haunting, intolerable spectre of Bianca making love to another man. The late autumn leaves blowing in Hyde Park seem to mimic his thoughts, drifting lazily one minute and lifting in gusts of anger the next.

Slowing his stride slightly before turning right into Hyde Park, Sebastian drops down towards the Serpentine Café, where people are enjoying afternoon tea. Taking care to remain inconspicuously out of sight, Hesketh copies him, patiently waiting, meanwhile embroidering his hatred and anger, allowing them to expand luxuriously, poisonously, to take hold.

'You alright, mate?' a stranger suddenly asks, noticing his agonised expression.

Hesketh gazes back at him speechless and uncomprehending.

When Sebastian eventually gets up to leave, Hesketh follows him. Keeping a safe distance, he watches his quarry's light-hearted skip towards Kensington Gardens, while keeping close to the Serpentine's edge, at one point stopping to enjoy the squabble of ducks and swans, the fierce squawk of wings on water. Hesketh's only plan is to follow. He has no idea what he will do when – if – he catches up with him, his mind a blank beyond the obsessive need to follow.

Suddenly, dark clouds threaten the afternoon sunshine. It starts to rain, gently at first, followed by loud cracks of thunder and zigzag flashes of lightning that send the ducks and swans scudding and flying low through the sudden eclipse, turning day into twilight.

The heavens open in tropical downpour, and the previously languorous movement of walkers through the park ceases. People, whether singly or in groups, find themselves stranded and ill-prepared. Huddling disconsolately under trees, they wait, hoping for the storm to pass, the trees, grass and soil all smelling fresh and brand new. Sebastian starts to run, making a dash for the pedestrian tunnel beneath the Serpentine Bridge. Hesketh hurries after him... Once in the tunnel, shaking himself dry, Sebastian turns good-naturedly, smiling at another survivor from the storm, about to engage in conversation, when he is struck silent by the distraught menace in Hesketh's eye.

Although Sebastian is taller, younger and altogether more athletic, Hesketh easily overpowers him with the blind fury of his anger. In his pocket, he is carrying the long-handled torch, heavy like a truncheon, that he keeps in the glove compartment of his car, barely noticing himself pick it up. Sebastian tries to back away, attempting to break into a sprint back into the lashing rain, but slips, half sprawling in a puddle of mud. Hesketh is immediately upon him, remorselessly, ferociously unforgiving, his attack brutal. He leaves Sebastian lying broken on the muddy floor of the tunnel, heavily bleeding and badly concussed. The attack had lasted only seconds... Through his miasma of fury, Hesketh suddenly hears squeals of laughter and fast-running feet... More people, about to arrive to take shelter.

Later, from their vantage point under a tall oak tree, three people recall having seen Hesketh fleeing the tunnel, in the distance through the heavy rain, but fail to describe him convincingly. They remember him as tall, with darkish hair and glasses, but little else. One said he might have been dressed in black tie, another that he was wearing an anorak and bent double against the rain. Later, in hospital, when quizzed by the police, Sebastian can only remember Hesketh's voice and the dazzle of light on his glasses, amplifying the terrifying menace in his eyes as he bent over him, after he had fallen to the ground, and immediately before losing consciousness. He also remembered, last minute, having seen him once before but could not remember where exactly.

'At the talk maybe?' the policeman with violet eyes probed.

'No, in the West End, near the gallery... on the street somewhere.'

He also remembered the man repeating a name, over and over again, but cannot remember what it was:

'It sounded like "anchor"... Yes, I'm absolutely sure my attacker was someone I don't know.'

'Do you have any enemies?' the policeman asked.

'No,' he replied simply. 'But my diplomat father does.'

* * *

Although Hesketh appears to have got away with the assault, instead of defiant, it leaves him feeling distraught and frightened. For two days, he cowers at home, not answering the doorbell in case it is the police. He has crossed a line, a threshold of pain that he had thought long forgotten; banished to a past, belonging to his murderous attack on Patrick all those many years ago. That time too, he had attacked from behind. A premonition of terror grips him, in which the urgency to speak to Bianca, even if only for one last time, becomes as acute as it was twenty-five years earlier; before the court case, before Bruno, before his marriage to Chloe and success in business. Daily, mentally, bit by bit, Hesketh is breaking down. His doctor's advice to use breath control to stabilise his moods deserts him. His mind plummets into sick panics from which there is no escape. No amount of pills or antidepressants stem his anxiety.

He now barely acknowledges Chloe's existence. There is nothing she can say or do to pacify him. Although he continues to make love to her, it is as though with a stranger, all the while talking to her as though she were someone else and muttering angry conversations with himself, his lovemaking abrupt and self-serving. He purposely sets up a tape recorder beside their bed to record their lovemaking, which he then insists on playing back to her the following morning... Just once, he had called her 'Bianca' again.

Each morning, in his den of an office, he plays the recycled tape of Bianca spitting abuse at him. Bruno, unobserved, intrigued by this new strain of music, listens from the other side of the closed door.

'Do you imagine we've all spent our time becoming more unintelligent like you?' she asks mercilessly.

Shocked by the change in him, Chloe arranges for a psychiatrist to call on them at home; Hesketh, ridiculing the man's impertinent questions, estimates he already knows far more about mind games than this poor, deluded innocent ever would. He throws the man out, refusing a second visit.

And all this time, Bruno is suffering ever more frequent epileptic fits, each following the same pattern – his slender, boyish torso suddenly going rigid, then falling forward heavily, like a felled log, his brutal impact with the floor opening and reopening the barely healed scars crisscrossing his tender bow of a mouth after his last seizure. Fear of falling is also making him physically timorous. Bruno is less and less inclined to stand, let alone walk. Slowly but surely, Hesketh and Chloe's mysterious, handsome riddle of a boy is becoming unrecognisable, the haunting beauty of Bianca's portrait already left far behind.

Once it is clear from reports in the press that the police are pursuing diplomatic connections to Sebastian's Nigerian father over the attack on his son, Hesketh ventures out again, his days and nights again often spent outside Bianca's apartment, having at last realised his mistake – her apartment not sold after all. Now more than ever determined she will never again escape him, he pays the young man he has employed in the past to keep vigil over her, whenever he cannot be there. Listening to the old cracked tape of her insults, he reels beneath the pain her scornful words inflict.

No more laughter. Her words have begun to sound true... He also writes to her every day... letters to which, as always, she never replies.

Dear Bianca,

If only I had your telephone number, I would ring and ask how you are. Are you the same person still? Have you really forgotten all that we shared? It was not a fantasy but something truly special and unique. I can't believe your feelings aren't just as strong and overwhelming as mine. My feelings for you never disappear... But your Miss Dior articles sit like a dangerously ticking time bomb, waiting to explode in my mind.

You once complained that I was clinical and cold. Let me explain.

I had overheard you telling someone in the kitchen in Putney that we were planning to separate and felt angry and shocked. No such thought had occurred to me. I was desperately hurt but, like an idiot, didn't try to change your mind. I should have made a joke of it. Instead, I asked when exactly you would be leaving?

How stupid I was... It wasn't at all what I meant...

But by then you'd gone. I lost you... leaving myself forever empty, lonely and desperate.

I love you,
Hesketh xx

One morning, having stationed himself there as early as 6.30 a.m., Hesketh witnesses Leonardo leave the building on his way to Soho, in a taxi. At lunchtime, Max arrives to take Bianca out to lunch one last time. Back briefly from Ireland, he has rung to say he needs to speak to her: 'There are things I need to explain.'

During the intervening five hours, the bus stop's weather alternates between boisterous squalls and dazzling, white November sunshine. Having barely slept the night before, Hesketh's emotions are as dogged as ever, but his nerves shot to pieces... Vaguely aware of the disapproving glances of passers-by, he occasionally walks to the nearby crossroads, lingering there a few minutes in an attempt to fool them by mimicking normality. A middle-aged woman sidles up to him: 'Nice to see you again, dearie... Can I help you? You look a bit lost?'

Hesketh scans her kind, plump face, blinking back sudden tears. But finding nothing there he recognises, he turns away, muttering: 'I need to be alone.'

He has forgotten to eat... Sitting back on the bus-stop bench, his head in his hands, he feels faint.

Looking up again, he sees Bianca emerge from the house with Max. She hovers mistily before his eyes... Instinctively, he pulls the hood of his baby blonde anorak over his ears, making himself unrecognisable. She and Max are talking animatedly, both casually dressed: Bianca in jeans and Max in harem pants, topped by numerous layers of jumper, plus a paisley shawl wrapped high about his throat. Careful to keep his distance, Hesketh trails them to a nearby Indian restaurant. Suddenly, he recognises Max, remembering the haunting humiliation of finding him in Bianca's seat that disastrous night at the theatre. Not daring to follow them inside, he waits patiently for them to reappear.

In fact, Max and Bianca talk only fleetingly before leaving the restaurant by a side entrance; Max, en route to an urgent meeting and Bianca taking a taxi directly to her studio, without returning home... Standing in the rain, not having seen them leave, Hesketh waits another three hours, panic and resentment building in him.

Between bouts of dizziness, Hesketh's fevered brain now imagines her making love to both these men too. All the old vicious, murderous feelings he had felt exclusively in the past towards Patrick, the violent sensation that he must, at all costs, separate him from Bianca, he now focuses on them, pleading: *Bianca is mine, all mine...*

His bruised mind again argues that if he could just separate Bianca from the nuisance attentions of Leonardo and Max, then naturally she would be his again. Meanwhile, his thoughts have become a playground of lascivious imaginings. For years, he has imagined Bianca solitary and waiting exclusively for him...

How can such a large cast of people have entered her life without my knowing?

He feels both baffled and annoyed. In comparison with these new complexities, dispatching Patrick had been relatively easy.

He starts to visualise her sexually with first one, then the other... and, last of all, with himself. Speculating bleakly, thinking of his wealth: *Perhaps I should arrange to have them both killed... That hard-up young man might help me, if I paid him enough?*

Briefly fantasising whether or not he should have Bianca killed too, he recoils in shock. Such a thought had never really occurred to him before. He shakes his head in despair... It would not do.

If Bianca were to die, I would have to also kill myself...

So inextricably are his emotions bound up with hers that, as well as his tormentor, she has become his lifeline; the essential life force on which his energies feed for survival. Another thought detains him. Without Bianca, the single thing he has most urgently dreamed of all these years would never take place: the reunion; the happy, forgiving conversations. Above all, the fierce lovemaking, face to face again with his dream that is Bianca. Briefly, his mind bows in thrall to the thought, still fervently believing that, if only she were to look at him, talk to him, she would fall irresistibly in love with him all over again.

He starts to plot a trap; to invent a way of isolating her in a confined space from which she cannot escape until all the conversations he so desires are fulfilled. He instructs his young friend to follow her but discreetly; maybe even try to befriend her, to discover her future plans.

Two days later, the young man follows her into a delicatessen near her apartment, where she is on friendly terms with the owner's wife. With head bowed, and on the pretext of not having yet decided what to buy, he stands to one side, browsing the shelves, seemingly indifferent to their chatter. Time stretches elastically until, embarrassed by his own loitering, he is about to leave. Suddenly, the two women start to discuss theatre, Bianca mentioning that she is going to a production of a Eugene O'Neill play at the National Theatre the following night.

'Will you get there by Tube?' the shopkeeper asks.

'No, a friend is driving me there last minute... I'll dash upstairs to collect our tickets while he parks in the underground car park. We'll be running late, as he can't get away from his office any earlier.'

The young man, whom neither of them had particularly noticed until then, surprises them both by suddenly making a pantomime of having waited too long to be served. Replacing the jar of pickle in his hand, he flounces out of the shop... Two minutes later, he is on the phone to Hesketh.

* * *

The following evening, Hesketh lies in wait in the theatre's dungeon car park.

Wearing his anonymous, duvet anorak, a peaked hat pulled hard down over his eyes, his body rests uneasily at an angle of thirty degrees. Waiting by the lift, he scans every car, but it is an impossible task... Bianca may yet escape him...

Then, suddenly, she is running across the brutalist concrete flooring towards him. She is alone. Turning abruptly to face the lift doors, one hand shielding a foolish smile, the other pressing the button to call the lift, he can hardly breathe. Circumspectly remembering to pull his cap low on his forehead, she must not recognise him.

With the very edge of her mind, Bianca half registers the lone figure standing by the lift doors and briefly hesitates. She usually avoids getting into lifts with just one other person, whoever they are. It feels too intimate.

But this is the National Theatre, for heaven's sake... Besides, we're running late.

Stephen, still driving around in circles, is searching for a parking space.

What can possibly go wrong?

As the lift doors open in front of her, she and the man both step inside, the doors instantly sliding shut behind them.

It is his voice that alerts her first; that familiar, low-gravel menace, with its ugly multi-layers of sarcasm. Behind its derisive notes, the arrogant defensiveness of a man, who bitterly resents being shunned.

'Hello, Bianca...'

She turns towards him in panic, her adrenaline-trained mind immediately searching for clues to his state of mind. More deranged, more transparently maddened perhaps, yet he is not so very different from the way she had last seen him, a few days earlier, at Robin's lecture. *Although more obviously rough and ready... she reflects.*

Terrified, she backs away into the far corner of the lift... but it is the wrong thing to do. Hesketh thrives on fear. She watches it act upon him like a poisonous elixir, turning him both happy and unhappy at the same time.

In a few seconds, the lift doors will open, and I'll be safe, she calculates. *Stall for time... Keep him at bay.*

But madness does not need time, its bite instantaneous. Hesketh crosses the floor to where she cowers, leaning his arms possessively against the wall above her head, his body rearing menacingly above hers... No possible escape... Lowering his face on level with hers, his scandalised golden gaze scans her carefully, about to kiss her...

In close-up, she again sees the broken veins and crepe skin around eyes, gorged in tiredness. A pulse, throbbing angrily on his forehead.

'Are you about to subject me to more of your incontinent emotions?'

He steps back, startled. This was not how things were meant to be. Up until that moment, his mind had been vaguely at rest, luxuriating in its peaceful proximity to her; revelling in the delicious nectar of her perfume and presence.

'You no longer wear Miss Dior,' he complains, sounding bereaved.

He appears not to have noticed her insult, yet remarks, as if in answer to some unspoken question: 'I've heard it all before... What shall we do now, my poor Bianca?' he asks softly. 'What would you like to happen next?'

She is too astonished to reply. Easing herself sideways, she slides

487

her back against the wall to escape the arc of his body. But he grabs her by the wrist.

'Let go of me,' she shrieks, pulling away violently.

Seeing the look of repugnance and sheer disgust on her face, he feels suddenly frightened. It is the same look as all those years ago, when he had confronted her outside the art school, where she worked.

What if this doesn't work? What then?

His fear turns to anger... Jeering, discordant notes of mockery infect his voice...

'Who do you think you are? What makes you think it was okay to discard MY LOVE, all these years?'

The tinnitus is back, drumming in his ears. He barely hears her reply. In her gaze is pure contempt.

'Is that what you call it? Your LOVE?' she barks at him. 'Why then does it feel like HATRED? Year after year, you have made nothing but a sad mockery of our lives, with your abhorrent, corrupt emotions... Both your life and mine!'

Hesketh feels dazed. Nothing about her words sounds right; they make no sense. Nor do they match her face. Perhaps they belong to someone else?'

He raises a fist to silence her... Somewhere in the distance, an alarm sounds. He has been caught on CCTV.

'Listen to me, BIANCA,' he shouts. 'It's not yet too LATE. We can still run away TOGETHER. Remember the platinum ring I gave you? It was meant for eternity... You and me, always, ALWAYS together.'

'I threw it down a London drain, so as never to have to remember it again,' she replies hysterically. 'I thought it was where it belonged... in the filth of a London sewer.'

Hesketh's right hand strays protectively towards his cheek in a sudden hopeless gesture of tenderness.

Behind them, the lift doors open... Security men in uniform are running along the corridor towards them. Hesketh casts Bianca one last shocked glance before fleeing down some back stairs, into the bowels of the car park, the distraught sound of the alarm shouting in their ears, enveloping them in sound.

Although he manages to escape without being caught, Hesketh scarcely knows what to do next, where to go. He hides for an hour in the men's lavatories at Waterloo station. When eventually he emerges, he washes and dries his hands twenty times, witnessed in fascination by the black female attendant there. Rather than return to his car, left parked by the Old Vic, he catches a train to Battersea Bridge and walks back, across the twilit bridge to Chelsea Embankment.

Letting himself into their building, he stealthily climbs the stairs, instead of taking the lift, to ensure neither Bruno nor Chloe hear him arrive, and steps silently into the flat. Chloe is having a bath, and Bruno sitting on the floor, listening to the music of the lift, his mouth and nose badly congealed with blood. He had fallen that morning onto their bathroom tiles.

While Hesketh changes from his jeans and duvet anorak into his new Yves St Laurent black suit, the phone rings, and Hesketh hears Chloe answer it cheerfully on their bathroom extension. She sounds almost happy. He notices a small, square, heavily wrapped package leaning against the bookcases in their sitting room but does not stop to unwrap it.

Once dressed, he scribbles a quick note, seals it in an envelope and quietly slides open the lift's grille doors, then, picking Bruno up bodily from the floor, he holds him, struggling, in a sudden fierce embrace as the lift shudders slowly to the ground floor. As always, the pentagonal hallway, with its dusty accumulations of mail, is empty. Bruno rocks violently in his arms, making threatening, ululating sounds, deep in his throat. Hesketh has no real plan. He still does not know what to do.

I cannot leave him… Bruno needs me…

He places his hand gently over Bruno's scarred mouth to prevent him from making too much noise, all the while making soothing, clucking sounds with his tongue, telling him how much he loves him. His hand, he suddenly notices, is smeared with Bruno's blood.

With tears streaming down his ravaged cheeks, Hesketh still

cannot decide. Everything is pressing in on him... The impossibility of it all...

Nothing is as it should be...

He feels like a maimed animal, disfigured by the harm he has done both to himself and to others. Finally, he sees there can be no hope of reconciliation.

I was caught on CCTV... They will know it was me... the police will come... No matter what I do or say, Bianca will never forgive me.

It is a moment of perfect clarity, when indolent thought flashes into pure feeling... Although not quite... There is still something within himself which he cherishes.

I'm someone special, someone unique... he thinks erratically, remembering suddenly the recurrent nightmare of his youth in which his father had tied him to a railway track, telling him to prove himself a good boy before he could be set free.

Have I not always been good and true? he salutes himself. *I'll show you all yet,* he pledges bleakly. *In the end, they will all have to know the truth.*

He falls briefly in thrall to his own majesty, to the glory of being someone to be remembered and reckoned with. Someone undeserving of rejection.

I have loved deeply and been treated like a pariah for doing so...

The tinnitus beats loudly in his ears. Bruno squirms, struggling violently in his arms, threatening to scream. Hesketh makes a rash decision.

I can't leave him... Bruno needs me.

Depositing him, still wrestling, on the hallway refectory table, there is a sudden moment of silence between them as Bruno ceases to struggle. For the first time ever, he looks his father directly in the eye. Hesketh smiles and kisses him tenderly on his scarred mouth, Bruno's blood mixing with Hesketh's tears... Holding him very close, ever closer, Hesketh slowly crushes the life from him, still cradling Bruno's youthful body in his arms, his sudden stillness takes him by surprise...

Sobbing, he lays him out on the table. He looks so very small and boyish now, his dancing hands finally brought to a standstill. From his pocket, Hesketh takes a musical score he had bought a few days earlier, for Chloe to play and Bruno to copy, and gently covers Bruno's face with it. He then kisses his son gently one last time and lets himself out of the building, darting to the post-box before crossing the road and climbing the embankment wall. Fully clothed, he starts to swim, fighting the Thames' night-time crosscurrent tides in his desperation to reach the golden Buddha opposite. The lights from Chelsea Bridge twinkle and dance like spangled necklaces before his eyes, illuminating his way...

I am all alone...

But the current is too strong; his black heavy silk smoking jacket saturates quickly, dragging at him heavily, rapidly tiring and towing him to oblivion. His very last thought is of Bianca's scared face, her frightened eyes pleading with him not to hurt her as he raised his fist to her, while simultaneously spitting her defiant insults.

So, at the very end, his dream had come true... Despite the long years of contempt, he had finally made her feel the indelible truth of his love. In the end, he had done her some harm, just as she had always claimed on the tape recording. It was a strangely exhilarating and comforting thought...

* * *

By the following morning, the press had got hold of the whole story, with the police finally making the connection between the three crimes, linking Sebastian to Bianca and to Bruno. It was on Cork Street, outside the gallery, in the early hours of one morning that Sebastian had noticed but not particularly remembered Hesketh. The press showed pictures of Chloe, emerging pale and grief-stricken from her Chelsea home, still dressed, despite the November cold, in her favourite pink dress, overprinted with white feathers... plus another of Bianca, looking ashen, taken outside her studio.

The parcel, when Chloe eventually got around to sending it, contained the missing panel from Bianca's triptych. Even before that terrible night, she had decided to return it to Mathew's gallery... Bianca's finished portrait of Bruno now all that she had left of her son. In his will, Hesketh had left Bianca the deeds to his house in Majorca, and to Chloe, the remainder of his properties and estate, including his magnificent collection of British paintings.

Two days later, the postman rang Bianca's doorbell, demanding payment for an unstamped letter.

Dear Bianca,

From the man that did everything wrong, and doesn't know why.
With all my love,
Hesketh.

CHAPTER 25

In the end, Bianca is obliged to miss her private view of Chinese watercolours at Matthew's Cork Street gallery.

That morning, at 9.30 a.m., the phone rings. She is again on her own, Leonardo having left for Paris two days earlier, to begin proceedings against Maria Chandos. Despite his English lawyers' advice that reclaiming the chateau will involve a protracted legal case, he is determined to pursue it. They had recommended coming to some sort of compensatory financial agreement with her instead. But it is the principle, the dishonour of the matter that offends Leonardo most. In all the years of their marriage, Bianca had never seen him quite so angry...

As she answers the phone, exasperation infects her voice. She expects it to be Matthew again, fussing over details. He has already rung twice that morning.

But instead, it is the voice of a stranger; a south London female voice, slangy and slightly combative, yet aiming to be business-like: 'Bianca Johnson?'

'Speaking.'

'I'm ringing from Dalley's Court.'

Bianca is puzzled. 'I don't know any Dalley's Court.'

'Yes, you do,' mocks the voice. 'It's where your mother, Anya Johnson, lives...'

Bianca's heart skips a beat... Holding her breath tight, her mind flees in panic: *Is this the phone call I've been dreading?*

'I'm the care-manager of her block of flats,' the voice continues.

'We've been estranged for twenty years,' Bianca blurts out.

Her voice stumbles over the unhappy words, as though making a shameful confession, her heart beating furiously now. Feeling faint, she waits for the final axe of misery to fall on her hopes of ever seeing her mother alive again…

'Your mother was taken to St Thomas's Hospital by ambulance this morning. She's in Accident & Emergency,' the voice rasps. 'I asked if there was anyone I could call, and she said she thought your number was on a birthday card you'd sent her.'

Bianca thinks dizzyingly of all the birthday and Christmas cards, not to mention unanswered letters and gifts, she had addressed to her mother over the years, care of Lloyd's Bank in Berkeley Square, futilely wondering: *Which card was it?*

She has not known Anya's address since she left the rented flat in Highbury where she'd first moved years earlier to be close to her sister, Lettie. Simply packing a suitcase one day, she had walked out on both William and the cottage; their marriage, by then, had become a battlefield. Although she may not have really meant it. She had flounced out several times before. William, dutifully catching rush-hour trains home from Liverpool Street each night after work, though knowing the likelihood of another row, was expected to chase after her, begging her to return.

In less than a year of her moving, both Lettie and her husband had died of heart attacks, each within weeks of the other. But not before Anya had also quarrelled fatally with her sister.

'You're a bitter woman,' Lettie rounded on her.

The last time Anya ever saw Lettie was from a London bus. Clutching a Swan & Edgar bag, Lettie stood waiting at a bus stop. Covertly shading her face with a newspaper, Anya had noted Lettie's grey pallor but decided not to get off. Two weeks later she was dead…

Anya later walked out on Bianca too… Nevertheless, until recently, William had always forwarded her a monthly allowance via Lloyds bank. Then, suddenly, he stopped, in part feeling resentful of Anya's haughty, seigniorial refusals to ever once acknowledge the monies he sent her but also to flush her out of hiding, for Bianca's sake. He himself had no desire to see Anya again. They had both committed unpardonable sins, but driving to the cottage one day to deliberately saw through the water pipes and tear up thirty of his paintings, that he would never forgive. People, with their vexed, wayward emotions might not be sacrosanct, but paintings most definitely were. Yet he and Anya had never divorced, Anya having made negotiations too painfully vituperative to ever proceed. Not even the most Rottweiler-like London solicitor knew how to deal with the tumult of Anya's fury in those first, early years of their separation.

The south London voice is talking again... the hurry in Bianca's thoughts instantly replaced by fear. *What will she dare to say next...?*

Bianca sobs despairingly. 'Just how unwell is my mother? Can I hope to get there in time... speak to her still?'

The voice quickens, awakening to a new sense of drama. 'I don't know...'

Bianca declares brokenly: 'I need to rearrange a few things... Then I'll go straight to the hospital.'

Thanking the woman, she replaces the phone in its cradle. An escalating, sick excitement envelops her; a desperate, desolate longing to see her mother again, coupled with sheer terror at the prospect of another bitter row... of being told, as in the past, to 'clear off'.

'You're no daughter of mine... you unnatural creature.'

Dialling Matthew's number, she hears the rise and fall in his guttural voice as he quells his excitement about her exhibition and cedes instead to the immediacy of tragedy. Knowing how deeply affected Bianca is by her mother's absence, he rejoinders sweetly: 'I'm just so very, very sorry, Biaancaaa.'

Even over the phone, she can hear his knuckles crack.

Next, she phones Stephen. 'What a thing... How wonderful for you, darling... You'll get to see her again, after all.'

Reflecting concern, his breezy words hope to conceal the truth... That he despises Anya for her ugly performance at motherhood. Nor will he ever forgive either her or William for interfering so jealously and boisterously in his and Bianca's own youthful plans to marry.

How different our lives might – should – have been...

He had been planning to join Bianca later at her private view, then take her out to dinner. Instead, he now asks: 'Perhaps I should wait to hear? It sounds as though you may not get there yourself...

Just ring me, darling, whenever you can… And if there's anything I can do…?'

'Yes, I do know…' she replies gratefully.

* * *

Rolling effortlessly through London's mid-morning traffic, her taxi hurries down Park Lane, swinging widely past Buckingham Palace, then onto Birdcage Walk, Big Ben now visible ahead.

The closer they get, the more Bianca's thoughts tremble with anguish, terrified of what she will find after twenty years. She has always imagined her mother's life one of blight and unhappiness, to the point of wanting to match her own to it, in acts of penance. Yet as well as fear, she also feels determined. The sun dazzles directly overhead, making it impossible to see.

Beyond Westminster Bridge, the taxi ducks left off the roundabout to pull up sharply onto the forecourt of Accident & Emergency. As she pays the driver, her hands shake. Pound coins escape from her purse to scatter to the ground. She turns away, indifferent to their loss. Sensing her distress, the driver eases from his cab to chase after the runaway coins and restore them to her. Smiling nervously, she whispers: 'Thank you…'

'Best of luck,' he says and smiles, driving off.

At first, she cannot find a way in, the forecourt full of ambulances but without drivers. No one to ask. Composing herself, she deliberately searches for signs and directions; her panic mounting. *Am I too late… even to say goodbye?*

A man in overalls emerges through an entrance of rubberised flaps.

'Accident & Emergency?' Bianca asks, consumed by fear.

'Yes, in there,' he replies, indicating the rubber curtains.

And yet, it seems unlikely…

'Shouldn't there be a sign or reception desk?'

Slipping between the nicotine-stained flaps, she finds herself in the old part of the hospital; in a barren room, with scored lino floors, and layers of cream gloss, covering ancient brickwork. Faded, medallion-print curtains, strung on to tall metal frames, roll on castors the size of tennis balls.

There is a terrible silence about the place. No one in attendance. Bianca stands irresolute and alone, about to retrace her steps to the outside world of driverless ambulances when a robust Irishwoman appears, her hips and breasts rotating seemingly independently of her starched blue uniform.

'I-I'm looking for my mother, Anya Johnson,' Bianca stutters breathlessly. 'I was told she was brought in here early this morning.'

Scrutinising the woman's face, determined to miss not a clue, she steels herself against the hangman's noose of irrevocable knowledge...

To Bianca's amazement, the woman replies, 'Yes, she's in here,' indicating a screen to their right. 'I'll just let her know you're here.'

Bianca's heart flutters, beating fast.

How strange... No reception, no forms to fill in... Just my mother, ALIVE...

No time to hesitate or worry... Just the immediacy of now, lying there beyond the primitive gathers of a makeshift screen. The nurse emerges smiling, ushering her in... Bianca walks in on tiptoe.

In the bed lies a miniature figure with matted, shoulder-length, white-gold hair, loosely wrapped in a robe of the same medallion print as the curtains surrounding her.

How strange, thinks Bianca, with her painterly eye, *to match patients to their curtains.*

'How have you been?' asks the darling, timorous voice from the bed.

At once so immediately right and unforgettable, Bianca tiptoes to her bedside, arms outstretched. Tenderly kissing a face streaked with grime, she looks into bright blue eyes, surfacing through tangled hair and nests of anxious lines... Anya looks like the once glamorous fairy from a Christmas tree, now grown a little dilapidated and shabby but still beautiful.

'I've been lying at home in bed, unable to get up, unattended for four days... The nurses burned the clothes I arrived in,' she explains shakily. 'What will I wear to go home? I feel completely suicidal,' wails the familiar, wistful voice, clutching at her daughter's hand.

'I shall bring you new clothes to wear,' Bianca says, smiling reassuringly.

How well Bianca remembers her mother's hands... hands that

had woven cats' cradles and made glove puppets for her as a child; hands that had made elegant, dancing shapes against the diamond-pane windows of the cottage; rarely still, always eloquently placed. The same hands that had stroked the length of her arm while adjusting the lie of a sleeve in some garment she was making for her, with her clever, dressmaking skills.

'But how have *you* been, darling?' Anya suddenly asks.

Darling... Her voice is like an elixir... Bianca can feel her whole being spooning it in like honey.

'But what's wrong?' asks Bianca gently. 'Why have they brought you here? What do the doctors say?'

'I don't know.,, The warden found me. Apparently, I've been ill for at least three days.'

Her voice is small and fragile. Starting to look agitated again, beneath her swathes of blanket, Bianca suddenly notices that one of Anya's legs looks much larger than the other.

'Your right leg is swollen,' she remarks. 'I'll find a nurse.'

Her mother's blue eyes lock painfully with hers.

'Don't worry,' she promises. 'I'll be right back.'

Finding the Irish nurse, she explains they are still waiting for the doctor to return with Anya's results... but that she almost certainly has an embolism, a blood clot in her right leg.

'How much danger is she in?'

'No immediate danger...' The nurse hesitates. 'Difficult to say... but her condition is, nevertheless, serious...'

Bianca dives back behind the screen to find her mother smiling joyously, welcomingly at her.

How strange and perfect it all is...

Exactly as she had heard countless people describe... All that pain and fear... all that terrible distance and hostility... yet suddenly as if none of it had happened. Seamlessly, rapturously reunited, as though nothing had ever truly separated them in the first place. Barely the need to catch up, their conversation flowing, as if the last time were yesterday, rather than twenty years earlier. Bianca pulls up a chair, settling as close to Anya as she dares, without leaning too heavily on her miniature frame, meanwhile resolving, *There can be no more misunderstandings...*

She decides to tell Anya everything about everything... but, above all, about William. Beginning right away, while they wait for the doctor to return, she starts to explain, thinking gloriously, 'My perfect mother... My adorable, darling mother... What heaven!'

* * *

'Tell me again about the woman who turned brown?' Anya often asked in the days and weeks that followed.

'The woman who turned brown' was William's secretary, who became his lover, and for whom he left Anya. Bianca was barely out of school at the time; it had also coincided with the break-up of her engagement to Stephen. All that had for so long felt fixed and secure dissolved within a matter of weeks into sheer chaos. Bianca remembers the increasing volatile bitterness and violence of her parents' fights, with knives produced and furniture thrown; had never forgotten her shock at seeing her father's chin weep with blood as Anya had jabbed at him with a kitchen knife. Just once, in her immense fury, Anya drove one of the baby Simcars at him. Eventually, Bianca felt she no longer had any right to intervene as peacemaker between them. Especially since she was herself about to leave home; her diplomacy, in any case, never achieving more than a few days' respite from their constant rowing.

At first, she knew nothing of William's affair with his secretary; William later claiming the last straw had been paying for a lavish holiday, touring the ancient, archaeological sites of Turkey, with Anya refusing, last minute, to accompany him, having declared: 'I never again want to go on holiday with anyone as tedious as YOU.'

At the time, Bianca refused to take sides. She loved them both. Anya, nevertheless, became increasingly unforgiving towards her. She wanted Bianca to condemn William out of hand; to cast him from her life too.

In the end, it was Bianca, who was 'cast out'. Not just by Anya, for being an 'unnatural daughter', but by William too, for being an irritant in his new love affair with a woman only a few years older than herself. He indulged this new passion by remembering that Bianca was probably not his child and therefore no longer his responsibility. Bianca, meanwhile, learned the cruel lesson that a refusal to take sides risks losing both sides. She was too young, too inexperienced, also herself a little too wilful, to know that Anya was right. Also, still too young to have experienced the depths of grief that might have taught her to recognise her mother's truth. Plus Anya's habit of losing her temper over every slightest thing had become simply repugnant. William referred to her as: 'My little dose of strychnine.'

Despite her immense capacity for charm, intelligence and femininity, Anya wilfully sabotaged any sympathy for her plight by making it almost impossible for anyone to like let alone love her. Her wonderfully rich, clever, varied personality had dwindled to a single, angry facet of itself... Yet it was sympathy that she both needed and deserved... Bianca knows that now.

Fifteen years after their affair began, the woman William fell in love with awoke one morning to find herself transformed into an Indian begum, overnight her skin having turned deep brown. Her new boss, having an international business to run, quizzed Bianca impatiently over the phone: 'You mean she has jaundice?'

But her condition was far beyond jaundice. Only the whites of her eyes shone bright, lemon yellow. No one, least of all William, knew she had been a secret drinker... Throughout it all, she had retained her super efficiency at work. Perhaps not even knowing it herself.

'Yet there must have been symptoms?' someone later remarked.

No one had ever seen her drink more than two glasses of wine... Only later did it transpire those two glasses had been laced with vodka. As her liver and kidneys finally rebelled, crying out for help, her body performed the strange litmus test of turning itself brown. It was a daring strategy but already far too late... Taken directly from her doctor's surgery to hospital, she died there three weeks later.

Stricken with pity, Bianca visited her every day. William, again based at the cottage, visited as often as he could. It was like watching a piece of fruit over ripen, then rot and finally decompose... A terrifying, cruel death... Yet Anya loved to listen to this tale, over and over again, like a child listening to a favourite bedtime story, her blue eyes full of starry wonder at the sheer mystery of life's reversals.

William, like Anya, ended up living alone, his retirement days spent in solitude at the cottage, where every morning he took a new sheet of expensive Whatman paper, bought especially for him by Bianca, and performed the magic of new wolf whistles at the Essex countryside. Once again, he became the severe bohemian of his Fitzrovian youth; a man whose only creed was the discipline of painting, and whose only craved audience was Bianca. The wolf whistles were intended exclusively for her; he felt no desire to exhibit.

William, the father and friend of Bianca's childhood, had finally returned to her. Although there were still odd days when he would turn towards her sadly and say: 'I think you have my eyes.'

Despite having counselled Bianca at the age of six, 'We don't believe in God, but you can if you like,' he now began to delight in daily readings from the Old Testament, the girl-next-door ambitions of his mother completely vanquished. The bourgeois dream, with its chimera of false notions of respectability, had revealed to him its feet of clay, just as he originally suspected. His new advice to Bianca was: 'Whatever else you do, don't try to be nice.'

* * *

Having moved Anya to Intensive Care, as a team of eager young doctors crowd round to examine her, Anya insists Bianca be allowed to stay, to watch in fascinated wonder as her mother's naked body gently unfolds before their inspection. Her skin is pearly and unblemished, neither withered nor creased; her breasts round and firm. Slender still, she looks like a young girl. It is only her extremities which give away her age; her hands, although elegantly gesturing, now gloved in loose folds of veined skin. With the blankets thrown back, there is also the shock of realising that one of Anya's feet is like a little cloven hoof, all those expensive high heels by Pinet having taken their toll. One of her middle toes had 'diverted', plaiting itself at right angles to her other more forward-looking toes.

Her rescue proves touch and go. As feared, the embolism in Anya's leg moves to her lung, where it is in constant danger of shifting position to ignite with her heart. In those first, early days Bianca cancels absolutely everything: work, painting, dinner parties, even her planned trip to Siena with Leonardo; Matthew's gallery and her exhibition equally forgotten. When, finally, Anya is discharged, she sets about nursing her in her own flat, realising that what Anya needs, above all, is the reassuring familiarity of her own surroundings.

The taxi delivers them to an address just north of Trafalgar Square, a street Bianca had unknowingly walked down numerous times before. And there, in Anya's student-like flat, are her clothes, left to dry, cooking to a crisp on the radiator next to her raspberry-pink chair, ready to put on, just as she had repeatedly described, while in hospital.

'My pink jumper and black trousers... I can see them now...'

Bianca smiles, the jumper bright pink, the colour of fuchsias, thinking fondly: *My precious mother... never afraid of colour.*

This had been Anya's home for the past seventeen years, Bianca remembering some of its furniture from the flat in Highbury; the same bright Prussian blue and turquoise of the sofa and curtains, the whitewood coffee tables and bookcases spilling with books and newspaper articles. Bianca picks up a sheaf of papers close to hand, only to find them written by Aubrey Byng. She also recognises the gigantic pottery vases in the shape of *Commedia dell'arte* heads she and Anya had bought years earlier together on holiday in Taormina. Above the television, is Anya's altarpiece of art historical imagery, crudely Blu-tacked to the wall.

Most poignant of all are the desiccated remains of dead flower arrangements.

'Your flowers have all died,' Bianca says, about to remove them.

Anya stretches out a hand to restrain her while lovingly tweaking the brittle stems into more satisfactory display.

'But they're dead,' counters Bianca, mystified.

'These are the flower arrangements you sent me,' Anya explains. 'I never wanted to throw them away.'

Bianca can feel tears welling, emotion rising hard in her throat, threatening to drown her composure. It was like touching a bruise, too deep to have known it was there. As well as having addressed cards and letters to Anya, care of her bank, she had occasionally, optimistically pressed a £50 note into the hand of some youthful bank teller, pleading with him to arrange for a lavish bouquet of brightly coloured flowers to be delivered to Anya's secret address, the notes representing simple acts of faith on Bianca's part. She had no way of knowing if the flowers were ever sent.

Perhaps the bank clerks simply pocketed the money?

It had hardly mattered… It was her attempt to send the flowers that counted for sincerity. And here, while her mother looks on fondly, is her reward. Their cherished, desiccated remains, having represented a talisman of mutual faith for Anya too. So much so that she refused to throw them away.

Bianca puts her arms around her mother's slender frame, hugging her tight, her ribcage as fragile as a bird's…

'What shall we do now, darling?' Anya asks brightly, looking about her, delighted to be back home.

That sound of her mother's voice, calling her 'darling' in that exact sweetness of tone, would never again desert Bianca. It was like a balm to an injury whose depth she had never quite known how to plumb.

* * *

Their happiness lasts precisely eight months, by which time it is high summer and the weather unusually hot, every day beginning with ferocious bursts of sunshine…

Much has happened… Leonardo's lawsuit trails laboriously through the French courts, he and his lawyers having mistakenly estimated Maria Chandos too poor to fight the case, it not occurring to them she might persuade a wealthy backer to sponsor her in return for a share of the eventual sale of the chateau. Leonardo, meanwhile, is determined to enjoy the chateau while he can, as well as to enhance his current 'nine-tenths' possession of it. Having changed all the locks, he has temporarily set up camp, using it as both his work base and principal home. Laetitia and Bertrand are with him, plus ill-assorted guests, Laetitia busily throwing the parties she always dreamed of. Yet all this in disguise of the single, most important thing… That the chateau must never be left unattended, at least one of them to always be in residence. To some extent, they are now little more than luxurious squatters.

Leonardo's new film is scheduled to be shown later in the year at the Venice Film Festival, its editing completed in Paris, where Leonardo travels regularly for meetings with lawyers, the eventual outcome of his efforts to repossess the chateau still uncertain.

Although also occasionally returning to London to see Bianca, he has never yet once invited her to join him at the chateau, not even for a long weekend. Since her mother's reappearance, he no longer fears her leaving him, knowing her too preoccupied to do so. Beatrice had phoned one day to explain that she and Robin were currently holed up in his Soho garret, while waiting for her divorce to come through. In the end, Byng had insisted on divorcing her. She and Robin then plan to return to America together. He has secured tenure for himself at Berkeley. She had also rung to report the tentative rumour that Solange may have spent a week, among other guests, at the chateau with Leonardo. But Bianca is not sure she believes it. She knows the rumour will have come via Robin, who had always hated Solange.

Meanwhile, La Casa, in Siena, stands neglected, despite pleas from its custodians, the Mazettis, begging them to come and stay: '*Venite, venite. Per carita, venite…*'

It is as though Leonardo and Bianca's marriage has taken a gigantic swerve. For Leonardo, that swerve has meant reclaiming the chateau; for Bianca, the all-important reclamation of her mother's love. Although Bianca occasionally misses her lazy evenings of domestic life with Leonardo, her daily existence is too focused on her mother to allow for much else. The one, true constant of her life is Stephen… and he, strangely, the only subject she has reticently refused to share with Anya, without even herself quite knowing why.

As for Max, Bianca had waved to him recently across the heads of a bustling theatre foyer, their eyes briefly locked in mutual understanding, before being swept aside by the clamour of the crowd… But their last proper conversation had been that day at the Indian restaurant near her apartment, when Hesketh had followed them.

That day too, Max's dark eyes had danced in fierce engagement with hers, while seeming to contain some mysterious plea, again instilling the unsettling sensation that he wanted – even expected – something from her. And she, as always, with no precise idea of what that might be had felt swept away on the tide of his misunderstood emotions. He was dressed as he had been that first evening they met in the hotel foyer, in a formal Armani suit, rendered last minute bohemian by his halo of tangled curls and the throwaway gesture of a bright red scarf, his mood throughout lunch emotionally demanding, yet curiously evasive, as though trying out various topics of conversation on her, as a prelude to the main course.

Eventually, simply confronting him, she asked: 'There's something different about you… Intangible, but different.'

He tried to defer the moment… remarking mysteriously: 'This is not what I intended.'

Slowly, reluctantly, he talked about Ireland… about falling in love with an island… about meeting a young Irishwoman… Until, finally, the truth: 'Sinead's carrying my child… Up until now, I'd never really considered children in my life…'

As he spoke, he watched Bianca closely, his eyes chasing hers for a reaction to his words, reluctant to let go. He clearly expected it to be extreme, distraught even… Long shafts of silver earrings danced lights either side of her pale, delicate features, her abundant gold curls tied back loosely with shoelace ribbons of black velvet. He could not remember ever seeing her look more beautiful.

'How slender you are,' he murmured.

Yet nothing could have been further from the truth… Briefly tearing her gaze from his, Bianca immediately returned it, serenely smiling. Offering him her congratulations, his eyes fell first beneath the faraway gaze of her scrutiny. Impossible to guess her thoughts, it was as though she had absented from the table, leaving only a phantom of herself. She then continued to chatter about other things, the whole episode leaving Max feeling vaguely humiliated.

Yet it was true that Bianca had felt nothing. Instead, a great cape of sorrowful misunderstanding had suddenly slipped from her shoulders, never to be picked up again. Her mind had performed a volte-face, turning tail on both Max and any thoughts of his child. Far from distressful, it felt like the last piece in a jigsaw. Everything finally in place. No longer was there any need to torture herself with a haunting sense of Max's expectations; expectations she only half believed in and never properly understood; his words releasing her from a strange, indefinable duty. Free, finally, to go on her way.

Even the idea of the child he was expecting left her strangely untouched. Her congratulations were sincere, her feelings very different from the hopeless dismay she had felt on learning of Leonardo's scattered nursery of infants. It was as though, on the question of children, her capacity for despair had already been exhausted... Nor did she mention his unfinished portrait.

It was Max who brought it up: 'Shouldn't we arrange more portrait sittings?'

Bianca studied him gently. 'Why don't we just leave it for the time being? There's no particular urgency, and we both have plenty of other work to be getting on with.'

A flash of dismay distorted Max's features; he felt summarily dismissed.

Bianca, immediately taking pity on him, said, 'Alternatively, I could finish the portrait using some photographs I took surreptitiously when you were last at the studio?'

Remembering Bruno, an involuntary sob suddenly invaded her throat; Max assumed the sob was for him.

'You could then review the portrait, just before its final stages... Wouldn't that suit your timetable better?'

Baffled, Max had nodded slowly, feeling numb, Bianca, meanwhile, remarking brightly: 'I hear your new play opens this autumn?'

A few days later, Max had found himself writing her a strange, impossibly difficult letter, almost one of condolence, on learning the news of Hesketh's death... yet failing to mention that Hesketh's death also represented the vanquish of a central character in his new play.

* * *

Meanwhile, with Leonardo ever more absent, Bianca and Stephen spend more and more time together – visiting art galleries, seeing films and plays and, most favourite of all, dressing up and eating out. They also spend long, luxurious hours making love. They are like eternal, unashamed survivors, forever ducking and diving, while remaining poised and ready to cede to the needs of others. Part of their secret with each other is honesty. No truth, no matter how unpalatable, ever banished between them. No dissembling allowed.

* * *

Since leaving hospital, Anya had never been back to The Society in Queen Square. Content to spend her days with Bianca, she sits in her raspberry-pink chair, eating smoked salmon and reminiscing about the cottage, while glancing fondly at Bianca. Rediscovering her daughter had been a revelation. Just as Bianca had falsely imagined Anya lonely and unhappy during their long years of estrangement, Anya had imagined Bianca weak-willed and living under the cosh of some tyrannical boyfriend or husband. She had once accused her of 'being frightened of life'.

How then to explain the immense surprise of meeting a woman who, to her maternal eyes, still looked girlish, who dressed elegantly and appeared serenely in control? It had been like falling in love again. Not with a man, but with her own daughter. She could no longer remember the reasons for their former hostilities. Every nuance of the great charm and femininity with which she had once caused men to fall in love with her, she now applied seductively to Bianca. Bianca's expectations were equally reversed… Far from irretrievably lost to anger and bitterness, Anya, in those absent years, had regained all the equilibrium, intellectual excitement and delicious charm of the mother she had so devotedly loved as a child.

Plus Bianca holds the key to Anya's other lost love, William… Listening to Bianca's tales of him, she starts to dream of loving him again; in Anya's mind, the story of her life, turning full circle.

507

Nevertheless, as she regains strength, Bianca is concerned that Anya might be missing old friends. Yet she has no precise idea who they are nor how to contact them. Anya's past twenty years remain a blank. Occasionally, letters arrive at Dalley's Court, addressed in primary-school handwriting, but to Bianca they are just names, with no reference points. Meanwhile, Anya argues dismissively: 'Besides, they aren't real friends.'

The more interesting letters arrive from abroad: Bulgaria, Mexico and Paris.

'I only need you, darling. Sitting here, reminiscing about the past... there's nothing more that I want.'

Walking arm in arm one day around Temple Gardens, Anya suddenly breaks free to talk to the young flower seller outside Embankment Tube. Standing to one side, just watching, Bianca is startled to hear her mother say: 'I'm unlikely to see you again, as I'm moving to the country.'

Catching her shocked expression, Anya blushes, explaining: 'I used to buy flowers from his mother.'

Still concerned, Bianca suggests accompanying Anya to The Society one Sunday, to reunite her with old friends. They catch a bus in the Strand, where Andreas used to wait for her; he, having months earlier, given up hope of finding her there. He, too, had written once but got no reply.

Both dressing thoughtfully for the occasion, with Anya neatly elegant in a black lace blouse over black slacks, and Bianca dressed for high summer, in a cream linen jacket and trousers, it is mid-May, ten days before Anya's birthday. Anya nods approvingly. 'That's right, darling. It's good to see you in pale colours.'

Fascinated just to observe, Bianca tracks Anya's progress among her old friends, hoping to fill in the blanks. Some are intrigued to see her, others plainly resentful of her reappearance. One or two more simply indifferent. Watching in wonder, as Anya sloughs off her recent pall of ill health to rise to the occasion, as beautiful, charming and sophisticatedly mondaine as ever, it is exactly how Bianca remembers her years earlier, dancing in William's arms in some nightclub or other. At the coffee break, following the morning's talk by a former headmaster of Eton, she notices how it is still the younger men who respond most to Anya's charms. As in the old days. There is something in her fierce mix of intelligence and femininity which draws them to her. It is not that they are deceived by her age but that she carries some indefinable spirit of youth with her.

She could deliver lessons in youthfulness to thirty-year olds, Bianca reflects admiringly.

Embarking on a fierce political debate with the young man with a caste in one eye, who habitually sits in the front row, so as to be the first to harangue any speaker, Bianca suddenly hears Anya state sternly: 'Define your terms…'

Giddy laughter from the past bubbles up in Bianca. This is Anya as she was in the old days at the cottage, before the tragic death of her own mother, when the precise definition of a word would occupy her and William in intellectual joust for an entire morning.

After the talk, despite her friends' protests that they should stay, Anya cedes to Bianca's longing for lunch. So they leave early, Anya remonstrating gently: 'You could have had some biscuits with your coffee, darling.'

That decision to leave early becomes one of Bianca's greatest regrets. As they depart, Anya asks the young man with a caste in one eye: 'Does Andreas still come here on Sundays?'

'Yes, always, but he was unable to get away today… Although he might join us all later for tea at the Royal Festival Hall.'

Wondering vaguely, *Unable to get away from what?* Anya smiles. 'Please give him my best wishes.'

During the two weeks that follow, the sun continues to shine, the heat of the days building into a furnace. Visiting daily, Bianca brings Anya lunches of smoked salmon, with crème caramels for dessert, returning in the late afternoons to her studio, where she has tentatively begun a new double portrait of a recent Lord Mayor and his plump wife. Her portrait of Max now hangs in the National Portrait Gallery. Occasionally, Matthew rings to scold her for being dilatory… It is seven months since she started devoting her days to caring for her mother, and during that time she has lost a lot of weight; partly out of joy, partly out of anxiety. Meanwhile, new commissions build up fast in Matthew's office. Not only for portraits but also for more of her miniature watercolours. Her exhibition had sold out within its first two days, abetted, no doubt, by the scandal surrounding Hesketh's death and her recent portrait, reproduced in all the press, of his son, Bruno.

Matthew's business, however, is no longer in jeopardy... Chloe had turned up unannounced at his gallery having decided to sell Hesketh's entire collection of post-war British paintings and asking Matthew to broker the sale for her, Matthew's commission for handling the sale promising the very rescue he most needed.

Bianca asks him anxiously over the phone: 'How did Chloe seem, when you saw her?'

'Not too bad, considering.,, a bit pale maybe. Certainly unhappy... But who wouldn't be? Yet she also seemed less jittery and altogether more steely than I remembered her... She's selling everything Hesketh owned, including that wonderful Chelsea Embankment apartment of theirs... Too many memories, I imagine... She plans to start again, modestly at first, by buying a house close to her mother, in the Cotswolds... When I visited her at Chelsea Embankment to view the paintings, I found her sitting on the floor, listening to the sounds of the lift, just as Bruno used to.'

Bianca feels tears welling again at the thought of poor Bruno.

'She left you a set of keys for the house in Majorca, by the way...'

Bianca hardly knows what to say. 'I've no idea what I shall do about that,' she exclaims sadly.

'And Sebastian, your young assistant?' she asks, deliberately changing the subject. 'What news of him?'

'He no longer works for me, sadly.' Matthew's voice drops several octaves. 'After a painful recovery in hospital, his parents arranged for him to resume his career at the Metropolitan Museum in New York... He's now a trainee curator of medieval manuscripts there... By the way,' he adds, 'I've just had another extravagant offer for your triptych...'

'But I don't want to sell it,' Bianca murmurs.

Matthew laughs, cracking his knuckles loudly.

Throughout those months, people repeatedly ask the same two questions: 'Has your mother ever apologised for the way she treated you?' and 'Are you sorry now that Hesketh is dead… Do you miss him?'

Bianca knows this last question implies a subtle criticism. *Could – should – Bianca have done more to prevent Hesketh killing himself? Was it her fault he had done so?*

Bianca has become the subject of the very song Anya repeatedly sang to her as a child:

'Twas in the merry month of May,
When green buds, they were swelling,
Young Jimmy Grove on his death bed lay,
For love, of Barbara Allen…

She had become Barbara Allen…

The truth? That of course she feels sad… not only for Hesketh, but sad and sorry for them all. Their story represents such futility and waste… Yet for the first time in twenty-five years, she finds herself free of fear, her mind no longer turning on wariness. Hesketh was a daily oppression she had taught herself to ignore… Suddenly, she feels a new lightness of being, as though a constant pressure had vanished. Although not remotely grateful for his death, she is grateful for his absence… Just as she would have been when he was still alive, had he ever had the wit to stay away. For the first time in her entire adult life, she moves about the world freely, no longer anxious of being watched. No longer hounded like quarry.

But that first question: 'Has your mother ever apologised for the way she treated you?'

Bianca considers it phrased wrongly and based on false assumption. She has no desire for her mother to be proved wrong, nor for herself to be proved right. All she had ever wanted was for them both to love one another again… no matter what the difficulties, the misunderstandings. Anything less would strike her of no value.

* * *

One morning, having been exceptionally busy, both at home and in her studio, Bianca arrives in Covent Garden to find Anya slightly unwell. The heat of the day is oppressive. She seems to have slept sluggishly, only to wake feeling breathless. On seeing Bianca arrive, she bursts into instantaneous tears, like the tears of a four-year-old. Putting her arms around her, Bianca hugs her close, asking: 'Do you know how adorable you are?' whereupon Anya's tears dry immediately.

Languishing together on the turquoise sofa, they spin out the remainder of the burning day, with Bianca making lunch and Anya eating very little. Once or twice, she seems to lose her memory, at other times as lucid as ever. Conversation between them becomes desultory, both weary with the extreme heat. After lunch, still dressed in her night clothes, Anya goes to the lavatory, some distant signal flaring unheeded in Bianca's mind. For the first time she can remember, Anya does not close the bathroom door. A small, irrelevant detail which nevertheless goes against the grain of Anya's normal fastidiousness. Bianca decides to call a precautionary taxi, to take her to St Thomas's Hospital, arguing: 'They will still have all the records of your former illness...'

But Anya refuses to go, declaring she would never again go willingly to hospital, unless her GP insisted she must.

So Bianca calls her doctor... But Anya's GP is an elusive creature, with manifold resentments of her own. Having once been a good and conscientious doctor, she had recently fallen prey to difficulties and subsequently become less reliable, her former sympathy for her patients now spiked with anger. Bianca, nevertheless, rings her secretary, to ask if the doctor would call on Anya at home. She gets an embarrassed, non-committal reply: 'She may not have time...'

Bianca again tries to persuade Anya to let her order a taxi, to take her to St Thomas's. Again, Anya refuses.

As day turns to evening, a gentle breeze infiltrates the open windows, dispersing some of the day's dense heat, Anya at last seeming quieter, her breathing less troubled, her mood less fretful. Bianca assumes she is starting to recover. Gathering up her things, she prepares to make her way home.

'Can I get you anything before I leave?'

'I'd like some ice cream... and a copy of the *Evening Standard*,' Anya replies brightly.

Bianca laughs happily. This is Anya back on form.

Disappearing downstairs to the local supermarket, Bianca also phones the GP's office once more. Still no promise that the doctor would call. Bianca leaves a message, asking the doctor to phone her immediately if she does plan to visit Anya. *In which case, I'll return and meet her there...*

Above all, Bianca asks to be told immediately should anything serious be suspected. She leaves both her home and mobile phone numbers.

'Is that ice cream nice?'

'Not particularly,' Anya replies dismissively.

'Do you remember that wonderful cassata, darling, the elderly Italian used to wheel from village to village on his bicycle, when you were still a child at the cottage?'

They both laugh fondly at the memory.

'Thank you for being you, darling,' Anya says suddenly, out of the blue.

Then, as Bianca picks up her things ready to leave: 'Are you coming back later?'

'Only if the doctor arrives or phones to say you need to go to hospital. Otherwise, I'll be here early tomorrow morning.'

She gives Anya a kiss; her cheek feels soft, like petals, beneath her lips.

'I think I'm probably fine now.'

Anya waves to her from the depths of her raspberry-pink chair, moved closer to the window to catch the evening breeze. As she says goodbye, Anya is still licking ice cream from a spoon.

By 10 p.m., already overtired, and the phone still not having rung, Bianca falls asleep with her mobile next to the bed. At 8 a.m., Stephen arrives on his way to work, and they spend an hour making love before he leaves again for a meeting. Ten minutes later, Bianca's phone rings. It is the south London drawl of the warden from Anya's block of flats, sounding slightly agitated.

'Your mother's not at home, and I don't know why? Did the doctor call last night and order an ambulance, do you know?'

The voice pauses. 'Hang on just a minute...'

She places her hand over the receiver, Bianca only able to make out a muffled exchange.

'A policeman has arrived about something or other,' the voice resumes. 'I'll have to call you back.'

Bianca is bemused but not worried. Anya had probably got up early and either gone to the local supermarket or to Trafalgar Square, where she likes to sit quietly, watching the morning rush hour of passers-by, interspersed with the arrogant, flurrying skirmishes of London pigeons.

Ten minutes later, the phone rings again, the south London voice now sounding very different. Gentle, quavering, no longer truculent... frightened even. The police had arrived with solemn news. Anya's doctor, having turned up late last night, had ordered an ambulance to take Anya to hospital but then left again, without either telephoning Bianca or alerting anyone else, leaving Anya to travel in the ambulance on her own, with no way herself of letting Bianca know. Anya had always refused Bianca's pleas to be allowed to install her a phone, arguing: 'No, darling. I wouldn't want phone calls to become your excuse for not visiting me...'

The ambulance men, when they arrived, were equally ill-informed. Instead of taking Anya to St Thomas's, they delivered her to King's College Hospital, where there were no records of her previous medical notes. Anya's GP, meanwhile, was no longer responding to calls. No one knew what to do. Once in hospital, agitated, frightened and alone, Anya again became amnesiac. Extremely distressed and constantly calling for Bianca, but without being able to remember either where she lived or what her telephone number might be, when asked for more details, Anya replied that both she and Bianca lived in the country, with her husband, William, at the cottage. In her distress, her mind had fled to thoughts of William for comfort, despite their not having lived together for almost thirty years. The nurses then called the Holborn police to help find Bianca. They were out all night, desperately trying to locate her.

And so it was that Hesketh wreaked one final act of revenge; one last, sorrowful legacy in his imbecile pursuit of Bianca. Since his death, Bianca had foolishly forgotten to have her home phone changed from being ex-directory. She was impossible to reach.

At around 11 p.m., Anya had grown a little calmer, enough to want to eat some supper. Then, at 2.15 a.m., she had had a massive heart attack and died. In her agitation and distress, the embolism in her lung had finally ignited with her heart, brought on partly by the excessive heat and not drinking enough liquids. She was suffering from hyperthermia. Bianca had had no idea. Up until that day, Anya had seemed relatively well.

And so, exactly as Bianca always most feared, a stranger had rung to tell her that her mother had died... with no more time to say 'I love you...'

If only I'd been there, I could have pacified her, Bianca's mind rails. *She wouldn't have felt frightened, wouldn't have become agitated and confused ... would NOT have DIED... I'd have soothed her... kept her ALIVE...*

On hearing the warden's monstrous words, Bianca convulses, doubled up in pain. She cannot stop sobbing, her mind in a rush, stumbling, trying to overtake the truth and reverse it...

Eventually she manages to dial Stephen's number.

'I'm coming straight back...'

Leaving work immediately, he returns to her side, holding her while she sobs uncontrollably in his arms for the next few hours.

For two weeks, Bianca is incapable of sleep, her brain fighting constantly against its verdict of permanent loss, her bruised mind condemned to chase impotently after her mother's lost presence. Anya had once said: 'I'm not afraid of dying, but I don't like the idea of not existing.'

In Bianca's mind, she would exist forever. By sheer act of will, she tries to overleap the truth, to live and share in her mother's pain all over again, just as she had always wanted to during their long years of estrangement. There was simply nothing Bianca would not trade just to hear the delicious sound of her mother's voice calling out 'darling' one last time. All that she had ever known of femininity, love and pain, Bianca had learned from her mother. Her mind would never stop calling for her.

In the days that follow, William's stern repudiation of Anya also turns to immense grief... He had refused her permission to visit the cottage, arguing: 'She did me great wrong...'

Sitting in her raspberry-pink chair, Anya had received the news sadly, stoically, gazing at Bianca with a mute ache of understanding in her blue eyes... Nevertheless, it was a savage blow.

But now, memory reverses on itself to become loneliness and pain. In the moment of her death, Anya had become his wife all over again... William finds himself remembering her beauty, her spirit, her intelligence, her smile... Above all, he remembers how very much in love they had once been... As so often with people truly loved, in death, he longed to reclaim her for his own.

* * *

The Sunday before Anya's funeral, Bianca returns to The Society to dutifully let Anya's friends know of her death and invite them to her funeral. Yet as she stands before them on the podium, they stare up at her strangely unmoved, one or two overtly hostile, almost shrugging their indifference.

Perhaps that is the way elderly people greet the news of death... when soon anticipating their own? she ponders.

Nevertheless, Bianca is taken aback by their reaction. *Perhaps studied ennui passes for intellectual elegance among this crowd?* she reflects.

Continuing to eye her coldly, only as she makes to leave do a small coterie of Anya's friends gather about her, anxious to know more details and fondly share their memories of Anya with her. All of them men.

Having left typed notices detailing the time and place of her funeral, Bianca escapes, almost with a sense of relief, into the long corridor outside... Ill lit and dismal with gloom, she walks its length lingeringly, sorrowfully. In the distance, a figure advances slowly towards her... At first, she cannot make out his face, but she recognises all too accurately the shape of his body against the sparse light. It is Hesketh...

Her breath stills in her throat... about to turn tail...

'Hello,' says the ghost, putting out a hand to shake hers. 'I was hoping to catch you. I'm Andreas.'

A terrifying doubt infects Bianca... A memory, long buried, surfaces vertiginously, of Anya lounging in a chair at her flat in

Highbury, talking animatedly to Hesketh, the hem of her skirt, meanwhile, riding indecorously high above her knee, and Hesketh, all the while, casting sidelong glances at Bianca.

Had that too been the reason for our long estrangement? Is that what my mother felt?

Andreas looks exactly as Hesketh looked twenty-seven years earlier, when she and Anya had first met him; the same lean, athletic build, even similar reckless, handsome good looks. But with a face swarthier and more chiselled, less reminiscent of a Brancusi bust. Terrifying thoughts spread themselves insidiously through Bianca's mind.

Had Anya herself coveted the company of Hesketh, all those years ago immediately following the break-up of her marriage to William... only to find her own attractions trumped by those of her own daughter?

Anya had once complained: 'Men no longer look at me in the street... They now just look at you instead.'

Had Anya not only lost William to Bianca, in some unfathomable way, but also lost Hesketh to her as well? Bianca remembers once confessing to Anya that she did not altogether trust Hesketh, and Anya dismissing her concerns. Had her own youthful instincts about Hesketh been more accurately far-seeing than those of her own mother? Or was it simply true that no one could have guessed how badly things with Hesketh would turn out? And had Hesketh deliberately flirted with Anya while setting about seducing her daughter, just as he had flirted with the French woman in Putney while carefully seducing her home from under her?

Bianca had always assumed Anya had rejected her because of her closeness to William, and her refusal to denounce the man who may or may not have been her father. But perhaps she had resented Bianca for stealing Hesketh from her too?

Later, sifting through Anya's possessions, Bianca finds a letter from Hesketh, written twenty-five years earlier; a letter loaded with emotional ambiguity.

It occurs to Bianca that if such a thing as 'evil' exists, then for herself and Anya, that evil had been Hesketh. Whether intentionally or not, he had poisoned both his own life and theirs. Far too late now... Bianca would always hate him. She could never forgive him for the things he had stolen from her. She still thinks of him as some dirty rag that had wiped itself indiscriminately over their lives... But her hatred does not disguise her belief in Hesketh's love for his son. She knows instinctively that Hesketh had only wanted to protect Bruno, rather than destroy him. And that, perhaps, Hesketh's own great tragedy and fate in life – to always destroy the very things he loved most...

Bianca stretches out her arm, to take Andreas's hand. 'I'm so very sorry for your loss...'

He hesitates. 'Did you know that I loved your mother too?'

ACKNOWLEDGEMENTS

My greatest thanks are to Tom Perrin at Zuleika, for deciding to publish *The Stalker's Tale*, but also for his swift, seamless intelligence and immense charm, which make him a joy to work with; every detail of the book resolved easily between us. My most grateful thanks also to George Tomsett, his editorial assistant, for his quietly supportive, unobtrusive, but always perceptively accurate editorial advice, and to Laura Kincaid, for her elegantly enhancing copyedit. Finally, to Jonathan Ross, who first introduced me to Tom, and so initiated all the great pleasures of participating in the proud adventure that is Zuleika.

More generally, my thanks to my vast circle of witty, intellectual friends, against whose backdrop of laughter and clever, speculative thought I lead my life. More specifically, my thanks to Jessica Douglas-Home for her constant championing of my determination to publish, after having written ceaselessly in relative silence for many years. My most grateful thanks to Lynda Samuels and Bill Rudgard for their many years of generous support, and Lynda's contribution to finding a distinctive voice for the stalker's letters. Lastly, all my thanks to my two newest and very best of friends, Mark Arena and Jason Arbuckle, for their great charm, delightful hospitality and ever affectionate enthusiasm for the publication of *The Stalker's Tale*.